PRAISE FOR MARY HOOD'S
FAMILIAR HEAT

"A prodigious talent . . . an ambitious novel. . . . Hood has drawn some excellent portraits and ventured down some uncharted roads."
—Detroit Free Press

"A delicious treat."
—Entertainment Weekly

"A writer well worth reading now—and watching in the future."
—Frederick Busch

"Languid, seductive prose. . . . 'How long does love take?' is the question asked at the beginning of the book. By the end, we know it is a lifetime."

—Miami Herald

"A book that trolls along at a leisurely pace, taking its own sweet time to tell a good story, reeling in the reader with skill and precision. . . . Mary Hood is a writer who has clearly observed human nature and sifted its essence."
—St. Louis Post-Dispatch

"Well crafted, satisfying . . . consistently interesting. Hood creates three-dimensional characters, almost any of whom could easily become the principal in another engrossing novel."
—Seattle Times

"Warmth radiates from Mary Hood's novel. . . . A number of FAMILIAR HEAT's chapters have the stand-alone integrity of short stories. . . . Hood's fierce compassion and affection for her flawed characters shine through, burnishing stories as sweet and tangy as Sanavere's salt air after a storm."
—Orlando Sentinel

more . . .

FAMILIAR
HEAT

ALSO BY MARY HOOD

And Venus Is Blue

How Far She Went

Mary Hood

FAMILIAR HEAT

WARNER BOOKS

A Time Warner Company

The title of this work comes from Book VIII of *The Aeneid of Virgil*, translated by Allen Mendelbaum.

Lines from Part I of *Versos Sencillos* by Jose Marti are translated here by the author.

Warner Books Edition
Copyright © 1995 by Mary Hood
All rights reserved.

This Warner Books edition is published by arrangement with Alfred A. Knopf, Inc., New York, NY

Warner Books, Inc., 1271 Avenue of the Americas, New York, NY 10020

Visit our Web site at
http://pathfinder.com/twep

Ⓦ A Time Warner Company

Printed in the United States of America

First Warner Books Printing: November 1996
10 9 8 7 6 5 4 3 2 1

Library of Congress Cataloging-in-Publication Data
Hood, Mary.
    Familiar heat / Mary Hood. — Warner Books ed.
       p.   cm.
    ISBN 0-446-67274-2
      1. City and town life—Florida—Fiction. 2. Cuban Americans—
Florida—Fiction. 3. Married women—Florida—Fiction. 4. Hostages—
Florida—Fiction. 5. Florida—Fiction. I. Title.
[PS3558.O543F36   1996]
813'.54—dc20   96-24323
                                        CIP

"Cupboard love isn't love," he said. "Is there any other? . . . Is there? . . . Have you ever known it?" "Yes," I said.

—G. B. Edwards, *The Book of Ebenezer Le Page*

Acknowledgments

Portions of this work were completed with the support and encouragement of the Hambidge Center, the Mac-Dowell Colony, and the Whiting Foundation. The author wishes to acknowledge gratefully Eric Ashworth, agent and friend, for laughing at the funny parts, suffering the follies, and hoping, always, for the best.

BOOK ONE

THE BLESSING

How much time does love take?
—E. M. Forster

FIRST THINGS FIRST

It was early in September when the whales came back, bringing sorrow with them. The Captain was away, far out in the Stream, a day beyond the horizon. Deep-sea charter. As he left, he had given Faye a list (the way he generally did) of little deeds to accomplish: to ask, to pay, to tell, to look for, to clean, to find, to write, to cancel, to call—that sort of list, a wife's list—and also to buy stamps and get to the bank. Definitely to get to the bank. He had underlined it.

So Faye had asked, and paid, and told, and found; she had written and called and canceled and cleaned; she had bought the stamps. Now there was only the banking left to be done and it was Saturday and the bank closed at noon precisely. Since there was plenty of time, and the weather was good, she walked.

That big house the Captain had built Faye out on the bluff stood about a mile from the village. A fine low modern house with a lot of glass, but dark, even at noon still dark and cool because of the sheltering oaks. The housekeeper bicycled away down the shell road to her own family comforts at night. When the Captain was late, or away overnight, Faye's mother worried.

"Come home," Mrs. Parry would tell her every time. She said it that September morning too. They'd talk on the phone at all hours, not long distance. Her mother had that to be thankful for. But there was that gulf between them, more daunting than open water, which Faye's marriage to what Mrs. Parry thought of as a "foreigner" had only widened.

"He was born here, same as I was," Faye uselessly pointed out.

"His mama don't talk to me," Mrs. Parry said. "She's got my number."

"She doesn't speak English!" Faye said.

"That's what I said," Mrs. Parry said. "He's foreign."

Faye had to laugh.

Mrs. Parry had been a naturalized war bride, convent-educated, with a French father and a Vietnamese mother. Her English was good enough for running a business, though she still counted and kept books in Vietnamese, prayed in Latin, and sang in French.

"Road runs both ways, Mama," Faye always reminded her. "You come here."

Her mother was welcome and knew it. But she had the shop to run—couldn't just lock the door and go flittering, as she called it. Still, if she had taken the notion to find Faye and spend the day with her, she could have been over to the bluff in a blink, by boat or car, both—thanks to the Captain—at her disposal. Leagues farther by land, of course, because of having to go around to North End and cross the gut on the drawbridge—sometimes raised, stopping the whole world for a bargeload of pine stumps or a dallying yacht or a string of luckless shrimpers—but even so, the causeway, the land, was her choice when she chose. Faye was like her in that, in preferring the land route. They both loved the water, and Faye even had a handful of diving medals, but that was in a pool, not open water. They weren't good sailors. Brave enough, but seasickly.

Through the pay telescope in the municipal park, Faye's mother kept a weather eye on things across the marsh and inlet. She'd walk down there after work most evenings, with far from random change in her pocket, to swivel the scope around like a pro, fixing the focus on the Captain's roof and sunset-shining windows straight across the sound. Madonna blue shutters, heavenly blue, Faye called it, matching it in the morning glories she planted on the back terrace.

"Everything the Captain has is touched with blue," Faye had told her mother early on, as an icebreaker, a casual remark to get the conversation on track. Her mother liked the color blue. "The name of his boat is the *Blue Lady*," Faye added.

"In Spanish?" her mother accused, leaning way into the dryer drum to haul out another armload for fluff and fold.

"No," Faye said.

They worked on the load together, efficient from long practice, eyes as blank and hands as quick as a bank teller's. They didn't talk, but this wasn't a quarrel. The machines were very loud back there, and Faye liked to wear her little pocket radio and earphones to drown it out. If her mother needed to say something, she'd reach across and touch Faye's arm—they worked that close—and Faye would drop the headset on her neck and listen. They had hand signals too, for when words weren't needed, and a light as well as a buzzer for the drive-through window.

Some sudden niceness, a deference to Faye's maidenhood, prompted Mrs. Parry to reach out, and sort the men's underwear from the heap and fold it herself, as though Faye might Get Ideas. Faye was grown, graduated, bound to marry someday, yet when Mrs. Parry studied her and thought, Soon, she shook her head no, and would go on shaking it. She was muttering to herself when she went to wait on the customer at the drive-through window, and she was still muttering when she came back.

"How do you know his boat's name is in Spanish?" Faye asked, about fifteen minutes later, not hostile, not defensive, but with that same friendly everyday open-faced look that had led her through high school to honors on the debate team.

"Lucky guess," Mrs. Parry said.

"Nope," Faye said. "It's in English same as our shop sign."

"How do you know?"

Faye smiled. "I asked."

"*Blue Lady*," her mother said. "All blue? Blue and white? Some folk paint that blue on sills and doors to ward off the evil eye."

"*Some*," Faye said. "You mean voodoo . . . That's not why, so far as I know," Faye said, after thinking it over. "He likes blue!" There was still a lot to guess about, but it proved true that the Captain was as proper a Catholic as a proud man—with no faith in luck or island mojo—could be. There Faye differed. She couldn't take things easy—as a matter of dealt cards, fated events, and *que será*. Susceptible to anguish over possibilities, prey to alarms for love, she believed in intercession, did what she could to prevent harm's befalling.

When they were newly married, she used to go down to their little dock and hold up the gas lantern to guide his launch safe home, even in bad weather, especially in bad weather, as though the light in her hands had drawing power amplified by love. It never once—that mote of faith and homefire—winked out in the wind, though the storm flags on the Coast Guard pole might be snapping flat square open: small craft warnings. Only a few nights that bad; the Captain was too keen a soul at his work, held his craft and crew too dear to risk them in critical winds.

Sometimes Faye's mother would struggle down to the park and aim the viewfinder of the pay scope across the whitecaps, trying to see Faye's lovelight. Abroad in weather like that, because driven by devotion, same as Faye. Simple enough to figure. If Faye didn't answer her phone, her mother knew what to dread, where to head, bundled against the elements. Faye's was the greater peril. The park at least had handrails and streetlights, and if you fell, you landed on earth.

"A mother's love is one kind of suffering," according to Father Ockham, Mrs. Parry's priest, "with the stages built in. Like the Stations of the Cross." Love like Faye's had precedents too, but no path. Like wildfire. Inviting backfire to keep it in bounds. "Oh, she can be a queen, no arguing with her," Mrs. Parry admitted. "Which is to say," Father Ockham agreed, "she's nineteen."

The Captain had a telescope of his own, but Faye couldn't see her mother's roof from there, because of the jog in the street and the trees, not because she had never bothered to look back. She wasn't ashamed of Parry's A-1 Dry Cleaning and Laundry, or of growing up over the shop. She even joked that it was the steam that kept her wavy hair—heavy, heavy, never cut in her whole life, caught in a barrette so it swung almost to her waist in back—from being as straight as her mother's. She would have gone on working there after marriage if the Captain had let her.

From the day Faye had been able to print both letters and numbers, she had helped in the shop. Her parents had set up a milk crate for her to stand on and she served as their counter girl, quick at numbers, and good at remembering faces and orders. She could make reliable change from first grade on, and could answer the phone sensibly when her father was out making deliveries and her mother was still learning to speak English. Faye was their only child.

The Sisters at Saint Joseph's skipped her forward across second grade and fourth, and she repeated the year in between, when her father died; Faye was only eight. For a long time they had looked up, she and her mother both, when the shop door opened and the little bells rang, expecting him to come back. The usual staggering and drift of sudden loss. Bankruptcy loomed, then receded.

Mrs. Parry—who had never learned to drive, and preferred to go by foot or on bicycle—hired a driver for the delivery van, but relied on Faye more and more. The business slowly righted, like their life. When Faye turned sixteen and graduated from her learner's permit, she took over the deliveries before and after school. That saved on payroll.

Mrs. Parry didn't just hand Faye the keys to the van and say, "Go!" Because she was small and plain, and because Faye was not, Mrs. Parry signed them both up for self-defense lessons—evenings—and together they learned precaution. As for the van, Faye had to promise seatbelt always, hitchhikers never, doors locked all around, no entering homes of strangers, and this: "Assume it's you or them. If they're going to kill you, make them do it first, don't let them drag you off somewhere and strew your bones in sawgrass so deep we won't find you till marsh hen season." Faye always laughed and promised. And kept the gas tank full, good rubber on the wheels. Practical paranoia. It wasn't retreads or blems that blew, front and rear curbside, and left her stranded out there on the dead end at Cedar Point with only one spare tire and nothing to do but knock at a stranger's door.

That time of day, no one was home. All the men off fishing or at the docks wishing they were. Wives labored in their hairnets and rubber boots at the crab plant, or were pulling linens and turning out rooms at the motels on the strip, or keeping books at the icehouse, checking groceries at the plaza, flipping burgers or waffles, whatever. Gainfully employed, every one of them. Grandfolks too. No old-timers sitting on their porches. All go-getters, not a thriftless soul around, just dogs, a cat on a window ledge, chickens in a backyard, a few gulls and grackles skulking around the garbage cans.

Faye was out of luck. She went house to house, knocking, calling. A quiet street, a shortcut, Faye had hoped, around heavy traffic on the boulevard heading to the toll bridge. A dead end, she now saw. A block from the river, the houses lichen-colored and some boarded up, sagging, next to newer little cottages of cinderblock and jumbo brick, so small they appeared to have burst at the seams and let life spill out into the grassless yards, toy-strewn, bright flowers in gaudy containers and beds outlined in shells. From the trees, like graybeard moss, the nets hung to be mended.

Finally Faye saw an open door, daylight spearing straight through an old two-story house front to back, through patched screen doors. She knocked and knocked. Calling hello, leaning against the screen, her eyes shielded by her hands, calling, "Someone? Anyone!"

At last, footsteps. Slow, heavy. A nightmare of a noise, unsteady, coming on. What had Faye interrupted? She almost fled. If she had!

He loomed, rumpled, wordless. "Big man," she told her mother later. Before she finished describing, Mrs. Parry said, certain, "Tom Rios." Not a bad guess; not a bad man. His brother was the one with the devil-in-a-white-shirt reputation, not Tom.

Faye didn't know any of them, or anything about them. Different parish. Besides, her mother never let her loiter around Lupo's, by the docks. Brought her up on Main Street, not the bay. Walked with her to parochial school, teaching her eyes down, no glancing in windows, no swaying or dawdling past those balmy doorways of the warehouses breathing out their exotic airs from bales and bundles and piles of hides and herbs, the sweet stores of vanilla deer-tongue, clover, coffee and tea and tobacco, spices, lumber, crates of plunder stenciled from all over the world. What child wouldn't stare and dream? But Mrs. Parry nipped her along, like a stock dog after a stray lamb in wolf territory.

Bayfront. Lupo's the capital of that rough ward. Where the Cuban captains and crews took their time over Cafe Bustelo—"Terrible coffee," Faye's mother complained, judging not by the taste but by the stains, having had the contract for those linens, weekly pickup and drop-off, couldn't *get* those stains out, had to agree about that from the first order—and read the newspapers and argued and bragged. When Lupo's rebuilt after the fire, they put in dinettes and booths, all Formica, and went to Styrofoam cups and plastic spoons. Paper napkins in little dispensers on the tables. "Flimsy, no class," Mrs. Parry decided. No more checkered cloths, no curtains at all, kitchen towels done by the linen service that did for the motels on the interstate. Progress. That was a major customer Mrs. Parry had lost, in the rocky years before Faye got her driver's license, so she had never gone in there, never knew who Tom Rios was till she walked up to his house and said, "I've had an accident. Truck dropped cinder blocks in the road and didn't even stop. I couldn't miss them all."

He didn't say anything.

Faye explained, "I blew my horn but he just gave me—gave me a gesture, and then drove on."

Nothing. He just stood there. She turned from the door and glanced back up and down the deserted street, pushed her bangs off her forehead, the bracelets on her wrist chinging slightly. She ran her finger over the eye-level patched place on the screen and read him the bottom line. "I need a wrecker, see?"

When he still just stood there, she wondered if he was drunk, or didn't speak English, or both. She tried out her B-plus high school Español. "May I use your telephone, please?" Not let me, or I must, but may I, and please.

He seemed to be thinking it over. Maybe he was Greek? Could be Greek. Fierce eyes, dark-circled like a panda's. She added, in all the Greek she knew besides Merry Christmas, "Good morning." And again, in English, "please." He turned and walked away, deep into the dark heart of the house. Left her standing there.

"Mister!" she called to his back.

"It's not locked," he answered tonelessly, in English as good as her Spanish. He vanished into the dim front room. She heard a chair sigh as he sank into it. The phone was on the wall in the hall. After looking around through the screen one more time, and breathing a prayer, she opened the door and went toward it.

The bird in its covered cage stared at her listlessly when she peeked.

Days of droppings were piled under its perch; the water was cloudy, the seed cup empty of all but husks. The bird was puffed, eyes almost shut, one foot retracted into disheveled feathers. Faye dropped the cover back.

Outraged, she called out, "What's the matter here?"

The man answered, "Dial six, then your number, not long distance."

So Faye dialed.

They put her on hold.

All the time she waited, she could see the outline of Tom Rios sitting there in the dark, his uncombed head. Everything in the house needed care, food, light, action. A stack of unopened mail lay on the table beside a couple of wilting dish gardens with florist cards attached: "In Sympathy."

Someone had died here. Faye didn't want to know who or why. The flurry and rites were over, and this was what remained. She just wanted the wrecker to come and let her go on her way; she didn't want to be involved, wished she had never walked into this, longed to be gone, to forget it all. And was ashamed for wishing it. For penance, she promised she would open that birdcage door and put her hand in and pour seeds and change the water dish, though she had never touched a bird before, and the possibility that it might flutter, or fly at her and try to escape, or, worse, settle on her hand, grip around her finger with its scaly little claws, made her spine ache, and her mind faint. But if she would do that much, it would prove she wasn't afraid of the grief and death in this strange house, that she wasn't just turning and running away. She could do that much, anyway, before she left that man alone, as the rest of the world had done.

Through the back door she saw the browning pots of funeral mums and a tub of sun-scalded poinciana, foil and ribbons still fresh. The pine-cone weights on the cuckoo clock on the wall behind her had reached the floor, and time had stopped at two-fifteen. Day or night didn't matter, that was plain enough.

No "what next" to the whole house . . . She puffed the chaff out of the feed cup and poured in a handful of seeds and a bit of stale muffin she picked up off the counter. The water sparkled when she put it back in the cage, fresh. All the time she held her breath, not only against the odor, but also against the possibility the bird might act wild. All it did was humbly begin eating with a tiny cracking and tonguing of the seeds. Relieved, she latched the door, leaving the cover half off the cage to let the sunlight in.

When she went into the dark parlor where Tom Rios sat, to offer to pay for the phone call, he was just sitting on the wallowed sheet on the sofa, as though he'd been sleeping there for weeks, or trying.

"Forget it," he said. To every offer—no thanks; about the blinds, let them stay down; no thanks about the coffee she could make in a moment; no thanks to toast or cereal or juice.

She swooped down on the dish gardens and took them to the sink and drenched them, set them on a sunny sill. That was the end of her good deeds, her nerved-up meddling. "I'll wait outside," she told him, almost whispering. Held her bracelets so they wouldn't chatter or bangle, just that bright little female noise seemed irreverent. She regretted her perfume, and her happiness. What sort of trouble were two flat tires and a snapped tie-rod, weighed against death?

Faye tiptoed to the edge of the porch and sat on the top step, her sandaled feet in the stinging-hot April sun. She decided it must be the man's wife that had died, because if a woman who loved a man were not dead, she would be here, right that moment, to help him get through this awfulness.

The porch offered a good vantage; she could see the road, hear the phone if the wrecker company had to call back. She was so intent on listening for that, she didn't at first notice the bird whistling. It was so important to her to believe that it was the caged bird, she didn't want to make sure, but she had to know, what good was believing a lie? She leaned against the dark screen door and stared; the bird sat in the sun-struck corner of the cage, preening and mumbling. Straight through the house were the parched flowers in the backyard.

Maybe she should go around back, see if there was a hose lying there, so she could water the poinciana. Somehow this didn't qualify as one of what her mother called Faye's Save the World Merit Badge projects. She had just got to her feet when Vic Rios drove up, the brother.

If he noticed Faye's van kneeling against the curb down the block, he never worried about it. The bad tires were not visible, the cracked headlight and grazed fender not extraordinary in that neighborhood.

When Faye saw he was coming to that very house, she moved to one side of the steps, and started down, explaining, "Leaving," off balance, flustered, as though she had been caught trespassing. As though Vic Rios—that devil-in-a-white-shirt—were the Law, arresting in brass and navy blue. Open collar, no tie, very, very tan. He came up the lower steps two at a time. Watching him, Faye fell.

"Whoa," he said. Reaching to help her up.

"I'm all right." Furious with embarrassment, angry, as always, at pain when it was her own. She never could bear sympathy, preferred to go off by herself to shed any tears. Did but most certainly did not want his hands on her. Brushed herself, and him, off.

He shrugged and went on across the porch and into the house without knocking. So he belonged, she knew that much about him, and that was all. He hadn't spoken another word, just "Whoa."

The wrecker came right away. The driver didn't know the people in the neighborhood, no. So Faye left, not knowing Vic Rios's name, or how they'd meet again, or if. She didn't let it obsess her; she had plenty to do, and more to think about. She didn't cruise around, seeking. Never had been goody-goody faithful at mass but took the slow way past the idlers in doorways—the sort that's a tart at heart.

She wanted what one often wants, but yearned no more than natural or seemly. Wanted it to happen, but never, till she met Rios, had she been sure. Cristo had gotten close to making her feel lonely, but none of those cocky, low-riding, beer-buzzed, night-prowling others in their crazy cars!—or the clam-baking, beach-dancing, golden-boy yearbook-heroes—no, not even Cristo, the National League's numero-uno draft pick bucking home from college in that army-surplus jeep—not a one prevailed. They took her spare time, not her whole heart.

So why him, the Captain, at first sight? It was that sudden. And of course they ran into each other again soon; fate doesn't need a map. It might not have been right but it was real. And they made plans, from the beginning. Mrs. Parry only insulted Faye once asking if she was sure.

Who made the wedding dress? Mrs. Parry. "Anything you can dream up," she promised. Graduated to bifocals sewing seed pearls onto cream. Three weights of peau de soie, clouds of lace, silk tulle veiling soft as mist; even the mitts were hand-fashioned. Hundred and fifty dollars a yard wholesale wouldn't begin it. Both mother and daughter shopped for fabrics with their fingertips, knew fabric quality by touch as much as by eye, in any light. They were unsparing. "Once in a lifetime," they agreed.

The shears through that night-chilled silk! "Like cutting smoke in a dream," Mrs. Parry marveled. The right ideas came to her, her hands moved with a mind of their own. Years of alterations, custom tailoring for others, had practiced her for this perfection. They worked mornings in the loft, shutters wide open for the land and sea breezes. Month of May, daylight savings, nine a.m. It was hot already.

"Like swimming naked," Faye muttered, "by starlight." She had her eyes closed and was drawing a cool scrap over her bare arm, up across her throat, testing it with her lips.

"Alone?" What mother wouldn't ask?

Faye's eyes blinked open.

"Alone!" She frowned, considering it.

Her mother stitched faster, thinking, *Sure as God, it's time.*

Through two rehearsals the Captain's mind wandered far from harbor, but on the actual day, when Faye hove into the chapel fully rigged, his attention dropped anchor. He stared like a statue. Faye's mother counted that a compliment and took at least partial credit. It is not easy to teach lace to cleave and flex decently on warm curves and hollows. The newspaper photographs, good as they were, didn't do justice.

The portraits succeeded better, so well in fact, the photographer was using an unauthorized copy of one of the hand-colored ones in his studio window, for an example of his finest work, he was that pleased; but the Captain put a stop to it as soon as someone mentioned it to him, in praise, a few weeks after the honeymoon: roared over to the studio from bayfront, during fishing hours, leaving his clients waiting at the dock, while he cleared it up once and for all.

"My wife's not bait," he explained simply. He was raging, but quiet. Very convincing. Customers in the shop fell back toward the door, in case it came to assassination of more than character. "I won't have her trolled as chum for suckers." He left the man's easel overturned in a cloud of tossed bills. It wasn't piracy, for he paid, then strolled calmly out with the picture under his arm. Faye's portrait wound up on Mrs. Parry's wall, a profile shot, backlit. Wearing her grandmother's earrings. That was her something old. Faye was glancing over her shoulder, side-to-back view, the button pearls and handmade loops highlighting her straight spine. Here and there Faye's mother could see little places she would've got perfect with one more fitting; it was all she could do not to touch up the dress anyway, afterwards, when Faye laid it off forever, to be cleaned and boxed for storage and posterity.

Faye wore a linen suit—blue to please the Captain—for going away. They hid their rented car, locked till the last moment, in a nearby garage, so no tin cans, no shaving soap, no balloons, no streamers. No posing. Toss the bouquet, duck and flee, his hand urgent and claiming. They were in such a hurry. That was the picture the FBI chose; they didn't keep it, but it came back marred.

About those whales: When they came back, the village pier stood deserted on its barnacled timbers, a fair Saturday in September, the post–Labor Day lull in no way accountable for the empty, the emptied landscape. A mild wind was rattling the palms and sending bits of litter rolling in the gutter like dice. The restless water, halfway between tides, surged and slapped against the pilings. Faye glanced at her watch: eleven o'clock.

Where were they? That usual weekend crowd of day-trippers in their tinseled hats and jaded resort wear. There was their ordinary clutter—bait pails, lunchboxes, beer and pop cans, sandwich wrappers and chip bags, poles and nets and floats—but the pier was deserted. Not a soul, native or off-rate tourist, stared openmouthed at the charts on the billboard by the cleaning sinks with the illustrations of record fish taken from the channel. No one crouched untangling nylon line. No child lay on his belly staring at the slap and pull of the water over dropped bait. Down the way on one of the concrete benches, a red sweater stirred in the wind. Fish heads, paper plates, clouds of monofilament line, folding chairs, crab shells, flies buzzing and crawling on a box of chicken-skin bait . . . A pole leaning against the rail rolled back and forth in the drag and ease of the currents; if there was a fish on the hook, it had caught itself. There was no one to reel it in. Gulls on the outer pilings mewed like abandoned kittens, and five brown pelicans flapped slowly along the channel, looking down. Faye watched them, and they led her eye to the crowd gathered into a clot way up the beach. A child on the periphery of the group was hopping and pointing toward the center of the dark mass. Faye shaded her eyes with her hands and stared.

The whales.

She too started down to see.

As she got nearer she could make out the dark beached shapes—a dozen or so—like logs motionless on the sand. A child went clambering up onto the dry back of one of the whales and after a survey from its height, began to bounce.

"Is he dead? He's dead!" the boy chanted. "Dead—uh—dead—uh—dead . . ."

"I thought they had dragged them all the way back out into the deep water," a woman was complaining.

"Twice already," a man near the center agreed, gesturing vaguely toward where. "But these are bound and determined to die."

A young man took a snapshot of his friend poised precariously, one foot on the animal's back in mastery, making a strongman gesture with his arms, clowning. Behind him the little boy kept bouncing, forcing a false breath out and into the whale's corpse, its blowhole shuddering without life. The man with the camera took out his knife and began to cut a souvenir. Under his blade the dark skin parted to the light.

"No." Faye looked away, out toward the horizon, then up and down the beach, but saw no help. Still she said, "No." She tried to tell them about the law—"a federal law," she insisted—that protected whales.

"Look, lady, they're already dead, what's your kick?"

"Dead or alive," Faye explained.

"This one is still alive," someone said, kneeling, passing a hand along the animal's side.

Faye knelt too.

"They said last night on the news they'd have to get a man with a backhoe to dig a pit and bury them. They'll mortify, you know." The woman saying this put her hand on Faye's shoulder and smiled down. "You know that," she said reasonably. Another woman, searching through the contents of the mesh bag on her wrist, added, "Or use dynamite," pronouncing it danny-mite; it was clear to her what the side effects of such a funeral would be. "No day to hang out wash," she chuckled, peeling her orange, tossing the rind toward the sea.

"These are whales," Faye said.

"They had their chance. Twice," another woman pointed out.

The man cutting the whale said, "If they want to commit suicide, who's to stop 'em, the Pope o' Rome?" He snorted into the general laughter. A little girl kept running to the surf and back, bringing pails of water to pour down the breathing hole of the one live whale, as though priming a pump. Faye took the sand bucket away and said, not unkindly, "Let them be." The child ran to her mama to accuse. Most of the people were just standing around, staring down, so they would be able to say they had seen them, in person.

"It isn't suicide," Faye said. "A disease of the ear, perhaps disorientation. They lose their way, others follow. Maybe out of concern." She glanced up again, the length of the beach, hoping for the experts, the scientists and hobbyists and specialists in their white coats and rubber boots and gloves, carrying medicine kits, the way they did on the news. New England, California, always the same earnest response and last-ditch efforts. "Federal law," she said again. "Marine mammals."

No one was listening. She pulled the jumping boy off the whale's back. "That's enough," she told him.

One of the women mentioned a pair of ivory earrings her grandmother had, claimed there must be a fortune in each jaw, and the real butchery commenced, the grapplings, the exclamations, the disappointments.

"Terrible," Faye told the newsmen who finally arrived. But this was an old story, and these weren't the large whales. They filmed a few minutes, then went away. Whales beaching themselves weren't hot; sharks were. A man washed ashore, his leg off, that would be something else.

Or maybe a big whale, or pregnant.

"Do whales have ears? Where are their ears? You said whales have ears. They don't have ears, do they?" The jumper pestered Fay to show him. He counted the corpses, pointing his finger like a gun at each one. "Fif-teen," he counted.

Faye noticed the sixteenth whale was a young one, only a calf, perhaps not yet weaned, stranded under its mother when the tide went out.

The hacking at the jaws went on.

"For nothing," Faye said.

"I want to take that one to my daddy," the boy told Faye. "That one." He pointed to the largest. "We'll have him for lunch. Mama'll microwave him."

When Faye heard that, heard him say lunch, she looked at her watch, looked again, alarmed. "Let me go now!" she cried, as though the mute and enormous immobility of the corpses anchored her there. She turned her back on them all and fled up the beach to the nearest steps and did not pause to empty the sand from her shoes. She had given her word to the Captain about the bank; there was no crisis except in that. She had never yet disappointed him. They had been married four months.

Now everything strove against perfection. The boardwalk itself was overwhelmed with drifted sand, slowing her. The traffic light turned red against her at the corner. She jaywalked anyway, right in front of the bakery truck, causing it to squeal to a stop. She swerved across the street on a diagonal and gained the sidewalk in front of Brittain's, where the repairman was blocking the way with ladders and pieces of rotted canvas from the awnings.

She plunged through the congregated pigeons at the hardware, scattering them with the vehemence of her steps. She did not again glance at

her watch, but ran on, saying under her breath, "I'll make it, I'll make it."
Like a game. She pushed open the door of the bank with three minutes
to spare.

It was dark indoors. She pulled off her sunglasses, blinking, and began
to fill out the deposit slip at the counter. She never looked around, so she
didn't notice the robbers.

But it was so quiet, and when she had finished writing, and turned, she
noticed that everyone was staring at her—cashiers, tellers, customers—as
though she were in trouble, or their last hope. The two men with the
guns stood to one side, as though politely waiting their turn. Faye swung
and started for the door, three steps, two steps away. The big man got
there first and put out his thick arm to block the way, saying, "No,
ma'am," and so she went and stood with the others. "Reality," the man
said.

The *Blue Lady* charter, with Captain Victor Rios, his two-man
crew, and clients Mr. and Mrs. Herbert Fortner, gently rocked a day beyond land, out in the Stream, deep-sea fishing. Light seas, light breeze.
It had been a good trip, as good as most.

The Captain looked amused. Mrs. Fortner had bet Mr. Fortner that
she would catch the prize fish of the trip, because this was her first trip.
"Beginner's luck," she claimed, "unless you count scooping tadpoles
barehanded as a child and tadpoles aren't really fish, not scientifically
speaking, are they?" She asked it again, told it again, the way she and her
brothers had gathered tadpoles. "I was such a tomboy! If I had known
they'd grow up to be frogs, and I'd grow up to be a woman," she said
each time, and the men would courteously agree frogs aren't fish, no,
ma'am, that didn't really count, so she'd conclude, "This is my virgin
voyage," with a quick look—not at her husband, but at the Captain, hoping to catch his eye for a wink. She knew he liked her; men like women
with spunk and get-up.

"I'm no faintin' Jane," she had said, baiting her own hook at sunrise.
But the day had passed and she hadn't caught anything to brag about, not
even the Captain's eye. "Let's get this show on the road," she said after
noon. Fishing was better then, and she refused help in playing and landing the ones on her line, though this wasn't a tournament and she had no

hope of landing a really big one and was only just learning how. But rules are rules, she agreed.

Mr. Fortner also abided by the rules. He had lost a world record once because he had failed to comply with International Game Fish Association regulations in one tiny respect: his rod broke while he was fighting the fish and the broken rod's length was less than minimum; it broke at the last moment—"an act of God damn," Mrs. Fortner said, "and I quote"—just before gaffing. Everyone said it was a near thing, and a real pity; just bad luck. Mr. Fortner felt it deeply, though years had passed. A forty-two-pound snook—when would he be that lucky again?

"Four feet long if it was an inch," he grieved, all these years later. He still carried pictures of it, showed them around the way some men show their children's. "But rules are rules," he conceded, and there was nothing to do but try again, just "Keep On Fishin'" as Mrs. Fortner's T-shirt advised.

The Captain did not believe in luck, bad or good. Skill and experience find and land the record fish, he said. He had the reputation among the charter captains to back that up. That was why Mr. Fortner chose him, because the Captain made his own luck, and always good. Two or three times a year Mr. Fortner reserved the Captain and his boat and they went out searching for the world records, because Mr. Fortner wanted his name in the book.

Mrs. Fortner had taken no pleasure in her husband's sporting ambitions until she met the Captain when she came to the dock to pick up her husband. After that she took an interest, began to read articles and books on fishing, and often found a moment to ask the Captain's advice or opinion on this or that piece of equipment, gifts for her husband. "What would a man who could have anything in the world want?" She had decided to go along with Mr. Fortner and his hobby. Really go along; this was her first trip.

She had not been the least bit sick, but she occasionally lost her footing and balance, would falter or brush up against the Captain, and once he had to catch her as she pitched down the companionway into his arms. Sometimes she ignored the Captain, but teased Mr. Fortner when the Captain could not help but see, yet the Captain never seemed to notice, nor Mr. Fortner either. Their minds were on the fishing.

This was Mr. Fortner's second wife, chosen—it might be argued—for her ornamental qualities. She had been in her youth much admired, a hard habit to outlive. She managed it by cutting herself off from her past; that younger self, with the platinum pageboy and the fire batons and tanned skin as smooth as a cabretta glove, was not herself, but her rival—her mother, her child. She disinherited them; she obliterated them. She no longer remembered them or those days. There was this *now*, this here and now, and in it she was in her prime, as young as she'd ever be and as good as she could hope to be, and no better than she ought to be.

When she had seen the Captain for the first time, everything had changed for her. These fishing trips had been so dismal; like a widow she'd wandered around in the shops on shore, had her hair done, her nails sculptured, gathered shells on the beach, dined exquisitely, written postcards, made phone calls. Now she didn't want to be left behind on shore anymore. Once she saw what she was missing, she knew what she was missing as she idly shopped in the village or read magazines in the motel that was more an outpost than a resort—no beauty makeovers, no spa, no pedicure, no jewelry boutique, no portrait painter, no tennis or golf pro shops where she could at least, so to speak, knock the ball around with someone who didn't smell like fish or look like poison.

The whole village seemed to go to work, or somewhere, every day; wherever they were, they had more to do than entertain her. How many times could she read the bulletin board at the library—faded clippings on Cristo somebody or other's World Series victories—was it baseball? soccer?—Mrs. Fortner hated both, and gnats, and bicycling on a rented wheel out to the sugar mill ruins and all these fishing trips of Mr. Fortner's too, oh, she hated them for the way they made her feel useless, pointless, and wasted her precious time. Then she met Vic Rios, and then she took an interest—whether in fishing or in the Captain, it made no difference—truth!—to Mr. Fortner, so long as it didn't interfere with his getting in the record books. Mrs. Fortner wanted to make time? Mr. Fortner wanted to make history. The odds and game for both improved dramatically on the fishing boat *Blue Lady*.

For their tenth anniversary, the Fortners' friends—meaning his, not hers, she'd left hers behind in St. Louis when they married—gave a reception at the church. Madge Keye was saying of her husband, just home after six weeks in the hospital, "One day more might have been too late, but they say now it's up to him. He just lies there with his male ego gone along with everything else they got," and Mr. Fortner agreeing, robustly, "He'll snap out of it, he'll be fine, let me tell you losing your male ego, as you call it, is a toughie," and taking out that pillbox—how could he!—how could he disclose and boast and shame her too!—"just one of these is all I need, but I have to choose—to live or to love. Can't have both . . . Takes a little adjustment, sure does, but the answer is easy. A man just has

to find something to live for. Hobbies . . . fishing . . . something . . ."
Mrs. Fortner walked away, with him in full spate, the vulgar little pillbox
still bright on his palm, shameless. "This little deal is my life," he was
bragging, clicking the lid; "I accept it absodamnlutely."

Mrs. Fortner kept on walking. They'd never miss her, not for a while.
She ducked into the lavatory and considered her face in the mirror, leaning into it under cruel and flickering light, to assess the ravages. She
couldn't help it, she liked what she saw, even though desperation made
her eyes look hard and wild. She unpinned the corsage from her dress
and re-pinned a single flower in her hair. Much better. Sassy. She ran
cold water on her wrists and slowly the scalding shame of her husband's
disclosures—hadn't she always pretended he was the big man, kept the
myth of the home fires going, and now he extinguished it all in one
thoughtless gust—leaving her cold. When the fire had gone from her
cheeks and throat and blood, she opened the bathroom door and went
out, not at all the way she came in. That was the afternoon she turned
the corner.

She ran out the back way, not slinking, but boldly. Smack into Dirk
Thompson's Texas cousin. She liked the down-home way he had, true
western, laughing as she crashed against him, his arms steadying her—
"Easy, darlin' "—till she got her balance. She had very nearly knocked
her breath out in the collision.

"You running to or from?" he wondered.

"From. It's that Christian punch they're serving. You try it? They left
out the main ingredient."

"I've got some Cutty in the car," he offered.

"I'm from Missouri," she said.

"Y'all don't drink scotch?"

"Show me," she explained.

She took paper cups from the water cooler; she didn't intend to drink
out of the bottle like some wino. She let him pour. And pour. Then they
drove around. He was staying at a motel out by the airport. They weren't
gone an hour.

When she got back, she offered no explanations, and the last dread and
scruple went when Mr. Fortner, idly, as they assembled for Polaroid shots
for the church album, fixed the hook and eye at the back of her dress,
saying, "Now smile pretty, Mama." She laughed out loud. It was the best
picture taken all day . . .

Once she knew how to handle her problem, she didn't go on the
prowl. She could afford to let things happen. Mr. Fortner had found his

hobby and regulations to serve, and she developed hers. When she first saw the Captain, she felt the lurch of both adventure and value, the way any collector and connoisseur feels before an object of rare virtu, a masterpiece.

When she asked, "Who is he?" her husband replied, "The best there is."

"I'll take your word for it," she said. It was not her first lie.

Faye's back ached, between her shoulders, as it used to ache while steam-pressing and ironing in her mother's shop. But now it was because she had to lean slightly forward away from the tall man's gun muzzle at the base of her skull. They were in the car now, and she was their hostage. She had refused to go with them, as though it were her choice. Her mother—whose early loss of her family, some by death outright and others by disappearance from the face of the earth as prisoners of war—had always told her, "Struggle. Don't let anyone carry you off . . ." Had told her to live and drive defensively, not to swerve if a deer or a wild boar ran out in the road in front of her. "Or a poodle, or a kitten. Yield to a train or a truck," her mother had told her. For the rest, "Fight."

In those self-defense classes when Faye was sixteen, she and Mrs. Parry had tumbled and tussled and kicked and punched and practiced and laughed. And Faye had gone confidently into the world, driving the delivery van without fear, but not because she knew self-defense tactics; rather because she knew most of the people in her world, and had no enemies. These bank robbers were strangers.

Even so, Faye tried to reason with them, before they tied her hands with her own scarf. Even so she punched and kicked and struggled. She had actually broken free and run, out in the street, but the big one, the one called Mackie, caught her and slapped her down and hauled her back, and a passing car had beeped its horn and the driver had waved, as though this were the usual beachfront hijinks and he approved. Mackie picked her up and carried her bodily to the car, folding her like a jack-knife and shoving her in under the steering wheel; he was the one driving. It was a rusted-out old station wagon that bounced and strove hard through the deepening sand on a narrowing track, nowhere Faye had ever been by accident or on purpose. Out into the noon-stunned marsh, silent and still.

"You missed the causeway," she pointed out. "All these little lanes dead-end, every one of them, at the water. Just for fishing. The ferry doesn't come here anymore."

Mackie laughed. He had strong teeth, long yellow teeth, a wolf's dentition. "Maybe you're lost," he said, and laughed again.

"Here," the other man said, leaning forward, and Mackie swerved the car onto a side path. Catbriers scratched at the fenders. They would have to force the doors open against the thicket; there wasn't room to turn around. Faye knew they weren't going to turn around, weren't going to go back.

"I won't tell," she promised. All the time trying to figure out what to try next, pretending to be calm, feigning candor and friendship, weighing her chances. Her heart was racing. "Just leave me here, who could I tell?" she promised.

"When you get to know me better, you won't mind," Mackie said.

Through the trees, a brightness, low—the river. This was the utter limit of land. The other man, thin as a mantis, slipped out the slightly opened door and took his briefcase with him. Mackie dragged Faye toward him, from under the wheel; he shoved the door wide, with two kicks.

"Let's go," the thin man said.

"End of the line," Mackie agreed.

"Please—"

"Now or later," the thin one called back, not looking around. He headed for the water. There was a boat waiting. Faye followed—what else could she do? If they killed her here, nothing. Her earring snagged on a bramble and she drew up, against the pain. Mackie, on her heels, gave her a push, and as she fell the gold ring tore from her flesh. Bad as that was, it gave her a chance. When Mackie bent to pick up the ring, Faye kicked. She surprised herself. She surprised him. He toppled over on his broad back and she whirled and ran back the way she had come, toward, then past the car, before he got to his feet again, puffing, shambling after. She plunged off that trail into the greenwood, so dense she vanished in a few steps, and there was only the crashing as she flailed through. She planned to run deep in, duck and outwait him, under a log; he would have to leave her, forget about her, because the thin man was already at the boat, revving it, and he had the briefcase.

Faye was so sure this would work. It would have. It very nearly did. Then she tripped over a grapevine as thick as her own wrist, and with her hands bound before her, she could not right herself, but fell facedown in the suffocating loose duff an armadillo had rooted that morning. Breathing hard, Mackie gained on her, caught her, hauled her coughing to her feet, slapping the debris and sand off her hair and face and shoulders untenderly. He had the earring on his thumb, jammed down as far as the first joint, as far as he could force it.

He didn't seem angry.

"You're worth more for trying," he said.

"That's my great-grandmother's earring," Faye told him.

He smiled, studying it. "Used to be," he said. "A little blood on it, don't hurt none." He raised his hand to her—Faye flinched and he laughed, "Don't rare up now"—and he took the other earring from her, then turned toward the river. He walked in front of her this time, with Faye in tow, pulled along by the silk scarf around her wrists. The boat's engine was revving, then stalling, sputtering, then revving again, ready.

"Please," Faye said.

But they had come to the boat, and the thin man was waiting. He looked disgusted with both of them. "I'd have left," he told Mackie, "but I have to kill you first."

Mackie took that as a joke. "You haven't got the guts. That's what I'm for."

"My husband—" Faye bargained.

"Forget about that," Mackie advised, lifting her down into the boat. Her hands were swollen; he couldn't get the wedding ring off her finger. "Later," he decided. With a sharp jerk, he broke the fine chain around her neck and pocketed the crucifix. They were already under way when he toppled her down the companionway below. He took off his belt and choke-collared her to the bunk. Her palms throbbed, wrist to wrist; she couldn't reach her neck to ease the belt; she had to rest slightly against the bulkhead, in a crick. The engine's vibrations tickled in her ears and skullbones. That and the foul air made her cough.

She'd never been a good sailor, and the diesel and fish fumes were already making her sick. She couldn't tell where they headed, except down the sound, against the tide, toward open water. Above, she heard them talking.

"About an hour," the thin man told Mackie.

"I never needed that long," Mackie laughed.

And then he came back down to her, stood by the bunk.

Against her will, she opened her eyes and looked at him. "Now," he said, "that's better. You be nice to me and I'll be nice to you."

Finally she realized it was a question of sorts. She nodded. He pulled the filleting knife from its sheath and cut the binding around her wrists, then sliced through the leather belt, freeing her. She sat up, her back to the wall.

"What's your name, doll?"

On his left arm a tattoo vaunted, "Here's Mine . . . Where's Yours?" above and below a bunch of red cherries. On his right wrist, blurred with a scar, "Bad Co." The knife he had used to cut swiftly through the cowhide lay on the table. She could see it out of the corner of her eye. She didn't move as his hand came toward her, took up her own hand, and turned it over to stare at the wedding ring again.

"Never seen one like it," he said. "You religious? He your first? Posted property, never had any but his?" He touched her face, ran his hands over her hair, smoothing. When she jerked away, he caught her throat in his grip, widening his grasp to encircle, one-handed, both pulses, ear to ear.

"I could kill you, just—like—that," he reminded her. He tightened the grip.

"No, sir," she whispered.

"You don't say no to Mackie," he warned, glancing over his shoulder. He reached for the knife. The tall, thin man still stood with his back to them, driving the boat. All the while, Mackie kept up that gentle killing pressure till Faye was lightheaded. He drew her toward him and she realized the tiny pressure on her ribs was the knife in his other hand, almost casual.

He wanted her to be afraid, he didn't want to hurt her, not yet, he was bluffing. That was what she decided, and that was why she held still, and let him draw her toward him, and seal his sour-mash-stinking mouth over hers.

That was when she caught at his arm, twisted aside, kicked herself free, got both feet on the deck, for leverage, and shoved him away. She thought he would fly backward, hit his head. Fade to black. But this was no movie.

A big, greedy, stupid man so quick! He ducked aside and the blade— his own knife—cut him. Cut but did not, did not kill him. A clean, deep slice through the flesh of that cherry tattoo. When she saw his welling blood, she sobbed, but did not try to help him.

He picked up the knife, stuck it in the bulkhead overhead, out of her reach.

"Too bad," was all he had to say about it. He tied up his hurt arm with a patience and thoroughness that frightened her more than any threat. He was blocking the way out, there *was* no way out. The only other thing she saw to hurt him with was the jagged sardine tin. She snatched it off the cluttered table and aimed it at his face, his eyes, while he was trying to tie his handkerchief around his arm while he was busy frowning, tugging the knot tight with his teeth. She drove the can lid at his eyes, hoping he'd reel away, and let her at the companionway so she could get up on deck.

"Just help me," she called to the tall one, but he didn't.

Mackie caught her arm, squeezed her wrist till she dropped the can lid, and held her at arm's length, out of kicking distance, though she kept trying. He seemed philosophical, like a breaker of horses who expects a certain amount of buck and balk. When he swung her around, he raised his boot, to kick, aiming for her stomach, but in the crowded cabin, unable to reach higher than her thigh. Shoved more than kicked, but still he flattened her, and knocked the breath out of her. When her head hit the deck, she began to scream, a shrill, last-ditch effort to unnerve him. Maybe she did. He hissed, "Shut up," and began to slap her, slap and slap till she lay still and a quiet twilight fell, with a lifeguard's whistle shrilling far off in her head. She lay quiet, listening to her own breath. She didn't want to lose consciousness. Mackie, straddling her, was all she could see in the world. That cleared her head like a whiff of ammonia. She shut her eyes so he couldn't see the will come back.

"That's better," he said, and began to peel out of his greasy jeans. That was when she sat up, so fast, so suddenly she unbalanced him; while he was still getting to his knees, then his feet, she was already across the cabin, catching at the railing, the steps, dragging herself up toward the sky.

He got to her with a lunge, grabbed her ankle in his iron grip, and dragged her back down into hell.

Mrs. Lockridge, his housekeeper, always kept a weather eye on the gate when Father Ockham was due back at St. Francis Xavier's rectory because she didn't intend to be caught drying laundry in the dryer in defiance of what she thought of as His Worship's Clothesline Decree. Of course she pegged his sheets out there in the salt air and sun, no way to fake that line-dried fragrance, but the rest—every towel, sock, hanky, collar, nightshirt, and Fruit Of The Loom went slyly through the forbidden rites of Maytag.

"What he doesn't know won't hurt me," Mrs. Lockridge had discovered. The dryer was so much easier! If she had her druthers, the clothesline—he cheerily called it "God's solar appliance"—would be converted into a grape arbor and she'd never have to lug another clothes basket down and up those seven back steps again. But Father Ockham, as he'd said more than once, was a good steward, and had been waging the moral equivalent of war on the power company since 1973, the year the parish installed central air. The priest had the old-fashioned idea that an indulgence, such as enjoying a heavenly indoor climate when outdoors it was infernally hot and humid, needs to be paid for with sacrifice if not mortification. Mrs. Lockridge had no quarrel with Father Ockham's spiritual or household budget and conscience so long as it wasn't at the expense of her varicose veins.

"Here comes Hell on Wheels now," she cried, hanging up the phone abruptly, no lingering farewells. Her cronies were used to it and to her; she'd get back to them later, and resume the conversation in good time, without a dropped stitch. For now, she knew from long experience exactly which jalousie to peer through to catch the whole show as the Father veered off the road, steered stiffly between the two gateposts, and aimed the purpling black Plymouth up the rise toward the rectory, three balding tires and one new recap spattering gravelly coquina as he braked, just in time, or almost, to avoid ramming the back fence. The chain link—he'd made a good impression on it over the years—welcomed the car with a perfect fit.

Usually he'd sit there, gathering the papers his panic stops all over town had scattered onto the floorboard. For Christmas, friends had bought him a briefcase—a fine piece of Samsonite—but he didn't carry it. Truth was, he'd accidentally locked it the first day and with both keys and the combination safe inside, the case lay void and impregnable under the knee-hole of his cluttered desk. He used it for a footrest instead, and thereby had some good of it. It was a fixture; he'd miss it if it were gone into more active service, but because he feared he might appear ungrateful if he didn't carry the briefcase (and he wouldn't carry the locked empty one—that would be hypocrisy—since he intended to secretly replace it and thus cover for his mistake), they were always teasing him for being unmechanical. But when he had priced a replacement on a diocesan business trip to St. Augustine during Lent, he was stunned, and felt guilty for all the good that much money could have done for charity. Or the Rotisserie League.

Sometimes he horrified himself at the things he did. This time, he did without. He didn't replace the attaché case. And what he saved thus seemed to be real, in hand, and not merely spared from the budget. He invested the "saved" money—that amount, as though it were actually an earning or windfall—in the baseball pool. He couldn't help himself, and besides, he had a hunch—the Cubs in the Series, in seven. Because of Cristo Montevidez, their ace pitcher, who was a member of his congregation, Father Ockham considered his bets an investment, not a risk. Anything he won would go to the youth activity fund, so he honestly felt he had been fair—not to replace the briefcase seemed a penance, and the money saved really felt like a windfall. But still, because it was not strictly charity—though certainly it involved faith and hope to back the Cubs as early as spring training—he left off going to the barber. That saved some more.

With the help of cuticle scissors and a Good News razor, he cut his own hair.

"More than a hundred dollars a year," he explained to Mrs. Lockridge as she stripped the cover off a Band-Aid and applied it to the accidental tonsure on the back of his skull where he'd shaved too close for comfort.

She really thought nothing he'd do would ever again surprise her, but he always proved her wrong. As on the evening he began wearing the surgical rubber glove as a nightcap to relieve his blood-pressure headache. She had to laugh. "You look like a crestfallen rooster," she told him. "And you're going to get gangrene of the brain if you don't take that thing off." Still, she didn't believe, as some did, that Father Ockham was "losing it." She made sure he took his medications; after that, if he felt like climbing up on the globe stand—so far he hadn't—and crowing, let him. "Whatever floats your boat" was her motto.

This time, though, when Father Ockham drove in, he scared her. He plunged the car as usual against the chain link, but he didn't pause to gather the scattered papers off the floor of the car. Instead, he instantly flung open the Plymouth's door and lurched out, disappearing from view as though he had fallen down a well. Mrs. Lockridge was thinking *stroke* as she sprinted across the kitchen to the sink window to see where he was, the emergency number already running through her memory, but he wasn't down, at least not fallen, as she expected to find him; he had been crouching—crouching?—and suddenly jerked upright again, both hands full of scrabbled gravels, which he began heaving—without windup or follow-through—into the garden at one of the neighbor's cats, whose trespasses weren't forgiven.

Stone after stone flew.

The cat trotted out of range and sat mildly watching as Father Ockham's face got redder and redder. Mrs. Lockridge forgot all about the laundry, left the dryer door open and a telltale sock hanging out. She ran to the side door to warn:

"Your nose!"

Too late.

The old priest had a nosebleed with more suddenness and generosity than he did most things. Mrs. Lockridge grabbed a dish towel and ran out. "Let me help!"

He did. He took the towel and gave her the remaining ammunition, advising her on elevation and windage. She had a strong right arm and came close a couple of times, close enough to drive the cat farther away. It finally turned tail and ran at the back fence, hit it running, with a bright *ching!* was up and over the top and in the other yard, unscathed.

Only then did the pastor allow Mrs. Lockridge to support him into the house. She grabbed a clean handkerchief from the dryer and kicked its door shut as they passed down the hall to his room. She didn't waste time unlacing his shoes, just shoved him flat on the bed, whisking the pillows out from under his head, pressing the clean cloth to his face, and sliding the morning paper under his feet to keep the coverlet clean.

"This doesn't count," he said, as though records were being kept against him. "I've always had nosebleeds."

In the time it took her to fill the icebag—not long, she had had experience—and bring it back to him, he was sitting tentatively up on the side of the bed, both hands on the sports section, lost in the news. He took the icebag and absently laid it atop his head.

"Father?" she said softly. Then, more alarmed, as he began twisting around and slapping at himself, twitching and lurching inside his clothes, "Father!" She hesitated then moved toward him. "What's wrong?"

He gave a cry of triumph and despair. "Found it, I hadn't lost it," he said pointedly. He offered her an envelope from his inside pocket.

She didn't reach for it, just stood staring at the chancery seal. Finally she waved it away. "Just tell me in so many words," she said. "I'm saving my eyes."

"It says Xavier parish is to welcome Mark Grattan here before Christmas."

"Who's he?"

Father Ockham reread the letter, folded it, and laid it on the bed. "My new assistant," he said. He looked beat.

Mrs. Lockridge crossed her arms, gripped her elbows, considering. For weeks they had been dreading such a thing, for months knowing it might be necessary, but now it had come, it was a blow to pride. "It's not Al Hammer's disease," he kept insisting, but it was true that Father Ockham's health had wavered recently; in the summer his head had shimmered with a recurrence of an old fever contracted in the tropics half a century before. His memory lost its place in time, and he had forgotten the intervening years. Vatican II wasn't all that slipped his mind. He was, in his head, young again. Had celebrated the Mass in Latin, invoked Saint Patrick, and tried to evict "that wild-eyed old man" he found in his room at night—wouldn't stay in the same room with him, finally wouldn't stay in the house at all, began to sleep on the screen porch. Mrs. Lockridge figured it out, and hung a towel over the mirrors, thus hiding Father Ockham's grizzled features from himself. He came back inside then, and slept in his own bed, fitfully, feverishly, for two weeks till his malaria cooled again and he was almost his old stout-as-an-oak self. But in the interim, the Bishop had heard, and come and seen, and perfected his plans.

"It's no shame," he reminded Father Ockham. "Even Jesus Christ needed help to haul his nets."

"Maybe," Mrs. Lockridge prayed of the new man, "he won't be young [meaning what she called "political"] or vegetarian [meaning that Father Ockham's low-salt, no-cholesterol, high-fiber, reduced-lactose diet was a god's-plenty to bother with] or a chain smoker." The old priest's occasional and forbidden pipes were always a peril to the drapes and Naugahyde.

"He damn well better," Father Ockham specified, "be a Cubs fan."

Mrs. Lockridge went to answer the phone. When she came back, before she could say what, the priest, working earnestly at his luncheon on the tilting tray on his lap, muttered, "Can it wait?" But the look on her face startled him. He put down his spoon and set the tray and the icebag aside. "Tell me."

"It's Tom Rios," she said. "He said to tell you Vic's wife has been taken hostage in a bank robbery. He wants you to be the one to tell her mother."

Faye fell to the deck in slow motion. It took forever for this part to end. "Hold still," he warned as he cut her out of her clothes, the blade cool against her belly. "You won't be needing these," he said, and she knew rape wasn't the last thing. She knew he intended to kill. That was next, when he had done with her. It meant something to him to know he was disgusting her now, hurting her, terrorizing her, it was why he did it, why he kept his eyes on her face, as he labored over her, his good arm corded and trembling, the point of the knife at her throat. She stared up past him to the square of sky framed by the hatch, waiting for it to be over, this now, waiting for the next thing, her next chance, her last chance.

When he rolled off her, she scrambled away from him at once, made it to the companionway ladder and up it rung by rung once again, into the light. Wasted valuable seconds at the rail being sick. It surprised her very much when she heard a laugh, and she turned to see the tall man step down from the wheel, complaining, "I thought you two'd kill each other off and save me the time."

He took the pistol from his belt and flipped the safety off. It looked like the Captain's gun, a blue steel automatic. He pulled the slide back and cocked it. His back was turned so he couldn't actually see Mackie, but they both heard him clumsily climbing, one arm useless to haul himself up with, the other hand gripping the knife. "She's mine," Mackie reminded him, finally topside.

"Your time's up," was all the other man said, and turned and fired. Faye watched the news—that these were his last breaths—slowly spread across Mackie's shirtfront. A last thought—impulse—determination—inspired Mackie, and he raised the knife, but the dark was already in his eyes. He fell at Faye's feet, still reaching for her. He seemed to grin, and his breathing stopped.

The tall man said, "Ol' boy never took one thing seriously, not even death threats." He stepped lightly across and eased Mackie's body overboard—an arm, a leg, torso, one last glimpse of his rundown bootsole as his dead weight dropped like a cut anchor.

"A few words of advice," the tall man told Faye then, pocketing the pistol. "You women all handle a knife like you were cutting cake for company. Thing is, you need to remember to cut *up*, you get a lot more out of it," he explained, gesturing with his hand in the air. "Like you're zipping up a jacket." The wind tousled his hair like flames. "Rip 'em *up*, now, remember that next time." His eyes crinkled, almost twinkled. He was close enough now to lay his cool, dry hand on Faye's burning bare back; she was turned away, all she could do for modesty's sake.

"I won't kill you," he told her when she flinched. "Not a nice lady like you. 'Course, nobody lives forever. Right?"

She jerked away from him but he caught her hands and bent her toward the sea. The rail was sun-hot. "Look," he said, pointing at the water.

A trick.

While she was looking where he had pointed, he brought the gun up, and clubbed her with it. A shadow alerted her; she ducked aside, took the blow on her temple and cheek. Her knees buckled and she caught hold of the rail. His laugh was like a cough. "You can swim, can't you?"

He shook his head, looking around. "No life preservers. We're in violation. Guess you're on your own." He was stronger than he looked. He looked frail, as gaunt as a mantis, but also like a mantis, strong. As courteous as an usher in church, he helped Faye overboard, backwards, because she had turned to struggle.

She sank, rising to hear his final advice: "Mackie's bloody, he'll draw sharks. Best stay clear of him."

He mounted the bridge and took the wheel again, gunning the boat, easing into a wide arc, and churning out over the deep blue toward sundown. On course for Mexico, maybe. Faye treaded water and watched him go. She paddled around, full circle. There was no land in sight. Miles of water in every direction and night coming on. Her endurance and instincts having been until this day untested in so many things, Faye now determined, as best she could, the position nearest to land, and set off swimming toward it, toward home, strong at first, too strong, putting into it too much of what she had left, in her eagerness. She would do what her mother had always said she should do: what it took.

The water made her feel cleaner.

She tried not to think about Mackie, about what his murderer had said about the sharks. She didn't want to run into him again ever, ever. The sharks could have him. They'd find him. Let them find him, not her. That was her prayer, the only prayer at Mackie's requiem. She gave a little cry as she remembered the earrings and cross, lost now, deep in his drowned pockets. In her vexation she faltered in her strokes, began to sink, took on salt water, a great gulp of it, and gave it right back up again, retching and retching as she thought how that water had Mackie's blood in it.

She had to cast him out of her thoughts, never think of him again— and the panic passed. She tried counting to steady her mind, she counted and breathed and stroked and counted and breathed and stroked, and in a few minutes she had a pattern, a routine her will could serve.

She gave no thought to time, pointless to keep looking at the sun as it headed on toward down. She knew she would be there in the dark, and she did not fear it, for she truly believed that every stroke was taking her that much nearer home. She had to believe that, to do what she could and all she could, for as long as it took. It was her obligation to hope, a sin not to hope. She could almost hear Father Ockham saying, "God does not ask the impossible, only the reasonable."

Faye didn't reason, she imagined: she was walking on the island, and it was good weather, a lovely evening, and she was walking down past the old sugar mill ruins; the little fox red owl in the chimney turned and looked at her as she passed down the avenue of plantation oaks, and the deer grazing in the grassy middles bounded just off to the edge of the dark woods as she passed; in an hour of strolling she would curve back home by the river road, down to their own dock where the gray heron stood fishing, and she would stand there too, and watch for the Captain's launch. If it was a land breeze instead of a sea breeze, she'd not hear the motor at all till he was almost there, so she would have to watch very carefully for the lights. Sometimes she stared so hard it seemed to her the dock itself was in motion, and receding, and leaving the shore farther and farther behind. But that was just a trick of the mind.

    Out in the Stream, the Fortners were quarreling like tired children over weights and regulations. Mrs. Fortner had disqualified herself from the record book by requiring help in playing and landing her day's big fish. She had called for help, hoping the Captain would himself come to her aid, but he sent Danny instead. A teenager, but strong. He would have assisted, but she stood back, let him do it all. She already knew this wasn't the trip when she'd land a world-record fish, or the Captain either, but she had caught the largest fish of anyone on the trip, and that was the bet she'd made with Mr. Fortner, so it looked as though she was going to win.

Then Mr. Fortner hooked a fourteen-foot hammerhead. Not a world record either, but larger than Mrs. Fortner's fish, and this was no tournament. Mrs. Fortner had wanted to come fishing; this was for her. He couldn't have stood it if it mattered, but it didn't, they weren't out far enough for anything special, though you never know, but anyway he'd won. When the mate raised the club to kill the shark, she looked away.

When they winched it up off the deck and hung it for all to abhor and triumph over, Mrs. Fortner said, "Very well, but a shark isn't a fish, not really, not scientifically, is it, Captain?" The same argument she had used against her tadpoles.

Silence. Everyone waited while the Captain considered her appeal. Mr. Fortner looked annoyed. He knew that the others held it against him, to let a woman like that aboard a serious fishing vessel. Might as well let her stand in the tower of a forty-one-foot Rybovich yacht during the bluefin tourney and blow bubbles from a pipe.

"I mean biologically," Mrs. Fortner pressed. She still thought it was amusing, still thought she was being charming. Thought she was fighting with Mr. Fortner the way he had fought the shark—for sport.

"Goddammit, Marnie," Mr. Fortner said.

"Let the Captain decide. That's what he's Captain for." She moved to his side, steadying herself against the swell with a hand on his arm.

"You should have stated any exceptions—biological or otherwise— when you made your bet," the Captain said. As though it were nothing to him. "A shark is a fish and isn't a fish, depending on how you feel about cartilage. Robins and Ray list it in their book, along with lampreys and hags." He shrugged.

"Hags," Mr. Fortner said. He slumped in his fighting chair, still catching his breath, still proud, flexing his hands where the shark's struggle against death had scourged blisters. "It sure as hell ain't a mammal, Mama," he said. He took a sip of his drink, squandering his two-ounce-a-day allowance.

Mrs. Fortner pushed her sunglasses up onto the top of her head. "I want to see that book," she said.

"Some folks claim the mullet's a chicken," Mr. Fortner went on, "just because it has a gizzard." He felt fine. He didn't care what his wife thought or did; he had his shark, and it was bigger than any fish she had caught. What difference if a shark's spine was soft instead of bony? "She reads too damn many *Geographics*," Mr. Fortner said.

Mrs. Fortner studied the book. "They eat shipwreck survivors," she said, turning to stare at the shark.

Mr. Fortner laughed. "How's that for luck?"

The sunlight was so strong, and reflected off the water too; Mrs. Fortner hadn't brought her reading glasses and was having to squint, and squinting wasn't pretty. She handed the book back and settled into a sweet sulk. She knew how to do that so it looked cute. Even if the whole trip hadn't gone her way, it had been worth it. Just when the ocean—its blue and green swells and the whole arch of heaven over them—began to seem boring, the arguing had begun to interest her. Even if the fishing was over for a while, they could talk about it.

Mr. Fortner's shark swung on its chain, the merciless eyes filming over as they dried. The animal seemed to have died disillusioned. As the *Blue Lady* rocked gently, the corpse swung on its chain so they could see all sides of him, so that his fearsomeness was diminished by the authority of the afternoon sunlight and the chance deed of death. Mrs. Fortner reached her red-lacquered fingertip toward the shark's belly and tested its texture.

"Sharkskin," she murmured, as though contemplating some amazing upholstery project when they returned home. "All right," she conceded—as though it were up to her!—"Call it a fish."

Just then the Captain felt Zeb Leonard's dark hand on his sleeve and Zeb said, "Cap'n," in a way that made him scowl, for although he liked to be called Captain, he did not like bad news, and that was how Zeb Leonard said "Cap'n," as though there were terrible news.

He went below and Zeb followed. Mr. and Mrs. Fortner stood for a moment reconciled, shoulder to shoulder in front of the dead shark, and Danny, the deck hand, took their photograph. Then the shark would have to go on ice, for safekeeping.

"The needle's not in the red, is it?" Mr. Fortner wanted to know, for it was his camera, and new, the very best, practically foolproof if you loaded it correctly and made sure that the needle wasn't in the red when you shot. Therefore Mr. Fortner asked it again, asked Danny the same question he'd ask himself, for that was all there was to it, as the salesman had explained, all you had to remember to get it right—fresh film, good batteries, and the needle not in the red. That was it. "All life should be so simple," Mrs. Fortner said, and Danny said, "Yes, ma'am," and then, "No, sir, not in the red," and the shutter made its satisfying flutterbuzz, quick as a wink, because the sun was so bright off the water. Then Mr. Fortner called out, "Just one more, just in case," and he had Mrs.

Fortner step aside out of the picture so it would be him alone with the shark, and Danny wasn't sure, so he suggested, "One more, for luck!" and again Mr. Fortner held still and proud while the shark swung slowly on the chain, too slowly to ruin the picture.

Below decks, the Captain picked up the radiotelephone receiver and said, "Sanavere Station, this is *Blue Lady* Flag Lima 5555 Victor Romeo—" and he listened, without saying another word while he heard about Faye and the robbery of the village bank.

Finally the Captain said, "So she's missing, she's not dead," and Zeb, standing by to be of any assistance, averted his eyes from the sudden quiet tension on the Captain's face, but there it was again, reflected back at him from the mirror over the little bar. Zeb went out and drew the curtain behind him as the Captain was specifying, yet again, "So you say she's missing, you don't say she's dead," as though a man could live with that, as though that were the sort of bad news a man could just bear to hear. But no more than that; no.

It seemed to Faye that she had been swimming forever in that twilight, as though her whole life had been spent never arriving at the unknown shore. No consequences, no continuity between her past and future, no landmarks at all. The moon, like her hopes, waned and set. Her eyes blurred and burned. She was cold. A tiny dot of light—she had been swimming toward it forever—probed out at her white and red, white and red, several times a minute, from the dark, from the land she could not reach, the beacon—visible fifteen miles in normal conditions (she racked her brain trying to recall the Captain's Light List) unplaceable. She did not know where it was, but no matter. She stroked strongly, counting, breathing, stroking, sobbing, but drew no nearer. She reckoned she made slight headway for a while, but now was barely holding her own against the tide.

Surely it was not fifteen miles, no. And how normal were these conditions? All she knew was that the tide would turn. It had to, it always had. She stroked three times, then rested on her back; three strokes, then rest. Now she increased the interval between rests to five strokes, but she could see she was losing ground.

She was numb. She gauged her remaining strength and wagered it against the tide tables she'd read in the morning's paper. Were they accurate for this shore? She didn't know how to adjust them, and had no watch anyway, no idea how to read the sky and stars. From time to time she bumped into things—or felt things slither past or nip, just tiny trial tastes—and she faltered, losing her rhythm, to struggle clear. If this were a movie, she thought, it would be near the end, and there'd be brave music, time lapse, and triumph. "Reality," Mackie had said to her in the bank. She heard it now in her mind, and it was so real she turned to see. She couldn't go on.

Resting on her back, just floating, she lay for minutes, unwilling to ease over again and face the water and keep swimming. She heard voices calling to her, down beneath the water. It was warmer under the surface, out of the wind. The voices promised warmth and surcease. She could feel the warmth around her feet, like sunlight. She longed for it, prepared to dive down into it, where the bright fish played and wonderful shells rolled, waiting. Death had her by the ankles, as warm as blood. Death had caught her ear, lulling her toward sleep.

Through her drowsiness another voice—her mother's—shrill as a gull: "Faye!" The voice her mother used to rouse her from dreams so she would not be late for school. Faye's heart pounded, and she lurched upright in the water, as though she had been caught in a crime. She began to swim again, still numb, but afraid now, afraid as she had not been before, that death would find the weak place in her, and win. It was so unfair. It made her angry! It called up the last strength in her in a surge, and she stroked faster, not resting at all.

At first she didn't notice when the breeze swept the scent of mangroves off the land and over her, as strong as sulfur. When she finally paused, exhausted, treading, openmouthed, the water running warm from her ears and trickling down her cheeks like tears, she heard the quiet surf on the shoals and acknowledged the distant boom of breakers.

In her joy she began stroking wildly, crazily; she had forgotten how to swim. Now her calf muscle cramped, then her foot. She caught at her toes, bending them back, almost breaking them to ease the pain. The spasm relented. Now she made herself count—five strokes, pause, five strokes, pause—every stroke perfect, to lose nothing of what she had left. Something large, heavy, sodden, brushed her arm. Shuddering away from it, thinking for a moment it was Mackie, she beat at it blindly, tangling in wrack. It was a log, a palm trunk. She caught hold, and hugged, letting herself float without effort, and rested.

Taking her bearings now, she could see that the beacon light, which had been on the horizon, now stood clearly above it. It flashed on her left, but now, despite all her efforts, the rip current was dragging her past it downshore. It was already well to her right.

"It's not going to be like that!" she sobbed, and raised her arm in protest. A man-o'-war stung her. She clung to the palm log, weeping. Ducked under it to come up on the other side, away from the jellyfish. When the wonderful thing happened, she didn't understand it; her feet brushed something and she recoiled, then slowly extended one foot downward—the toes, full-stretched, her chin just on the water—and touched sand. She bobbed, letting go the log, and felt firm ground underfoot. Bounce-walking, her chin, her neck, then her shoulders rose from the sea as she walked along the ridge that the ebbing tide was exposing. The breeze struck her wet skin like frost. She stood on a sandbar, shivering, exulting. She had made it!

She had only to cast herself toward shore, a few hundred yards more, floating, almost wading. "I'm safe as a coconut," she rejoiced, and as the beacon probed across the night toward her, she held both arms aloft in triumph. The diamonds on her wedding ring scintillated minutely into the void, like fallen stars.

The *Blue Lady* put hard about as soon as the Captain got the news from the FBI. He did not tell the Fortners why he was heading in, or why it required such speed. He did not mention Faye at all. He gave them some other reason—any reason would do, he was Captain—weather or some such excuse, not the real reason, which to him was a terribly private matter.

There were clouds massing, thunderheads, but they seemed to be flowing away from them. The Fortners grumbled like children called away from a pleasant game just at bedtime, but Mrs. Fortner wasn't really sorry to return to port early, and Mr. Fortner did have his shark.

It was dark before the *Blue Lady* drew in to its moorings.

Mrs. Fortner, still barefoot, carried her silly shoes till she was safely ashore. She wasn't barefoot for fear of falling from their height, but rather because the Captain had made what she thought of as An Issue of them. She stood now, balancing on one foot on the concrete pier, trying to strap them back on.

"Do you mind?" she asked the dockhand who had taken the tossed cable and tied the boat up. She had dismissed him with one look, but now she put her hand out to him, almost absently, to steady herself. He said, "Crissake, hurry up." She stared at him, but couldn't make out anything that gave him the privilege of talking to her like that. Without her glasses, and in the uneven light, she couldn't manage to buckle the straps on her sandals, but I'll be damned if I hurry now, she decided.

Perhaps he read her mind, perhaps that was it, but suddenly he knelt and fixed them for her, first the left, then the right. She looked down on him, on the top of his dark hair silvered by the dock lights. He was swift, his hands used to unknotting things, making things right.

"Teak decks," she explained to him, now that he was at her service.

"Yeah."

The Captain had said to her, "These decks are teak," first remark he made as she boarded. She had smiled and glanced down, not understanding what he was getting at.

"I bet they cost a fortune," she agreed.

Mr. Fortner had laughed, and the Captain had appealed to him with a glance, man to man, but Mr. Fortner, who saw no reason for beauty to be wise, had merely shrugged. "Can't tell her anything," he laughed, denying any responsibility. "Just lay it out to her in basic English."

So the Captain had asked her, "Didn't you bring deck shoes?"

She hadn't.

Then he had told her either the high heels must go, or she would have to. He left it entirely up to her.

After a minute of sulk and bluster—she had given him time to take the shoes off her feet and fling them overboard if he intended to, it seemed worth trying for—she had taken them off, descending from their stilting height to the flat deck, saying for Mr. Fortner or anyone's benefit, tossing her head so her thick hair swung, "If you talked to me like that, you'd get what you deserve!" and Mr. Fortner had sighed from long experience and said, "No, I wouldn't," and everybody had laughed. She had laughed too, and soon they had headed out into deep water, in high spirits.

Ashore again, buckled onto those wooden platforms, restored to her accustomed height and hauteur, she regained charge of her life, giving—not taking—orders, bestowing her various luggage on Danny and the other hands, directing them to their car in the municipal lot. Only Danny went. When he returned for another load, shortcutting across the seedy lawn to the pier, Mrs. Fortner said to her husband, who joined her now from the lockers, in a last little tableau of farewell-and-see-you-soon,

"Thank the boys, Herbert," for her husband was an absentminded tipper. She leaned to his ear and whispered how much, for she knew, if anyone did, what a man is worth. Danny took his without embarrassment, but the other man, who had buckled her shoes for her, scowled, "What's this for?" and shoved it back, saying, "I don't work here."

Then the Captain swung ashore. To that insolent hand, he said, "Tom?"

"*No hay de nuevo,*" the man replied. "Nothing new." After that, neither of them spoke. The Captain had brought his blazer ashore, and drew it on as he stood there. One of the monogrammed buttons dangled by a thread. Mrs. Fortner, who always managed one last look, one last word, put out her hand to that dangling button and teased, "Why, you'd think he had no wife!" and plucked the button like a ripe berry and dropped it in his pocket and settled it with a proprietary pat. The button clinked on something metal, and when Mrs. Fortner gave the pocket a pat, she felt the outline of a pistol.

"Why, Captain," she said.

"She's not dead," he answered sharply. His remark dropped inexplicably, snuffing out the bright little goodbye that Mrs. Fortner had been currying up for show. His dark mood was so obvious, it silenced her. She stepped back, more surprised than offended.

Tom had his keys out, rattling them against his jeans leg.

"We're gone," he told Danny when he drove the Fortners' car up.

"Next time," the Captain promised the Fortners, a traditional parting phrase.

The Captain and Tom got in an old truck and Tom drove them out of the lot, fast. The Captain never looked back.

"He wouldn't work for me long," Mrs. Fortner said, "unless he learned some basic manners."

"Tom?" Danny shook his head. "He don't work for him, that's the Captain's brother."

"They don't favor—" she began, interrupted by Zeb, running down the gangway to Danny, with a look on his face.

"Wait!" he called, but Tom's truck didn't stop. Zeb just stood there watching it go. "Take it easy, man," he said. A prayer. He knew what it was to love a woman, to have a wife you'd break bones for, yours or anyone else's. He knew too that the Captain had papers for the gun, but not for carrying concealed.

Danny was wondering about that gun. He waited till the Fortners had gone to ask, "He take it?"

"Nobody live by the rules anymore," Zeb said.

"I'd lay in a ditch if I had to. I'd find 'em," Danny said.

"What man wouldn't mean it?" Zeb agreed. "But you better give the Law first chance. FBI don't miss many."

At the nearby ice house, someone heaved a crate of stone crabs onto the scale and dumped them. They rattled like thunder, like bones. Whoever it was tossed the empty crate out into the dark on the heap, broken. Someone would fix it. There's a whole enterprise in mending.

Faye knelt on the beach, finally ashore. Knelt not in jubilation, but in exhaustion. The tide surge on the last full moon had cut hard terraces into the beach, perfect bleachers. She took a place in the front row, well behind mean waterline, higher than sea level for the first time in hours. Her thoughts cleared. She moved her head around, tilting, to try to empty the canals of her ears. She felt deaf. "I," she said in her own voice, unsure of the pitch.

She was hungry, not starving. Parched. She idly licked the salt off her hands, her lips. Her hair was as tangled as wrack, strange-textured, clammy, coarsened, rubbery as she wrung it out; she wondered if there were bits of shell in it, or trapped fish. She took inventory and gave thanks. She was alive, not just barely alive, though she was bare. Certainly she was bare. She did not know a thing to do about that, either, except to be glad it was night. But the night was more horrifying, because she must wade through it without shoes. Everywhere her mind turned, something unthinkable lurked. Things sang and shrieked and scuttled on all sides. Was this an island? Was there a bridge? Was there any habitation near? If a government range, were there security devices? Was it merely a wildlife preserve with no roads or traffic? Every pulse pounded with the irrefutable logic of the survivor: there is no fate worse than death.

She stood stiffly up and began walking. After staggering, she righted, and ratcheted on.

There was just enough light to detect the scurry and furtive commerce of nocturnal crabs. Downwind, a raccoon, paddling in the surf, turned and stared. Ahead of her, a heron battled into the wind, slowly lofting, circling out over the water to land behind her. She thought she heard the bird's wings, then realized, far off—a helicopter was chopping along.

Coming her way? Frantic, she scanned the sky till she picked up the little lights blinking.

Then she ran, shouting. The run, wasteful; the call, futile. Her feet prey to every sharp shell and burr. She staggered down to the water's edge, then back up the hard sand to the soft dune edge, lurching along crying, "I'm here! Here I am!" but the helicopter, on routine patrol, never slowed. She faltered, slowly gave up, dragging herself coughing up the dunes and over their top into the lee. At once she knew she'd done the right thing: the surf roar was muted and the wind ceased. She lay back, gasping, almost warm. Almost asleep.

Should she sleep? Could she sleep? She was already asleep. An hour passed, a second hour, before she stirred. She came to herself slowly; she didn't know where she was, then she knew that she didn't know where she was.

What if she had overslept her last chance, the one chance, whatever it might be? She forced herself to rouse, to sit, to stand guard.

Footsteps. She thought she heard footsteps, slow, clumsy. She held her breath. Whatever it was, it wasn't human. Snorting, clumsy, it trundled on by, hastening a little when it caught her scent. Armadillo, perhaps, or possum.

She felt strong enough to walk. Setting off, she listened, to the point of delirium, for footsteps—that slow animal's return, or other wild things making a living in the night. She breathed as quietly as she could, to hear beyond herself. She walked softly, trying not to dread where her feet might step.

In a sudden gust, the wind rattled the oaks, the oleanders, tousled the bay trees, shivered the myrtles, shook the oats and grasses and vines. It was like traffic, like a squadron of jets or a train. She crouched, head on her knees, hands over her ears. When the gust passed, the noise went on. She looked up, around. Not the same noise, a different noise, a traffic noise, rubber tires on a paved road, a solitary vehicle, going fast. She tried to fix the location, began running toward it, tripping, tumbling into the yaupons, screaming, scrambling up, torn like floss in a gin.

Where was that road?

Deep in the scrub, a lorn bird complained as she thrashed by. Under the trees, there was not enough moon to guide by; it seemed to her pitch dark. She ran toward a faint gray line, a break in the cover. Didn't look down, didn't see the ditch full of black water. It rose up and smacked her in the face. Not drowning depth; she pushed herself up on hands and knees and listened.

All her life she had lived near the marshes and beach, played in the surf, cherished the trees and birds and moody weather. She felt absolutely alien now, as vulnerable and wild as some lost household pet. Schoolroom maps and family picnics hadn't prepared her for a sudden detour cross-country, guided by folly and nerve. Faye didn't know how she was going to live, but she knew she was going to. She splashed upright, listening. Cupping her ears. Nothing. The vehicle must have passed and gone while she was thrashing around in the ditch; she never heard it again. She crawled out, shuddering at her handholds on slimy plants, trying not to think of snakes and God knew what else in the murk around her. By the time she once again stood on dry land, she had her priorities straight: first deliverance, then salvation. That was her agenda. Behind her the reeds swung and settled, curtaining off the scummy slough.

Silence.

She couldn't do anything but listen, harking for some clue. "There was one, there'll be another," she reasoned. Mosquitoes settled on her flesh, as silent as snow, as thick as fur. She squatted and scooped up handfuls of mud and smeared it on her body; that partially worked. Outrunning them, her next ploy, didn't. They swirled around her in clouds, singing one song. She breathed them in and coughed them out. Frenzied, she didn't notice she had come out onto an unpaved road, hardly more than a sandy track with grass in the middle. She bent and felt it with her hands, to be sure it was true; the sand was pale enough to stand out dim in the starlight: a road offered the promise of destination. It had to begin somewhere and go somewhere. She reckoned as best she could that it ran roughly north-south. She chose arbitrarily—north—counting her steps.

After about ten minutes, as she guessed it, she came to real pavement—a crossroads—and turned eastward, she thought. Not long after, she came across a roadkill, still warm, not yet defaced by carrion eaters. Cheered, for that meant traffic had recently passed, she kept on walking. The road surface was a smooth macadam, not tar and gravel. Easy on her raw feet.

If she fell, she got up. Always she kept the same stars over one shoulder. When she felt something crawling on her leg, she slapped it; surprised, she drew back a bloody hand. She didn't even know when she had cut her knee, but it was her own blood, and the flap of skin wouldn't stick in place. She let it hang, and walked on, a little lopsided now, because she had to reach and wipe the insects away from the bloody gash.

The next time she stopped to rest, she felt, before she heard, a slight vibration, a tingle in her tenderized soles. No energy to waste on any more false hope, she waited, straining to hear or see. Cupped her ears, scanned left to right, uproad and down. And the sky. But she didn't want a plane now. She wanted four wheels and headlights.

"Please," she prayed. "Please."

The FBI agent told the Captain, yet again, "We don't believe it's a matter of ransom, sir," preparing him for the possibility that "no further contact"—as they put it—would be made. He explained the Bureau's four categories of "missing" adults: "endangered," "involuntary," "disability," and "catastrophe." Big words; little hope. And the Captain said, as though money were all that would be necessary, and that he'd sack the world for enough, "I'll pay whatever it takes."

"It is increasingly unlikely that—" the agent began to explain, but Tom, sprawling on the other end of the ratty leatherette couch, growled through the puff of blue smoke from his pipe, "Too soon to haul that net, man."

The lawman, the brothers Rios, the old priest dozing in the other chair, they were the four in the temporary and shabby headquarters. On the borrowed desk, Faye's wedding snapshot lay smiling. Its silver frame stood empty on Mrs. Parry's sideboard.

From time to time as he paced, the Captain's prowling, restless glance sought Faye's face among the official debris on the cluttered desktop, then he'd look away at any other thing instead, light another cigarillo from the leather case in his pocket, and check his fine watch against the clock on the wall, a generous civic dial with emphatic numerals. It got later and later on the wall, though time seemed to have stopped. The second hand clicked forward with an electronic economy rather than swept; it sounded as though it were dryly kissing the seconds good-bye.

The hours wore on, going nowhere, never mounting up.

The phone rang again. All along it had wrung their nerves, tested their poise and pulse. The FBI man jumped to answer it as Father Ockham flailed awake, crying out to prevent the worst, "Godalmighty no!" The agent shook his head—no news—and turned his back to them, sat on the corner of the desk, chatting low into the receiver. There was another line open. The agent played with the phone cord; behind him, it tap-tapped across Faye's serene and shining eyes, her honeymoon smile.

"Goddammit," the Captain exploded. "That's mine."

The agent turned, startled, and took the photograph from the Captain and laid it down again. "You'll get it back. Cherry condition," he assured him. "Our word on it." He was still on the phone, trying to concentrate on the call. He waved the Captain away.

Tom got to his feet and laid his hand on his brother's arm and said, "Don't." That was all. When he felt the hardness and flex in his brother's arm relax, Tom subsided again, resettled on the rump-sprung vinyl, and relit his pipe.

In his side chair, flat-footed, upright, making the best of it, Father Ockham nodded off again, in that sudden, shallow, catch-up sleep of the insomniac.

The FBI man hung up the receiver and went out, jingling his pocket change. He'd be back, he said. Just listen for the phone, he said. There was a clatter of talk and machine noise as he opened the door; when he closed it behind him, the hermetic quiet was like dead weight; they couldn't push their voices out into it. There was nothing to say.

The silence settled like frost.

Traffic. Oncoming, unmistakable. From beyond sight, coming Faye's way.

"Yes, yes, yes," she crooned, lurching along, one hand holding that flap of skin to her knee, the other upraised, waving. She picked up her pace, heading toward salvage at a lope. Now the headlights—it was a cattle truck—probed into view, swept the tops of the trees (one-half mile), down their trunks (one-quarter mile). The shadows in sudden commotion around her confused her, and she had to struggle to hold her mind on the one thing needful: to be seen; not to be missed, to be saved. She slowed to a walk, then just stood, in the oncoming glare, in the center of the un-marked road, shading her eyes. At the last moment she flung out her right arm, imperative: stop.

The driver braked. Braked harder, leaning on his horn. The tires smoked and the truck skidded, slid a little, fishtailed, slewed to a stop not five feet from her. She had held her ground. Fear did not enter into it. She stood righteous in the full high beam of his insect-moted headlights.

The hot breath of the grille and radiator washed over her; she moved closer. The driver stared.

She turned a little, hunched, her arms doing what they could for modesty's sake.

The driver kept staring, his right arm almost casually moving to the seatback, as though to rest, but within reach of the shotgun on the rack. He suspected some trick. Hijacking. Motorcycle gangs. Drug dealers. General craziness. He rolled his window halfway down.

"I'm the one," she announced, shivering. "Alive."

He checked the roadsides for accomplices, vehicles or bikes hidden in the bushes, some clue to this whole thing.

"You all alone out there?"

Faye crept to his door and crouched, just her head visible, and her bare shoulder. She put up a bloody hand and closed her fingers on his mirror brace. He could see her face now, the bruises, welts, mud. Her eyes tracked his, unblinking. She looked mad, that far gone.

"Looking for me," she said again, a hoarse whisper. He leaned to hear.

"Police?" He shook his head in wonder. "You—you, uh, escaped, ma'am?" His cab doors were locked; he checked again to be sure.

Crazy situation. No Riders, his decal said. Still, he unbuttoned his shirt and handed it out the window to her; it was warm from his own body heat. She buttoned it on crooked, her hands inept, her eyes shining, vacant, feverish. The sudden warmth and light pressure on her skin started her trembling and jerking. The sea had washed all salt from her; her puffed lips were white and cracked. She was having trouble speaking plainly, just kept nodding her head, nodding and trembling. She couldn't stand anymore. She eased down and sat on the running-board step, her back to his door. All he could see was the top of her matted hair.

"Lady," he said. "You gotta move." If he opened the door, he'd brush her off. She didn't seem to hear. He set the brake, and slid across the cab bench and got out. Couldn't leave her there, crazy or not. He walked around the truck.

"All's I got's this horse blanket," he told her. He rolled her up in it, lifted her into the cab like so much carpet.

When he picked her up, she just let go, no more striving, no more vigilance. It was up to him now. She couldn't even keep her eyes open, though she wasn't unconscious. And all the time those convulsive shivers and shudders.

"Got no coffee left," the man was saying. "Nothing to drink. Some oranges is all . . ."

She peeled it, scratching at the rind with her broken nails like some wild animal, ate savagely into the sweet, wolfing the juice, moaning a little when the acid burned her cut lips.

He stared, weaving all over the road, as he watched her eat. Another orange, and another. "You must've had some hell of a Saturday night," he said.

She rested against the door. Her eyes flickered, but didn't glance his way. Just flickered and flickered.

"Ma'am?"

"Hurry," she whispered.

"Nearest help, fifteen miles. Patrol station at Cyrus."

He watched to see if the mention of the Law would scare her. They hammered along, as fast as the truck would go, and so what if the troopers pulled him over? I've got something to show the Law, he thought, turning the heater on, and up, full blast on her. The shivering gradually stopped.

He didn't know what she'd escaped from. Mental case, probably, was how he figured it. "I been up to Perry," he told her. "Sold off a load of heifers." She seemed asleep.

They crossed the county line. Five miles to Cyrus.

The heater was roasting them both, but she wasn't sweating. By the time they reached the Highway Patrol, just outside town, she was so deep asleep or gone he wondered if it might be drugs. He leaned on the horn as he swung off the road and in at the patrol's gate.

A corporal looked out from the barracks door. Another from the office.

"This lady here says she's escaped," the driver yelled.

The one on duty came over and looked in, scowling. The cattle truck smelled like cattle.

"She's partied out now," he decided. "I gave her my shirt, found her nekkid as Eve in the middle of the highway. Bleeding all over, looked like."

The corporal went around to Faye's window and tapped. "Miss? Ma'am?"

Reluctantly, she roused. Struggled to focus. Watched, stupid, as they unlocked the door with the driver's key. When he jerked the door open, she rolled out into his arms, in her blanket cocoon. He stood her on her feet, taking stock.

"I'm Mrs. Rios," Faye murmured. "I made it."

"Sarge! Hey! Holy Christ, Macafee!" the corporal called, when he finally figured it out. Lights came on. From the distance, all around, came the pleasant official sound of running feet.

Midnight.

The FBI agent answered on the first ring; listened; turned and held out his hand, flat, flexed all the fingers at once, a funny little wave that meant, "This is it."

Father Ockham sat up, yawning.

Tom and the Captain stood.

"Aw-*right!*" the agent said, punching his fist at the sky. "Alive!"

Faye had been moved from Emergency to a private room and was speaking on the phone long-distance with her mother when the Captain arrived, courtesy of a flight in a coast guard helicopter. Just the Captain. She wasn't expecting him so soon. Through the heavy door, heard him in the corridor outside. "I suppose the whole goddam world knew it but me," he was shouting at the woman from the Rape Crisis Center who had stepped forward at the elevator door and handed him her card.

It seemed to Faye it was a very long time after that before he opened the door and came in, stood at her bedside, looking down. He didn't say anything. He looked so tired she tried to take his hand, raise it to her cracked lips. The IV tube in her wrist rattled the bottle on its hook. She collected her voice, pushed the words up out of her, determined on strength, but she quavered, "It's okay."

"Take it easy," he said.

He sounded different, kin to himself but not himself.

She wanted him to look away, to cross over to the chair and sit, to check the view from the window, or the numbers on the monitor. Something. Anything. But not to stare. What she said was, "I'm sorry."

After a moment she thought of something good to share: "I didn't lose the credit cards. I left them in the bank! They must have found them . . .

my pocketbook . . ." When he didn't say anything to that, she added, "Didn't get my rings, either."

The IV bottle shook as she lifted her hand to show him.

"Just take it easy," he said again.

She felt shy. "I have to stay till tomorrow." She struggled to sit up, found the button and slowly elevated the head of the bed. She tried to show how good she felt, but after resettling, she lay back, her eyes shut. Remembering.

"Did they find my wallet? My purse? I left it on the counter."

"All right, Faye." He sat down at last. Just out of reach. She could almost touch his knee.

"My sandals. They made me take them off, threw them out the window on—on Delary Road." She sighed. "They won't find my shoes. Did they?"

"For God's sake, Faye! I said all right, didn't I? We'll buy you another pair, okay?"

"Have you had anything to eat? You could go down to the—"
But he wouldn't.

She showed him how the TV worked, everything right at her fingertips, volume, channel change. She kept the sound down, and cycled through the channels. CNN had a feature about the whales. Excited, Faye said, "Look!" knowing that she would not appear in the clip, this was file film, there'd be no brief glimpse of herself on the beach, sidetracked on her way to the bank. Even so, it was strange.

"I can't believe it all happened in one day," she said. She covered her eyes with her bandaged hands. "It's because I'm dehydrated I can't cry." Her eyes felt like burnt-out matches. He wasn't listening. He got up and paced over to the window, stared out at the roof below, the trees beyond. Somewhere in town, a train mourned over a grade crossing.

The Captain looked bored, tense with wanting to be somewhere else, doing something more rewarding. The way he'd acted when he visited Mrs. Parry in the hospital when she had her first surgery, as though marriage and kinship might require that he be there, but that was as far as he'd give, as though sickness were an embarrassment, an indiscretion, an affront. Infuriating.

Was he angry with Faye? How could that be! If that were so! She racked her brain. "Did you have to refund the—the Fortners' money?"

He swiveled on his heel, and stared at her. Blinked. Sat. His fingers tap-tapped on the chair arm. "No," he said. That was all.

"The sign says No Smoking, but it's up to the patients. I don't mind if you"—she was saying. He stood up again, scowling.

"I'm not smoking, am I? Do you see me smoking?"

"Vic," she said. Just "Vic." The sort of utterance, like a spark, one makes in the absolute dark, to reassure oneself that one is safe from solitude. She moved closer to him. He stepped over to the window and fiddled with the blind, opened it full, narrowed the sifting light till not a star was visible. He stood there looking at the closed blind.

Finally he said, "I'm flying home tonight. State Patrol's offered me a seat in their plane. I drive back down tomorrow to pick you up. Me, or Tom or somebody."

Instinct prevented her from mentioning Mackie, but she had to have clothes. She told him, "I'll need things. Mama can pick something out. Anything."

He had started to touch the side of her face, below the black eye, when she added, "Everything. I'll start out fresh."

Scowling, he took hold of the sheet and snapped it off the bed. It settled onto the floor in a gust, deflated in a sigh. He stood there looking down on her, from her bloodied toenails to the stitches in her knee, to her black eye. In that cold, estranging glare she tugged the hospital gown down on her thighs, shamed. Shut her eyes against the murderous look on his face.

She kept trying to make things right, normal. "I—I got the stamps. Commemoratives."

"Goddammit, Faye," he said.

She opened her eyes. He was gone.

PART II

LAST RITES

Vivian Lockridge had been more than once a fool for love and twice a widow, when she came to her senses, swore off, and went to work for St. Francis Xavier parish as Father Ockham's housekeeper. Twelve years now she had been exactly what they needed when the ad ran in the *St. Petersburg Times*. She was from the first a fixture; and by her muttering loyalty and righteous labors had seen herself through silver-crowned midlife and Father Ockham around the corner into deep golden age.

It had taken, as it sometimes does, a hair of the dog to cure her of romance. She had been, from girlhood, rash in her blushes, and when that tendency wore off (long before her twenties), there was Tangee rouge. Truth, a phrase spoken by a stranger—her fiancé—during a Bicentennial Election Oration cured her of him, and took about as long as lightning does, a mere flash, more sobering and instant than a mug shot. Charged with being susceptible. It wasn't that she saw him suddenly so plainly for what he was—well she knew—but something worse, saw herself—a bag of bones and flesh jacked up with Spandex and underwires and Clairol, caffeine-jazzed and trying so hard to believe that the show must go on that she could feel the sweat running down her bare ankles. Too hot for pantyhose, so why had she painted bronzer on her legs? It was like being dipped in plastic.

New meaning to the term "hotly contested race." She'd been in the sun on the dais for less than an hour, but looking at it another way, she'd been arriving at that moment for almost fifty years. If she had worn a hat, or been seated in the shade with the wives of the senatorial candidates, would history—her story—have been changed? There she sat with the dignitaries in her hometown, staring across the faces of the crowd, out beyond the fringes, the tardy picnickers still tidying up their tables and straggling over to hear. The invocations were under way, had been for some lordly time, two ministers—one black, one white, a fundamentalist chiropractor (one of the sponsors), and a rabbi, to cover all the bases. The bases were covered too by the temporary grandstands set up for this historic occasion, the playing field—American Legion–sponsored—

churned up by all the foot traffic, rake marks and limed baselines obliterated and carried away on the feet of the milling generations, the Bermuda grass outfield littered with sprawling, cagy latecomers who also planned to leave early, through a gap in the right-field fence, to drive out to the mall for the concert and fireworks. Beyond the honeysuckled chain link, sallow second-growth pines glittered in the sun, too flimsy to screen the bleached markers in the city cemetery, some of which, in marble, in granites gray and pink, in military bronze, commemorated her parents, her first beau, and two husbands.

"Lifetime achievement," the master of ceremonies was saying.

She looked down at her hands. She could feel them freckling. Senator Thornbush had given her a garnet dinner ring upon their engagement. "No use in this diamond solitaire business," he said. "We're not children. We've been to town, the both of us, wouldn't you say?"

When she sighed, the silk of her dress stuck to her damp back. Her attention wavered and focused and wandered, as the rules of the afternoon's debate were explained. The loudspeakers boomed and crackled and bounced back. The flags on the pole stirred, almost lifted, in a puff of breeze. Mrs. Lockridge was being introduced. Was she? She thought she had heard her name. She wasn't sure. The Senator (the southern colonel sort) was seated in the row ahead of her, and turned in his chair, beaming. She slightly rose, dropped her gloves from her lap, and stooped to retrieve them. She felt quite dizzy. When she slid back into her chair, the Senator was at the microphone, saying nothing new, as fervently as possible.

Aides had prepared him, and media consultants had honed him. He knew what not to say, and how to circumnavigate the global issues. He would win the debate, win reelection. He promised.

"It is incumbent upon me," he was saying.

If only the day had been overcast and the sun not quite so oppressive, and if the master of ceremonies had not used the phrase "lifetime achievement." She couldn't help but look across the field to the graves beyond. It was too far, of course, to make out individual names, but she could see certain landmark angels from her great-grandparents' generation, and that single broken column of grayed marble that the UDC had put up over the "unknown hero" the crews turned up on the right-of-way when the train derailed. Not much to go by but buttons and buckle, but those miscellaneous bones were, as the United Daughters said, "one of ours."

Mrs. Lockridge's first husband—Bunt Thompson—had died a soldier in Korea, his second war. But when she met him, he was between wars, and lively enough, a rolling stone with a GI Bill law degree, an open car and face, and, after a few weeks in town, a reputation.

He leased office space over a storefront near the courthouse, and hung out his shingle. He couldn't afford a secretary, but he needed a part-time typist, and advertised for one. Vivian saw it as the opportunity of a lifetime; it was either that or return to schoolteaching. Vivian did not want to spend the best years of her life in the fourth grade. Only one problem: she couldn't type. "If you know how, you'll have to," her mother had advised early on. But Vivian had a diploma, and much to offer. She was tired of the "classy chassis/nice knockers" brand of courtship she'd received from the local swains, who wanted to take her, but not far, or seriously, just to the movies or the steakhouse, or to the lake to swim. She was a long-legged late bloomer whose height and religion worked against her small-town chances—which she'd further ruined by getting a college education.

Vivian borrowed a Smith-Corona and a ten-day typing course, and played the little type-along records night and day for a week—"A contract is valid if legal. A contract is valid if legal. A contract is valid if legal . . . &c."—and got the basics; she never did learn the number row. She did some reading in *Britannica* and made a few long-distance calls to law offices in Atlanta, to know what she was in for. A counselor at a vocational school gave her some advice as well. When she appeared at Bunt Thompson's law office with his week-old ad in hand, she wasn't winded from the run up two flights of dark stairs, but if she had been, she'd have had time, plenty of time, to let her pulse rate settle before she got her chance to speak with him. There was a coltish young woman at the front desk when Vivian came in; she glanced up and rose, with her cosmetic pouch in hand, and headed down the hall past the Coke machine, as silent as snow except for her hoofbeats on the wooden floor.

Vivian waited.

When the phone rang, no one answered it. She could hear, from beyond the closed door of the inner office, the slow shuffle of pages turning, papers being sorted, punctuated by the thump as a book now and then was closed and laid aside. About seven minutes passed. Vivian had no appointment, she'd allowed all day; she had as long as it took, and she had what it took. The young woman came back from her break, tested her fresh fingernail polish for dryness, and settled at the desk again. She ran a legal form into the typewriter and worked furiously for almost a minute, then sat back, to thumb through a small reference manual. "Anybody call?" she asked without looking up.

The courthouse clock struck noon.

Vivian said nothing.

The phone rang. The young woman answered it with "Yes?" then, less businesslike, "Oh, honey," a pause, then, "Sure. Where you parked?" She looked out the window. "Is it gonna rain? Looks like it's just a few sprinkles to me. Okay . . ." Before the courthouse clock finished bonging noon, she was already lifting her jacket off the back of her chair, shooting her arms into it. She switched off the typewriter and drew its canvas cover over, askew. At the inner office door she paused, tapped, and went halfway in. "See you tomorrow," she said, and ducked out.

When she had gone and the clatter of her high heels on the stairs echoed and died away, the office was very quiet.

Vivian got up and went around to the desk chair and adjusted it up, laid off the typewriter cover, found the switch on the machine, and powered on. The half-finished form was still rolled into the machine. Vivian stared at the copy and data on the holder, and began to type. She knew nothing about tab settings; she had to use the space bar and count. She had been working for several minutes, she didn't know how long, before the lawyer looked out, clear-eyed, shrewd.

"What?" he said, not unreasonably. "Who—" he began.

"I'm your typist," she explained, standing up.

"I already have one."

"No, you don't," she said. "I've been here almost two hours and she typed twenty-one words, three of them misspelled, has had a coffee break, painted her nails, failed to answer the phone once, used your work line for personal business, and now is gone till tomorrow."

"Wednesday's her half day," he said.

"Your idea or hers?"

"I think that's entirely my business," he said. He had a little accent, Midwest maybe. They were about the same height; she could look him in the eye. She did.

"Of course, if she's kin to you," Vivian said. Not a question, but a challenge.

They studied each other.

After he'd thought it through, he said, "She's nothing to do with me at all."

"I can spell, or look it up, am familiar with how a law library works, I can drive, serve papers, and run title searches, and I am not afraid of anything else I might be called on to do," she said, "in the name of the law."

"How fast can you type?"

"I'm fast," she assured him.

People talked. About her being a Catholic and his not being anything (which was the only thing more suspect); about the age difference (a dozen years), the fact that he had no local family or connection at all; and about that convertible of his with the well-used picnic blanket folded in the trunk, his speeding tickets, the wine bottles in his trash, the silver flask he carried in the pocket of his seersucker jacket, the three days he spent in jail for contempt of court, and the way he won the civil suit for the little country A.M.E. church against the right-of-way company and the State of Georgia.

He took some heat for that; had to have his windshield and a couple of tires replaced and his car repainted. Hate letters came to the office penciled on pulpy Blue Horse tablet paper. Local postmark. They were always delivered to him, though there was no other address, just "Nigger Lover."

Winning that one case, he lost clients. When the army recruiter came by one day and talked to him about going back into the service because of Korea, he didn't say yes right away, but he didn't say no, either.

When he asked Vivian to marry him, she did.

Her aunt sacrificed a hatful of fresh eggs for the wedding cake. They had a civil ceremony; couldn't get Bunt into a chapel, he was so far lapsed. He did not invite any of his family to stand with him; he said he had none left. He said he was starting over. He said it was about time for some happily-ever-after. They drove to Key West on their honeymoon, took a month off. While they were gone, there was a fire in his office. Arson suspected but never proved. When they came back, Bunt was restless; the office was boarded up, the salvaged books and files crated in the cellar at Vivian's aunt's. They set up a little office in the front room, but business was slow. The clientless days stretched long. He called the army sergeant at the courthouse on the next recruiting day, asked him to stop by the house for lunch, and bring papers.

"No desk job this time," he specified, signing his life away.

They had talked about her flying to Japan for one of his leaves, but it never worked out, and he was killed before rotating home. Buried with full military honors in her family plot in City Cemetery. No one knew—no one in town ever would know—that he wasn't actually buried there at all. People who knew Vivian said she was never the same, but no one could have suspected why.

When she had been notified by the army, she rode the train to Atlanta. There was some mixup in the paperwork and when it got straightened out, about the benefits and next of kin, she had released and relinquished all claim. She had the body shipped back to Michigan where (all this was news to Vivian) Bunt's undivorced, deserted, but legal wife and their children lived, so that they would have somewhere official to lay their roses, and end the story.

Vivian, not surprisingly, felt more than bereaved; she confided in no one, arranged—at her expense and for propriety's sweet sake—a masquerade. A casket, sealed, was shipped back with her, to lie in state, and laid, with its freight of sandbag and boulder, in the plot beside her mother and father. Much was made of her final gesture, at the grave. The few who attended stepped forward at the last, as the flag was folded and handed over to Vivian, and dropped single flowers upon the casket. Vivian, almost in afterthought, when the first few handfuls of earth were rained down, slipped off her wedding band and tossed it in.

Mrs. Lockridge knew how to keep a secret. "Oh, she talks," Father Ockham said, "but she doesn't tell anything." High praise from a man inherently suspicious of the feminine principle. They got along from the word go. He hired her over the phone, long distance, her dime.

She had been, for several weeks, utterly distraught, had even thought that very word about herself, and wondered if it was an alternative spelling for *destroyed*. She wasn't shamed because she had stood up at the senatorial barbecue, approached the microphone during closing arguments, and announced, "I have made a fool of my life," and adding, "but better me than you," before handing back Senator Thornbush's engagement ring right then and there. No regrets. He had just said, "Friends, I fasted during Lent, and went meatless on seven Tuesdays and meditated deeply before coming to this conclusion: ERA is the work of the Antichrist." Vivian rose. She went to his side while the crowd was still roaring. She didn't think to cover the mike when she told him off. At least, she thought, I ended this one before the funeral. The Senator was too much. So was the heat. She in no way diluted the sensation of her remarks by adding, before she fainted—diagnosed as slight sunstroke—"I seem to be susceptible to matrimony. I've been widowed twice. Perhaps I'd be luckier at cards."

There was a strong sympathy vote for Thornbush in the primary, a feminist backlash in the runoff. On election day in November, while the Senator was winning his third term, Mrs. Lockridge was migrating south in a Skylark loaded to the gunnels with what remained of her past, headed for Sanavere rectory and what remained of her future.

She hardly noticed when she drove across the Sewanee; it must have been subliminal: miles later she found herself singing, ". . . far from the old folks at home."

What if she had not smoothed out the newspaper packing—Boy Scouts were having a paper drive—in the vitamin order her aunt received from the Retired Persons' Pharmacy?

What if she had just clipped out the crossword and left the rest unread, stacked it with the *Local* for charity's sweet sake?

Classifieds. From March of that same year, eight months stale. A small notice in the *St. Petersburg Times* offering housekeeping employment for wage and free rent on efficiency apartment for a sober reliable female in good health. Must drive own car. The phone number was at the chancery in Miami. She phoned there first, thinking every moment she would back out, it was too crazy. But when they gave her Father Ockham's number, after a few preliminary questions (he had asked them to screen applicants, which they did by simply forwarding all inquiries to him anyway), he said he thought she would do, and she said she thought he would do, and, sight unseen, she was hired. Father Ockham wasn't very good at that sort of thing, and his questions had tended to be vague, evasive, or euphemistic. "Is that *Miss* or *Mrs.*?" She read him very well. "Widow, forty-fiveish, Catholic, Celtic on my mother's side, Slavic on my father's."

She had decided one very important thing—that "widow" wasn't the same as "single," and she had resumed wearing the wedding band that Alton Lockridge—her second husband—had given her in faith and love, neither of which had failed, but only his health, rather soon. He died the September after Nixon resigned. He kept staring at the hospital's TV screen and saying, "Who is that?" about Gerald Ford. She had decided to wear the ring to defend herself, but she felt reasonably sure—and the years at Sanavere had borne it out—that she, Vivian D. Lockridge, was cured of romance.

"Dependents?"

"None."

"No pets either," he hoped. "It's just that—" he began, afraid to hope after so many disappointments.

"No allergies, no genetic predisposition to addictions or insanity, no felonies, no misdemeanors, two parking tickets, one paid under protest, one deserved."

"Ah," he said. "Ah." His mood fluctuated wildly between righteous cheer and abject endurance. It had been, as he told Mrs. Lockridge, simply dreadful what they'd had to put up with. By which he meant slovenliness, cold meals, misplaced and forgotten messages, and rifled expenses. There had been two hired and fired since the ads ran in the major South Florida papers. Though Miami was their cathedral city, Father Ockham had thought perhaps they might attract a steadier type, a retiree perhaps, from the St. Petersburg area.

Father Ockham was the sort of man who wanted things settled, for good and all. The past year had been, with its vicissitudes, deeply "unsettling," as he told Mrs. Lockridge. One woman had drunk the sacramental wine; her replacement had been a faded flower child who seemed to be opening a way station for her friends on the road to Key West. After a few weeks she split too, leaving behind Contact-paper daisies on all the cabinets and appliance doors. Her replacement was simply the most horrendous cook: an earworm and silks in the Bishop's corn, steel radial flank steak, water in the meringue, black bean soup like pebbles. A Diocesan guest broke a tooth. "I expect your cook salted too soon," Mrs. Lockridge said. "What?" Father Ockham said.

Mrs. Lockridge said, "Do you like pot roast? Soda bread? Leek pie with potato crust? Shortbread? Chowders? Cioppino? Those little sausages with garlic and peppers? Lime marmalade? Do you prefer tea for breakfast or coffee?"

"Ma'am," he said, "ma'am?" He pulled himself together, to ask, "Do you know how to iron, dust, defrost, all that?" He wasn't sure he wanted to go through it again. If it didn't work out, after such promise. Like the rest. He was no good at this. He had to steel himself for the probability of failure. Like God, he must require only the reasonable. "Can you read and write the English language?" he asked. "Can you remember messages?" He turned fierce Inquisitor: "Have you experience . . . and all that?"

"I do," she vowed. "I certainly do."

Something about Mark Grattan—not just the heavy wool suit so far south—marked him as "foreign" or "renegade" or "rehabilitated" or otherwise vulnerable, perhaps a recent parolee. He didn't know what the other passengers thought or speculated; it never occurred to him to wonder. He rode lost in his own thoughts, which were vivid enough to keep his dark eyes open and quick even when the rest of the riders, through the long night, dozed all around him. It wasn't unusual for him to keep vigil, it was part of his job, though it wasn't his duty now.

When is a priest "off duty"?

God knows, Grattan thought.

"Go fishing," they told him when he admitted during a Lenten retreat that he was considering leaving the priesthood. "Take a couple of weeks; think about your vocation." His vocation was not shaken, but he had lost his vigor, his enthusiasm, his will for sixteen-hour workdays, and the long dark nights on call. Canadian winters were part of the problem. Nothing heroic, no "greater love hath no man" accolades or challenges. Just weather. He had collapsed shoveling snow and had lain unconscious for an hour before someone found him, delirious with fever. He'd had a cold all winter, a cough that sounded serious. He bought a sunlamp at a jumble sale and took vitamins, and pressed on. He was shoveling the snow off the steps on Boxing Day when he fell.

When he woke, in hospital, he was amazed to discover that he was being treated for tuberculosis.

"You weren't sick and tired of it," his confessor told him triumphantly. "You were just sick and tired!"

Eight months to cure him; rest and medication. When he was ready to return to active duty—"More of the same?"—they told him he could be reassigned.

"Could be?"

Would be. Their decision: United States. His to choose: New Mexico, or Florida.

He had been born in the maritime; had served twenty-two inland years in Manitoba, but had never lost his taste for salt. He could not imagine being high and dry for the rest of his life. He chose Florida.

. . .

He could have covered the distance in one day by air, but at the last minute decided to stay at ground level, less because of the head cold he was getting over than for the chance—once in a lifetime, maybe—to see America. He had ten days, and he took them all, buying one of those bus passes that allow unlimited miles. He liked the window seat.

Till he checked in with Father Ockham, he considered himself "off duty." His sacred and other books were stowed in a taped, twine-trussed Cutty Sark carton in cargo, his collar and kit in a Nike duffel in the bus's overhead rack out of sight for the duration, yet a threat, always, on the tight Kentucky curves, to tumble down. He rode braced.

He almost lost his window seat in Alabama. Not because his breakfast took too long; he ordered it "to go" and carried it with him, ate from the paper sack as he walked around the block: tea—which the waitress had poured over ice in a waxed cup rather than serving hot in a foam mug as he'd expected—and stale doughnuts he finally bounced in pinches to the pigeons and sparrows. He recognized those mendicant birds, their appeal is the same anywhere, but the thick morning light, the soft sky, the sweet cold tea musky as though brewed in a pumpkin, the rounded-off accents of the workers lounging in doorways, the fact that doors were open, this late in the year—all said "different," "southern."

There had been no frost yet, nor storms lately. In the dust at the feet of the tubbed trees, and in sturdy civic window boxes—attempts at urban renewal—soldierly marigolds and mums waited on the tardy rains. After hours of riding in the diesel coach, Grattan could have walked on and on in the fresh air. He strayed too far, legging almost down to the silt-clogged river under its scarves of mist. The passengers had all boarded by the time he sprinted back; he was the last one up the steps. The air inside was stale, a sturdy blend of nicotine, Pine-sol, body oils, and human exhaustion.

There were a few empty seats. Relieved, he saw that he would not have to ride beside anyone. He was always glad of that; he didn't want to talk, and he had heard it all. One more good reason to choose the window— not as much room to stretch his legs, but he could always turn away, look out at the countryside, rest his head on the cool pane, feign sleep or deep interest in the program coming through his Walkman headphones. That would be a lie—the batteries had died miles ago, yet who would know? He kept them handy; the silence was as good as a symphony to him. He didn't want to hear anyone else's problems, for just this while, these precious remaining miles; his batteries were as dead as the Sony's.

Still Alabama, but the land had changed. Live oaks stood over their shadows in wide, flat fields. The creeks were slow, brown, and sandy. A few white egrets lifted off in the pastures, flew low, settled again, high-stepping among the grazing cattle. Not dairy stock, but moon-pale, exotic-looking Brahmas.

All defenses for privacy failed after noon, as stop by stop the bus filled. He was on the main line now, the bus that took the interstate. Some of the riders were workers heading home for the weekend; others were travelers on their way to a holiday at the shore. Finally there were no more seats. Grattan and several other men stood. He saw that he had ceded his place to a stout, pursy matron with a dreamy wisp of a child in tow. Several gallant riders swayed for miles in the aisle, but little by little, guilt and decency gathered offspring and burdens onto laps and made room. The stout woman's breath whistled as she decided to hold the little girl on her lap and give Grattan a seat; she hauled the child over the armrest and grudgingly patted the aisle seat—she took the window—in invitation. He had been the last one standing.

"If this was a spellin' bee, you'd be the winner!" she exclaimed. Was she waiting for thanks? He shed his jacket before he sat. His shirt, which he'd washed out in a motel sink on a layover in Chicago, looked as though it hadn't been ironed, which it hadn't. When he turned the cuffs back, they were clean. He saw her noticing every detail. He thought of the cleanliness-is-godliness inspections in school when he was a boy: red dot, white dot, blue dot, and gold star, depending on how clean your nails were, your ears, your teeth. Gold star only if you got a blue dot on everything for a week; in short—perfection. And that freckled girl— Charlotte? Charlene? his first sweetheart—with a smile ruined by tetracycline, saying on every inspection—"I brushed, Sister Levitica. It's not my fault they're yaller," but never getting credit until he sent her the valentine constellated with the ones he'd stolen from the chart on the back of the door. Peeled them from beside his name, not really stolen. He'd drawn a singing cat: "2 mi-mi-mi you're purr-fect." He had found her reply the next day in his speller, on gray pulp tablet paper, a hand-drawn heart, a flowerpot and two flowers. Signed,

I LOVE YOU
Carlie

"Hot enough for Popsicles," the woman riding beside him said cheerfully. So loud and near he jumped.

"Everyone's been talking about the unusual weather. They say since November. I say all year. They blame this drought and everything on the Niño. That's Baby Jesus," she said. "You'd think he was a secular humanist."

When he didn't say anything, she continued louder and clearer, having noticed the oiled cotton in his left ear, "Bad for sinus, weather like this. My neighbor, she had sinus and that sugar blood and she don't fly either. Me? I just purely caint afford it. Not sinus trouble, flying."

He knew then she would comment on every living thing as though the world—every atom in it—had shown some particular interest in her opinions, which she must return at once and more thoroughly, possibly religiously. She probably talked in her sleep. He was sure she would talk in his. He pretended to doze off, but held out little hope for the ruse to work. She was muttering to herself as she rummaged around—shoving aside the child's dead weight in pink and rattling ruffles, even her socks were ruffled, and there were bells on her shoelaces—sorting through, around, among, and beyond her various shopping bags wedged at her feet, filled with what appeared to be yard-sale booty.

Staring at him, the child drew her stick legs up to her chest to give the woman room to lean over. Her bright young glance was a trespass. Grattan took out his sunglasses and put them on, then tried again to sleep. . . . Almost. Jerked back from the brink by the woman's voice.

"Well, I caint reach my shoe buckles, that's all they is to it." She straightened up, catching her breath. The silver roots of her hennaed hair were stark against her scalp; she was very pink in the face. A pause while the child's lolling body rose and fell with the woman's gusts. He found nothing to say. What was there to say?

The air conditioning wasn't doing much good with so many passengers to cool. He unbuttoned the second button of his shirt.

"You're pale," the woman accused him, leaning close. He could smell her powder, her Dentyne. "Feeling icky?" She gave the window a try and a tap. "Stuck," she said.

The bus rocked on down the highway, making time.

"Watch that black man," she said, nodding to the rider across the aisle, two seats up. He wore faded blue work clothes, the sleeves cut out of the shirt at the shoulder, with cement splashes on his boots and pants legs. Big man. Legs sticking out in the aisle. He was pressed back in his seat, sweating. His eyes were shut against the flicker of sunlight picketing through the stark, storm-denuded pine trees—"Hurricane Frederick," the woman explained, "not Camille. You'll think, at first glance, that fire rather than a gale of wind was what went sweeping through. The wind's why the young ones are bowed over. See? Some this way, and whole sections back the other. Because of the eye."

The laborer moaned.

"He's going to fling a fit," the woman predicted. "I've seen it before. Epilepsy."

The child riding on her lap came to crisp attention. "Elvis Presley?" she murmured, craning all around. When she didn't see anything, she lost interest. Sat staring sleepily at a second laborer, who, because the bus had been so crowded, was not able to sit with his friend, and who now moved forward to the big man's seat and crouched, talking low. A dark stain of sweat dyed the center of the second man's shirt. He was cement-splashed too.

The child on the woman's lap turned bratty, squirming, lashing her guardian with her ponytail, whinnying for attention. "Are we there yet?"

"Miles to go," the woman told her automatically, as she had told her several times before. She didn't even look out the window.

The woman's shoe-leather patience was finally beginning to crack; she couldn't carry on her monologue with the constant interruptions and distractions.

"I was Fovver Time in the Pageant," the child reminded, with some calculation. It worked.

The woman hugged her. "You were the star," she emphasized, planting a waxy smack on the child's forehead, instantly brailling the lip print off with her tough fingertips. "The best."

When Grattan had nothing to say to that, the woman narrowed her smile and glanced out the window a moment, not even having to look down to tug the child's socks up and straighten her own creeping skirt. She seemed discouraged. Desperate for a topic, she fell back on the personal, once again spoken at large, an announcement, not a gambit.

"My feet's gonna swell to bust. I knowed better than to ride in ankle straps, so why did I?" She glanced at Grattan's shirt and shook her head. "It don't matter what you look like traveling, so long as you don't stink. My mama, my grandma knowed that, my cousin Sieburn knowed that, and he didn't have the sense God gave a goose." For emphasis she spanked the armrest with the flat of her hand. The child jumped.

"They was room in this handbag for my scuffies," she mourned, sorting through, as though they might have packed themselves. No such mercy. She drew out a tract from the side pocket, stared at it in dawning recognition, and began to read, with a frown and sigh, in dutiful concentration: "Peace in the Valley." That didn't last long.

She stared out the window, and hummed.

The little girl began to sing—"A, B, C, D, E, F, G . . ."—and took the booklet into her own hands, trying to decipher it, offering it back to the woman for help, pointing randomly at this letter and that, till she had picked out her own name scattered across the pages, squealing, "No, Mamaw!" when the woman, to tease her, said "crooked letter" instead of "s."

"Susan's my grandbaby," the woman explained. "I'm raisin' her. Second chance for both of us."

The child mooed out the window at a Brahma bull in the faraway field, then looked up and down the highway. She glanced across the aisle at the man crouched beside his sick friend. She quivered with boredom. "Soon?"

"Little while yet," the woman reckoned. A billboard flashed by, something about the beaches. The child turned her back on the landscape, collapsing into her grandma's lap with a thud that made the woman grunt. "You a big girl now," she reproached the child.

"Christian day care since September," she told Grattan and anyone who cared to know it, and many who didn't. "Already knows 'Jesus Loves Me' and 'Caint Wait' "—they beamed in unison—"and her alphabet—"

Startled, Grattan removed his sunglasses and slowly turned and beheld the child, who had just kicked him in the ribs. Perhaps an accident.

"—and vowels and blends, and can count to twenty."

He stared hard.

"To fifteen," the child corrected, and looked away first.

Across the aisle, the big man's sweat stood out on him, as Grattan's seatmate pointed out, "like water on a Simonized car hood." The friend crouching beside him looked wildly around. "Maybe some gum. Somebody loan me a stick of gum?" The whites of his eyes were ochre from sunburn and weariness. "Sometime chewing gum make it all right. Ben just need a little something. Just outdone himself in that sun today, you know?"

Half a fragrant pack was scrabbled up from a purse, and handed along.

Ben struggled to take it, got it unwrapped, tried to chew it. "I be fine if I just—" he explained, with great dignity, twitching. He reached between his feet, fumbling with the lid of a little cooler. His friend helped him fish out a drink, pop the top, hold it to his lips. The bus driver looked sharp in his rearview mirror, let up on the accelerator, decided okay, nonalcoholic, when he recognized the label. The ordinary and pleasant sound of the icy water sloshing as the remaining soda cans resettled themselves charmed the pasengers' overheated minds for a moment, like a glimpse of something beautiful.

The sick man's hands were shaking too hard to hold the can. His friend held it up for him, but he was beyond needing it; eyes darting, his jaw clenched, he flailed it away. The can rolled back and foamed against Grattan's shoe.

"All day long he been lifting cinder blocks," his friend explained. "Four at a time, both hands full. He just outdone himself in the heat. Veteran. Got a plate in his skull. This be over in a minute now, y'all all just let him be."

"Don't you pay the least mind," the woman told Grattan as he picked up the empty can. "I worked with in-surance for fifteen years, and I can spot a phony sure as God."

The man was thrashing halfway out in the aisle now, beyond hauling back. At that point some of the passengers expressed their alarm, and began forming a committee. The ones from the seats to the rear stepped across the man's body and presented their case to the driver: he should stop the bus right there—they pointed ahead to the exact place they preferred—on the side of the road, and put the sick man off. Them or him. That was their plan.

Others—these kept their seats and called out their votes anonymously—thought the driver ought to press on, as fast as the law allowed, toward official aid, the highway patrol or nearest town on the interstate where there was a doctor. A few simply offered medical advice. Most just sat there, embarrassed or annoyed, pretending it wasn't happening, in dread of any anguish, checking watches, reading the newspaper, or determinedly chatting. Someone in the back of the bus preached and prayed; Satan got a lot of air time. The cardplayers in the very last row of seats cut their laughter, then the cards, and went on dealing.

Suddenly rising, Grattan said, "If you don't get the goddam Juicy Fruit out of his mouth, he's going to choke." It took both Grattan and the man's friend. When they succeeded, no one cheered, but there was general relief, for the man, and for their schedule. They eased him to the floor, where he lay rigid, his eyes rolled back. Finally he seemed to sleep.

In a mile or two more, the seizure passed and he stirred, looked around, sat up, lucid, uneasy. "Shamed," he said. He took his seat again, not looking around. He rested his head on his great dark hands. His friend dipped his bandanna in the ice water and handed it to him to wash his face. "Naw, man," he reassured him, "it wont too bad." He retrieved his friend's cap, set it on his head. The seatmate, a stranger to them, did what he'd done from the beginning—look away, look away. The little crowd that had bothered to strain to see, to witness, watched his friend lurch back to his seat again, showering thanks on the passengers indifferent and kindly alike, trying to give back the remaining sticks of gum, but no one claimed them; they swerved their eyes front again, turned to commuting stone again, and the bus rocked on, surged on, south, south, south.

"So much for that," the grandma said, offering Grattan a Wash 'n' Dri. When he didn't imediately accept it, or even comprehend what it was, she nipped the corner of the packet with her teeth and tore it open, unfurled the towelette, and presented it to him with a lemony flourish. "You not used to any of this, are you?" she marveled.

They were on the cooler side of the bus, behind the driver. The declining sun was striking full on the opposite windows, but the billboard— and the little bump onto smoother pavement—were plain enough.

"Welcome to Florida!"

"He made us miss it, made us miss the state line," the woman cried. "That was gonna be the highlight!"

The child on her lap shot upright out of near slumber, prancing on her grandma's soft lap, foot to foot, slapping at the smeared window glass, gazing back at Alabama receding fast. Her bleak face slowly and sincerely puckered into a wailing; she grieved terribly, but even so, she was harking for consolation, some trade-off or candy-on-a-stick promise. It came, rash as a rainbow and worth no more.

"Darlin' Sue, just stop that snubbin'. We'll catch it on the flip-flop. Beg the driver to set us down right at the line so we can walk across, and that's better anyway, 'cause it'll be Sweet Home Alabam' and they's no place like it."

All the time she was saying this, she was smoothing the child's back, patting and soothing and lulling. Susan subsided slowly, leaning full on that broad, baby-talc-ed bosom, and, mile marker by mile marker, wound down toward deep sleep. At last. "She's finally down," her grandma said. Low, so as not to wake her.

Now that they were, so to speak, alone, the woman leaned toward Grattan and confessed, "I had you picked for outlander." She almost winked. "You know: speaky-speaky. Immigrant. And here you can roar as good as my old man!"

Mrs. Lockridge couldn't make up her mind about Father Mark Grattan. Was he or wasn't he going to fit in? She knew people who had sled dogs and malamutes for pets, even this far south, but they had coat problems, and shed. Father Grattan had come from almost that far north, and he shed his coat too. Also his shirt. He'd go out into the back garden, out of sight of the world, an hour a day, with his book and lawn chair. Late in the year as it was, it took some time before he made any progress weathering that baby-pale skin. Every day, though, he seemed stronger. Before dawn he was up, dressed in sweats and sneakers, and off running along the roads toward sunrise; an hour later he'd be back. He was always showered and dressed for the day before Father Ockham started competing for the hot water.

He was no trouble to cook for, Mrs. Lockridge found. If he liked it, he ate it. If he didn't like it, he ate it. If he needed or wanted more or different from what she was serving, he bought it on his own. She'd seen him at the Bluebird—doughnuts, coffee—and coming out of Lupo's with a sack of something to go. He didn't keep food in his room, though; she didn't have to worry about bugs and mice. Really, she didn't have to worry about anything, but she kept her eyes open, just in case. She was no snoop, no meddler. She didn't go through his things while he was gone, or make lightning raids to surprise him when he was home. He had a lock and the only key. It was up to him to say when she could come in and clean, change the linens, pick up and drop off his laundry. But he never did! He took care of all of it himself.

He was no trouble.

"The ideal pet," she muttered, one morning after he had gone out. "He even walks himself."

"He has to," Father Ockham reminded her. "He can't drive."

That was their one major disappointment with the new man, until they saw Father Grattan fraternizing—there was no other word that would do—with the enemy of Father Ockham's peace of mind and row crops. As though it made not a bit of difference to anyone in the world, there the new man stood, holding that black and white cat from next door, speaking kindly to it, petting it, feeding it something from his pocket! When he set the beast back on the ground, it trotted after him. The very cat that had dug up the baby beets, wallowed the celery flat for a nap bower, and fought all night with another tom, leaving enough belly fur blowing around to line mittens. They'd hoped he'd died, but here he was back. And against all rectory policy, being made welcome.

Mrs. Lockridge tore outside to more than explain.

Father Grattan looked up, startled. He was working on a shady little triangle of unused sour earth, turning it into a bulb bed. No use telling him tulips don't like the climate. He had the lifelong habit of planting them. She had even offered to store them in her crisper for six weeks, since he'd already bought them, but he thought planting shallow would work the same. Wait till he worked the bone meal in. They wouldn't be in the ground ten minutes before the cat and the chipmunks would have them out.

She sniffed. "That cat—"

"Oh, are you allergic?" he wondered. He stood and brushed sand off his trouser knees.

"Worse," she said. She turned one of the patio chairs and sat. She glanced back toward the house.

"Ah," he said. "All cats, or just that one?"

"Any, but that one especially. Moreover," she began . . .

"Lives next door," he said, squatting, taking up his trowel again. "What can you do? A tomcat isn't going to sit around when he can get around."

"Surely you have noticed . . ." she continued.

The booby traps? The electric rabbit fence strung along the row by the wall so if the cat lands astraddle, it gets a nasty hello? The ritual gravel toss? He sat back on his heels. "Quite a show," he agreed. The cat came and sat by him, rubbing its left cheek, then its right, against Grattan's outstretched hand. But looking at *her*; gloating, Mrs. Lockridge would say. Smirking. Purring so she could hear.

"He ruined my angel-food pan," she said, bringing heavy charges against the purring animal.

Father Grattan thought that over. He tried not to smile. "And how would that have been?" He couldn't picture it. He was willing to.

She said, "He went sauntering by the window with a bluebird in his mouth, and I threw it at him, if you must know. It was empty. There's a dent the size of a guinea egg. In the pan, not the cat. I missed."

"Blue jay, you mean," he hoped.

"Bluebird," she said firmly. "*Sialia sialis*. Female, I'd say, larger than juvenile."

When he looked about to challenge that, she added, "Hunched posture, eye ring, blue in wings and tail."

"Ah, well," he said sadly, glancing at the cat. "The one bird now and again . . ."

"They mate for life," she said.

"Best go," Grattan told the cat then, clapping his hands and pointing. The cat went. Picked its way daintily over Father Ockham's rabbit wire, scaled the wall, and vanished through a gap in the stonecutter's hedge.

"What's his name?" he wondered.

"Otto Schimmelpfennig."

"No, really," he said.

"Gospel," she said.

"Who'd name a cat—"

"Not the cat, the man next door."

Father Grattan considered.

"Have you—"

"He's deaf," she said. "Save your breath for your oboe."

"A letter, perhaps."

"Tried it twice. Postcard reply, by return mail. Beautiful old-world script, like Black Letter: Care taken, he promises. And the next full moon, they're all back here at it again, howling and tearing. Choirs of 'em!"

"How long has this been going on?" Father Grattan asked. She took his meaning very well.

She laughed. "There's nothing 'going on!' Just cats."

Father Ockham's bedroom office faced the garden. He appeared at the window now, seemed to be trying to get it open, gave up, knocked at it furiously to be sure he had her attention, and yelled, through the double glazing and sun film, what sounded like, "Yellow haste abate the sleeves zord?"

"So you see," she concluded, as she rose to go hunt whatever it was, "he's got to be considered."

Cristo Montevidez's homecoming parade was proving to be imperial, a triumph. "You've drawn more people than Santa Claus," his mama told him, reaching into the convertible he'd received as MVP in the Series, for one last proud hug before the motorcade started.

"Ride with us," Cristo offered.

"No, sugar, this is your day. Besides," she added, giving Connye Marlowe, Miss Marine Fisheries Comeback and first runner-up in the regional Vanna White look-alike contest, a knowing look, "two's company, three's a crowd."

Miss Marlowe made an "okay" sign. "Ready," she said. She wore an improvised safety belt, and sat up on the back of the car, on the folded-away convertible top, her feet in silvery shoes resting on the Mustang's backseat. They had rigged a strap for her to hold on to, like reins, but she ignored it, it clashed with her color scheme, looked so clunky and barbaric and stark, and besides, she had practiced, and perfected, two-handed kiss-blowing, and wasn't about to miss her chance. Her outflung arms were elegant in above-the-elbow kid evening gloves borrowed from Cristo's mother. Between the gloves and her neck there was nothing but bare shoulders. She had a lapful of roses—two and a half dozen, one for each day they had known each other—courtesy of Cristo himself. He was driving. After all, it was his car. And he liked being in charge; he never balked about signing autographs, he even held up the parade en route, when fans ran out with scorecards or baseballs or scraps of paper for him to sign, but he liked being the one to drive that new car, what was the good of having it if you couldn't drive it?

Connye Marlowe was glad he wasn't in uniform. She secretly thought baseball uniforms were tacky, and if he had worn his, and she were in her elegant gown, it would look as though they were going to a costume party. They had stopped again, for more autographs. Only the girls asked for hers. Except when they were actually rolling along, Cristo was the one getting all the attention. She adjusted her crown, played with the little pearl buttons at her wrists, hiked her gown up under her armpits, re-settled the sheaf of roses. With the very tip of her silver shoe, she nudged Cristo.

"Almost through," he said. "Are you chilly?" He was about to shrug out of his jacket and hand it to her. How would that look, speaking in a fashion sense? As for the proprietary nature of it, of his kind—however distracted—attention, she was all for it. In fact, she had designs, as she had told his mother. But it was plainly not possible to consider (should the matter arise) marriage. Connye was trying for Miss Florida, and then Miss America, and for that you could be engaged, but not married. There wasn't much that Cristo's mother could do about ambition like that except admire it. (And thank God.)

Connye had caught Cristo's eye at the Miss Marine Fisheries Comeback pageant; he was one of the judges, and when she performed her talent, she had danced around—"Very elegant, very Ginger Rogers," as her coach put it—while sketching a rose, quite nicely, in a matter of minutes, in William Alexander oils. Her palette and easel were clear acrylic, like crystal; she painted the rose on a great, dark panel of velvet, while singing what was billed as "a Manilow medley." When she had done, she keyed her smile and eye contact right at Cristo, central behind the judges' console. Through rehearsal and exquisite foreplanning, the spotlight on the easel went out at the exact moment she pulled forth a real, long-stemmed American Beauty red rose, which she offered to the crowd with a flourish and a deep bow, as she sang her finale, "This one's for you." Oh, it was magic, the more-than-applause telling her that the coach ("You've got it, kiddo") was right. Cheers. Even before they announced she'd won the crown, an ovation. And every day since, not one day skipped, like DiMaggio and Monroe, a fresh rose from Cristo no matter where he was, no matter where she was, and "This one's for you" on the card. A standing order with Floradora's. Almost legendary by now.

All around the car was a surf of excited young people, calling, "Yo, Cristo!" "Me!" "Here!" He signed and signed. Listened. Replied. Gave and took fives high and low. Thanked them all for coming, and rolled on for another block. Did it all again. Ahead of them, in back of them, high-school bands played conflicting songs, marching in place with a chumpf, chumpf, chumpf.

When she thought about it, Connye Marlowe didn't really mind the delay. These rides never lasted long enough anyway, and the crown for only a year.

Faye had not forgotten Cristo's homecoming parade, but she had almost missed it. The Captain was away. He had been gone all night. He wasn't supposed to leave till morning, but he had left after dinner, rather than quarrel. He had been getting some things together for his overnight, and she was helping. He wanted a particular shirt—he was particular about his shirts—and socks that matched the one he was already wearing, and when she went to his dresser, Faye found the socks, finally, and a packet she thought at first was matches, and took them out because she didn't want the sulfur to ruin the silver cufflinks he kept in the same drawer. She didn't even look at the packet, just set it aside and went on helping him pack.

They had been talking about Zeb Leonard, the Captain's mate, a good man who had just given notice. He had shrimp-fished with Tom as striker and mate, and had sport-fished with the Captain as deckhand and mate, but now he wanted to go off and fish for himself.

"And you can't blame him, really," Faye was saying, idly fingering the little packet. She had had nervous habits like that since her ordeal as a hostage. Folding her dinner napkin smaller and smaller, squares to triangles to squares to triangles, or like a fan, always smoothing along the crease, pleating, unpleating. Raveling a string on a fray, or peeling the bark off a green twig, or folding scraps of paper in her pockets. Once she found a penny in her jeans pocket, wrapped like a gift in an old grocery receipt. She didn't remember it at all. Perhaps she had done it as she was doing this—while she was talking, just turning whatever object it was over and over, as though it were an idea. Then she looked at it.

There the Captain stood, reading a chart by the touch-on light, when she held it out to him—no more sense than that!—and asked, "Oh. Are these for us?"

Rubbers.

For a moment he stared at her as though her guileless question were mocking. She didn't know better, wasn't sophisticated enough to be defensive, jealous. He told her the thing that would most furiously punish her—the truth.

"No," he said.

He put them in his satchel and left.

. . .

They had had problems, before that. Silences and tensions that had become part of her life, like her height, her brows, the tic below her left eye that fluttered like a finch in a sack, so persistently that she was no longer aware of its flaring up and exhausting itself on the periphery of her consciousness. If it was a warning signal, or plea of some sort, the Captain did not respond.

A couple of times Faye had looked in the Yellow Pages for some sort of counseling service, but she never kept her appointments. How could she talk about it? How could she tell anyone what she could not discuss with her own husband? Faye had had to take an AIDS test—because Mackie may or may not have been infected, and there was no way to tell except by waiting to see—and the test couldn't even be administered for ten weeks or so, during which time Faye and the Captain stayed apart. He seemed glad enough to be away; he had tournaments and other charters. It was easier for him not to be near if he couldn't be close, he said. But he sounded glad to go. Seemed relieved. When they were together, they were miles apart. No hugging, no kissing. No touching. It felt more like punishment than precaution.

When the AIDS test came back negative, they had another one, by a different lab and procedure, to be absolutely sure.

Things should have been wonderful for them, a second honeymoon, if they could have gone away together, in some special way, instead of his being chartered out for blue marlin. He didn't know how long he'd be gone. When you fish for marlin, it is more a matter of finding than of fighting. The playing and landing can take several hours; the hunt can take days. Faye had spoken to the Captain on Saturday night by ship-to-shore telephone, and she had no idea he'd be in the next day.

She was up on a ladder, hanging wind chimes outside the bedroom window, when he came home. She never heard his launch, because she had been hammering. And then the chimes were playing their pentatonic scale in her ear. He heard them too. He came around the house and across the lawn. Not sneaking. It wasn't any kind of attack, just a surprise. If he had just called out her name. But he crossed over to the foot of the ladder and grabbed her by the ankles and slid his hands up her bare legs and dragged her down into his arms.

He expected a squeal perhaps, a little fake frost and shyness—it had been so long—but she was as crisp as kindling in his arms, and friskier than he thought. It was all he could do to hold her.

"Please," she said.

What was he to think?

Housekeeper's day off. Complete privacy assured by hedges and fence. He rolled with her to the ground. Spectacular results. She clung to him, but when he kissed her, she beat at his face and clawed a terrible brand down his cheek and neck. He lay back on the grass, stunned. She kicked free and ran to the house.

He was puzzled, but far from sympathetic; he didn't know why she was acting like this, and he didn't care. When he got to the door, and it was locked, he didn't waste any time arguing or pleading with her to come open it. He went to the next door, and it was locked also. So he found an open window, kicked in the screen, and stepped inside.

He could hear the shower running. She was crouched under the stream, fully dressed, hag-ugly, a disposable razor in her hand. She shook it at him. It was almost funny.

"Leave me alone!" she screamed.

So he did.

And he had, ever since. She had tried to explain, when she figured it out herself, but it hadn't made any difference to the Captain. Night after night they lay in their bed, dreaming separate dreams. She tried to reach him, but offering herself didn't do it. What tenderness she gave, he took, but he made no reciprocation.

She went to confession and admitted she and her husband had not had intercourse since the bank robbery. The priest—it was Ockham, she was sure—recommended a book—*Happiness Is a Choice*—and delicately directed her to read page 150. When she did, she discovered that, according to Saint Paul, a husband and wife have a right to each other and should never turn each other down for sex except during prayer.

But what is the good of knowing the answer if no one asks the question?

Faye got more out of her romance novels. She had begun reading in the evenings, to fill the hours before the Captain came in; she never could sleep till he was home safe, even if he crashed on the couch and never said a word.

On one such evening the Captain was in an especially bad mood; a shark had that day taken a thirty-pound bite out of a tournament strike. A big billfish wasted. Trophy fish. Not worth one point with a hole in it.

Faye said the wrong thing. "Why can't they just stuff and mount it going the other way, so the hole doesn't show?"

"In tournament fishing, any hooked fish so much as grazed by a shark is a wipe."

He couldn't stop thinking about it. One thing for a fish to get away; another to lose a trophy to thieves. Twice this season it had happened.

First time, one of those hotshot poet-journalists wrote it up on the sports page. Under his photo, the caption "Old Man and the Sea Redux?" Sure, they mentioned how he'd caught sharks while his client was in the fighting chair, three in one afternoon, on squid, hauled them up and clubbed them to death to keep them off the fish his client was fighting. But the headline hurt, made him sound unlucky. Bad for the legend. Bad for business.

On top of that, Faye had forgotten to buy more of the little cigars. She'd promised. His pocket case was empty; he went to the humidor in the den—not empty, but very nearly. And she'd promised.

He brought that up later, when he saw the chunky paperback on the bedside table. "Female crapola," he said, hefting it. He fanned through the pages, studied the embracing couple on the cover—" 'She hated him for lying but couldn't live without his loving,' " he read in a sneering voice—and threw the book on the bed. "Something missing from your diet?"

Before she could reclaim the novel and put it away, he took it up again, saw that her bookmark was about halfway along, and said, "I'll tell you how it comes out. Save you some time for something useful."

"Don't," she said.

But he read her the last page. Then he threw it down on the bed again. She picked it up. "You missed the best part," she said. And pitched the book at his head. He was too surprised to duck. It hit his shoulder and bounced off, lay on the rug flat open, its spine broken. They just stood there, the bed between them, glaring at each other. "I'll leave you with it," he told her. "Don't wait up."

He took the car, not the launch, so she figured he was headed for the Moonglow or one of the other lounges on the shore road where the tournament fishermen let down. Faye left the porch light on.

"Don't wait up," he used to tell her, but she'd always been there when he got back, on their little dock, holding up the lantern. And all the lights on in the house as though for a victory party, or a search party. "Christ's sake, Faye, why don't you hire klieg lights?" But pleasure, then, not anger, in his face.

Faye didn't sleep much, or eat right. Her mother thought Faye was pregnant. She tried not to ask, to pry, but her hope forced her to say, "Is everything all right? You need a checkup?"

Faye read her mind. So bitterly it stayed in Mrs. Parry's ear forever, she said, "I haven't been exposed."

The morning of Cristo's homecoming parade, Faye overslept. She had sat up till almost three, thinking about the condoms, and the way—she couldn't get it out of her mind, finally took one of the sleeping pills the doctor prescribed after the kidnapping—he had just reached out and taken the packet and dropped it in his kit as he said "No." There was something so final about that. It slammed like a door. He had dropped out of sight with one syllable, and she did not know if she would ever find him again. She did not know if she had ever known him at all.

She had never been jealous. It hadn't occurred to her that during the weeks of waiting, he hadn't waited at all, but had found and taken comfort and pleasure elsewhere. She had enough barbiturates to cure more than insomnia, but she took only the one.

The pill knocked her out for six hours. When she awoke, groggy, it was hard to put her life in gear and drive on. Her mother phoned and said she was going to close the shop for the hour the parade would be tying up traffic. "I always miss everything. This time, front row."

"See you," Faye said.

But she didn't. She got there so late they had already closed off the streets and turned traffic onto detours, and she had to park on the far side of the courthouse and walk back. The sidewalks were cluttered with booths for the street fair later, and a dance that night. City crews were stringing lanterns in the plaza. There was a billboard of the *Time* cover. Cristo, looking older but no wiser.

When his bright red car came by, she overlooked him. She had thought he would be riding, not driving. She noticed the beauty queen first; Connye Marlowe was throwing roses now, not just kisses, stripping the wilted flower buds from the wired stalks and tossing them right and left.

Faye edged up to the curb and stood in the gutter, studying faces. She was still expecting Cristo mounted high, like the hero he was, not driving along, till he swerved gently over to the curb on the wrong side of the road, to hold out his hand to her. It was such a surprise, and the kids all mobbing around, before he could say a thing or she could think of anything better, she curtsied, and was swept away in the crush.

For her, that was the parade. The rest was so much crepe paper and oompah and confetti and cuddly sharks on roller skates. She went back to her mother's shop before the last units of the parade were past; all afternoon she helped her at the drive-through window and the folding tables. One of the machines had flooded, and she did the mopping up. When she got back from rolling the bucket out back, there was a large box on the main table—lying open, ready for long-term storage, acid-free tissue lining it.

"Wedding dress," Faye said.

Mrs. Parry brought it back just then, over both arms. "Second try," she said, studying the skirt front for wine stains. "Very damn fussy customer."

Faye swept the box and lid down the table to leave folding room. It was a lovely dress, but not so nice as her own.

"It's never what you think, is it?" Faye said. "That's why women cry at weddings."

Her mother looked at her, pointed that finger with the leather thimble. "Men cry too." She made an invisible mend, turned the skirt a quarter-turn, and began working on the ripped hem. "Some party," she commented.

Faye was just sitting there, winding a thread around her finger. Unwinding. Winding.

She jumped when her mother reached across to her and put her hand along her cheek and said, "What have you got to cry about, Missy?"

Faye pulled away, but Mrs. Parry caught her face in both hands and gently held her. They looked at each other till Faye's tears welled. That tic fluttered and fluttered below her eye. Tears wouldn't short it out. Hadn't so far.

"Nothing," she said.

"Then I won't tell you mine, either," Mrs. Parry said.

But she did.

Faye stayed till closing time, and then went upstairs with her mother and cooked a little supper, which neither ate. It was first dark when she left. For a few minutes she couldn't remember where she had parked her car: an odd feeling.

There was so much to remember.

When she crossed Bayfront, she looked sharp in both directions. Not for traffic, but for the Captain. The sound of the street dance wafted in the damp air; a foggy-soft drizzle with gale ambitions. She had on her raincoat, her purse tucked under her arm, out of the rain, so it wouldn't spot. She almost ran. She wasn't in any hurry, but she never liked walking alone after dark. From time to time she glanced around. Still, she didn't see him till he stepped right into her path and caught her by both arms.

"Cristo!"

"Didn't you hear me? I've been calling for two blocks."

He pulled her into a doorway out of the weather and caught his breath. "Where's the Captain?"

"Bonefish tournament, out of Islamorada," she said.

"That can't be," he said. "One of my friends won. Weeks ago."

"Oh," she said. "That's right."

She shivered.

"Coffee," he said. "Come with me. Just one cup."

"Where?"

"Lupo's."

"You're missing the dance," she said, when they had their coffee. They were at a table up front. They could see the lanterns, hear the music, the slow boom of amplified bass. She knew how she looked, scarf over her hair, no makeup or earrings; she didn't need a mirror. She didn't need those sunglasses either, but she didn't want to take them off.

"Who's back there?" he said.

She turned to peer toward the kitchen. He meant behind the lenses. While she was off guard, he took her glasses and laid them on the table.

"So who died?" he wondered when he saw her red eyes.

"Does he beat you?" he teased when her only answer was a nervous shake of the head.

"Listen," he said. "I read about you in the paper. What happened to you. The trial. Life ain't nothin'," he said. "If he gets out in any seven crummy years, I'll give him death. Trust me."

She stared at him, feeling better. "Flex, flex," she accused his male ego. They both laughed. Like old times.

She looked guiltily around.

"What?"

"I've never been in here before."

"Crazy. Ever?"

She thought. "Never. My mama thought it had a corrupting influence on the pure of heart. Plus rotten coffee." She shook her head. "Coffee's great."

"They've lightened up a bit," he agreed. "Now you can cut it with cream instead of a machete."

She saw people looking at them, recognizing him. Who knows, maybe even her. She wondered what she'd do if the Captain walked in. Or his brother. She had been about to touch Cristo's World Series ring, perhaps try it on. She knew it wouldn't fit, not even on her thumb. She had worn his high-school ring on a chain around her neck. Three years. She was wearing it the day she met Vic Rios on Tom's front walk . . . This year. All in one year.

She put her hands in her lap instead.

"Congratulations on your wonderful season," she told him.

The beeper on his belt went off. He ignored it. When it beeped again, he cut it off. "They can find me at the hotel later," he said.

He reached across the table and put his fingertip on that fluttering nerve under her eye. "Faye," he said.

The fluttering stopped.

Then she began to cry. He laid her coat over her shoulders and led her outside. It was really raining now. The dance had broken up, and celebrants were scattering. "My car," he said, dismayed. "I left the top down. Where are you parked?"

They ran.

Every step of the way she felt a lightning fear and dread. She staggered once, from the shock of thinking she saw the Captain at a table in a restaurant as they ran past. With a woman. The woman? Some woman. Any woman. His glass lifted in salute. She thought she saw him again at a window in the hotel, the drape pulled back across his arm as he leaned sternly, judging the world. She imagined him everywhere, in passing cars, beneath the theater marquee, lighting a woman's cigarette. In the cabin of the *Blue Lady*, with no lady.

She outran Cristo, and stood at the locked car beating no no no on the glistening roof, but when they got in, she wouldn't tell Cristo why she was upset, except about her mother's cancer, and what the doctor had said.

Of the Captain she only said, "I'm not his type."

Cristo was worried about her. He would drive her home. She wasn't very wise, but she knew enough to be wary of that, not because he was bad, but because of his affection—sweets can corrode and decay. "I'm just going over to Mama's," she told him. After she said it, she meant it, it wasn't a lie. She didn't have to go home to that empty house, why should she? She wouldn't. Relieved at her plan, she dropped Cristo off at his car. No kiss. No embrace. Just "Take care." Mutual.

The Mustang was parked in the hotel lot. The valet attendants—for joy, not a tip—had raised the top. Cristo started to go after Faye, but decided to take care of business first; the lobby had the usual crowd of well-wishers, kids who had missed their chance for an autograph, accompanied now by parents to see that things went right; a few boisterous drunks and the *pièce de* no resistance: on the bench beside the elevators sat Connye Marlowe. Different gown, same tiara. Long day. The rain-out at the dance had cost her a little—her bright smile was trembling now, a little weary and uncertain. The gloves—gray-palmed from hard wear—sagged below her elbows, her paste bracelet had dulled in the salt air. Her tiara was askew. Half of her hair had slipped its pins and spray, and lay in loops on her shoulders, which were quite as bare as they had been in the morning. This time she did not refuse his offer of the jacket. He laid it over her and signaled the doorman to call a cab. When she protested, he said, "My treat."

He had a complimentary suite, best in the house. He went up alone, with the evening paper and the latest *Sport*. He had a shower, and plenty of time to think. Room service brought him a steak and some beer. He answered his message light, returned some calls, spoke with his mother, told a joke to his father. Sleep well, they told him. A good idea, he agreed. He was in bed when he dialed Faye's number. On the island, not at her mother's.

Three rings before she picked it up.

How did he know that's where she'd be? She had had every intention of going to her mother's. Had gone by, and sat awhile, but had then felt she must go on home. She didn't know if it was because she didn't want to be in town, so close to Cristo, or if she had hoped—her voice sounded desperate when she answered—the Captain would come home. But Cristo didn't need explanations; he knew, that's all. He had "just one thing—" he tried to say.

"No," she said.

"Just let me say—"

"No," she said.

"It's just that—"

"I know," she said.

"Good night," they said, simultaneously.

Three cups of coffee shouldn't have kept Faye awake or troubled her heart. Or conscience. Especially since they were drunk on three different days, in a brightly lit public place—window table, not a booth—with an old friend.

But every time, afterward, Faye told herself and Cristo, "Never again."

The first cup—it wasn't even her idea!—the evening of the homecoming parade, she had had no ambition, no ulterior or secret motive. When she had glanced around Lupo's to see if the Captain was there, or Tom, it had not been a guilty glance. What she had been afraid of was finding out, not being found out.

The second cup—she was still persuaded of her own innocence, yet she felt she was being somehow vengeful, imprudence her concealed weapon. If someone talked? She had done nothing, but let them gossip anyway; let the Captain worry a little. She herself suggested Lupo's, because it was so public. She pushed open the door with a dainty dread—not for discovering the truth so much as for revealing it. Not that she was even sure what that truth might be; but she felt furtive. In a bold way. She knew she was somehow "getting even."

What did they talk about for two hours? Cristo, mostly. His winter life—he was in and out of town, flying to benefits and roasts and clinics; he'd even been on a telethon. And was in New York for a week, making endorsements and a TV promo. It went so fast. She hardly even touched her coffee, a sip of coffee, a sip of water. More laughter than tears, this time. The other customers left them alone. A wave maybe, a called greeting, a joke. "Let's get out of here," Cristo kept saying. "Let's go somewhere." So they drove around, his car this time. Not very long; when he cruised past the church, she looked away. To her horror, before she could even classify the heat in her face as shame—for what?—he was making a U-turn and heading back. Father Ockham was out in the side yard, heaving something across the hedge. Cristo got out and offered to help.

"One thing I can do is pitch," he said.

The priest hadn't heard him come across the soft lawn. He jumped. Then caught Cristo to him in a bear hug. "If I had your arm," he said, "that cat would've been bait years ago. Ah, stay for lunch, there's plenty to share and more to talk about, but if there were none, you could have mine for the sheer pleasure of your company." Then he saw Faye in the car.

She had her hand up to her face, hoping she might not be recognized.

"What are you two up to?" he asked innocently, walking over to the curb.

"A flat tire." When Faye lied, she felt the balance tip in Cristo's favor. She saw him studying her, interested, surprised by what she'd said. Something made her say, looking down at her hands, picking a bit of cuticle, fraying it into the quick—it would throb for days, if she needed any reminder—"Not true. I was just telling an old friend all my troubles."

She managed a natural enough laugh. "A flat tire wouldn't be such bad news," she confessed.

She didn't look to see Cristo's face now.

The priest reached into the car, gave her shoulder a rough grip, and said, "That's what we're here for, to listen. You pay us to do the worrying. And best of all, it's tax-deductible."

"Yes, sir," Cristo said.

They didn't stay five minutes more. But it was sufficiently awful that Faye really thought she meant it when she said, "No, never again," the next time Cristo called.

The third cup was the most upsetting. It scalded her for days. And nights. Since she had to be in town anyway, for her mother—whose treatments were outpatient, daily—it was almost impossible to say no to Cristo. Even if she had, he'd have found her—as Father Ockham put it about the sway of destiny in general—"by hook or by God." But this time she said a definite "No" to Lupo's. Completing the cycle of motives from her own jealousy, to hoping to make the Captain jealous, to fearing she would. She had chosen the public place as a neutral ground; then as a weapon; now as a defense. She feared being alone with Cristo because of what she might allow, because of the way his gentle slightest touch that first Saturday, no pressure, had healed the flickering nerve below her eye where she had been pistol-whipped by the bank robber.

But there wasn't anywhere else, she realized, quite as safe as Lupo's; somewhere new would be a signal for a new phase. She wasn't ready to decide. The night before, she'd lain alone on the Captain's side of the bed, trying to think. He hadn't been back, except for clothes (and had made those arrangements with the housekeeper, not with Faye, scheduling his drive-bys while Faye was out), since the Saturday she found the contraceptives. She had heard he was living on the boat.

Christmas and the old year passed; the new year brought them, day by day, nearer spring training, when Cristo would leave for Phoenix—and, if he could have his wish, not alone. He hadn't asked. But he hadn't had to. He knew she knew. He didn't court her; hadn't he tried that once, for years? All he did was be himself, and be indispensable, which is to say, he made himself necessary by listening, and caring about what he heard. She did a little listening too. It wasn't all Faye, Faye, Faye.

But still, she lay at night alone, thinking how it couldn't be just a little wrong; it was either right or it wasn't. And she knew which it was. So she said no, no, to Lupo's and that third cup of coffee.

But where else was there? *What* else was there?

She stood Cristo up, twice.

Then called to apologize, ruining her whole resolve. They met at Lupo's after lunch. It didn't go well. They were too near the final act for the tension not to be killing. She kept changing the subject, or deliberately missing his drift, as though she moved the target after he let the arrow fly. She got up and left, and he caught up to her on the street. In broad daylight he caught her by the arm and swung her around and cursed her. "This is life, not high school," she told him, very coolly. He let her go, but he didn't let her pass. To her horror, he began to cry. Six foot three, national hero, the killer instinct in his eyes enough to dwindle any batter's ego if the fastball didn't. He shook the tears off, like a bad sign from the catcher.

"I love you the way you love him," was all he said, his final argument. The prosecution rested.

They adjourned.

She had no defense. His remark bored itself through every distraction she could devise. This time she knew she meant it, and knew he knew she meant it when she said she would not see him again; they might meet, but not on purpose, or for any purpose of her own. Had she been using him? Crutching along with Cristo till the Captain came home? Horrified, she went to confession but could not offer pure contrition, for she still felt part of it was the Captain's fault. She lingered in the booth, after absolution.

"Is there something else?" Father Grattan asked finally.

She said, "What do you mean?"

"You mean, what have I heard? Nothing. Except your sighing."

"It isn't about me," she said. "It's a friend."

The priest said, "You believe that?"

She said, "Why can't my husband—" and broke off. Fled the booth, amazed at what she had been about to say: "—love me like that?"

There are two kinds of things to wait for. The one is a count-down toward its event, whereas the other's likelihood decreases day by day. Would the Captain return? Which kind of hope was that? Faye didn't know, but all along she'd think, If he will, this day brings that day nearer. At dawn she'd think that, in her garden. Then, in the evening, watching the sky darken, she'd feel the other thing—that she'd lived and was a day farther away from him, rather than toward.

Hope is better as a breakfast than as a supper.

It was like a tide in her, from full to empty and back again. Perhaps twice a day. She thought of him sometimes at fullness, sometimes at ebb.

If he were just staying on the boat, or at Tom's, that would be bad enough. That would tell the world he didn't want to be with her. But she found out he had rented an apartment, downcoast. That meant he wanted to be with someone else. After a time, she found out that it wasn't any one person, but she couldn't decide whether that made it better, or worse.

One good thing: she didn't have to fear running into them by accident. And one place she knew she would never see him was in church. But still, she left off going to Mass.

Father Grattan paid a call at the shop one day; she worked there full-time now. Her mother was upstairs resting. "We've missed you," he said.

"I pray all the time," she told him, a little wildly beside the point.

"Come back," he said. "Just come by. We'll talk."

"When I can," she promised. "Pretty busy."

She attended the Ash Wednesday morning service, but she hadn't been to confession; she didn't move forward for the Host.

On the steps, after, Father Grattan called her aside. "Is it something you're holding against yourself or someone else?"

"I'm making up my mind," she said. That was all.

Spring-training road trips brought Cristo home several times, but Faye didn't see him. They spoke on the phone once or twice, long distance, but still too close for comfort. He had won the season opener, a shutout. They talked about that, about the weather. Her mama, his folks, local news. National highlights. He mentioned a movie. She hadn't seen it. He said, "See it with someone you love."

"Did you?"

"What do you think?"

"Your chances are about as good as mine," she said.

"I could improve the odds," he said.

"I don't think so."

"I'm coming home for the Blessing of the Fleet."

"No, you're not," she said.

"Crissake, Faye, you don't own the whole island."

"You have a game that day."

"Night," he said. "Atlanta. Blessing's at eleven at Sanavere. Josh Powell sings the hell out of the national anthem at what, seven-twenty-five? Thirty-five? Same time zone. I can take the afternoon flight up, be there for warmup and BP. No prob . . . Let me tell you something," he said.

"Did you say a day game?"

He knew she had heard him right; he wasn't going to say "Night" again, just like that, because then she'd say, "Night" too, and hang up. A trick. He had a few of his own. Like the bedtime stories he said he read on the road, when he couldn't sleep. "Let me tell you," he said. "Once upon a time there was this weaver called—"

She broke in, "Don't start with another one of those magic-mushroom Apache—"

"She's Peruvian," he said. "And besides, I haven't ever told you this part. Where she saves for a dowry but has to spend it on—"

"Surgery for her grandma."

"No."

"Bail for her father?"

"No. You'll never guess."

"A little white goat?"

"All right, you heard it. But not the part where she finds the emerald and the nun on the burro comes along and—"

"Cristo," Faye said. He always did this, when it was time to hang up, some ridiculous stall.

But she wouldn't.

"The point is . . ." he was saying when she hung up.

The Blessing of the Fleet fell on the last Sunday in May. The week before, she had made up her mind; she would go to confession and acknowledge what she had not been willing to admit before. "I have been tempted not unwillingly." When she realized it was Father Grattan behind the grate, she was relieved. If it had been Father Ockham hearing, she could have told by his labored breathing, that whistle, familiar all her life. The pauses—had he fallen asleep?

Father Grattan never made her wait. Quickly he said, "In what way?"

"My vows. My marriage," she said.

A silence, a shifting. "Recently?"

"Last winter," she said.

"What did you do?"

Did you give in or did you dig in? One of Father Ockham's well-known Lenten homilies. She thought of how Cristo had made her feel desirable. She had neither given nor resisted. She had played dead because she felt dead. And Cristo had brought her back to life. She knew where it began; she knew where it would lead; she didn't know where it would end. "My husband has left me and I don't know if he will ever be back," Faye said. More to the point.

"If it were happening to someone else, how would it look to you?" he asked her so fast she thought it must be a standard get-in-touch question.

"Don't make it a game," she said desperately.

"Marriage isn't a game," he said. "It's a sacrament."

I might as well have gone to Father Ockham, she thought.

The last Sunday in May wore the best weather of the year. A few pretty clouds strolled across the sky, no threat to the morning's festival. There was breeze enough to make the flags and pennants stutter. The gulls rose and soared. Sanavere Bridge was crowded with dignitaries and tourists and local people who were for whatever reason boatless. Most of the action was in the water, though. You could walk across the river shore to shore, by stepping from deck to deck. The boat jam thinned a little as the procession lined itself up. The craft to be blessed—the fishing fleet mainly, and smaller pleasure boats—had been decorated for the day in streamers and flowers on mast and rails. The river itself bobbed with wreaths and garlands and individual flowers cast in. Shortly after eleven the long dark diocesan Buick parted the crowd and paused. Doors slowly opened.

"Let the games begin," someone yelled.

The Right Reverend Dennis Patrick O'Daniel heard and paused, raised a slow hand in salute. The crowd cheered. Warmly welcome, and already too warm in his holy layers, he appeared to acknowledge the crowd by raising his hat. He wiped his forehead and reset the black headgear, firmly enough so he'd not have to worry about sudden gusts. When all the priests were gathered, they made their way up the arch of the bridge to the very central span. The Right Reverend moved to the rail, laid his hand on the rough concrete to steady himself from a sudden dizziness when he saw the olive waters of the river sweeping by below. Every motion was slow. The crowd, too far away to hear, watched the ballet; from the boats below, the glint of sun off binoculars twinkled back at him. His claret cape furled and unfurled around his shoulders; he put a hand slowly up to still it. The acolytes moved to his sides and the one on the right raised the brass cross high. The signal. Choir. Prayers. The beautiful old routines.

The boats began their procession under the bridge, to be blessed.

The first drops of holy water missed a boat called the *Legal Hours* and sprinkled the river instead.

"The shrimp need Jesus too," one of the deckhands said.

One of the fishermen, who had seen three bad years in a row, growled, "I hope He's on our side this year." It was Tom Rios, captain of the *Legal Hours.*

Cristo rode with his father. Faye was nowhere in sight as they passed under the bridge, but when he looked back, to the ones on the upstream rail, he waved. Perhaps he saw her, before she ducked back behind the crowd, or perhaps he was just waving in general. He was the most famous net-mender's son in Sanavere. The people on the bridge showered flowers down on him when word passed that he was home.

The *Blue Lady* didn't pass in review. Faye saw Tom later, and almost had the courage to ask him why, but not quite. She went by her mother's and cooked their lunch. Mrs. Parry was feeling better; had her good days, and more than before. She prided herself on having gone through radiation and chemo without having missed a day's work. "Of course, I didn't do a day's work," she added, "but what are friends for?" She hugged Faye and invited her to stay over. "Just this once."

"I should," Faye said. But she didn't.

It preyed on Faye's mind, how her mother had said, "Please. Just this once." Was she not telling her everything? Was Mrs. Parry better, or did she just pretend to be? How many more chances would they have, either way? Faye decided to drive back. She packed her overnight case with such a lightening of heart that she began to gnaw at herself about it. Was she just using her mother as an excuse? Was she leaving today so she need not ever come back? The fact that she could even think it. She started to unpack.

She was so tired, all the wrangling, the to-and-fro, the hope after hope deferred. She left the case on the bed, yawning open, and went out on the patio to sit and think. Lay back on the chaise in the sun and fell within minutes asleep. When she woke it was over an hour later. She woke with a start, dry-mouthed. Her heart pounded. When she walked back into the house, she was weak-kneed. It was probably from sleeping in the sun, but she wanted to make sure it wasn't the stir-fry she'd fixed for lunch. She phoned her mother.

"Just all right," Mrs. Parry said. "Why?"

"I was feeling a little shaky, that's all."

"It's the weather, maybe. Winds out of the east. Gonna rain. My stitches itches," she said. An old joke, something one of the customers used to say.

They both laughed.

"Come home," Mrs. Parry added. She said it every time.

"Well," Faye said, "I have been thinking about making a change. But you know me. I took three months just to choose a shower curtain. Look, I'll see you in the morning, okay? But if you need me, just call."

"Ditto."

"Mom—"

"What?"

"I love you."

Sometimes Faye thought she was losing her mind. She would be completely decided about something, then do just the opposite of what she had planned. It wasn't fifteen minutes after she hung up from speaking with her mother that she decided to drive back to town. She changed her mind after a phone call; she didn't know who it was. Someone looking for the Captain, prospective client. "He's not here," she said. "May I take a message?" "Well, when do you expect him back?" the caller persisted. "I . . . I don't expect him back," she said, "right away." Whoever it was hung up.

"How do you think *I* feel?" she said to the dead line.

What was she waiting around for, papers to be served? She had already packed once; the things were still lying on the bed where she had unpacked. Before she could change her mind again, she hurried through the house, locking the patio doors, adjusting the shutters and blinds, watering the plants. She stood for a long minute at the security console, then set it to leave one light on at the dock, and one on in the foyer.

She had her keys to the deadbolt, the little overnight case in the other hand. She opened the door.

Cristo stood there. Of course she jumped. Not for joy.

"I don't think so," she said, shaking her head.

"I haven't said a word! I came to ask you a favor. No big deal."

"What?"

They stood on the steps; she did not invite him in.

"Drive me to the airport, and bring my car back. I don't want to leave it in the long-term lot."

He looked at his watch. "Right now, no foolin'."

"All right," she said. "I was just on my way to Mama's. I'll drop you off. I can do that."

They were already walking toward his car; he had backed in, ready for a quick getaway. He had the top down.

"You drive over, I'll drive back," she said. Still feeling a little shaky. He looked at her.

"I'm not afraid of the gears," she said. "I know how."

"You better."

"When did you say your flight is?"

He reached in his jacket pocket and drew out the Delta envelope. Handed it to her.

"There's two. Which?"

"Both the same," he told her. "Side by side. You can have the window seat if you want it. More room in the aisle for my legs."

While he adjusted the volume knob, he looked to see how she was taking it. "Playing our song," he said.

"You had all this planned," she said.

"Easier than I dreamed," he admitted.

"What made you think—" She fluttered the tickets at him, stunned. "What have you done?"

"I was going to leave it with you, for whenever. Good for weeks, or trade it in for cash. Come by bus. Taxi. I don't care."

All she felt was sad.

"Poor Cristo," she said finally. He didn't want to hear that. No. They had come to the first bridge. They had come to the final act. She told him so. "Didn't I tell you so?" Something about the way she said it, the way she spoke at ease, persuaded him. He had had his second chance, and he wouldn't get a third. He reached for the tape deck and clicked it off, pulling the cassette out before it had quite cycled off, tangling the tape, unreeling it. Jerked it free and threw the tape out of the car. She heard it bounce off the road.

"Cristo," she pleaded. He was driving too fast.

"I can't hear you," he said. He was like a little boy in a rage.

"Maybe he won't come home," she said. "Ever. Even if I knew it, for sure, I wouldn't go with you. But not because of you. Because I promised."

"Like hell," he said.

"I'd go to hell for him," she said.

"Perfect!" he said, disgusted, pulling off the causeway onto the berm. The sky had been purpling up all afternoon as the morning's clouds packed into each other; now there came the first ragged lightning behind them. A fast-moving, grab-the-picnic-basket-and-run-for-the-bus storm. The first few drops were falling. A spring squall, nothing serious. Exhilarating, rather. Together they raised the convertible top, sealed themselves in safe. Sat there a few minutes while the storm drummed down. The oleanders thrashed in the wind, and the stubbornest grackles held fast on their summits, rocking back and forth before they flew to cover.

"In case you hadn't noticed, this is the modern world," he said. "There is such a thing as divorce. The 'get thee to a nunnery' days are over."

"Nobody's telling me what to do," she said. "It's how I feel. It's not just a decision; it's what I am. Married. I gave my word."

"That's holy shit," he said, so robustly it made her laugh.

They just sat there in the rain. Behind them it was clearing; a beautiful sky beyond the roil.

"It's over," she said.

"Damn," he said. Quietly. When she looked, he was crying, not the kind of tears he could shake off, but like an exhausted stubborn child, finally broken to rule. She put her arms around him and held him, both of them softly crying while the rain moved on. The wipers cut wedges and let the world in, squeaky clean, as she rubbed the fog from the windshield so he could see to drive, her wedding ring tap-tapping as she scrubbed. He caught her hand and hushed it. "Enough," he said. And let her go.

"I feel old," she said.

"Grown up," he said. "This is it." He started the car and put it in gear. Checked his mirrors. "Got a plane to catch," he remembered.

"Can you pitch tonight?"

"Like a sonofabitch," he said. "My fastball's wicky when I'm feeling mean."

They drove on, exceeding no known or posted limits. Just before they came to the third bridge, Faye was saying, "I could look at this forever," meaning the marsh in that golden light. She wasn't looking ahead, and didn't see the little deer trot out into the roadway, attracted by the tobacco in the cigarette butts passing motorists had tossed out. Cristo lay on the horn. Too late. The deer was dazzled, the pavement oily.

The State Patrol said later that the car rolled five times after it left the causeway.

The deer and Cristo were killed instantly.

Rumors about the two Delta tickets and the overnight case—not reported in the news stories—nevertheless made their vicious rounds. Faye was the only one who could have set the record straight, but she was in a coma with a fractured skull, and the surgeons said she wouldn't remember that day, or possibly anything, when she awoke. She would have to start over, "from diaper and drool, crawl and coo" as one put it, "if she lives."

Father Ockham was at the hospital as soon as anyone, but he couldn't—wouldn't—wasn't able to administer the last rites. Not even for Cristo. He had to be sedated—they feared stroke—he was "beginning to be in danger of the peril of death" himself.

In Emergency, Father Grattan stood by Faye. "*In nomine patris et filii et spiritus sanctus . . . Amen.*"

BOOK TWO

MATCHES

Desire moves. Eros is a verb.
—Anne Carson

The day Cristo died, his mother's secret life ended. She used to take off her wedding ring to wash dishes, and drop it into Cristo's baby cup on the windowsill while she worked, and when she had finished at the sink, and the counters and the stove were wiped clean, she'd smooth almond lotion onto her hands and massage it in, then slip her ring back on, always doing this, every time, except when she fled on one of her musical and sexual fugues, taking nothing but the northbound bus, no luggage, no ID, nothing pawnable, just cash in her pocket for bus and concert tickets, coffee and cigarettes and incidentals—someone else would pay for the drinks and meals and room, if it came to that, and that's what it usually came to, and her staying gone as long as her mood and mad money held out.

She'd leave her ring in the cup then. For safekeeping. Not forgotten or denied. Leaving the ring did not mean she was leaving her husband, Agapito, though it took suffering for him to arrive at a faith that these adventures had nothing to do with their marriage and that she was actually leaving the ring as an earnest for her return, dropping it safe in the cup like a wish in a well or an anchor on high seas.

Unpremeditated. These were crimes of passion.

It was as though she were two different people, or living two different lives. When the spell broke, and she started back, she never felt quite safe till she was home again. Riding on the bus gave her time to resume herself again, not harden—like an animal after a molt—but soften into whom she really knew herself to be—Agapito's wife, Cristo's mother.

She talked about it—or around it—once, only once, to a priest. She didn't know he was a priest. It was on the same bus ride that brought Father Mark Grattan to Sanavere. She didn't know who he was, or what, but from the first she noticed, in a manner different from her noticing of strangers when she was outward bound toward whatever musical and sexual interlude, as a candidate, a destiny, a lapse. She was not noticing him wantonly—but she noticed him nonetheless. Something about him made her glad she wasn't quite home yet, and hadn't missed this connection, had been able to catch the Gainesville-bound bus instead of the Daytona, and upgrade her ticket to be in the same place and time with him. They did not exchange names; she learned his later.

At Tampa she stepped off the bus a few minutes to stretch her legs and breathe a little fresh air. It was a beautiful night. She was glad she still had a few cigarettes left. She searched her pockets, but no matches. She said nothing, but her look inquired.

"I can't help you there," Mark Grattan said. He had taken his overcoat and jacket and rolled them, tucking them into the luggage compartment just as the driver closed and secured it for the next leg.

"Are you sure?" the driver asked, hesitating.

"You mean, is it safe, or is it going to get cooler?"

The driver laughed. "Your skin either way." He slammed the hatch. It was time to get back on the bus; no time to run buy some matches or a lighter.

"I'll live," she said. Mark Grattan stood back so she could board first. She took a seat on the left, and stared out the glass as though it didn't cross her mind he might sit with her. Or not.

He didn't. And that was that.

Cassia used to buy Cristo a toy. She would always bring him a candy bar or a toy. When he got older, she might bring a book or a magazine—something about sports—or a music cassette. Sometimes she selected the same thing she had brought the last time. She noticed that once when she was cleaning. Cristo had cached the little piles of balsa gliders, plastic harmonicas, KitKat bars, baseball cards, key chains, and cassettes on the shelf in his closet. There was a stack of T-shirts also. She recognized them. They had not been worn. The most horrible part was the candy—that he had not eaten it. He liked candy. He had laid it away, though, untouched. She went in one day with a garbage bag and cleaned it all out, shirts, toys, and candy. Just cleared it all, as though the tacky little remembrances had been as likely to draw mice as the food. That had been on a Saturday morning, while Cristo and Agapito were at Little League. In the evening she went to confession, and, the next morning, communion with its fresh start. After that, she didn't bring him anything. She might think of it, while she was in Jacksonville, or even in the bus stations along the way home, staring guiltily at the display of snacks and newspapers and pastimes, but she'd tell herself, "Just something else to dust," and let it go. He was asleep when she got home, anyway. She always took the late bus.

She fell asleep, her head against the window. She didn't wake when the bus stopped. "Ma'am?" someone was saying. And touching her on the arm. She woke in a moment of absolute disorientation. Her terror showed.

Mark Grattan was not the one who had awakened her. She had been dreaming about him. When she opened her eyes, he was standing there looking at her. In fact, several people—strangers—were standing looking at her.

"Home?" she said, looking around.

"Something's wrong with the bus," one of the women began to explain. They all were smiling at her. The way people think it is amusing to catch someone napping. Cassia touched the corner of her mouth. She had not been drooling. Her forehead felt funny where it had been pressed against the glass so long. She rubbed it. She stood. Now they were all standing, filing off the bus.

"We're not in danger?" she asked. "We're not on fire or anything?"

"No fire," a man said. "No lights. No nothing." The driver helped them all down into the dark. They were somewhere in Collier County.

One of the riders had a flashlight pen and a *Rand McNally Road Atlas*, checking for side roads. None. Many of the passengers were in the same tour group, with cruise connections in Miami which they were not likely now to make.

"No way in hell, Mother," one man told his wife.

"Not even if the bus they send for us goes on like gangbusters?" she hoped. They were already sorting out luggage by flare light and what few flashlights they had among them.

"They aren't taking us on," another man reported. "Says we're going back to Naples!"

"Who said!"

"The driver said."

Mutiny.

"You can drive it," a woman urged her husband. "I know you can. Just pull him off the seat and leave him in the road when he gets here. We'll go right on. We can make it!"

"Driver's got a gun?"

"They've got radios."

"Then let ours use his now. Tell him to call it in. We want to go on, or we want a plane."

The driver had walked up in the dark and was listening. "Am I being hijacked?" he said. He didn't sound worried. He was smiling.

"Sir—" a voice began somewhere in the dark.

"It's all right," he said. "The company understands the problem, and we're trying to address it. How many of you need to make the boat in Miamah tonight?" He sighed, and counted.

"Let's get your luggage, and you and it stand right over here." When that was done—and the relief bus hadn't come—he sorted out the remainder of the passengers. "There's going to be a flight," he said, to a general groan of relief at this news. "That's the good news."

"Uh-oh," someone said.

"The bad news is we are going to have to go back to Naples, and the rest of the bad news is there's only room on the commuter flight for twenty people. No luggage."

There were more than twenty passengers on the stranded bus, but fewer than twenty headed for the cruise. A bit more negotiation, and they voted to let the cruisers go on the plane, with their luggage in the extra seats. The rest of them could ride the relief bus back to Naples, stay there all night—accommodations provided, and a chit for a meal—and resume their trip the next morning.

"Or?" one of the men not going on the cruise wanted to know.

"Or you can wait for a van." Which would take them on to Miami. The van would not be there for another hour or so; the bus back to Naples was on its way. In fact, they saw its headlights.

When it all got sorted out, and the relief bus had gone again, and the van had not yet come, or the wrecker to haul the bus to the shop, there were seven riders left who chose to press on toward Miami.

One of the ones who stayed, waiting for the van, was Cassia. Two of the others were Zeb and Ben. "I'll walk if I have to," Zeb said. "Done it before. Feel like doin' it again. Bad luck to turn your back on personal progress."

"Glad I don't have to walk it tonight," Ben said. He was one of the ones with a flashlight. He played it out across the dark, looking in the ditches for the glowing reflection of gator eyes. Something splashed. Night things cried all around. It was never quiet, not even in winter.

"They're out there now," Cassia marveled. She and the woman with two children exchanged looks. They moved toward the broken-down bus's door. The seventh van passenger was Mark Grattan. His luggage— the boxes tied round with twine—were still in the overhead rack, that's how sure he had been he wasn't flying, or backtracking. The man with the map had gone. The woman with the children helped them back on the bus, to wait. The little girl was asleep already, heavy on her mother's shoulder, one limp arm trailing. Mark Grattan reached across and wiped a mosquito off the girl's arm, just above the elbow, lightly, gently, and the child didn't wake.

Cassia liked that, and the way he asked, "State bird?" in that accent of his.

"You've been reading those tacky postcards," she said.

The bus driver stepped down from the bus again and said, "The van is a little delayed. Make yourselves at home." Ben decided to try to sleep, and Zeb boarded also. Everyone did, except Cassia. She paced back and forth, and finally vanished. Mark Grattan napped, woke, then reached his luggage, swung it and himself down the steps, and set it with everyone else's. He remembered his stowed overcoat and jacket in the cargo bay, and when he stooped under its open hatch to retrieve them, he found Cassia sitting in the luggage bay, the door over her like an awning. "Awake," she said, as though he had asked her. "I don't sleep just anywhere."

"May I?"

She turned, swung her legs down; there was plenty of room. He did not sit close to her. He had to duck his head. He leaned forward and studied the ground, decided to take a chance, spread his jacket and sat on it. "Much better," he said, stretching his legs out. He looked up at the sky. His view was cut off by the cargo door, and by the black silhouettes of cypress and fig-strangled palm, darling-plum, dahoon, fiddlewood, mahogany, and other vine-tangled trees in the hammocks beyond. They were on a kind of causeway, with black water between them and higher ground. Not that any ground was high. The shoulder of the road was not wide enough for the bus to be completely clear of the pavement itself. Where Mark Grattan sat, the roadside already curved down toward the ditch.

The swamp had a rich odor. The roadway was built up, and there were the trees beyond, but there was that dark, teeming water all around. When something splashed nearby, he drew his legs up. "Was that a—"

"Probably," she said.

"Are they afraid of fire?"

"They aren't afraid of anything," she said.

"Then you can have all the matches," he said, handing her a book with only a few left. "It's all I could find. Someone left them. Not many, but it doesn't take but one." She offered him a cigarette, and this time he took it. He lit from her match. It set his cough going. "I shouldn't," he said, but he did. He coughed some more, and finally just tossed the cig-

arette out into the water. It sank in a churn of bubbles as something rose
to meet it, snapped it up, and sank again.

They watched without a word. Finally she said, "Anything. It could've
been anything. So I'm going to imagine something pretty. A pretty fish,
not—not the worst it could be. Now you know that about me."

"Tell me something else about you," he said.

She considered.

"I don't like games either," he said.

"No," she said. "It's not *if*; it's *what*. I could tell you anything. How
would you know if it was true? But it will be, and it'll be pretty. I'll tell
you something pretty. I was named for a tree. Up until this exact moment, did you know anyone named for a tree?"

"I had an Aunt Willa. Does that—"

"No!" She mitigated her vehemence with a sigh. "They're always pulling that one on me. Willa," she said. She never told him her name.

She lit another cigarette from the first one, then tossed the butt of the
first one far out into the water. This time nothing came up for it.

"One was enough," he said.

"They've got more sense than I have." She had been wearing her
jacket draped over her shoulder. Now she slid her arms through the
sleeves. There was going to be dew; it was already beginning to con-
dense, and a cool breath rolled slowly from the swamp. She stared east,
toward the false dawn of Miami's skyglow. "My watch stopped yesterday,"
she said. Before he could tell her what time it was, she began, "There is
a family of trees called tree-of-heaven." As though he were about to
guess, she added, "Not my family tree, I mean not my namesake.
Though I am"—she laid her hand softly on her chest, then turned it outward, palm up, and nodded—"yes, I am tropical."

She exhaled smoke off to her right, away from him. He had not
coughed again. "The paradise tree and the bitterbush are in that same
family," she said. "Isn't that just the way?"

When he still didn't say anything, she added, "I know my trees."

"Tundra and prairie my whole life. Traveling at night like this," he
said, "when the sun comes up, I won't know anything except the
language."

Rather out of the blue she exclaimed, "I need to be home tonight! I
don't know what might happen!" A terrible sorrow flooded her. She
pressed her hand to her throat. Her skin and clothes gave off a cinnamon
and lily scent. And cedar and sandal and camphor—not rough and

commercial, but like the sweet woods of a temple. Her agitation stirred the air.

"Perhaps the driver would let you use the radio."

"Oh no," she said. "No. It's not a matter of hearing. It's a matter of . . ." she seemed to lose her train of thought, turning her attention to bending and rising out of the cargo hold and walking the length of the bus, stepping carefully in her nice shoes, staring toward Naples, hoping for the van, pacing back.

"I'm sure it will be here soon," he said.

She finished her third cigarette, the last one in the pack, tapping it out on her upturned sole, field-stripping it, casting it to the wind.

"There," she said, noticing how he watched her. "No evidence." She slipped the matches down into his shirt pocket and patted it. For a moment she left her hand there; she mistook the pulse in her own fingers for his heartbeat. "You're my witness," she said. "No sparks flew."

She turned away, walked back to the luggage bay, pulled his overcoat out, shook it, and drew it around her. "Please don't mind," she said. He didn't. "I'll share," she said. Again he shook his head.

"Is fire a danger, with all this damp?"

"The insides of things smolder for years," she said. She came and stood beside him, and they both stared into the velvet dark. "Lightning, usually," she said. "Somewhere they can't dig it out or drown it. Not always," she added. "Sometimes it smothers. Of course it does. Of course. Otherwise, the world would be—" A car was coming. They turned to see. It wasn't their van. It slowed, then went on. "Would be—" she said, having lost the thread.

"Troy," Mark Grattan said. It startled her.

Perhaps he had meant it as a joke. He couldn't know her. Of course he didn't know her! She was glad he didn't know her the way she was away from home. And glad, too, he didn't know her as the person she was at home.

"You're a teacher, aren't you?" she said.

"I . . . have taught," he admitted. "Not presently. I'm between assignments." He stopped abruptly. "I'm rather starting over."

"I didn't mean to get personal," she said hastily. "I really didn't intend to ask anything. People always do. They think they can say or do anything on a bus because—" She broke off and turned to stare at oncoming lights. Again, not their rescue van. Totally distracted, she cried, "Wait!" as the sedan slowed, then whooshed on past. She ran out in the road after it, waving it down, but the driver kept on going. She stood there sobbing like her heart—and not the heel of her shoe—was broken. She limped back to the bus.

She balled her hands into little fists and hammered against the bus, by the driver's window. "I have to get home! Make them stop and take me!"

"You will," Mark Grattan said, touching her shoulder, pointing toward an approaching vehicle. It was the van. "Now get out of the road before this turns into a tragedy instead of a detour." Inside the bus, the sleepers were waking, scrambling.

The driver asked Cassia, "Luggage?" and her chin went up. Mark Grattan handed her one of his boxes, and smiled. He chose the seat beside hers. "Better?" he said. She had dried her tears on a scrap of tissue that she kept turning and turning in her hands. "I'll have a headache tomorrow," she said. "I'm amazed that I did that. I can't explain it."

They rode awhile before she added, "If this were the movie of my life, here is where I'm running through the firestorm."

"Toward, or from Troy?"

"It's always both, isn't it? I mean with Troy." She didn't look at him. "I don't like that story," she said. "There's literature," she added, holding out one hand, "and life," holding out the other, as though balancing the two on her palms. "I mean, really," she said. "If the story had gone on— and life would have, must have—don't you think one day she'd have gone home?"

"That would be a different book," he said. "But she did go home, eventually."

"That's it," she said. "She wanted to go home. She'd have to. But that's Life, not Literature."

"Is the movie of your life Life or Literature?"

"A work of imagination," she said after a time. "No one could write it if no one knows. How could they know? Only God knows." She sat back, triumphant. As though she had escaped a trap. The driver had the radio on, a jazz station, low. She had felt chilled through, and now she was getting warm again. Not drowsy, though several other riders had fallen asleep again. After her last remark, Grattan had said, "Well, that's the thing, isn't it?" and had fallen silent. She thought he might be asleep too.

She glanced out the window for landmarks. There was nothing, not a billboard or mile marker, nothing to encourage her about their progress. She always had needed the time, coming home, but this time it was taking more than she needed. She wished she had gone back to Naples, insisted on flying. If only she could fall asleep again, too, and wake up to find they had made the turn south from Miami.

He always left the light on.

"Please, darling," she prayed, unaware she had spoken aloud. All around her, slumped, silent, the riders slept. Eighty-three miles more, across the Everglades. She thought Mark Grattan was asleep also; she thought she never would sleep. She was wrong about both of those. And she was never more surprised in her life than when, at Mass on Sunday, in full clerical regalia and poise, Mark Grattan assisted Father Ockham. After church, she could not pass him on the steps. Had to stand in line and shake his hand. All she could think to say was, "I don't smoke," to which he gravely replied, "I believe you."

At the curb, she looked back, to find he was watching her. He excused himself, came down to her, looked up the street, then back at her, shrugged. "I was between—" he explained. Agapito had gone to the parking lot, was bringing the car around, was idling—double-parked—in the street. She waited; Agapito was coming around to open her door. He and Father Grattan shook hands. "You like?" Agapito's gnarled hands indicated all of Florida. "Some good, some bad?"

Father Grattan smiled. His eyes shone dark and quiet and deep; he was not the winking or twinkling sort. "I am glad to be here," he said.

"Is scenic on the maps," Agapito agreed. He walked back around the car and got in the driver's seat. Father Grattan leaned down and said, low, just for Cassia, "I don't smoke either. The heel of your shoe is in my coat pocket. All was well?"

Her eyes stung with tears. She fastened her seat belt, looking up toward him. "I got home in time," she said.

That, in fact, was the last time. Before she left again, they got the phone call about Cristo's wreck, about the accident with the deer on the Sanavere Causeway. Somehow, though she was not to blame, she knew she was not blameless. She became obsessed with the details of the day, with how she and Agapito had lived every moment of Cristo's last day with them, how a moment more here, or a moment less there, might have sped or delayed him so that the awful intersecting of his path and the deer's would never have happened.

As he had been leaving to catch his plane, Cristo had turned back. One more hug. His kind of hug, gathering her entirely into his arms and powering her up onto the stone wall in Cassia's garden.

He had been moody all spring. This trip home he had been restless and a bit short with his family, silent, reclusive even. Had stood for a long time pitching shells into the creek after blowing off a little steam at the parish supper. He'd always been generous, even gregarious, with the hometown fans. This time he had barely been civil, had pushed his way past the little crowd gathered around his table and stalked to his car. Left rubber smoke in the air as he peeled out of the parking lot, and never looked back.

Fans had always said that Cristo had gone away but had never left, he was still their down-home boy. After a moment of embarrassed silence, the party had gone on, and before it was over, Cristo came back, apologized, and stayed till the end. It wasn't that he felt better, it was that he knew better, Cassia realized. She appreciated the way he had returned to make it easier for her and Agapito. Especially Agapito. He had not been entirely well in some time.

Agapito was the first one Cristo apologized to. They walked back to the center of the hall, arms across each other's shoulders. Cristo clowned around a little with the band, sang a song, by special request—"Mine," he said, and they laughed, and that helped too. They sang "Two Dollars in the Jukebox." He didn't know all the words, but stepped to the mike each time on the chorus about the lady on his mind, driving him crazy.

His moodiness had lasted all winter, and now, with spring training, seemed worse, even though he had plenty to occupy himself with. Some blamed fame, said it had turned his head. Some mentioned the *Sports Illustrated* cover curse. No one—not even his confessor—knew the trouble was Faye.

After they got home from the church supper, he had not gone out again, except for a few minutes when he bought the extra ticket he hoped Faye would need. He kept that secret also. Cassia and Agapito saw the light under his door; they could hear his television any time they walked down that hall, but he didn't want to talk. Cassia had knocked and asked. So they went on to bed. From the look on his face, the edge to his nerves and the circled eyes, he had not slept much, but his mood was good. Even cheerful. By the time they rode in the boat to the Blessing of the Fleet, he was in high spirits, and they had not flagged at all. So when he set Cassia on the wall, she didn't scold, she endured, with a flutter of gladness that he seemed happy.

"Don't mama me, Mama," he said. "Okay?" He glanced at his watch.

"Your plane doesn't leave for two hours," she said, wondering what his hurry was.

"I'm outta here," he said. The sun stood behind him, cosmic splendor; he eclipsed the very center, outlined in fire. It was one of the memories burned in forever.

The screen door opened. Agapito had the instruction book for the VCR. He shrugged. "Had eet, but lost eet," he said. "What is about range? All I get is *canal* fourteen over and over."

Cristo waved the book away. He legged back inside, was kneeling before the TV and recorder, his hands quick, deft, not desperate, flipping this switch, wheeling that wheel, tuning to the station that would carry tonight's game.

The picture cleared.

"*Hombre,*" Agapito said.

Then, in a hurry, a flurry, he was out to the car and standing there, waving in that silent storm of their pride and prayers, safely in the driver's seat with plenty of time, his eyes on the mirror as he backed down the long drive. He backed with one arm on the wheel, and one out the window, waving. They stood on the step, side by side, till he had gone.

Cassia liked to keep busy when she felt low. She took her sack down to the boat and began undecorating the streamers and paper flowers from the Blessing parade. She harvested them one by one. Agapito had made the sack. It was like the ones the Greek sponge divers use, yet not exactly like them, for the Cubans had different knots from those the Greeks used, and both Cubans and Greeks had a pride of origin and originality. The old-timers could tell, at a glance, not only if the net or sack was Greek or Cuban, but which netmaker and mender had laid hands on it. Agapito's work was famed. Some Greek captains brought their nets to him. Agapito liked to say his work had been to college, and it had—all through school, Cristo had used one of the sacks for his laundry.

Agapito worked on the boat while Cassia took down the decorations. He was older than she. He had already been out in his grandfather's boat in Cuba, fishing for a man's share, when she was just getting born, a navy brat, at Norfolk. He never talked much about his life before he met her; he always said it began—when he thought it was over—the very hour they met.

That was how she had felt about her own life, and meeting him, but she had never said more than that, and he had never told her what he feared most—which she never suspected he knew at all—that her will kept her alive in this world, and she might break the tether and slip free if her will broke, or her heart. He felt that he had been destined to keep her heart from breaking, only that, and yet they had discovered so much more than that.

The bus trips north had been another story, not their story. Since she believed that, he had to. Because he loved her from the first as an act against death—something to lay his life down for—he believed her. In time, her pain—about those absentings from their home—was all the pain he knew from it; he suffered *for* her, not because of her. And that was why she loved him, and why she left her ring in the cup, and why she always came home.

On the afternoon Cristo died, while they were still putting the picnic things away, Cassia kept her eye on Agapito. From time to time she came to the window and watched as he moved back and forth behind his net racks and frames. He had put the ice chest away and retrieved the grass trimmer. He vanished a moment and she heard something thump in the workshop, then he was back, kneeling on the grass, tending the trimmer. He fiddled with something, then tried to crank it. He pulled on the cord and pulled again. Finally it cranked. He unbuttoned his shirt and set to work, moving surely, leaving the yard tidy in his wake. He looked fit. Very browned by the years in the sun. Only slightly bent to the healings of the broken places. He had great strength in his arms and hands from lifting the nets.

Once he had been able to do the mowing and trimming in a morning; now he considered it two different chores. He had time and he took it. But he was not old, not yet old. He would not be old for an hour or so more, until the phone call.

Afterward, Cassia could not bear to hear the phone ring. It didn't matter when it rang or who made the call. She reacted with total adrenal terror. Even though it wasn't the phone's fault, she blamed it. Blamed it and everything she could blame, including the deer that had wandered out on the road to nibble the cigarette butts, blamed smokers too, blamed baseball for giving Cristo that car, blamed Little League for teaching him how to play, and blamed Faye and blamed Agapito and blamed herself. There was enough blame to go around and around. There was plenty left over for God.

And though time might mitigate those other rancors, she never overcame her dread of the phone, as though if they had not answered it—

But who, when death calls, lets it ring?

Cassia would have done anything to save her son's life, would have been willing to undo anything, sacrifice, take his place even, to give him another chance. She mentioned this, in a carrying tone, at the hospital, more than once.

"You believe me," she said to the doctors, as though persuading them would make it possible. As though negotiations were under way. As though negotiations were an option.

The hospital chaplain did what he could, of course, but what of that? Reminding her that tragedies are redeemed by God, not intended by God. "There is that which is ordered—and perfect—and that which is allowed—chaos," he told her, holding out his empty hands to her. God might allow chaos; Cassia couldn't. She slapped his hands away, walked up and down the hall outside the room where Cristo's body lay after it had been "pronounced." He had been "dead on the scene" but still had had to be examined, as though one might keep on hoping, past hope. Now they were rolling him away somewhere else. Pathology? And after that, the hearse.

Agapito had braved it first, going in to see Cristo. Had done that for Cassia, to see if Cristo was too broken for Cassia to bear, as though there were something worse than dead. But Cristo was beautiful, intact. And though Agapito was surprised and glad of that, he was also very sorry; it seemed more terrible somehow; there was that much more to be angry about. Agapito did not know how he could open that door and go out in the hall and tell her; he sat down on a little metal stool for a moment and rubbed his heart. He could hear Cassia through the door.

"The thing is," she was saying. "The thing is . . ." But she couldn't finish it, didn't know what, couldn't think. Agapito came out and walked down the hall, claimed her, and walked with her slowly back to that same impossible door. How could he say "It's all right," when he knew better? He didn't speak at all. He was crying. Not sobs, just tears in the creases of his weathered face. His shirtfront and collar were damp. She noticed the glistening on the silver tuft of hair that escaped above his undershirt neck, where the crucifix nested. Everything was strange; they both seemed to have disconnected from meanings. Objects presented themselves, and they could name them, but there was no grammar, no motion, no point. Cassia moved closer to Agapito, and like a kitten putting its paw on something, marveling, she reached out and touched that hair on Agapito's chest.

They caught hold of each other then, she not tall and he not taller (and their Cristo such a fine, big, tall, strong man) and right there, in the corridor, knelt, praying for the impossible to be untrue, praying for another chance, or for the mercy of hope. Not wanting comfort, but wanting instead not to need it. They asked for help, and they rose together and went in, hand in hand, the way they always held on to each other at takeoff and landing when they flew to see Cristo play ball, and the way they held onto each other at Mass, during communion, that they might be truly one flesh, and God not loose or lose them.

The hospital staff gave them time, guarded their privacy, but the pathologist was waiting, and there was work to be done.

Father Ray, the hospital's chaplain, helped them into the family room, out of public gaze. He had taken Holy Orders late in life and had been chaplain at St. Joseph's for three months, a great reassuring bulk of a man moving along the halls in his white vestments, not quite at home in their splendor. He had a lifelong tendency toward candor, toward the bottom line, and though he accepted that the world could be disappointing and miserable, his faith and confidence gave him cheerful energy that was hard to mute. He was still fresh enough from seminary and clinicals to quote teachers and statistics.

"Those who break late break hardest," he told Cassia, who was a textbook case. "Cry," he told her. "It's all right to cry. It's healing."

"Healing!" Her surprise scalded deeper than scorn. Stony-eyed, Cassia studied the buffed floor.

Father Ray, with a priestly creak, knelt on his best knee, courting her heartbreak, trying to woo her soul into its proper season. The plaque on the wall between the windows announced, "The righteous must suffer many things, but the LORD delivers him out of them all."

Cassia said, "All right," indifferently, meaning she heard. The same way she answered Carlo, their old dog, when he petitioned for food before suppertime. "All right," she'd say, unpersuaded. Agapito kept hold of her hand.

Father Ray nodded. He spoke of the long term, rather than the local. "We inherit mortality. The rate has always been one hundred percent. 'After the first death, there is no other,' " he said. "Thanks be to God for that!"

Cassia slowly raised her head and looked at him.

"I always say, 'If God meant us to keep a stiff upper lip, He'd have put a bone in it.' " Instantly he added, "I always say that at the wrong time," and fell silent at last.

He engulfed both Cassia and Agapito in his big warm hug, his white garments crinkling and rustling. He held them beneath his starchy white

wings and laid a hand on the head of each of them and said, "God's blessing come upon you, you darling God-creatures. May you be renewed,
and held, and restored in peace, for you belong to God your Creator.
He will help you bear this, for who better? His own blameless Son
mangled . . ."

Cassia had been quite still until she heard that word. Not mangled, but
blameless. Then she jerked herself free and struggled up, crossed to the
window, trembling. She would not weep. To weep would be to admit it
was so. To accept. To resign or reconcile. To take comfort, for in taking
comfort, they who mourn are blessed. Hadn't the chaplain just said so?
Why should she seek a blessing? Why should Cristo's death profit her
at all?

Father Ray waited with them till Father Grattan returned. He had delivered the brief message Agapito had written out for the reporters downstairs. The press had begun to converge.

It had been less than two hours since the phone call with the news of
Cristo's death, and already the word had traveled around the world.
Cristo was famous, and he was headlines once again.

"I won't leave him here," Cassia said, furious when they suggested she
and Agapito leave before the news media arrived. Downstairs in the waiting room, on the pavement outside, and in the entrances, well-wishers
and reporters had been gathering, not unkind. A few close friends came
too, and were permitted upstairs in the waiting room, poised or unpoised,
trying to help. Some wept with Agapito, some spoke with Cassia in gen-
tleness and love. She concentrated very hard on what they said. She listened intently. But they seemed to be speaking in code, and no matter
how she listened, she could not understand.

A nurse brought pills for later—doctor's orders—and the offer of a
shot for now, but Cassia warded everything like that off. All medicines
that would dull the pain, turning it into a blunt instrument to beat her
senseless. She wanted her wits about her and her eyes open, for if she
shut them, left her vigil, something else terrible might happen.

She saw Agapito in the hall, speaking with the doctor and the nurse.
She wondered if they were conspiring. She saw how they were all watching her. She backed away, even from Agapito, turned her back on the
whole lot of them who seemed to think that there could ever be some an-
odyne, or that it could be easy. When she had backed all the way across,
and bumped into the wall, she had the dark fortune to turn to the window just as the hearse bearing Cristo's body drove away. A dark, plain,

awful vehicle, as silent as a shark, purposeful, unhindered. Fascinated, she ceased breathing till it had gone out of sight, out from under the canopy at Emergency, and slowly away down the street.

"It might be anyone. It might not be," she said at large, "anyone we know."

Agapito joined her. She looked quite calm, but when he put his arm around her, he could feel her trembling. Father Grattan had delivered Agapito's brief message of gratitude to the reporters and fans, with thanks for their concern and a plea for privacy. Father Grattan and Agapito flanked Cassia as they rode down in the staff elevator; they ignored all shouts and flashbulbs and appeals on their way to the car. They powered Cassia through the crowd and into the car. She might have been a condemned prisoner being escorted from court.

Because it was Cassia's wish, Agapito and Father Grattan sent everyone away when they got home. A crowd had gathered there, also. Church friends, fishing friends, clients, fans, heartsick and stricken. Cassia went into the house and did not come back out. Father Grattan stayed a few minutes longer, after the others left. When he left, Agapito rode down with him to the road, to thank him, and to stretch anchor chain across the drive. They didn't have a gate; it would have blocked the view across the marsh. A strong barrier, the chain was practically invisible. A couple of fluorescent streamers hung from it, to warn traffic.

Agapito stood there in the twilight, wondering if he ought to hang the little sign he had made when Cristo got famous. Tourists and fans had come, seeking, at all hours of night or day, even in winter, and always during spring training and the regular season. The sign was never intended to protect Agapito and Cassia's privacy, but rather to spare the fans and well-wishers the futility of a long wait if Cristo wasn't in town, or likely to be.

NO ESTÁ.
—CRISTO—
NOT HERE.

Then Carlo, their old dog, came up from his evening run along the creek and his evening swim. The dog knew where the sign went. He sniffed the edge of it, looked back down the drive, looked up at Agapito. It settled Agapito's mind. He told the dog, in Spanish, how it was. How their boy would not be back. He gave the wood a little knock with his knuckle.

Agapito's eyes were tired. The twilight didn't help. He needed three tries to adjust the notice—this seemed important—to the exact center of the chain. He counted across the lane, link by link, to make sure, as though he were praying a giant rusted rosary.

A mullet jumped in the creek. Carlo responded with a bark. Often he and Agapito went out with the cast net at the turn of the tide, and fished off the dock. Carlo didn't know any better this night than to hope. He looked around. Agapito walked with him a few paces toward the water, then stopped. Listening. A heron quaarked, but that wasn't it. Agapito turned his head. The general marsh racket had set in, but Carlo heard it too—something behind them, toward the house. Carlo's ears perked.

Cassia. Cassia had begun to throw things, smash things. Even this far away they could hear glass breaking. Agapito ran.

He was glad now he had retrieved the little vial of pills from where she had slapped them into the corner of the waiting room, out of that nurse's hand. He knew how to use them, had no doubt or regret that he must use guile. Cassia liked her coffee strong, Cuban thick, and sweet, so this part was easy.

She never suspected a thing. She drank. Took several little cups to ward off sleep. She had no intention to sleep. She would keep pacing and making wild and dry-eyed plans forever. But the sedative worked. She finally sat in a chair, not leaning back, but drowsiness overtook her, and she asked for more coffee. She was asleep when he brought it.

Because there was no one there to help him watch her, when he got her into bed he strung a little bell to a piece of thirty-pound-test line and tied it to her ankle. Loose. She never stirred. No harm in it, only a hindrance. An alarm if he dozed off and she woke and decided to wander. Like belling the cat.

She slept several hours, and woke before Agapito. Before she could slip past him where he was sprawled in his chair at the foot of her bed, the bell called him to action. He toppled her into his arms, gathered her, and headed her back toward bed. She was wild, wild. Like a bat in a parlor. And groggy from the medicine, confused, trying to shake off whatever it was on her foot. She broke things. Smashed the mirror and a lamp. Ripped the curtains down from their rings and took a tumbling, cunning run over the bed itself to get to the door. No use, he'd locked it. She slid slowly down and sat, hard, on the floor, crying like a baby till she had no more tears.

"Please let me," she said.

"I regret," he told her, when he saw her finally comprehend that the little bell wasn't something she had stepped into by accident, but was intended, done to her, on purpose, and by his will and wile, exempt from causal extrication. Her will could not break that tie. She stared at the bell blank-eyed, blinking.

"You should have done this sooner," she said bitterly.

"Who are you to take blame like glory?"

He sat down beside her, and put his arm around her, drew her close. They talked then, made real plans for Cristo's honoring and laying away. Settled all that could ever be settled with talk. They went upstairs to Cristo's room and sat on the floor with their backs against his bed, looking through his scrapbooks, verifying dates and honors for his obit.

Cassia did not object when Agapito mentioned taking another pill. She reached for it eagerly and drank it down so gratefully, so thirsty for oblivion, for not-thinking, for peace, that Agapito made a mental note to hide the rest of the bottle. She would have been very surprised to know that Agapito had always known she had once tried to kill herself.

That was in fact how they had met, by accident, truly, and despite Cassia's proven susceptibility, it wasn't love at first sight. She hadn't been looking. She had plunged out into the street from between parked cars and darted into Agapito's path, exactly in front of St. Francis Xavier Church, in rainy twilight, Cassia's first winter in Sanavere City.

"Like cat," Agapito told the policeman. "Head up. No left or right, full speed." It sounded as though he had said "fool speed." The policeman shook his head, and wrote it down. Agapito showed him the way it had been, the quickness of it, the flash, with his hands, whisking the palms. "Like trains passing," he said.

So that first sight had been Agapito's, barely an instant before they collided, just enough time for him to jerk the steering wheel hard left and brake for dear life. He almost missed her, perhaps he could have, but when he swerved out of his lane, to try, an oncoming ice truck clobbered him and drove him back, and they all wound up news in the February rain. It was the first day of Lent.

When he'd kicked his way out of his jammed truck door and got to her, lying there with the breath knocked out of her, dead pale in the streetlight, the penitential cross of ashes on her forehead as stark as the bruise of a mortal blow, he thought she was dead; he thought he had killed her.

Then she coughed, gasped, and her breathing resumed. She was still unconscious. Her face, after the little spasm of coughing, was serene.

She had been carrying a leatherette case of organ music, and in the accident the loose papers had spilled. Bystanders began picking up the sheets, mixing and confusing the scores of the requiems—some Mozart, some Verdi—and one leaf washing down the gutter and into the storm drain. Agapito and the driver of the ice truck knelt beside Cassia, holding their jackets above her to keep the rain off her face. Help was on its way. Even now, Xavier's priest was there, kneeling, the very one who had drawn the cross above Cassia's brows, murmuring, "Remember your humanity." Now he took her hand, telling her, "All is well, all is well," gently, talismanic. Her eyelids flickered and opened. Sirens were piping far off but coming on.

Where did she think she lay, heaven? For a moment an uncomprehending radiance lit her face, then as suddenly faded. She struggled— fought them!—to sit up. Disappointment, panic, chased the look of joy; it fled like a bird startled from its shrub at night, flying wild and forlorn to God only knew what perch or doom.

While Agapito was answering questions, explaining to the Law, he left out his strictly personal eyewitness conclusion that she had thrown herself in front of his truck. It wasn't so much that the young woman had not looked to see oncoming traffic; it was that she had not cared. But of course this was only his opinion, a mere suspicion, darkened and not in any way relieved by the way she looked when she regained consciousness. It may have been a matter for the priest, but if so, then it was between her and God, not the police. Agapito kept his opinions to himself.

While the officers wrote down what Agapito told them, the ambulance came and took Cassia away. Agapito never thought to ask her name.

The hospital didn't keep her overnight. Couldn't. She refused to stay for further tests and observation, and was released after a lecture and a note on her chart: AMA—"against medical advice"—with a sheet of instructions to follow in case of serious symptoms. She was not in the hospital when Agapito came the next evening to visit her with a hard-gripped tissue of carnations and fern. He had scrubbed down twice to get rid of any fish scent, and had dressed for Sunday. He had used a potato brush on his hands, and a razor—midweek—on his cheeks. He was not sorry that his crew and friends were not around to see the results.

All of it for nothing, including oiling the tops of his shoes and buffing them—while he had them on—till his toes burned. Not to mention the price of the flowers, a considerable frivolity.

The duty nurse had sympathy, but would not tell him where Cassia lived. Policy. He next tried Admissions. They were closed. So Agapito left, drove around, thinking. His old truck flapped and trembled. One headlight goggled; one fender was nearly sheared and the other one had been crunched. The windshield was spidered and a stunned axle (on the side the ice truck hit) led the truck steadily rightward. He had to cut the wheel against its will, but he hardly noticed. He kept asking himself, Why does this stranger matter? Every light was red.

Then he thought of the accident reports. The light turned green. He drove directly to the police station and asked to see the records. "Is public," he kept saying. But they had no objection.

Now he was glad the officers had asked all those questions, had filled in all the spaces on the forms. He looked through all the pages. Her name was Cassia Campbell. Campbell. Anglo name, but she didn't look it. In fact, she was first-generation Greek-American, her father having shipped to the States on a common sea-ticket on a freighter, at seventeen, and taken as his "American" name the red and white trademark he had seen on a billboard for tomato soup. He had liked the sea well enough to make a career in the navy. They had moved around so much, they had never put down or dug up roots, but Cassia had, over the years, gathered bits of Greek culture. She had been glad enough, however, changing schools so often, to have a name that was familiar and not "foreign," and she had always worn her hair in that sleek cap, so that she did not have the tendriled profile of a statue. Her music teachers had always insisted that it was better to wear no jewelry—not even a watch—for auditions and concerts. She was not wearing a ring that day she ran into Agapito's path.

He thought about that, tried to recall. He did not remember any rings, but there was a great deal else to notice, so perhaps he had not seen what was there. He did not remember a wedding ring. But when he saw that her name was Campbell, he wondered. Married name, maybe? He scowled at the pages. He could speak English and understand it spoken much better than he could read it. If there was some clue on that report—single or married—he couldn't decode it. He did learn that she was employed as church organist, Xavier Parish. No home phone listed, no next of kin. Agapito copied down her address and filed it in the pocket of his shirt.

He would go see her. Married or not, he'd take his chances. He had to know. This very night.

She lived in a ground-floor apartment in a two-story, flat-roofed, stucco shoebox building he had never before noticed, though he had often driven that street on his way to Lupo's. On the main drag, down toward the old section, bayfront. There was a light in one window, no car in the drive, just a bicycle—woman's, he noted—by the front walk, chained to the porch column. It had a big basket, like a paperboy's, or a retiree's, big enough for groceries for a week, if you lived alone. A sign in the front window said PIANO. And he could hear music, but too good for lessons. This was not a lesson. It was Cassia playing, or the radio.

Agapito's heart lifted a little with these discoveries. He glanced back at his truck. He had parked it out near the curb, in her drive but with the tailgate almost in the street, saying "temporary" to anyone who wanted to raise objections to his being there at all. Just in case there was a husband, Agapito had decided to leave the flowers in the truck.

He hadn't considered what he would say. It wasn't far enough to the front door along that narrow walk; he needed more time. He turned and paced back and forth. Took his hat off and stuffed it in his pocket, smoothing his hair. Then changed his mind. Hated to be without his hat. She'd see—first thing—the silver in his hair, especially if she turned on the porch light, and of course she would. By now he was to the first step and was looking up at the ceiling to discover if perhaps the bulb was burned out or, next best, might be one of those yellow ones, dimmed to discourage bugs.

Before he could ring the bell, she flicked on the light and opened the door.

The rusty screen, one more layer of dark between them, was latched. He saw her look to make sure.

That wonderful, grievous music was playing behind her in rooms lit golden and gentled with bright rugs. Immediately he decided that she was too fine for him, completely beyond him. He stepped back, not recoil but relinquishment. His hat surprised him by being rolled tightly in his hand; he didn't remember having taken it off again. He shook his head.

"Yes?" She waited.

Her hands were ringless.

"Agapito Montevidez." He slightly bowed.

She didn't say anything, just stared uncomprehending.

"Was my truck . . ."

She glanced past him, toward the driveway and the battered Ford.

Her eyes, fugitive, fled from the truck to his face and back to the truck. "I will not be able to pay for it all at once," she began explaining. She dropped her chin to keep her voice steady and unshrill, a trick she had learned early, in choir.

Agapito waved his hands, no, no. His vehemence, the gestures, sent her back a step into the dark.

"I have the insurance," he clarified. "Okay by them."

She stared at him, wary. Dark circles under her eyes.

"Gesture of respect," he said. "With respect," he said. He bowed, set his hat back on, and fled.

She was still standing there, silhouetted against the screen, watching him back out into the street and drive off. Later she shut the door and turned out the light; not long after that, he coasted back, his one functioning headlight turned off. He ran across the grass, silent as a rabbit, and left the flowers on the stoop.

In the morning, when she went out to get her newspaper, she'd find them abandoned on her doormat like an orphan. By then, if he applied himself, he'd be two hours gone, fishing the sound, and if it was a good enough day, and he could master his imagination, he'd not be troubling about Cassia at all.

It was good when the work was hard, when there was so much to do. What was it his grandfather had always said? Every man has his own way of killing fleas. Agapito worked. The fish came into his nets. But still, the fleas kept biting, little thoughts he could not quite drown. He knew from the police report that Cassia was half his age; his boat was older than she was! He hadn't worried much when he passed fifty, because he had to pass it alone. But now he started looking around, looking back. Measuring. Subtracting. What was left. What added up.

"Something on his mind besides shrimp," his striker muttered when they ran into trouble. "Jellyballs!" he hollered, but Agapito didn't do a thing till their nets filled with jellyfish and the weight almost pulled the boat to a standstill.

"Cut!" Agapito called, then. He concentrated on jellyfish then. It was a mess; worst job there could be, clearing those nets. Yet he didn't hang back; he plowed right in with the crew. While he worked, there remained—remained to sadden (for it would eventually heal and be gone)—that bruise on Agapito's chest from Cassia's collision. Muscle, bone, or deeper, internal. Something hurt. They dropped the nets twice again that day and each time, hauling them up, a tenderness would catch him.

Would she be at the dock when they came in? She was not. Of course not. Even if she had known when, and who, and where—of course not. But still he looked, a quick survey his instincts argued against, and his experience. He drove his workers by their lodgings and cruised from there to Lupo's. The back way, not down that main street past her building. He told himself to forget all about that. Later, Lupo's was reeling and riotous as usual, the atmosphere a blend of *mojo criollo*, *sofritos*, fried bananas, nicotine, and coffee. He sat alone. Ordered a supper plate and didn't plan to linger. No cards tonight. No dominoes. No arm-wrestling. No stories. He ate without appetite. He found the food a little cold, and absently oversalted it. He shivered when Concha breezed up and began to clear off his plate and bring more coffee. She brought cognac too.

"Medicinal purposes," she said. "On the house." She'd been watching him. "I think you're coming down with something."

She studied him a moment and laughed, not unkindly. "Pray to God," she said. She reached for the cognac and offered her traditional toast: "My liver don't exist!" and knocked it back in one long gulp. "Agapito," she said, offering her verdict when she had her breath back, "a man too old to wish is too old to fish."

So there he was—no breakfast or coffee—the next Sunday, kneeling in Sanavere's grand old deep-vaulted St. Francis Xavier, with its whispers and echoes, not a large church, no cathedral for sure, but with its own cloister, elementary school, and cemetery. To him, accustomed to the chapel-like dimensions and motel-modernity of Nuestra Señora de la Caridad, this seemed papal and magnificent. There hung a glamour over everything. He felt a little giddy, having fasted since midnight.

He was talking to himself, but not arguing himself out of being there. He kept looking around, a little shy. Maybe they thought he was praying out loud. Maybe he was.

Everything here was generally familiar—words, prayers, standings and sittings, colors, scent of beeswax and incense—and everything was different, too, most especially the music. There were two choirs, facing each other. Beyond them? Below? Somewhere there was the organ. He could feel it in his feet, through his shoe soles, and under his hands on the pew back, and in his chest. He studied the pipes, imagined them as so much plumbing, and tried to trace them back to the source of that sound, but for the life of him he couldn't see the organ or organist. So he didn't know if it was Cassia or not. Whoever it was twinkled hands and feet over key and pedal like someone fighting off fire ants. Dancing. He tried to imagine how many notes were on a page, how the pages looked. Were they the same ones he and the others had collected off the street the night of the accident? He had the idea that the faster the music went, the more notes there must be on a page, like so many fish in a net, as though the lines were a net to catch song. He imagined these pages almost black with notes.

He had fasted, but he had not been to confession, so he did not move forward for the Host. As a boy, he had served as acolyte. He had learned the names of everything. So many words and names. Now he thought in English about it, in American terms. He thought about it in restaurant terms: napkin, plate, cup. No utensils, but when the sacring bell rang, he thought, dinner bell. He wasn't paying attention now that the organ had stopped.

They ate with their hands, he was thinking. Those fishermen of Jesus's. One hundred fifty-three fish, and the net did not break. *"Ascuas puestas y un pez . . . y pan,"* he was remembering, from Saint John. He nodded, thinking of the scene on the beach, how their hands looked, strong and a little stiff from hauling that net.

"Beeg feesh," he said.

Everyone else said, "Amen." They were kneeling, and then they were dismissed, and he left, to find a vantage out front to watch for Cassia. He waited a long time. He waited almost too long. Then he thought of the side door. By the time he walked around there to see, she was already gone. He picked out her dark cap of hair a good half-block away. She was walking slowly, and she stopped at the driveway in a group of other pedestrians while a string of cars peeled out from the parking lot.

That gave him the chance to catch up.

He had to dodge his way through and past whole loitering families on the sidewalk. Finally he stepped onto the strip of turf at curbside and ran. She didn't hear his footsteps on the grass, couldn't have, but she turned, warned perhaps by the jingling of his keys and his hard breathing. Again that look of wild hope on her face, fading when she saw it was Agapito, or, rather, when it was only Agapito.

That might have discouraged him, if he had had time to think, but he reacted to her paleness by reaching out. She seemed about to faint, and he caught firm hold, guided her through a gap in the oleander hedge onto a bench in the parish house's front garden. He tipped her over and shoved her head between her knees. Same cure he'd used more than once on deckhands, no time for questions asked, practical in the extreme. She rewarded him by retching on his shoes. Same as a deckhand.

Miserable as she had to be, all she could do was laugh.

They were in plain view of the house and street. The hedge was a psychological rather than a physical barrier, but no one paid them any official mind, or offered to help, or asked them to leave. There was a small fountain, a dingy plum tree, and a bird feeder in a circle of choking turf lilies. Sparrows and grackles flew in and out, taking sips or bathing in the water. Baby birds begged from hidden nests. Petals drifted from the gone-by plum.

For a moment, as Agapito dipped his handkerchief in the water, he forgot many years and family losses, two revolutions, his world war, much local history, happiness and regret. The cheeping of sparrows, splashing of water, and cloistered peace hypnotized him. He was a child again, playing on his grandmother's terrace.

"I'm all right," Cassia said. "Are you?"

When she had freshened her hands and face, he used the handkerchief to wipe off her shoes, then his own.

"My grandmother had a garden," he explained. "Bees. A fountain." There was room on the bench beside Cassia, but he did not sit.

"Maybe I scared you?" He pronounced it *ess-carid*.

"I—no breakfast. Missed supper, too."

He shook his head. Sighed. "I think I scared you."

There was a pause, a silence that seemed reasonable, not ghastly. They were both considering how much truth to tell.

"I just wondered who, that was all. When I heard—"

"Agapito Montevidez," he said.

"I remember."

"Permit me to walk to your car?"

"I don't have a car."

"Permit me to offer you mine? Is yours. Remain for lunch. Let me get my—"

"You have a lot of—" (What? Confidence? Nerve? She couldn't think.)

"Keys," he said.

They talked about those keys during lunch. They ate hamburger sandwiches, and they ate in the truck, drove out to the marsh, and parked in the shade. She got out and walked around. She seemed distracted. When he followed, she took the keys from his hand and hefted them. He told her what each one was for, their color codes, the rings on rings. Various engines, padlocks, compartments, tool chests, bank boxes, post-office boxes, ice lockers, foot-lockers, closets, gates, doors, rented rooms, his truck, the truck before that and the one before that, keys to houses that no longer existed, in a homeland that no longer believed in private property at all. "I no part so easy with things," he told her. "I no lose things or forget."

"Where in Cuba?" she wanted to know. "Where was your grandmother's beehive?" As though she knew all about Cuba, and honey. But she didn't, and she admitted that soon enough, and he told her all about everything. She had thought Isle of Pines was in South Carolina.

He considered it before correcting her, as though that too might have changed, like the name of the island itself, since the revolution. Then he said, "No," and drew her a little map on the back of an envelope, marking where—and there, and there too—with small, quick, dark *x*'s all along the north coast, and one on the Caribbean.

"You were rich?" she wondered. He considered that, too. Did she mind, either way?

"All gone," he explained. "Here is how it happen." He told her about the storm of '33 and the way everyone had had to start over, how he'd never gotten back to school though he'd helped rebuild it.

"Instead?" she wondered.

He told her about his little wife, their child. About the storm in '53.

"And that's where they're buried?"

She wasn't playing with the keys now. She held them perfectly still.

He turned his right hand palm up, helpless to explain. Finally, "Only their bodies," he said, and shrugged. He was not a man ready with words; he hooked them one by one and played them and fought them and landed them in English with gaps and pauses and frustrations. He had not had such a long conversation in years. He was better at listening.

"I am going to learn Spanish," she realized.

Even with difficulties, they found things to say and more occasions to say them. They met midweek. And again after church. And the next Saturday after that, she went to the docks to meet his boat. But they were very late coming in. It was past dark.

She had walked down. When he did not come, she sat in the cab of his truck. Even fell asleep. He knew, even before he found her note, that she had been there. Some personal spice or attar left in the air, clean and light, woodsy and pleasant, an uncloying essence more and more essential to him.

The note surprised him, to see her handwriting, her name. The pleasure of it overcame his regret at having missed her. He walked around into his headlight to read it.

I ll be
back wait if
you please
Cassia

All of it written in that same breathless way she spoke, her handwriting round and open-looped and unpunctuated and hunkered-down and slant-ing left.

She wasn't gone long. When she came back she had two little paper cups of hot tea. His whole life he had hated hot tea. Except for that cup of it. While they were sipping, they walked back down the dock to his boat. She hadn't seen it before. She had brought a little dictionary in her jacket pocket, took it out now to try to unpuzzle the name.

C. Viento y Marea.

"Is that a family name?" she wondered.

Agapito laughed. "*Dicho.* You know. Saying. *Contra viento y marea.* Bat-tle cry. 'No matter what.' You understand?"

"Come hell or high water," she said.

He liked that. "Come hell or high water," he agreed.

He had dropped the keys on deck. She picked them up, laid them on his palm. Held her own hand flat over them, lightly, gravely, as the priest blesses the wine. She would always surprise him, but this time he sur-prised them both. "If you like these so much, I can have another set made."

They stood like that, almost touching, doing nothing, settling every-thing. Father Ockham insists that before any wedding the marriage—the actual God-joining—has already taken place and the ritual of sacrament is simply the seal on the deal, a celebration and performance of the earlier moment. At any event, Agapito wasn't too old to fish or too proud to pray, first in hope and soon in thanksgiving: he and Cassia celebrated their marriage as soon as Lent ended, and he and his friends counted him the luckiest man on land or sea.

He only got luckier. Their son was born, a little early but fine, the week of Christmas the same year. By then they had finished building a simple two-story cinder-block and coquina house, perfectly square, flat-roofed, white, out on the sunset side of Dunbar, between the Sanavere River and U.S. 1.

"The sugar cube on the edge of the marsh," Cassia always said, when giving directions. They planted royal palms and a cajeput, camphor and red bay. Cassia's first little clearing of garden grew year by year. On their first anniversary, Agapito paid for a truckload of stones to be brought for the garden wall. The statue in the fountain came from the sea—he hauled it up in his net one day—a voluptuous fragment, very sea-worn, possibly a broken piece used as ballast in a sailing ship that never made it back to harbor. Whatever she was, she was no ordinary saint. Cassia called her an angel, furled. Agapito studied books and figured how to make the water spray and ripple around the statue's feet. From the first, the garden was a sanctuary for family and birds. Life was sweet.

It wasn't until Cristo was five and safely in kindergarten that Cassia ran away for the first time. Too soon it turned out that first time wasn't going to be the only time. The best luck that Agapito had ever had was beginning to look like no luck at all. A lesser man would have left her, or left her as dead as Desdemona. Not Agapito. How could he not take it personally, unless he felt he deserved it? And how could any man love that way unless he wasn't man enough, or man at all?

No note; she didn't know she was going to leave. No luggage; she intended to come home. A moment of melancholy, some low cello note sustained in her soul filling her with a cordial melancholy, turning her fugitive, not furtive. Rebel against the desolation, not life. It began that first time with an empty moving van rumbling down the road high on its axles and empty; she knew it would come back by on its way out, carrying within it a household, a home in its dark hold.

It brought her whole childhood back to her—all those moves as she grew up, a navy brat, base to base, her mother and sister and she following along, breaking camp, making camp, riding between temporary housing with the unsparable and fragile things balanced on their laps. Keeping personal life and items spare and tidy, always sorted and sifted and unaffixed—no pictures or posters hanging, just leaning. Their father did not like to repaint or plaster before the next move. They had nothing—beyond what they could hold in their arms—that could not be parted with. More than once, things were lost in the shuffle. They kept glue handy, to fix what could be, when it came out of the packing crates in pieces. Something always broke, with each move. "Even my mama's punch bowl was plastic!" Cassia told Agapito. For their next anniversary he bought her a crystal punch bowl with cups as thin as paper, a grandeur and burden she lived in terror of, whose beauty laid grave responsibility upon her, whose fragility she could imagine running back into the house to rescue while storm flags warned of imminent peril and evacuation routes were jammed with people who were wise enough to travel light, grateful for life itself.

Cassia was not ungrateful for life itself. She just wanted to make sure of things. She could never mail a letter without taping its flap against the undoing of weather or havoc, and now that she could put pictures up on her wall, she always nailed an extra nail. Applied glue in two coats. Went over every stitch in their clothes when they bought them, so nothing could come apart at the seams.

Agapito, with his lifetime collection of keys, was no match for her saving ways; he could lock or unlock, but Cassia could and did label and order and alphabetize everything they owned. Nothing was ever lost or misplaced or left to chance. Everything in her life, in her home, had its shelf, file, rank, value. Even time, measuring itself out by quarter-hours. She wasted nothing, wanted nothing.

And until that first time, when she so suddenly left, she would never have believed it could happen, and after it had, that it would ever happen again. Yet she could not have lived without the possibility. That was what she saw first. Jacksonville had never crossed her mind. At the ticket window she had seen the poster for the Mayport Jazz festival. When the agent asked "Where to?" she had pointed, and had taken her ticket and found her bus. Riding north, she felt a hot, fierce defiance and contempt at circumstances she could not even name or reasonably describe that had sent her—she felt driven—on this pilgrimage. Her ticket took all her pocket money, but she wouldn't turn back, wouldn't look back, or imagine life at home without her, the daily adventure, or life ahead, for however long, without them. She just rode knowing in her marrow that this going was essential and that any budget that allowed no squandering—and she did not mean money—would be bankruptcy continually. Something in Cassia's nature had saved up for this spree. Months and years had passed in absolute happiness. She was not faithless all along, but all at once. She was as surprised as Agapito.

This first time—when she phoned him from Jacksonville when it was over—he could say nothing after he said "Yes" to the operator about the collect charges. He listened. She had had her sister call him the first night to tell him Cassia was with her. True only for the length of the phone call.

After that, without plans and making no promises, Cassia had gotten in a taxi announcing she had an audition (she had no music with her), and had vanished from official records for five days, reappearing at the end of that time on the police blotter, rousted for vagrancy, having been arrested in the botanical garden at five in the morning for "trespass and behaving in a manner dangerous to herself and civil peace."

She had been found singing in the upper reaches of a Coral Shower Tree whose sign announced,

> There are many Cassias throughout the tropics.
> This coral-flowered one is first to bloom.

Tests made at the time of arrest subsequently proved her to be intoxicated, but without any trace of controlled substances in her blood. Her sister had told Agapito about Cassia's "audition." The first thing he asked Cassia, since there had to be a first thing, was, "Did you get the job?" This was her "one phone call." A lawyer, they told her. But she called home.

"I'm in jail," she whispered, as though making it harder to hear would explain why it was impossible to understand. Her own sister across town—the very one who had alibied for her—she didn't call, but Agapito. Long distance.

He heard her. "How much?" As though it were all simply a matter of money.

That was the only time he ever had to bail her out. When he got there, he had Cristo with him. He set the boy in the lobby while he and Cassia stood at the window and paid. No court to it. A perfectly civil transaction, like paying taxes. Cristo was looking all around, not ashamed or afraid. If Cassia was, she didn't show it.

As they were walking out, hand in hand in hand, Cristo asked, "Where are we going next?" And Agapito looked at his watch as naturally as ever, as though it were a matter of when, and echoed, "Where to?" yet making it an offer, not an ultimatum, allowing for whatever else Cassia might have on her mind or agenda. He'd brought her some clothes in a little suitcase, and extra cash, if she chose to travel on.

"Don't you have to see a man in Fernandina?" she asked. "That's on our way home."

They stood on the curb a moment, then crossed the gutter and headed for his truck, still all three holding hands. "On our way," he agreed.

He dropped off the captain's net—Agapito had already begun to have a reputation as a mender—in Fernandina and bought some ice cream, drove out to the beach.

It wasn't nice enough for swimming. A little cool. There were waders and shellers and walkers.

"I want to change!" Cassia said suddenly. She went into the bathhouse and showered and put on the clothes Agapito had brought her. She threw everything she had been wearing—even her shoes—into the garbage. A complete molt. She walked out barefoot, fresh, and ran to where Agapito and the boy were dancing with the skirts of the surf, forward and back, forward and back, laughing as the water and foam came close.

When they got home, Cassia would've sworn she wasn't at all the same woman who had left.

Agapito would've sworn nothing could have been worse that that first time, because he had no idea a thing like that would ever happen. Later on, he decided that the worst was the second time, when he saw that it might happen again. But finally he came to see that the most awful moment of all was after the third time, the fourth time, and the fifth, when he knew it not only could happen again, but would.

She never again needed to be bailed out. And she never again needed five days. She got better at it as she got worse. She'd go on weekdays while Agapito was out fishing and the boy was at school, and she'd get back to the bus station—wherever—with enough money left for a ticket home and a phone call. If she didn't make the fare, she'd call Agapito to come get her. He always did. She never took money out, hoarded up, or planned ahead. Not the slightest provision. Between these fugues, she never thought of going at all, nor did she think of what she did as straying. She looked neither forward with appetite nor back with remorse, performing immediate private acts of contrition and penance required by her confessor and conscience and living thereupon in composure, an honorable wife to Agapito Montevidez, untouched by time (a simple genetic blessing that kept her youthful and trim) and scandal (Agapito's lifework of chivalry and redemption).

She preferred to ride the bus home. Most of the times, she did, decompressing slowly back into her domestic personality. Her confession, on Saturday evening, neither elaborate nor detailed, was always sincere. She felt that since God knew everything, the priest did not have to.

On Sunday they attended Mass as a family and sat together. Someone else was organist now; after she had missed a few weekday rehearsals, she had resigned. Agapito had built her a music room at home, with a wall of windows, a Chinese rug, cases for her books and music, good chairs, and a baby grand they were still making payments on. Cassia had declined when Agapito wanted to buy her a car. "That's my car," she said of the piano. "The music takes me away." That was before she left the first time. The room always gave Agapito that same feeling he had had on her porch, the night he paid his respects after the wreck, when she had seemed too impossibly fine and beyond his hopes.

She'd play the most wonderful things, her small hands pouncing on the keys, her body tense as she leaned forward, her face as blank as the statue's in the garden as she concentrated. He admired her. Sat witness. His mind appreciating. She always played something new for him each time she played. She used to tell him the title and something about the composer. But he did not mind about all that; he liked it best when he simply played. She chose lieder, lullabies, nocturnes. Once, on one of her trips, she returned with a new book of such music, but he couldn't bear to hear those, the only time he ever walked away.

When Cristo was killed, Cassia believed that God had suddenly remembered her sins. She believed that God had somehow walked away. She understood then how God had witnessed every one of those mornings she had awakened in an unfamiliar room so displaced in her own thoughts and reality she couldn't for a moment recall what year of her life it was, what city, what day. When Cristo died, she had that same sense of a sudden return to reality, a terror of comprehending what she had risked, what she had thrown away.

When she was away from home and felt this way, nothing to do but dress and go. Knowing herself exactly, knowing the fullest, bitterest measure of herself. Powerless beforehand to prevent this mania and ruin, yet, in the very moment of realizing her degradation, taking her only victory—closing the door quietly behind her and slipping away. Knowing where she really belonged, who she was and whose, if he'd have her back. And Agapito had never yet failed to meet her more than halfway. Because he never faltered in honoring her, the people in town could do no less.

Early on, if anyone pried or asked ill-timed questions, he'd answer, "And how is your business?" and pitied the fools who pitied him.

When Cristo had been dead thirty-nine hours, Cassia woke. She didn't thrash around; for a moment she didn't do more than take inventory. Item by item she figured out the room, assessed the damages she had inflicted on its windows and walls, built it into reality and placed herself in it. There was Agapito at the foot of their bed, his head on his arms, resting only momentarily. Immediately he woke, as though her mere gaze had been a cry of his name.

Her eyes were matted but lucid, dark-circled but not wild. She was home. She sat up and he helped her to the bathroom. Together they washed the salt off her face, combed through her hair. She leaned into the mirror, close. "Is it white now?" She tried to see the back of her head, the crown. She felt so old.

Her hair was as black as ever, a sleek cap as glossy as a grackle's back.

As she stepped into the shower, the little bell on her ankle jangled. Agapito knelt and tried the manicure scissors. They were like a child's toy against the monofilament. He went to get his pliers. He nipped the line with his side-cutters and took off the bell, laid it on the sink. She brought it out when she came back to the bedroom and laid it on the arm of his chair.

He was just sitting there, looking out the window.

"I wish it was just any day," she said. "What day is it?" She thought. "Did I miss—"

"Funeral? Is today. Is time for coffee, then we dress." He led her to the kitchen; he had already set out spoons and cups. He had set those rooms back in order, swept up the broken things, restored the curtains to their rods and rings. He opened the curtains now to let in maximum light. It made the white kitchen stark, dazzling.

While Agapito turned, pouring the juice and coffee, setting things on a tray, she left. She was always so quick and quiet. He looked over at her chair to ask if she wanted toast, and she was gone. He whirled toward the door, which hadn't swung shut yet. She was standing there looking down toward the creek. Not full tide, but drowning depth, even at ebb, for the determined. Her hand lifted from the porch rail and for a moment he imagined her leaping from there, as though the intervening lawn were no obstacle. He imagined himself outrunning her, having to, tackling her. Or worse, because she knew he would never, with that bad leg, outrun her, fishing her out of the water dead, if that was how far she intended to go. He let his mind run that far, speed of light, in perfect shape for it, years of practice. He began to form the syllables of her name, if that would do any good; she would hear that, the last thing she ever heard . . . him coming after her, calling her back.

All this in an instant, between the time she raised her hand from the rail and stretched it out to signal to Carlo. The old dog hauled himself to his feet, trotted up and came on in, wagging and thumping and making glad. She knelt by him and held him close. "Oh, Carlo," she said to him, "did anyone tell you about our boy?"

She looked around to see if Agapito would nod yes. Agapito was leaning against the sink, the rush of relief about Cassia bringing an old pain to his heart. He managed to cross the room fairly chipper and straight and set the tray in front of Cassia, but the cups were trembling against their spoons and saucers and she noticed it. Looked up at him, surprised, then stricken.

"My Agapito!" She shoved her chair back and reached for him.

He didn't fall. He sat. Wouldn't lie down. Almost laughed, he felt so foolish and all gone, his long bones and arms like water.

She crouched beside him, clasped her arms around him. "Ill? Agapito, are you ill? Is it bad? I'll call someone. Help me think! Senses, help me!"

He could almost have laughed, really, at her total disarray and fussing, except that she was frightened. He didn't want her to suffer for his sake. "No, no," he apologized.

But she stayed frantic, so finally he explained, "You scared me. That's all."

"I scared you!"

"I think you maybe going down to the creek—"

She looked at him, puzzled. He put his callused hand to her cheek, the tip of his index finger, lost in youth, the only thing missing from his total tenderness.

"—and not stop."

Comprehension and outrage dawned together. She pushed herself away from him. She would not be accused. So many things he could have accused her of. But to be told she made him suffer for something she never—

"Why would you say that!"

He was sorry he had, very sorry.

"Why?" It felt good to be angry; for this little while, it drove out the grief. It felt like action, as if something was getting done.

"Maybe you leave something in boat," he said.

"That's not what you meant! Why don't you say what you meant!"

"God knows," he told her then, "we should have talk of this in beginning, or never."

She couldn't think of anything to say to that. She went over it in her mind, word by word. He couldn't mean what she thought he meant. What if what she thought he meant wasn't at all what he meant, and she betrayed herself by some hasty remark? But what could he mean, if not that? That couldn't be it!

The tension of the unsayable thickened as it had the moment before he had told her of Cristo's accident, when he had listened and said, "All right," and come to her and stood and said nothing, so she knew it would be something impossible and she had said, "Tell me!" when what she meant had been "Don't tell me."

She said it now. "Tell me!"

"All right," he said. "Every moment of our life—and the boy's life too—was stolen back from what you hoped was death. Can you deny?"

Stunned, she didn't say anything. In her astonishment an absolute alienation occurred. She felt betrayed, felt he had harmed her all those years. That life itself had played a joke. She couldn't grasp it. She kept sorting it, sorting.

"Will he be here today?" Agapito didn't look at her when he asked.

"Who?"

"The boy's father."

That was the thing that left her totally speechless. All these years, she saw now, Agapito thought she had been going away like that to— Would it be better if he knew the truth, knew it had always been strangers? That Cristo's father had been just one more? For a moment, in her own hurt and amazement, she had a glimpse of what Agapito must have been going through, was going through now.

Would it help him at all if she said, simply, no? But she couldn't even say that. She had believed that all her life she had kept the good and washed the bad away. She had thought she could do that. They seemed to be total strangers; she dressed for the funeral Mass in a separate room. They rode together but said nothing. The crowds helped, the busyness of the funeral, the pictures the world pressed into her eyes momentarily overcoming the inner chaos. Every once in a while a phrase would seep through, some kind-intentioned person leaning close, offering comfort. "It takes time."

"That's what hell is for," she said.

From time to time the words of the Psalm broke through also.

according to thy great mercy

She tried to shut it out.

ever present before me . . . against thee alone have I

She stumbled

and what is evil before thee I have done this I confess

and Agapito caught her arm, helped her up the steps. They stood at the door, the chant going on within and without the walls

and in sins did my mother conceive me. Behold, thou lovest loyalty! The hidden and secret things of thy wisdom thou makest known to me

while the pallbearers

a spirit chastened, a heart broken and crushed

eased the casket through the doors.

"Oh, Agapito," she whispered, when they followed it in and saw that the church was full.

During Communion they did not hold hands, but Cassia laid hers on the rail, near him, if Agapito chose to. At the last moment he covered her hand with his, and when they rose, they rose in unison, together again though there were all those miles she had ridden, the length of all those beds between them, but somehow they held on.

The funeral procession was three miles long. Afterward they went home, left the supper and drove back alone. It was almost dark when Agapito paused inside the gate to stretch the chain across. When he got back in the car, Cassia almost had the question formed, the one she had been trying to answer on her own all day. "Why did you let—"

But no, that wasn't it. She shook her head. Couldn't speak around the constriction in her throat.

"Why I let you trick me, you mean?" He piloted them up the lane to the house. "You think you not worth loving if I know? You think I don't see it be me or just some other damn fool you tricking, once you decide to stay?"

But that wasn't it either. They sat there in the twilight while she tried to say it. Finally she exclaimed, "But why didn't it make any difference?"

Did she not know? Why did she not know? His head hurt. He went inside then, found the aspirin, sat in the music room with no lights on. The leaflet missal in his back pocket crackled when he sat. He leaned forward and pulled it out, laid it on the table. He was too tired even to pull his necktie off, or his shoes.

He could hear her in the kitchen, running the can opener, feeding the dog. She set the dish on the back terrace by Carlo's water pan. The phone was ringing. She didn't answer it. Wouldn't. No intention of ever answering it again. Agapito hauled himself up and moved toward it.

Didn't answer it, either. Unplugged it from the wall, and then went looking for Cassia.

She was standing in the garden, by the birdbath, filling it with fresh water. When Cristo, as a little boy, had asked why the lady was standing in the birdbath, Cassia had told him, "She's washing her feet of clay." After he began to play baseball, he'd say that, from Little League on, after a game as he headed for the shower. "I'm gonna go wash these feet of clay."

"You weren't 'just some damn fool somebody,'" she said. "You have been my life."

"The boy," he reminded her.

"No," she said. "Think about it. He didn't change my mind toward living; you did."

They sat in the garden till late. Talking. Thinking. She told him she had never seen Cristo's father again, had never gone looking. Explained how that had been.

He was thinking about the accident. About the ice truck, how it had knocked him back into her path. "I almost missed you."

Toward morning they drove over to the island, to the cemetery where Cristo had been buried. She rode the last quarter-mile with her hands over her eyes. "I don't think I can bear it," she said.

"*Mira,*" he told her. And she looked. The flowers covered the entire plot, ringed it, overflowed. There were little candles in cups, still flickering.

They stayed till daylight, till the last candle winked out.

When they got back to the house, Father Grattan was there. He had brought mail—a sack of it. While they were away florists had delivered more tributes.

Agapito went to make more coffee, though Father Grattan said he would not stay unless he could help with the mail or something.

Cassia invited him to sit, just for a moment. "One cup," she required.

He sat. Agapito didn't have much to say. He actually dozed a little. The silence lengthened. They didn't speak because of Agapito. They did not want to wake him.

"How many days has it been?" she whispered, counting them up. She had lost a few.

Father Grattan counted. "Five," he said.

"Will she live?" She found she could not speak Faye's name.

For a moment he didn't understand her question.

"That girl in the car."

"She may, yes. It looks as though she will. Faye, yes. They have her sedated. Coma lasts for a while. It has only been five days," he said, as though that were not so long.

"And nights," Cassia added.

Father Grattan cleared his throat. "Father Ockham ate a little breakfast this morning. He may even get out in the garden this afternoon a few minutes."

Agapito didn't wake. Cassia walked the priest to the door. "Come back," she said. "Come back in a few days. Sit in a chair, on the terrace. Make my Agapito come to rest—he will be working, my Agapito is always working. He will sit down then, and listen, even if he doesn't talk. You talk. And that way he will rest."

While Agapito slept, Cassia cleared away the few dishes and ran the water to wash them. She squirted liquid detergent into the pan and the suds rose, crackling. She started to take her ring off, slide it idly off, unthinking, and bank it in Cristo's baby cup on the sill, when she paused. Didn't. Just didn't. Not couldn't, but wouldn't. Would never take it off again.

Later that evening she was sitting at the piano, touching the keys but not making any sound, when she realized that the thing she had been listening to, and for, had ceased. Agapito had been driving the belly mower down and back along the lawn and field by the creek, to keep the marsh at bay. She rose and went to the window to look out. Didn't see him, though the tractor was there. She poured a glass of lemonade and walked out to find him. She was halfway around the house when she met him. He had got as far as Carlo's doghouse and was leaning against it, bent over. He didn't hear her even as she called his name, but after a time his eyes noticed her shoes there in front of him, and he slowly looked up. Not lifting his eyes, but his whole head.

"Something?" she cried. "Phone?" She scanned him for blood. He did not seem injured. "Heart?" He did not seem to understand her. In her panic she could not think of the words in Spanish. She touched her own chest, over her heart, and then gestured as though making a telephone call.

He nodded.

She ran. It felt like slow motion, but she was back in no time. He didn't fall. He never left his feet till the ambulance arrived, and he helped himself up its step. Finally he lay back, and the oxygen washed the blue from his lips immediately. Every heartbeat of the siren-screaming way, Cassia was beside him, not letting go.

He did not lose consciousness. Every car they met pulled off the road to yield way. He lifted his hand, as though brushing off all the trouble they were taking. She caught his hand and held it to her lips.

For Cassia, for Cassia alone, he said the last English words he'd ever speak. "Not—sorry—damn—fool—was—me."

BOOK THREE

FIREWORKS

But the longing persisted, and when it grew weary, the longing for this longing.
—Eugen Herrigel, *Zen in the Art of Archery*

PART I

LONGING

Zeb Leonard was not the sort of man to trot to his wife for permission before doing what he knew was right in moments of destiny, but he did rather expect her praise for the results. When the three rode out—Zeb and Palma and their boy—that Sunday afternoon after church, she didn't know that they were headed for a tidal creek off and up Sanavere River to see the boat Zeb had already signed for. She thought they were in a celebrating mood because of her being pregnant again and because it was spring. They had half a picnic with them, the other half to be brought by Ben and his wife and kids. Zeb was the first one to arrive at the site, and he soon found out this wasn't going to be any picnic.

"How do you like it?" he asked. The boy was already out of the car, running toward the bluff, enjoying himself. Staking claims before the other children got there.

Palma looked all around, smiling, thinking Zeb meant how did she like the location. Smiling, remembering that she'd been there before, years ago, no, not there, not even close to there . . . couldn't be the same creek! just somewhere along a creek that looked the same. That time had been in Georgia, and had been, as it transpired, the last wild night of her misspent youth, a turning point on the road to her own destiny. That was how she thought of Zeb, that was what he was to her, and she had known it their first hour together.

"Well?" Zeb asked, and Palma brought her thoughts up to date, still smiling.

Then she noticed how he was staring at that shrimper weathering in its cradle above high tide. Elven was out there chasing something, in and out of the shadows.

"Do you like it?" Zeb asked again.

Palma shivered as the first chill shadow of a doubt crossed her mind. "I hope you mean the weather," she said. "Or the locale. Or anything in the wide world except that wearying boat."

Zeb had stepped around to open her door. He helped her out. "Come see," he urged. "She's ours. Done done."

Palma's shriek turned their boy's head. She had to sit back down, fast, with her head between her knees. She spoke faintly into her skirt. "Signed and sealed?"

"Optioned," he explained. "Deposit nonrefundable. I think we can get a ninety-day rollover on the truck loan."

" 'We'? You and who else?"

Zeb hesitated. It had seemed so simple, that day the old Cuban told them, "Decide with calm," and he and Ben had driven away, around the block, down the next block, and back, parking for fifteen minutes so they wouldn't look too eager. But they were sure. They knew. Zeb told her, "Ben. Me and Ben."

"My Bennie? My brother?" She sat up, looking around for him. He and Cliffie were late. Just as well. Palma wouldn't set foot on that boat till she had reasoned it all the way through.

"Cliffie's Ben," Zeb reminded her. "She has a say in it. A stake in it, too."

"Does she know? She getting to vote the way I am? *After* the polls close? Has she seen this boat?"

Zeb looked around. "I don't know where they are," he hedged. "Supposed to be here already." He didn't let his crest fall yet, but he was having to work at it.

Elven came up, swung on the open car door, announcing, "I'm hungry."

"There's a little galley. Table and everything. You bring a tablecloth?" Zeb was tired of her teasing and stalling. "The boy and I'll be on board," he said, signaling Elven—one long whistle that worked wonders—and left her in the car. His shoulders were set in an I-know-you're-watching-but-I-don't-give-a-damn brace, and he covered the distance to the dock and its weathered length in long, determined strides. Elven hopped innocently along beside him from plank to plank over the gaps. She watched the expression—not on the boy's face, they were too far away for that, they were silhouettes, dark against the glare off the water—but rather the boy's whole body and Zeb's too, as they discussed the boat. Anticipation, enthusiasm, excitement, delight, fraternity. The boy broke and ran. Toward the future. It might have been Christmas and he was the first up.

She felt left out.

They vanished up a ladder over the side, and she was alone with her first impressions and second thoughts. She rolled the window down, trying to catch their voices, Zeb's low rumble, Elven's happy young piping.

"I can see daylight not just underneath that boat," she pointed out to

God, as though offering a defense for her hanging back, "but also through it. I can see right through it!" She eased out of the car, left the door open, began the long, slow walk down to the dock and ways. She studied the ladder for some time before she put her hand and foot on it. She stopped from time to time and tapped her strong finger on every weak spot she saw in timber and steel, in case God hadn't noticed, and begged His protection if not his mercy, on foolish men and their dreams.

When she poked her head over the rail before boarding, Zeb was standing at the wheel, happily explaining to Elven, "The danger signal is five or more short blasts." Zeb looked even happier when he saw Palma.

"I told you I was going to be a skipper someday, me," he reminded her. He gave her his strong hands to help her over onto the deck.

"That's right, mister, you did," she agreed, "but I thought you meant seagoing."

Palma was a little older than Zeb, but he was years ahead of her in knowing how to live his life. Palma let things happen; Zeb made them happen. Sometimes she thought about the difference between them, and what she was doing, growing up in Georgia, while he was growing up in Alabama, out in the field with a hoe, while she was running wild on the island—not a door in Birdwhistle Hammock closed to her, not a turn of path strange to her tough bare feet.

Twelve years before she set foot on the mainland's downtown except at Christmas. When it happened, it was the end of summer, not the end of the world, wild grape leaves turning gold in the oak tops, little mushrooms like thumbtacks in the damp ditches, and the cattle gate—cool to bare feet—lost to her touch in school shoes, and Palma crying like it was death and taxes. All it was was junior high.

"You got something for do beside trifle with a cast net and run around free from day to dark. Don't know how I know, but I know," Nana Ada said.

"I be come back?" Palma wondered. She knew. She just wanted to hear Nana Ada laugh. "I be right here watch you step off the ferry," Nana Ada promised. "Every day."

Palma left, wintergreen sweet and crisp-ironed, with starch, on that yellow bus, rode and rode, looking through a rain of tears. The next fall,

Bennie—who'd been held back a year—went too. No tears from him. Natural as a melon parting clean from the vine. He liked new ways, and even played football, but he was no scholar. Palma never shamed herself with her marks. But her specialty was home economics—all those appliances in that "lab"! Machines do all that work. She set her heart on having a washer for Nana Ada. Two years of part-time work and she did.

After graduation, Palma stayed in town. Made a good enough living, supporting herself and her "appliance habit," for six years operating the elevator at the grand old bank downtown, shopping at Sears, and furnishing her grandmother's house with Kenmore everything. Never in all that time needed or took a sick day for body or soul. Liked how things were going, just going up and down. Then Nana Ada died, and Ben got drafted. When she thought about it sometimes, Palma couldn't figure where those years went. What she had to show for them she could carry in both hands—her "admiral" uniform and an engraved badge: AT YOUR SERVICE PALMA STEVENSON. These they let her keep, when they remodeled the bank, modernized the elevators, made them self-service, and brought Palma down to earth forever. Not fired. They had another word for it: "severed."

Where would she ever again need that double-breasted blue serge with its brass buttons and silky epaulets? She handed over her ring of keys and wrote her name on the official papers, sheets and sheets of them that all added up to "the end," and walked out of the third-floor office after shaking several hands. That was it. No ceremony. She was just the next one, after the last one, and there were plenty more—black and white both—waiting their turn on the little chairs in Personnel.

Palma knew everybody by sight, if not by name, but no one was feeling conversational. There was a bright gloom under those flickering fluorescents in the ceiling, a dreamlike torpor. They still belonged, for just a little while longer.

Palma walked out into the hall, severed.

That's just what it felt like. Lopped off. Like dreaming some terrible thing and the most awful part was not feeling it. It made her want to yell, run wild, anything to break the spell.

Her elevator was chained. OUT OF ORDER, the sign said. It wasn't. But they'd told her on Saturday they didn't need her anymore; all those jackhammerings and drillings and mysteries and rumors finally came clear. She vowed she'd never use the new elevator; climbed all those stairs in the fire exit—"Why not the *fire* exit?" she said, "I'm being *fired*"—and was planning to use them now, but the guard wouldn't let her. Herded her back up half a flight to three, and pointed down the corridor to where.

"Yeah, sir," she said. He watched to make sure she did.

She walked down the hall to those stainless-steel doors shining like a new saucepan, poked the button whose arrow pointed toward hell. The bell rang bink-bink almost at once and the doors smoothed open, a cool lady-robot voice from a grid overhead in the car warning, "Watch your step . . . Going down."

"You telling me," Palma said. She hated it in there, being out of charge where she had once been in charge. Those solid walls, no little window so you could read the numbers as you came to the floors. Nothing to hold on to. By habit she stood to the left front, in the driver's position, staring at the self-service button panel. The car stopped gently, no lurch or sink of arrival.

When the doors opened—no jerk, no rumble, just pure glide—she stood there, though there was a little crowd waiting to go up. She started to welcome them, then realized it was not her business, as of now, forever. Overhead the robot voice warned, "Watch your step . . . Going up." Palma pushed her way out, stepped onto the solid terrazzo of the lobby, into the free world of what-came-next.

That smolder of wildness fanned up in her, with the breeze from the street. She stood a long time on the steps, then turned herself around, looking at the sky, the street, the Monday workday traffic. Everything looked just like itself; only person out of place in the whole wide world was Palma.

Two white boys in a revved-up car idled at the light, yelling, "Where's the rest of the parade?" as they tore on away down Gloucester Street, leaving a trail of smoking rubber. Because of her uniform and the little hat. She had never been ashamed of her uniform, wasn't ashamed then, either, but then was when she wanted to cry. Because the jacket, with its brass and braid, now meant nothing. It lay heavy on her shoulders, but she wouldn't take it off in public, and she walked as tall and haughty as she could, so that if anyone was spying from that third-story window in Personnel, they'd have nothing to report in the way of sagging morale.

Everywhere she went looking for work, they told her, "No luck, sorry." Motels, the loan company, cafés, packers, bus station, five-and-dime, schools, all had all the help they needed. Maid and bus work was in short supply, nothing much was happening in Georgia at all on the coast. Even the navy had gone.

Palma fished the want ads out of the trash. *Jacksonville Sun, Florida Times-Union*. Read them all, letting her feet cool out of her shoes, giving herself a break, sitting on the St. Marks steps. Nobody said Boo. Not even Keeter, driving by slow, not noticing her, even though she called out, and who else was there but Palma sitting in the sun in her soft yellow sweater that accentuated the positive?

She wadded up the papers—plenty of jobs, if she would just relocate—and stuffed them in the trash can again. That was when her LUCK CHANGED. That's what it said on the bright orange handbill that wafted out and skittered along the gutter, teasing Palma along after, like a kitten after a string. She caught up and stomped it, picked it up and read,

> Money? Love? Work Worries?
> Let Madame Hortense Try.
> Reader and Adviser. Adept.
> Interdenominational. Lowest Rates.
> Cardiff Street . . .

Madame Hortense's place was dandy. A green and yellow block bungalow with a blue plywood star nailed to the point of the roof, and matching new moons cut in the shutters. Not a blade of grass or flower in the yard. Sand. Garlands of jasmine vines twinkling like stars in the pine tops. Blackbirds strutting around, making their rusty remarks to each other, eyeing the two women standing on the bottom step. Palma suddenly changed her mind, never mind her luck. But the cab had already gone.

Pretty little boy opened the door and stared out at them. Not white, not black. Something else. Dirty neck and no buttons on his shirt. Hot eyes of a practicing terrorist.

Palma's friend Toby nudged at the door with her sandy sneaker.

"Madame Hortense herownself," she required. Bold as a sheriff with a writ. The boy ran inside hollering, "Grandma!" Door ajar.

Toby pointed to the mat under their feet. " 'Welcome,' " she read. "In we go."

Nothing special to look at in the dim light. Smelled like wet dog or something wrong, bad wrong, under the carpet. Aquarium leak, probably. The fish tank was nearly swamp black. One pale fish stared desperately out from a tangle of weed. The whole contraption bubbled like a cauldron. Palma caught Toby's arm. Footsteps coming their way, the sniff and slap of house shoes with a loose sole. Breezy sound, like taffeta on taffeta, came next. In brisked Madame H. She was impressive, big enough for two, as glorious as a funeral. Ankle-length skirt, plaid blanket shawl askew on her shoulders, head wound round and round in gold brocade. Gold clanking and chiming and chattering everywhere, neck, wrists, fingers, ears, even on her ankle. Strung with silver necklaces too. And some charms made of wood and what appeared to be turkey feathers and squirrel fur. Saints and totems and coins rattled on their chains. Earrings heavy enough to anchor a boat. She gave them time to take her in.

"Difficulties?" she suggested, when they had taken stock.

Palma held out that orange flyer she had retrieved from the trash. "This stuff true?"

Madame H. nodded, almost shy. Held out her hands, hennaed palms up, as though apologizing for such skill. "Frankly," she said. And that was all she said, till they had settled the matter of her fee.

"Five dollars per hand. Spiritual rendering, ten. Change your luck, fifteen. Change of heart, seven-fifty. Oils and herbs and incense, dollar on up. Aerosols extra."

Palma hesitated.

"Full-court treatment," Madame said, "thirty-five."

"Needs it. Ain't got it," Toby explained.

"Today only, the works, twenty-five."

Palma gazed into her purse, muttering, "Cab fare."

"We'll walk," Toby said.

Startled, Palma thought she meant right then. She turned and headed for the door. When she caught on, she laughed along with them.

"All I got is eleven dollars and some change."

Madame scowled. But took it, pennies too. "I'll see what I can manage," she said. "This way."

Through a red plastic curtain into a flamingo-pink, tobacco-smoked room with Martin Luther King on one wall. Madame H. adroitly flung her shawl over another picture, a soldier in gray, on a horse. AND TRAVELLER, announced the unmuffled half of the little brass plate on the frame.

"Seated," Madame H. directed, and they sat. Madame studied them. Pointed to Palma. "You're the one with the jinx. Who put it?"

Palma and Toby looked at each other, high beam. Then Palma looked at her hands in her lap and said, "I lost my christening cross out fishing with Keeter, then I lost Keeter, then I lost my job."

Madame H. said, "Mess," in a speculative way. Took up her Tarot cards and riffled them. Brought the deck to her lips and tapped. Then blew her breath over them.

Palma didn't like it. "I never come here to cut *cards*," she said, shaking her head.

Toby elbowed her to be still.

Madame H. smiled. "Tools, not sporting, not a matter of chance, a matter of fact," she said. But she laid them aside and went into the other room and brought some tea. Toby sipped cautiously; Palma just stared into her chipped cup at the punk liquid.

Toby explained, "Cards like this be like medicinal alcohol."

Madame H. seemed alarmed.

"Just herbs, that's all it is. Refreshment even a baby could take." Madame wiped her lips on the hem of her blouse. No way they could have seen her, in the kitchen, door shut solid, splash a little bourbon in her own cup. "Now then," she said, "let's see those hands."

It was almost five o'clock when they got away from there. Toby hardly hit the sidewalk before she was fretting over her family, how they'd be as hungry as sharks, and if she'd known she was going to do all this, she'd have left the slow cooker on. They'd used up cab fare, and a little more too, on Madame Hortense's oils. At Pea Street they got a ride with someone they knew, and parted ways at Jackson. Pretty time of day in the prettiest time of year—redbuds and dogwoods and azaleas bright in the sun.

Palma felt young and new as she stepped along. It wasn't Wednesday, but she headed for the Better Life Mission Club anyway. She could smell fish frying. Knew in her heart she'd find Keeter, and he'd buy her a plateful. She was hungry-hungry.

She went card-playing with Keeter after supper, squatted there beside him, thigh to thigh, and played out on the marsh in a high-and-dry boat, saying, "This just my lucky night." Of course she won. Won and won. Claimed her share and stood up when Keeter did.

It was late. She didn't know how late it was. Didn't care. "Evening all," he said, leaving. They tried to call him back, but she and Keeter were up the ladder—Palma first, Keeter right behind with his hands on her hips— and gone, with "business in town."

In the car, he told her, "You not the same gal." They drove past the Abyssinia Baptist with its PRAY marquee. "Where you been?"

"Where you been looking?"

The late train crept on across Gulf Street. She put her head on his shoulder while they waited at the grade crossing.

"What you want, gal?" he teased her. "What you gone do with that money you win tonight?"

She was in a squandering mood. "If you could have anything in the whole world, any wish, what would it be?"

"Like what?"

She felt so quiet and full. As if they'd been fishing all day and had a brimming basket to show for it. "Oh," she began, but decided to rest her mouth a bit longer, do a little listening, a little dreaming. If she had all the money in the world, she'd put enough to the side for some more schooling, so she'd never again have to wear her shoes out begging for wages. Send a little to her mama and stepdaddy upriver, buy every one of the half- and step-sibs bicycles and skates. Buy her own Pap a bass boat, little little one, or maybe just a new motor and a fish finder. Put a marble stone on Nana Ada's grave, with a little looking-up angel. Buy Ben a truck, if he still wanted one. Pay his tuition at the Vocational.

What she wanted for herself didn't take money, though. She thought about that, how she wanted happiness, no, something bigger than "okay," something tremendous but quiet, a life, that was all, just a life on any street, in any house, with neighbors to look out and see her husband walking out in the morning satisfied, on his way to his wages, striding along peaceful-like in clean clothes, fresh-ironed, a sweet orange in his left hand, his hair in her comb, his child in their bed till school time, his kiss sweet on her mouth all day long, her brother calling him friend and her family calling him sir, her old Pap sharing the bench with him, as they sat in the yard and smoked.

Palma shook her head. Wouldn't say all that. Not just yet. Shy, she asked him, "What *you* want?"

They were back in town now, back on their side of the tracks, paused at the red light. The billboard on Hogg's boarded-up grocery proclaimed THE COME TOGETHER STATION—WADN RADIO—VOICE OF THE MIRACLE COAST. A poster next to it, sun-faded, offered stylish black faces staring nowhere past each other's eyes selling cream? cigarettes? beer? Bottom half torn away, pasted over with store ads and handbills for last year's fair. Keeter idled right there, studying the ad.

"I want me a diamond ear stud," he decided, gesturing toward the man on the left in the poster. "Like that dude's there. No more cubic damn zirconia."

Palma waited. "Is that all?"

"Eh, so." He nodded, satisfied. "Got everything else." He studied the billboard again, checking out the fashions against his own.

The light went from stop to go and Palma took the whole next block to move. Then she let out her breath, slow. Eased over to the door on her side, and reached up to her neck to untie Madame Hortense's High John kernel. She dropped it out the window. It landed in the sandy gutter along with the litter of pop tabs, cigarette nubs, dry leaves. She thought she could see it, shining like something slowly winking out.

"What you looking back for?" he asked.

She untwisted herself and faced the future.

"I don't know," she said. God's truth. "Nothing, I guess."

There was a little half shell no bigger than a baby's fingernail still lying on his dashboard where she'd put it the day she got laid off at the bank, and they went fishing. She noticed it and reached for it just as they hit a pothole. The shell went to dust under her fingertip.

He started to turn in at the All-Nite for her to buy breakfast groceries. But she'd changed her mind.

Four years then, after that moment, not caring about courting any man. Couldn't stand the sight of her same old self in those same old mirrors. Moved back to the island that summer, was living there when they got the news about Ben. He needed help she didn't know how to give when he came home from the VA Hospital. She saw how she could be of use. Took the practical nurse course at the Vocational, got her license and worked steady helping with Ben and Pap, one getting better and better, the other losing out all along. When Pap died, and Ben got a job in Jacksonville, Palma moved on, too. Not trailing along after him, no. She went all the way to Miami, signed up for registered nurse's training, and working as an LPN till she got her cap. Catholic hospital. State certificate. Two more diplomas Nana Ada would have been proud to see.

Anywhere in the state she could have found work, larger hospitals, or specialty clinics. She was drawn to obstetrics, but wanted to do something about saving life as much as welcoming it into the world. And because she had specialized in Trauma, she answered the ad from Sanavere Regional for an emergency-room nurse. She was working her first full-moon weekend when Tom Rios brought in his net striker with a rived-open foot.

Palma helped cut that ruined boot off. The blood on her two hands was warm and real and steady.

She always tried to say something to help them keep their nerve, make them a little proud of themselves, how they were handling it. Hard on a strong man to be hurt and lying so public, unable to do more than bleed and sweat.

"Strong heart to pump like that," she said, trembling a little, trying to find the exact place to press to stem the tide. There. She looked up at him, to reassure him. Part of her never looked away again.

Lady intern and the orderly laughing and busy with themselves, getting him ready to be stitched up. What's your name? they kept asking. What happened to you? Not to know, they already knew, wouldn't be back there in that cubicle if papers hadn't been filled out. His wrist tag said ZEB LEONARD. She checked his blood pressure again. Cuff barely wrapped his black, black arm, not so big a man, but built up from hard work. Like something carved out of wood. Or will. No shirt, just jeans and shoes and socks.

"Doin' fine on this end of the table," she reported. The doctor finished irrigating the wound and began to stitch it closed.

To distract his brain from the needlework, Palma asked him, "Mister Leonard, you a pirate?" Meaning that little gold hoop in his left ear.

"I'm a peon," he told her when he could, "but I've got plans."

He caught her hand and held it hard while they set his ankle. No blaspheming, no meanness, no thrashing around like some or most. She thought he'd forgotten all about her being there till she tried to move away.

"Stay with me," he said.

And she had. Was with him yet, as though there weren't but one soul between them. The more she learned about him the better, day after day after day. A man like that after all she'd been through God be praised a man like that.

Before Zeb Leonard came to be mate on the charter boat *Blue Lady*, he had served as striker on Tom Rios's shrimper. In fact, Zeb's first seagoing miles had been spent trying to prove to Tom Rios that he was man enough for the job. He'd talked himself into Tom's life and a percentage of Tom's *Legal Hours* haul with nothing but native wit and determination. He was a runaway kid, an Alabama eighth-grade dropout with no kin to speak of but aunties glad he was gone, and he'd been working as a dishwasher at Lupo's down by the docks, watching for his chance. When he saw Tom Rios's notice on the bulletin board—DECK HAND—he answered it on his first break, eager to exchange sudsy water for salt.

"Shove off," was Tom's reaction to the damp-sleeved, swaddled-in-a-hash-cook's-apron applicant. "I don't need galley help."

"I know what you need. Hiring a deckhand. Me. For striker."

"I please myself as to that," Tom growled. Rios had a pint of varnish in his hand, gestured toward town with his tousled brush. "Move on."

Zeb looked around the dock. At that moment, before the season opened, things were slow. A few gulls paced through a sheer puddle in the deserted parking lot, their white reflections the only clouds in the mirrored sky.

"Who else but me? Don't see any throng of applicants beatin' a path," Zeb pointed out.

"*You* beat the path," Tom said. "Beat it." He ducked back inside the cabin. Interview over.

Zeb didn't leave. Of course he didn't leave. He stood on the dock and waited. Thinking what next, and how. When Tom didn't reappear, Zeb's common sense told him not to go on board to pursue the argument, and not to toss gravel at that spattered window. But nothing stopped him from yelling—half cattle call, half crazy. When Tom poked his face out the window, Zeb said, "This your man."

Unpersuaded, actually annoyed, Tom said, "I don't need you, keed, if I need a man."

Zeb shook his head. Kindly, he explained, "Now rightly, mister—"

"No, I don't need you. I told you."

Zeb heard a little something persuasive in that. Nothing he wanted to hear. He didn't believe it. He sank down, rested on his heels, ran both hands over his head back to front, scoured his eyes, took a handful of the smallest gravel and began lining it up. When he had five in a row between his sneakers—each stone a reconsideration, maybe this wasn't the day, or the boat, five little stones for courage and patience (David needed no more for Goliath)—Tom Rios looked out again, and saw him still there.

"What you say is your name? Say it. Say your name, keed." Sudden as gunfire. Zeb jumped up.

"You change your mind?"

"No, goddammit," Tom roared. He looked wildly around for something to throw.

"When you do, you find me at Lupo's. Ask for Zeb. Offer me a basic wage and any standard share of the catch."

"I wouldn't offer you cup of coffee."

"Seawater'll do."

Tom scowled. "Why? Why all this gotta have it? Why this here and now? Why *me*?" There were other help-wanteds on that bulletin board.

"They say you one of the best. You can teach me. For my own boat one day."

"What else you hear about me?"

Zeb considered. He'd heard plenty. "Hard to please; even harder when I don't please you. Hate late. Won't truck with slacking off early. Can't keep help. Temper like a—"

"And?"

"When you lose it, you yell in Spanish, louder when you don't come clear. Hire and fire, and the ones you don't fire quit. Driving so hard you drive even your friends away."

"Only need six for pall bearers," Tom said. "What if—if it's true—all that stuff you hear?"

Zeb shrugged. "I learn soon enough."

"You such a student, why don't you go to college?" Tom thought of something. "You planning on beating the draft or something? Maybe using this job to plead hardship or necessity? Won't work. They've tried it already."

Zeb saw he was going to have to tell the truth. Truth he never told the police when they picked him up as he wandered into town across the Duck River bridge out of his mind with fever, no more sense than to walk right on the roadway in traffic, unaware of the pedestrian catwalk. Just mingling himself in rush hour, dodging the morning shift on its way to the pulp mill. They thought he was drunk till they tested him.

"I been in jail for vagrant," Zeb told Tom. All that first few days they kept asking, asking, asking who he was. Prints didn't match any on file, and no missing persons either. "They let me go," he said. The truant lady came and talked to him. But he wasn't breaking any law. "So long as I have a job and keep at it, I don't have to go to school, me," he said. "I tell them I'm sixteen already."

Tom listened.

"Tall enough," Zeb went on. "And strong." For proof he looked around for something to lift, or throw. Nothing.

"You don't miss by much in inches," Tom agreed. "How much you lack in years?"

"I be about fifteen."

When Tom didn't say anything, Zeb added, "When I hit eighteen, I register the draft. They call up my number, I go fight the war. Finish all that, legal, I come back here, you teach me some more. I be captain one day." In case Tom got the wrong idea about that, if it sounded like mutiny, Zeb added, "My own boat. Nobody else's. Long time off, but no dream. Bound to happen. Born for it."

"Who knows where a bird will land?" Tom said. He thought of something else. "You read and write?"

Zeb's turn to be wary. "Can. But I won't sign papers. Won't. This the merchant marines or just a lousy shrimpboat? Say a handshake's enough, if you meet the right man."

Tom sighed. "Relax your mind on my account." First time he smiled. He got over it instantly, but Zeb didn't miss the message.

He whipped off the apron and wadded it into a ball. "Maybe I take this goddam apron back to Mr. Lupo and tell him to find another fool."

"I've got mine," Tom agreed.

They shook on it.

Zeb had reminded Tom of himself. Only a couple of years difference in their ages, actually, but Tom seemed already far beyond his teens. He'd had the same dream, too: his own boat, and no boss to please. He had been impatient, and driven, and hard-driving, and he took chances when he had to. He couldn't make allowances for those who didn't or wouldn't. The fact that Tom wasn't yet twenty-one was not generally known; he had kept his beard since he was eighteen, to mask himself, and he came to Sanavere to be on his own, no one to remind him he was still a rookie at most things. He knew boats, and he knew shrimp and weather. He married a little Cuban woman a couple of years older than he was, a bookkeeper at the ice house. Nola was quick of mind and slow of temper, a natural foil for Tom's impulsive ways. They lived with her parents the first year, and every penny went into the bank for the boat. They never developed the habit of wanting things, except a baby. And they didn't want a baby—as so many did in those years—to dodge the draft. Tom registered, but his number didn't come up. Twice, in those early years, Nola and Tom had the joy of hope, but she miscarried.

Tom's mother offered at that time to send him to law school. "Is not too late," she said. When Tom said no, his mother blamed Castro. And perhaps things would have been different, if they had stayed in Cuba instead of coming to the United States.

"His father was an educated man, not a fisherman," Señora Rios had told Nola more than once. "Opera, not galoots." She pronounced *galoots* with scorn and precision. The scorn was typical, but the precision came from long practice; it was her favorite word for country-and-western. It took all her effort to break it off at the final *s* and not say *galootsy*. She always finished, breathing hard, as though the effort had been enormous, aerobic.

Nola loved the word, and when she got her little bird—an anniversary extravagance from Tom—they named him Señor Hoot Galoot. By then they had signed papers on that old house in South End, and were fixing it up room by room. They offered Señora Rios a room of her own with them, but she couldn't imagine it, no. Not because of the bird, though she didn't like birds. She had her own life, her own job, and her own agenda, none of which fit Tom's. "But I had to offer," he told her.

"As I had to refuse," she said.

For a time, however, Tom's brother, Vic, had lived there. And for a shorter time than that, Vic had even tried working for Tom. "Like oil and water," Nola tried to explain, after the parting of the ways.

"Like powder and match," Tom said. What Vic said was "Adios, and don't wait up."

Tom was eight years older than Vic, and Vic's whole life and attitude—from junior high school on—had been to catch up and go farther and do it in a bit more style than Tom. Tom had been six years old when Castro triumphed over Batista. Señora Rios had held back from the general rejoicing. "That beard is hiding something more than his smile," she said. "I do not like the look of those teeth," she said. Tom was almost eight when his father was detained, questioned about a thoughtful series of letters in the Cuban press, and sent to a work camp for "correction" of certain counterrevolutionary tendencies. The Rios home was broken into, and their books rifled and scattered. He was released, but they lived their lives under suspicion and sanction.

Surprise searches had never discovered the ham radio hidden in a false-backed closet. Rios taught Tom how to work it. They did more than listen.

Then came the Bay of Pigs. Tom's father was arrested. Prominent enough he could not simply disappear without a trial. While awaiting trial, Tom and his mother used what was left of the household's pawnable worth in efforts to bribe or to win Rios's release through official channels. Failure after failure; finally, through unofficial channels an escape was arranged—from the prison and from the island itself.

What went wrong, by whom they were betrayed, they never knew, but Rios and three other men—two priests and a university professor—were discovered before the farm truck they were hiding in had gone five miles.

Tom and his mother, who was four months pregnant with Vic, were waiting in their dark, empty house, curtains drawn, doors and shutters locked, bags ready for fleeing. It was all arranged. But it wasn't freedom or opportunity that knocked at their door that night; it was a summons to the hospital—"an accident" was all they'd tell them—and it was endless terrible hours more before they were admitted to the morgue to identify and claim what remained. There had been, they were told, an accident with the truck, a subsequent fire. The truck was not damaged. The fire had not completely done its work of obliteration of clues. The body was almost intact. It was apparent that Señor Rios, his wrists bound by wire, had been killed by a bullet fired into the back of his skull.

"*Padre mío,*" Tom said. Marcela, his mother, made him look. "In time you may forgive," she said. "But you must never forget. He would die twice." He was to be buried the next day, in the churchyard. Few friends dared to attend. A furtive Mass.

One of the curates, who was brave enough and of a height to pass for Señora Rios, offered to wear her widow's weeds and veil and stand in for her at graveside so she could complete at least part of the plan of escape. She didn't want to go, but they couldn't stay. For her son and the unborn child she would leave, and because their escape would be a victory, in some small way. There was no time, and no way to contact family. Betrayed once, they dared not risk open farewells. The priest helped them. They left in broad daylight, traveling on "borrowed" papers, to Mexico, then to Miami, rather than to France. Tom's last memory of his homeland was of the island in its sea, framed by the wing of the plane. While his father's remains were being lowered into the ground, Tom was whole and healthy, being lifted far above it. He could pick out the steeple as they banked and rose.

When he turned to see if his mother was looking too, her eyes were shut, her hands busy with her rosary. They had disguised her as a nun; he was supposed to be blind. He had a collapsible cane and dark glasses. Their papers listed their destination as Lourdes. She stirred. "*This,*" she prayed to God, as though she had him by the buttonhole.

"Look," Tom urged her, interrupting. The island was fast receding below them, the plazas indistinct now, the towers and roofs blending.

Thinking of the priest, at graveside, hearing their engines droning over-head, Tom said, "They can see us though we cannot see them?"

Thinking of something quite else, she agreed,

> *Todo es hermoso y constante,*
> *todo es música y razón,*
> *y todo, como el diamante,*
> *antes que luz es carbón.*

> All that's precious and steady,
> all that's sung or true-sworn,
> and all, as diamond, or body,
> before there's light, must burn.

Tom Rios was not sentimental. If Zeb had not worked, and hadn't worked out, he would have been gone. Soon enough, though, Tom had seen that the kid meant business.

He practically grew to manhood on Nola's cooking. Ate standing up in the kitchen, never could get him to feel easy in the house, but it had been quite a day when they finally got him to come in the kitchen; he'd pre-ferred to sit with his plate of food out in the yard, his back against the big oak, alone, alert, like some wild creature poised to bolt. He'd slept in the storeroom at Lupo's; when he left that job, he had no place to call home. He used to walk, just walk, till late; when the coast was clear, he'd slip through shadows and jump over onto the deck of *Legal Hours*, sleep there. There was canvas if the weather was foul. He managed for weeks like that, unsuspected. He'd wake early enough to get off the boat, and be uptown and walking back, as though just on his way to work, when Tom drove up in the mornings. It was always very early when they put out; shrimpers can fish legally from first light to last light, and it always took some work and willpower to be out on the grounds in place, before daybreak. One morning Zeb overslept, and Tom found him lying there curled up on deck, the crummy tarp pulled over him.

Tom figured it out, before Zeb could scramble to his feet denying any trespass. "I got here early," he claimed.

"*Hombre,*" Tom said. "Let me think of an idea." He wasn't mad. That was the main thing; before Nola died, Tom's temper had more fair days than foul. Zeb relaxed a little when he saw he wouldn't be fired.

Tom's offer, of a room in their home—he talked it over with Nola first—came that night. Zeb ate supper with them, or almost with them. They could see him sitting out in the dark, on that oak root, hunkered, scooping up black beans and rice. *"Moros y cristianos."* Moors and Christians. Zeb knew what the dish was called. And it was why he ate outdoors in the dark. Nothing they could say moved him from that root. No, no, ma'am, no, he would not sleep under their roof.

So they offered him space in the shed; gave him a blanket and pillow. Gave him permission to sleep on the boat, but in the cabin, not out on deck prey to every mosquito and squall.

Every week he took all his wages, never asked Tom to hold any back for room and board, and every week he paid three ten-dollar bills into his savings account, and two tens onto Nola's kitchen table, "to help defray," as he shyly said it. When she realized he would never take seconds, and yet growing so fast must often go away hungry, Nola found a larger plate, and heaped it the first time. When he realized what she was doing, Zeb added a five-dollar bill to the two defraying tens.

Out of scraps of lath from a crab crate, Zeb built a little locker; in it he kept his worldly goods. Tom gave him an old Yale lock and key. He wore the key on a string around his neck.

Once a week he took his change of clothes—he had two sets from the skin out, one to wear and one to wash—to the public showers, and scrubbed himself and his laundry. When he turned sixteen he started shaving, out of need. When he turned seventeen, he had his left earlobe pierced and a little gold ring curved through. When he turned eighteen, he registered for the draft. Before the year was out, his number came up, and he went. First to Georgia, then to Alabama, then to Vietnam. Before he left, he returned to Sanavere. Unexpected. Knocked at Tom's back door, like old times. Tom was out on the water. Nola was the one he wanted to see, anyway. He and Tom had already said what and all they intended to, and Tom had promised to save Zeb's place.

To Nola, Zeb said, "In case something happens, or I send you anything to keep safe," and gave her the locker key. There was something pretty and gentle about her unlined face, her pulled-back hair, her shining black eyes; she reminded him of his mother. "Don't worry," he said. "I have a future, me." They shook hands. She wouldn't let his go.

"Son, son," she said. "I believe you. *Momentito,*" she said.

So he waited, leaning in the doorway, while she went into the house and wrapped up a guava pastry and a loaf of Cuban bread, some sausage, a thermos of milk.

"They feed me," he protested.

Then they just stood there. She found the courage to say, "Don't let them kill—"

"Me? I told you, I be back."

"Don't let them change your mind about things," she said. She lightly touched his marksman's qualifying medals, and stepped back. "Don't let them kill your heart."

Two years later he was on the water with Tom again, in the *Legal Hours*. But he rented a room then, over on Kirby Street, and he had little PX niceties—radio and alarm clock and rabbit-eared TV, hot plate and icebox, table and chair, cot, bookcase made of crab crates, and the little locker he'd built when he was fifteen. He had company over sometimes, but they, like the room, were temporary. The only thing that never changed was his work. Little by little his bank balance grew. Not enough for a car, not enough for a lot of things. Certainly no way he could have seriously considered a boat, but he was as confident as he had been when the police arrested him for vagrancy his first day in town, as he staggered across the Duck River bridge.

At first he had thought this was the sea, it was so wide a water. He saw his first fishing boats tied up to docks in the marsh. But he knew this couldn't be the sea, for no bridge could possibly span it. But it was a great deal larger than any water he had ever seen. Wind enough for whitecaps. Gulls huddled on the pilings. Smoke and stink from the pulp mills blowing his way. He just walked out on the bridge, staring down at the water, wishing he could taste it, to see if it was salt. He didn't hear the police car.

"Nigger? No fishing from this bridge, y'all know that."

Zeb had turned to run, but there was nowhere sure to go, just into the water, and maybe he would have jumped, but the lawman put his hand on his pistol and said, "Whoa now, son" and Zeb let himself be taken, for how far could he have gotten if he'd thrown his shoes, hanging on their laces around his neck, at the lawman's eyes and jumped into the marsh? He didn't see any real chance.

He let himself be taken, but he announced, "I'm going on, not back," as the police bent him to fit the backseat of the car.

The lawman answered, not unkindly. "You're not under arrest yet, if you're sick, not drunk."

Zeb gave blood to prove that he was sober.

He wouldn't talk as they booked him into Juvenile. All he said was, "This is temporary."

He had made up his mind, he'd run away as often as it took, all his life, till he got a chance to live it his way. They emptied his pockets. He had no billfold, just his age, more or less, in loose change.

"I'm here to buy a boat, me," he had told them when they asked. So what if they laughed. He knew what he knew. What he wanted. And not a day had passed in all the years since that decision had been reached that it had not been uppermost on his agenda.

Born so far inland, baptized in fresh water, and raised on pond fish, where did Zeb get his saltwater ideas and knack? Blame that able-bodied daddy of his, wandering the seas on a merchant ship, sending home platter-sized pressed flowers from the Canal Zone, Philippine straw slippers and tropical stamps and sevenseas currencies as bright as butterflies. Sometimes his old man came by the schoolhouse on his way home on leave, filling the sunny door with a dark silhouette, casting a long shadow. Zeb never asked permission, he'd just rise and follow, proud, stretching tall, trying to measure up.

His daddy left him with a riddle, every time, the last morning home; he'd ask it, and first thing, when he got back, he expected to hear the answer. Not easy riddles, not *Weekly Reader* or bubble-gum jokes, but hard ones that got harder as the years went on, giving Zeb something to think about, and keeping alive the give-and-take between them over long distance and time.

When his daddy asked him, "How do you thread a needle with two eyes?" Zeb didn't need any time at all to say, "Shut one."

So his daddy had laughed, and asked, "Well, then, how do you thread a needle with one eye?"

And Zeb had thought only an instant before saying, "A needle only has one eye!" And he thought he had triumphed. Couldn't be stumped.

But then his daddy asked the one that would take years to figure out, a lifetime to solve. And as it turned out, it was the last riddle his daddy ever asked. Asked it as he was leaving, and died before he could return to hear Zeb's guesswork. "What three sons live my father's life?"

And Zeb thought that over as they walked to the store where the bus would stop and take his daddy away. He didn't understand this one. He protested, "But your daddy have only one son—you!"

"That is why it is a riddle."

Zeb wouldn't quit. Kept pecking at it, trying to make it easier to solve, hated to be set back after such a smart beginning. "And your daddy was a farmer, and you are a sailor!"

"A riddle isn't much if you can figure it quick as a sneeze," his daddy told him. He swung him up against him, chest to chest, man to not-yet man. Big hug and farewell, Zeb's mama next, the new baby in arms, a whole little crowd of them at the roadside, hurrying up all that love and packing it in for his journey.

That year Zeb turned eleven. And that year their little snuff-stained neighbor hobbled to the schoolhouse and fetched Zeb home to help his mama bear the bad news. Zeb wouldn't go with her, couldn't understand. Kept holding out for better news. "Overdue?" he said, trying to fathom it, for he did not yet suspect the depths to the sea, only knew the pictures of its pretty face. Such storm tales as he had heard told in his daddy's voice, always ended in happiness and calm.

"Not overdue, overboard," the woman said. "Drownded."

"Not so!"

"Prob'ly. Him and the rest. Say they ain't founded nothing but oil and trash. Thing's hit you mama wors'n a thunderball, like to sour her milk. Her and the baby both crying and threshing around like they been scalded."

Zeb ran.

Bad as that was, there was worse ahead, and they wound up on the margin edge of someone else's life, just penciled in, barely tolerated by his daddy's mother, who called them to live with her and her daughters and their families, and the old woman died and the aunties and cousins resented them, but they were stuck, Zeb's mama unwell and the new baby dwindling. When the baby died, the earth took her in and healed over the little grave and there Zeb and his mama were, living cross-state, cross-purposes with in-laws, almost strangers. No one close by heart, just kin to kin, obligated, not obliging. Welcome in a tepid way till their benefits ran out.

No privilege, no acre, no dog, no handnet or tool fell to Zeb, just his daddy's name and frame. He was strong, and they set him to work their will, that holy confusion of women in whose headwinds he learned to tack and turn his back on, for any personal progress at all.

Where was Zeb's mama? Failing and failing in the flesh, bed-bound, nothing to be done to ransom her. After a time she rode to town in a hired car, and after a few weeks more she came home to die, not right away, not suddenly, but too soon.

For that long last summer, Zeb had been sleeping out in the yard within earshot of her call, on the ground in good weather, and under the porch in bad. He wouldn't stay in that house any longer, sleeping on a pallet in the hall, being stepped around by those poking, teasing, spying cousins of his.

If it weren't for his mama, Zeb would have been long gone from there. "When her funeral's over," that was the secret line he drew across his life for *before* and *after*. That wasn't rushing it, or hoping for it, or contemplating some child's game of "running away." He made his plans for leaving.

Zeb had been out in the field, working, when his three girl cousins came to the end of that row and called him, just two words, in just that spiteful way they had—"Poor Zeb" so he knew. She was dead at last.

"Don't run," they teased, laughing at him even then for caring about what they didn't value at all. They followed him home, badgering his heels, as he hastened to honor all that was left of her, so light the pine box would sway on the ropes over the burying hole in the littlest wind.

When the funeral was almost over, he slipped away. Took precautions not to be stopped. He never suspected his kinfolk might actually watch him leave and look away, not sorry. Every heartbeat he was thinking they might be coming after him to try—they'd never succeed!—to call him back, to keep him—"awarded by the court," as he thought of it—to do their fieldwork forever.

He kept to the woods beyond town. He was used to striding, but not so used to hard shoes. He preferred barefoot to Sunday leather, so he paused, shed them, strung them by their own laces around his neck, no use wearing them out on byways and local dirt, miles before he needed them. Then he made tracks in the dust, gaining back the time he lost when he went back, one last time, into those stifling rooms. All because he had forgotten the fish scale his daddy had sent them from some island in the Stream, a scale as big as God's fingernail, mailed home in a Prince Albert can.

If Zeb had just remembered it sooner. He couldn't leave it to them. He had to go back, double back past the churchyard and cut through the pines toward the house he had sworn he'd have no more to do with. They were still praying over the grave. Let them think he was moody and heartless not to stand there with them and pray too. He saw one of his cousins stamp her foot, a little puff of dust rise from under her white pump as she looked right at him.

Nobody home. One last time into the room where his gentle mama, full of good wishes and heartsong, had lain sleepless, as patient as a bird, brooding death. The Prince Albert can was hidden behind a loose wall board. Zeb slipped it out into the light of day, looked inside, slid the can and all into his pocket. By the time he got out of there, got back to the graveyard, the place was deserted, the new little mound, with clumps of propped-up flowers, some real, some fake, lying in wait for him. He faced it alone, standing at the foot. Finally knelt, laid his palms on the heaped cool clay, listening, but not a voice, inside or outside of him, said, *No. Don't go.*

He glanced around for some wildflower tribute of his own to leave there, a farewell offering. Something to last, to outlast the ones piled and already fading. When he remembered the fish scale, he knew that was right. It was hard, but it was right to leave it. "Living right's almost as much trouble as living wrong," his mama always said. Didn't the scale belong here? His own daddy had never had a resting place; this would somehow do for both. Much as Zeb wanted to have the scale, being able to give it was better, not just something handy, but the only treasure he had.

He couldn't just leave it lying there, bait for common curiosity. He mined the clay with his bare hands and settled it over where he reckoned her heart stood still. He didn't dig all the way down, just deep enough to make sure no one else would come along and dig it up. Patted it smooth again, erased signs of his tampering.

When he rose, dusted his knees, he was ready for the rest of his life. Probably he'd never come back here, ever. How he would live, not where, was the way he would honor his heritage. When he thought of that, he remembered the riddle, the last one his daddy ever asked and left him to solve alone. Now, suddenly, he knew the answer because he'd earned it, lived into it, learned it. A harvest of truth he paused to give thanks for.

"What three sons live my father's life?"

"My gran," Zeb figured, "who was his own father's son, and my daddy, who was his son, and the third son to live that man's life is Zeb Leonard. Me." He almost shouted. "Me!"

He went along then, happy. Not grieving anything left behind and buried, but rather taking along with him all that cannot be lost to death. A sufficient treasure, but no burden. He walked fast, the September sun burning on his right. When it finally sank, miles later on, the familiar stars rose. He kept on walking.

When he finally stopped to rest, he scratched up a bed of dry leaves and slept curled in his own warmth, like a deer. It was six weeks till frost, and he knew he'd be where he was headed long before then. He had less a destination than a destiny in mind—the sea.

When the sun rose the next morning, his first morning on his own, Zeb saw he was still in cattle land, no ocean in sight. Familiar land, and days and nights of marching before it even began to look any different. But he knew what he had to do, and he did it. He was going down to the sea to make his living, his life, catching big fish. No one was so patient, so cunning as Zeb with a fishing line, didn't they all say? He told the Brahma bull across the rusty barbs of the sagging fence, "I'll have me a boat, what I'll do. A real one. Not some river skiff with muddy oars. Seafaring. Going to be captain, me."

Besides the Prince Albert can, and the clothes he was wearing, Zeb had taken nothing from out of his aunties' house except a quarter round of cornbread, his day's fair ration, cut with the fire-black knife. A thief would've claimed the whole pone, and the knife too, but Zeb was no thief. That cornbread was all he had to eat, for days, but when he raised it to his mouth, it smelled like he was back there among them, any old day, eating his field fare. He had choked. Cupped up ditchwater to ease his thirst, but if he had longed for the first taste of brackishness of salt and tide, he was disappointed.

Miles and days to go, a lifetime ahead, but still there was that hurry-up in him, so he couldn't rest long anywhere, sick of the lingering sun, hoping for night to come on so he could travel boldly, never looking around or back. Almost a week like that, county to county, south by east along creek to river, living on what fish he could catch on a pin, and what he could find in the fields—a broken melon, onions, peanuts, raw dry corn. Never enough to make him sick, never enough to cure his hunger.

It rained one night, so hard it drove him away from the river, out of fear it might rise from its banks. He holed up in an old curing shed; hung his wet clothes on the tobacco sticks, broke other sticks up and made a fire, risked the smoke in the fog and rain. He roasted windfall apples from the hedgerow, gathered that morning and pocketed against need. When he finally fell asleep, he didn't dream at all, and when he woke, it was late in the morning, the sun was already high, and yet he noticed something very fine—he had quit running *from*, and was now running *toward*. He didn't know how many miles it had taken, but he finally felt safe and free. He knew it, deep. The way he had known which direction to take. Now he would travel in daylight as freely as in the dark, and his pace would be his own, unobliged by fear.

The river was up in the fields. He set off due south now, and walked till he began to notice stranger creatures to his eyes. The river was darker now, slower, running on sand instead of clay. On the telegraph poles, watersnake birds sunned with their wings open to the east, like crazy fierce things. Cattle stood in dark huddles in the parasol shade of the oaks. Egrets prowled among them.

He climbed through the fence and picked up one of those white feathers, for his mama's sake. If she had been alive, he'd have mailed it back to her, for her Sunday hat.

The cattle were uneasy with him, but he talked low, moved slowly. He knew how to talk to cows. They let him come near. He laid hands on a nursing calf and when the cow turned, he caught at her, calling, "Co', boss, co'." Wooing her back to him. Soothing, patting. She let him have some milk; held still while he crouched and aimed the stream into his mouth. She flicked her tail at flies, the green and yellow ear tags rattling. He thought that meant her milk was safe. He thought those tags meant he wouldn't get fever if he drank that body-warm milk.

And maybe it wasn't the milk; maybe it was the ditchwater, or some of the raw food he'd been eating. Fever set in, though, and came near to driving him off course. He wandered a whole day in a great circle. Lost sight and scent of the river. Came at last to picked-over soybeans, acres of them on land as flat as a deck. Beyond and far, across the heat-shimmering acres, he could see the tops of cars as they went along a paved road, some coming, some going, all fast. By the sun, the road ran east and west. Zeb thrashed through the bean stubble, deciding the road would do as well as the river. The ditches were filled with strange blooming plants, as strong as leather in their leaves, with white and purple flower spikes in a haze of bees and gnats. The snake-doctor dragonflies flew up and down the water lanes, more than he had seen at any time in his whole life. He knew they would bewitch him; he held his mouth shut against their charm.

There were butterflies too, and in the turpentine thickets the cries of unknown and unseen birds. He walked faster for a mile or so, but the fever was winning. His clothes prickled with his spent salt. He got crazy, strength wavering and mind confused. He staggered out onto the highway itself. When a log hauler passed too close, he tumbled, dizzy, into the ditch. He found presence of mind enough to flail out and into the palmettos to hide from the motorist who stopped to see if he was hurt.

"It's your funeral," the man said finally, giving up, walking back to his car, driving on.

He never knew how long he lay there, or wandered, out of his mind. When he woke clear-headed, he pressed weakly on. Was still knee-knocking weak when the county police stopped him on the Duck River bridge, and hauled him in to Juvenile. He had nothing to tell them, about his past or his identity. The only lies he told and had to remember were his age—"seventeen"—and his name. He called himself Zeb Leonard. Leonard was his daddy's name, rightly so, but his first name, not his surname. So if it wasn't the truth, it wasn't really a lie. As for his age, what are a few years added on at the beginning, when you need them most?

The barnacled old rib-built shrimper Zeb and Ben signed for had none of the glamour of a boat-show purchase, but they couldn't have loved her more. She had lain in drydock for several years, lost in weeds before they found her. It was Zeb who found her. It wasn't what she was now, or what she had been, that caught Zeb's eye and soul; it was what she might be. He and Ben had been looking for such a long time, without eagerness or tension, but rather as birds in winter, long before the days lengthen toward spring, will begin to be interested in knotholes and snags as possible nesting sites. It was hard on Zeb to work inland, away from the sea. But he had left Captain Vic Rios a few months back, when the *Blue Lady* began to stay downcoast. Ben found them a good job in construction, and even though Zeb had to be away almost as much as if he'd gone with Vic, the pay was better, because of overtime. He'd left boats so he could buy one. Now the job was about done. That didn't break Zeb's heart. He always felt his spirits rise as they neared the marshes. Something in him quickened. And then he saw that old shrimper. He recognized it, like fate.

A beautiful old hulk. Past prime, and scraped down past prime, and weathered into insignificance. He spotted her from the window of the bus the evening of the day Ben had the seizure, when Father Grattan helped him from his seat into the aisle.

That boat had been there all along, and he'd ridden past it—the bus crossed high over the marsh at that point, on the Interstate, and the view unblocked, the last gold-dusty light almost signaling in its slant, drawing his drowsy eyes to the skip-planked dock and barnacled pilings. He'd always sat on the other side of the bus, or was dozing, or talking, or getting things together for when they got to town. There the boat stood, his future, shining in the raveled fringe of the marsh, the sungold as thick as pollen, every blade of grass burnished, and the creek with that same gold in its reflected sky. The weathered wood looked gentle, gracious, elegant in its curves, in that light. He loved the boat at first sight. He marked the spot, for when Ben could come back with him. Only one glimpse, and it had him talking to himself, like love at first sight. He forgot all about Ben's seizure, his embarrassment, the long, hard days away from home all week on that construction job. He stepped down from the bus smiling, and whistled home.

First thing he did after kissing Palma, roughing up Elven, and tousling the stray dog, before supper even, was to phone the number on the For Sale sign, and then to phone Ben. They were closer than brothers-in-law. They were what Palma had always hoped her husband and family would be—friends. When Palma settled in Sanavere, it looked for a time as though she wouldn't have any family nearby, but she and Zeb persuaded Ben and Cliffie—after five bad shrimping years in a row in Georgia—to come south. Cliffie got a job right away, in the local school district, in town. Ben hacked around, doing day work and part-time, until he heard of the wages he could get in Alabama, working as a mason. He'd done some of that, knew how, felt he had to give it a try, even though it meant being gone all week, commuting, and living in a kind of strain and weariness he hadn't known since the Tet Offensive.

When Zeb dialed Ben's, the little girl handed Ben the phone out the window to where he lay on the porch. Just flat on the concrete, too dirty to sit on Cliffie's upholstered and fringed glider. Not that she would have minded; she came out and slid a pillow under his head and kissed the frown lines on his forehead. Set a glass of iced tea on the porch beside him.

She couldn't hear Zeb tell Ben, "Get up off your wallet, man, I've found us our future home away from home."

When he heard the asking price, Ben said, "What's wrong with it?"

"Everything, probably, but nothing we can't cure."

They decided not to tell their wives "for sure" till they *were* sure. That is, till they had the loan.

When they finally tracked down the owner, he turned out to be an old Cuban in South Point Nursing Home, the very place Palma worked. Agapito Montevidez, Cristo's father, owned the boat. At first he didn't really want to sell. He wanted to talk, even though they didn't speak Spanish, and also to remember, but not to sell. Zeb went and got Tom, to help translate. Tom and Agapito were friends from way back. Cristo's death hadn't changed that. Agapito's reluctance was more than sentimental attachment to the old boat; Agapito played fair. Was sincerely concerned at the boat's condition. His advice was frank. He wanted to take a ride, to show them, and his nurses checked, came back saying, "One hour." And so he rode out to the marsh with them. They helped him down to the dock. He told them she was poorly laid, not timber-built and slim, but rounded, pregnant-looking, built rib on rib. He had hauled her out of the water to fix her when he was recuperating from a broken shoulder. Fishing accident. He had decided then that it was time to work on nets, something that kept him on shore, but still involved in the life of the fishermen, because he had taken so long to heal. Then he'd had surgery: hernia. And after that, ulcers. He had wanted to travel too, to see his boy play ball . . . A few seasons passed, and he didn't get back to the boat. He had sold off the engine, planning to buy a better. Never had. He told Tom to tell them, "No guts left to either of us." He even laughed. He seemed better, just to be out. Zeb and Ben wanted him to take their retainer, that day, that hour, had the checkbook out, for the holding fee, the down.

"No, no, decide with calm," he told Tom to tell them.

They drove him back to the nursing home. His wife was waiting at the door. She and Tom helped him to his room. He didn't need a cane; he was just a little slow. He had had a stroke, but now was better. He needed therapy, but that was soon to be as an outpatient. "I won't be here long," he said. When Tom explained that to Zeb and Ben, they thought he meant Agapito was dying. Tom told them no.

"*I* don't need no more time," Ben said.

"He the one," Zeb agreed, then he thought of something. "God knows, I hope he won't mention this to Palma till we sure."

"He know Palma? I mean, know who she is compared to you?"

Palma worked part-time, another wing, but she knew everybody. That's just how she was. This was her day off. They had planned this day around her.

"Truth be told," Ben said, "unless she speaks Spanish, ain't nothing he or anyone can do to mess up this deal. As for bein' sure . . ."

"That's it," Zeb said.

"But we *sure*!" Ben protested.

"Yeah," Zeb agreed. "There's 'we sure' and there's 'she sure.' And there's 'bank sure.' "

"That so," Ben agreed. "Even when God's dealin', a wife and a banker always ask to cut the cards."

Three tries before they found a bank that would listen seriously. That wasn't so many, but the cold results were so conclusive, Zeb had second thoughts. He went back to Tom Rios and asked him about a better way. Asked Tom if he would speak for them. Not co-sign, no, just testify to their character and chances, since Tom knew the boat, and he knew the Cuban owner, and he certainly knew Zeb.

They'd continued as friends even though Zeb jumped boats, going over to Vic Rios to learn deep-sea fishing, not for the sport of it, but for a better wage, a better chance, to make the dream of his own boat come nearer, season by season.

It wasn't crawling back to ask Tom for help now. It was natural. Tom had seen Zeb married, stood right there in the little crowd applauding as they ran out into the sunlight. But sport fishing beat market fishing, for wages and tips. When the Captain came to him with the offer, Zeb never thought of that before, never trolled for it, and went with the offer to Tom first, before he even asked Palma.

"You're a married man, with hopes of children," Tom agreed. Shrimp were going for plenty, but as usual there weren't so many of them. Always something to make it even out. When they were scarce to catch, they paid well enough to try; rest of the time, you could find them, but they hardly paid for your ice and fuel.

Zeb needed a steadier income than a wage of shares in whatever might or might not come up in Tom's net. Tom said, "Go on, go on and do it, man." Tom saw it the way Zeb had seen it. But he knew it would be hard, that matter of tips, a matter against Zeb's pride and manhood. That was just how Zeb was. He said so, "Tips widen you' wallet but cut down you' height." Tom said, "Let Palma count it, see if she minds." Not to knock Palma, but a woman gets tired of even shrimp for supper every night when that's the wage.

So Zeb wound up learning baits and methods for Vic Rios, and learned the ropes and reasons. Learned the rules for the contests and tournaments. Vic had said he was the best mate ever, and Vic didn't need to say it unless it was so. And trip after trip they'd come in and Vic would say, "Fine work, Zeb," and Zeb would say, "Next time, better," and every time as he left the boat, he'd say, "Cap'n, you tell you bruddah, you tell Tom hello from me," and they never lost touch, not really.

It was Tom whom Zeb went to for advice and courage at the banks, when the time came, not Vic. Considerably galled by the results of his own efforts, he didn't feel the least bit set back to ask for help from Tom. Tom told him and Ben both, "Be here on Saturday morning, just come on in."

When Ben and Zeb got to Tom's, they were suffering in high style in ties and coats. Tom took one look and asked, "Who died?"

"Legal undertakin's," Zeb said. "None dead." It was his common knowledge that you have to show up at the bank asking for money looking like you don't need what they've got.

"Lose that rag from around your neck," Tom told them. "Lose those horse blankets, too."

Right then Zeb was thinking, Oh, no, he won't help us either. But Tom was already opening the door for them, wider than the welcome mat, for both to come in, and saying, "I'll make some phone calls."

Zeb told him again he wasn't asking for a signature on anything, just for a word for their character and chances; they wouldn't use him as a reference without asking him first, wouldn't take his name in vain.

They found a bank that would listen! No time at all, with Tom's help. Tom's own bank, where he did his business. Not another halt to their hopes, done in no time at all, so the next step was off to the nursing home for the Cuban.

They drove to the boat in Zeb's crew-cab truck, Ben and Tom riding in the jump seats, stuffed in, and Zeb and Agapito—wild as the east wind—up front. A terrible day of weather, bone-aching weather, with a full gale of wind whipping and lashing the rain. Nobody out and about.

Streetlights were still on, dark as evening, and noises of everything loose on the move—palm leaves, litter, signs on their hinges. The neon at Lupo's sizzled like a steak on a grill. Zeb stopped them by there by special request. Agapito wanted coffee, first thing.

It was strictly contraband, that caffeine stimulation, and even dangerous for a man not well, but such a good old soul, lively in his hopings, his guile, his gambits to make the morning last, and to keep from letting go that boat a little while longer.

They indulged him like a child.

Everywhere he said go, they went. Zeb followed hand signals, didn't even wait for Tom's translations. He could see which way the old man pointed. Had to lean forward in that smoky rain to navigate. Ben and Tom sat in back, cramped and bulky, as cheerful as though they had lived their whole life thus far just hoping for such a ride and day as this. They toured the streets of old town, and Zeb got the truck through flooded storm drains and onto a higher street. Agapito wanted to see the graveyard. Tom didn't say which one, so Zeb agreed, then found out it was on the island! An hour passed in that escapade, and it was too rainy to see anything anyway. The old man wanted to get out, but Tom argued against it. Finally Zeb pulled a poncho from under the seat and Tom held it like a tent fly, and Agapito went back and forth in the graves till he saw what he wanted, satisfied himself. The poncho hadn't done any good, except to their feelings. Tom and Agapito were both wet through when they got back in the truck. Their dampness steamed up the windows. After they got back to town, and for a wonder the bridge wasn't up, no extra pause there—Zeb had begun checking his watch, afraid the adventures would put them past the bank's closing—but Agapito asked if he might go by the church. Said he needed to pray. Not the Mass especially, just pray.

No great crowd at the church. Nothing going on. Wasn't a thing to be afraid of, but Tom wouldn't go in. Old man went in alone. Tom wouldn't go get him, either. Zeb checked his watch again, and hopped from the truck. Motivated. Saying only, as he left Ben and Tom, "Cap'n, you wors'n me about church," and went on in.

Zeb hadn't attended Tom's wife's funeral. Had never been in this particular church before. Zeb and Palma had attended the laying away, as Palma put it, but not the praying. "Do my own prayin," she had said. Palma wasn't Catholic, in her tastes or in her venerations.

Zeb didn't know what to expect, but he went in after Agapito. He figured there'd be someone up front, saying something. Wasn't a soul. Church looked about like most, to Zeb's eyes, a bit more Christmasy, with the dark and the candles. Flames leaned way over like wind in the grass, from the draft Zeb let in. Door gave a bump, pulled itself right out of Zeb's hands. Agapito roused, looked around. Zeb thought he might still be crying, as he had at the graveyard, but he looked dry enough for a stormy day, just sulky.

"Tom say come on," Zeb said, as clearly as he could, as though the English would soak in that way. Agapito finished up, prayed a little more, cut his eyes around at Zeb, like a child postponing bedtime. One more thing, one more thing he thought of to tell to God.

Zeb was not a churchgoing man himself, but not a scoffer either. A deliberating sort of man. His daddy's old gran—an Indian woman—had prayed on beads, learned it at a mission school maybe, the best way he could remember the story. But she was the only one. It hadn't passed on down in the line, only Catholic he knew he was kin to. And the beads had gotten gone, those trifling cousins of his had scattered them in the Alabama clay in a quarrel over them years ago. Had to be. They got so completely gone. Zeb shook his head. Didn't hock them, never hocked a thing, but he was as sure as he had ever been—a rancor that never went stale—that he'd rather a pawnbroker had got them than those ransacking girls of his aunt.

"I'd a rather the *hogs* et 'em," he said out loud. Didn't know he said it. Agapito looked around again. Held up his hand, *cinco*. Five more minutes. Zeb checked his watch. He sat on the pew beside the old man and waited.

Zeb hadn't cared a thing for church since those cousins of his had showed him about hypocrisy. Palma and Cliffie weren't like that, and neither was Tom's wife, Nola. But till them, he hadn't had a good feeling about righteous females. Except his mother. Zeb's mother, of course, had been how he measured the rest. She had been the touchstone. And those aunts and cousins had proven their brass on her till she died. They'd used her up and she'd died. They had no respect for feelings, for a man's feelings, that unholy confusion of womenfolk—begrudging, belittling, interfering—all sizes of females, and him the only man (still a boy) on the place to withstand them.

They'd set him back in his natural appetites for a few years, and that had saved him—with his good looks and quiet appeal and strength—a great deal of trouble, as much trouble as pleasure. He saw now it might have been a plan somehow, to keep him free for Palma, to help him see her worth. He thought of that, sitting there by Agapito. He thought it might be he ought to say so, to God somehow, but he didn't know the Catholic way. He looked to see how Agapito was doing it. He knew about Agapito and his sweet little wife. They'd had to plan around her faithful visits to the nursing home with as much care and guile as it had taken to evade Palma. This didn't say anything bad about womenfolk, either. Men and women had different ways of being heroes.

Zeb had simply fled his cousins in hard work, the one place he knew he'd never find them. He'd spent a year or two in the fields, never minding it. Preferred the way-off fields, away from the house, out of sight and hearing, clean clear of trees and encumbrances to this view. Just row crops and sky. He could see trouble coming. Folks. Storms. Some came slow. Some came fast. He liked the sea for the same thing, for the open vantage. His mama's dying had been a long, slow storm, with time for plenty of dread to build up. She'd died too soon and too slow.

Zeb's daddy was the one who had gone fast—so fast it spun everything around and they lost control. He was lost at sea. Him and all hands. Him among many. Nothing left, nothing. Just what the airplane reported, flying over: oil and trash. No rafts, no cargo. Nothing.

Long time for them to believe it, believe he wasn't just out on a ticket, merchant marine, able-bodied, maybe due any day. Or at least someday. Long time to accept that it was never going to happen.

When the old man put his hand on Zeb's arm, he jumped like gunshot. Had forgotten all about where he was, and why. He helped Agapito back out, up into the truck. No use in fighting it, they both got soaked on the walk. Agapito got himself settled and asked, once more, "One time to the boat. To look. Maybe you need one last time." When Tom told them what he wanted, he laughed. Zeb didn't. He felt like he was going crazy. Ben felt that way too. "By then the bank be closed tight as a duck's butt. And that's waterproof."

Zeb pulled them up under a railroad bridge, let the rain rain down. In the silence, in that sudden abatement, Zeb and Ben just breathed. The truck windows fogged from their steam. They could hear their two watches ticking.

Tom leaned forward and laid his hand on Agapito's shoulder. Said something in Spanish. Not hard or mean. Laid it on, not out. Gentle. More like a poultice than a lance. Back in the church, Zeb had thought about how his daddy would be at least as old as Agapito. Agapito wasn't like him except in that one thing, but he had never thought of it, had never imagined his daddy old. Swallowed up by something besides the sea. *"No,"* Agapito said.

Zeb said, "Tom, I don't mean this hard, but it's time we got on. Make him see it. We've got forty minutes left."

Tom and the old man talked some more. Back and forth it went. "It's their turn," Tom said, in English. Then in Spanish. Then a pause. Then the old man said what Zeb thought sounded like "SOS."

Might have been something else in Cuban talk, Zeb was thinking. He surely hoped it wasn't a cry for help. No disaster, please, Zeb was thinking. The rain let up, and he rolled them on out from under the train bridge. They pulled off into the parking lot at the market. Tom got out and went in to buy pipe tobacco. Came back with a brown bag with cognac in it. Didn't keep it to himself, but passed it all around. Rapid fire. Finally the old man nodded, yes, yes, and pointed down the boulevard; said, as Zeb and Ben heard it, "Dolly." Not eager-like, but determined. Zeb thought, now, not that, not dollies! Again, the old man said it, this time hitting Zeb on the arm. "Dolly!" Staring straight at Zeb, waving him on.

"I don't know nothing about no dolly," Zeb told Tom. "How long that goin' to take?"

Tom told Agapito what Zeb had said. The old man laughed till he cried. Grabbed himself, so as not to pee. "Dolly!" he yelled, wild and firm.

Tom said, "It means 'Give it.' What and all you got."

Ben said, "Okay to that."

The truck fully responded. They booked it through two caution lights and stopped at the bank. Just in time. A notary named Angel ("Honest to God!" Ben marveled) conducted the paperwork. Signed and sealed, no waiting. They left there just at noon, went and bought sandwiches, Cubans, something else for Agapito to remember if he could, and live down in his digestion that night. They took the food back to Tom's boat. Didn't take Agapito back to South Point. They sat around the cabin, emptying the rest of that cognac into their coffee. Tom's gray and white cat slept in the big bowl on the table, never did even offer to get himself up and let them have the whole place.

They talked as though it were all one language, everything flowing back and forth, and Agapito seemed to keep up. Talked in Spanish about women, storms, snow, jokes, happenings. All the time the short-wave voices were going spit and sputter, nobody out in the weather, just boat to boat up and down the coast.

Agapito raised a toast. *"¡Jesús y cruz!"* Tom explained it as "Happy trails."

Ben looked at Zeb. Saying what Tom had told the old man in the truck, under the bridge, finally getting him moving. "Our turn." Time flowed on.

Tom topped off Zeb's cup with coffee, knowing him to be more of a coffee man than a brandy man. "Drink up, Captain," he said.

Took Zeb by sweet surprise. "Me!" he said. First time it ever got said. "You!" he said, tapping his mug against Ben's.

"Finest kind of day," Ben agreed.

     The electrical system was buggy, there was rust and condensation in the fuel tanks, the tough old Allis-Chalmers diesel engine they bought thirdhand needed complete overhaul, but the main problem was tightening and sealing for leaks, so they could haul her downriver to the municipal boatyard, nearer help and home. Evenings and whole weekends of spring and summer went as they raked out dried caulk from the seams, priming and resealing the hull. Ben's construction job still took him away from town Monday through Friday, so the weekday-evening stints were all Zeb's. Sometimes Elven went along with him, and sometimes Palma too. But mostly Zeb worked alone out there at the edge of the marsh, late into the night, by lantern light. He kept a little transistor radio tuned to the blues, but he was happy enough.

After he left working for Vic Rios on the *Blue Lady*, because he couldn't count on regular hours, he went back to Tom's shrimper. Not forever, just till he could get his own boat launched. As soon as *Legal Hours* docked, later and later as the season wore on, he headed for the bluff where the boat lay in its cradle, crying for attention.

For her anniversary, Palma bought Zeb a secondhand generator. He had it working in no time, and, after that, was able to use power tools. Though Palma had been going to use that money—a month of overtime in the last of her full-time and moonlighting work; she was having to slow down some, because of the baby on its way—for nursery furniture, as she said, it was worth it to spend it on power tools if they'd help get Zeb home sooner at night. Ben and Zeb were away so much of the time that Cliffie and Palma began to call the still unnamed boat "The Other Woman."

There was no official or ceremonious relaunching. The manufacturer's recommendations for the antifouling paint were to get the boat back in the water before the coating dried. So they did, using a borrowed sledgehammer to knock the underpinnings out, on a high tide. It wasn't a matter of greasing the ways and cracking a magnum of champagne; they simply knocked her free and dropped her sideways into the creek. She splashed wonderfully and righted and stood rocking. They had already been pumping salt water through her bilge for days, accustoming the long-dry wood to sea conditions. Only one through-hull fitting leaked. All the seams held, once the wood swelled.

"Looks a lot smaller in the water," Cliffie said, "but it's haunting my sleep like it was an aircraft carrier."

Party time.

They mowed back the marsh, strung Christmas lights in the low oaks, and pumped up the gas lanterns. Had a fish-fry that Saturday night, for friends and well-wishers. They danced and celebrated. Wives and children and dogs and the more than occasional gull hawking scraps. Tom brought the old Cuban by for a few minutes. They had a chair for him, in the thick of things, but he wanted to step on board, and made it up the ladder and over onto the deck as spry as Elven. He checked out the instruments, kept testing the wind, looking at the sky. Only a slight easterly breeze, but he predicted rain. When he learned they were planning to move the boat downriver the next day, he said, "No day for it."

"Because it's Sunday?" Palma had her own charts to go by.

"A calm day would be better," was all Agapito would say.

He was right about the weather. It set in to rain before dawn, with fresh enough winds to slap the river into whitecaps.

They used the day to align the power train, but it meant being in the rough water, in and out.

Zeb had had a hot throat for a week from paint and sealer fumes, but after Sunday he had a cough too, and the hot, dreamy eyes of fever. Still, he didn't miss an evening's work on the boat till Friday, when ague and chills overtook him and Palma didn't have to argue to talk him out of going.

Then it was Ben's turn to work alone. He repaired the clutch and

pulled the prop, sent it to the shop for rebalancing. Cleaned the fuel fil-
ters, de-gunked the tanks. They still needed a valve-and-rod job, but
when the prop, and Zeb, came back in working condition, Ben decided
to try what he could, right there, on the overhaul, so they'd not lose
much time. They were hoping to be sea-ready before the autumn gales.
That meant pushing themselves hard.

The first time they cranked the engine, it idled noisily and ran cold.
The sheer roar and racket were magnetic. Elven was drawn from his tree
nest, down the rope, across the acre to the dock, and onto deck. "We going?" He was dancing with hope.

"No," Zeb said.

"How far is it, man? Two, three miles?" Ben argued for trying it, argued against—ignored and abhorred—the weary valve springs, eager to
get on the way, even if it meant limping downriver. Just to be going, after
all these months of moonlighting.

"More like six," Zeb estimated, staring down the creek toward the
river, wondering about the draft. The tide was setting in, would be high
within hours, their best chance.

"We keep wide to the middles," Ben suggested, "we be fine as frog's
hair."

"What about the truck? Just drive off in the boat and leave the truck
here? Then what?" Zeb checked his watch. "Supposed to pick Palma up
after work in an hour, get some groceries, run by the bank . . ."

"Drive down," Ben urged. "Get her. Bring her back here to drop off
and send her home, tell her to do chores and then meet us downtown at
the pier. At"—he looked at the sky—"sundown."

"You crazy?"

"Okay, Elven there, he could drive it down," Ben suggested. The boy
jumped up, ready. Hadn't he driven the truck around the yard at home?
And down the sand road fishing and back, easy on the gears, a natural
hand.

"The boy's eight years old," Zeb said.

"Almost nine," Elven said. "Tall for my age. Willing."

"Both of you are crazy. Nothing but," Zeb decided. Elven heard that
and slumped down again.

They sat there subsiding their hopes as the tide rose. Blackbirds whistled in the marsh, squeaked and whispered *weee*. Zeb said, after a time,
"Truth be told, I'm feeling a little crazy myownself . . ."

Elven hopped up again, his hand out for the truck keys.

"Not you," Zeb said. "Not this year. Not yet. Not that crazy."

He crossed his arms, bent at the waist to stretch. "I'll go get her to drop me off, be back in little while."

While he was gone, Ben and Elven gathered and piled everything they'd scattered in the long months—tools, jackets, tackle, rags, cooler, the gas grill, the debris and clutter of living on junk food. Fiddler crabs moved out in armies from the cleanup. Elven used the rake while Ben moved back and forth from the land, stowing gear, making fast.

When Palma and Zeb drove up, they were ready, two piles were now one only. Everything that needed to be on the boat had been carried aboard. All they had to do was load the truck. Elven took his stand. Please and thank-you had no part in these negotiations. "I'm not riding back in that ve-hicle," he announced. Not a dare, a fact.

"Listen to the child," Palma said, unimpressed. She stood to one side, peeling a tangerine. Her uniform looked very clean and fresh, even at the end of shift. She was still in her everyday clothes; hadn't gone to maternity wear yet, but was beginning to need a little more breathing room.

"Kiss but don't hug," she warned Ben when he came over to greet her. He was grimy to the point of waterproof in those same coveralls he kept on the boat. She popped a section of tangerine into his mouth without touching him.

"You call Cliffie for me?" He spat the seeds to one side and signaled for another slice. She gave him the rest of it, shaking her head at the state of his hands. "Her and the kids out buying school shoes. Labor Day's Monday."

Zeb laughed. "Not around here. Every day's hard labor."

Elven and Zeb had the last of the stuff loaded into the truck, and now they all stood by the open door. Palma checked her watch. "Got to get on to the bank," she said. She turned and beckoned Elven.

Oh, he was reluctant, his "What, ma'am?" a little more sharp than civil.

"Right here and now," she explained. "Fast forward."

Elven flinched when she put out her arm. Not expecting a blow, no, never had been treated like that at all. It was this maternal custody he dreaded, being told what and where and how and when. Like his daddy, just exactly like him, a head as solid as an oak board and a will to match. She laid her arm across his shoulders and drew him in for a side hug, righteous and tender.

"Listen here now," she told him. "I'm going to let you. But you have to wear a vest." He tried to pull away. "Have to," she said simply and absolutely. "Have to promise and have to do it."

"I hear you," Elven said.

"More than hear," she required. "Promise."

"Trust me," he said, looking away. Mr. Cool.

The men were already working at the lines, down on the dock.

"Elven?" She could wait all afternoon and the bank could close—could fail!—and night could fall and the stars burn out before she'd swerve off course. He was the one to have to come to the end of the tether, like a running dog, jerk around, and trot back, humbled. Palma had a lifetime of practice at being stubborn, and the tether was as strong as love. It wouldn't break.

He studied her shoes. He nodded.

"Don't just *have* to mind me," she hoped. "*Want* to."

He looked up into her eyes.

"Trust me," he said.

She smiled.

"When I'm grown up," he wondered, "and have five Olympic medals for swimming, then will you let me fish without a life jacket?"

They stared into each other's eyes. Neither blinked. Palma told him, "Maybe."

He twisted away, and ran toward the boat, and Palma got in the truck, shoving the seat back to fit her pregnancy and her legs, longer than Zeb's. The men were on the boat, the engines revving, roaring. Palma had to yell to be heard. But no one was listening. She backed around, headed for the road, just barely heard Elven hollering, "When I'm twenty-five?"

She leaned out the window and yelled, "If your wife lets you. Maybe then."

In the rearview she watched him lope up the gangplank. She shivered. "Lord, keep 'em safe," she prayed. Something—nothing—called her back. She almost turned around to see if they needed something from the bed of the truck, something she was hauling away. A tool or rag. Or was that just an excuse, her mind offering up an excuse, so she could go back and make sure? She considered a U-turn, checked the sides of the road for a wider place to swerve around in, the truck being so hard to steer. But she didn't.

Zeb and Ben and Elven had gone about half a league downriver when the valves gave a death rattle and offered up their last motion. For a few busy minutes Zeb and Ben tried everything to revive it. Finally, Ben said, "That's all she wrote."

There they were, floating on the high tide, in the middle of nowhere. They watched their last ripples widen and vanish outward. The silence was vast.

Elven broke it. "This thing got oars?"

He was studying the life raft lashed outside the cabin. Underinflated, it lacked enough buoyancy to support either of the men. Elven saw his chance. "Just tell me who to call," he said, "when I get there."

They scrabbled up pocket change and some bills.

"It may be I'll hit shore at somebody's house," Elven said. "First place I come to, I'll phone in for the tow," he promised.

He lowered himself down a rope and dropped gently into the raft. It buckled, then popped flat open. He was fine. He was able. He knew how. But still it seemed to take forever for him to draw away and diminish down the river. He watched them steadily as he pulled on the oars. A quarter of an hour and his orange vest was out of sight around a bend, his ripples lost, finally, to distance.

A fish jumped.

"Lookit that!" Ben jumped too. "Cliffie loves a nice fresh mullet."

"Net's in the truck," Zeb remembered.

Ben sat down again. "Oh."

They sat and discussed the ancestry of those failed pistons and valves and the man who'd sold them the engine. Ben took out the service manual from the locker and began to search it again for some clue, some miracle cure. Anything he'd overlooked. From time to time he turned a page, or grunted when another fish, or the same one, jumped. All around them the marsh stirred and whirred and hummed and buzzed. Zeb cleared a space on deck and stretched out, tipped his hat over his eyes. "Take me a little rest," he said. He had the soldier's way of dropping off when and where he could.

It was after six when their tow hove into view. The water was broad enough to turn in, that was one good thing. They knew the captain, at least it wasn't some stranger called away from some other job, arriving with a chip on his shoulder. Because the electric system had failed too, the pumps weren't working, and they had taken on enough water to ride low. By seven they were hooked up and in tow, headed for their reserved berth at the municipal. Ben wasn't too concerned on the subject of "wife," because he'd had the sense to have Elven phone her and let her know he'd be late getting in. But Palma didn't know; Elven hadn't been able to locate her. "Y' mama's gonna be fit to be fried," Ben told Elven.

" 'Specially if she bought frozen food," Elven agreed.

"We be there soon," Zeb reckoned. He'd been saying that for several hours. But now they were actually under way. "All we have to do is arrive."

They were in sight of their landing when the accident happened. Ben was below, his turn to work the hand pump. The tow vessel crossed strong turbulence from another boat's wake, drew them sideways so they caught the full thrust of the breaking wave. It broke over the bow and ran the length of the boat, down the open hatches, and, in a matter of seconds, swamped them. An eddy. A turbulence unpredictable and unforeseen and deadly. The boat—as the newspaper accounts reported it—"turtled." Belly over. Sank. Like a toy pulled down under a lake.

Palma was standing on the docks watching, had been pacing back and forth for over two hours, watching. When they came into sight, she had raised the little American flag in her hand to wave and show them she was cheering them on, proud. Had bought the little flag at the market at the checkout, all they had, no time to shop for a larger. She watched the towboat drag them up across the river in silhouetted slow motion, saw the dark wave crest and fall on her family, and screamed, her scream as much as the sudden anchoring drag on his lines alerting the tow captain. They cut free instantly. Cast off lines and cut the rest. But it didn't help. Nothing was going to help. The shrimper—Zeb and Ben's boat—sank slowly down, bobbing under, as though the water were taking it on, not the reverse.

Palma ran the length of the dock, shouting for help from heaven or earth. First Elven bobbed to the surface, in his orange vest. Then Zeb shot free, vestless, but a strong swimmer. There was a crowd by then, strong arms to hold Palma back from jumping in herself, for she wanted to, had to, intended to cast herself into the dark water as a life preserver.

"Ma'am, ma'am, in your condition . . ." someone pleaded. But it took two grown men to hold her back. Nothing they did stopped her screams when the shrimper—with a horrible sigh and belch—sank out of sight.

Elven was safe ashore by then, dripping beside her, spent, on one knee, then both, retching. She crouched beside him, to hold him, her attention divided but no less intense, on him, on the events in the river.

When Zeb appeared, Palma's relief lasted only a moment, till she heard his report. "Ben's down there."

She wouldn't hear of it. "No!" She beat at him, not to drive him away, but he went. As soon as he had his breath back, and a waterproof lantern, he dove back in. Elven struggled to go too, but Palma held on.

The rescue units came, one after another. Divers suited up and went down, again and again, all along the hull, coming back up to report: they heard Ben tapping. Someone was tapping. Maybe with a wrench or something. Tapping in an air pocket, where he could breathe. An air pocket. There was that much time, not much time.

Night fell.

Zeb and the rescue divers worked on and on, but they couldn't get to Ben.

From time to time they'd yell "Silence!" and the world would hold its breath, listening for the tapping.

After a time, it stopped.

"My brother!" Palma accused. Accused them all—the boat, the rescuers, the water, Zeb, and Ben himself and herself too. She wouldn't leave. Couldn't be persuaded to leave before they found him. Had to see him to believe it. To put an end to human hope. Maybe then she'd believe it.

"No, no." All she said. Quieter now, Cliffie the only one to hear her, pacing with her, pacing beside her, arrived in a police car, sobbing quietly through the hours and hours it took the searchers to send up their empty bubbles.

They recovered Ben's body around midnight.

Grudgingly, Palma had consented to the boat project in the first place. Now she was completely set against it. It never occurred to her that Zeb would not feel the same. When she realized he intended to salvage the boat—they pumped air into the hull and floated her up in a matter of hours—and shoulder the whole burden of finances and go on with the plan to fish, not default on the co-signed loan though it meant using up their savings, the special fund set aside for Elven's education—she gave Zeb a simple and very clear choice.

"This is family," she explained slowly. "All that other is is seafood. Show me one fish that's worth kinfolks."

He contradicted her in the worst possible way. He laughed.

She knew he'd loved Ben and she knew he loved her and Elven and the baby-soon-to-be. But she could see he hadn't a clue to the core issue. She clarified it in so many words: "You can't love me and that boat both."

"Yes, ma'am, I can," he said. As though it were up to him!

Palma had plenty to say about that, but it all boiled down to "Not here you can't."

So it was that the night after Ben's funeral, Zeb slept in the yard. The house and Palma were that inhospitable. Zeb blamed it on grief and maternity, and didn't mind all that much resting under the sky. It brought back memories of his boyhood.

The second night, it rained. He slept in the cab of his truck. The third night he cleared out the junk and tools on one side of his truck bed and made a pallet there, under the camper top.

After that he began to take their difference of opinion seriously—a lasting climate change, not a squall. But thinking it over didn't change his mind. He would campaign hard for a chance, but he wouldn't beg for it. He had a life to lead, a day job, and plenty to do after hours. As soon as he could, he moved his headquarters to the shrimper, which lay moored and needy. He steered clear of Palma for a few days. She could locate him if she craved conversation. For what he needed, he waylaid Elven on his way to or from school. "Bring me . . ." or "Put this cash in the coffee can," or "Tell—you tell your mother . . ."

Sometimes he drove by the house, left gifts on the steps or back porch. The compliment of a fine mess of fish in a cooler on ice. She couldn't have missed them, but there they were the next day, untouched. Flat ignoring him and his peace offerings, a rude slap. It woke him, brought his pride up. After that, he made provision, fair provision for her and the boy, but as for the rest, she was on her own.

He traded his truck, emptied the tools and junk onto the dock, and covered the mess with a tarp till he could sort it out. Traded the truck for a motorcycle and a good-hearted old clunker of a station wagon. The station wagon was for her; he drove it over to the island and left the keys over the visor, and a note—"Yours"—with the title in the same envelope and the extra keys and a money order for groceries and gas.

The motorbike was a quiet little one, just to run about where he didn't have time to walk. Wouldn't have to worry about how she was managing; she'd have wheels, and so would he. And if he wanted to ride by some night, and see for himself, he could. No law against it except Palma's. But he'd have to want to pretty bad before he did. He didn't look forward to wanting to.

Sometimes it almost surprised Palma out of her resentments to discover secondhand the good things Zeb was up to. Surprised her as though time had stopped in the world with Ben's burial and Zeb's going, and Elven wasn't getting on toward his birthday, and the year was ticking along only in her body, where the babies grew. Twins, hard to imagine and impossible not to think of, two good reasons to call Zeb back to her. "Come home where you belong," she could have said at any time. Never a day passed that he wasn't in the neighborhood, or near. Hoping.

She hadn't told him about the twins, yet.

She hadn't told Elven. Or Cliffie or anyone. And she made the doctor and his staff promise not to tell it either. "Right now it's nobody's business but my own," she said. Not to keep Zeb from worrying, but to keep him from rejoicing. That was the truth. To deny him that pleasure, and the joy of seeing the babies on the ultrasound screen. She even had that Polaroid picture of them, blurry, like bunnies curled up in their nest. At least one was a boy; they could see that, could see his wee manhood as plain as a statue without a fig leaf.

When Ben's widow stopped by and had words of praise for Zeb, a pang like the onset of labor racked Palma. She had to lie down.

"Woman, it's your heart, not your water, that's breaking," Cliffie scolded. They had been out in the yard, just visiting while Palma pinned up a short line of wash, man-clothes conspicuous by their absence. Their various kids were everywhere, in and out of the shed, gathering supplies for an expedition, a voyage on dry land in the johnny boat. They were using her broom for an oar.

Going back across the yard to the house, Palma said, "You had a flat," noticing the new-blue tint on the white sidewall.

"Zeb fixed it for me. Third time it went flat, he said wasn't any use in fiddling with it, just do it right. Said he didn't want to worry about me and the kids out in the car maybe at night, stranded. Ben always took care of things like that. I'm learning how. I can even pump my own gas and pour in oil when I need it. Not the same hole," she added, laughing, thinking how dumb she'd been at first. That's when Palma doubled over, not in amusement but in that sudden pain.

"Let me call him," Cliffie offered.

"No way," Palma said, easing herself onto the bed.

"There's no way, or you mean I better not?"

Palma considered the options. "Both," she decided. Almost smiling.

"Girl, girl," Cliffie grieved, at the window. Maybe she meant her daughter Mary J., who had the three boys harnessed to the bateau by various ropes and was primly seated, calling "Row!" as they valiantly hauled her over the sandy side yard through ripples of shade, but Palma took it personally.

"I'm not wrong," she said.

Cliffie shook out the afghan, sailed it high, and let it fall over Palma.

"He put you up to this? Sent you over here to nice me up? Work me around? Waste of time." She crossed her arms, but it was hard to maintain fierce authority when lying down.

Cliffie pulled the rocker over to the window so she could keep her eye on the children in the yard. "Pretty day," she said. "Always did like Saturday mornings." She draped the curtain out of the way. "Only day we let them watch cartoons. Insisted. So we could lie late in bed."

Palma turned over on her side so she could see the sky too. First thing she noticed was a cloud.

"I can't believe I'll never see Ben again," Cliffie whispered. She put her hands over her face and drew a deep breath. "Sometimes I get so angry!"

Palma misunderstood. "That's it," she said. "How can Zeb sleep on that boat!"

"Badly, I imagine," Cliffie said, "to look at him."

"Try to tell him," Palma dared. "Explain till you're blue in the face that that boat is a Jonah's ark."

Cliffie *laughed*! "Do you think that accident surprised God?" she asked. "Since when are you so rich you can waste your chances?"

Palma rolled over the other way, turned her back on the window and the widow. "He put you up to this," she said.

Always *he*, not *Zeb*. Wouldn't say his name aloud in rage or prayer, just *he*, always, first person accusatory. "*He* sent you."

"No," Cliffie said. She thought for a long time before she dosed out this bitter medicine: "We were so happy fishing and talking and having the cookout supper and fun with the kids, Zeb never mentioned you at all."

Zeb's motorbike was nothing flashy, and though it was far from the ideal winter or all-weather vehicle, he rode it daily over the causeway and down the village road to Palma's. Sometimes if he made the trek in the morning, he'd take Elven to school, but only on nice days, and never straight from home. "No use in poking that hornet's nest just for sport," Zeb said. When he stopped by the house, to bring Elven something or to work on the woodpile—he'd split and stack for hours, and never lay eyes on Palma, though he could hear her talking on the phone, or singing to the radio, or running water in the sink—he could tell she was vigilant by the twitch of the curtain at a suddenly dark window. Weeks went into months with the only words passing between them relayed through Elven. Hers to him were lists of needs, rebukes, rancors, never gratitude. Elven did what he could to mellow them out before delivering them. Zeb's messages to Palma were always the same: "Let me hear."

Every time, when Zeb hugged him and swatted him and parted, saying, "This situation's only temporary, boy, but I love you full-time," Elven would hug and swat right back, and agree, "Any day now."

On toward Thanksgiving, as Palma's due date neared, and Zeb still hadn't heard a word direct from her, he stopped by the nursing home during her shift. She was back on duty full-time till full term, because of the insurance, maternity leave, and day care benefits. She was holding up. She was looking fine—busy and glad of it.

"Can't help you," she explained, brushing past. "Can't help you." Dismissing him as though he were a salesman. He just stood there, turning his hat in his hands.

Startling to see her close up, after so long. Months of imagining her, behind those dark windows. She was carrying the baby low, but hadn't gained much extra; it was all baby, he decided, studying her trim, hard back as she stalked away. Her righteous shoes squeaked double-time and bore her away. He was left rocking in her wake, unexplained to Palma's co-workers, unintroduced, just "some man," as the receptionist had announced him.

He left.

When Palma got off work, she never thought she'd come across him again so soon. Twice in one day. There he was, slumped against the passenger door of her car. Asleep in the sun. For one instant she thought the worst—suicide or heart attack—thought he might be dead. That lurch— "Please, no!"—was hardly over when she saw him stir.

Drunk?

Zeb wasn't the sort, definitely not. Yet what sort was he? Did she even know? She was angry enough not to be afraid of him—what if he had a gun? sometimes men did things like that—and she opened the door and got in with him rather than turning and going back inside, to the phone and her friends. It was courage, not love, that was how she explained it, as she got in the car and slammed the door, clumsy with pregnancy, that hard cannonball that had weeks ago required her to shove the seat back as far as it would go so she could clear the steering wheel.

Zeb jumped awake. Almost bailed out before he remembered where he was, and with whom. Her familiar voice was saying the familiar thing. "Unless you've sold the boat and have been to the bank to sign it over, I don't need to hear your news." That was hello.

She had to adjust herself to breathe more easily. Blamed that on child-bearing, not dismay. Wouldn't even admit to dismay, though that had to be what it was—to see him so derelict, in need of home cooking, running water, a bed long enough to stretch out on, and a decent haircut. His hair looked wild, funny—a half-grown-out barber college special. And there was grizzle, frost over his ears. She blinked twice, squinted, almost reached out to touch, to be sure it wasn't the way the sun was striking him.

He had taken her greeting to heart, and didn't say a word. Finally she said, "Well?"

He shook his head. "Everything I do or say makes you mad."

"No, just one thing," she said.

"I want to know it when the baby comes. I want to be there," he said.

"You know what it'll take."

Again he shook his head. Just a little. Just once. Sighed. "Harder to say no than yes," he told her. "How you going to get to the hospital?"

The old rage flew up in her, and all over. She felt it in her toes, in her fingers, in her claws. Her ears pounded and that little skip in her heartbeat caused her to catch her breath. She wanted to hurt him now, wanted to see his face, but he was standing outside the car, at the open door, leaning down to hear her answer. She couldn't see his eyes.

"Friends," she said. She shrugged. "Maybe Cliffie, or my folks, or even Elven. Maybe a neighbor. Somebody. Anybody handy. 'Better a stranger who is near than a brother far off,' " she said.

"Amen," he said. She thought he was being sarcastic, thought he was smiling till she saw the tears roll down. If she had bent just a little, she could have seen him clearly.

He handed her an envelope.

"Another money order?" She laughed. "What did you hock this time, your gold tooth?" She handed it back to him. "I have insurance, sick leave, maternity benefits. I'm absolutely fine, rest assured."

He must have nodded. He had nothing more to offer. He turned aside to take out his empty wallet and fold the envelope into it and pocket it again. "I'll buy something and send it," he said. "Just thought you might care to please yourownself." He walked over to his motorbike and set the anonymizing helmet on his head. He could have been anyone then, nobody she knew. He kick-started and puttered away down the lot and paused at the street. He didn't glance back or offer a farewell wave, though she found herself watching for it. He looked very solo, and as he chugged down the boulevard, his diminishing over distance gave her no pleasure. What if she never saw him again? What did Cliffie mean by those "last chances" she was always preaching about?

She wondered then if she ought to have told him about the twins. She could still catch up to him; he wasn't going fast, or far. She could always find him and tell him. But she couldn't make herself do it, fumbled in her purse for her keys, stalling. Soon enough, she decided, finally. Twins, like murder, will out. The sense she got of retribution and justice from holding out on him stiffened her spine a bit, not much, but almost enough to cancel out the memory of those new patches of silver at his temples.

It wasn't till later, way on into the night when she woke with a start, that the reason he looked different to her, besides the haircut and natural frost, was his left earlobe—it was naked of that gold ring, the little one that matched his daddy's, to give him sharper eyes for the fishing. That was what he had pawned! That was where the money he had offered her had come from!

Agitated, she couldn't sleep. Rose and paced. Then, to keep from wasting so much time in empty exercise, she did some ironing. Cleared it all, right to the bottom of the basket. Still wasn't sleepy or calm, so she mopped the kitchen and hall and laid on wax. While that dried, she read the newspaper, cut coupons, studied an article in her nursing journal, opened her Bible and looked for a long time at the page for family records. Nothing had changed. Ben's name was still there, and the blanks filled in for born—same day as hers, her own twin, the two of them like the two she carried now—and married and children and dead. She stared at that page till her mind swam and sleep began to come. She didn't even go back to bed, just lay on the couch with the afghan over her. Briefly she prayed for her soul.

"Why did you make me so sure, God, if I am wrong?"

The breeze as the tide turned freshened and shook things in the world beyond her walls. Leaves scuttled and scraped on the roof valleys, and the telephone wire tap-tapped against the side of the house. She dreamed again of the night in the falling dark when Ben's wrench signaled the last moments of his flickering life. She woke yelling. She woke Elven. By the time he found her—he ran to her bedroom first—she was back in control, her doubts and second thoughts healed. She had almost caved in to those old feelings for Zeb. Best not to see him, if the sway was that great. She flipped open her Bible and read the verses again on what to do when a man offends you. Tell him, and if he repents, forgive him. As often as it happens, as often as it takes. But not until he repents.

That seemed clear enough by daylight. And lovelight wasn't worth a second glance, Palma decided. While they were eating breakfast, she asked Elven, "Next time you see your daddy, ask him what happened to his earring."

"Already did."

She made herself wait till she had cleared the table to ask, "Well?"

"Well, *what*?" Mr. Cool. Making her beg.

"Don't you 'well, what' me. You know very well what."

"Said he used it."

"Used it?"

"For bait."

"For bait?"

"Yep. What kind of fish he after, take that kind of bait?"

"None I know."

"Maybe he just joking. Something else you want me to ask him?"

"Not a thing," she said. "Not one thing."

Every year for his birthday, Palma granted Elven a wish, or a permission, or a right. He had cake, too, and a few traditional store-bought or homemade presents, whatever they could afford or invent. But Palma's annual contribution of a "grant" was not necessarily cheap, even though it was intangible. And it was meant to make Elven feel responsible for a lifetime, not just special for a day.

"To teach him how the years build not just *up* but *us*," as Palma put it.

Sometimes Elven knew well in advance what to expect; other times the bestowal came on the very birthday itself.

This year, because he was staying over Friday and Saturday night at Cliffie's with his cousins in South Point, and Palma was going to be home doing some wallpapering in the nursery, she had to phone the grant in.

Called Elven just at bedtime on Saturday night to ask, "You know where a kitty cat keeps his spare change?"

"I—I'm not for sure," Elven said.

"Then I reckon it's time you learned," Palma said. "Don't you?"

That was how this year's granting went.

Sunday morning, Elven was up at dawn to enjoy every moment of his day. While his cousins were still piled in sleep, he dressed and went to the kitchen for some Alpha-Bits and apple juice, ate the cereal dry, pocketed a slice of bread with peanut butter on it for later, and headed for his bike, stored around the side of the house. He rolled it out and waved to his aunt and the little old dog Shin; she had to hold the little mutt, he was still eager. They watched Elven speed down Acorn toward the west, toward the docks. Cliffie knew where he was headed—to his daddy, docked near Tom Rios, chipping paint in the off-season, making *Legal Hours* ready.

All Elven was thinking about was the day and his promised gift. He wanted to share the news and enjoy his daddy's advice on the subject. He went over it in his mind as he rode along. *My mama say I can have me a cat now then. Not just any cat to come at his name and eat cheese, no, I want me a real wildblood bobtail cat maybe.* The river was pretty and quiet. The streets had a holiday stillness and specialness that early. The little rain was drying off, sparkling on the leaves and grass. Elven swung off the street onto the walk, rode swiftly past boat after boat, on the concrete rolling as silent as an owl flies. So quiet, so sudden, he startled Zeb with just a simple, "Hello, hello."

Zeb jumped. Cried, "What?" Laughed, then, when he saw who, but low. He was putting paint around the wheelhouse windows. It dripped onto the fresh white door when Elven startled him. For a few minutes Elven did not mention it. Just watched it run, watched his daddy smear it with the rag. Only then did Elven suggest, "Maybe you should have paint the door last."

Zeb gave him a look, kept on working, concentrating on making a straight, clean edge across the top trim. He was steady; he had a rhythm to the work—brush brush slap. "Door needed a second coat anyway," he said. "And do not be chattering. Folks asleep."

Elven yawned and looked around at the next boat. Didn't see anyone. Risked asking, "Boss Tom drunk again?"

"I tell you h-u-s-h, boy!" He paused, took his pipe out, aimed it at Elven. Meaning be quiet but meaning don't be impertinent also.

Elven took up a little sash brush and began working. Not slow, but not wild either. Zeb studied him, didn't object.

Only then did Elven remember why he had come. "When we finish this, you help me find a cat?"

"Whose ket's lost?"

"Nobody's! Not lost. Mine. One for me to get and keep."

Zeb paused again, to repack and light his pipe. "You mama don't crave no ket, boy."

"She say yeah, okay, fine."

Zeb shook his head. "Stuff," he decided.

"No stuff," Elven protested. "She *say*. For my birthday." He looked sideways at his daddy and sighed. Maybe Zeb had forgotten? So many disruptions. "Today," Elven added.

"I know what day," Zeb said, smiling in such a cunning way that Elven couldn't tell if he really always knew it or had only just been reminded. Zeb reached for Elven's head and pushed down. "You getting too big for yourself," he said.

"Not me," Elven said.

"You just about right," Zeb agreed finally.

Together they painted the rest of the wheelhouse trim. Cleaning the brushes, Zeb said, "We finish this up, we go find us a ket."

"How long?"

Zeb paused to consider. Held out his green-splashed hands. "Usual size, I suppose. Four legs. Whiskers. Tail—"

Elven said, impatient with the teasing, "How long till we find him!" A little loud.

Before Zeb could shush him, the cabin door of Tom's boat eased open and a familiar-looking lady popped out, saw them, and vanished inside again. Only thing she said was "No." Definite. Couldn't miss hearing it, or seeing her. But in case Zeb overlooked her, Elven mentioned, "Boss Tom got company." Elven was pretty sure he knew her name.

"You keep it to yourownself," Zeb warned.

Just then the man himself came along from shore, Tom Rios with a little brown paper sack of café cooking.

"Anybody bother her?" he growled, but low, the way Zeb had been talking too. As though he thought she was still asleep.

"Not a one," Zeb said. He went right on stripping off masking tape.

"I saw her," Elven said.

Both men looked at him.

Nobody said a word.

"It's my birthday," Elven explained, sensing something more was required of him.

"Seven?" Tom guessed.

"Goin' on ten."

"Nine," Tom said, considering. "Next summer you be working for me?"

Elven looked at his daddy. Zeb said, "Now wouldn't Palma fling a fit on that one?"

Both men laughed, so Elven figured it wasn't a serious offer. Tom knocked on the cabin wall, yelling at the same time, "Breakfast!" He asked Zeb, "She dressed yet?"

Zeb wadded the old tape into a ball and tossed it toward the trash. "You asking me, man?"

Elven picked up the bigger brush and whisked it against his thigh, fanned the bristles against the sun, studied the world through that dark fringe.

"I spent last night in my truck. Put that straight in your brain," Tom said.

Elven thought they might be about to fight, but no, they laughed again.

"I been there too," Zeb agreed. "Motel Chevrolet."

"Zeb," Tom said, checking the cabin to see if she had appeared yet. She hadn't. "She needs to anchor. Out of sight. A few days, a week."

"Fugitive?"

"No crime," Tom said. "Maybe your place?"

"My boat!"

"No, on the island."

"Palma be the one to ask about that. She the one in charge over there. You know how it is with us. Nothing happening."

"Ask her, then," Tom said. As though that's all Zeb needed. Just to drop a coin in the phone and dial her up and chat!

"Ask her, man," Tom said again.

"The Law—"

"Not a legal matter. They won't bother you. She's got money for rent. Help out Palma to have someone around, wouldn't it?"

Zeb argued against it. Didn't want to get involved. Knew all about who that lady was in Tom's cabin. Vic Rios's wife, that was who. "Ah, man," Zeb said. They kept talking, planning, imagining every emergency, while the coffee cooled. Steam rose in the bright air and was gone. The lady did not reappear.

Elven brushed the brush dry, slapped it clean, and laid it on the deck; settled beside it. "When?" he wondered. "What about my cat?"

"Come with me," Zeb said, raising hopes. But he and the boy only went as far as the pay phone at Lupo's. Zeb fished up a quarter and dropped it in. He dialed. Clumsy, he messed it up, hung the receiver up fast, hard, rested his head on the wall, got the quarter back from the return, and tried again. When it rang, he panicked, dropped the receiver, then shoved it into Elven's hand and said, "Ask her if she'll listen to me for a minute. Tell her it's not my fool idea."

Of course, Palma overheard all that, from "ask" to "fool idea," and before the day was over, she heard a great deal more as well.

PART II

THE LONGING FOR THE LONGING

The woman on Tom's boat was Faye, but not as she had been. She hardly resembled her wedding portrait anymore. After the wreck on the causeway—Cristo had died instantly, unmarked, a slight bruise on the back of his neck, Cristo whom she did not now remember, or know as living or dead—the surgeons had shaved Faye's head. Cut the hair first with scissors, then with electric shears, then shaved her egg-bald with a razor. Drew on the broken skull, with antiseptic skill, computer-reckoned life lines. Various operations. Drillings. Drainings. Bone-settings and pinnings. Her left leg and pelvis as smashed as her skull. There were plastic surgeries, easements, approximations, and fierce therapies. She wore a traction "halo" and a body brace for months. Lay in a coma and then woke to simple infancy, with everything learned now unlearned, her mental slate wiped clean.

A year of hospitalization and nursing-home care before she had been ready for a place in the Lauderdale rehab center. By then, Faye had re-learned the basics of personal hygiene and table manners, could leave her wheelchair for several hours a day, could move about in a walker. In a few more weeks she had graduated to braces and a quadcane. Though she could not—when she had arrived at the rehabilitation center—read or write, her brain was functioning on a kindergarten level in attention span, vocabulary, and emotional maturity.

As they weaned her from painkiller and mood-managing medication, she had tantrums, became acquainted with the "time-out" room, the padded, quiet womb of a room where she could be safe from herself and the constant pressure to catch on, to fill in, to resume herself. Sometimes she cried, sometimes she raged, from frustration or for no reason at all, for just having to take someone else's word for everything.

Faye's mother, in her final contest with her own illness, was too frail to move on with Faye to the rehab campus, and spent her energy and remaining weeks recording onto a series of cassettes all that she thought might be of interest and use to her daughter, for later, when questions might arise that no one else could answer. All those Christmases! A whole childhood of memories, firsts, joys, griefs, pets, dishes, bedspreads, arguments and makings-up, pals, passions, crushes, fads in food and dress. Relatives—Mrs. Parry's whole life in Asia, her courtship, the coming to America. Mrs. Parry tried to think of everything, spent hours, after she closed and sold the dry-cleaning shop, and moved from above it into a nursing home, sorting clippings and old school papers, filing and arranging and reliving and taking leave. There was money enough from the sale of the business to put in trust for Faye, for later, when she had graduated from rehab. When she could handle it. Not much, just a little nest egg. The large things she sorted and saved in a steel trunk. The small and core items and the keys to the trunk she secured in the bank vault.

Faye came home for Christmas, Mrs. Parry's last, Faye's—as far as she was concerned—first. Father Grattan arranged it, took charge and custody for the furlough; rode the bus to Lauderdale to pick her up and rode back down with her.

Faye was on her feet full-time, then no more wheelchair, no more walker. One brace on that left dragging foot. Conversationally, still a child. Chattering and enthusiastic.

Faye didn't know her mother, Mrs. Parry, was so changed. Didn't remember her from before the wreck, but knew her from the hospital time onward. She had been at rehab only a few months, but she had made progress, had kept in touch with cassettes mailed back and forth. Her mother had sent cassettes too, and that was the familiar thing, the voice. Faye's hair was still cropped. Mrs. Parry's was now long, twisted up, loosely pinned.

When Faye came to the door, she had her arms full of gifts she'd made for Christmas presents—kid stuff, paste and paper items, mostly—and she didn't knock, just shouldered the door open, backed against it to push it wide, and entered sideways. Mrs. Parry was lying in the bed, staring at her upraised hands, the fingers as thin as twigs, all the old calluses on the palms, from ironing, softened but ineradicable, as were the thimble ridge, and the needle nicks and scars from a lifetime of tailoring fast, While-U-Wait.

"Mama?" Faye said.

Mrs. Parry lay very quiet, looking at her hands. She stretched them toward her daughter, gathering her in. "It's Faye," she said.

As soon as the presents were scattered across the foot of the bed, the room looked cheerier. They had their party beginning right then. Mrs. Parry's gift to Faye—the box full of the cassettes she had been recording—"for later," her mother told her. "Now let's see what you brought me." Among Faye's little gifts, the most labored-over was a calendar illustrated with twelve pictures she had drawn. "Just what I needed," Mrs. Parry said. They spent an hour discussing the pictures, month by month, months Mrs. Parry would not live to see. Not that Faye understood that. Her innocence was like hope, like mercy. Her love was real, not learned. Mrs. Parry had camped in Faye's room. They bonded from day one, from ground zero. Faye didn't understand about her mother's illness, that it was a countdown. What did Faye suspect of death? Only what her instinct for life told her. She picked up the shoeboxes full of cassettes and sorted through them. "Christmases," one was labeled.

"I know a carol," Faye said. But her mother had lain back, was asleep.

Later, Faye would listen to those tapes, even the ones in which Mrs. Parry had lapsed into Vietnamese and French, trying to find herself. They were no mirror; they were behind the mirror, the dark side, not the silver. After her mother died, long after, Faye would think of herself as two people, and the one that lived first—the used-to-be—was "she," and the one that lived now was "I." She tried, for a time, to be both, to take it on faith, and proceed in imitation and parody. She was always making mistakes, saying the wrong thing, doing the exact opposite of what was expected, or normal, or required.

At her mother's funeral, at the Mass, she did not recognize people. Tom, yes. Tom Rios. He had visited her. Had sent her a ticket home from Lauderdale, had offered to meet the bus and drive her to Sts. Joseph & Ann convent school, where Father Grattan had arranged for her to stay. But Faye's counselor drove her home to Sanavere. Tom chose after the funeral Mass as the best time to reintroduce Faye to his mother, Señora Rios, who lived with him now. A tall, distinguished woman in black and scarlet, with a scuffed handbag, and searching eyes like coals. Faye shook her hand and said, "Did I know you before?" and when Señora Rios nodded gravely, Faye hugged her.

The woman, startled, could say nothing at all. She went out to the porch where the Captain, Vic, who had not been home or to confession in a year, stood smoking. He had seen Faye once, the day after the accident, to sign papers, consenting to her treatment and giving Tom custodial power of attorney in his absence. Vic had not seen her since.

After introducing Faye to his mother, Tom left Faye on the steps. He did not say good-bye. Shocked by daylight, accepting condolences from the few remaining, Faye saw Tom get in his truck and leave; Señora Rios was still on the steps. Had Tom forgotten her, left her there?

"Do you have a ride home?" Faye asked her. Faye's therapist had a van; there was room.

Señora Rios looked startled. "My son Vic is waiting." She said it "son veek" and at first Faye thought she had said "convict."

"Oh. You have two sons?" Faye asked. Not sarcasm. The irony of ignorance. "I know Tom."

The Captain, who had been standing on the other side of the pillar, did not step out into view. He actually withdrew. Faye's ride came, and she went. She stepped on Vic's shadow as she left.

She had no idea, none, that her friend Tom had a brother Vic, and absolutely no idea that she had once been or was in any way still connected to him. That rude awakening came later in the week, when she used Tom's bus ticket for her first furlough, a day trip, solo, no overnight privileges yet. She was sitting in the vault at the bank, sorting through her mother's personal effects—a modest lockbox of deeds and dealings and receipts, certificates, warranties, old report cards, Faye's medals from swimming, family passports (the faces in the photos were just more people she didn't know), an envelope from the hospital dated the afternoon of Faye and Cristo's accident, containing her watch, earrings, wedding ring, neck chain, and coral charm. Faye didn't recognize any of it except her name on the envelope and her initials. She was reading at above the fifth-grade level now. She stared at her own name with a thrill—For me! she was thinking—and at her wedding ring with utter unrecognition. On the inside, engraved, her initials and a date and VXR. She laid it aside and looked at the clippings, all kinds of clippings, a lifetime of them.

"Tell her no more than she's ready for; answer no more than she asks," the doctors had said from day one.

When she got this furlough, her counselor had gone over every possible exigency; together they had practiced the list—numbers to call, priorities, and plans B, C, and D if something went wrong or Faye came across a situation she had not practiced for. Faye unfolded the list and looked at it. She ruled out dialing 911. She ruled out asking a policeman. She ruled out going to the emergency room and showing them her ID card from Greenhill, and her Medic Alert tag. The only thing she saw on the list that seemed at all comforting and useful was Tom's phone number. It was an odd number, and she had to get help from the bank to put the call through. It went ship to shore, or in this case, shore to ship.

Only it didn't. She had to tell a message to the machine. So she said, "What's VXR? Who is Cristo? Oh, this is Faye. I'm at the bank. I don't know which bank, do you? Let me—" And the machine clicked off. In just a few minutes, Tom phoned. The woman at the bank came and got Faye. She had to take the call in the main lobby. He sounded as if he was shouting, as if he had to, because he was so far away. He also sounded busy, and she wondered if she should not have bothered him. He told her to stay right there, someone would be there as soon as possible. She took that to mean, not Tom. He was miles away, out in the *Legal Hours*. But he did what he could—he phoned the church. Father Grattan was out, so it fell to Father Ockham to backfill the sacramental and passionate gap in Faye's reeducation.

"Of course I can," Father Ockham said, reaching for his hat—he was wearing it—and his keys.

"Not too fast," Mrs. Lockridge called as he left.

"High time," Father Ockham said.

Father Ockham's attitude about Faye and her marriage and difficulties was, for the most part, his Church's own, served in classic style on the usual untarnished monstrance, yet garnished with his own personal sprigs of bitter rue, because of his lifelong affection for both Cristo and the Cubs. He felt—as many did—that "if Faye had just left Cristo alone, the boy would still be alive." Faye had been very discreet in her Ascension penitence, saying, "I have been tempted," not "I am being tempted." She had not elaborated. She had not named her tempter. But what did it all matter now? She could not, would never, remember any of it.

"God does not forget," Father Ockham explained, picking up Faye's wedding ring. The metal was vault temperature, cold enough to burn. He rolled it between his palms till it was warm and handed it back.

"Tom got mad when I asked who was VXR," she said.

Father Ockham said, "That's his brother. You saw him."

"I saw him?" Faye said. "I never saw him. Which one *is* he?" She thought about it. "I like Tom better," she decided.

"Suppose," Father Ockham began, "suppose you were married."

"Me and Tom!"

"No."

"Tom and I," she said, correcting herself.

"To someone else. To—"

"I don't know anyone else," she said. "Besides, I don't think I'll be married for a while yet."

"But you already are," he said.

"No," she said. "No!" Feeling cheated of something; she couldn't even suspect what it might have been, but cheated, of planning, of choice, of hope, of time. "How can that be?" she said, starting to cry.

He saw then it wasn't going to be easy. It would never be easy. Truth wouldn't be one simple, single, petty coin he could drop in a parking meter and ring up and bring her up to date and legal, and say, "Here you are." He must build the city, the street, mix the paint for the lines, and, as it now seemed to him, get out and push the car every inch of the way back from the wilderness. He felt so tired already. He went back to the beginning. He tried to explain, as to a schoolchild, about the nature and meaning of the sacraments. "You learned all this for Confirmation," he reminded her. "Father Sebastian taught the classes." He had looked it up. They were sitting at the little table in the vault, between them the open lockbox with its mysteries plundered yet unfathomed.

Faye said, "That was before."

"Those vows," he said, "your first Communion made at age seven? You were that young, but sure. You were ready."

She shook her head. "Maybe I ought to do it again?"

"The sacraments leave an indelible mark on the soul," he said. "One doesn't—" He had begun to get agitated, impatient. He shoved his little chair back and began to pace.

"I'll take your word for it," she said, not impertinent. Trying to reassure him. An act of good faith.

No matter what he did, he couldn't make her understand about her marriage to Vic Rios. "The Bishop will allow you for a term, a specified term," he explained, "to live apart."

"A part of what?" she asked.

"*Listen* to me," he said fiercely. "A grant until these conditions cease."

"What conditions?" The whole notion of having lived with someone now a stranger was not as appalling as having to live with someone who was now a stranger. "I don't think I'll be married till I can—till I can cook a whole meal without looking anything up."

"Out of decency," Father Ockham said, "Someone ought to have been offering advice and instruction."

"There's a movie," she said. "We'll learn that next time. Home cooking. I already signed up for checking account and meal planning." She began gathering up the clippings.

"You don't understand. You don't have to," Father Ockham said. "It isn't a choice. You see? It's done. *Done*."

"Over?" She tried to comprehend him.

"Not over," he said, making plans.

Father Ockham believed in "the evidence of things not seen," but he also and mostly believed in evidence that *could* be seen. In Faye's case it was circumstantial: those two one-way airline tickets in Cristo's pocket and the little overnight case filled with Faye's things, among the strewn contents of car and passengers at the scene of the wreck. There was no mystery to him in all this; prior to the accident he had been from time to time hearing Faye's—as he now saw it rather unforthcoming, un-candid—confession, and he was not without opinion, then or now, concerning causes or remedy. Marriage, being instituted by heaven, must be saved.

Father Ockham had a few more things to say to Faye about the sacra-ment of marriage. He was highly suspicious of the doctors' consensus that it was all news to Faye; he didn't see how she could be simply *tabula rasa*, as they said. "Mighty convenient for her," he said. Subtlety and pa-tience were not his long suits, but because of the medical advice and the specific orders the hospital gave, he bided his time, gaining her confi-dence in a series of brief visits, gradually achieving—or resuming, as he thought of it, stubborn to the last—authority.

He had dealt with pagan penitents on death row who had more spir-itual knowledge than Faye now did. He found her neglected rehabilita-tion in matters of religion greatly to be lamented—they were teaching her to walk, talk, and count, but had not said a word to her about prayer. Thus, from time to time, he and Father Grattan drove over to the rehab center when the hospital released her into intensive therapy. They watched her through the reinforced glass windows of the therapy room. She didn't recognize or notice them the first few times, but they became less unfamiliar. After she knew they came there on her account, it made her shy, but she learned to work on, even as they watched, her frustra-tions and angers never because of them, yet made worse by their witnessing them. She spent a lot of time in time-out on those days when she'd look up from her struggling and see them there, dark-suited and all-knowing, like judges. Sometimes she hung there weeping, the parallel bars under her armpits, or she'd drop to the mat and lie inert till they carried her out.

Always when things went wrong she lost her temper. Twice she had to be sedated. After a while Father Grattan had explained to Father Ockham that it would be wiser and kinder to wait to talk to Faye till she was farther along. Father Grattan didn't go back. But Father Ockham knew the way by then, and he simply drove there on his own. It took about an hour when he got all the turns right first thing. He didn't tell anyone he was driving that far.

He could not have explained his continuing interest, this making a project of Faye. It wasn't persecution and it wasn't pity, and if it was love, it was the kind of love God asks of us but seldom sees us accomplish. Father Ockham felt many things about the death of Cristo, but not responsible. He didn't hold Faye entirely responsible either. This accident was not punishment. But he had deep sorrow over it, over not having found a way through to her in that long season of her discontent. He could not reach her this time, either; she had no sense of need. Everything at rehab turned on goals; his offerings and remarks seemed irrelevant, her responses trivial. They were kind to each other, as though dealing with different species.

"Thanks to you," she said when he brought her the rosary. "Keeps?"

He nodded. Then frowned as she put it on, or tried to, over her head as a necklace.

He spent that afternoon's visit explaining it to her. "You don't remember at all?" he marveled. She studied the beads, the links between, the cool little crucifix. She said, "He's Jesus. They already told me. At the hospital."

"You were at St. Joseph's," he said. "And?" He took a sip of the tea they'd brought him. He nodded encouragement.

Faye studied him, troubled. Seeking clues. Trying to find the thing, the idea, the words, the idea and words together, and not give up fitting, like putting a puzzle together on the table in the game room, every bit of that blue sky clueless and blank.

"And so?" he pressed.

"And so on," she decided.

Immediately released from the tension of something being required, sorted, placed, figured, guessed at, and everybody else's knowing it already, exercising her for their—for their what? Entertainment? (Father Ockham laughed. "And so on," he echoed.) For their collection? The doctors had notebooks. The nurses made out papers. She was always taking tests, being examined, asked, and indulged—she could tell that much!—when she measured up, or down. In an instant—and this was one of those occasions—she could go from "and so on" to pure blind rage and frustration.

A nurse came. "Think of something else," she told Faye, seeing her agitation. Father Ockham had stood, seeing the change, and rung the bell. Now he turned his hat in his hands as though steering the car, swerving from a hazard.

"Sing," the nurse said urgently. "Think of a song, think of something else. Remember the one I taught you?"

Faye couldn't remember. She rocked back and forth, not singing, but making ugly noises. She had something else to be bewildered about. She didn't remember the song; she hated herself, hated everybody for not being able to remember the song. Father Ockham standing there troubled, saying, "Perhaps I—"

The nurse began the song. Soothing, simple. Faye's mind caught the melody like a lifeline.

> Row row row your boat
> Gently down the stream
> Merrily merrily merrily merrily . . .

Faye had a beautiful voice, as clear as a child's. She closed her eyes as she sang, and when she opened them again, Father Ockham had gone.

Only after Señora Rios had interviewed Faye did she decide to go on with her plan. Tom thought it was his idea for his *madre* to move in with him, not just while her shoulder—which she had broken in a fall—healed, but longer, as long as she cared to live there, as long as she cared to live. The house was too much for one person, and Tom had never given it much attention since Nola's death.

Señora Rios didn't want to be in the way. She had said that over and over. She said it so much that Tom was glad to see her disappear into the basement to plan her suite there—extensive remodelings allowed her to anticipate independence for as long as she lasted. She used up her small savings, and she used up Tom's patience, who thought she had a morbid interest in cataclysm. Every imaginable future accident or frailty or impairment had to be considered and accommodated—wheelchair ramp, chair lift, safety rails in bath and halls, no carpet or scatter rugs, lever handles on doors and appliances, a little alarm bell she could ring for emergencies (Tom called it "the panic button"), and a hospital bed, with ports for oxygen and suction. The ascetic bleakness of her rooms and her cheerful preparedness, like the gathering of a trousseau for the grim reaper, all so she wouldn't be a burden, burdened their first months.

And then she got well. She was utterly able-bodied and full of energy again. Her sling and cast were off, her shoulder healed, and she was fit for walking seven miles a day, which she often did. She even cut down on her smoking to a pack a day.

In the new year she soon became a feature of Tom's neighborhood, a walking landmark as she made her brisk and upright way along the sidewalks toward town to fire off her latest squibs and editorial rockets. Her typing campaign had resumed with the discarding of the sling. She dropped off books at the library and picked up more. Biography, history, revolution, heroes, villains. Her reading skills in English kept on getting better, though she didn't try to speak better. And she never borrowed poets. "A poet deserves to be bought," she'd say. Poets she bought through the mail and at obscure readings and in the newsstands and at the mall. Poets she read like scripture. She stacked them along her shelves, piled them on tables by her bed, left them open as though their pith exuded a lively air, a vitamin she could breathe which her eyes themselves could not take in. She marked the fine pages with sprigs of bitter herbs and candy wrappers; she scribbled, on receipts, calendar pages, clippings and absurdities from the newspapers, the titles of books yet to be purchased. She objected to politics, raged against policies, but from the poets she took notes and heart. Her husband had—among other things—been a poet.

Never did she leave off the fiction that she had come to live with Tom at his urging rather than from some ulteriority of her own. If time would tell, she'd let it. Time was in no hurry, and neither was she. She regretted only one thing about her life with Tom: she missed the view she had had from her apartment in Key West. She had lived as close as she could get to Cuba. In Spanish the phrase for having a view of was "give on to."

Señora Rios had to find another way for her heart to give on to Cuba. In her mind's compass, memories of Havana—true spiritual north—needled her endlessly that way.

But Tom's basement had had no window on the southern wall. Now it did: a porthole he bought at salvage and installed in a hole his sixteen-pound sledge had left in the poured foundation. It was Señora Rios's favorite improvement, even better than air conditioning, the planter's fan, the grow-light garden shelf on the dark wall with the trays of orchids— her husband had grown orchids—from the mountains, the Cuban mountains! "Don't ask," Tom had said, the night he brought them in in a burlap sack, wrapped in damp, musty pages of *El Diario* dated from before Playa Girón.

Señora Rios aligned her bed to face that porthole. From bed she could reach—on the right side—the table with the phonograph player, and on the left, her Hallicrafters radio. It was not for music. She decorated her walls with framed newspaper articles about her husband and with photographs. On a nail, in plain view always, the nun's habit she had worn to freedom. Her rooms gave an impression of severe and temporary residence reproachful to loiterers and pleasure-seekers. She was a revolutionary, not a hedonist. In many ways she considered herself a prisoner of war. The suitcase lay open on a bench at the foot of her bed. Her clothing—that unrelieved black with a shock of red somewhere—the colors of her revolution.

Tom found her a filing cabinet for her correspondence with other refugees and editors. She had a drawer for her husband's papers. She had carried them from Cuba in that same suitcase. Over the years she had managed to quote him in every major periodical and many minor ones. The letters she wrote to editors she signed with her full married name. She liked that way of writing it, American-style, so that his name, in full, appeared in print. He seemed in that way to be making little tracks into a future he had not lived to see. She accepted every publication of her writing as a tribute to him.

To Castro, she may have been less a threat than an irritation, but she ran her risks with courage. Governments did not have to seek her; she remained a constant and very public irritant and stimulant among readers of the Spanish-language reviews.

In Key West, and now with Tom, she found energy to gather the younger generation—"the university-age children of the lotos-eaters," as she called them—recruiting a few chips off the old blocks to kindle into revolutionary flames. She often read her husband's poetry at cafés and coffee houses.

Sometimes she lay in bed and thought over the many parts of her life her children knew nothing at all about, and the springs shook with the humor of it. Sometimes they found out, and weren't amused. Once she had been arrested in a demonstration at Miami International Airport. Tom, waiting at home, saw her on the eleven-o'clock news and came down with bail.

"What else does she have to do?" Vic pointed out, when Tom complained. Not about the bail, but about the general wear and tear on his expectations and even tenor.

It was long distance to Vic—Tom's dime. Vic was still downcoast, anchored off Marathon Key, mostly sleeping on his boat. Months till the autumn tournaments out of Islamorada, but Vic always found excuses to anchor there, midway, where he could run either way.

"Well?" Tom asked again, on the subject of Señora Rios and her energy and sublimations.

"Put her on a bus to Hialeah, she always loved dogs and horses," Vic suggested.

"You know she doesn't gamble."

"Jesus! It was a joke," he said. In the background Tom could hear talking. In English. The sound of music and laughter.

"Send her a card or something," Tom said. "Birthday's coming."

"Sure, right," Vic promised. He hung up then, and Tom hung up too, listening to his quarters and the rest of the change fall deep into the silence inside the phone.

"Down a rathole," Tom muttered as he walked away.

Vic had never asked about Faye.

Actually, Faye's mother-in-law had been unhappy for three decades, restless, disapproving. Her rancor toward Castro turned every heartbeat into an act of rebellion, resistance, and revenge. There was only one thing she could say about Fidel that was affirming: at least he was Cuban. When Vic Rios had married Faye, Señora Rios's mood had not lifted. Not because Faye's mother was Eurasian, not because Faye was not one-hundred-percent Caucasian, but rather because Faye was not any percent Cuban.

Señora Rios enjoyed—as much as she could enjoy anything—American citizenship. She had studied and taken her oath. Her sons were American citizens—Tom by naturalization, Vic by birth. Señora Rios loved

America and was grateful to the United States, but this was a matter of the body politic—her actual body, as she saw it, not her soul—not personal or religious, no. Her heart was alien; she had left her young husband in a fresh grave in Cuba, and her spirit flew the flag he died for; she would never strike her colors. She had been in the States for almost thirty years, and she had never yet unpacked her suitcase. She kept it open on a chair; all she owned—that dark wardrobe of furious mourning—she kept to hand, as though she might be called upon at any moment to mobilize and return. Some soldiers return from their wars and find they cannot again sleep on a bed, but must rest as they can on the floor, or out in the yard or in the woods. Some veterans, forty or fifty years later, lying in hospital, require a warning sign on their headboard: DO NOT TOUCH THIS PATIENT WHILE HE IS SLEEPING. CALL HIS NAME IN A LOW VOICE AND REPEAT IT UNTIL HE WAKES. DO NOT TOUCH THIS PATIENT UNTIL HE IS FULLY AWAKENED. Señora Rios was that sort of survivor, the sort whose trauma cannot be laid off or lived down, but has bored into the marrow and becomes a part of it, and self-replenishes. Señora Rios was the sort who would never forget.

The nun's habit in which she fled Cuba was the first mourning she wore, a getaway costume that protected not only her identity and the unborn child in her belly, but also the other child she drew by the hand along the tarmac and up the steps into the airplane headed for Mexico, and after that, supposedly—according to her hastily arranged and illegal papers—on to France, to Lourdes on a medical pilgrimage, to try to restore an urchin's sight. They had shaved Tom's head as though clearing him of lice, dressed him in rags, and shoved a pair of smoked lenses over his quick eyes to make him look like the part his papers said he must play—a blighted orphan from Pinar del Río. In Mexico they changed planes, and plans.

For Señora Rios, the passage of the years counted in a special way: one day, and sooner every day, Castro would meet his maker and face the judgment. Also, each day that she must live in exile would be laid against her enemies. She didn't mind as the years mounted up. Castro would pay and pay and pay. The more the better. Meanwhile, she occupied herself with keeping her martyred husband's name remembered on both sides of the Straits. And she played cards.

Her cardplaying was not a widow's game of patience. She had her hands full with canasta, sitting at tables with people as intransigently transient as she. The younger generation assimilated, acculturated, and moved on. These little groups remained, the original expatriates, their

die-hard groups closed to the *marielitos*—the second wave—whose motives for exiling themselves had been misery, not outrage. It was not that
they were intentionally unfair; in the inundation following the boatlift,
the old-timers began to seem obsolete. Their stories, their shrines no
longer caught the public imagination. They saw it as the same war, and
the new refugees as proof of their predictions and hopes coming true—
the *comunistas* had spoiled everything and their programs were doomed.
But the world treated them as veterans of another time and place; they
might as well have been heroes of the War for Independence! Around
these tables, there was much to be regretted but nothing to be explained.
Their shattered fortunes and identity were completed in each other's
memories. Here was where they felt most at home.

And then Señora Rios fell.

Though at first she could not see it, Señora Rios began to believe that
it was the hand of God himself that pushed her down the steps from the
boardwalk to the beach and broke her shoulder. In the first shock of recuperation, she struggled to continue as she had done, on her own and
fiercely independent. She had gotten to her feet and found a cab to take
her to the hospital. She had not even told her sons of the overnight stay
in the hospital.

"For what?" she said. "When I need, then."

To her friends she said, "My brain and my legs did not break." She
showed up for the card games as usual, but had to admit things had
changed. She couldn't deal, and she couldn't manage, and she got drowsy.
She blamed the pain medicine for that, and left it off after a few days. She
left off typing letters to the editors of magazines and newspapers. She
dropped out of her shift at the petition tables. For six weeks, then eight,
when she thought her arm would be healing, she geared back, guarded
her stamina, and did what she had to to manage her light housekeeping.
She took a break, and she took stock.

During the eighth week of what she had believed to be recovery,
she learned about soft-tissue X rays, ligament tears, and the nature and
use of tendons. "My bone has healed," she told Vic the next day when
she stopped by the laundry to pick up her fluffed and folded clothes, and,
without expecting to see him, ran into her son in the street. Actually, Vic
saw her first, and pulled his car to the curb, called her name. He had a
woman with him; he usually did.

Señora Rios held the bundle of laundry to her chest, and turned away
from the car, hoping he would not notice the sling, but he did.

"What?" he said. In that way he had, as though she had done something cute, something to be indulged, as though never in his life had he seen her as she saw herself—as though her strength and pride were whims, quixotic, and her needs and crises quaint little contretemps.

"You are looking good," she told him, taking in him, the car, and the woman in one instant's high beam, then she doused her gaze to low again.

"Do you need anything?" he said.

To her surprise, she had started to weep. She was mortified. "My bone has healed," she said again. "But there are"—she couldn't remember what the physician had called them, all those little bits of tissue that were separated and hard to heal—"other things," she said.

He could not hide his alarm. He took her by the good arm and turned her and they walked up the sidewalk a few paces. He kept his head tucked down, as though the woman in the car could read lips. "You have cancer?" he asked. It sounded like Tom, asking, "You voted for Reagan?"

Señora Rios laughed. "Not cancer," she explained. She tried to make it clear. "I have come untied." She shifted that hurt shoulder toward him.

He surprised her very much by exclaiming, relieved, "Rotator cuff!"

"Yes, yes, how you know this?"

He shook his head. "Read the *Sporting News*." He walked her back toward the car. Señora Rios thought he was going to introduce her to the woman. She was going to have her good hand full of laundry, and not offer to shake hands. But Vic hugged her, gently, and said, "There goes your fastball," so that the woman in the car could hear it and laugh.

"Soon," Vic promised, and drove on.

He was the one who told Tom. Señora Rios would never have done that. But when she heard Tom's voice, concerned, and his offer, she felt she might again disgrace herself by crying. So she told him, instantly, no, and hung up. Then sat there, thinking hard, and reaching some interesting conclusions. She faced facts: the time had come to give up this place and move on. She believed if it was right for one, it would be right for all. It was without regret and with a certain species of hope and excitement—she felt younger, as though that little surge of optimism and intention had begun to knit her back together—she picked up the phone and dialed Tom.

Just as though it had been weeks, not hours.

She tried his number twice before she reached him.

"You know what is?" she began. In English, a major concession. It made him suspicious rather than conciliating him.

"Everything all right?"

"Is Assumption."

"I'm not assuming, I'm asking," Tom said, exasperated after only two words. "Lord God," he was thinking, "what if she had said yes to my offer!"

"Is Assumption. You go?"

Now he understood. "Guess I missed it," he said, in Spanish.

"*Existe Dios,*" she said fiercely. "You don't even pray for your mama like I hope?"

"I'm not an atheist," he said. "I pray."

She didn't speak, but he heard something. She didn't cry, she never cried, the heat of her angers burned her dry. When she wouldn't speak, he called her back on the line with her own name, harsh, like a warning. "Marcela?" Nothing.

"*No entiendo,*" she said.

"*Demasiado coño,*" he said.

"I don't—"

"Oh, yes you do, oh *sí, sí, señora,* you sure as hell do understand." Tom said. "You just give it to me straight; I can stand it if you can."

"Did I ask you to come rescue me?" She steadied up her voice.

"You never ask, you command."

"Not this time," she said, and hung up. So of course he went.

By the time he got there, she had everything packed. She met him at the door with her black scarf tied over her hair and another scarf—a red one—tied over her black sling. She reminded Tom of a storm flag—full gale—and for some reason that made him laugh. "Truth in advertising," he said.

"What?"

"I am glad to see you," he said.

It took Tom a week to persuade her of what she had already decided to do—remain with him permanently. During that week—at every meal they took together, at every bedtime, at every arising, at every going forth and return—negotiations proceeded, adjustments and recitations of principles and pride. During that first week, Señora Rios did what Tom never found out—she went to see Faye in rehab. She took a hundred dollars out of her savings and called a cab. She bargained with the cabbie as though she were still in Cuba, as though the meter were an ornament, a roadway saint's robotic statue. The cabbie won, but Señora Rios—after the visit—rejoiced in money well spent.

"I remember you," was the first thing Faye had said, when she saw Señora Rios in the visiting parlor.

When Señora Rios looked startled, Faye said, "Don't you remember? You were at my mother's funeral."

"It was only right," Señora Rios said.

"Do you come here often?" Faye had not seen her, but there were many floors and wings.

"I come again if you like. I bring my son."

"I like Tom," Faye said.

Señora Rios's eyes flickered. She pressed her mouth into a blank. "You lonely? Miss your friends?"

Faye frowned, trying to discover an answer. She gave it up, shrugged.

Señora Rios put out a hand, touched Faye's cropped hair. "It'll grow," she said. Caught Faye's upper arm, ran her good hand down it to the wrist, like the witch testing Hansel for frying size. "You need a little fat," she said. "Just a *little* little. You not what is a picky eater?" She examined Faye's fingernails, short but unbitten. Healthy looking, the anesthesia ridges already growing out.

"You on medications?"

"I don't like the soup," Faye said suddenly. "I won't eat the soup. Or the liver either."

Señora Rios held up Faye's hand to the sunlight and stared at the red. "You aren't *anémica*, are you?"

"What's an amika?"

Señora Rios studied. "You bleed okay but not too much."

"I'm not bleeding!" Faye pulled her hand away from Señora Rios's.

Señora Rios reassured her, cagy, "You do, though? Every month?" (She pronounced it *moonth*.) "Baby business? They tell you all about it, explain you why? All okay?"

Faye blushed. "Oh." She said, "I saw the movie. I know about that. There's nothing wrong with . . . It's for—"

"I know what is for," Señora Rios said. "Now tell me what's what. You do it? Like calendar? Like moon?" She cycled her hands through the air between them, the left one free and smooth, the right one constrained by the sling, Faye stared.

The longer she didn't answer, the more intense Señora Rios became. Her dark eyes burned below her shrubby brows and she did not blink.

Faye could not look away. She did not know what the woman was talking about, what she wanted, but she knew the answer, so she said, "Yes, ma'am."

Immediately Señora Rios smiled, rewarded her with a firm grip of her good hand on Faye's wrist with the hospital bracelet.

"I knew all okay," she told Faye. "Pretty girl like you very healthy. Lonely, too."

"I'm not lonely," Faye said.

"Ah," the woman said. She laughed her rich laugh and gave her a wink. "You want again the husband, pretty girl like you."

Faye tried to get up and leave.

"You take my advice," Señora Rios said.

It's about VXR, Faye realized. She said it aloud: "VXR."

"*¿Qué? ¿Quién?*"

Faye thought of the last time she had seen Señora Rios, on the church steps, saying she would ride with her son, saying she had two sons, Tom and the other one, the shadow across her path. She drew back.

Faye tried to leave the day room, but Señora Rios had her by the arm.

"Tom?" Faye called. It was like a prayer.

"I came in taxicab," Señora Rios said. "*Sola.*" She looked in her purse and bought out a little box. Wrapped with gold paper and a ribbon. "For you," Señora Rios told her. "You see? Something pretty for you."

"You knew me before," Faye said.

She opened the gift. It was a gold flacon of perfume. Monogrammed.

"Is this what I liked?" She sniffed it. "Who liked this?"

Señora Rios said, misreading Faye's reluctance, "No trick on you. Store-bought, no magic. You like it?"

"Do you have a picture? A photograph of you and me?" Faye thought about it. "A photograph of you and me together. Smiling."

"Next time," Señora Rios promised. She took the little flask from Faye and spritzed some in the air, then turned it toward Faye—toward her elbows, ears, wrists, cleavage, knees.

Faye backed, swerved, flung her arms and stamped. Blinked. Coughed.

Señora Rios coughed too. She handed the perfume back to Faye. "Every day," Señora Rios told her. "Spray. Spray."

Señora Rios had dynastic ambitions. Tom and Vic had her husband's name, but after them, what? She saw her husband's career as a flight cut short, though while he flew he flew as straight and purposefully toward his brilliant destiny as an arrow toward the heart of a target. But his flight had been no natural and gradual downcurving toward earth and rest, nor had he struck, so far as she could tell, any target he had aimed for. His protests, his resistance, his arrest and murder had accomplished what? A man who lives for something does not live in vain, and a man who does not live in vain does not die in vain, yet Señora Rios wanted somehow a reassurance that though he had been stolen from her (as well as from the world), he had somehow prevailed. Heirs, that was what she wanted. Generations to rise up and call him blessed. The line of his broken flight to pass into the lives of his children's children.

She had kept scrapbooks for years; now she worked on them for posterity; not a library or an archival posterity, but a living one. The poems and writings came back from the printers custom-bound. She laminated certain things, photocopied others, and kept them with a few photos in a plastic bag in her purse, bound round with rubber bands; the rest of her treasures she banked in a safety deposit box. Now she no longer dreaded accident or theft or loss, as she had when she first came to the United States, when she had felt uncentered and unsafe and at risk everywhere. She had carried all her treasures with her; she would draw these out and offer—clippings, diplomas, transcripts, evidence, poems, letters, and photos (even diagrams of the way his body had been seen, in the ditch, beside the truck, and a cassette of her own impassioned testimony before a distracted and indifferent Dade County notary, who spoke no Spanish, concerning the condition and markings and wounds on her husband's body in the morgue, which cassette she would remove from her attaché-type handbag and play)—on the bus, on the beach, in cafés, in the post office, to anyone who could bear to listen and to many who simply did not know how to flee.

When she first came to the States she carried her grudges the same way she carried her case—hauling everything out, including her wedding rings and the locket on the chain around her neck, pulling these up from beneath her clothes, their gold as hot as her own unshed tears. Those who came to know her dreaded her—fled, as from the Ancient Mariner—her carefully honed points, her indefatigable righteous wrath. If Tom was with her, in the early days, she'd drag him forward too, as evidence—a grade-school exhibit. She had the baby carriage mined with other exhibits, including Vic, orphaned infant of the martyred father/hero. Perhaps she thought repetition would create heroism in her sons; perhaps she thought their memorizing of their father's poems would make them poets as well. Tom mastered English, became confident in it if not competent, within a few months. Vic spoke both languages from the first. They grew fast and found their own passions early, and didn't stick around helping her type and translate. They did not love history, they did not care to care about what they increasingly came to file, in their minds, as "all that." Señora Rios thundered and flashed and rained down reason. "You escaped Castro, not Cuba," she told them over and over. "And Castro will not escape."

As the years passed, Señora Rios's methods changed, her expectation of early vindication moderating into patience for an ultimate victory. Her testimonies moved from raw reports into shaped history, her intentions from simply being heard to being understood. She never sought a thing for herself, not money, not fame; she wanted her husband's name not to die out from living memory.

Neither son—though both possessed the wit for it—had the passion for law. She had hoped they would study and work for justice in the courts, as well as through them. Had there been the money for such educations, they still would not have chosen law. Both loved the water, and found their life and future on the very seas that separated them from their homeland, yet they plied them to go forward, not back. When they had left her, made lives for themselves—Tom marrying Nola and Vic making a name for himself on the charters—Señora Rios looked around for a way to help her dreams. She began studying law herself, reading it at night, and though she took courses, she realized she would never pass the bar exam because of her poor English. She took English-as-a-second-language so many times the ESL instructors finally told her she and they had reached their limits. It was at this time that her project—translating Martí—moved to the back burner, too, as she reassessed her talents. It was also at about this time she fell and broke her shoulder.

Before she moved upcoast to live with Tom, she had a few weeks—and free time away from the card table—to review and reorganize her hopes. She sat on the bench in the park and talked with Don Salvo Rodriguez. He had free days, being a janitor in a bank. His credentials and degrees and licenses had not transferred, in the relocation to the new country. They had met one Saturday evening in the law library when she was trying to comprehend tort law, and he was simply visiting the books. Though he did not expect ever to practice law again, or to hear himself called "Judge," he felt a kind of peace being surrounded by the shelves of thick tomes with their holdings and upholdings of each other. They fortified him; he did not regret them, or see them as his enemy.

He had lived a quiet life, before coming to the States. His wife had been an invalid for many years. They had escaped with only the clothes on their backs, in an open boat. His wife had died a few weeks after their rescue by the coast guard. He felt the same sense of loss and peace here, among the laws of the new land, as he had when he visited her crypt.

He noticed Señora Rios first. After several evenings watching her work at the table, retrieving books and searching them, scowling, making copious notes, he stepped up to her in the elevator and introduced himself as they both left the building. When he learned her name, he lifted his hat and made a slight bow.

She experienced a wild hope. "You have known my husband?"

"My loss," he said. He had read Señora Rios's letters in the papers. He had from time to time read pamphlets and poster quotes. He had seen her reviews. Before they met again, each had looked up the other in the reference section, in the biographies and histories. They made no appointments, but when they met they shared a mutual respect for, as he put it with no bitterness, "who we once were." She won his friendship with her spirit.

"This isn't shipwreck," she had said, "this is war."

They never met for meals, only for coffee. They enjoyed the park. He read his newspapers there, in the afternoons. When he and Señora Rios chatted, they never used their christening names or *tu*. Their subjects were classical and civic. They did not meet regularly, but when they did, the formality of their conversations—in a world where manners and customs had become barbaric and informal, and courtesy nothing but cynical manipulation—offered great pleasure and surcease. At times they did not bother to open new ideas; in fact, after a time their conversations themselves became ritualistic, one's remark about "how many laws there were in the world and how little justice"—a gambit such as chess champions recognize and counter with the best they have—provoking the other's predictable and necessary reply. He was perhaps a dozen years older than she, but because of her deep mourning, she seemed to have caught up. They saw eye to eye; she was cranelike in her height and gauntness, sudden, impatient, whereas he still had a fencer's grace. His knees failed him often enough that he carried a cane. He used it to effect, sitting, looking out to sea, his hands propped one on the other atop its ebony curve. He listened to Señora Rios without looking at her. They sat side by side, never closer than the width of his hat, which he set on the bench between them. There were pauses, some days, of minutes at a time when neither spoke at all.

Both Don Salvo's fame as a jurist in Cuba and his need to flee sprang from his championing of impossible causes. His name appeared in more than one headline. Coming to a freedom that meant hands-and-knees floor scrubbing had not broken his spirit, only his heart, his diplomas and experience guaranteeing nothing in the United States, where much law was based on precedents and one's knowledge of them, whim and decree and royal grant and all the exquisite flourishes of Caribbean jurisprudence washing up on this new shore like so much broken crystal.

"Which Castro broke the most of," Señora Rios would point out, as though on cue, but with great and sincere passion. Sometimes a shadow would cross her own broken heart as she considered what might have come of her husband, had he been able to reach her that last night, and escape with her to this new land. He would have had to start entirely over, like Don Salvo. As though she had suddenly and actually seen her husband on his knees scrubbing public floors, fresh outrage would rise up in her; Castro would still have ruined their lives even if her husband had lived. She must never forget, death was not the enemy.

She said it now. It was time. *"Bien de morir, en tal caso."*

As though he had been freshly inspired by her very thoughts, Don Salvo, who forgot nothing he could remember and forgave nothing he could not forget, would rock to his feet and stand staring across the water. Señora Rios would rise also. *"Nunca,"* she'd vow. "Soon," she'd vow.

"Is not so far," he'd say.

One afternoon she missed her cue. Came to herself and realized that Don Salvo had been on his feet, for the finale of their ritual, and she had been sitting there, who knew how long, following a very different path to victory. That was the afternoon she had thought of Vic and Faye together again, of how much simpler a route to grandchildren that was going to be than a divorce, which would require negotiations and extrications both civil and religious. It would also take time, and suddenly Señora Rios was in a hurry.

Children were playing on the rocks and beach, running back and forth like peeps, their shrill cries and laughter blowing on the wind. "The future," Don Salvo was saying, as though making a toast. Señora Rios stood, dazed. She felt faint, swayed, and accepted Don Salvo's hand on her arm for balance. "We are not young chickens," Don Salvo said.

"Is not too late," she said.

He turned to her in astonishment, a thrill of apprehension, of misapprehension sending shock waves of an electric and unaccustomed nature across his circuits.

"The revolution?" he said, to clarify her intentions before hope's high horse bolted or threw him.

"Children," Señora Rios said, having no idea how her mind's turn had turned his.

"Is not unheard of," he said, considering medical articles he had read. He also considered—in American legal fashion—certain precedents. Biblical precedents. He was thinking it would be more likely he could do his part than she hers, but gallantly he said, "It might require"—he paused to find the most delicate word—"assistance."

"For my part—" she began.

Again, with greatest gallantry, and a slight bow, he murmured, "For all parties. Only a fool would resist to try."

"That's it," she said definitely. Joy creased and then cracked her usual sobriety; she turned her back on the sea and faced him, her smoldering eyes kindling his.

"Can it be?" he wondered.

"I'll find out," she vowed, and grasped his hand, clasped and shook it. It was the end, not the beginning, of their times together, but even after she moved to live with Tom, she received letters from Don Salvo, beautiful letters that, had she not known him so well, might have astounded her into either hysterical laughter or crisp, formal rebuke; certainly she knew how to ridicule, to scathe. In her whole life she had let no fool unsuffer. But as it was, she accepted his wild protestations and hints as metaphors—she thought he was making some sort of trope: apostrophizing Freedom, courting the revolution with ardor and expatiating on the bliss and glories of violent overthrow. She thought it was politics. She thought he wrote in code, so that Castro's agents—there must be some, and they must be brutes—could not comprehend. Because she believed that he believed that, she believed it too. Thus, she answered in kind, and they corresponded fervently till the end of his life, and she always replied to his ritual closing—"Is not far"—with one of her own—"Soon"—handwritten at the end of her typed letters. They never met again, and when he died, a few months after she had moved in with Tom, she saw the obituary in the Miami paper.

"They left out so much," she fumed, seeing the scant two inches of column space he had been given. She wrote a letter of correction, pointing this out to the editors. Calling him "a buried treasure," she said the United States had entertained an angel unaware. She added, after re-reading all his letters, "He might have been a poet."

On the day before Señora Rios moved in with Tom, she made a final pilgrimage to the Martí memorial. She had not managed a statue for her husband—not yet—but she left a wreath of greens—no blooms, evergreens, as she had told the florist, bay and palms. She visited the library, touched again the spines of the books in which her husband's name and words appeared, including a recent bilingual textbook.

She gave the librarians her new address and phone number. "Not before Monday," she specified, since Tom hadn't asked her yet. He would. After some thought, she decided to continue as the regular Spanish-language reviewer for a Latin sub-coast weekly; the pay would keep her in stamps and cab fare, and the review copies—if she didn't keep them—she would pass along to the library in Tom's neighborhood.

Señora Rios did not—as anyone who knew her could see—waste anything, especially time. Even the cardplaying had been a form of journalism, making contacts, keeping (as she defined it) current. Certainly she did not need Vic's offer of bus fare to the horse and dog races. Tom's beleaguered call for Vic's help had not been because their mother was idle. Nor was she so intellectual she despised sports. She loved the jai alai courts and the beauty of all men and animals straining for a prize, but she was not a betting woman. Still, if she had had to bet on anyone, it would have been on Vic and Faye.

They might have been considered a long shot by some, but Señora Rios did not waste a moment in considering or lamenting the odds. She went, that first week she was settled under Tom's roof, to interview Faye in the rehabilitation unit. The week after that—the very first Monday Tom was away fishing—dressed in her usual black, a few carefully chosen pieces of evidence in her handbag, her lips carmined in that to-and-fro stroke uninfluenced by looking glass or any fashion consultant, and armed with her umbrella—clutched in her fist, as though if the weather threatened her, she would threaten it right back—she walked, gathering directions from strangers along the way, and before nine o'clock she was knocking at the door of St. Francis Xavier rectory, asking for Father Ockham.

Father Ockham was still driving in daylight, in good weather. His health had been better, but at this point it was better than it had been recently. He considered Señora Rios's visit and the plan she suggested very interesting. They wasted no time coming to an agreement, having, as they did, compatible if not mutual interests. As soon as they could, they made a trip up to Greenhill to visit Faye. Father Ockham had a catechism in his pocket, and Señora Rios a refill for the tiny bottle of perfume she had given Faye.

The special diet that was driving Mrs. Lockridge crazy had begun to show results; Father Ockham's collar was a bit looser, and his neck less flushed. On his red cheeks a three-day grizzle bristled. He hated the electric razor, and they no longer permitted him a blade razor because of the blood-thinner he took.

As he got in the car, he tossed his hat on the backseat. His silky white hair rose toward the car's headliner from static. When he put the key in the ignition, he grounded that charge through his fingertips. The audible *skik!* of the shock provoked his temper, but nothing could spoil his mood. He felt a little off center, a little furtive, and altogether fine—in charge, ready for anything. He loved to drive.

As he accelerated onto the frontage road, his own spirit surged with the turn of the season. Even in a subtropical climate, whose weather could never be said to be wintry, one could feel—as Lent came to its stately close—an intensifying, a sap-rise. Father Ockham liked that: sap-rise. Sap-rise, surprise. He repeated it in his mind's ear, and began to imagine where he would toss it in. His idea of homiletics was something old and familiar boiled down, even the toughest thing, into tenderness, with little nuggets thrown in for spice. Lost in thought, he had let conversation lag. He had even forgotten Señora Rios was with him until he started to signal—as he had already begun the turn—onto the tollway.

Señora Rios made a noise. Not a scream, not a reproach. More of an entreaty. Then she covered her eyes. The car swerved violently, the tires puffing smoke as Father Ockham jerked it sideways to avoid the semitrailer full of Easter lilies also headed north.

Señora Rios opened her eyes. " 'Wide turns,' " she read, from the re-frigerated truck's warning sign. In her heavy accent. Father Ockham thought she had asked, "Why turn?" which suited him just as well, and he veered back out of harm's way. He had been, in the confusion of the moment, racing the truck up the ramp, side by side on the one-lane access. He did not notice his half of the lane was running out. He braked and came to a stop on gravel and grass, not in the least unnerved.

"Certainly," he agreed, and put the car in reverse and began to back, sometimes fast, sometimes creeping, down the on-ramp. He had no peripheral vision; blood pressure had blinkered him. He never even thought of anything oncoming, just backed out onto the frontage road, and aimed north, gunning it ahead of another truck. The blast of air horns gave his spirits a boost. "Get out and come on in!" he hollered out his half-downed window, full of good cheer. Spring was definitely in the air. He felt like a kid again. Three blocks later he glanced in his rearview. He didn't at all like what he saw.

It wasn't what he had expected. There was a roof rack of blue lights strobing and flashing and a siren—punched once so it growled into silence. Father Ockham pulled over to the extreme right, across two lanes of traffic, to let the car pass. It did not. It cut in right behind him, and the driver motioned him over.

"Now what's his problem?" he wondered, easing off the pavement, and rolling to a stop.

"Sir?" the officer said, glancing in the window at Señora Rios. "Ma'am," he added. She never looked his way, just sat with her hands folded, staring straight ahead.

"It is unlawful to back up on the Interstate."

He asked for Father Ockham's license and studied it, comparing the frailer reality with the robust photo. He did not overlook the collar. "A warning this time," he said, writing in his book. He had Father Ockham sign, tore the page out, handed him his carbon. "Another warning," he added. "If you don't like the direction you're headed, there's an exit and interchange up ahead, they build them in all along, and plazas. Don't back up on the ramps."

"God allows U-turns," Father Ockham said, his twinkle rallying.

"Not on the West Dade Expressway." The officer did not look amused. He leaned in and looked, frowned.

"Sir, would you step from the car?"

Señora Rios crossed herself.

Father Ockham opened the door and got stiffly out. He had not taken

Tylenol that morning; in the rush to get away before questions were asked, he had forgot.

The officer knelt by the driver's seat and gave a little tug to the seatbelt, extricating it from where Father Ockham had stuffed it out of the way. It sawed his throat, and he refused to wear it. The officer had to work a kink out of the belting, and then ease the slack back into its proper place. He untangled bends and twists so the mechanism would work properly. He removed the two clothespins and the rubber bands. "Here you are, sir," he said. Father Ockham put the things in his pocket. He got back in the car, and the officer waited, watching. Father Ockham put the seatbelt on and snapped it safe around him. He pulled the shoulder belt across and clicked it into place.

"That's Florida law also," the officer approved. He stepped back. Saluted. *"Vaya con Dios, Padre,"* he said. Grinned. "Keep it between the lines." He held up traffic so Father Ockham could swing safely and easily back on the road. He followed them for over two miles, Father Ockham noticed. After that he forgot to notice, so he wasn't sure when he—as he thought to it—"lost him." He was checking the rearview one more time when they came to the rehab driveway and he missed it, drove right past it. He wasn't about to admit it, so he just swung up over the curb and jolted them across the grass and down into the employees' lot. He parked past the Dumpsters, in the very back of the building. Señora Rios had to step in a puddle of mop water to get out of the car.

Father Ockham was already at the side door, hammering for admittance.

They had an appointment with Dr. Grayson. Faye had not been told of their visit or intentions.

A worker was stapling a border of shamrocks around the bulletin board in the hall. The chart by the dayroom door announced, at wheelchair level,

TODAY IS	Friday
DATE IS	March 1
TOMORROW IS	Saturday
YEAR IS	1991
WEATHER IS	Sunny
NEXT HOLIDAY	St. Patrick's

"Where do I go? Where do I go?" an old woman in a wheelchair called. She looked up at Señora Rios. Held her hand out—Halt! Señora

Rios wasn't sure what to do. Father Ockham took the extended hand and shook it, and said, "We just got here. Were about to ask you." And Señora Rios agreed, "Choost got here myself, me."

"Well, it's a grand place, they'll treat you right, just all right," the woman said kindly, searching their faces. "Don't you worry about a thing, honey," she told Señora Rios. She ankled her wheelchair around the corner and began moving the chair along with her sock feet to propel her on. Her hands lay in her lap, at peace. "See you at lunch!" she called back. They could hear her, farther along the hall, asking anyone, no one, everyone, "Where do I go? Where?"

A nurse taking medications into a room saw the looks on Señora Rios and Father Ockham's faces. She shook her head. "Don't worry about it, she's fine, she's not lost, she just keeps finding herself all the time, that's all, she's much better, actually," she assured them, ducking into a dim room from which a thrill of organ music and a broken voice calling "Ramón!" indicated a *novela* in progress on the television. They could hear the nurse saying, "Come on, now, sweetie, let's sit up and have a little sip of *agua*, there you go, *bueno*." She brisked the empty cup back out, tossing it in the trash sack on her cart, then rolled on to the next door.

"Is not rehab!" Señora Rios said.

The nurse heard that, came back out, and pointed. "Down the hall, through the double doors, and left."

When they finally came to the door marked Administrator, there was a nice lobby, chairs and sofas, a good rug, paintings, and pleasant drapes. There were also public rest rooms, and while Father Ockham availed himself, Señora Rios sat and watched cars drive up under the marquee out front, discharge passengers, and swing across the alley to the parking deck. She glanced at her watch; they were fifteen minutes late.

"We came in wrong way," Señora Rios mentioned as they stood in front of the receptionist's desk.

"So long as we leave," Father Ockham said.

When they did leave, they were not to take Faye with them, although they had naively believed that would be possible. Dr. Grayson had heard their proposal with some interest but not enthusiasm. "Soon," he told them, "but not yet. She needs continuity."

"What is?"

"She's still on a rollercoaster temperamentally."

Señora Rios thought about that and drew her own conclusions. "You mean ess-tubborn?"

"Stubborn, no. I mean easily frustrated. And when that happens, and it can happen for things that you or I would see as trivial"—he consulted the chart—"not getting her jacket unzipped, forgetting the name of a common object, or just being tired—she has no resources, no resistance. She improves every day, but she is still brittle, fragile, and vulnerable."

"Throws things?" guessed Father Ockham.

Dr. Grayson sat back and looked at them. "Tantrums, yes, sometimes, but if you are thinking about control, or about being embarrassed in public, you are thinking about the wrong person. She needs, those are the very times she needs, to feel that someone else is in control, when she can't be."

"Time out," Father Ockham said, remembering the chair in the kindergarten class at St. Francis Xavier. "Is she still at kindergarten level?"

"She hasn't gone to time-out in several weeks," Dr. Grayson said, "and when she did, she walked there on her own. She has setbacks, but her progress has been remarkable. She's come calendar pages, pages and pages, some weeks." He glanced at her chart again. "She's come a long way back."

They thought about it.

"I don't mean to frighten you. In general she has progressed past kid stuff, but she has her days, like the rest of us. Every advance has its shadow and regression, then she moves forward again. Her moods are steadier, but they still swing. She has jags of crying, of exaltation. She's learning how to manage her emotions all over again. Imagine you're dealing with infancy, childhood, and adolescence all at once, not to mention learning a new language, and struggling with physical humiliation and pain in therapy."

"Crying?" Señora Rios said. She had never had any use for crying women. That was one of the things she had liked about Faye. If this was a new tendency, she'd have to break her of it.

"Her emotional age is playing catch-up," the doctor said.

"So how old is she now?" Father Ockham asked.

"How long it will take?" Señora Rios wanted to know.

Dr. Grayson laughed. "For what? This is life. She's living it now. This isn't a detour. How long does it take for any of us? What is maturity?"

Señora Rios let him finish. Barely. Then, "How long before she comes live with Tom and me? I teach. I know what she needs to know!"

"You can afford to be generous with her," Dr. Grayson said. "Indulge her tempests, answer her questions. You have the advantage of her in every way. Are you patient?"

"Yes!" Señora Rios said.

"Is she—might she be—" Father Ockham wondered, "a danger to herself?"

"Her depressions are not clinical. They pass."

"Is not ess-tupid," Señora Rios said with approval.

"Teachable," Father Ockham prayed.

Dr. Grayson made a note on Faye's chart and closed it. "I see you are deeply involved in this project of yours. It's a good one. We need a little more time here, daily therapy, but when she is ready, she will need sheltering, she won't be able to live independently all at once. As a halfway measure, why not, if she agrees. It ought to be up to her, you know. When will you discuss it?"

"She has nowhere else. No one," Father Ockham said.

"She married to my boy," Señora Rios said. She handed Dr. Grayson a photograph. Faye had asked for one in which she and Señora Rios were together, smiling. The photograph had been taken at the wedding reception. Everyone was smiling.

"Look, for all she knows, her life began with the wreck," Dr. Grayson warned, handing the photo back. "Like a newborn, she adds on daily. She sleeps a great deal. She needs dream time to process. It won't be at all in her best interests, in my opinion, if you suddenly unload a lot of old history for her to sort. That's luggage she doesn't need for this trip."

Señora Rios said, "Truth!" She said it in such a warm way that the doctor thought she was agreeing, when in fact, she spoke from her own experience and inclination—truth for her was all the luggage, and only the luggage. Where would she be if she forgot? Oblivion was the fate worse than death.

"What do we tell her, then?" Father Ockham asked.

"Don't tell, let her ask. She will, when she can handle it. She'll ask; answer then."

"Will she catch all the way up?"

"This isn't amnesia," he told them. "A word of caution here, please—this isn't a pet you're adopting."

"I'm not adopting," Father Ockham agreed. "I'm translating."

"Not adoption," Señora Rios said. "Already Rios."

The doctor shook his head. "You understand it isn't a matter of filling in blanks? This isn't amnesia. There was massive damage. Paths were destroyed. Portions of tissue gone. It isn't there to 'get back.'" He shook his head, marveling. "Can you imagine how it would be? Innocence."

"Just because she doesn't remember doesn't mean it never happened," Father Ockham said.

"God's truth there!" Señora Rios stood. It was time for lunch. The receptionist had already clicked on the answering machine for the hour. Dr. Grayson always took his meals with the patients.

"You're welcome to stay for lunch."

But they didn't.

Residents moved in a slow stream toward the dining room. Some lurched, straggled, or rolled in chairs. They saw Faye pushing another patient in a wheelchair. It was the woman who had asked, "Where do I go?" They were talking, laughing. Faye pointed something out in a side room, and they both waved.

"That doctor was not very—" Señora Rios began.

A stout woman pushing a linen cart down the side hall paused to speak. "Lissen. I been here. Seen it all. Been seeing it for years. Don't you never give up. You caint out-dollar patience. Patience. Patience. Just set right by 'em and talk talk talk . . . Love. Never wasted a second I squandered on love . . . Is it your mama we talking about? Stroke? Seen 'em in their nineties come on back to life and joy and Merry Christmas."

"It's Faye," Father Ockham said.

"Faye?" the laundress said, trying to think.

"Faye Rios," Señora Rios. "There." She pointed.

"Me?" Faye turned when she heard her name. "That's who I am." She came toward them as though summoned. She was smiling, hardly limping at all.

Señora Rios visited Faye every few days. Father Ockham was sometimes busy, and couldn't accompany her. On the weekends, Tom drove. She preferred Tom's driving to Father Ockham's, or to the taxi or bus, but she did not like Tom's conversation or radio music. She preferred to hear the tires humming along over the concrete highway rather than listen to Tom's Afro-Cuban jazz, his country-and-western; his sports.

"Your father was educated man," she would say. "You look like him, but Vic—"

Tom would shut off the radio.

Señora Rios liked opera. She liked it when Tom was able to drive her to see Faye on Saturday afternoons early enough so that she and Faye could listen to "Live from the Met." Sometimes she brought old Havana playbills to show Faye. Tom did not like opera. He'd drop his mother off, and as soon as the orchestra began tuning its reeds and strings to that concerted A, he'd make smart talk and ease out the door. He might take a walk, or a drive, but he wouldn't be back till it was over.

Señora Rios arranged a pass for Faye so they could attend a champagne concert. *Tosca.* It was one of Vic's favorites, but Faye didn't know that. In fact, she didn't know that Vic enjoyed opera at all. And she certainly didn't know that Señora Rios had purchased two tickets for Vic and whomever he might bring. Señora Rios had had enough sense to make sure she and Faye would not be seated anywhere near Vic. But she had also arranged it so that Vic and his companion would be seated behind Faye and his mother.

As it turned out, they ran into each other in the lobby during intermission. Faye didn't recognize Vic, wasn't looking for him or for anyone, just looking around. She had stepped out of one of her high heels, very relieved to be letting her left foot—which still swelled from the break and setting pins and surgery—find its own shape. She stood out of the traffic flow, sipping a fruit ice. Señora Rios arranged herself between Vic and Faye. When she saw her son, she went over to Vic and spoke, of course, but very briefly and casually, and she did not draw Vic and his companion over to be introduced to Faye. He never got close enough to have the advantage of the perfume Faye was wearing, but Señora Rios, as they took their seats again after intermission, felt Faye had shown to good advantage. Señora Rios had brought Faye a rather sleek blue dress, a bit too sophisticated for her, perhaps; she didn't flex into curves as she once had. The wreck and healing had made her more angular, a little thin, and she walked on those high heels like a colt finding its legs for the first time. It all made her seem younger, as the doctor had said, adolescent.

Faye was very concerned about behaving properly, and her self-consciousness made her shy. But above all, she was pleased and delighted to be at the theater, to be moving among such fine people. The excitement had put color on her cheeks.

From time to time she raised her hand to her hot face and touched it with her white glove. She wore the gloves because she was still ashamed of the scars on her hands, but she didn't flap her hands around like a gawky child at Easter; she sat with them folded in her lap, and they remained quite clean. From time to time she checked to be sure.

At intermission, when Señora Rios worked her way across to speak to Vic and his companion, she did not mention Faye at all. She spoke only of the music, the performances, the weather, and was altogether charming; she even lightly shook the hand of the woman with Vic.

The truth was, it hadn't caused Vic a second glance for Faye to be there. Their lives had been long separated; he said, "Pity our seats weren't together," and Señora Rios said, "No, no this is perfect, trust me."

She turned to see him and to wave, just before the house lights went down. Faye was already seated. Señora Rios spoke to her so Vic would be sure to notice them there.

To Vic, it didn't look like Faye. He didn't like a short haircut on a woman. He wouldn't have known her. When they had married, she had never had her hair cut, not once. The weight of it—gone now—had let what was left curl. Not tightly, but with great life. She looked like a dozen other women there. Nothing to make him want to know her, if he hadn't already.

At least that was what he thought. Señora Rios rather hoped that would be his reaction. She believed that if he believed that, he wouldn't be suspicious or wary. He would be able to visit with Tom and Señora Rios and not have to dread encountering trouble, petition, or appeal. Without awkwardness, then, Vic and Faye could become reacquainted. It would only be natural for Vic to notice certain changes in Faye, some of them all to the good as Señora Rios made her into what Faye could always have been if she had been given a few lessons—the ideal Cuban wife.

Of course, it was also part of Señora Rios's plan that Vic and his woman friend be seated behind them at the concert. So that Vic could see Faye without having to seek her. Perhaps seven rows ahead. This was why it had taken Señora Rios so long—and so much money—at the dress shop. To find the perfect dress, one with the back just bare enough that the birthmark on Faye's right shoulder, half-revealed, would remind. So that it would take great concentration on his part to forget what the rest of that birthmark looked like.

Faye liked Señora Rios, or at least she didn't mind her. She thought of her as "Tom's mother." She still had—or again had—the innocence of a young mind, which thinks that if it chooses not to entertain thoughts or realities, then they aren't real to anyone else either. To Faye, Vic was part of the unremembered and unrecoverable past; Faye still thought of herself as "she"—the one before the wreck—and "I"—the one living now. She trusted people who were good to her, the only people she knew, the ones she had met in the hospital and rehab; she remembered the weeks she had had with her own mother, as her mother was dying, but she did not grieve for her mother or for herself as adults normally grieve.

Because she had no memory of her childhood—or of her father or her school years or a Christmas or a birthday or a heartbreak of puppy love, or even of a puppy or other childhood pet, or of her prom, her swimming medals, her courtship and marriage—and because her experience with emotions in rehab so far had been as something to control or be destroyed by, she dealt in facts. Faye loved facts. Facts added up, or stood alone. They were what the world had and she could get—one at a time or in gulps. They were recoverable. Her schooling with private tutors and basic reeducation in therapy gave her the most pleasure. She could see daily progress. She learned to read, to count, to spell. She worked at a computer and would have stayed before it into the night except that the little lab closed at nine. She learned to tell time. Tom gave her a watch at Easter. Tom's mother gave her a book of Jose Martí's poems. That afternoon they invited her to a movie, and let her choose. She looked at ads in the papers and decided on *Volver a Empezar*, because of the title: *Starting Over*. She knew nothing about the film itself. Neither did Señora Rios, who wholeheartedly approved the choice. Tom from the beginning scowled. Faye and Señora Rios, in over their heads, left the theater scowling too.

Afterward, they stopped for an ice, and Tom bought a kite and they went to the breakwater to fly it. Faye had her Easter shoes on, not rubber soles, and she had trouble clambering down the riprap to the beach.

"Shoes!" Señora Rios—who had bought them—cried.

Faye turned back at once and took them off, handed them to Tom, who set them on the grass beside Señora Rios's bench on the promenade. She had chosen not to risk the beach. It was halfway between tides, and Faye went running on the hard, smooth, damp sand, running fairly well, running for joy. She drew up, suddenly, and walked more soberly, trying to get as close as possible to a flock of gulls standing on the sand. The birds turned, eyeing her, and when she was no more than her own shadow's length away, they rose, lifted, swirled around Faye. Cutting low and high through the air around her, shrilling, circling. Faye stood absolutely still and the gulls settled again. Tom and his mother watched. They could see Faye's mouth moving, see her talking to the birds, see her laughing.

Tom knelt to assemble the kite. While he was tying the line to the keel, Señora Rios was rolling and unrolling the nylon tail ribbons. They made a rustle like taffeta. When Tom glanced up to see why his mother had not replied to his question about the illustration on the kite package—there were no instructions, just a diagram—he was dismayed to see his mother's eyes shut, and tears silvering her cheeks. She looked withered, somehow; not at all formidable. The kite, taut and trembling in the breeze, eager to try itself, blew against her black stocking. She opened her eyes and saw Tom looking at her. She shook her head, no, and he didn't. Not a word.

"Kite's ready," Tom invited. But she waved him away.

"Go. You've got the good of the wind now."

"Let me get the truck, let me—"

It wasn't a cold wind, but she was ruffled by it, and hunched against it. She shook his concern off. "I wait here. I watch."

Tom started directly down the rocks as Faye had done. Just before he jumped to the beach, Tom's mother called out in English, "I was not born old woman."

Tom looked back and waved. Faye came up to him and he handed the kite to her. When Tom jumped down, his shoes sank in the sand past their tops, past his ankles. He wavered a moment, then pitched forward, had to scramble up, dust off. He and Faye were both laughing. The wind blew their words away. On that same gust, Señora Rios cried out, "Was girl once, me, with ribbons!"

She opened her handbag and began searching. She pulled out her crushed pack of cigarettes and lit one. Took out her book and found her place and began reading as she always read, with a hope for poetry, an eye for human folly and error. This was a history, so she had plenty of the latter and none of the former. Her mind steadied itself, and her mood lightened. Her eyes dried. From time to time she looked up from her page and stared out across the water, or up and down the beach. Then she read some more.

Now and then the kite's shadow passed across her hands and page, but she didn't notice. Engrossed, she had forgotten where she was, forgotten all about Tom and Faye. She didn't check on them. When she remembered, she picked them out far down the beach. The kite was down. Faye was carrying it in her arms, like a broken bird, and Tom was winding the string. They stopped once, heads together, figuring out a knot, then they came on toward her. For a moment Señora Rios experienced a twinge of dread. She shivered. The day had turned the corner toward evening, and the tide had come way on in. She buttoned her sweater and watched Tom lead Faye to the narrowing strip of dry, loose sand above tideline. There was no real danger at all.

Faye had made such progress. Dr. Grayson had told them they could ask her—and they would, today—if she would like to go home with them and live at Tom's. Soon. As soon as she wished. To stay. Señora Rios made a small prayer of intention and thanksgiving and crossed herself.

Faye looked so fresh, so happy. Her hair had grown a bit longer and the wind wouldn't leave it alone. Her skirt blew hard against her legs and looked like slacks, and the great pink ruffle around her peasant blouse's neckline fluttered. Faye did not like dressy clothes, and chose things too young for her. Señora Rios added that to her mental list to correct. Vic had a taste for tailoring and detail; if a garment was casual, it had to be somehow outrageous or unique. Faye dressed like a commune hippie who hadn't gotten the word that the war—and the Age of Aquarius—had ended. At the tidewall, Tom climbed up first, then turned to help Faye. He lifted her by the wrists to stand beside him, then caught her around the waist and set her over the sharp edge of the rocks onto the grass. They were laughing so hard Faye had hiccups. Every time she hiccuped, it set them off laughing again. Everything seemed silly and funny. Señora Rios wished she had brought her camera. She wished Vic could see Faye now.

The idea of leaving Greenhill startled Faye only a little; she had been thinking of what the next step would be. The therapists had already begun offering her some ideas. And yet, at this moment the idea made her stomach lurch and her heart race. They were in Dr. Grayson's office; there would be paperwork, but they had to make sure Faye was sure.

"Where would I go?"

"You could come with me," Señora Rios said. She took Faye by the wrist, less a tender gesture than a power move. As though she were the one to say. Faye considered. She pulled her hand away and stood alone to consider. Dr. Grayson was nodding at her, with raised brows. "Yes?"

They both seemed so pleased. Why wasn't Faye pleased? She looked around. "Tom?"

Tom had gone out on the front bench, to smoke. But he heard Faye the second time she called his name. He had hoped not to be in there, had hoped not to influence Faye, had wished with all his heart that he could believe in his mother's intentions, whatever they were, and had been trying not to care so much what Faye's answer was.

Which was yes, emphatically, only not immediately, because she wanted to hear from Tom. She was young enough in her experience to think that he would say something she really wanted to hear. And naive enough not to factor in Vic or that wedding band with VXR into her own expectations. VXR was long gone; how could his shadow keep eclipsing her joy?

"What should I do?" Faye thought that if you wanted something and someone else wanted the same thing, and your motives were clean, then theirs were also. Tom scowled. He looked at the doctor, and at his mother, and at Faye. He shrugged.

Faye said, "Okay with you?"

The doctor got up from his chair and went out. He touched Faye on the arm, reassuring, as he left.

"Is—it your idea?" Faye still hoped Tom would tell her something wonderful.

Tom glanced toward his mother.

Señora Rios went to Tom's side, gathered up his shirtcloth over his ribs and twisted it, hard. "You make her!" She whispered, but Faye could hear it.

"Why don't you want?" Faye began to think of all the things she got wrong every day, all the lessons she still had ahead. But she was learning all the time! "What—"

"Goddammit," Tom said. "My reasons are no better than hers."

Señora Rios drew her breath in a hiss.

"She's not thinking of you," Tom warned. "Nobody is."

This had been interesting to Faye; now it was scary. Tom was sitting. He wouldn't look at her. "I thought you were my friend," she said. "Friends."

"Other places you could go," Tom said.

Señora Rios stood up.

"Those others," Faye said, "aren't so good." She was afraid she would cry. She wasn't going to cry. That was baby stuff. She remembered to count her breaths, count four on the out and four on the in. She remembered to think of the lovely blue pool, its stamplike clarity, her perfect poise above it. She regained calm. Ready to dive.

"Is it what I do? What I did? I'm—I could pay a little. I have some. I am going to get a job, too, it won't be long."

"Tell her," Tom said. Señora Rios looked at Tom. Faye noticed that look, that anger. "Tell her what you want."

Señora Rios came over to Faye and knelt, put her hands on Faye's, her thumbs nailing Faye to the chair arms. "For family." She raised her hands to her lips, made them into the composure of prayer and petition, over her lips, then spread her arms wide, outreaching, gathering, generous, grand. "Family," she whispered. Her eyes shining with tears. It looked like love. It looked like truth. It was a brilliant performance.

Tom got up and went out.

The slamming of the door broke the tension between Faye and his mother. Faye accepted Señora Rios's embrace, and when they had hugged, the woman told her, "Go tell Tom." She stood and brushed her knees.

Faye caught up with Tom halfway down the hall. He didn't stop though she called his name.

"I won't bother anything," she told him. "I won't get in the way. I will learn."

"You'll learn," he agreed. He had scrubbed his face raw with his callused hands, trying to rub the trouble away, trying to get back to the morning's mood. He had made up his mind he would stay clear of her, that's all. Out of sight, out of mind.

"You have always been welcome," he said.

"Her," she said, desperate, desolate, the way she said it when she meant the Faye she used to be, the one she could never live up to or live down.

"You," Tom said.

So he finally said it, but it wasn't nice, the way she had hoped it would be. He didn't make her feel the way she had on the beach when she picked up the shell and put it to her ear and he said don't but she did anyway and the hermit crab inside the shell had come out and touched her face and she had screamed and almost fallen and had thrown the shell back into the water and dipped her hands and washed her face and he had used his handkerchief to get the salt off her cheek.

She wanted to feel cherished; welcome was one thing, but cherished was the best. The way it felt when he had brought his mother to see her and she had been in the hobby room, and was trying to clip off a broken fingernail with the florist's wire cutters and he had taken out the little clippers he carried on his key chain and fixed it, without asking, without thinking. All the time talking about something else. What? Lilies. She had been making arrangements of flowers for the chapel, and there was pollen on her shirt, on her arm. Pollen like iodine, and he had teased her that it would not wash off, and she had flicked some on him also. And they were laughing. She liked laughing. She liked the way, when she had let the kite spin around and dive into the surf and a bird had flown up, squawking, Tom had said, "*¡Lástima!*" about the papalote, the kite, but had laughed about the bird, and had not really minded so much about the kite. She was supposed to have done something very simple to the kite so it wouldn't crash but she had not known what, he had not told her. The kite had been broken but could be repaired. "We'll fix," Tom had said. "Next time maybe it'll fall on a chicken and we can have a cookout."

And that was what Faye wanted, a next time.

The life at Greenhill was not complete; it was orderly and disciplined, and yet it was not all there was to life. It was halfway. That was its name: Greenhill Halfway Home. And now Faye wanted the next step. All the way home. Wasn't she ready? "Tonight," Faye decided. Señora Rios joined her; they packed. Tom went to get the truck.

"People do things like this," Faye said.

"All the times," Señora Rios agreed.

Because Faye was going to leave Greenhill, she did not stay for dinner. They were loading the last of her things on Tom's truck when the first bell for mealtime rang. They had to walk down the same hall as the residents who were on their way to the dining room. "I'm going home," Faye said. She had many friends. She shook hands that shook; she spoke to everyone. She did not cry. She introduced Tom. She was proud to introduce him. She had practiced introductions in class. She got it right every time. Tom was not having as much fun as Faye was. He slipped away when she knelt by the little woman who asked, "When am I going?" and gave her a kiss. When she looked for Tom, he was talking to someone across the hall. A man in a hat, in a wheelchair.

Faye knew the man. It was Mr. Montevidez. His son—Faye turned to explain it to Señora Rios; she whispered, "His son was driving the car in my wreck."

"No, no," Señora Rios said, to hush her, not to deny.

"Yes," Faye said, forgetting to whisper. "I read it in the paper clippings."

Señora Rios waved one hand and with the other gripped Faye's elbow, turning her aside. "Not for now," she said urgently. When she had guided Faye around the corner and into another corridor she added, "Boy of theirs, you no love heem?" As though *no love* were a verb.

Faye peeked back around the corner. "You mean *hate*?" She searched everywhere, but found no clue in her mind. "Do you?" she asked, instead of answering.

Señora Rios didn't answer either. She shook her head and let Faye's arm go. She stalked outside. The way she shoved the door open, the way she hit the bar to make it open . . . Faye ran after her.

"You mad?"

"Smoking," Señora Rios said. She pronounced it *ess-smoking*.

Faye thought she meant she was *very* angry. She said, "If I don't hate him, why should you? Anyway, he's dead . . . He died." Faye broke off. "You know that?"

For some reason Faye could not fathom, Señora Rios laughed, darkly and briefly. And waved her away. Walked on off down the lot toward Tom's truck.

When Faye went back inside, Tom was still talking to Mr. Montevidez and his wife. Faye did not think of them by first names. She walked over to them. They were laughing at Tom's story, which had involved a bird, Faye thought, and a fish. She had heard the word *fish* several times, and had seen Tom's hands flying as he talked. He was talking too fast for Faye to understand much. When Faye walked up, she was smiling too, because they were. Their laughter stopped, and the bright look on Cassia's face flickered and dimmed. She pulled her husband's wheelchair back a little, to make room, but Tom rebuffed Faye, didn't turn to include her, and said nothing, just gave her the hand-sign for "five minutes" in a way that made her feel absolutely extra. Tears stung her eyes, and her face got warm. Sometimes Tom is cold, Faye thought. Sometimes he is hard. She saw how Mrs. Montevidez looked at her, stared at her, pitying: as though she were someone who couldn't keep up? who couldn't be included? who had to be told what to do, where to wait? who was a pest? Faye's chin came up. She put out her hand to shake with Mr. Montevidez. "Goodbye," she said in Spanish. "I'm going home."

When she said "home," he looked up at her, peered into her face from beneath his cap brim. His eyes were very clear and piercing and as she looked, they filled with tears. "Oh!" Faye said, addressing his sadness. She had never spoken directly to him before. She had been wanting to say this. Now in her simple Spanish she said, "I'm sorry about your boy."

He was an outpatient, but took meals—as part of therapy—in the main hall. His table had every item labeled. Patients were to try to say the words, not just point. Faye had not sat at that kind of table in months and months; she had been able to speak and feed herself when she came here. Sometimes Agapito and his wife were the only ones at that table because it was labeled in Spanish. Sometimes Faye sat at that table, but she thought they liked to be by themselves. She thought they were sad. She had never seen them laugh till Tom got them started today. Faye thought, sometimes Tom can be kind.

Tom said, "Go pack, Faye."

"I'm packed," she said.

She offered her hand to Cassia, thinking the woman spoke only Spanish too, since Tom had been firing it off so fast. She said, *"Me llamo Faye,"* as Cassia touched her hand briefly and let it go. *"Lástima,"* she told Cristo's mother. *Pity.*

"Lástima," Cassia said.

Faye was glad there was time to run back down the hall and say goodbye to Mr. Firthwood. He took his meals in his room. He was not on the rehab hall; he was in the unit the staff thought of as "will to live." He was not going to get much better. He was very old.

She had met him when she was delivering beadcraft valentines to the "shut-ins" as part of social and small-motion therapy. They had gotten along from the start. The door to his room and all his walls were decorated with baseball items. One poster announced "Bad Henry", and showed a player swinging hard. It was framed and signed, "Your friend, Henry Aaron." It hung on the wall facing Mr. Firthwood's bed, and it was the first thing he saw when he opened his eyes.

Faye often stopped by. One day she had asked him about the Cubs. This was shortly after her mother's funeral, after Faye's trip to the bank vault to open the lockbox. She still had those clippings very much on her mind. Mr. Firthwood wasn't a Cubs fan, but he said, "Everybody knows about Cristo."

"Do they know about me?"

He said, "I don't." He studied her, adjusting his bed upright. He pointed to the chair at the foot. She sat. "So tell me," he said, "what have I missed?"

She excused herself and went to her room and returned with the clippings. Every now and then, as he read, he'd look up at her, consider, and then go on reading. "You're *this* Faye?" he said.

"I'm just Faye," she said.

After he read them, he gave them back with only one comment. "You're lucky."

Faye considered. Sifted. She didn't know if he meant lucky to have known Cristo or lucky to be alive. When she asked him which, he said, "That's one to ask the Umpire."

He was an expert on baseball. He was a Braves fan—"From way back," he said. He remembered when the Braves were in Boston. "Beaneaters," he called them. He had scrapbooks labeled "The Boston Years," and "The Milwaukee Years," and was keeping one on "The Atlanta Years." Faye helped him cut and paste things from the newspapers and magazines. "This is history in the making," he told her. "This is the year. Our year."

He taught Faye as much as she could learn about the game.

Greenhill had cable TV, and Faye and Mr. Firthwood had watched all the games of spring training. Faye hated to have to tell him she was going to miss the season-opener game with him because she was going home with Tom and Señora Rios, but he was happy for her.

"Traded to a new team," he said. He was all right about it. He shook her hand. "You like your manager?"

Faye thought about it. "Yes." She had to go.

"Swing for the fences," he told her. "Watch for the curves."

"Rally," she told him.

She had stayed a long time, talking. She was afraid Tom might be waiting for her, or getting mad. Señora Rios was in the truck already, but Tom wasn't mad. He was still visiting with Agapito and Cassia. When Faye came up to them, they quit talking again. Faye said, "Hello."

They were done talking. Tom said, *"Hasta,"* and took Faye's arm and they left. Faye looked back once. "Do I know them? I mean really know them? I mean, did I?"

"Someday," Tom said, "you might ask them. They know you don't remember."

Faye slid across to the middle of the front seat. Señora Rios had the window down. She was smoking one of her strong cigarettes.

"Those two don't ever talk to me," Faye said. "Or anyone. I think they are very sad. Sometimes he cries. I think they need their friends to come visit more often. I think you should visit them again soon."

"¿Quién?" Señora Rios asked. She flicked her cigarette away half-smoked, and rolled up the window.

"Montevidez," Tom said. "Agapito, Cassia." He shrugged. His voice had a little edge, a warning. Faye looked at him, and then at Señora Rios, who started to speak, then sniffed.

"You already knew them," Faye said. "Did you notice how they seemed younger when you talked to them? Your visit did them good. I think you ought to go see them again soon." Faye turned to Señora Rios. "I think Tom told them a big joke."

They were heading south now. Tom shifted gears. Faye leaned toward Señora Rios, to keep out of his way. She was still a little miffed.

"I was telling them about Father Ockham's tri-parish egg hunt," Tom said.

"¿Pasó?" Señora Rios said.

Tom slowed, then rolled on through a caution gone to red. He checked the mirrors to see if he had gotten away with it. "Fiddler crabs," Tom said. "Someone put fiddler crabs in the prize eggs. He was carrying them in his pockets down to the field to hide them when they broke open."

"What are fiddler crabs?" Faye said, forgetting her vow to be "cool." "Are they real crabs?"

"Real," Tom said. "You know, the little ones. You've seen them. You used to—" He shook his head. He had been about to say, You used to have to sweep them off the steps every morning before you went outside, and if you left the door open while you were sweeping, they just came on in the house. Vic's house out on the marsh . . . "Used to see them every-where," Tom said. "I'll show you one sometime."

"I think you should visit that man again. Next week," Faye said. "And I can visit Mr. Firthwood."

"I'm fishing next Sunday," Tom said. "Season's short enough."

"Every Sunday? Every Saturday?"

"Every day for a while," Tom said.

"Don't worry," Señora Rios said. It sounded like "wary." "We will think of things to do. Be very busy. You like school?" She pronounced it *ess-cool*. Faye had to think what that was, but she would have given the same answer; she was not going to cause them any trouble.

"I like everything," Faye said. "Really."

Faye did not remember Tom's house in South End. She did not remember those steps from the walk to the porch where she fell for Vic the first time she ever saw him. If anyone had told her about it, she would have thought it silly, that anything like that could ever have happened to her. She didn't think it could. She knew accidents happened like that, but not fate. Not that she thought much about fate. The concept was like God, only God was bigger. So she thought about God when she thought about things like that. That's what she told Father Ockham. She always asked him, when he told her about the people in the Bible, "Is it true?" Faye sifted for facts. Facts were the fuel for the engine of the world, visible and invisible. Wasn't God truth?

Father Ockham's lessons took a lot out of both of them. One day he asked her in what percentage did God interfere with human affairs. She couldn't answer till he explained *percent*. She said, "We had fractions, but not decimals so far."

"Of one hundred pieces, how many pieces of the hundred?" Father Ockham prompted.

She stared. "Pieces of what?"

"Pieces of anything. Of everything."

Faye didn't get it. She didn't see how it could be a matter—with God—of voting. She was afraid to get it wrong. She wouldn't say. Father Ockham blessed her, and told her to think about it, and said he would see her again soon. He was already out Tom's door, leaving, when she ran after him.

"One hundred!" she called.

Startled, brittle, he barked, "What? What is it?"

"One hundred pieces, if that is all the pieces. If that is not all the pieces, then all the pieces there is . . . I mean *are*. Or he's not God."

Father Ockham suspected she'd had help with that answer. He glanced toward the house, but he couldn't see anyone to blame for prompting her. He asked, "How do you know?"

Faye darted her hand out and touched him on the arm, a quick little touch. "I'm one of the pieces," she said.

Father Ockham found their conversations interesting. Early on he saw that the catechistic approach was best for Faye, question and answer, and brick by brick she could rebuild course on course. Rebuild. The bricks were old. Some were mossy, crumbling. He passed those with care, and she accepted them with a caution that he took as reverence. She excelled in saints; she learned them day on day, each on his or her own day, as the year went round. Sometimes the facts were startling, but they were facts, and Faye loved facts.

It bothered Father Ockham that she made no distinction between the facts of the lives of the saints and the lives of the stars. Or of the birds. Or beetles. But in any case, Faye did not take the things she learned personally. That was why facts were so soothing. They filled in and defended against feeling, against the unknown. Chipping away at the dark, one spark at a time. The one place she never dug or chipped or sought was in her own past. She had a horror of the personal. In fact, she often failed to question the people around her, or their pasts. She took for granted.

She liked the library. She and Señora Rios would go there, each with a notepad and pen and their card. When Faye discovered that she already had a card, and they were going to reissue it to her, same name, same number, she insisted they change the number. She wanted the books she read now to mount up against her new ignorance in some clear way. She knew the old number. They had shown it to her. Now she'd look at the book's circulation record to see if she had read it before. If she saw that old number, she'd put the book back. Even if it looked interesting.

Book by book, she mined out notebooks of facts, and carried them home. In time, she was sure, she would have the whole world. The scattered approach, and then at times the extreme focus on a particularly interesting subject, made her absentminded. Yet she was giving the world her fiercest attention. She did not try to interpret. She catalogued in her undermind. She took in and took in and took in. She drew no conclusions. She had not begun that, yet. She was still gathering evidence.

There were times, though, when her past intruded. Generally it intruded on her senses. That part of her brain had not been completely cut off from access; in general it would be a texture or a scent or a sound that left her puzzled, frowning, or rapt. She could not recall what it might be that the senses were reminding her of; she did not even know it was a memory. To her, the reverie was another experience of learning, or of not-knowing. The first time Señora Rios saw this happen, Faye had found the birdcage that Tom's wife used to keep in the hall. Señora Rios and Faye were in the upstairs room that served as an attic; Señora Rios was looking for bookends.

And when she had turned to show them to Faye, triumphant, her daughter-in-law was standing by the cage, which still swung on its hook from the floor stand, and her eyes were shut, her forehead touching the bars, her right hand on the latch, one finger and her thumb holding the little knurled brass knob. Señora Rios was alarmed.

She forgot to speak English. She gave Faye a little cuff to the arm, to rouse her, and caught her into her tough hands and set her down on a dusty trunk. Faye, startled, cried, "What is it?"

Señora Rios saw she was perfectly fine, not fainting. She resented it somehow. "What is it?" she agreed.

Faye said, "This is a birdcage?"

"No birds," Señora Rios said. Slamming that door before it could open.

Faye looked up at her. "Whose?"

"Tom's wife had a bird," she explained.

"Tom's *wife*?"

"Ah," Señora Rios said, seeing that it was news, irritated that Faye never suspected anything she didn't know. She reminded herself to check that child development book on mental stages to see at what mental age conclusion-drawing begins. "Tom's wife, Nola. She died already the long time. Her little parrot."

"A parrot?" Faye wondered. Parrots live for decades. Like humans. A parrot would still be alive. She told her that.

"*Papagayo*, no," Señora Rios said. "Not parrot is dead. Is Nola." Not clarifying things much. "Leetle bird, Tom let him go . . . Made me cough."

"Maybe Tom will get another—"

"No more birds!" Señora Rios said.

"Wife," Faye said.

"*Quién puede decir*," Senora Rios laughed, "on which tree that bird will land."

Later, downstairs, it was Faye who brought up the subject of marriage again. Yes, Señora Rios thought, this will be easy, and was glad to God. She and Faye had the house to themselves. Tom was away, fishing. He didn't stay away just on account of Faye—though he thought that was a good idea—but ever since Nola's death he had found reasons not to sleep there. More nights away than home, sleeping on the boat rather than push himself through the empty rooms. He had not made any changes since the funeral. A cleaning woman came in once a week, and a neighbor's child stopped by in the afternoons to feed the bird. It was Señora Rios who got things moving again—ceiling fans, furniture from room to room, drapes pulled down and cleaned, shades opened, windows polished, the lawn mowed. It was Señora Rios who opened the cage doors and let the bird fly. It *could* fly; it did. It still knew how. She knew it would. She told Tom it escaped. Didn't it? "Instinct," she told Tom. She believed instinct, like Father Ockham's sacraments, endured. "The important things are built in by God; we do not forget!"

Tom left the bird's food on the patio table, hoping. But every night his mother reported, "No, nothing." Yet during the days she had to keep the windows shut, and the doors too, for over a week, as the little bird kept flying back into the house, or trying to. It had always gone to roost in the trees by the time Tom got home at night. After a week he quit grieving for it, and after a few more days Señora Rios could leave the windows open again.

It was not a bad little bird, but she dreaded things like that in the house with her. Her grandmother's house had had bats. The women in her family had never been rational about certain things—pet cats, snakes of any sort, bulls, and bats—all unpredictable and a nuisance to the nerves. Who knew what they resented? Or when they would repay?

Señora Rios was glad the little bird was gone. She washed the cage herself, and set it in the sun to dry. She planned to use it for an ornament, place a container with a vine in it, one with bright blooms.

But the bird found it first. Actually flew back inside the cage! It was then Señora Rios had her idea. She phoned the pet shop. They agreed with her that a little bird that smart was worth something. But when Señora Rios went softly out and tried to shut the door to the cage, to capture the bird to sell, it had flown again. She watched for hours, and the next day too, but did not see it again. She looked around for feathers, but she saw no evidence of a cat having gotten it. She left the little bowl of seed on the cage floor for another day or two, and after that, when the bird never returned, she flung the seeds onto the lawn and hauled the cage upstairs to Tom's lumber room.

Faye and Señora Rios were just sitting down to lunch on the patio when Faye mentioned marriage again. Not directly—which would have been too good a luck, Señora Rios thought—but wondering about Tom's wife. "Were these hers, or yours?" Referring to the dishes they ate on, the linens, the basket with melons and grapes, the frosty glasses. Señora Rios was about to answer when the little bird came back. Flew around, then settled on the table itself, marching with its crooked little feet. It walked right up Faye's sleeve and sat on her shoulder. Faye began feeding it bits of cut-up grape and crusts of her sandwich. Quite naturally, as though accustomed.

"*Que nunca,*" Señora Rios objected, as though it wouldn't be possible, not that it wasn't allowed.

"At Greenhill we could have pets," Faye said. "If we wanted." The little bird looked well. "I love animals," Faye said. She touched the bird's pink cheek feathers. Its eye blinked bright. It ignored Señora Rios completely.

"Some people call these lovebirds," Faye said. She looked around for its mate. She used the same hand with which she had fed the bird to raise bread to her own mouth. Señora Rios handed Faye a napkin, managing as she reached across to give the bird a little brush-off.

"*¡Za! ¡Zape!*" she hissed, and it flapped up into the tree, sidling back and forth, watching down at them, first with left eye, then right.

Faye protested, "Oh!" and tried to lure the little fellow back down to her. "If we hold very still," she suggested gently.

"*El pan comido y la compañía desecha,*" Senora Rios said. "Faithless brute." She accused the bird of "cupboard love" and made a fly-away gesture with her hands. She decided to stack the dishes. She did everything except what Faye hoped—which was to sit quietly and reassure him back into their hands. No. Señora Rios wanted a cigarette. Would have one. She needed matches. Had none. She had to go into the house. When she came back, she had something else in her hands to keep them moving briskly—a manicure kit and bottle of nail enamel. "They dry in no time, this breeze," she told Faye. She handed the things to her.

It worked. Faye was distracted from the bird. She knew how to shape her nails, but she had no luck with the painting. Señora Rios helped her with the left nails first. The hypnotic little dabs of the brush, the light taps, the scent of the polish made Faye drowsy. She touched Señora Rios's rings with her right fingers and said, "I was married."

"Careful!" Señora Rios might have meant anything. Faye took it as some kind of warning for tact and prudence. Faye said, "It's okay. I don't remember."

"Will all come back," Señora Rios said, raising both her own rope-veined hands and gripping Faye's face between them, as though making memory was like making diamond, with heat and high pressure. Gripping so hard that tears came to Faye's eyes. The sight of that salt water looked to Señora Rios like tenderness, like progress. "You want to remember," she said, "you *will*."

"Of course not," Faye said. Utterly simple, utterly free. Utterly sure. The doctors had showed her the chart, had showed her the CT scans, had explained how her brain had been ravaged, cut, tidied, and sewed and plated back, and the skin of her skull knit back over it. She guided Señora Rios's hand to feel the seams, the little holes where the drill had bored. When she noticed the look on Señora Rios's face, she said, kindly, "It's all right."

"You are too thin," Señora Rios told her. "You need to eat, eat, eat."

"I ate," Faye said. The empty plates were still in plain view on the table. There was not enough left to feed a bird.

"A woman needs little fat, just a little," Señora Rios was saying. She had read it in the newspaper. Dear Abby? A magazine. The waiting room's *Buen Hogar*? Somewhere. "Listen," she told Faye, gripping her hand, applying a second coat to the nails. "A little fat for hormones. Not so much. Just little bit. Maybe ten pounds."

She took the other hand and painted it, nail by nail. Faye could tell that she would not be able to pull her hand away even if she struggled. She could feel Señora Rios's pulse beneath her own. She held very still. Señora Rios finished painting. The color was a deep, warm pink. She gave Faye her hand back.

"*Sandía*," she said. "Melon. Very ripe, very *deliciosa*. Little little bit wicked-sweet. Some men like it like crazy. What you think?"

Faye didn't know. "What men?"

"I'm telling you," Señora Rios said. "Like crazy."

The next morning Faye was up early, before breakfast was begun. She helped set the table, and was pretending to look for the salt and pepper in the cabinet. "What are you doing?" Señora Rios wondered. "Cold cereal. No salt. No pepper." Faye was trying to find the food coloring; she knew about it from Easter. She had helped make Easter eggs at Greenhill, and she thought every kitchen had the little colors. She needed blue. She could not think of anywhere else to get blue. She had to have it. She was terrified when Señora Rios noticed that Faye had ruined her manicure—paint chipped off, several nails broken, and one torn into the quick. "What have you done?" Señora Rios asked, amazed.

Faye amazed her further by bursting into tears and running from the kitchen up to her room. She locked the door. Señora Rios heard it, before she was halfway up the same stairs, but it didn't matter, because Señora Rios had Tom's keys. It took her only a moment to sort the right one from the ring in her pocket. All the time she was calling through the door, not angrily, but with dread, "What is? What have you done?"

"Go away," Faye said. "Please."

Señora Rios could smell chemicals. Bleach and God knew what all else. It smelled like a lab. When Señora Rios got the door open, a great roil of humid air came out around her. Señora Rios gasped.

Faye's bed was stripped. In the center of the beautiful new mattress— bought just for Faye, the first payment on the revolving charge not yet due—was a bleached-out area the size of a dinner plate. Faye had the food color mixed in her sink glass and was about to try to daub it onto the ruined area. Señora Rios did not need any explanations. Señora Rios didn't want any apologies. Señora Rios did not tell Faye, "You have to go back to Greenhill." Señora Rios laughed.

She was shaking her head, but she laughed.

"Peroxide," she said. "Cold water," she said. "Salt," she said. *"No bleach."*

Faye set the glass full of blue water on the night table.

"Where are sheets?" Señora Rios asked.

Faye had balled them up and kicked them under the bed when she heard Señora Rios coming. She knelt and pulled them out.

"Give," Señora Rios said.

Faye put them in her arms.

They walked down the hall to the laundry. "We are all witches," Señora Rios told her, "about stains." She sent Faye to the kitchen for the box of salt. "Every woman has her own recipe. Mine is so good I could murder and never leave clue."

Faye watched the ancient formula work its magic. Sun drying did the rest. By afternoon the mattress was dry enough to turn, and they remade the bed together. Señora Rios brought Faye a calendar and told her to keep up with things. She told her to plan ahead. She told her it was up to her. But all the time she was telling Faye these things, she was looking ahead two weeks, to the heart of the next month, when Faye would ovulate. She was already planning how to get Vic home, and what Faye would wear for the dinner, and how Tom would have to be away that night, and Señora Rios herself as well be out of the picture. She did not need to inform Vic of her plans, or Faye either. Nature, Vic's and Mother Nature too—would do it all. Faye would look her best. Not like this, miserable with cramps, lank-haired, circle-eyed, and a bit clammy.

Faye was slump-shouldered, curving, curling forward around her discomfort. "A cure for that," she told Faye, handing her the tumbler with brandy in it. But what Señora Rios was thinking was, *A child*.

A week later Faye was down at the seawall at the city docks with her field guide and a hand lens. She concentrated on keeping her footing on the breakwater's jumble of broken pavements and old ballast. She was waiting on Tom. She had spent the afternoon at the main library, and he was going to drive her home. The *Legal Hours* was in for repairs, and Faye was enjoying his being home. Tom was delayed, talking to some man. She could see them, at the other end of the docks, and Tom had his arms crossed over his chest. The other man was standing with one foot on a crab crate, gesturing easily. From time to time the gold braid on his hat glistened. Faye thought he was trying to sell Tom something and Tom wasn't going to buy. Once they both looked her way, and she decided to turn back, then, make her way back down to the water's edge, with the turnstones and the peeps. She knew who they were. She had her book. There was a heron standing on the very last heaped rubble, as silent as a stump, staring out toward the channel. She knew he saw her. He let her get quite close. She sat where he sat and watched where he watched. She could almost have reached out her hand and touched his head.

She read her book, and the bird fished. They passed several minutes so, and then suddenly the bird opened his wings, stepped forward into the air, and flapped away. She could hear the feathers pushing through the air. The bird landed thirty yards away, on the beach sand, and turned its head to look at her. Past her. She turned too, and saw Tom and the man walking toward her. Then she saw who the other man was—Tom's brother.

"Faye," Tom said. That was all, just "Faye," so she stayed, she didn't run away. Tom looked tired.

Faye offered her hand. Vic took it and shook it quickly and let it go. "Hello, Mr. Rios," she said, awkward but not embarrassed. She was squinting into the sun. She put her hand up to shade her eyes.

"Is your ship here?"

"Boat," Vic said. "No."

Vic reached out and gave Faye's book a tap. "Whattya know?" She didn't know if she was supposed to say, or not. She had been learning so many interesting things. "A heron's temperature is one hundred five point eight degrees," Faye said. "A hummingbird's brain is proportionately the largest in the animal kingdom—four point two percent of its body weight." She paused. "Percent—that's how many in a hundred. That's divide the top by the bottom, that's how to get it." When no one said anything, she added, "It's an average. Every hummingbird is different."

"Hell you say," Vic said. He started to laugh.

Tom gave him a look. "Tell him about the robins."

"Robins?" Vic said. He glanced at his watch. When Faye saw it flash at his wrist, she lost her concentration, as though she were about to think of something else.

"On their last day in the nest," Tom said.

Faye looked at him. Tom was making funny gestures, pulling his hands far apart, as though measuring something long. "Help me here," he said.

"Oh! On their last day in the nest," Faye said. "That?"

"Yeah."

Vic looked bored. Vic looked around. He had his car keys. He lit a little cigar. Faye put her hand on his arm and said, as though presenting him with something wonderful, "On their last day in the nest, a young robin can eat fourteen feet of earthworms."

"Come to supper with us, *hombre*," Tom said. He was smiling.

Vic said, "I have plans. I always have plans." He shook his keys.

Tom said, "I'll think about it, you think about it too," and Vic said, "I already have," and walked away. He went across the public lot to his car, and backed it out and drove in a tight circle so he wouldn't have to come back along the lane where they were standing, but they could see, they saw even from that far, that he was not alone. There was a woman in the front seat with him, with a scarf tied around her hair and big dark glasses, like a movie actress.

Faye started to wave. Tom caught her arm and turned her toward the water, said, "Look," and she looked, thinking pelicans maybe, or a skimmer, or even the little whisk and scuttle of ghost crabs digging out after the tide, but she didn't see anything. "What did I miss?"

"Nothing," Tom said.

"Pining away," was what Tom had said, explaining Señora Rios's need to see Vic. But Vic was in town for business, not family. It was purest accident that Tom had not been out fishing. Vic had assumed he would be. It was accident they had met at all. But Tom tried, for his mother's sake.

"Pining?" Vic said. That's when he put his foot up on the rail. "She has company," he added. "And so do I."

That was when Vic crossed his arms.

"Listen," Tom began.

"Look," Vic said. And they both turned and looked. When Faye saw them looking, something in their attention, some seriousness, sent her back down the beach to the heron. That wasn't shyness, she didn't feel it was herself they were discussing. She was afraid that if she came closer to them, they'd stop talking, that her presence would change the subject. She wasn't self-conscious then. She didn't know it was Vic. And she didn't know Vic. But when she found out, she was glad he didn't come to supper. She was glad it would just be Señora Rios and her and Tom.

Señora Rios would have liked to see both her sons at table that night, but she did not consider the evening a failure. Vic was buzzing around town; Vic was happening to run into Faye? Vic was— "He'll be back," Señora Rios said to the two people in the world who did not hear that as consolation. Faye, in fact, hardly noticed. She was trying to finish her meal and be excused. Tom had promised to work on the bicycle she had found in the shed in back. They had stopped on the way home and bought a new wheel and two new tires.

Faye had scrubbed the rusty basket with steel wool and was spraying it with flat black while Tom worked on the chain. In the house they heard the phone ring and Señora Rios answering it. She came to the door and said, "Tom," and she said it in a new way. He got up and went to her. They talked through the screen, low. Faye wasn't trying to hear them or not. The spray paint made her sneeze.

Tom came back.

"Faye," he said. He always said that when he needed her to brace something or hold something or hand him something. She hopped up, put the spray can down, and was ready. "What?"

"It's about your friend at Greenhill."

Tom wasn't sure they should tell her; Tom wasn't sure he ought to say a thing.

"He wants to talk to me?"

Faye started for the phone.

Tom was still standing on the step. "He's very sick. He wants to talk to you. To see you."

"All right," she said. "Are we going now?"

But Tom didn't move. "He's out of his head," Tom said. "Maybe he won't remember it when you get there. Maybe—"

"He's *dying*?" She thought she knew what that meant. She knew enough of what that meant to deny it. "He's old. He's just old."

Señora Rios said, "I don't know why he want to see you, old man don't need secret, need to be telling to priest." Señora Rios wouldn't go with them. She did not like Greenhill. It was bad enough when Faye was there; then a visit made sense, but for a dying stranger, no. Señora Rios did not entertain such thoughts.

And yet. And yet. She wasted nothing. Like a bird that can't find a snakeskin to weave into the nest, she'd use a strip of cellophane. Whatever she had, whatever it took. She had what it took. She saw an example here; she could use it. As it turned out, Mr. Firthwood, Faye's baseball friend, did not die. Faye sat with him for several hours, and when he was better, she left. Tom and she got back about midnight. Señora Rios was still up; they saw the red tip of her lit cigarette glowing on the porch as she inhaled.

"He's going to live," Faye said, explaining the good news and their evening.

"Not forever," Señora Rios said. Following Tom into the house, she made him promise: "You tell your brother," she said, "tell him, Wednesday night, dinner." She turned aside to cough. When she spoke again, there were tears in her eyes. "Tell him I don't command, I beg." That's what she had learned from Mr. Firthwood. Tom peered at her in astonishment. "That oughta do it," he agreed.

"Tell him I have been to the doctor and I have a heart," she said.

"Do you?"

She came back down the steps to stand eye-level with him. He saw the flash of her smile, so like Vic's. Before she could answer, Faye was out of the shower, and crossing the landing above them. "Good night," she called down, waving. Her white robe and the towel on her hair gave her a ghostlike aura.

"Dry your hair!" Señora Rios called up. "Completely."

Tom turned and started back down the stairs.

"Where are you going?"

"To finish the bicycle," Tom said. "It's supposed to rain."

"It's your deal," she said. "But if it rains, she won't be riding."

"I'm sleeping on the boat," he said.

"I don't get," she said. "Is connection?"

"I have work to do. This is the last chance here for a while."

"Why are you so—"

"I *have* to go."

But that wasn't good night. The cuckoo clock had just chimed one when Señora Rios came back downstairs an hour later, as Tom was finishing the bicycle, and putting the tools away in his truck. She had been watching from the living-room window. It had begun raining. When he noticed her there, Tom had thought, with a little lift, that it was Faye. But when she didn't come out, he knew it was not. It was the first time he thought it, thought the word *love*, connecting it to Faye. He thought, I love her for that, for being the sort of person who'd come out in the rain to me. But it wasn't Faye, it was Señora Rios, and she waited till Tom was ready to leave, and then she ran out onto the porch and called, in that dire whisper she had, "Don't forget to tell your brother." Tom was thinking about that, about how he was supposed to lure Vic back to Faye, and how his mother now has a heart, and why, above all, Tom felt he was running away. He wouldn't even see her take her first ride on the bike, unless the weather set in and stayed sour a few days. Riding along through it, Tom thought the rain looked pretty good.

Vic, like a miracle, showed up on Wednesday. Faye wore the dress Señora Rios had chosen, and Tom wore a heavy-weather scowl, something they were all getting used to. Señora Rios laughed enough for them all. She filled in the gaps. There were many gaps. It was her birthday, and neither Tom nor Vic had remembered. That gave Señora Rios the edge, morally. She used that edge subtly, tactfully, simply hoping that their guilt would make them—and it did—more pliable and agreeable with each other.

Señora Rios hoped her sons would do this again—put their feet under her table and break bread together. She said so. She forgot for the moment that it was actually Tom's table, but she never forgot for a moment, or let anyone else forget—especially Vic—that it was Faye who had baked the bread. "Real Cuban bread," she said. "Would you look?"

They used candles for their light, and little flames sparked in Vic and Tom's dark eyes. Señora Rios looked around at them, on her left hand, on her right, and wished, not for the first time, that Tom were more like Vic and Vic were more like Tom.

When Faye brought in the bakery cake, with candles lit, her face aglow, Señora Rios was watching Vic. Faye set the cake down in front of her mother-in-law, and as she leaned over, the little crucifix swung away from Faye's throat and passed through the flames of the candles, then swung back against her flesh, and it was Tom who noticed her flinch, and knew why. Vic was looking at his watch. Again.

Señora Rios closed her eyes and made her wish.

She was disappointed.

Tom couldn't stay after dinner, and Vic wouldn't.

"I have work," Tom said.

He helped clear the table. He and Faye. They waited in the kitchen so if Señora Rios were going to tell Vic about the doctor's report, she could do it now. When Vic had noticed the little bottle of white pills at his mother's place at dinner, he'd looked inside, and asked, "Saccharin? Since when do you count calories?"

But she hadn't explained; she hadn't said, "No, it isn't." She had simply taken it from him and said, "You don't need," making it into a conversation about him instead of her. Making a comparison, yet again, of Vic and Tom, and as usual, in Vic's favor. Vic was in fact leaner than ever, never gaunt, but angular. Hard and tanned. But with new dark circles under his eyes.

"You're not sleeping," she accused. "You ought go to bed sooner."

Vic pulled back from her hand as it reached to touch his face. He laughed. "I get to bed sooner," he said, "or later."

"Don't drive back down tonight," she offered. "Sleep here."

He took that as a joke. "Yeah, sure," he said.

After dinner, she tried to keep him longer. He wouldn't hear a word of it. He stepped out on the patio to smoke. As he lit his cigar, she joined him, but refused a light for her cigarette. She held it unlit. "I'm trying to cut down," she said. "Is a habit. I don't need."

"Maybe later," he said, and dropped his lighter into her hand. "Keep it," he said. "Happy birthday."

He embraced her lightly, turned, and started down the back gallery steps to his car. As he passed the kitchen, he rapped on the window and waved to Tom. Faye wasn't in there. She was in the dining room, gathering the last dishes onto a tray. She glanced up as Señora Rios came in, walked through the dining room into the parlor, and sat.

Faye watched her take out the little bottle and tap a pill onto her palm and put it in her mouth. She sat there a moment, then turned on the light. She seemed to be studying something gold. Faye didn't know it was the lighter Vic had presented. But she saw Señora Rios turn and turn it, stare at it closely, then suddenly throw it into the fireplace. Faye heard it land. She heard something smash.

It had broken one of the candle cups. Señora Rios had wanted a fire, but of course it was too warm, so they had lined the fireplace with votive candles, dozens of them, and they were only just now beginning to wink out.

The next day, as Faye was cleaning, she remembered the broken glass and knelt to pick it up. That was when she found the lighter. She wiped it on her shirt hem and polished it between her hands till she could read the inscription—EN UN DECIR AMÉN—and a phone number. On the other side it said, in English, *Satisfaction Guaranteed*. Faye thought it was gold; it seemed very nice. It worked. She polished it some more and laid it on the mantel. She swept up the broken glass. She was going to ask Señora Rios what *en un decir amén* meant, but she forgot. She thought of it later, when she was riding home with Tom from the *mercado*.

"*En un decir amén*," he said. "In a heartbeat."

"Oh," she said.

"Something quick-quick." He made a gesture with his hand like a finger-snap, twice.

He was in very good spirits. His boat's repairs were finished. He could fish anytime now. About time. He snapped his fingers again.

Faye tried that. She couldn't make them snap. Tom said, "Easy, look," and he took both his hands off the wheel and did both at once like castanets. They almost ran up on the curb. They swerved back. A horn blew. Their groceries spilled and rolled around in back. Grabbing the wheel, he blew the horn. They zigzagged home, laughing. A policeman stopped behind them in Tom's own driveway. He and Tom talked. Tom was not drunk. The policeman drove away.

Faye and Tom carried in the rumpled sacks of groceries; they were still laughing.

"What is?" Señora Rios came to see.

"Nothing, *madrecito*, just a little joke, a little Spanish lesson." Tom ducked back out the door to get the rest of the groceries. Some were for him, some for the boat. Faye started sorting the potatoes into two piles. When Tom came back he helped.

They had gotten everything on the list—which they forgot to take with them—except for scouring pads, shoelaces, and matches. "You won't need S.O.S.," she decided. She could not do a thing about the shoelaces—besides, he didn't need them with rubber boots—and for the matches suggested—an inspiration—the lighter Tom's mother had thrown away. She retrieved it from the mantel and handed it to Tom. "It works," she said. "Señora Rios thought it didn't, but it does."

"What?"

"She threw it away, but it works. All right now."

Tom didn't say anything. He just looked at it. Read both sides. *En un decir amén. Satisfaction Guaranteed.* And the phone number engraved below.

"So that's it," he said. "Jesus." Not *hay soos*, the way he usually said it, but the way men on TV in trouble said it. Anglos in trouble. Tom looked angry but he didn't say anything else.

"Is it yours?" Faye was trying to figure why he could be mad.

"No," Tom said. "Hell no!"

He read it again, and again. "So that's where you got that," he said.

"It's got Vic's number," Faye said.

"She sure as hell does," Tom said.

He looked the way he did sometimes when he was reading the newspaper.

Faye knew Vic's number. She had seen it often. It was posted by the phone, underneath 911, to notify in an emergency. The dialing order was 911, then Vic, then Tom. (Because Vic had farther to come.) It wasn't that number of Vic's on the lighter.

"An old number," Faye decided.

Tom made a noise.

"Is it the fishing that's in a heartbeat, or the satisfaction?" Faye wondered.

"Goddammit," Tom said. "It's not his number! Can't you figure anything?"

Tears stung Faye's eyes. She wouldn't cry or answer back. She was that much better. Her face got very warm.

Señora Rios was coming with a mesh beg for the onions and potatoes Tom would take with him on *Legal Hours.* Tom slipped the lighter into his pocket and said, quickly, "Hush now," and it wasn't an apology, it was a warning, including her in something and not including Señora Rios. She felt a strange thrill as she realized that, that there was now something between her and Tom that she and he could know alone. She felt okay again. She liked having a secret with Tom. She turned her back to them, pretended to get a glass of water. She had no thirst, but she filled it and sipped. As she turned off the tap, her hand was shaking.

She sipped again. Thinking, I do not know if I am glad it is against Señora Rios or not, this little secret, but I am glad it is with Tom. I won't ask any more questions. She felt the weight of the secret without understanding a thing about its need or cause. She hadn't a clue. But if Tom wanted it like that, then that was what she wanted. Faye's feelings were not complicated. Yet every moment for the rest of that evening she felt furtive, complicit.

Was this something she must confess? How could she explain it to a priest? "I was saving something that someone else had thrown away." Is that a sin? But her problem became altogether different that evening when she went to her window. She had heard something in the yard. Looking out, she saw Tom on the bottom step, smoking. She started to raise her window and speak, but she recognized Vic's gold lighter in Tom's hand just as Tom hefted it and threw it away, as hard as he could, overhand, toward the tangle of briars and vines along the back lot line.

Immediately she thought, He did that on my account. Against me. That was something she was not to have seen or known. That was the closing of something against her; she was not meant to be a part of it either. What did all of it mean? Señora Rios had thrown it, and now Tom. Now everybody had a secret. Why was there such a mystery? She knew that the lighter was gold; you don't throw away gold.

She let her curtain fall back and stepped away from the window. She remembered what she had decided in rehab, that heaven would be knowing everything. She had not believed Father Ockham when he told her, on hearing her idea of heaven, "My dear, *that* is *hell*."

"If truth sets us free, how can that be hell?" she had rejoined. She would never be that sure again. She didn't recall what the priest had answered. What would he say to all this? Of her standing at a curtain, spying. It made her feel horrible. She went back to bed, and in the morning, when she heard Tom up hours before daylight, getting some coffee and going to the truck to go out fishing for three days, maybe five, she didn't even get up and run down the stairs to see him off. She had never missed, but now she had to. She thought he would be able to see, somehow, into her soul and discover this division, this disloyalty, this . . . *what*? She didn't even have a word for it, didn't know what she felt except confused. And determined. She was going to find the lighter when daylight came, search in those brambles till she found it, and this time, when she did, she wasn't going to show it to anyone, she was going to keep it, and when she had thought what to say, she was going to dial that phone number, SAT-ISFACTION GUARANTEED, and see who answered.

PART III

PERSISTENCE

It was a very bad idea for Mrs. Fortner to go fishing with her husband. Now it wasn't so much a question of her having quarreled with Mr. Fortner, but of her having quarreled with Captain Rios. Whatever idea she had of reconciliation—with either of them—became less and less likely as they drove farther out in the Stream. Now that Mr. Fortner had retired, he had moved to the coast so he could fish every day he was able. No matter what had happened with his wife and the Captain, he still preferred Vic Rios and his boat for fishing. He had tried several others. He had tried most of the others. Mr. Fortner could reconcile himself to a bad marriage, but not to a bad captain. What neither of them needed was Marnie Fortner along for the trip. Marnie Fortner was the sort of woman who as a child had thrown rocks into the pond just to see the ripples. She wasn't about to stop now.

Mr. Fortner was after white marlin, but would be glad of a blue. The mate was busy sewing baits. Not mullet or mackerel but squid. Mr. Fortner had been reading about squid. The source for the article suggested squid, and on this trip, for the first time, Mr. Fortner had told the Captain and his mates what baits to use. Captain Rios didn't normally use squid. "Billfish aren't gourmets," he said.

"Your boat, my money," Mr. Fortner had replied.

"Your call," the Captain had said. But he was annoyed. At both of them, at Mr. Fortner for thinking squid would do what skill and patience had not—bring Mr. Fortner a world-record fish to the side of the *Blue Lady*. He was irritated with Mrs. Fortner for being there at all. For the whole mess between them, the three of them. Mr. Fortner didn't care? Mr. Fortner didn't care. Mrs. Fortner was too sure of herself, of the trouble she had caused and could still cause. What usually happened was what usually happened. The fun had gone out of it a bit, and now she wanted to needle Mr. Fortner, to distract him from his game, and force him to notice how her game was making a fool of them all.

It was late May. The weather was perfect. The fish were on the move north.

"Are you afraid?" Mrs. Fortner asked the Captain when he told her to stay home.

When she showed up at the docks, when she got out of the station wagon and started for the boat dressed for the charter, the Captain had said nothing. He tried ignoring her. Everybody knew about them. Had to. How big is the ocean? Word gets around. His mate and hand both grinned. Audible grins. It turned the Captain's head. He muttered and stepped back as Mr. and Mrs. Fortner came aboard together. They were even dressed in identical shirts and hats. If the Captain was surprised to see them back together, he didn't show it. Was he relieved to see them reconciled? He didn't show that, either. Mrs. Fortner couldn't tell if the Captain's irritation had a thing to do with her at all. She always had trouble reading him; that was part of the fun. He said something. Under his breath. In Spanish. She couldn't make it out, wouldn't even be able later to look it up in her Spanish-Inglés.

"Eat your heart out," she said as she brushed past him, her arm in Mr. Fortner's.

"Welcome," he said to both of them. "I can stand it if you can." That was all he said.

It had been rough for three days, but was good weather now. Still, it was rough enough to take the joy out. There might even be clouds later on, but they'd blow their tops and scatter. The morning would be fine. The sea had a slight chop and turbulence. When they hit the Stream, the Captain was already in the tower, and less than fifteen minutes later he spotted a fin. "Blue!"

Mr. Fortner was using fifty-pound-test line and expected a fight. If he hooked a blue of any good size, it would be hard fishing. If he hooked a small white it would be too easy, but a small white was no record, either, and he'd just tag and release. "Lord, I know how to do that," he grieved. Still, this might be a monster. He always trolled for a monster.

Then Mrs. Fortner came up and took the other chair. She chose thirty-pound test. Mr. Fortner laughed. "You a better man than I am?"

She just looked at him.

The Captain could tell that something had happened between them. Something had changed. Captain Rios didn't much care.

Mrs. Fortner glanced up to the tower where he stood. He was looking out at the seas that rocked them; his face was dark under the brim of his hat, and his eyes were hidden behind dark glasses.

"What would it take?" she asked. Maybe she meant it for him, maybe for Mr. Fortner. It blew off in the wind. Mr. Fortner turned and studied the baits. Making sure he got what he was paying for—squid. Mrs. Fortner didn't like to see them sew the terrible hooks inside. Mr. Fortner took one of the cool squid and tossed it right at her chest. She didn't touch it. She didn't slap it away, just let it fall. Then she nudged it with her shoe. "Reminds me of something," she said, looking right at Mr. Fortner. Trolling for a fight. When he didn't take the bait, she picked the squid up and tossed it over the rail into the water. "Freebie!" she called, as though the fish were right there, circling, hoping for largesse. Maybe they were.

"Fin!" the mate called, and "Blue!" the Captain called, and both Fortners hurried back to their rods. The blue struck Mr. Fortner's bait and took off. "Doggies!" Mr. Fortner cried, in that old, old joy. He bent to his work. It took over an hour, with what turned out to be light tackle for such a big fish on, to get him boatside for a look. It plunged up out of the sea and did some looking of its own. Mrs. Fortner screamed sincerely when she saw that huge white eye like a baseball. It judged. It never blinked. She covered her face with her hands. The next time she dared look, Mr. Fortner had the marlin's head up and mouth open, dragging in water.

"You're drowning him!" Mrs. Fortner protested.

"Never seen that before? Where you been? That's how, little lady. You thought they just raced back and forth till their batteries wore out?" He shook his head. "Fish on!" he crowed. He was strapped into the playing chair, in deference to his bad back, and his gloved hands blurred into action, the drag lowered to seven pounds, and the kidney holster dark with sweat. Right at the two-hour mark he had worked the fish up to the transom, the leader in sight, ready for clubbing or gaffing. Whatever it took.

"Record?"

The Captain looked, reckoned. He was fair. It wasn't good news, except for the marlin. "A lot of fight, but on light tackle," he said. "No."

"Tag him," Mr. Fortner said. The mate and Captain and hand shook their heads at Mr. Fortner's decision; it was a good decision, but it had been a good fight, too. Mr. Fortner had not been well. He had been recently in the hospital. "*Tag him,*" Mr. Fortner said again. "In a year or two he'll be big enough to break somebody's back—or heart." He sprawled in his chair, wiped the sweat. "Gimme something," he said. "Damn Lasix leaves me dry enough to spit cotton." The very same thing he said in bed. Mrs. Fortner had never seen him work that hard before, not for any fish, and certainly not for her. She took a bucket of cold water and dumped it on him.

Mr. Fortner was in such a good mood, all he did was howl.

That afternoon it was Mrs. Fortner's turn. While she was still using that thirty-pound test, a reasonably strong fish came up on the baits. She was alone on the fishing deck at the time. "Fish on!" she called, and began what took almost three hours to finish. Not a blue, but a white. Mr. Fortner had been hoping for such a fish. At first they thought it had to be a blue, the way it fought and ran, but she managed to work it up to the boat and Captain Rios saw the lateral line and rounded fin.

"Are you sure?" Mr. Fortner couldn't believe it. You don't ask the Captain, "Are you sure?" but Mr. Fortner said, "It's that big. Are you certain?" Oh, his heart was sore; Marnie was always the one. "I've never had much luck," he mourned. He sat in his chair and watched and offered advice.

"Don't you touch me!" she screamed once when it looked as though he couldn't stop himself from offering a hand as well as advice. He was even pulling on a mate's glove.

"This is *my* fish," she said.

Mr. Fortner worked the glove on anyway, on his right hand, ready to do what he had to do, if he needed to. "Let it go," he said, an hour into the fight. She wasn't big enough to hold out. "Look at you!" Her arms, he noted with some satisfaction, were already trembling; she wouldn't listen.

"You couldn't stop me with a gun," she said.

"You'd think it was community property on the other end of that line," Mr. Fortner said.

"Get his head up," the Captain said. But Marnie wouldn't do that, oh no, she would not be robbed of this moment. She let the slack go out of the line and run free spool. Letting him bolt. Sound. Leap. He did it all and she stayed with him. Cussing. Mr. Fortner stared. Where had she learned all that? Not the talk, the fishing. Was she crazy? She fished like she was crazy, like this was it, all or nothing, life or death. How much longer did she think she could hold out?

"*Get his goddam head up!*" Mr. Fortner yelled when she had played him back in.

"I'm going to let him wear out, not drown," she said. "I'm going to bust this bronco. I want to see just how long it'll take to get him housebroke."

"One of you's going to be housebroke," Mr. Fortner said. He leaned back a little in his chair, tried to relax. "If you've got the money, honey, I've got the time."

"Is this fishin'?" the mate marveled in the next hour as Mrs. Fortner cursed and cried her way through the fight. Tears ran out from under her sunglasses, washed the suntan lotion off her cheeks, left her mouth bitter and hard-set.

It would kill her, the mate thought. She would surely die before that fish ever did. The Captain did all that was legal for him to do, and all the things he knew, what he would have done for anyone fishing with him. Turned the boat to run with the waves instead of against, and backed down on the fish to give Marnie a break. Every break made Mr. Fortner say, "Amen." Captain wisdoms, things that would not spoil the record, if there was one, and this looked like a record fish. "Don't lose it now," Captain Rios told her quietly. That set her attention completely on the fish, and she did not see the sharks.

Mr. Fortner had seen the sharks, but hadn't said anything. What he was hoping he could not have said. Maybe he was rooting for his wife, maybe for the sharks. Maybe for the marlin. All at once, all three. This was almost as interesting as if it were happening to him. The Captain moved astern and fired the rifle at one shark, fired again at the other one. Took out both of them. The mate had the gaff ready. Mrs. Fortner kept on working the fish to the boat.

She saw the third shark, then. She had reached her limits. "Now!" she screamed. "Now!" and the mate leaned over with the gaff, and the Captain leaned over with the club, beating the third shark away. Mr. Fortner leaped up and took the club away, laid it on the hatch. He took the gaff, and the mate stepped back, surprised, wary. Mr. Fortner had the knife, was going to use the knife instead. Much more dangerous to get that close. He always wore the knife, strapped in a holster on his leg, a diver's knife. It had looked pretty harmless on a man who wore socks with his sandals.

"Do it!" Mrs. Fortner screamed, pressed back in her chair, taut, using up her last strength to hold her own. Mr. Fortner leaned over the transom and for an instant they all thought he was going to use the knife for gaffing; no one suspected what he had in mind, no one could have stopped him. He did something perilous beyond belief, in a domestic sense, not in a sporting sense. He cut the line and let the marlin go. The sudden release of pressure threw Mrs. Fortner around in her chair. She didn't know what had happened.

The fish didn't swim off. It stood in the water there, in that clear sweet blue-green Gulf, and waited for something awful to come next. It was exhausted. It seemed almost humble. Then it gave a little shudder and swam ten yards out in front of the boat, where Mrs. Fortner could see it. It seemed to be thinking it over. Suddenly it sounded, dove and vanished. A moment later you couldn't tell where the huge billfish had been or gone. There was nothing.

"Like snow on the water," the mate said.

They all looked from Mr. Fortner to Mrs. Fortner with awe and dread.

"I always wondered what it would take," she said.

She was breathing hard, from the fight with the fish. She didn't have energy to do what she wanted to do right then. She flexed her hands, stripped the gloves off. Her palms were raw, bruised. She brushed the wet hair off her forehead. No one said anything. No one offered any help. When she lit her own cigarette, her hands shook. Not in vibrations, but in wild uncontrol, spastic. It was something to see her light that cigarette, but everyone held back from helping; they were afraid of her. She was shivering now. She was soaked. She pulled her windbreaker on. She was bound to do something. Finally Mr. Fortner said, "You know how much that monster would've cost me to have mounted?"

"As much as the lawyers? As much as you've got? That's about what it'll take," she said. She sounded fairly chipper. She stretched, worked the tension in her shoulders, stepped down from the chair. She walked as though her legs were very light. She stepped lightly. A puff of breeze could've blown her over. Just before she went belowdecks, she turned and looked at her husband. "What's that the grouper crews yell to the monkeyboats? Yeah, 'Keep ya pole up!'" She gave Mr. Fortner a tweak on the crotch.

After she had gone below, Mr. Fortner said, "Damn, that was a beautiful fish."

"Still is," the Captain said.

Mr. Fortner's mellow mood began to erode. He flung the knife over the rail. "Should've done it sooner," was all he said.

When they separated, Marnie Fortner kept the phone number. She found an apartment and settled in. Anything she wanted or needed for decoration or comfort she had ordered, and had the bills sent to Mr.

Fortner's lawyer. So far, this was working. So far, things were friendly, or at least civil. "Give it to her now," Mr. Fortner had said. "She's not going to get a penny after I'm gone." He had changed his will.

Of course the Captain and Mr. Fortner didn't fish together anymore. "I'm sorry," the Captain said. They shook on it. "See you in the record book."

"Damn right," Mr. Fortner said. "Keep on fishin'."

A couple of weeks after that, Señora Rios had another attack. This was not a pretense. She lay in the front room, bluelipped, hurting. Faye got her flat on the couch and ran to the phone. She dialed 911 first. Then Vic. He wasn't in phone-reach. Next she called Tom, shore to ship. Then she tried Vic again. She kept running back to the parlor to see how Señora Rios was doing; she had the front door open so the medics could come right in. She wiped Señora Rios's face, then ran back to the phone, because she had just remembered the lighter. She dialed that number.

Faye had had time to think about this a little. To guess. So when the woman answered, she asked, "Are you the woman who was in Mr. Rios's car?" as though that made perfect sense.

"I still am," the voice answered, cool.

Faye couldn't think what to do next. She wanted to hang up, but Señora Rios needed Vic.

"Is Mr. Rios there?"

"Who the—who *is* this?"

"His mother needs him."

"Is this some kind of joke? Listen, this number is private, unlisted. How'd you—"

"I found it in the weeds."

The woman hung up.

Faye hadn't heard the ambulance yet. She ran back to reassure Señora Rios it would be all right, it would be soon. She lay as Faye had left her, eyelids fluttering, not open, not closed, like someone dreaming. Her chest labored, and when Faye touched her hand, it was cold. Faye ran back to the phone and redialed 911. They told her the unit was on its way, did Faye need instructions in CPR?

"She's breathing, she's breathing," Faye sobbed. She hung up and dialed the SATISFACTION GUARANTEED number again.

"*Please*," Faye said.

"I'm warning you—" was how the woman answered that.

Faye said, "If you see Mr. Rios, will you please tell him his mother is very bad sick, I found her on the floor and she is going to the hospital when they come, soon as they come. I'd take her, but I don't drive a car. I have a bicycle," Faye said, as though that part, and only that part, needed explanation. She took a deep breath. "I dialed nine-one-one."

When Mrs. Fortner didn't answer, Faye said, "Please," but Mrs. Fortner didn't hear her; she had gone to tell Vic. Faye said into the open empty line, "If you see him is all." As the silence continued, Faye hung up.

She ran to the door. She could hear the siren now. She clicked the porch-light switch on and off several times, to let them know this was where, then she knelt by Señora Rios, and held the woman's cold hand.

When Señora Rios came home from the hospital that time, she checked herself out against medical advice and rode home in a taxi. Tom and Vic had both been with her daily, but they weren't there then. Both had stayed till late the evening before, left only because she insisted. They'd left scared. They knew this was not a case of the shepherd boy crying wolf. Somehow or other, that made Señora Rios glad. She was not glad to be ill again, or to "have a heart." But she was very glad to discover that in her crises, both sons ran to help and stood by ready.

Well, of course, she added that to her bag of tricks. It was not to be used trivially, but it would be used. She didn't need anything extra for a few weeks; Tom and Vic showed up for Sunday dinner without being begged at all.

"Just what the doctor ordered," Señora Rios said, wrinkling her face at the vegetable plate, squeaky-clean heart portions on her plate. No salt. She tried to get salt. "Pass it," she said.

"Isn't any," Tom told her. They had foreseen this. They'd all do without rather than tempt her.

"Is cheap. Go buy."

She pointed at Faye, at them all. "You need! Go buy!" She crossed herself. "I give my word I don't eat it."

She began to get agitated. Tom decided to do as she asked. Faye rose to go with him. Señora Rios told her, "You sit." As Tom left, she handed him a new prescription to be filled. When he had gone, Señora Rios said, "We've got an hour," as though the medicine and salt required vigil. Vic started to light a cigarillo. Faye said, "Oh." Not knowing how to signal him he should go outside; the smoke was bad for his mother. But somehow he caught on.

"Am I tempting you, *madre mía*?" He put his cigar case away.

"Better men have tried," Señora Rios said.

"I hope so," Vic said.

Faye said, "It's the smoke."

Señora Rios agreed. "Is bad for breathing. And for babies." She smiled at Faye.

"Listen," Vic said, partly to Faye, partly to his mother. Nothing had ever been said about that call to Marnie Fortner, no explanation or excuse. It had been awkward; Vic did not like awkwardness. "I've got a service," he said. "Answering. Beeper. Don't—you won't have to—one number does it all." He handed his mother a card with the new number on it. She held out her fingers for another one. "For Faye," she required. He slid it between his mother's scissoring fingers. "You won't be needing it," he told her. "You're going to be fine."

"Already." Señora Rios started to get up.

"What? We'll take care of it. What?" Vic got up too.

Señora Rios smiled at him. "I want my coffee now. Make us some coffee? Maybe a little cinnamon."

Vic went into the kitchen. Faye said as he left, "Decaf."

"Help him," Señora Rios told Faye. "Tray—on top of cabinet, he doesn't know where is anything."

Faye had hardly gotten into the kitchen when Señora Rios called her back. "Little cups, little spoons," she required. "Fancy best."

Faye got the little napkins from the top drawer. She counted out the little spoons. She set the sugar bowl and creamer down and filled them. When she went into the kitchen to get the tray from the top of the cabinet, she leaned on the stovetop to balance. She put her hand down on the burner Vic had turned on by mistake. She didn't cry out, just stamped her foot. Vic thought she was mad about something. She ran to the sink and leaned over and let her hand catch the full stream of cold water.

"Cut yourself?" Vic looked, didn't see any blood.

"Burn."

He swung around to the freezer. "Ice cream?"

"She can't have it," Faye said, thinking of Señora Rios's heart diet.

Vic was rummaging. He brought out a bag of frozen peas. "This'll do," he said, and took her hand out from the water, looked at it a moment, then slapped the bag of frozen peas on the burn.

He could tell it helped. She relaxed. It looked as though she might be about to faint. She pulled away from him, ran out onto the back porch, still holding the peas on her hand. She leaned over the rail and lost her lunch. She came back in. It was his fault, but she didn't want him to worry about it. "It's a lot better," she said.

By then he had figured out what had happened. He had an ice cold towel for her; he even wiped the back of her neck, her forehead. She wouldn't look at her hand yet. She had heard the flesh sizzle. She had felt it pull away as she jerked her hand back off the burner. He said, "Let me see it." He took the bag of vegetables off her palm, examined it, and frowned. He put the peas back, told her to keep them there till he fixed a bowl of ice and water. "Do what I say. No scar, I promise you, I guarantee it," he said. He sounded sure.

She took the bag off and dared to look. "What do I care about scars?" she said. He told her, "Just keep it cool." It was miraculous; no torn flesh. And for the moment, no pain.

Their coffee was made. Señora Rios could smell it. She braced in the doorway, leaned in, looking. Their backs were to her, their heads together. She drew a deep breath, savoring.

"Is more like it."

The next weekend, Faye's friend from Greenhill, Mr. Firthwood, was buried. He had died on Friday evening. Faye had not been to see him that week. She understood from the last visit she had made that he was not going to get better again. He was drawn up, very thin, and did not know her. Faye had seen only one other person dead, her mother. She stood for a long time in the hall at the funeral parlor. Finally, Tom went in and looked at the body in the casket and came back out to report.

"It's okay. He looks like himself."

Faye decided she would go in, then. She stood a long time by the casket, looking at things. She liked the way he looked in a suit. She had never seen him in anything except pajamas and robe. One thing scandalized her. She whispered to Tom, "He doesn't need his glasses!"

"He wore them always?"

Tom didn't like being in the funeral home. It made him jumpy. He remembered things. And he absolutely couldn't stand the smell of the flowers.

Faye was talking to people, and after a while she noticed Tom had gone. She found him outside, sitting on a low wall. He seemed to have a cold.

"Some people are allergic," she said. "Some people sneeze instead of cry." When he didn't say anything, she took his silence for doubt or disapproval.

"I read it in a book!" she protested. She sat on the edge of a planter and picked a sandspur off the stocking toe that showed through her sandal.

"You're not afraid about your mama, are you?" She could tell when Tom was depressed. "She's just got a little heart, the doctor said."

That made Tom laugh.

"Come," he said. He started for the truck, to leave. But Faye wouldn't go. Not yet. The funeral would be held there in the chapel on the premises. She wanted to be there, to do that for her friend.

"It's not supposed to be easy," she said.

"Then we're doing it right," Tom said. He relit his pipe.

Faye sat beside him on the wall. They were in the shade, but their feet were burning from the heat of the pavement. Suddenly she knew. "You're thinking about Nola, aren't you?"

Tom didn't answer. But Faye knew, suddenly, that was it. She had several feelings at once. She didn't know how to sort them. There was a feeling of pain, but not like sorrow pain. It made her want to growl like the pharmacist's little dog when you took its leather bone and hid it. Forlorn and angry and having to behave about it in front of company.

Saturday afternoon at confession, she told her suspicion. "I think I've been jealous," she said.

"Did you want what someone else had, or did you think that someone else had what you deserved?" Her confessor tried to sort *covet* from *envy*.

After a rather long pause, Faye said, "Can that something be love?"

"God's kind of love gives; man's kind of love takes," the priest told her.

Faye was trying hard, but she didn't feel they were making much progress. "What about woman's kind of love?" she wondered.

And, more or less, that was what her penance was for.

Father Ockham could not, of course, violate the privacy of confession, but he did tell Señora Rios, "Progress," mistakenly attributing Faye's pain to Marnie Fortner.

Señora Rios took Father Ockham's hint of "progress" and ran with it. She had been planning, but now she had to make it happen. When Tom asked, "Anything? I'm outta here till Sunday," Señora Rios had her list ready. While Tom and Faye shopped, Señora Rios made a phone call, dialing the number on Vic's new card. When the answering service operator spoke to her, she hung up. She had forgotten that was how it would work.

She did some figuring. Went to Faye's room and considered. Faye's room was nice, but it wouldn't do. Twin bed, for one thing. She looked at Faye's calendar inside the closet door; she had taught her to count the days, mark her cycle. She counted to *catorce*, fourteen, and the day fell on Saturday. Perfect. Tom would be away. And Faye would be at her prettiest. Señora Rios knew the numbers; she had been married fifteen years and had never done a thing the Pope would have forbidden, but she'd still managed to have only two children. She left Faye's room smiling. Faye would be at mid-month. And prettiest. Nature does that much for us, Señora Rios thought. She made plans.

She made the bed in the guest room downstairs. She took out the wedding picture from its tissue wrapping and set it on the dresser. She knelt at the prie-dieu and asked a blessing and offered up her hopes. She crossed herself and went out, softly closing the door.

She was sitting in the parlor, resting, thinking, when Tom and Faye drove back with her groceries. She didn't get up to go see or help. Tom took a couple of items for the boat, and came through the room to speak with her before he left. He wasn't going to stay the night, just go on to the dock and be out in the channel before first light. It was already late.

She turned her face toward him. The light shone in her eyes. "You are so quiet," he said.

"No pain," she reassured him. "Go-go-go along." She saw that if she didn't perk up, he might not leave, and then all her plans would spoil. She stretched and yawned.

"What you thinking?"

"Cigarettes," she confessed. "Sitting here fighting temptation."

She pulled him down to her, crushed him to her, and took a deep breath of his clothes. Pipe smoke. She inhaled again. "See how I am broke? I settle for cheap pipe tobacco, secondhand." She beat him good-naturedly on his back and let him go.

"Go catch a fish," she said.

"Don't—" he started to say.

"I'm determined."

"Proud of you," he said.

"Proud of me too," she said.

. . .

They got through the week, Faye and Señora Rios, without Faye's ever suspecting anything unusual was on its way. Faye did the Friday chores. They ate fish for dinner. Faye took out the trash. Saturday afternoon, Faye attended catechism class and went to confession. After supper she took a satchel of books back to the library—three blocks—light till after eight this far into summer. The catechism class was for little kids; she had to learn the answers again, but she wouldn't be baptized or confirmed again. "God remembers," the nuns told her. She understood, but she wished she were done with class. She could have an extra hour in the library then. She had promised she'd be home by eight-thirty, and she was, but when she got there, she wished she had skipped the library completely. She found Señora Rios on the floor by the sofa, reaching around underneath it to find her pills. They had spilled. Her breath was coming in awful gusts.

Faye ran to the phone.

"Already called!" Señora Rios said it again, "Already."

Faye came back and knelt and helped her round up the nitro tablets. She tried to put one under the woman's tongue. Señora Rios battled her hand away. "Already," she said again.

"Tom," Faye was saying under her breath, like a prayer. It steadied her to think he was already on his way.

Señora Rios said, "I call him first this time, not so bad this time. Now you call Vic." She lay back against the couch. "Vic," she said. Faye said, "Are they coming? Is nine-one-one?" She ran to turn on the porch light.

"I won't go with them," she said. "No. I don't need. You tell Vic."

So Faye dialed Vic, spoke to the service, and had him beeped. Vic called almost at once. He was not at home, but he was not at sea either.

"She's crying for you, won't go to the hospital."

"I'm sort of—"

"Says she'll die right here," Faye told him. "Tom's gone. It's just me . . . Tell me what to tell her!"

"I have to stop at the Amoco," Vic said. "Give me an hour."

Long before the hour was up, Vic was there. But before he arrived, Señora Rios had made a remarkable rally if not a recovery. Faye didn't know what to think. The medicine had never worked so well before. Señora Rios was on her feet, walking around, telling Faye to do things with wineglasses and fresh flowers. Faye thought *delirium*; she thought *overdose*. She couldn't tell. She looked into Señora Rios's eyes. They were bright, almost wild with hope.

"I won't leave you," Faye said.

Señora Rios told her, confidently, "You have what it takes."

To Faye's surprise, Señora Rios darted down the hall and checked the guest room again. When Faye saw it was freshly made up, she said, surprised, "Are you sleeping here tonight? Let me go get your gown."

"No, no, all for Vic," she told her. As usual, she pronounced it *Veek*.

"Vic's sleeping here tonight?"

"That, my love, is up to you. And nature. We give nature a little push." She winked.

Faye hadn't a clue.

"Unbutton," Señora Rios told Faye. "Top two." She had a little bottle of cologne in her pocket, and started to spritz Faye with it, then decided against it. She had read about pheromones in a magazine in the cardiologist's waiting room. "Permit nature," she said.

Faye was sure that Señora Rios was experiencing some kind of drug reaction. As they returned to the parlor to wait for Vic, Señora Rios's energy waned, and she drooped into an old age and feebleness her pride had not before been willing to feign, even for the sake of her schemes. She pulled the afghan around her and curled up, wizened, her bright eyes burning, seeking, intent, intense. She watched for the glide of headlights across the ceiling. Vic always drove around back. To Faye, Señora Rios looked like the granny/wolf in "Little Red Riding Hood." The cuckoo chimed and retreated. Señora Rios took Faye's hand and crushed it. "Permit nature," she said again, with that same intensity and significance. "Recall from Father Ockham? Said *is nothing bad*. 'Spose has the right. Every right."

Faye didn't know what she was talking about. She was sure the woman was delirious. She told Señora Rios, "I'll make some toast, some coffee," and eased toward the kitchen, determined to dial 911, no matter what the woman said. She put the coffee on first. Before she dialed the emergency number, Vic's headlights finally swept across the backyard. They were like the beacons in a prison, seeking out the strays. Suddenly Faye reached for the dictionary, Spanish-English, which she kept by the cookbooks so she could use the same recipes Nola and Tom's mothers had used.

'Spose . . . Faye couldn't find it. Vic was opening the door to the main hall. *Suppose*. That didn't make sense. So what was it? *Toast*, like *toast*. *Spost, spoast*. Nothing. She went into the room where Vic and his mother were talking. Faye thought about what Señora Rios had said, it was up to her if Vic slept . . . She ran back to the kitchen and looked in the dictionary for—but for what? Maybe it was a nice dictionary, and there was no word like that allowed in it. Maybe it was a bad word. Faye thought maybe it was. Maybe it wasn't a Spanish word at all. Maybe it was the way she pronounced an English word . . . She found it . . . She didn't even bother to shut the books or lay them back on the shelf . . . esposo . . . spouse . . . Didn't turn off the stove. Didn't say good-bye. Didn't look back. Just tore the door open and ran.

She didn't even go down the steps. She swung under the railing and leaped to the ground. Behind her, all she could hear was Señora Rios calling her name, and Vic's good shoes on the kitchen linoleum. "Hey!" he called. She crouched in the dark till he turned from the door and receded into the dark, deeper into the house.

She ran and ran.

Father Ockham was watching the videotape of Cristo's perfect game. He didn't push the pause button for any reason, and he didn't fast-forward through the commercials even though the World Series was over, and history for almost a year. To pause or fast-forward would be to admit that the game was taped, not live. Then Cristo wouldn't be alive either. This was Father Ockham's way to celebrate things he would otherwise mourn. He didn't surrender the control for the TV remote. He set it, and laid it out of reach. The conditions of his happiness were that for this couple of hours he was not to be intruded on by any temporal clue that would break the moment into past tense. He played it a bit louder than usual, since his hearing-aid battery was now almost a week old. He always put in a fresh battery before Mass on Sunday morning. Still, loud as the TV was, the noise in the yard was louder.

Some unexpected and unreckonable racket. "Sounds like someone's losing her virtue," Father Ockham said.

"It's taking a long time," Mrs. Lockridge said. She had been in the kitchen and had heard it, had come through to peer out the front window, guessing, "It's Schimmelpfennig's saws." That was to defuse any accusations the priest might make that it was Schimmelpfennig's cats. The saws were bad enough, but Father Ockham would never suffer the cats gladly.

She didn't see how Father Ockham could have heard anything over the TV.

"It's the cats," he said.

"No, the saws," Mrs. Lockridge assured him. She shivered. Just the idea of it, of metal burning its way through stone, chilled her. She couldn't bear the sound of a rake on a sidewalk, let alone the thought of the mason's diamond-tipped blades screaming through granite.

"It *is* taking a long time," Father Grattan said, unplugging the rechargeable flashlight lantern from its socket and going toward the door. Father Ockham irritably waved him away from the front door, and sent him out the back. "No," Father Ockham said. Just no. It was a plea, not an order. He required peace and absence of distractions.

Father Grattan stepped out into a night with an almost full moon. Very poor fishing, because of the light, but for land dwellers, wonderful to move around in moonlight so bright and stark it cast shadows. He walked around the side of the rectory and swept the light back and forth across the hedges and garden. Nothing. He turned toward the street again, the arc of the light playing on the ground ahead of him in the shadow of the house. It moved along like an animal straining on its leash.

He patrolled around to the other side of the house, away from Schimmelpfennig's wall and hedge. He saw and heard nothing like the noise that had brought him out. He was about to go back indoors when the sound came again. It was a scream, not a saw's, not an amorous cat's, but a human scream, female, terrified, not outraged. Authentic. It brought the hairs up on his neck and arms. He turned in the direction it came from, across the valley. He listened. Nothing. He brought up the lantern, steadied it, and aimed it across the sandy lane into the thicket on the far side.

It was a strip of uncultivated garden on property the church had plans for in the next century. Mockingbirds and scrub jays and catbirds and grackles knew its ins and outs. His light startled one of them now, sent it flying. For a moment he thought of the mockingbird. Could it mimic a cry like the scream he had just heard? No, he decided. He wished he did not know—he had been reading nature guides—how the little green snakes draped themselves over the vines, how the ants, beetles, and biting things scurried along every surface and leaf and frond of blackberry, brier, and palmetto. He wished he did not know there were rats, armadillos, rabbits. He stood facing the moon, the flashlight held chest high, aimed at he knew not what, and commanded, "Come forth!"

The thicket rustled. He did not see what. Then she was standing there, her hands up, as though this were cowboys-and-Indians.

"Don't shoot," she said.

It was Faye. For some reason, Father Grattan was thinking, *of course.*

"Are you hurt?"

She sniffed, wiped her eyes, rubbed her hands on her skirt. "There was something in there. A horse?"

He almost laughed. "No, no," he assured her.

"It snorted," she said.

They stood there and thought it over. He aimed the light at the ground between them. "Come to the house?"

She backed up a step.

"Faye," he said, "you were the one who screamed for help."

"Where is this? I was running away . . . ah . . . away off . . . I got lost."

Father Grattan thought, Well, she can't lie, she's a terrible liar, it won't be hard to know if she's telling the truth. "What are you doing out this time of night?"

She looked at him. He did not have his collar on. She caught hold of a bit of limb nearby; curled her hand around the branch-end and held. She looked as though she was about to turn and run. "You know me," he assured her. He turned the light up onto his face. The light, cast upward like that, made him look very strange to her. "Father Grattan," he said. "Father Mark."

"I know your voice." She let go of the tree and stepped onto the road, her sandals crunching on the ground shell and sand. One strap squeaked. She came right over to him and looked at him, took the flashlight from him and pointed it toward his eyes. "I know you," she said.

"Come along to the rectory?"

"You know who I am, too," she said.

"Yes," he said. "You're Faye. Faye Rios."

"I—If I wasn't!" she cried. "I won't . . ." She drew a deep breath. "I won't be going back," she said evenly.

They walked side by side to the rectory, around to the back door. They could still hear the ball game. Even though the front porch light was on, and Mrs. Lockridge was watching for them, for whatever this was, back door was it.

"Bad luck to go in a door you didn't come out of," he said. "You ever hear that?" He was just making small talk, trying to keep her from bolting at this last moment. "My grandmother always said that."

Faye wondered if he was trying to teach her something. She didn't understand why he told her that. She had run out of Tom's back door. When she went to live there, she had gone in the front. How did he know that? How bad a luck was that?

"You ever heard that?" he said.

"I'll know it for next time," she said.

They were to the steps. He sent her ahead, shining the light so she'd see the worn edges and miss the pile of gravel Mrs. Lockridge kept to toss at marauding cats.

"Did I know your grandmother?" Faye asked, as she got to the top step. "I mean, before?"

He pushed the door open. "No," he said. "I'm new around here too." The porch sounded hollow under their feet.

"Thank you for saying that," she said. Then they went into the kitchen, and Mrs. Lockridge, taking one look and drawing swift conclusions, said, "You missed supper." She began rattling saucepans. "Spaghetti? Sliced apple? Jell-O?" She was already putting dishes on a tray. "Five minutes, tops. It's leftover." As though Faye had run all that way just to eat supper. Faye still hadn't said a word to all this welcome. "You haven't eaten?" Mrs. Lockridge repeated.

Faye shook her head. "I'm not—"

"Yes you are," Mrs. Lockridge said.

Father Grattan stood behind Faye, making shrugs and hand gestures such as admit mystery, plead tolerance, and require no words. For official explanation, he said, "Faye's been out walking and got herself lost."

"It was dark. I cut through the woods," Faye said.

"Woods!" Mrs. Lockridge exclaimed before she could stop herself. She never could.

"She's not from around here," Father Grattan explained gently. Faye turned and considered him. Her eyes filled with tears.

"You like to wash up before you eat?" Mrs. Lockridge suggested. Faye looked down at her skirt. She had torn the pocket half off and she was holding it on by balling her fist in it, hoping they wouldn't notice. She thought she must look very rough if they would ask something like that.

"Yes, all right," she said, as though it had been next on her mind to do. "Certainly."

She was gone a long time. She was gone so long Mrs. Lockridge began to fret about the Jell-O losing its shape, and the noodles congealing in their sauce. Fifteen minutes passed. Then twenty. Then twenty-five and Faye was still in the bathroom. Father Grattan had gone back to the parlor to watch the game with Father Ockham, who had said only, "Stray cats?"

Father Grattan said merely, "No, sir." He would have said more, but it was Cristo's turn at bat in the eighth inning, and he was about to hit the double that drove in the game-winning run. "Don't need but one!" Father Ockham hollered. This was Cristo's perfect game, but of course you couldn't mention that, that would be a jinx. Three outs to go to perfection. "Come on, kiddo!" Father Ockham rocked forward, kicking the recliner shut, inching the volume way up; it rose, typically, with the old priest's blood pressure. At this point, both were booming.

Cristo connected with the ball. "Not only pitches, he hits! Godalmighty, did you see it go!" Father Ockham shouted as the ball skidded into the outfield.

Mrs. Lockridge came in at that point and laid her hand on Father Grattan's shoulder and said, very low, "She's still in there. What was in the medicine cabinet?" He got up in a hurry and followed her, leaving two men on base.

Father Grattan and Mrs. Lockridge stood in the hall outside the bathroom and imagined, and tried to think what to do. Mrs. Lockridge said, "Just ask her! Ask her if she's all right! Maybe she's . . . maybe she's sick." They could hear the water running and running. Both of them wondered about drugs in the medicine cabinet, razor blades. Who knew what, if one were desperate enough?

Father Grattan stepped up to the door and tried it. Locked. Tapped. "Faye?"

Nothing.

Rapped harder. "Faye!"

"A minute," she said. "Occupied."

"With what?" Mrs Lockridge muttered. She sighed. Deeply relieved to hear Faye's voice. She jammed her arms farther up her sleeves, left to right and right to left, and gripped her elbows, hard. "*Do something*," she hissed. Father Grattan considered his options. He scratched most of them. He raised his hand to rap at the door again, but before he could connect, the door opened. They could hardly savor their relief for their astonishment. Faye's head was wrapped in a towel, and her clothes—she had washed them and wrung them out and put them back on—were almost dry. She had, it was obvious, taken a bath and washed her hair as well as her clothes.

It was too much for Father Grattan, and he started laughing. "Well, all right," he agreed. "We *did* ask her if she wanted to wash up!"

Mrs. Lockridge turned away. Not amused, and pretty sure he ought not to laugh. "Supper's ready."

Faye got a little warm. "Did I do it wrong?"

Mrs. Lockridge said, "I'll find you something to wear; we'll dry your clothes while you eat, how's that?"

"I don't understand. I don't even understand English! I never—"

"Put this on," Mrs. Lockridge interrupted. She gave Faye her raincoat and had her change in the laundry room, had her do her own putting in the dryer and setting of the timer. Faye came back a bit calmer, and utterly swallowed up in Mrs. Lockridge's coat. Faye had rolled the sleeves up, then thought she should ask permission, and rolled them back down. "May I?"

"You let me," Mrs. Lockridge said. "You eat." She rolled Faye's sleeves as Faye sat at the place set for her. Faye ate idly at first, just picking. After she started on the apple, she ate it completely, slice by paper-thin slice, and then set to on the spaghetti. She ate ravenously. Father Grattan sat at the table with her, drinking a glass of tea. When Faye was done with it, Father Grattan reached for the core of the apple and studied it. "What do you call these things?" he asked Mrs. Lockridge.

"Seeds," Mrs. Lockridge said tartly.

"No, the clear stuff, the seed holder." When Mrs. Lockridge didn't have an answer, he said, "Granny's toenails. You ever hear it called that?"

"Must've been *your* granny," Mrs. Lockridge said. "Mine had hooves."

Faye looked up from her plate and said the first thing she had said since she began to eat—"Hoof . . . Hooves. It's irregular."

Before Mrs. Lockridge could find a reply to that, Father Ockham gave a whoop in the other room and came powering through on his way down the hall to the bathroom. "Did you see it? Perfect!" he crowed as he shot through. When he saw Faye sitting there at the table, he stopped short. He pointed. His face got red. "What?" he said, as though someone had already explained it and he just hadn't heard.

Faye got up and backed into the porch door; she was about to run. "I won't go back," she said, to explain everything.

Father Ockham sat down on a side chair and blinked. His color went from red to purple. He husked, "Call—"

Mrs. Lockridge had the phone. "I am," she said, punching in 911.

"No!" he barked. "Call—" He shook his fist, trying to remember the name he needed.

"Tom," Faye said simply.

"*Yes!*" Father Ockham said.

So they did.

. . .

Father Ockham retired for the evening. He had not finished the day's office, and it was almost midnight. He was gone only a few minutes. Came back out and looked. Faye was still there. He went back to his room again.

Tom was not so easy to locate, and was far enough out that he would not get back, even if he came directly in, for several hours. Faye said again, "I don't want him to come get me, just talk to me."

"But where will you go?" Mrs. Lockridge was about to offer the sofa bed in her apartment. She didn't want to make it harder on Faye. She said, "You're not a ward of the state or anything, are you?"

Father Grattan said, "Let me call your—let me call Tom's mother."

"No!"

"But they are worried about you."

"She may be worried, but not about me," Faye said.

Father Ockham came back out, saw Faye, and overheard this last. "In all decency, they must be told."

Mrs. Lockridge said, "They *may* call the *police*."

Faye looked so alarmed, Mrs. Lockridge added, "Missing person, that sort of thing."

Faye seemed to comprehend the trouble she was in, her homelessness. "What am I going to do?"

"Let me call them," Mrs. Lockridge said. "The Rioses don't know me, don't know my voice. I'll tell them you are safe, you are with me and everything's all right."

"Would you?" Faye said. They could hear a siren, far off. Faye said, "Do it now!"

Mrs. Lockridge picked up the phone. Faye told her the number. "Don't tell them where I am," she said again. Father Ockham and Father Grattan shook their heads.

"Don't stay on the line long. Don't let them trace it!" Faye said.

Father Ockham said, "You watch too much television, young lady."

"Yes," Mrs. Lockridge was telling Señora Rios. "Yes, she's safe. She's quite all right. She's among friends." She listened to something. "Yes, good evening, hello," she said, as though Señora Rios had passed the phone to someone else. They all knew who. "Absolutely," Mrs. Lockridge said. "Good night."

She hung up. "That's it," she told Faye.

"What did she say?"

"She said—" Mrs Lockridge paused, considering. "She said they missed you."

"I left the coffee boiling," Faye said.

"She never mentioned that," Mrs. Lockridge said.

They had left a message for Tom. Boat to boat, the word passed. They did not know when he would hear and return the call. Father Ockham went back to his room again. Father Grattan went into the other room and rewound Father Ockham's video. He turned on the news, watched the weather.

An hour passed. Faye had on her clean, dry clothes. Ready. The phone rang. Father Grattan answered it. It was Tom.

Father Grattan talked to him a moment, then handed the phone to Faye. She sat on the edge of the footstool and talked. Listened. Talked some more. Father Grattan went into the kitchen with Mrs. Lockridge.

She looked a question at him, but he couldn't answer it. He shrugged. "It's an opera," he said. Father Ockham came back. He was in his pajamas now, and barefooted. He thought Faye had gone when he saw just the two of them at the table, drinking coffee. Then he heard Faye's voice from the other room.

"Is she spending the night here?"

Faye hung up and came to report. "He's coming. Tom's on his way." It would be a few hours at most. "He promised. He was—"

"Fishing?" Father Ockham guessed. He shook his head, marveling. "Called him off the water?" He pointed at Faye with his whole hand. "Helen launched a thousand . . . You just drive 'em in like a storm at sea."

"Helen Who?" Faye asked.

Father Ockham took that as wit, and went back down the hall to his room, chuckling.

Tom's truck growled to a stop at around two-thirty. They had heard him, roaring along, a block away, pushing the dark world out of his way. He stumped across the front porch like thunder; he hadn't even taken off his rubber fishing boots. He jerked the storm door so hard he almost tore it off the latch; the latch would have to be replaced. He forgot to knock. He just plunged right in through the door, confettied with moths from the porch light.

His eyes picked out Faye and he went straight to her. "All right? All?" He caught her to him, side by side, not heart to heart, and they did not kiss. Never have, Mrs. Lockridge thought.

All Faye was saying was "Yes," over and over.

"What the *hell?*" Tom asked, surveying them all.

"She can come home with me," Mrs. Lockridge said.

Tom turned to Father Grattan, hoping for some clarification. Father Grattan explained without prejudice or length.

"Is this a police matter?"

"Not at all."

"She free to go?"

"Free."

"Have—who else knows?"

Faye ducked clear of Tom's shelter. She went over to Mrs. Lockridge and embraced her and thanked her. "For the raincoat, the spaghetti, the apple, and the Jell-O and everything."

"Goodness!" Mrs. Lockridge laughed. "Don't be thanking me for the noodles one by one," she said. She had watched Tom's arrival with interest and their reunion with greater interest. As Faye released her from the thank-you hug, Mrs. Lockridge whispered, "He's who I'd call, too."

"We're going," Tom said. Half a dare, if anyone planned to interfere. Father Ockham, for a blessing, slept through the whole thing.

Mrs. Lockridge stood at the front door and watched them go. She waved. They ran out into the storm of insects and Tom had his shirt pulled up, unbuttoned, holding it as a filter against the bugs as they ran across the porch. Faye looked around and waved, but Tom never looked back. He helped her into the truck and then ran around to the other side, jumped the clutch, and drove them away into the dark.

Mrs. Lockridge closed the door. She left by the kitchen, usually; they locked the front door, but the back one stayed open. It was odd how much energy she had. She wanted to sing. "Crazy night," she told Father Grattan. He was going through the rooms, turning out lights, powering down for the night. "Full moon."

"Your day's over," Father Grattan said. "Long over."

"When the sun's straight up, it's noon. What is it when the moon is?" she wondered. She took the spooner from the center of the table, refilling it with spoons from the dishwasher. After that she culled the flowers, taking out the faded ones and freshening the water. She couldn't say what had gotten into her. Maybe it was the moon. She suddenly had the need—not impulse, but need—to polish the copper bottoms of the pans; she worked on them till they were as pink as new. She cleaned out the vegetable drawer, sacking the bad squash and a cucumber so soft she put her fingers through it when she tried to pick it up. She got her jacket and purse and started down the steps toward home. Father Grattan had already said his official good-night. She had pulled the door shut; now she had to ease down the steps in the dark. The moon was casting the house's shadow on her path. She walked out into the garden, to put the discarded vegetables in the compost pile. She could hear the cats in Schimmel-pfennig's stoneyard; she couldn't say what got into her. She took the squash first, and flung it. Then the cucumber, over the wall they had forced the mason to raise as a sound baffle. The squash vanished. The cucumber flipped out of her hand and struck the Rogation Cross. She heard it hit, saw it shine as it dripped.

She had to open her purse and find tissues and crawl around in the dark and wipe the stuff off. "God and Harry," she said, creaking to her feet again. The cats had left off their wailing, or taken themselves elsewhere. It was very quiet. She could hear traffic on the bridge a mile away. The tires buzzed across the drawbridge grid. It wouldn't be Faye and Tom, she thought. They'd be long across, but for a moment it seemed that it had to be—riding along through the night, the grid all that stood between them and the water with that moon spilled on it and the tide—she considered the moon, calculated the hour, and extrapolated for the river—yes, the tide running toward full.

That was the Saturday Faye slept on Tom's boat and Tom spent the night in "motel Chevrolet." She slept late, and when she poked her head out on Sunday morning, there was Elven Leonard. His daddy, Zeb, and Tom were talking over coffee from town. She hadn't even thought, during the night, about what came next. She had intended to; she had not planned to lie down and sleep and not wake till morning. She had imagined she would be restless, keyed up, even seasick from the rocking of the boat and the aromas of fishing and the diesel and low tide. She had thought the strangeness of the place, the odd color of the night sky filtering through the amber dock lights, the tilting shadows of insects and the cries of night things—she had thought all these would keep her wide-eyed all night, listening, brave.

Most of all, she had thought she would lie there listening for whatever sound might mean Tom's mother had come to take her back.

But Tom had told her she was safe. He had swung her over the rail and set her on the deck of *Legal Hours* and said, "Whatever you need. Yours." He hadn't come aboard. He had left her there. Then he had driven the truck up onto the public walk, across the dock access. If anyone came by, he'd know.

He didn't want a blanket or a pillow?

No.

Or anything?

No.

He rummaged behind the seat and found a can of compressed air, tossed the siren down to her. "For pirates," he told her. She took it below and set it by her bunk. For a moment the bunk made her remember—or almost remember—something. She felt a wave of panic rise and wash. She might not ever remember Mackie, but there was something that almost made her lose her mind in the way that bunk rail felt as she leaned against it.

No, she was not going to sleep well. She chose another bed, the bench at the very back, with no upper to close it in, just the flotation cushions and a blanket. She sat there, the air siren in the hand, and breathed and counted, breathed and counted, as the rehab doctors had said to do, against fear. She sang "Row Row Row Your Boat." One of the dock cats came and sat at the hatch, paws tucked, listening. Tom could hear her too, not that she sang loudly. He had his windows down and his cab door open as he finished his pipe.

In the night a shower came up, and Tom eased down to the boat, onto deck—the tide was in now, and the *Legal Hours* was riding high, deck and dock about level—and, sock-footed, he crept to the cowling and pulled the skyhatch cover shut. It was too high, from inside, for Faye to reach, and if it stayed open, she'd get drenched in any kind of blow. He tiptoed back, side-vaulted the rail onto the dock walk again, and trotted to the truck. He felt young. No, he felt younger. Than what? Than he had for a while. He didn't like to figure why. The rain wasn't hard or stinging. The first drops had been large and pelting on the truck roof and hood. Now a finer rain fell, misty, local, not the lasting kind. The moon was already in the clear as the storm passed on through. Tom tried to get comfortable, and finally rolled the passenger-side window down and stuck his feet out. That's how he slept, stretched across the cab, his socks rinsing clean in the last of the shower.

When he woke, it was just dawn, and there was no blood in his feet past his ankles. He was cold, stiff, and, for a moment, completely disoriented. When he pulled his boots on and stood, he got so dizzy as the blood plunged into his legs he almost fainted. He had to stump along, lurching and rolling, to wake the feeling. The cowlicks in his hair had sprung into full riot, and his old sweatshirt was sagging off one shoulder. His watch had stopped. His beard had not. He ducked into the public men's at the city park and freshened himself up. No hot water. He washed his face and shook himself dry; the wall-mounted hot-air hand dryer was broken.

He strode on up the street, his damp socks squealing in his deck boots. He was Lupo's first customer, and he was whistling when he pushed the door open into that bright harbor.

Tom took two hours to read the paper, drink a pot of coffee, and eat breakfast. He ordered another breakfast to go, and took it, paid without explanation, and left. When he got back to the docks, there were Zeb and Elven. Which suited Tom just fine, because he had been making a plan. Faye needed somewhere to go, and it wasn't going to be anywhere near Señora Rios. Zeb was used to hearing anything, but this took some getting adjusted to.

"Now you know," he began, "Palma and I haven't—"

"Ask her," Tom said.

Palma listened to that with some interest, and no response. But she asked for an hour to consider it. And that was a lie, sort of. She had no intention of waiting an hour to decide. Not saying no, first thing, had been a yes. That's what Tom thought, but Zeb was afraid to hope. Palma could always surprise him.

When Palma hung up the phone after Zeb's call, she started for town. She would do her thinking en route. She got to Lupo's sooner than she'd promised to arrive at her decision. When she walked into the café, Zeb and Elven were enjoying their big breakfast in a booth at the back. They weren't expecting her in person, so they had their booth near the phone, not their eye on the door. She had the advantage and pleasure of total surprise.

Zeb scrambled to his feet.

Palma, in her late-stage pregnancy, was as majestic as a ship of the line. She couldn't fit in the booth, didn't even try. This wasn't a social occasion. She drew a businesslike chair over from the table across the aisle, and sat. Zeb subsided back on the banquette. Elven just watched and chewed.

"The boy says you say okay to a pet tabby ket."

Palma nodded, impatient. "Look," she said, "about that gal. Okay, you fetch her here if she wants to go home with me. Up to her."

Zeb hesitated.

"I'm never setting footstep on those docks," Palma said. It was true she hadn't been back since the night Ben died.

Zeb still hesitated. "She's—"

"Trying to keep a low profile," Elven said, bottom-lining it. He drank the rest of his milk and set the glass down precisely on its ring.

"Trouble with the law?" Palma scowled.

"Mother-in-law," Zeb said.

Palma laughed.

Zeb took offense. "You never had no trouble with yours," he said. "Done you good to get to know her, if she'd of lived."

"She stubborn too?" Palma said. "That where you get it? Bound to love her as much as I love you."

They glared at each other.

Elven dusted his fingers on his napkin and scooted out of the booth. "Wait here," he told them, pointing at both. "I'll go get her. We'll be back in ten." He left them before they could either object or ratify.

Palma licked her lips. She was thirsty, but wouldn't satisfy Zeb by asking for a thing. Only ten minutes, she thought. Those ten minutes stretched like a desert all around her. She couldn't imagine what there might be to talk about. Zeb poured water from a beaded, frosty aluminum pitcher and handed her a slender glass. No, her mind was saying, but her hand reached out and took it and sipped. The glass in her hand gave her confidence; she gripped for dear life.

"City water," Zeb warned her. She didn't have to be told. She didn't like that sulfurous taste, never had gotten used to it. But because he had remembered that, she couldn't let it make a difference. She was that contrary. She had to praise it if she could, and not for his sake, either.

"It's wet," she said.

"It is," Zeb agreed. Not too eagerly, just for something to say. He checked his watch, sighed. "You care for some breakfast?"

"No."

"Done eat?"

"I didn't come here for eatin'," she said.

"Piece of toast left," he mentioned.

"Half a piece," she pointed out.

"Sure you don't—"

"No," Palma said, a little loud.

Zeb counted money onto the check and change atop the bills. He checked the time again. The sweep second crept imperceptibly around. "Only been five minutes," he said.

Customers came and went. There was a continuous clatter behind the kitchen doors. Three more minutes passed with no word form either of them, then Zeb said, "You want a tangerine?"

Palma looked around. Not a tangerine in sight anywhere. The old mood reared up in her. "Where you gonna get a tangerine!"

Wrong season, wrong everything. Zeb said simply, "I remember you like them."

"You kill me," she said.

Another pause. No Elven, no runaway Faye. Six minutes more gone by. Way past the ten minutes Elven had promised. Palma said, "All right, coffee. Decaf."

Zeb leaped into action. When he brought it to the cluttered table, no tray, no room for one. She took it black. There was no place to set it; she held the cup and saucer, perched it on her eight-month belly, a natural shelf. "Only thing it's good for," she said. The cup and saucer rose and fell as she breathed.

"Won't be long now," he said. Did he mean for delivery or for Faye and Elven to come?

When Palma didn't answer, Zeb found one more something to say. It surprised him when he heard it. It slipped past the barricades he'd put up for safety's sake around the gap in their life. "You need somebody around. Tom's right about that. But what you doing making her welcome instead of me?"

What irritated her more, his bringing it up now, or her noticing his earlobe minus the gold ring? Seemed as though he kept his head turned that way, so the sun would strike it and show her it was gone.

"You want me to change my mind?"

"Not about her," Zeb said.

He leaned forward. "I had a dream about you," he said.

"Sweet dream or nightmare?" She looked away. She looked wildly around. Where was that boy! What was keeping that boy!

"Sweet," Zeb said, not looking at her, and then, looking at her, "Real sweet."

She stared into his eyes. "I had a dream too. Dream it all the time. It's a sound, not a sight. You heard it too."

"What?"

He laid his hand on hers, first body contact in months. She didn't flinch, but he did, when she said, in two merciless syllables, "Ben's wrench."

He pulled back as though slapped. She was almost sorry, in her triumph. Shouldn't even slam an outhouse door that hard, she chided herself, but since she was telling the truth, she acquitted herself and gave in to gloating, feasting righteously on Zeb's hurt look and recoil. She was relieved the mood had changed between them and this cozy parley was over, the truce flags struck and the battle flags raised.

For his part, Zeb didn't say anything, just sat there, as silent as a sundial. Picking through the collapsed house of cards, trying to salvage an ace. Considerably set back.

Elven returned. Didn't come in. Stood tapping on the café's front window glass to get their attention—a dull sound eerily like the one Palma had dreamed of. It took a moment for them to realize it was a true sound, not their memory working on their nerves. But there he was, on the sidewalk, semaphoring for them to come outside.

"She's waiting in the car," Palma deciphered, hastily and gratefully uprising. She didn't even look back.

Hours later—when Palma and Faye were long gone across the causeway and getting used to each other, and Elven was entertaining his cousins with birthday cake and yard games, the quest for his promised cheese-eating cat postponed for another day—Zeb, alone on his boat, finally answered Palma. Took him that long to think it up, to get it right. "You guess you the only one hear that tappin'?" he said. Later, in the night, suddenly waking, desperately listening, he added, "Silence is worse."

Faye liked the idea of island life, liked it that there was water between her and Señora Rios. Faye agreed to the move.

Palma and Faye hit it off right from the start. Palma was in a teaching mood, and Faye had a lot to learn. Sewing lessons, for instance, something Señora Rios had not had the slightest interest in. Neither did Elven, who finally got his cat. He and his cat were out in the yard, on the trails down to the creek, or up in the live oaks, or digging around on the bluff for Indian shards all day long. The cat was all Elven had hoped for and all that Palma had feared—"He's not coming in this house," she kept saying, every time she found him on Elven's windowsill, or curled up napping in a chair.

Elven named him Bob, because of his tail. They couldn't decide whether it was gone from an accident or genetic. "More of a stub than a nub," Elven said. "I *know* his daddy was a bobcat. His eyes catch the light red, not yellow at night."

"I might have known your daddy would pull something like this," Palma said.

The cat—not a weaned kitten but a half-grown cat, already a hunter with ideas of his own—had been on the top step in a cardboard box, the lid weighted down with a basket of tangerines, the second Monday morning Faye was at Palma's. No note, no apology, no explanation—a bobtail cat and a basket of tangerines. "Both out of season," Palma said.

Elven knew right from the first it was going to work out. He trained Bob to come to his name with rewards of cheese. By that time Palma's sewing lessons had advanced. She had taught Faye how to hemstitch and pleat and make French knots (the project was for the nursery, which was being worked out in peach and natural live-oak green—nothing to remind anyone of the sea or boats—"earth tones," Palma insisted).

In the afternoons, Faye and Elven and Bob would take a walk. Sometimes the cat would dash toward the weeds or the water and, after a furor and tussle, fetch back a lizard or crayfish and once a whole little fish. He carried his plunder in his mouth, trotted along beside them, and when they stopped to sit on the overturned bateau, Bob would stretch out sphinxlike and hold his prey to the ground under both front paws.

Elven liked walking with Faye, because she didn't know a thing and he could tell her about the boar wallow and swamp cats and coral snakes and every thing in the world that might be out there. She didn't require proof, and she didn't raise objections to going farther along, the way his mama would have.

At the Indian camp on the west side of the island, he showed her where the best pieces of broken pots were. She crouched there and dug and sifted. She found a big piece of worked clay with a lip and curve and some of the painting still clear. She even found a bit of something metal with a hole through it. But she wouldn't take them. Left them there, right where she'd dug them up.

"Why?" Elven wanted to know. He'd already told her the university people were coming, going to cut a road and dig it all out and haul it away.

"They're not mine," she said.

"Whose are they?" Elven said.

He had found a spear tip, and what did she think he was going to do with that, leave it? The next rain might wash it into the creek and down into the sea forever. Then who'd have the good of it?

He handed her that pretty curved piece of clay and said, "Here."

"I don't need it," she said.

He thought it over. "I found my arrowheads before the professors made their claims. That's my thinking."

They started back. Bob had vanished. Elven whistled for him and they turned home. The trail was so narrow through the grass and briers and palmetto that they had to keep one hand in front of themselves, to push the way open.

"Bound to cut them a road, first thing," Elven said. "Swamp ket'll go, swim on off to the mainland, and they'll tear things up some, scrap and build a little house to keep their stuff in, lock it at night, won't be a berry left for a sparrow's supper."

He stood and looked back, rubbed his hand over his head, from the nape of his neck forward, and rubbed his eyes. He took the piece of flint from his pocket and looked at it, then at nothing, overlooking nothing. Finally he said, "Tom Rios says a man got enough to do without supporting a conscience."

"My Tom?"

He looked at her then. Weighing that too. "Ain't but one," he said.

He flung the flint back down the road, as far as it would go. It sparkled in the light, in its arc. They didn't hear it hit.

"I don't want God watching me all the time," he said. He picked a berry off the brier nearest him and aimed it at the sky. When it fell back, it almost hit him.

"Shoot," he muttered. He and Bob walked on ahead.

"Tom was joking," Faye said to his back. "Wasn't he?"

Elven shrugged. They had come to the crest of the little hammock, and he was just put out enough to stand where she'd be looking past his shoulder at the blue-roofed house way off on the edge of the marsh. Last time, she had asked what it was. Wanted to go there when he told her it was an abandoned house, but he had known better. Palma had warned him not to say anything. He didn't. Still, he hoped Faye would notice it.

She didn't. That's how he knew she really didn't remember it. Her own house! They walked on back to Palma's. She was summoning them—beating on a pan lid with a spoon and calling, shrill as a bird, "Tooey, tooey!" They started to run. Faye was getting faster, but Elven still won, every time. She didn't have breath for answering, even if she had thought of something to say, when he asked, "What are you gladdest you forgot?"

From day one, Palma worked to get Faye out and on her own. Not right away, but one day. "Sooner than you think," Palma said. She had changed her mind about wallpaper, after the first wall. Now they were painting the nursery. Everything was piled in the middle of the floor and covered with a bedspread while they cut-in the corners and rolled the ceiling and walls.

"Where will I live?" Faye wondered. *Where*, Palma noted, not *how*. A good sign.

"Find you a little place, live on you' own," Palma said. She aimed the brush right at Faye. "You not scared of the dark?"

Faye said, "I'm not afraid something's there. I'm afraid nothing's there."

Palma laughed. "Gal, you brave if you afraid of nothin'!"

Faye didn't think it was so funny. She felt ashamed, not entertained. She said, "Nobody knows that but you."

"You afraid of ladders?"

Something stirred in Faye's insides, a little leap in her stomach. Nothing connected to it. Just an idle, random leap and then the ripples settled. She shrugged. "Not this time around," she decided.

"Then you paint the ceilin'," Palma said, and pointed her to the far corner.

It had been raining all day, and the lights didn't do much, even without shades, to brighten their work. Palma knocked off at three for a nap. There was a break in the weather, and Elven took his chance, went out along the usual paths to try to find Bob. The cat had been gone all day. At the last moment, Faye went along too.

"He's not missin', he's hidin'," Elven said. But he was looking along the roads first, in the ditches. The cat hadn't been in all night; he always slept in the yard under the porch, and he hadn't come for breakfast and hadn't come for lunch and now it was suppertime, almost. Elven had some cheese in his pocket. "Way he like it, you think his name is cheese," Elven said. "He always come to cheese."

Faye went along because she was afraid of the same thing Elven was, but didn't say so either. They pretended they were just out to stretch their legs.

There came a break in the dark skies—almost a blue rip through the gloom, toward the west. "Now it's stopped thundering, he'll come on out from hiding," Faye said.

"Reckon so," Elven said. "It's built in they know how to care for themselves."

It was Faye who saw the little dark pile of fur on the side of the road, down past the turn toward the village. Elven saw it at almost the same time.

"No, don't," Faye said, trying to hold him back, but he had to know, had to go. He raced ahead, calling, "Bob!"

He sank to the road, relieved. The worst thing would've been if it *was* Bob, but it wasn't. The animal was a rabbit. But after that, it was about the worst thing Faye could imagine because it was hurt but not killed. It lay there, broken-backed, bright-eyed, looking up at them, trying to run, hardly able to flop, and otherwise strong. "It might make it," Elven said.

He knew better; he was saying that for Faye's sake. Here came the rain again. Heavy rain.

"Best not to move him if he's got a spine injury," Faye said. She'd learned that on TV, on a police show. "We need something to carry him on."

It was pouring now.

"We gotta go on home," Elven said.

"We'll come back," Faye said.

Elven looked. The light in the rabbit's eyes glinted, unblinking. "He's not going anywhere," Elven said.

They memorized landmarks, and laid a tuft of grass on the edge of the road to mark the place, then turned and ran for home. The blue rift in the sky had filled with emptying clouds.

When they got to the main road and started down the lane where Palma's cottage was, they stepped off the road to let a truck go by, but it didn't swerve to pass them. It slowed. It stopped. It was Tom.

"Everything all right?" they all asked at once, then laughed. Not a rich, good laugh but a frightened laugh. They were worried about Palma, and Palma had been worried about them. When Tom stopped by to check on things, and bring Faye's mail, Palma sent him on again, to try to find them.

"Storm warning's up," Tom scolded.

They got into the truck. Elven wanted the door seat, so Faye slid over to the middle. She took the opportunity to lean close to Tom's ear and whisper, "Do you have your gun?"

She said it too softly, and he couldn't make it out. He almost jumped out of his skin when she got that close; she was soaked through, cold against his dry arm, but he was willing to try that again. "What?"

Faye shook her head no, because Elven was paying attention now. She was trying to let him know about the rabbit; she thought it would have to be killed. She thought Elven didn't think so. And Elven was trying to do the same, on her account. He pretended he saw Bob.

"We gotta go back," Elven said. "Turn back here."

"Gotta?"

Faye agreed. "Please?"

"We're looking for Bob," Elven said. "He was out in the rain all night, but he's okay."

Faye tried to ask Tom about the gun again, but he still didn't understand. So Elven, who heard it plainly, asked it out loud. "You have the gun with you?"

Tom braked.

"Let's see what we're getting into here," he said. "For what am I driving fifty miles an hour into 'do you have your gun?' "

"There's this rabbit," Elven began.

"So turn here," Faye said. Tom turned. "There, over there it is," Faye said, pointing. She didn't see the rabbit, she saw the clump of grass they had left to mark the place. Rain had washed it down the road a few feet. Elven started to get out. "I'll show you." Faye caught his arm. "No," she said. It sounded so much like his momma, it made him mad.

He said, "No," right back, to cancel hers. So Faye got hold of him with both hands.

Tom said, "Both of you hush. I see from here." He drove across the road into the other lane, rolled his window down, and looked. Rain blew in. Tom backed up till the headlights—it was that dark—shone on the rabbit. He thought that over and then decided against doing it in the spotlight, if it had to be done. He drove past, parked, walked back to see. Knelt and put out his hand (they were watching him in the side mirrors) and they could see him talking. He came back to the truck.

"Still alive?" Elven wanted to know.

Tom didn't say. He reached behind the seat and got his pistol.

"Guess so," Elven said.

Tom carried the gun under his jacket to keep it dry. Faye wouldn't look in the mirror. She shut her eyes. Tom's window was still down. She braced for the noise. Elven had turned around on the seat, looking out the back window. "Here it goes," he said, excited.

The gun misfired. Just a click. Faye heard it. It misfired again. And a third time. The fourth time it fired. Just once. Faye crossed herself. When Tom came back, he broke the gun, emptied the shells, saving the good ones with the others in his pocket, and threw the spent casing away. He handed the gun through the window to Faye. Her eyes were still shut. He nudged her with the gun and she opened them and stared at it. She wouldn't take it. She wouldn't touch it.

"It's empty," he said. "And it is raining out here."

She took the gun, laid it on her lap. When Elven reached for it—of course that was next—she pushed his hand away. Elven turned to the front and faced the road. Sulking. He hadn't been a baby in years. "Years," he said.

Tom took the shovel, walked to the rabbit, turned it under. He cleaned the shovel in a puddle and put it back into the truck bed. When he got in, he noticed the color of Faye's face. "Didn't feel a thing," he told her.

"Thank you," she remembered to say. Elven's eyes flashed.

"Was he bloody?" Elven asked.

"He looked more like a rabbit yesterday," Tom agreed.

"I coulda done it, I had me a gun," Elven said.

Tom handed the gun across to him, from Faye's custody. Elven sat up, proud. "He's not afraid," Tom said.

"Not me," Elven said.

They were rolling toward Palma's. The storm was just overhead, the lightning silver, neon pink, and loud. It struck the old tower on the dead-end bridge lift, the one the fishermen still used. "Pow!" Elven said. The mill smoke was blowing back over the river, away from them. The trees lay over too, and the grass. The squall seemed to be pushing them along toward home.

Faye could smell brimstone. She wasn't sure whether it was the marsh, the lightning, or the gun. Something about it made her sick. Made her shake. She thought she was going to be sick. As soon as Tom stopped the truck in Palma's yard, Faye scrambled out and ran bent over to the weeds on the land line.

Palma didn't see that. She was standing on the top step with news. "Look what found me! What'll you give me for this ket?"

There he was, perfectly dry and groomed like a gentleman in a tux, his white paws and bib gleaming and dandy.

"I was about to adopt me a broken rabbit," Elven said, still playing the macho fellow whom nothing fazed. But he got his arms around Bob Cat soon enough and held him like a baby while he fed him cheese.

"Faye," Tom said.

She thought he was going to tell her she had been stupid about the gun. She was ashamed of getting sick like that. "I guess I'm just a person who throws up," Faye said. "Did I before?"

Tom shrugged. "Not on me."

She wouldn't laugh. "I shouldn't have—we—the . . ."

She took a breath. "You did the right thing. I mean, I knew the rabbit had to be killed. I just didn't know how. We shouldn't have bothered you. Should we have just left it? I didn't know."

The rain had almost stopped again. There was only a light mist. Things were beginning to steam, and the sun was trying to burn through.

Palma came out to see what was keeping them.

"Can you shoot?" Tom asked, handing Palma the unloaded gun. Palma clicked the cylinder open and spun it, made sure it was empty.

"Been tempted. Forebore," Palma said.

She looked from Faye to Tom, puzzled.

"Faye has fear," Tom said. Elven had told his momma about the rabbit, so she knew why the gun. But she wasn't sure what Tom was getting at now. Obviously he wanted her help. She said, "When you get you a place of your own, you going to need—"

"No!" Faye said, covering her ears with her hands.

Tom and Palma exchanged a long look.

"Sometimes," Palma told Faye, "you scream out in your sleep. Holler right out."

"I wake up afraid," Faye said.

"Same effect on me," Palma agreed.

"You saw a man killed," Tom said. "Anyone ever tell you that?"

"In that wreck," Faye said.

"No, ma'am, I mean with a gun," Tom said. "News to you?" Faye nodded.

"I think it's why you have the fear," Tom said.

"Your brain remembers that noise," Palma said. "No memory, no scenery, just noise."

"You need to fire the gun," Tom told her. "I think that is what you need."

"Momma! Telephone!" Elven called from the door. Palma put the gun in Faye's hands. "*Now,*" Palma said.

They were out there only a few more minutes. Palma made Elven stay in. He was sorely tried. He stood at the window, watching. Faye let Tom load the revolver. She did what he said, tried to do everything he said, and above all to listen. The first two shots seemed nothing to do with her. They were accidents. They terrified her. The third shot she was able to aim and hold steady. The fourth she managed to place near the target—a bit of an old invoice Tom had impaled on a twig at the edge of the yard. She blew a wild plum limb clean off. The fifth shot struck the wet paper. The sixth was a misfire. She kept her stance, and tried it again. Almost in the middle of the target! Tom took the gun, emptied the casings, flung them over the hedge into the marshy field beyond Palma's lot. Faye came on into the house then. She was smiling. Tom didn't stay.

That night it was Elven who had a dream, woke the whole house with it. He wouldn't say what it was, said he didn't remember, really, just "It was so bad," over and over. He wanted his daddy. He wanted everybody. Faye had never seen him cry. She had never seen anyone wake in a sweat like that and keep on suffering, not even in the hospital. She sat by his bed and talked with him. Palma went to call in Bob. "Just this once," she said, the kitty could stay with him the rest of the night. While Palma was gone to fetch the cat, Faye told Elven, "Just turn your pillow over, the bad dream won't come back."

Elven was ashamed of how much he needed to believe that. "You sure?"

"It's how I do," Faye said.

After Palma brought the cat in, she walked back out to the hall and stood for a long time by the phone. Once she even picked up the receiver, but then cradled it again. "Lord Jesus, Lord Jesus," she prayed, "send my boy back to sleep right now."

She didn't know what she might have done if that crying kept up.

Faye and Palma couldn't get back to sleep. Faye still slept on a cot in the soon-to-be nursery. She knew that there would be another crib where her cot now stood; she knew Palma was going to have twins. Palma had shown her the sonogram. She had explained all about it. Faye had sworn not to tell. "Not even Elven," Palma insisted. "*Especially* not Elven," she added.

"Not even Elven," Faye had agreed.

"Nobody at all name of Leonard. I mean Zeb."

"All right."

"No Rios."

"All right," Faye said.

Palma had the extra set of everything bought and laid out of sight under her bed and in the back of her closet. She had posted her room off limits to Elven till after the birthing. "Oughta send him on to Cliffie's till I get over with all this," Palma said. "He bound to find out, and he worse'n any chile I ever saw about telling the truth to any soul he meet."

"You don't want Zeb to worry," Faye said.

Was she being ironic? Sarcastic? Palma studied her; decided no. She shook her head. "What you gonna be when you grow up?" she asked Faye. They had their sewing project out and Faye was trying once again to embroider the duck on the little layette jacket. Palma had helped her place the pattern and cut and sew the shirt parts. Faye still did not have great fine-tuning skills on her hands. And she hated—there was no other word but *hate* for it—sewing. She had tried and tried. She wadded her work up and shoved it back in the bag with her scissors and notions. "I'm not going to be a sewer," Faye said.

"Seamstress," Palma said.

"That either." She put a book on top of her sewing bag so the cat couldn't get into it. "You can buy those little shirts already finished," Faye said.

"Machine work," Palma said.

"It's one job I don't want, even if there's a machine."

Palma brought two mugs of herb tea. Faye's mug said JAVA. Palma's was the Happy Anniversary one, the one Zeb always used to choose. You had to read it off both sides: "When it's good it's very very good . . . and when it's bad it's still pretty good."

"What job do you want?" Palma asked, when they got settled again. She wasn't being pushy; it was the kind of talk Faye needed.

"That diploma of yours," Palma said.

"I don't re—"

"Nobody remembers high school," Palma said.

They sat for a few minutes thinking about that. Palma said, "I had my first job in high school."

"Candy striper," Faye guessed.

"Good God, chile," Palma said.

"Didn't you want to be a nurse?"

"Lord, no, I didn't want to be no nurse. I wanted to be queen of England but I didn't have the—what you call it?—documentation." She rolled back against the pillows, laughing. She had to turn herself a little to the side to see over her stomach. "They are sure-fire kicking tonight," she said. It was true; her nightgown and robe almost rattled as the babies stretched and played. "Elevator operator, that's what I was. Good little old job even if I did have to wear a monkey hat."

Faye tried to think. There were no buildings over two stories tall on the island. She said, "I could babysit."

"Anybody can," Palma agreed. "Lissen! My first job! I told a tale. It wasn't elevator, that was *second*! You know what I did? First thing I ever got outside wages for—scrubbing heads at George O's Mighty Soul Finger."

Faye considered it. "Cleaning toilets? . . . I know how," she said.

"Shampoo gal," Palma clarified. "Shampooing! Washing heads of hair!" She sat up and looked at Faye. "Whattya say? This could be it."

"I—"

"Right. It's perfect," Palma said. "Let me ask around."

"Don't I need a license or something? Don't I need lessons?"

"Directions on the bottle," Palma said. "Temporary permit or something, maybe, nothing too rough, you not planning a career of it, just get you started."

"I'll go tomorrow and ask," Faye said. She was excited. She liked the idea.

"No, not now, wait now, I be leaning on you for the little while of it longer if you can stand to stay. Besides, we got to find you a place. Been lookin' . . . Still lookin'."

"Me too."

"Been prayin' about it."

"Me too."

"Gal, you shinin' like it was Christmas."

"I'm not scared," Faye said. "I'm not scared of anything."

"Rightly so," Palma agreed. She had just one other subject to bring up for review. She hated to spoil Faye's good mood, and she said so.

"Go ahead and try," Faye said. She didn't think anything could.

"What you doin' the Fourth?"

"I don't care. What?"

"Lissen, don't you answer it yet!" Palma urged her. She struggled to her feet. Had to roll to her knees and grapple herself upright. She brought Faye an envelope. The letter Tom had brought that afternoon. "Been holding this back; he said do what I think best, up to me."

"Who?"

"Tom."

"So, what is it?"

"Old Mrs. Rios been sick again."

"No way," Faye said. She got up, walked around the room, and came back to her chair.

"Nobody told me," Faye said. She was thinking, I never asked. I never even asked! As though she didn't exist as soon as I forgot about her! "Sick?"

"Ten days in ICU this time."

"I can't go live in that house. I can't," Faye said. "Please don't ask me why. She knows why."

Palma said, "I hear that."

She eased herself down in the rocker, just laid the envelope on her stomach in plain sight, but never mentioned it again. Faye seemed to be looking at a magazine. After a page or two she looked up. "Did she die?"

"I'm glad you asked that," Palma said. "And I'm glad to be able to say no, she did not."

She rocked awhile longer.

Faye finally laid the magazine down. Had to ask, craved to know, had to know, "What's that envelope?"

"For you." Palma handed it to her. "Feels like an invitation."

"Faye," the envelope said. She hadn't even put Faye's last name. Señora Rios's handwriting was usually bold. This looked a little withered, uneven, and had no flourishes or underlinings.

Inside, a single folded, typed note. No flourishes there either. "Look here," it began. "I never mean to scare you away from this your home. All good pleasant day Fourth of July God willing it we make a picnic, see you again one more last time, okay? You no have to come here, I come there! South Beach. Big day for America. Big day for every body. Do me the favor? Last request, your meaning well Marcela." All that was typed. After it, handwritten, one word more. Faye couldn't believe her eyes. "Forgive."

Faye picked up the phone.

"It's three a.m." Palma warned.

Faye laid the phone back down.

"It doesn't sound like her," Faye said, showing Palma the note. Palma read it twice. "Is she for real?"

"This sounds just like she talks. Like a phone call. Except for that last word."

"Tom told me what she wanted," Palma said. "You going to do it?"

Faye couldn't figure how to answer. "A picnic?"

"It's only a picnic," Palma said. "You can bike up there from here and just coast on home if you hate it. No big thing."

"What if Captain Rios—"

"Vic?" Palma shrugged. "So what? Whole island's going to be there. This is the biggie for us, it's our Macy's Parade and Santa."

Faye looked blank.

"Thanksgiving? New York?" Palma clued. She could see that Faye didn't know anything about it. She said, "From now on I'm gonna pretend you an exchange student from outer space."

Faye didn't think that was funny. "I am doing what I can," Faye said fiercely. "I read books and books. I read newspapers. I read *Time*." This was the first time, at Palma's, that she'd lost her cool.

"I think you should go," Palma said.

Stunned, Faye didn't reply. She just got up and went to the closet where her little suitcase was stored. She headed for the nursery to pack. Amazed, Palma rocked herself forward and launched herself out of the chair and into hot pursuit. "Chile! Chile!" she cried. "Listen! Not *go away*, but *go to the picnic!*"

Faye set the suitcase down and started to cry. Not dainty tears, but huge, racking sobs of relief and frustration.

Elven woke up with all the commotion. He came to the door of his room. When he saw the lights on and the little suitcase in the middle of the floor, he ran to Palma, excited, solicitous, disoriented, disorganized. "Is it time? You hatching out?" He headed for the phone.

"Don't you dare call Zeb Leonard!" Palma said, slapping the receiver out of Elven's grip. That woke him up. She grabbed him and hugged him and said she was sorry, but no, no, it wasn't time. "Everything's all right, no babies tonight," she crooned, then clapped her hand to her mouth when she realized she had said *babies*. Plural. Elven didn't notice. Neither did Faye.

"Not that you could call him, this time of night," she said, her mind tracking in old grooves. "Not that I would if I could," she grudged.

Elven said, "Momma, you know he say call him at Lupo's. Somebody go fetch him."

He stood by the rocker, where Palma had settled again. He touched her on the shoulder. She absently laid her hand on his. "Good night," he said.

Faye walked him to his room so she could see how Bob Cat was curled up on the foot of the bed. But Bob had stretched, and now he blocked the bed diagonally. Elven slipped in, and parked himself parallel to the cat. Faye helped him arrange his pillow. Then she went back to put her suitcase away.

Palma was still sitting there rocking and muttering. She looked up at Faye and sighed. "I wish you could drive a car," she said. "Been planning it all the time these babies goin' to be born in daytime, on time, in due time, but what if the Lord play some kind of prank on me?"

"I can't drive in daytime either," Faye said.

"I'm not due till the seventh. Gives us three weeks. Who knows what you can learn in three weeks?"

"Never," Faye said.

"Don't do no good to say *never*," Palma said. She sounded regretful, like someone who knew.

PART IV

THE FOURTH ITSELF FROM
CAN TO CAN'T

When Señora Rios woke on the Fourth of July in her good mood—as good a mood as she ever had—she was up early enough to make the coffee, scooping decaf into her MOKA pot and Bustelo into Tom's. She hummed. She ignored the wheelchair. When Tom woke, he heard what he thought were moans (Señora Rios was not a soprano) and thumps: the quad cane had bold rubber tips that she got the good of as she stumped it back and forth across the kitchen. Her song was vaguely operatic, but mainly monotone. She trilled, from time to time. She was trilling when Tom double-timed it down the stairs and pushed the kitchen door open. Gave it such a shove it swung open and hit the wall and rebounded. He didn't even feel its slap on his shoulder, he was so busy looking for trouble.

And there she stood, peering down into the crock of *escabeche*, crooning as she tucked its calendar towel back over it.

Tom's first word of the day—"Damn!"—came in a gust of relief and exasperation, and then "What goes?" with a chip on his shoulder.

"This goes," she said, sliding a basket along the counter. She had several things already gathered for their picnic. Tom looked at the various things she had prepared. He looked around for things he had expected to see but didn't.

"What else?" he asked, suspicious.

She was truly sad. "No *pulpetas*," she told him.

"I believe you," he said. But he looked anyway, in every pan on the range and in the refrigerator. She was not to have boiled eggs on her new diet. "You didn't have to cook anything," he told her again. "I know we can get everything at the market."

"*Escabeche* last week," she explained, as though the rules had been entirely different then, in June. She handed him the list she had made. All Cuban things; he wasn't going to be able to run by the mini-mart except for ice. Because she knew him, knew his American tastes, she specified, "No hot dogs, no deal peekle, no cheeps." She excused herself, touching her chest, reminding him that such things were bad for the heart. "Very corrosive," she said.

They had decided to grill fish steaks instead. While Tom was gone, she went out in the backyard—down those steps one by one--and gathered a windfall harvest of avocados. It would not be a picnic without a salad of *aguacate*. Avocados were forbidden too, but she knew better. *Aguacate* has much good, she was muttering as she picked them off the lawn. Good as aloe for the skin. She rubbed the peels of these across her face, as cool and smooth as a smile, and if it was good for the outside, it would be as good for the inside, and if it was good for the inside, wasn't that where the heart was? *"Cierto,"* she said. Case closed. She made a splendid salad.

Señora Rios had been so ill and now was so very much better. She liked being home, being back on her feet. She still had the wheelchair, but she used it as a kind of walker, pushing it along ahead of her through Tom's house. Sometimes when she had done a little too much, she'd sit in the chair and walk it along, digging her slipper heels into the floor and using her hands on the wheels only at the doorsills and edges of rugs, to help herself over the humps. She did not need the chair. She was supposed to rest on her bed when she rested and walk on her feet when she went. Every day she was to walk; every morning and afternoon she was to rest. She did not need the chair, but Vic had rented it for a month and she would have the good of it. She intended, in fact, to take it on the picnic. She believed it might help the day roll smoothly. She was feeling so well she thought she might by her healthfulness lose the leverage of pitifulness, and she dreaded seeing Faye again without some mitigation or appeal to Faye's mercy.

The quad cane just didn't have the charisma the wheelchair did. She remembered seeing Faye in the hall at Greenhill, kneeling beside someone's chair. Yes, the chair was a good idea—an ingratiation, a buffer, a silent plea—and, if all went well (and it would, Señora Rios thought, with the confidence of a saint having said her prayers)—a throne.

She wanted to wear her red-flowered shawl, red on black, with a red silk fringe. It was downstairs. So were her hair color and comb. She had promised Tom before God she would not go down those stairs. She had had an aunt in Pinar del Río who had a little monkey who'd fetch things. Not always the things they sent it for, but sometimes things from other houses! That gave Señora Rios an idea. She thought, I am as clever as that little monkey. She went out the kitchen door and down those steps, about which she had made no promises, and eased herself, balancing with the cane and with a hand held against the boards of Tom's house, around to the door of the basement room. The door was locked and chained. She had done it herself in a time that now seemed as distant as childhood. She still carried her keys on her belt, but she couldn't do a thing about the inside security chain. She tried everything. She finally used her cane handle to break a pane in the door. She reached through and let herself back into her own life. She kicked the glass out of the way. She would have the pane replaced next week, when Tom was away. He need never know.

She had a strong urge to lie down on her bed and take that morning rest, but she resisted. She felt a little keyed up anyway, from excitement for the day and that thimbleful of Tom's real coffee she had sneaked. Mostly *espuma*, she had told herself, mostly foam.

She rummaged in her cabinets till she located the cosmetics she only occasionally used. She didn't want too many today, just enough to look better than she did, but not enough to look as good as she might. There was still some hair color left from the bottle she had tried on Faye. There is, she mused as she worked the color through to the ends with her special comb, a fine cosmetic line between valiant and pitiful. She wanted a look that blended both. She smoothed on powder, avoiding the circles under her eyes. Powder would only turn them into fish-skin change purses. She opted for sunglasses instead. She sharpened her lip-liner and applied it, set it with powder, then leaned toward the mirror, frowning. She had never liked to paint herself. She always thought of Jezebel going to the dogs. But she admired Jezebel, too. For going in style.

She filled in her outlined lips with care and bright color. Not with her usual straight-across Zorro strokes, but patiently, a tender, full-court Gioconda smile, as bright as the roses in her shawl. Done. Now she considered her options: she had promised Tom she would not descend those stairs; she had not made any promises about ascending them. She decided to lock and chain the door, filling the broken pane with a shirtboard. The curtain covered it. Then she went upstairs with her shawl in her lap, sitting her way upwards, step by step, her heart light and humming its opera of indestructible plans for the future of the Rios family, her words a hymn of recuperation, a game, as usual of words and wit and invincibility: *Vuelvo en mí . . . unh! Vuelvo por mí . . . unh! Vuelvo atrás . . . Unh! Vuelvo sobre mí . . . unh!* And with a laugh, *Vuelvo a la carga . . . Unh-huh!*

She reached the top step none the worse for wear. She stood, brushed the back of her shirt, and swirled the shawl around her. She was seated at the kitchen table, writing a letter to the op-ed page about Indian Ocean shrimp, when Tom got back with the food. There she sat, all black and red. A storm warning on a perfectly clear day.

"Ready," she said.

   South Beach Park, midafternoon, Fourth of July. That was the plan. But even though Tom had figured "no sooner than two-thirty," which would allow the morning crowds, the parade crush and traffic jam and overload parking to clear, and the picnickers to have begun to pack and go on to other events of the day, Tom had figured wrong.

"Was good plan," Señora Rios said again, as they inched along in Tom's truck—no air conditioning—but her enthusiasm had begun to wane. The traffic was impossible, there was no parking, and every table under the oaks had a family entrenched, enjoying the day, the food, and the breeze from tide-turn. There was no place even to double-park to wait till someone cleared off. Señora Rios saw no one she knew. Certainly she did not see Vic, and she did not see Faye and it did not please her to have nothing to do about it but sigh. They had circled the main lot by inches, and the additional lot and the police-taped, one-day-only overflow lot too. Tom said, "Let's go to other side." Not of the lot, of the island.

He stopped, set the brake, and stood on the running board to look around. Hoping for someone he could leave a message with. Traffic piled up behind him; his old green truck was the olive in the bottleneck.

After the first person tapped the horn, another joined. Soon a chorus. Tom seemed to be deaf. When he finally spotted Elven, he slipped back into the cab and drove the truck up onto the sandy grass just past the last handicap space (full) and stopped with his front bumper just touching the tow-zone warning post. Cars began to roar past him to fill the gap he'd left. Some made comments, some made gestures. Tom waved. He said, "Right back," to Señora Rios and left her the keys, as though if she needed to she could move the truck. "In an *Ave Maria*," he promised, and was gone, loping off through the crowds, whistling for Elven.

It was already hot. It got hotter. Señora Rios opened her door. She stepped to the ground, and looked around. She fanned herself with a map. Fanned herself even faster when she spotted the mounted policeman moving through the crowd, headed her way. Tom's truck did not have a handicap decal or plate or anything, and besides that, it was in a forbidden zone, not a handicap space. Señora Rios felt her heart tighten. She stood looking in at the picnic things in the truck bed, all of them packed with such happy hope. The grill for the fish, the coolers, the folding chaises, and her wheelchair. That gave her an idea.

She climbed up onto the running board and tugged at the wheelchair. She couldn't lift it over the side. But she thought it could be more conspicuous. She got it to its wheels; it just fit in the channels in the truck bed. She had to move the other things around to make room. The mounted policeman was getting closer. She had hoped he would turn and patrol the other way, but he was definitely coming in her direction. Señora Rios climbed up over the side of Tom's truck and seated herself in the wheelchair. It faced outward, its rubber handles squeaking against the cab window. The sun was stern. She wrapped the shawl over her hair and folded her hands in her lap. She sat motionless behind her wraparound sunglasses and watched the policeman come on. He did.

When he was exactly alongside Tom's truck, his pretty brown mare rolling the bit between her teeth, Señora Rios and the policeman were eye to eye. The policeman had on sunglasses, also, but his were silvered. She couldn't see past them. The horse bunched and backed, at the policman's slight tug, then he let her head come back down. He studied the contents of the truckbed, including Señora Rios. He opened the lid of the nearer ice chest, saying, "What have we got?" He peered in. The fish to be broiled peered back, their icy bed steaming in the sudden sun.

"Sorry, buds," he said, and shut the lid on them. He was smiling. "How you gonna fix 'em?"

"*¿Cómo?*"

"Yeah, how?" He tapped the grill with his mechanical pencil. "Broil? How long? A little oil? A litle *mojo?*"

He pronounced it correctly—Cuban soul, not *norteamericano* voodoo.

"You ess-speak it?" she said.

"High school," he said. "Still learning. My girlfriend," he explained.

Señora Rios looked at him. She thought he sounded sincere. She thought he might enjoy her grandmother's recipe for *sofrito*. Just the one little extra thing that made it the best. She explained how it was the simplest thing. She explained—she didn't remember how this got into the story, but as she told it, he listened, so she was not sorry she thought of it also—how her grandmother had washed the crabs. "Optional," she said. She saw he did not know the word for crabs in Spanish, that was the part he did not understand. She said, "Craps!" and he laughed, and she said it again, "Craps!" and made hand gestures, like great claws, and he seemed even more excited, and said, "Craps!" and laughed and made the gestures too. She showed him how the crabs fought, as her grandmother took them one by one and scrubbed them in fresh water. He took out his book and began writing. He was shaking his head. "That's a good one," he said. His pencil clicked its lead out and he wrote. His pencil did not have an eraser.

Here is a man, Señora Rios was thinking, who either makes no mistakes or else makes a great many.

She was sorry she had told him about the crabs. How unpredictable they could be, how they strayed. She feared he had only been indulging her, teasing her along, so she could make a fool of herself in this hot sun. She feared he lacked *sinceridad*. She had thought he had *sinceridad* when he took off his sunglasses; but now she realized he had taken them off and hung them by their sidepiece in his pocket only in order to see what he was writing. Not to appear less menacing.

She looked out to the sea. She did not turn her head back to him. "How much is ticket?" she asked.

"How long you been here?" he said.

She watched a fly settle on the little bundle of American flags he had in his saddlebag, their tops just poking out. The fly settled on the very tip, on the gold plastic knob. It flew off and came back and settled on the same flag again. "How much is ticket?" she asked again.

"No ticket, ma'am, Fourth of July is free, parade, parking, everything except the barbecue, and you're not going to need that with those fish. Fireworks tonight, they're free too."

She turned and looked at him then.

"What I'm asking, ma'am, is not how long you been *here*, but how long you *been* here!"

Was he crazy! She listened in her head to the question again. She couldn't find the trick. She couldn't find the answer. "Fifteen minutes," she said, shaving it only a little.

"I mean in the States. *Los Estados Unidos*."

Oh! She took off her sunglasses and looked at him in the killing light. "Since Playa Girón."

He whistled. "Bay of Pigs," he said. "Jesus. I read all about that."

"Is twice as true!" she told him.

"Damn," he said, considering.

"*Americana,*" she explained, tapping her chest. "*Naturalizada.* Taxpayer, whole bit," she said. "Taxpayer," she repeated.

He said, "Ma'am, ma'am," and shook her hand she had flung out. Respectful.

He was finished writing.

"You want me to sign book?"

She was still suspicious. She knew a signature was required, even on warnings. The officer said, "Sure," and handed her his book and pencil. When she looked, she saw he had been writing on the back of the ticket, he hadn't filled in anything on the front. He had been writing down the recipe she gave him. When she realized that, she put her sunglasses back on.

She had trouble with the pencil. It was slender and swift. He helped her steady the book. She was surprised to see that her writing was trembly. She handed it back. "I smutch it," she apologized. He looked at her writing—bold in size, intense in slant, and amazing in message: "Sofrito de Gracia García de Rusto, abuela materna de Marcela Consuelo García de Rios, by grace of God wife and witness to Oscar Carrasco Rios, hero." And below, in all the remaining space, "Marcela, QBSM."

"Okay," he said, taken aback, pleased. He said so. "Pleased to—" and then pointed to her signature. "What is this?" He thought it might be an order, like a knighthood or medal.

"Marcela," she said, thinking he meant her name.

"No, this: kay bay essie em . . ."

"QBSM?" she laid her finger on the initials.

"Yes," he said. "*Sí.*"

"Is gesture," she said. She could see Tom coming. Not in fact, but in reflection in the policeman's sunglasses. "Who kiss your hand," she said, "*Quien besa su mano.*" She showed him.

Tom stepped up at that exact moment, seeing his mother, shawled in roses, seated like a festival saint in the back of his truck, in the wheelchair with five more days to go on its rental, a small bright American flag in one hand, the officer's hand in the other raised to her carmine lips.

"No ticket needed," she said to Tom, as though that explained everything.

At South Beach Park, Elven did what he had promised Tom—to keep a sharp eye out and to wave 'em on . . . Vic got the message. He arrived a long time before Faye. Elven knew where she was, and why she was late (cooking a pie and cooking a second one when the first one didn't work out), but he had promised his momma—and Faye—he wouldn't tell. It made Palma uneasy to leave Faye cooking, but she and Cliffie and the children—and Zeb, he was included too—had made plans for an early start. All morning long, Palma had kept looking back toward her house beyond the near village, afraid she'd see smoke or a firetruck.

When Cliffie argued for calmer nerves and confidence, Palma said, "Woman, she burnt that first meringue black as ashfault."

They sent Elven, finally, to see. He met Faye walking. She had the pie in a box. A tall box, the kind of used carton people give away puppies in, or try to. Elven lifted himself up on his toes and peeked over the edge. It looked good. Bits of sugar dew had begun to bead on the peaks and dales of the meringue. Elven said, "Wish you made two."

"I did."

"I mean, and didn't ruin the first one."

Faye looked down in the box, pleased. "It looks okay, doesn't it?"

"Did you turn off the oven?"

"I did."

"You sure?"

"Yes."

"Then that saves me a little time," Elven said, and turned back on the road. Faye walked beside him.

"They waiting on me?"

Elven remembered Tom's message. He said, "You may want to go back and get your bike."

"We're almost there," Faye said. "I'm fine."

"Tom moved the party on around to the river. Over by Sweet Chapel." Faye stopped walking.

"It's more than a mile," Elven said. "Will that pie keep?"

Faye turned back to Palma's, to get her bike. "It'll keep," she assured him. "I'm the one keeping it."

"While you're there, check that oven again," Elven said. Then he jogged on back to South Beach.

Señora Rios didn't see Vic when he finally drove up. She had set her chair where it faced the green, the handles pointed toward the shimmering river. Vic parked in the chapel lot, but on the other side, and came across the turf so silently she didn't hear him, or suspect. She had stood up to watch Tom light the grill. He was not patient with charcoal, and used a great deal of the lighter, so the first *whoompf* and roar were followed by a tower and roil of black smoke. The leaves overhead, twenty feet above the flames, shook in the updraft. In a moment things settled down. Before Señora Rios could find her seat again, Vic grabbed her from behind. Señora Rios cried out, but she knew him; she was pleased, not startled. She beat at him unstrenuously, joyously. And turned so she was embracing him, dancing a little, always a bit of the coquette with Vic. Over his shoulder she saw Marnie Fortner coming carefully on—picking and choosing where to walk in preposterous heels, as usual. Marnie was carrying flowers, a tissue of them. She paused, waiting politely till Vic had finished greeting his mother, then came on.

"Where's the fatted calf?" Vic asked, stepping over to where Tom was tending the grill.

"You have said it," Tom agreed.

Vic was a little tense, because of Marnie. Señora Rios had said, "*Nunca,*" refusing all hospitality, but that meant indoors; no roof here. "Sky's the limit," was Vic's motto from way back. He was relieved that Faye wasn't there. She made him nervous too. What he thought of as "that whole business."

"See how much better I am?" Señora Rios was saying to Vic. "Last month this would kill me." Maybe she meant the picnic, but she was looking at Marnie when she said it. Marnie had on an excellent Panama hat, flat-brimmed, not on her head but swinging over her arm by a bright scarf. She obviously did not need the hat to protect her from the sun; she had sought it, on every apparent—and most of it was—inch of her skin, which was tanned like leather beneath the freckles that still showed on her back, her arms, and her hands.

Señora Rios looked away from that advertisement of bare flesh. She appeared to sway. Vic rolled the wheelchair up behind her, in case she fell, an offer, not an opinion. He knew his mother's pride.

"I no need this," she said. Maybe she meant the chair. Her smile smiled on. Her sunglasses hid the rest. After a moment she did sit in the chair, but without emergency, queenlike, without looking around to see if it was back there at all. When she was thus enthroned, Marnie handed her the flowers. A tiny paper flag, such as might decorate a cupcake, stood hilt-deep in a carnation on its toothpick pole. Señora Rios studied that particular carnation, then laid the sheaf aside, in the sun. "Thank you," she said.

Marnie said, "Let me."

Señora Rios looked at her, surprised. Even from behind the sunglasses, it came out high beam.

"They need water," Marnie explained.

Señora Rios nodded, as though this were a major point well taken. "*Bueno*," she said, "they suffer," and with her bare hands she seemed about to put them out of their misery. She wrung the flowers from their stems, halfway up their length, and stuffed them in a plastic cup filled with ice. They were not ugly, but the cup was.

"One thing I never expect," Señora Rios said. "I think I plan for everything. Then you bring flowers." She put the accent on *you*, not on *flowers*.

Marnie was no amateur at hardball, but she sat down, having struck out for now. She leaned toward Vic, but didn't touch him as he did something delicate with the radio and its batteries. "Wrong size," he said.

Tom had some in the truck.

"I'll go," Marnie said, leaping up. She took her shoes off for speed and set them on the bench beside Vic, as though saving her place. Tom's truck was on the far side of the clearing; he'd dropped off his mother and the food and the grill, and driven it back to the road. She ran for a little bit between the tracks his tires had left on the grass. After a while she walked.

"Is Faye?" Señora Rios was looking toward the chapel, where some people were walking around outside. A tour-bus load, and a folk tram. They could hear the guides, amplified.

"No," Vic said, scanning the crowd.

"*Where?*" Marnie yelled, rather than run all that way back. She was on the far side of the truck, on the running board, sorting through the debris on Tom's dash. Tom went to help.

Before he got there, Marnie had opened the cab door and begun looking in the glove compartment. She had the gun in her hand when Tom walked up.

"Is it—"

"Not loaded," Tom was about to say, but Marnie had already pointed toward Vic—across the hundred yards of intervening centipede grass—and pulled the trigger. Five, six times, nine times.

"Don't have to fire a gun to test it's not loaded," Tom said.

"I'm the sort who does."

"You wouldn't have missed, if you were closer."

"No lie," she agreed. "If we were closer."

He found the batteries and gave them to her. He wouldn't let her get the box of ammunition open. He put it back in the glove box and locked it. Along with the gun.

"You don't like me," she said. "What makes you think I care?"

She and Vic had already been drinking. Tom didn't argue with her. "I am sorry for you," he said.

"A free country," she said. "Six more weeks, I'm free, too." A hard wild look came into her eyes.

"I heard about that," Tom said.

"He doesn't love me," Marnie said suddenly, desperately.

Tom didn't ask who. Tom didn't say anything. They walked back to the picnic. Marnie stopped to comb through a weedy patch of dollarweed and clover. She thought she had seen one with four leaves. "If there is one, I usually see it right off . . . I don't need it," she said, straightening and catching up with Tom. "I was born lucky."

"You will live a long time," Tom predicted.

The coals were ready. Vic had his little knife on his keyring open, and was cutting the seal on the wine. Marnie had a corkscrew in her pocketbook. The cork pulled with a slight pop. "Let it breathe," Vic said, setting the bottle in the shade. Marnie held out a plastic cup. "Pour," she said. "I'll do the breathing."

Tom helped Señora Rios set the places. "Is time," she fretted, glancing from the gray coals toward the lane.

"Maybe she had a flat," Tom said. He had taught Faye how to fix one, had made sure she had a kit and pump.

Señora Rios had her opera glasses, always carried them. She took them from her handbag and scanned the chapel area. Looked like a wedding party. They were posing by the bronze gates. One of the children rang the bell, climbed the wall to catch the rope, and jumped down with it. Marnie turned to see. Vic didn't.

Tom checked his watch. "She knew," he said again. "Elven wouldn't have missed her. He found her. She'll be here."

"She promise?" Señora Rios asked.

"Yes."

"Then she be here soon," Señora Rios said. "Start cooking," she suggested.

"*Justo*," Tom said. Impressed by her faith. "That's fair." His mother's certainty cheered him.

Marnie leaned over and whispered in Vic's ear. He pointed toward the chapel. "Rear door. They won't mind," he said.

Marnie stood. The bench had left marks on her thighs below her tennis-length skirt. Her panties, they all knew it now, were high-cut and ice blue. She laughed in false mortification, and gave her clothes a settling shake. "Oops," she said. She was a little drunk. She tied her hat under her chin, made a flustered exit. "It's a long way," she said, hoping, but Vic didn't go with her.

When she had gone from earshot, Señora Rios said, "Faye knew Vic would be here?"

"I told her," Tom said.

Vic didn't say anything. He looked away.

"Maybe she come already and see *la Señora*—"

"Fortner," Vic said.

Vic didn't look away from the marsh. Just sat staring. Blind as a statue.

"She don't give a damn about that Marnie," Tom said easily. "Why should she?"

That brought Vic's head around. Just in time to spot Faye walking her bike across the grass from the nature trail, an obvious shortcut it had never occurred to any of them to check. Faye had balanced the cardboard box with the pie in her newsboy's wire basket. She had her house key dangling from a ribbon around her neck. She wore a look of triumph. It had been a bit bumpy on part of the trail, and she had feared the meringue would crack. It didn't.

She set the box on the grass. She had kept the pie chilled with ice cubes in a plastic bag. She left it in its cool nest atop the bag, and tucked the flaps of the box in. Not a word of greeting till all this was done, then, "Tom," she said, and "Captain Rios," she said, and "Ma'am," she said, as Marnie came back drying her hands on her skirt, straddling her place on the bench beside Vic, and resting her bare back against Vic's arm.

Faye greeted Señora Rios last of all. Knelt by her wheelchair and tried to see past those dark green glasses.

"You need my comb!" Señora Rios said.

Faye caught Señora Rios's hand where it was trying to smooth Faye's hair. Low, between the two of them, for no other ears or eyes, she made as private an apology as possible. "Palma told me if I say I'm sorry you will forgive me?" Before Señora Rios could speak, Faye said, "But I'm not sorry I ran away, I won't say I am, but I'm sorry I hurt you, that's what, and I'm sorry if—I'm sorry I wasn't there when you got sick and sorry if I made you sick, but I didn't know you were—I mean *again*—I mean, *really*—"

"Faye," Señora Rios said. "*Me alegro, me alegro* . . . you making me happy now, is enough, I feel it too, I tell you."

"Then we will be all right?"

"*Compañeras.*"

"If I don't go back?"

"Go back, *no*," Señora Rios said. "*Adelante.* We go *on*."

She got to her feet. She and Faye embraced. They walked off together, deeper into the shade beyond the first trees. They paused near a strangler fig. Señora Rios again put her hands to Faye's face. Touched the hair, the cheek. She gave Faye something—it flashed white in the gloom. Again they embraced.

At the picnic table, they made no effort not to stare. Marnie said something she thought was funny. No one laughed. Vic said, "I don't know how to dance to this! I thought—"

"Maybe she hypnotized her," Marnie said. "Like a snake and a squirrel." The image struck her as hilarious. She laughed and laughed. She picked up her cup, poured more wine, and drank to her own wit.

When Faye and Señora Rios walked back, the grilling fish were almost done. So was the picnic, if they had just known. Faye didn't have a pocket for Señora Rios's gift. She set it by her place at the table.

"Oh, an angel wing!" Marnie exclaimed, reaching across to pick up the shell. "That's the biggest one I have ever seen."

Señora Rios reached it first and picked it up again, casually; she did not snatch it away. It wasn't awkwardly done, or pointedly, but Marnie's eyes narrowed. She took the hint. Instantly she said, "When a woman starts giving things away, they say she's getting old, or ready to die."

"Have heard so myself," Señora Rios agreed. "Must not be true. You no give anything away."

For a moment she thought it was worth it, then Vic sighed and stood, without haste, but with a certain dignity. Without a word, he took Marnie by the arm and collected her shoes, and they began to walk off. Tom sighed, and took the fish off the coals.

Faye had been about to sit down. She paused, halfway, as Marnie came back.

Marnie pointed at Señora Rios. "If you were a man," she said.

"Even then, especially then," Señora Rios said, "I never be interested in floating rib like you."

Vic got a closer hold on Marnie's arm.

"*What?*" Marnie said. "*What* did she say, may I ask?"

"Start without us," Vic said. They left. Marnie kept looking over her shoulder. Vic didn't look back at all.

Señora Rios had nothing else to add. She stood at the head of the table, fanning flies off her avocado salad. She was still smiling. Faye eased down onto the bench. She kept going over it in her mind, trying to figure and file it. "Will they be back?" she asked, finally.

"All these food," Señora Rios said, beginning to realize what she had done. She was pale. She sat. Not in the wheelchair now, but on the bench, and not to rest, but to reach. She didn't hurry. She took up the paper cup with the flowers in it and looked at them one last time, then flung them behind her into the shadows. They lay brightly strewn. Blackbirds came at once, and grackles, and a gull, quick as that, to see. They pecked at the blooms, looking for easy food.

Señora Rios got up again. For a moment they thought she had changed her mind, when she stooped by the carnations, but then she retrieved only the little American flag on its toothpick. She stood twirling it between her fingers. Tom reminded her—with the grill now covered and the *pargo* on its platter—"He said, 'Don't wait.' " He ate some of the fish and bread.

"*Seguro*," she said. "Is true. But he will be back." She sounded very confident.

Tom shook his head. "*Madre*," he said, not unkindly.

"Oh, yes," she said. She held up the proof. "He forgot his car keys, him!"

Obviously, Tom didn't want Vic to come back. He held his hands to his face and whistled. It carried. The second time, Vic turned. Tom took the keys from Señora Rios and held them up and shook them.

"Meet to him at the halfway," Señora Rios said, handing the keys to Faye.

"No," Tom said. He intercepted the keys. He hefted them. It looked as though Vic wasn't coming back for them, but was sending Marnie—or wasn't able to stop her from coming. "Maybe I'll throw them," he said.

For some reason, Faye hoped he would, and not toward Vic, but into the marsh. Just to see what would happen then. Amazed at herself, and repenting, she said, "Tom, I'll run," trying to reach the keys. Tom held them higher than her head, and was already on his way.

Still, Faye said, "Me."

Tom said, "Me."

Señora Rios said, "Tell him . . ."

"I'll tell him," Tom said. "You bet I'll tell him." He did not intend to hurry. When Vic saw it was Tom bringing the keys, he called Marnie back and they sat on the shady cemetery wall, smoking, letting Tom be the one to roast in the sun. Vic lit Marnie's cigarette from his cigarillo. They sat laughing. Marnie said something that Vic enjoyed very much. When Tom got close enough to hear, she hushed and Vic stood. "Dead in the water," he said. "Couldn't get out of sight," holding out his hand for the keys. But Tom gave them to Marnie instead. "Crank it up, turn on max air," he suggested. He had a thing or two to say, and that ought to keep her out of it while he did. But Marnie said, "We've got plans."

Tom looked at her. "Cool off," he said.

If he was hoping to make her mad so she'd just put it in gear and drive off, leaving Vic, he was disappointed. Tom and Vic walked as they talked, around the far side of the chapel, to be out of sight of their mother. "Why didn't you just stay home?" Tom asked. "This was a nice day."

"Elsewhere, maybe," Vic said.

"Don't ever bring her anywhere near where we are!" Tom said. "You insult your mother, your family, your—"

"Wife?" Vic said. "That accidental virgin?" He laughed. "Fashions change."

Tom knocked him down.

Just like that. Flattened him with one punch. Vic's head almost hit the wall, but he landed safe on the turf. It wasn't so bad. He waited for Tom to give him a hand up. When he was on his feet again, Marnie had driven around the lot, to find them. When she saw what was going on, she reached over and opened the passenger door and said, "Get in!"

Vic brushed off his clothes.

"*Momentito,*" Tom told her. He slammed the door. She rolled down the window.

"Vic," she pleaded.

"Drive it around the lot," Tom said. "Slow."

She looked at Vic. He nodded, once. She managed the gears without a nip or bark. Tom thought that was what Vic was thinking about. He braced himself for Vic's attention, when it returned. He figured Vic had a turn coming. Neither brother had ever been afraid of a fight, though it had been years since they'd fought each other. As it happened, Vic didn't need his fists to floor Tom; he did it with the simplest truth, plainly spoken.

"You love her, that's what it is." Not accusing. Still watching Marnie slowly circle the lot. Comprehending it as slowly as that, as though it had taken Tom's clip to his chin to knock the light on.

They stared at each other.

Finally, Tom said, "She's married."

"Well, that's the problem for both of us, isn't it?"

"Can't see it holding you back," Tom said.

Vic laughed. "You can have—"

"Don't say it," Tom said. "You don't give and I don't take."

Marnie was back, easing the car to a stop in second, clutch in. She stalled the engine. They could hear grit falling off the tires, oil dripping back into the pan. She cranked it again, tapped the horn. Not a blast, a little tap. She was leaning over, looking at Vic's face. She couldn't see any place bruised or broken.

"All your life, such a Boy Scout," Vic told Tom. He walked around to the driver's side and Marnie slid over. Vic adjusted the mirrors, tilted the wheel his way. "This is rich," he told Tom. "This is biblical. This is one for the Pope!" No other farewell, just a sinister salute, two fingers to his right brow, thumb up, sighting down their barrel cool and slow, aiming right at Tom's heart.

When Tom got back to the picnic, Faye and his mother had broken camp. They had chucked it all into Tom's truck bed once again. Faye had driven the truck over the grass to their table. Tom always left the keys hanging. She had had a couple of lessons. Palma's car was automatic. Faye couldn't change gears yet, so she backed it, all the way. Faye would never have tried it, but Señora Rios kept saying, "Please." She did not seem at all well, but she wouldn't let Faye do all the packing. Finally she got in the cab and lay back, eyes closed. She spoke to Faye without opening them. Finally, Faye rolled her bike around to the door by Señora Rios, and stood vigil. Because of the way she had parked the truck, she couldn't see whether Tom was coming back.

All Señora Rios had said, as they cleared the table, was "Pity." It seemed the day's epitaph. She had taken one of her heart pills. There was a breeze. Señora Rios's thoughts drifted, connected, dispersed. She'd say, "Faye," and Faye would say, "Yes," and that was how she knew she was not alone, that Faye had not gone. Señora Rios had told her to go.

"He's back!" Faye said suddenly.

Señora Rios's eyes broke open wide. It was Tom, not Vic. Señora Rios roused herself to ask, using the plural *you*, "Apologize?"

Tom got in the truck, considering. He had not said a word to Faye, or even looked at her.

"We agreed," he said finally.

Faye hoped Tom was not mad about clearing the picnic, or about her backing his truck over. She said, "You will have a good supper tonight. All on ice, now. I made a pie. Key lime! The salad is still beautiful . . ." She fell silent in the face of his. He checked the rearview. "I'll get my pan later," she said.

"*Esta noche?*" Señora Rios said suddenly, her eyes flashing open again.

"No," Faye said. "Another day."

Tom glanced Faye's way, then out the windshield. He had his fist on the ignition key, ready.

"Please could I have my shell?" She had set it on the dash out of harm's way. Tom handed it to his mother, who presented it to Faye.

"Unless . . ." Faye offered. Tom cranked the truck.

"Is yours," Señora Rios said. She held Faye's hand for a moment, wouldn't let her go. Turned that hand over and inspected Faye's fingernails, not painted, not long, but not bitten, and clean except for bits of paint from Palma's nursery stenciling project, which they had been working on the night before. She pinched Faye's hand between her own gnarled thumb and index finger, circled Faye's wrist with her own grip, testing. "Five more pounds," she told Faye. She tapped Faye's right cheek with her finger. "Not an ounce more than. *Perfecta.* But you must do something about that hair."

It made Faye feel sad. Like seeing that rabbit on the side of the road, paralyzed, but still running with its front feet.

Tom pulled the truck into gear.

"Fireworks?" Faye called, hoping. They were leaving without one word from Tom.

"Already," Señora Rios said. "Enough," Señora Rios said.

Faye stood there a long time after Tom's truck rattled out of sight. She started to pedal back to Palma's along the nature trail, but she met joggers wall to wall; the Fun Run had begun. She turned and pedaled back across the field. She could see Tom's footprints in the dry grass. She was thirsty. She didn't feel hunger. She paused at the chapel garden; there was a drinking fountain, artesian, and she drank it, though it was sulfurous, and tepid. She splashed it on her face, and sat for a few minutes on the bench made of wrought iron shaped like oak leaves and acorns. The paint had weathered off, like the color on Señora Rios's lips.

A family posed by the chapel door for a snapshot. The child pushed his face against the grillework, pretending to be a lion in a zoo. He roared. He ran around, looking at everything, not staying on the paths, tearing through the flower beds, calling, "Is there a cannon?" When he came in sight of Faye, he stopped. His mother grabbed him by the hand and hauled him away. "Shh," she told him. "Can't you see she's praying?"

Faye stood up at once. She started to say, "No, I wasn't," but how would that sound?

"*Is* there a cannon?" the little boy asked when he saw Faye was done.

"No cannons," Faye said.

"We honeymooned here," the woman told Faye. "Would you?" and handed Faye the camera. It was a simple one, no focusing, one button, built-in flash if needed. Faye waited while the woman got her husband to come stand by her. Faye took the picture. They wanted another one, with all three of them, the whole family—"So far," the woman said, and giggled—so Faye took that one also, with the little boy tilted forward, hands on knees, scowling at a line of ants trekking across the pavement. In the photo, his mouth would be open, his eyes shut.

Just after Faye clicked the picture, he stood and pointed. "What's she doing?"

Everyone turned to see. A woman in a man's hat—a baseball hat—knelt on all fours on the far side of the graves, digging. "Is she going to bury that dog?" the boy asked. His father laughed. "That's no dead dog." The dog, in fact, raised its head and looked their way.

The man checked his tour map. He studied the monuments and sections. He said, "That's Cristo Montevidez's grave." He had already been there, paid his respects. He'd already had his photo taken there. He had a pebble in his pocket from the mortar in the coping. He explained—as Faye kept staring, her hands to her eyes as a visor—"People all the time leave stuff there, tributes, you know. Like at the Wall in D.C."

"Cristo Montevidez," Faye said, in a wondering way.

"Ballplayer," the man said. "You had to be a fan."

She walked off while he was talking. She didn't go straight over to the grave. It surprised her that there was a grave. It didn't seem real to her. She had read about him in the clippings. Of course there would be a grave. Faye leaned her bike against the outside wall and waited, hoping whoever it was would finish at the grave and go. She wanted to see what it said. She knew part of the story. Why didn't she think to ask the rest, why was she like that? She said, "I am not stupid," as though that were the issue. The woman at the grave did not go. There was a lane around the back of the cemetery, so a hearse wouldn't have to run onto the graves and back and turn to leave. Faye walked from the far side, hoping the woman would go soon. There was a car parked just past the tunnel of trees, near the grave. All its doors were open; it was parked in the shade. There was an old man in it.

Faye recognized him. Agapito, from Greenhill. She went over to the car and spoke to the man. Approached from the front so she would not surprise or frighten him. He had on a little hat. He touched the brim when she came up. "We were at Greenhill," she said. She remembered how Tom had knelt by the chair he sat in, so he could see eye to eye, how he had talked Spanish, how he had made this sad old man laugh. Agapito didn't seem to remember. He searched her face.

"I'm Faye," she said in Spanish.

She knelt also, as Tom had, so he didn't have to bend his neck to take her in. He scuffled his feet on the floorboard. Looked fierce. Finally tilted over toward the steering wheel. Reached the horn button and leaned on it. Blew and blew. Strong, the crabbed fingers curved like the sisterhooks on a block and tackle.

"Sir!" Faye said. He wouldn't let go the horn.

The woman at the grave came running. The old dog ran too.

"I'm sorry," Faye said.

The look on Cassia's face, helping Agapito to sit up again. "He has been ill," she said. "All right, all right," she crooned.

"He has forgotten so much," she explained, as though Faye might get the wrong idea. "There is no bitterness. It is always like this when he has forgotten, and then remembers. Sooner or later, they tell me, he will forget it all . . . Everything."

"Oh," Faye said. She picked up Cassia's gardening gloves from where she had tossed them down as she reached to help Agapito. They were stained with dark soil.

"It won't come out," Cassia said. "It's clay. From the Delaware River." She studied Faye's face for recognition. Shook her head when she saw Faye didn't get it. "They rub new baseballs with it," she said. "That's what they use. The team sent me a whole bucketful for the planter. It's right," she said. "It's so right."

She was crying.

Faye said, "I'm sorry."

Cassia wouldn't hear of it. "No, no," she said. "He was driving. But he *was* sober, it wasn't *that*, I can be glad of that. I've been meaning to see you," Cassia said. "Wanting to meet with you and talk. But *today*? Today I never thought. *Not* today," she decided. The way she decided, every day.

. . .

Vic turned north off the island road. He and Marnie drove in silence. Not even the radio. This was no argument, yet by some instinct he had turned onto the only road home that would take as long as they needed. To settle everything. After an hour he stopped at a tavern where they were both strangers. She didn't want anything. He didn't either. They didn't even go in. They circled the lot and drove on.

"What happened back there?" Marnie asked once. Or thought she asked. But Vic never replied, so she decided she hadn't said it out loud. He turned toward the west, and they rolled past groves and farms and ugly, new-scraped land. They knew the place.

After they'd parked, they walked along the river, down to the dock where pleasure boats tied up for ice and supplies. They made their way back across the sandy yard to the riverhouse, hand in hand, as long-married couples approach a doctor's office with great dread, to hear test results, knowing that things will never be the same after this hour.

They chose the deck. They were early for dinner. They ordered coffee. Vic chose their meal and asked for a bottle of rum from the bar. The waitress brought glasses, but Vic didn't open the bottle. Marnie was no longer tipsy. They behaved with great courtesy toward each other. From time to time Vic touched his chin where Tom's fist had left a shadow.

Marnie spoke pleasantly. They found things to say. When the food came, they ate with appetite.

"Captain," the manager said, as they were leaving. "Come back again anytime."

They rode for a way along the unpaved road south. Old bridges hummed past under their wheels. They crossed the looping river three times, and each time nearer the mouth, the bridge got longer.

"All I want to know," Marnie said, "is why you invited me. I didn't crash that party." They were crossing the bay bridge now, the final bridge. She lived off the harbor road. Three more blocks. She did not sound bitter or aggravated. "Who were you trying to hurt?" She wasn't the sort to cry at times like this. Not that there'd ever been many like this. She pushed the lighter button in, clawed a cigarette from her pack, and lit. Exhaled with a mighty gust. "Just—"

"Marnie," he said.

"Or was it—you were afraid—what were you afraid *of*?"

Here was her apartment.

"I won't ask you to come up," she said.

She got out, reached back in, set the bottle of rum in her seat, snugged the seatbelt and shoulder harness across it, turned the label to the front.

"*Añejo*," she read. She shook her head. "Is that a verb? First person?" Her voice broke. She took a deep breath. Again Vic said, "Marnie."

"*No*," she said sharply. "Don't get out, I mean it." She rallied. "*Adiós, muchacho*. It's been swell." She tapped the bottle with her trademark acrylic claws. "Pace yourself," she warned him. "This stuff'll kill your butt dead if you rush it." She shut the door. Stepped back.

She stood on the curb till he drove off. A better exit would have been her walking up that exterior flight of stairs through the terrace garden, the skirt of her dress ducktailing as she ascended, step by step, out of his life and reach forever. The shoes she had on were great skirt-flippers, but she was afraid the seams of his tuck-and-roll car seats had imprinted themselves on her bare thighs and back.

There's no use losing it in extra innings, she thought as she took her shoes off and trotted up to her door.

She was surprised at how early it was. Several more hours of daylight left. The door of her apartment was baked with the day's heat. It seemed very hard to push that door open. When she laid her keys down, her hands shook. She suddenly felt very weak. It took her several minutes to remove Vic's key from her ring. She considered it:

Plan A: Flush it down her toilet; swaddle it in tissue and send it south into oblivion, out of temptation. The advantage there was (1) she couldn't change her mind and (2) he'd always wonder if she might. But she chose Plan B: Mail it back. Classier. He'd know she meant it, and she got to have the last word.

After several tries—her notepaper had MARNIE embossed across the top—she decided on a simple, declarative, unsigned, apparently hastily scrawled sentence:

You'll need this.

That prophecy would be all her revenge. There'd be others—Vic was no monk—and after a time (Marnie was confident) comparisons would be made. In her favor. Too late.

She walked down to the marina, to the mailbox out front. It was beginning to be twilight when she dropped it in the box. She started home. All the traffic in the world on land or sea, it seemed, was heading in the other direction.

Elven darted down to the docks as soon as he saw Zeb's boat nose in. The sun was about gone. A few bright streaks danced along the channel, in the water roughed up by boat wake as pleasure craft began anchoring for the fireworks show. Most of the sparkle on the water was already from the pier lights. The coast guard vessel stood off, surrounded by the smaller boats, bobbing in the slight chop. Fireworks would be launched from the coast guard's deck.

Zeb tossed Elven the stern mooring line. Then the bow. Elven tied them fast. Zeb hopped over to the pier to take a look. He wanted it just so. He wanted the light to fall directly on the gilding on the boat's name-board. He'd had it specially made. Coats and coats of spar varnish sparkled. Elven stood by Zeb and shared. Leaned out and over, to touch. Paused. "Dry?" he wondered, because of that deep shine.

"Waterproof and guaranteed for a hundred years," Zeb said. The words, carved by Otto Schimmelpfennig with the same style he used on granite and marble and sandstone, were finger-deep, in cypress.

"Look," Zeb said, jumping back onto deck, and pulling a beribboned bottle from an ice chest.

"Champagne?" Elven jumped down beside him, to see.

"Cider," Zeb said. "You see you' Baptis' momma going near any champagne?"

"How you get her down here anyway?" Elven wondered.

"Well, I could lie or I could tell the truth," Zeb said. "Those my choices. I'm prayin', that's what it is," he said. "Prayin'." But he didn't have a clue as to results. "Somethin'," he said. "It'll happen."

Elven knew his daddy wasn't going to tell a lie. And he had no confidence in the truth's appeal. "I believe you," he said. He looked around in the pilot house.

"My daddy, Captain Tom give you any firecracker sparklers for me? Say maybe he will."

"What makin' you such a general favorite?"

"'Cause I'm cute and smart and just like my old man."

"Tell you momma that all along."

"She the one told me," Elven said. He didn't see the look on Zeb's face. "We got to hurry," he said. He could see a star or two. Nothing going on on the coast guard's deck, but soon.

They secured the boat and climbed the dock ladder up to the pier, just to have the adventure of it. Their movements were exactly in sync, choreographic. "Momma never do *this*," Elven said.

"Won't have to. Tide's coming. Growing moon, too. Be a fine old tide, fine old tide tonight. Level things up so she can step her foot right across," he said, "just like this." They stood on the pier and pictured it.

Elven still had doubts, looking down at the shrimper, but Zeb couldn't afford to. Zeb had even strung up Christmas lights and he planned to plug them in as soon as he got back to the boat. Christmas lights and the nameboard sparkling in the dock light. Palma couldn't miss it.

"Beautiful," Zeb said. "She's beautiful."

"Momma?" Elven said.

"Is her name Palma?" Zeb said.

Elven smiled. "Better be."

They started for the park, where Cliffie and Palma and the other children had already spread quilts.

Cliffie was testing one of Palma's fried pies. She broke off a little piece of the crust and tasted it. "You put any salt?"

"Salted the skillet," Palma said. "Need more?"

"It'll do, it'll do," Cliffie said. She held the pie on her hand and looked at it, turning it this and that way in the streetlight to inspect. Made Palma nervous.

"Look a lot better tonight," Palma said, "they sure do," she confessed, "than when I cook them this morning. Burned the first batch black as radial tires."

"Steel radial pies," Cliffie said. "I have that recipe myself. Raised on it. Et it many a time. Had to. Glad to. Y'hear me?"

Grateful for that, Palma said, "Get you one from under."

Cliffie squealed. "You put the pretty ones on the bottom? Ugly ones on *top*?" Realized what she'd said. "'Scuse me," she said. "They look all right to me."

"Ugly ones on top and get it over with," Palma said, "that's my motto. Helps to finish with something sweet."

"Speak of the devil," Cliffie said, as Zeb came up. Elven was hopping from clear place to clear place between the blankets, beach towels, and tablecloths spread on the park lawn. Zeb just came on, didn't seem to look down, yet avoided all hazard. Cat eyes, that was what Palma always said he had. Cliffie's children were sprawled one to a quilt, but made room. Palma was reclining on a lounger.

"I wish this was a hill," Elven said. "So steep I could just lie on it and not even have to look up; I'm gonna get a crick."

"Not likely," his momma said, because of the way he kept jumping up and checking on everybody else, and the boats, and Zeb's watch, and the sky.

Elven had an inspiration. "The ferris wheel!" He bolted upright. "Right at the top. Could maybe cotch 'em before they quit burning!" He imagined that. Cliffie's children began to agitate for the ferris wheel also.

Palma didn't vote no, she just took Elven in hand. Reached over in the dark and found his head, grabbed it in her hand, and pushed him back down into reality. "No way," she said. "Don't mention it again."

Cliffie's kids subsided after that.

Zeb hadn't sat. He wasn't sure where. He poked around in the picnic things and found the pies, pulled one out and ate it. "Miss Cliffie," he said, "you outdone yourself."

Cliffie laughed.

Palma ratcheted the back of her chaise straight up and looked to see what Zeb was eating.

"Didn't you recognize your own wife's cookin'?" Cliffie teased.

Zeb said quietly, "Well, it's been a while." He was close enough that Palma could smell that sun-dried laundry smell he always wore from being on the water, in the sun and wind. He smelled a little like fresh paint, too. He was always fooling with that boat. Annoyed because she was pleased, Palma said, a little curtly, "Sit down. You dropping crumbs on my hair." She brushed at herself. Accidentally touched Zeb's arm. He was standing nearly behind her chair, the only clear spot near her, but if he moved the picnic basket there'd be sitting room, half on the quilt where she sat. Half off, too. He smiled. He was used to that. He folded himself down beside her. Elven had belly-flopped on the ground in front of them, so they were more or less all on the same quilt. Elven pushed up to his knees, then turned and waddled toward his daddy.

"I've thought of something," he said, excited. He winked. Palma saw that, but couldn't imagine what he was talking about, some secret between the two of them. She saw the white of Elven's eye flash, and the pupil gleam in the dusk-to-dawns. Then everything went black. The show began. Tier on tier of lights dimmed till the crowd sat in darkness. Boats rocked in the channel, in the harbor, all aimed toward the coast guard, the epicenter. With a *whoosh*, a ripping boom, and the traditional *aaahs* and spattered applause, the first rockets went up and sent down freshets of falling fire.

Vic didn't even look up. He was moving along the back of the throng, trying to get to the kiosk that sold sundries before it closed for the show. He didn't make it. But after the show started, it was easier to get around. The people coalesced on the lawns and left the paths clear.

There were cigarette machines in the casino building. He smoked the last of his little cigarillos as he walked there, a handful of change ready. He almost ran into a baby stroller parked on the edge of the path. He stopped short, and when a particularly loud firework had gone off, low, bits of the wrapper floating down, its falling splendor giving enough light that he could see, yes, he had enough quarters for the vending machine, and he glanced up. There was Faye.

The shock—a physical sensation of electric intensity—like terror or guilt stopped him violently in his tracks. His instinct was to flee. He never felt that way about anything, and it made him angry. He didn't want her to see him, and he didn't—for some reason—want her to see him alone in this paired-off crowd with its families and lovers and summer pals. He decided that he simply would not see her. Cut and run. Before he could process his feelings into action, he noticed Faye's terror. Not of him. She hadn't seen him. She was looking up, walking backwards. She feared—and he saw that it was truest terror—the fireworks themselves.

She had brought her hands to her ears to cover them against the noise, to fend off the falling ashes, whatever they could do to save her, and she was backing slowly away. She passed directly in front of him, on the path where he stood. He said nothing. He held his breath till she had gone. He watched her. He tried to see what it was Tom saw in her. But all he saw was the outside. Just one more undergraduate in the school of hard knocks. Not his type. Her coltish walk—from the rods and pins in her broken legs—her arm-swinging and gawkiness and sincerity of countenance unlayered by inhibition, unlovelied by paint or guile.

He could have said "Boo!" and he longed to, for that one instant, just to see her response. She crept sideways now, up the little slope toward the casino wall. The sky was dark between flares. She moved slowly till she touched the wall itself. Pressed her back into it, her arms at her sides like someone about to be shot, her fingertips brushing against the stucco.

She looked like a painting. Flat. Like something blown against the wall.

Yet she kept looking up.

She shook with dread, yet she kept looking up, kept her eyes open to the full fire-flowering of the sky. Not her fear but the beauty of the thing she feared compelling her courage.

You'd think she had never seen fireworks, Vic thought.

Faye's rehabilitation—from what to what—Vic had never quite comprehended till that moment. He'd listen to Father Ockham or a doctor on the phone and say, "Yeah," and he'd phone Tom and ask, "Is this covered," because Tom was handling all that for him, as though insurance were the bottom line. Vic had never before thought of himself as a man crippled by his own self-interest . . .

Her first fireworks, Vic thought. Allowing that, knowing in fact it wasn't so, but seeing for the first time the difference between history and reality.

We all duck the first time, he grudged. He looked again. Surely Tom was around somewhere; would be spotted coming along toward her with both fists full of snowcones or something that had taken too long to find, and left Faye at large till his return. But she was alone. Absolutely alone in the dark with her back to the wall.

Vic approached her slowly. If she had seen him coming on, purposefully, she would have fled. He knew that much about how she thought. He wanted to stand a little nearer her, though. Close enough to exchange words, to hear each other under the noise of the show.

"Oh," she said. She noticed him.

"They always burn out before they hit the ground," Vic told her. "No danger of fire."

"I wondered," she said.

"I'll stand here," he offered.

"All right."

"Today was not so good," he said.

She considered that. Meanwhile a rocket with bright green, red, and gold bursts seemed to come right at them. Then from within all that light, a huge chrysanthemum of white brilliance burst. It covered the whole sky. Fingers of light grappled down toward the ground, like lightning.

Faye put her hand to her mouth, but did not recoil. "How far is it?" She turned her face for a moment toward him, then back to the sky. "How far down does it really come? Does it come as close as it looks?" Her eyes gleamed.

Before he could answer, another rocket went off. Wobbled up, fizzled out, and dove headfirst into the sea.

The crowd laughed. Faye laughed too. She crossed herself, as though the little drowned firecracker had a soul, like a shooting star. She was a step away from the wall now. He moved back as she moved forward.

"At the end of the show," Vic told her, "they send up the very best ones. The sky is filled with them, pow-pow-pow-pow-pow. It doesn't stop. You hope it never will."

"It will be beautiful," she predicted, looking up.

They stood there, shoulder to shoulder now, watching. They didn't talk again. When the finale began, Vic murmured, "Now," so she'd know and not be afraid, or somehow miss it. And he was thinking how she had said, "It will be beautiful," and considering how it was the same with fireworks as with fishing, with finding the good fish for his clients, how the other person in your boat appreciates, and so the thing is better. He wasn't sure how it worked. He thought it over again. He wanted to tell her. How her pleasure had instructed his. How his pleasure had fed off hers. He studied her face in the flickering light—familiar and yet unknown. He suspected there might be enormous truth, about nature and the world, which could be gotten from and developed out of these ideas he was having, and these exact conditions—and these only—the weather, the lighted sky, the crowd, and themselves looking. This is good, he thought, this needs to be more generally considered. He imagined a diagram. X (here) and Y (there) and object (Z) . . . dotted lines . . . possibly angles and arcs. Like celestial navigation, only sighting toward a moving object. He liked that. Said that aloud. "A moving object." How do you fix a moving object? he was wondering. Of course, he thought. Of course.

"Someone should get a picture of all this," he was about to say, but when he turned to tell her, Faye had gone.

When Zeb heard Elven's plan for getting Palma down to the dock to see the boat, Zeb said no. "Oh, it's a good plan," he agreed, when Elven argued, "It'll go," but Zeb pointed out the one flaw: "I'm not a plannin' man." Meaning *no tricks*. The lights had come back on after the fireworks ended, but as Palma had said, seeing the crush of people trying to leave, it would be hours, especially if the drawbridge had to go up for river traffic.

"Might as well," Cliffie agreed, sitting down again.

"Shoulda come in a boat," Elven said, never one to give up on a good plan. Especially one of his own.

Zeb ignored him.

"You-uns just *set*," he told the children, his boy and Cliffie's three. But they still wallowed and wrestled on the quilts.

"Mary J. Stevenson!" Cliffie said. "Mind yourself."

Mary J. sat up.

"Be a lady or at least act like one."

"La-di-dah-dah," Drew said.

Mary J. fell across the boys, pinned her brothers to the ground by main force.

"Mary J.?" Cliffie said. Very quietly. She got to her feet, dragged at the girl's shirt and belt, and hauled her up.

"Crowd control," Mary J. explained.

"She gone be a great teacher," Palma said. "They ack out, she sit on 'em, leave 'em flat."

"Gone be a lady paratrooper," Mary J. said.

"Bomber," Drew said.

"She the bomb," Jondi said. "Stink bomb."

"That's it," Cliffie said. She pointed to their quilts. "You—here. You— there. And *you* . . ." she shook her head at Jondi.

"Military school?" Elven suggested.

Zeb said, "Mister—" and Elven folded. Sat.

For a moment everyone was behaving. Zeb stepped to the middle of their attention and cleared his throat. "I wanted a better time," he said, for openers.

"Won't *be* one, you do it your way," Elven muttered. He made a ha-ha-ha grimace, but he left off. He had already pushed past the reasonable limits and he knew it. Zeb didn't look his way but once. That was all it took. The others, seeing that, quieted too. Cliffie and Palma looked at each other, shrugged. They had no idea what this was all about, they were telling each other.

Zeb took something out of his shirt pocket and handed one to Cliffie and one to Palma. Bank books. Savings-account passbooks. They looked identical. Brand new, blue. Hard to open. The buckram covers cracked when they tried. Palma said, "This one's Cliffie's." And shut it, quickly. But not before she had read the balance. Cliffie said, "Well, this one's yours, but that one's *not mine*." She handed Palma the one Zeb had given her first. She wouldn't take the one Palma was giving her now. "No," she said. "Some mistake at the bank."

Zeb said, "Just listen to me."

"What?" Palma shifted in her chair. She couldn't get comfortable. Her response lately to anything was aggravation and impatience, as though carrying twins to term was more than enough for life to ask of her at one time.

"It's from the boat," Zeb said.

"You sold it," Cliffie said, aghast.

"You sold it," Palma said, astonished.

"Never," Zeb said. "As to that, never," he told Cliffie. "As to that, it's worth more and you know it," Zeb told Palma.

"A ransom more," Palma agreed darkly.

Zeb took a breath. "Not discussin' that," he said without rancor. "Not goin' to discuss that. And any further more, subject's closed. Been covered. Long covered." He gave a slow chop with his left hand, ear-level, palm up, like the old deacons giving their *Amen.* As though this was the final word.

Palma couldn't believe her eyes and ears. Where'd he get this *tone*?

"Preach, suh," she mocked. Oh she wanted a fight tonight, you could see it. She was almost out of her chair.

The children all rolled to their knees now, watching back and forth.

"This—this—" he couldn't think of the word. In his extremity he made two fists, knocked them together knuckles to knuckles, to show what he meant. "Can't go on," he said.

Right out in public! Dressing her down! Palma looked around, but no one was staring at them. Zeb was firm, but he wasn't loud. Never had to be.

"Mockin' my undertakin's," Zeb said. "*Let* the chirren hear it, God know it for the truth: never said or done a thing against *you*."

"Undertakin's," Palma echoed with some malice. "I hear *that*."

"Palma," Cliffie said sadly. "Now don't. Don't now."

"This can't go on," Zeb said again, quite reasonably. "You know it. Need a little relief from it, all of us." Zeb knelt beside Palma's chair and folded the bank book into her hand. "For the boy," he said. "For our chirren's educations, just for that, nothin' but that."

He gave Cliffie her book too, and gave her hand a pat. "Your'n too." He stood up. "Every bit of fishin' I do, from now on, they get their share as much as woulda been Ben's. Half for mine, half for his'n."

"No!" Cliffie cried. She got to her feet too. "You bought that boat, bought out Ben's share. We don't—you don't—"

"It's fair," Zeb said. "It's right. It was his dream too."

Cliffie started to cry.

"Now don't," Zeb told her. "Don't."

Mary J. took the book from her mother's hand. "How much is it?" They all gathered around to see.

Cliffie hugged Zeb, hugged and hugged him. "Not for the money," she told him. "For the dream. You know that."

"As to that," Zeb said, "you know the boat's been prayed over."

"And for," Cliffie added.

Zeb smiled. "And against." He didn't get a whiff of a smile from Palma's direction, but she was listening.

"I just like the two of you to be there for the christen," Zeb said. "Tonight."

Palma jerked her chair-back forward, straight up, in one violent motion.

"It's not champagne," Elven said, "it's cider."

Palma stared at them. "Help me up outta here," she said. She held up her hand to Cliffie. Elven took it instead.

"Takes two," Elven said. So Zeb took Palma's other hand, and they pulled. When Palma was on her feet, she said, "Enjoy yourselves." She headed off up the path toward the public rest rooms.

Cliffie decided not to ignore the hurt look on Zeb's face. "I was hoping," she said gently.

"It's gone happen," Zeb said. "Bound to." He sighed. He indicated his son. "Boy had a plan," but without much bounce.

"Let's wait," Cliffie said. The kids were already on their way, pelting down the path along the seawall toward the pier. Elven led the way.

"No," Zeb said. "I been waitin'. About done waitin'. She didn't say wait."

"You don't mind?" Zeb said, helping Cliffie down the catwalk to the bow. He jumped the rail and landed hard on deck. Flicked on the Christmas lights and brought the bottle of sparkling cider to her, its ribbons trailing. The children lined up, calling advice. Cheering.

Cliffie stood there. Just stood there. Zeb thought . . . He didn't know what he thought. He never thought Cliffie might be praying. He asked again, "You don't mind?"

"I'll probably miss," she said.

"I mean the name."

"Oh, darlin', who better!" she cried, with infectious joy. She intended this for Ben, too, somehow this was part of Ben's life, not his death. She swung the bottle with all her strength, for all of them.

"Make a wish!" Jondi called.

"Already have," Cliffie said.

They all held their breath as Cliffie went around.

Missed! When she didn't connect, her momentum carried her all the way around. She couldn't hold the wet bottle. It slipped from her grasp and smashed on the seawall, its foam mingling with the breakers.

"Oh no," Cliffie wailed.

They all stood there.

Zeb thought about it.

"It's in the water," Zeb reasoned, "and so's the boat."

"Is that it?" Jondi said. And when Zeb said, "Yep," Jondi said, "Then where's the refreshments?" And they all rumbled down the catwalk and boarded the shrimper. Cliffie had been on the boat several times, but not at night. She went aft on one side and forward on the other, looking, touching. Zeb had Ben's picture in the pilothouse. He'd asked Cliffie for that, but it still surprised her, to see it enlarged, framed, and at eye level. Zeb said, "It's a good picture."

"It's a good boat," Cliffie said. "Ben never was the quittin' sort."

When Cliffie stepped out onto deck she saw answered prayer: Palma her own great self steaming down the quay with a paper plate of fried pies. They were her excuse.

"Zeb!" Cliffie called, not turning back, just beckoning him with her outstretched hand. "Come on here, man." When he stepped up behind her, Cliffie moved aside so he could see. "Hell's not gonna hafta freeze over," Cliffie said. "Thank you, Jesus."

Palma was almost in full view. Plate in one hand, other hand holding to the railing. She hadn't seen the boat yet, hadn't picked it out, peering this way, that, and seeking on the wrong side of the pier! Soon she crossed and started the search on the near side, big as life.

"Gettin' warmer," Cliffie called.

Palma's head jerked around. "I see you," she said, but she didn't, she hadn't made them yet, she just didn't want them to have the advantage of her. "That's Palma," Cliffie said. "Nothing surprises *her*."

But it did.

When her eyes raked across Zeb's grand old rib-built shrimper she swept it from stern—where the kids were playing on the piled nets and doors—to bow. She stepped from the pier to the catwalk, leaning way over to get a look in the clear, to be sure she could believe her own eyes, her own . . .

PALMA FOREVER, the nameboard announced.

"Ah!" she cried. Her face contorted. She clutched at the rail. "Zeb!"

The boat rode a harbor swell, and then dropped again. Palma tried to make that step across, that final step onto the deck. Failed. Had the oddest look on her face: a reckoning and astonishment and alarm. Not a cry for pardon, but for help. She held her hand out. Zeb gripped it in his.

"Babe—" she muttered through clenched teeth.

"All yours," Zeb said. His heart was pounding in sweet triumph. Joy. One step more and she'd be on board.

"Babe—" she whispered, sinking.

"Lord!" Cliffie said, beating Zeb on the arm. "Can't you see? Her water's broke. Baby's on the way!"

BOOK FOUR

EYE OF THE STORM

And I cannot say, how long, for that is to place it in time.
—T. S. Eliot, "Burnt Norton"

PART I

LIVING ON THE EDGE

As soon as Tom had helped Faye move from Palma's, he vanished from her life like salt in water. She didn't have a phone at first, that was one thing. Water service and electricity were all she could afford. She had made a strict budget, just as they had taught her in rehab, and she paid cash for everything. She even bought the house outright; it took most of the money in the trust fund from her mother's estate, not that Faye had been an heiress. Nor was she bankrupt afterward; she simply was on her own.

"I'm a thousandaire," she told Palma when she had consolidated her own little savings with what remained of her mother's. The bank offered her checks and a charge card, but she wouldn't. "Cash or nothing," she said. She wouldn't charge anything. "I'll only owe my friends," she said on moving day. "I'll be paying them back the rest of my life."

"That's how I feel about Sears," Palma said.

The burden of Faye's household goods barely set Tom's truck down on its springs, but still it took them all day to get everything settled in her little cottage. She kept rearranging things.

She had been working at Raquel's, the hairdresser's, since August, nine till nine on Fridays and Saturdays, with Sundays and Mondays free. Minimum wage and a few tips. Another job at the all-night market mornings before she went to Raquel's, and on Sunday evenings and all day Monday. Three nights a week she went to school. The rest of the time, whatever time she had, day or night, she worked on her house. Everybody had advice about that, too. From type of brush and paint to where to start and what color. The women at Raquel's were after her, nonstop.

"I heard about a woman who got arrested for paintin' her house pink," Dawn said.

"Sued, not arrested," Faye said. It was in all the papers. "And besides, she won," Faye added. "And besides that," she felt obliged to point out, "it isn't pink. I mean mine isn't."

"A rose by any other name," Tracey said. One of her favorite remarks; she even had a T-shirt. Tracey's real name was Rose, but she thought that sounded too square. She hadn't liked her last name, either. She had been married and divorced twice. She had a son in the navy and a daughter with children. She never called them grandchildren. She never called them at all. They were not her reason for living and they didn't have much to do with her life, judging from her conversation and plans. She read a lot. She often pointed that out. She read the Sunday paper from cover to cover, as she put it, and that was where she'd learned all about how to paint a house. She didn't live in a house; she and her boyfriend— her term for it—lived in a condo near the waterfront in town. He was harbormaster. She mentioned that too. "You ought to start painting at the front. It'll look great from the beginning, and if you never finish, nobody passing by on the street will know."

Faye said, "I'll finish."

"What if you fall off that ladder? Break your neck, place'll look like nobody cares. Plus they'll never look for you till the flies swarm." She pointed her nail file at Faye. "Start with the front, girl."

"If I knew how," Faye agreed. "But I don't know how. So I am starting at the back and learning. That way the best I do will be what shows."

One of the others, a customer getting a haircut from Sandy, said, "Makes sense to me."

"You brain-damaged too?" Tracey said.

Faye was sweeping up the hair around Sandy's workstation. She paused a moment, and for a startling instant she felt the customer's gaze, a knowing gaze, pass over her. The customer held up her glasses and studied Faye.

"Well, I didn't know," she said simply, as though that changed everything, including the customer's mind and vote. As though Faye needed either. Sandy was still snipping at the woman's crown. In the awkward pause, Sandy said, kindly, "Things work out."

The customer put her hand up to feel the length of her hair. "Oh!" she said, startled.

"It'll grow," Sandy said. "Let me finish, okay? I'm working on a concept here. Let me finish. If you don't like it, I promise you . . . it'll grow."

The customer, a fifth-grade teacher and Girl Scout leader, sighed. She folded her hands in her lap, her glasses tucked into her palms. She spoke to Faye with a different tone. "A word to the wise," she said.

Faye finished sweeping, gathered the hair onto a dust pan, and took it to the trash. She sat for a moment in the shampoo chair, and tied her shoe.

"Faye?"

Faye came back.

"Talking to you," the customer said a little severely.

Faye said, "Me? To me?"

"Yes, ma'am, I am. I just want to know if you're the sort—ouch! Sandy, I told you I have a tender head I don't want that hot curl thing I told you that!—the sort," she went on, "who finishes what she starts?"

Surprised, Faye said, "I hope so." She meant to sound more sure than that. She shrugged.

A simple little question. But Faye wasn't sure. She suspected they knew something she didn't, about her intentions, or her past.

Faye ran to the back, in tears. They could hear her putting in a load of wash, and taking towels out of the dryer. They could hear her humming "Row, Row, Row Your Boat" as she worked. She sniffed loudly.

"Well, who rocked on *her* tail?" the customer said.

Faye was back there a long time. Sandy had finished with her customer and the woman was looking at the back of her new style in a hand mirror, when she saw Faye's reflection in it. "No hard feelings," she hoped.

Faye said, "I've got a class." She started for the door. "I've cleaned up," Faye told Sandy. It was Sandy's shop, but she didn't use her own name for the name of the shop. "Sandy Hair Designs," she had laughed; "I think not." So she had chosen "Raquel's" for her shop sign; it had the sound she wanted, plus she liked the way the *R* looked, the long trailing serifs and the little flowers the painter had added to the spine.

No one working in the shop used her given name except Faye. Even Dawn had begun life as a parochial-schooled Donna Sue. "So fifties," she mourned. "Might as well have been Peggy Sue." It was Dawn who picked up the worksheet that fell from Faye's portfolio. "A class in *what!*" she exclaimed. She made her eyes round and big and gave a little hoo-hoo-hoo of fake shock. She waved the paper as though it were hot. Faye reached for it.

"No, no, now wait a minute here," Dawn said. Sandy's customer fitted her glasses onto her face and peered over Dawn's shoulder.

Tracey said, "Where did you get this?"

"Church," Faye said, trying to retrieve it. "I have to go now. I'm almost late."

"Things have loosened up since I lapsed," Tracey said, ignoring her.

"It's not Catholic," said Faye. "It's from the Singles Mission."

"Part of a series," Dawn read, pointing to the line on the bottom of the sheet. "Life on the Edge."

Sandy took the page then and read it. " 'The Twelve Steps to Marital

Bonding. Session Four . . .' " She frowned. There were eight lines, numbered, and four lines after that. The numbered lines were blank. "_____ to _____ ," they said. Sandy shook her head. "So what's the big deal?"

Dawn tapped the last four lines. Not numbered, they were a statement only. " 'The last four stages in intimacy are related to sexuality in marriage, and God intended these to be reserved for a marriage relationship . . .' " Sandy read aloud.

"Yeah, yeah, yeah," Dawn said, "read on past all that Sunday-school crap."

" 'They are hand to body, mouth to breast, touching below the waist, and—' "

"Oh, my God," Tracey said. "Look at Faye."

But they had to look fast, because she snatched the paper from their hands and left. She hadn't gone fifteen feet down the sidewalk when she ran into Vic.

Ran flat into him, so violently she almost scattered the rest of her papers. For a moment she didn't realize who he was, then she said, "Oh, Captain." She bent to unlock her bike from the rack; flustered, she didn't remember the combination. That gave her time to compose herself.

"Of all people," she said. She stood and backed her bike out of the rack, slung her bookbag into the basket, and turned to go. But Vic was in no hurry. He gave the satchel strap a flip and said, "You off to school?"

"I've finished," she said. "I mean with the equivalency. I'm sure I passed. I haven't got my results yet but didn't have to worry about anything except algebra and I think I got it this time." She had had a tutor. "I could do x and y," she told Vic. "It was z that—" She broke off. She didn't look at Vic. Couldn't. To her horror he opened the book bag and reached in. Took out a travel book. She breathed again.

"I'm going by the library on my way," she explained. "Geography's my favorite." She took the book from him and buckled it into the bag, turned the whole thing over so it couldn't be got at again. Her hands were shaking. She turned the bike. "I'm going to be late," she said.

"Nice bike," he said.

"Tom helped me fix it," she said. He looked as if he hadn't heard her.

"Geography," he said. She put her leg over the frame and settled her right sneaker on the pedal.

"I'm going to set my foot on every island in the sea," Faye said, and pedaled off.

She was late to the class at church. She missed the video portion. That was session four, so she'd never know how to fill in those blanks! "Eye to eye," she decided the first one must be. She had decided that during the week, before the fourth session. And now she would never know!

Not that she had need. She had not known the "Preparing for Life as an Adult" lifestyle series would cover marriage at all. The church listed it in the programs for singles. What did that have to do with marital bonding? Besides which, she had to look up *marital*—she thought it had to do with war. That's why she thought "hand to hand" might be another answer for those blanks from one to eight. But that last paragraph—those last four levels of intimacy—completely befuddled her, left her walking into walls. One of the reasons she was taking her books back to the library so early—she had only had them four days—was because suddenly they didn't interest her at all. Or they interested her in ways she did not know how to profit from. The book on the Masai, with the sweethearts standing on each other's feet as they danced—"heart to heart"—as she thought of it, that close—another of those phrases that might have fit in the blanks on the questionnaire for "Life on the Edge." But somehow, Faye knew, or at least suspected, that the blanks would be filled by stranger phrases than she could think up on her own.

She went on back to library and turned in the books—on Africa and Australia and the Argentine pampas. "Already!" the clerk said, when she saw they were back so soon. Faye had requested them from inter-library loan.

Faye thought of the lady in Sandy's beauty shop asking, "Do you finish what you start?" The heat rose up her neck and toward her scalp. She stepped back.

"I didn't have to read it all," Faye said.

"I see," the clerk laughed. "I'm that way myself. Nice tune, but you can't dance to it, right?"

Faye laughed too, but she wasn't sure what the woman meant.

"May we help you find something else?"

"I just want to look around. I'll browse," Faye said. For a moment she wanted to ask her how to find a book about bonding, but she wasn't sure what she'd say if the clerk required her to be more specific. Faye had looked it up in her student dictionary. The definitions hadn't been much help. She now checked the library's big unabridged version, on its oak stand. Not a bit clearer. She felt she was committing trespass of some sort. She turned the pages away from the one she had consulted, so no one could see what she had been reading. She went to the card catalog next, and looked and looked. Finally she went outside to the pay phone and phoned the desk, keeping her back turned so they wouldn't notice it was she calling. She looked way out past the shade of the trees into the sweet dusk. Across the channel, the little lights began to come on on-shore. The gulls were all heading back in-water from the open sea for their night roosts. She leaned a long time, as though she were talking, be-fore she actually dropped her coin in and dialed the desk. She didn't turn to see; she knew they didn't have a clue it was Faye. She disguised her voice. She tried to sound like a child. Then she thought, they might not tell a child the truth. So she tried to quaver like an old lady.

"Can you tell me the difference between bonding and bondage?" Faye asked.

"What? Is this—" The clerk drew a deep breath and said firmly, "Pranksters will be prosecuted to the full extent of the—"

"No," Faye said, "I just wanted to know the difference between . . . be-tween love and sex," she said. She flung one arm out, measuring such a tall order. She realized she had turned and was looking at the clerk through the glass. The clerk caught her eye and smiled and made a cir-cling motion by her head with her free hand, as though sharing with Faye that this was a kook call. "Let me connect you to reference," Faye watched the clerk's lips say. Faye turned her back, as though she had other things on her mind. She pretended to be talking into the phone. The clerk said, "That line's busy, will you hold?" and Faye forgot and in her own voice answered, "Yes," but later, when the clerk came back, on the line and asked, "Still holding?" Faye wasn't.

On the way home, Faye stopped at the pier and walked out to look at the water. She wished she had not ridden her bicycle; then she could walk home by the beach. The tide had just turned, and there would be shells. She still needed a few more for her walk. She wanted large ones, whelks and conchs. She wasn't making a path out of crushed shells, as some did. Her path was cement. She didn't choose it, it had been done before she bought the place. Old cement, with stains and cracks. But she had bleached it and scrubbed it till it was as white as she could get it. Then she had edged it, on her hands and knees, using a butcher knife to cut the dollarweed and turf back in a neat line. She took all that out, laid in a strip of white sand one foot wide, and put the shells on the far edge of that. It made the path look wider, and it gave the yard a sort of—she thought—necklaced look. She had used the inside of one of the shells to match for her house paint. Not pink, not gold, not salmon. The pal-est dawn-on-white-sand color. She had paid extra to get that custom-blended.

She had not yet finished painting the back of the house. She was going to trim out in white as she went. Then the sides. Halfway along the sides, she would stop and move to the other side and paint that far. She had a plan. Then she'd finish to the front, then the other side to the front, and then the porch trim and shutters. The shutters were a deep, rich rust color. It had a name, garnet something; she knew what she wanted. She didn't trust her memory. She took the little paint chips with her to Tom's boat and found the exact match for his wet anchor chain. She did that color-matching on moving day, disappointed she hadn't gotten the exterior painted before she moved in. She and Tom had driven over to the municipal docks to get a crab crate. Tom had said he didn't see how she came up with her ideas, but if that was what she wanted, that was what she'd get. As to why she wanted it, "I'll tell you later. I'll *show* you!" Faye had said, excited and sparkling. She hadn't explained about the anchor-chain/paint-chip adventure either. He saw her leaning down and comparing and said, "Nobody paints their chain."

She had looked up, surprised. "Of course not," she agreed. Then she folded the chips and pinned them in her pocket and didn't mention them again. The button was gone from her pocket. She used a safety pin.

Faye didn't spend money on clothes. Her jobs all required uniform tops, and she had sandals, sneakers, and a Sunday pair of shoes. She couldn't imagine shopping for shoes or clothes as a sport. The money she made went into the bank, touched down and flew out again, to buy building supplies, but she kept within her budget. Sometimes she got lucky and found things on the curb, left for the garbage men to haul away. She shopped that way for her dinette chairs, a gateleg table with warped veneer, a card table, and, best of all, an archback cedar garden bench. It was covered in layers of horrible patent-leather-looking enamel paint. One of her friends from night school saw her dragging it along the street, trying to get it home on foot. Together they shifted it up into the back of the friend's weathered old station wagon. Faye had her friend unload it in the yard, so she could strip it. "How hard can that be?" Faye said.

She learned not to ask that, after a while. After gallons of stripper, sanding, scraping, bleaching, and sanding again, then a sealer, Faye had her bench ready. It would serve as her sofa. It was ready on moving day.

Tom took one look and said, "No way."

"Yes, way," Faye said. She had a tape measure and showed him the bench would fit through the door if they took the door off its hinges. So of course they did. They had to take it off its hinges again for the crab crate. That was to be her coffee table, with a glass topper. The glass was new; the fair-trade price made her a little lightheaded. She was used to yard-sale and Joseph's Attic prices, but she liked the effect so well when Tom finally got the cardboard packing off it and set it on top of the crate that she forgave it.

She enjoyed finally having all her ideas and goods in one place; all day she kept changing where things went, seeing other possibilities, aiming the chairs toward other views, or putting the rug on a diagonal. Her favorite piece of furniture was the old rocker, and she hadn't even foreseen it; out of the blue, two weeks before, a woman had walked into Raquel's after Labor Day and offered to give Faye back the chair she had bought at Mrs. Parry's estate sale, when Faye's mother closed out and headed for her third and final chemo. Then the woman said, "Your mama told me she rocked you as a baby in that chair. Haven't felt right about having it ever since I heard that you were back out and on your own. Is that true? Is what I heard true?"

Faye had not known what to say; she had begun to test every remark for hidden meanings, undercurrents, or innuendo.

"Mrs. Parry was my mama," Faye said.

"They say you don't remember a thing—" Here the woman broke off and glanced around the shop. Kindly, she took Faye by the arm and they walked out back, to finish their conversation. "But I remember you, and your peppy little mama too! Folks still caring about you. Rooting for you! Glad to hear you're getting back on your feet. When I heard that, I said, 'Well, the chair's here and she's there, so what am I going to do about it?' It's more yours than mine. If I can do your mama a favor now, let me. She's done me plenty. Miss her like a front tooth."

She wouldn't take a cent, wouldn't hear of it. Brought the chair by Faye's little cottage one evening when Faye wasn't even home, and left it and a cardboard box with some plants in it on Faye's little porch. Wrapped in newspaper, dampened, wilting only slightly, the plants— some lilies and an angel trump with enough dirt on the roots to keep it going—had been labeled "Don't thank me." That was all.

Faye had no memory of the rocker, not by sight, but she liked the way it fit, the way it felt, its deep seat and smooth arms on either side of her, the worn surfaces and curves pleasing to her touch. Her wrists lay just where the finish was worn away. She set the rocker in the house, in what would be her main room. Besides the bath, there was an alcove where she would put her bed. There was hardly room for the steel locker trunk that her mother had collected full for her, with the memories—scrapbooks, photos, tapes, toys, tools, figurines, bits of fabric—she hoped would be of use to her daughter someday. "A different kind of hope chest" was what she had called it. Faye had not liked to look inside it. It made her feel the same way the lockbox at the bank had—wishing she could ignore the past, just leave it all behind and go on forward. She wished that reading something was the same as remembering it; but even if you ended with the same facts, the two were not at all the same. She knew she didn't know what she was missing, but when she had looked in the bank box, in the trunk, in the library's old newspapers, and she had braved and read and read and read between their lines, how was she to find what got left out? Above all, she had decided that if she was never to be the same, then she wasn't going to pretend she was. She wasn't going to pretend at all. She believed that she could not miss what she could not remember, but after the rocker came into her life, and she opened that trunk of her mother's careful choices, packing it full as she unpacked into death through her last days, Faye grudgingly found treasures—and a new way to look at things.

She began to make a habit of exploring the trunk toward evening. Always, of course, pretending that the person she had been was "her," as Faye always thought of her former self. A sister, maybe, but not a self.

One night when she had been moved into the house for a few days, and she was still having trouble sleeping through, Faye got up and opened the trunk. She was looking for a photo of herself and her mother in the same snapshot. There wasn't one. Except the ones where Faye— who could have been any baby since the world began—was held in Mrs. Parry's arms, presented to the camera, bundled, bonneted, to be authenticated and adored. Finally, Faye found two photographs in which she and her mother were approximately the same distance from the camera. They were never in the same photo after Mr. Parry died, because there had been no one else to take the photos, and either Faye photographed her mother or her mother photographed Faye. Still, in this set of pictures, Faye could compare; she (and Faye thought of herself as "she") did not look at all like Mrs. Parry, but their posture, the way they tilted their heads, the ways they arranged their arms, their very joints and joins, were similar.

Faye studied them. She considered how much of a height they were, and how it must have been her mother's hands and arms that had rubbed the finish off the chair as she sat working, sewing, reweaving, and altering for the cleaners. There were dimples where it might have been Mrs. Parry's work—perhaps pushing a needle through heavy fabrics—that left its mark. Faye had been considering repainting the chair, but after that night, she chose to leave it as it was. She liked to rub her wrist along the smoothed arms and feel where the finish gave way to the bare wood below, satiny from long use. Under her pulse the unvarnished areas were smooth and cool.

The rocker's arms were broad enough to set a glass on; Faye used them for her desk. She set her shopping pad on a slant and made her list. She had plenty of things she wanted, someday. But after that evening, she had added—at the top, not the bottom—"Learn French." And she had begun to play her mother's dictated tapes that night. The woman who had given Faye life—"given *me* life," Faye was thinking by then—had hoped to save it for her. Faye had never before cared to hear them. Now it mattered, and she dragged the trunk over to her bedside and set the tape player on it, dropped in the first cassette, and listened. Strange sounds—sometimes in Vietnamese, sometimes in French—her mother sang and talked. Faye listened till she fell asleep. In the night, waking, she turned the cassette over and listened some more, sleeping and waking to that low voice telling, telling, telling, and singing its indecipherable words. As her mother had neared the end, she had forgotten to speak in English, but Faye somehow heard what she needed to in the voice itself. It was like the murmur of the sea; it was like the turn of the tide when everything quickens after the long pause, and the grasses stir, and the essential salts.

"I'm ready," Faye had assured Tom when she'd decided to buy the cottage. He was one of the many who didn't think she was ready at all. "I am," she had insisted.

"You'll have to prove it," Tom had warned. "You're on your own."

He wanted her to fail. What could she think but that? That was another reason she hadn't put in a telephone at first. She was afraid she'd find reason to use it, to call and complain or fret, to cry for help. She'd told everyone to tell everyone she was doing fine, anyone who asked, just fine, but in the night, when she couldn't sleep, she'd play those tapes. Her mother's voice. Faye hadn't a clue to what Mrs. Parry was saying, but she knew what it sounded like: she was not on her own; Faye was not alone; she could make it.

Faye's house was a handyman's special, a one-room cottage as hollow as a garage. In fact, it had begun life as a boathouse garage. It had a good tin roof, a wonderful cupola and seagull weathervane, a wall of windows added when it had been converted into an artist's studio, some fairly modern if utterly basic plumbing, and was structurally sound. It suffered from neglect but not termites. Vegetation had already begun to swallow it, but digestion had not started yet.

"And the price is right," Faye said, fending off advice.

Anyone who dared to or cared to offered advice. All told her not to do it. Some thought it simply wasn't the place. Others said don't buy it outright, consider the tax advantages. Some warned about resale, neighborhood values, the unpaved street, the pitch blackness beyond the last streetlight up on the paved road.

"What if you—"

"A storm could—"

"It won't always—"

"You won't always—"

"Hardly room for one, let alone two—"

To all of which Faye could only say, "True." And then she had added, urgent, completely at a loss to explain it better, "But." That was all. Just, "But." And a shrug. As though that explained not the case, but *her* case. She pitied their prudence, their ability to hold themselves back from joy, from life, to live *toward* that life, someday, rather than *in* it, *for* it, right now.

They teased her, called it her halfway house, because it was so much a hybrid of what it had been and what she intended to make it. She went over every evening after work the first few weeks, working. Shoveling out the inside, painting over the scrubbed-down walls. Everything white, every surface, including the bare trusses and rafters. Not a sophistication of taste but a simplification of budget. "White's cheapest," she said. "Brands don't even have to match," she said. But that was the first week. After sad experience she knew better about that. There were too many choices. Too many arctic names for the rainbow of snow. She trained her eye, and settled on a brand, and after that she could select by number and not have to deal with "quite white," "off white," "antique white," "desert white," "polar white," "cool white," or "warm white." It taught her eye something. She began to look at things differently. And she decided to sign up for a watercolor class during the winter session at the community center.

"Why watercolor?" Palma asked her, when Faye announced that.

"Water wash-up," Faye said. "Only way to go. You taught me that, remember?"

It was true that the only paints Faye had worked with were the marine paints Tom had used for her bike, and the latex and acrylics at Palma's, when they had painted the nursery.

In fact, that was what brought Faye over. "I want to borrow the stencils, please. For my bathroom."

"Noah's ark?"

"Just the whales and starfish," Faye said. "I see a little blue and gold, you know? And maybe a few stars on the floor." She sensed Palma's next objection. "I know, but I'll seal it with urethane, it'll do. That's how they seal bowling alleys."

"Bowling alleys are wood," Palma said.

Faye said, "That epoxy is stuck, I guarantee you. I put it on just the way they said, label directions." In fact, she had sealed the whole house's floor at one time, battleship gray onto the cement slab, wall to wall. Budget-pleaser and eye-pleaser too.

The plump little spouting whales sailed around the bathroom windows, with a gold starfish between, and across the floor, as planned, random starfish. White canvas liner for the shower; she had no tub. Whole bathroom the size of a Pullman water closet, but somehow airy and pleasant with the white, blue, and gray.

The Friday before moving day, Palma and her boys stopped by. "Place as fresh as an old maid's porch first day of summer," Palma approved.

Something flickered across Faye's face.

"What?"

"Nothing," Faye said, not meeting her eye.

Palma studied her. Shook her head. Finally let out that live-oak laugh of hers. "Don't you fret yourself," she told Faye. "You not the old-maid type."

Faye went to the window and wiped at a speck. No curtains. "I'm not a *type*," Faye said. "I don't care what kind."

Palma ran Elven out in the yard with the twins in their stroller.

"But if I was—" Faye added. Then she stopped. Shook her head. Couldn't go on.

"Reckon why she didn't want curtings?" Palma asked the house. Faye could answer or not. She didn't. No curtains and no kitchen either. Just a studio-size sink and a counter on wheels for appliances. No doors to the cabinets, just shelves, open. Faye already had a few items in stock. Cocoa, soup mix, spices.

"Oh. Almost forgot." Palma took out a little bottle from her pocket and handed it to Faye. "Goin' to give it to you later. I'll give it to you now."

"What is it?" Faye opened it and sniffed. Sneezed.

"Lots of folks saying something besides 'Bless you'?" Palma asked.

Faye tried to read the label. "Is it snuff?"

"I say bless you," Palma said. "You doin' fine. I say go, girl."

Faye looked at her.

"Is it magic?"

Palma said, "You know I don't hold with that stuff! Naw!"

She took the bottle and shook a little onto her palm and rubbed her hands together and then blew the dust toward Faye. "It's marjoram and oregano, my special blend. Let me tell you," she told her, "it's good. Since Egypt times they been putting it on beans."

"For happiness?" Faye said.

"For flavor, darlin', for flavor!"

"Oh," Faye said. She tried to sound interested.

"You remember it," Palma told her. "And remember, they's always beans."

"Beans?" Faye said.

"Beans," Palma said definitely. She sounded sure.

Faye wasn't disappointed, but she had expected something . . . She didn't know what she had expected. But she was feeling that threshold fear and energy which come when life is about to change. She was feeling that hope for talisman or truth that would carry her over and carry her on. But beans? She tried to make the best of it. "I didn't know beans," she said.

Palma stuck her head out the door. "Elven? Now!"

Immediately he appeared with a gift-wrapped package.

"Oh," Faye said. It was heavy.

"Open it now," Palma urged. Elven and the twins watched.

It was a slow cooker. "Look inside," Palma said.

Faye sat on the floor and tugged the packing materials out. The twins rustled around in the wrappings. Inside the cooker Faye found a sheaf of hand-written recipes, and a certificate for an orange tree. "That's for someday," Palma explained, "when you've done what you mean to to this yard. You know Zeb says you can borrow any of his tools to cut and dig with, and I say you can even borrow Zeb, if you can catch him."

"And me," Elven said.

Faye reached into the slow-cooker crock again. She pulled out a bag. And another. "Beans," she said, beginning to make sense of their recent conversation.

"Soak 'em overnight," Palma said. "Then put 'em on first thing tomorrow and you'll have you something good for supper." She scrabbled around in her baby bag. Pulled out a foil-wrapped something. "Here's you a hambone, too," Palma said. "I'll put it in your cooler."

She came back, to warn, "Now you know that'll feed a crowd?"

Faye shook her head. "A crowd," Palma said again. "But there ain't no way in this world you can manage on those two little bitty ice-cube trays! Make sure you and Tom pick up a bag of ice somewhere . . . and when you forget, just run on by my place, I keep extra, as you know."

"I'm not having a party," Faye said.

She had been firm about that. No housewarming, no bid for gifts, no cry for help in moving.

"Guess I shouldn't have wrapped it," Palma said, pointedly.

"I'm glad you did." Faye felt tears sting and glitter. This felt like farewell, like a moment. Palma and Elven and the twins were going back to their house, and Faye was going to sleep in the cottage. She had a sleeping bag. Tom would help her move the secondhand bed from St. Joseph's Attic on Saturday. She was crying. "I'm glad," Faye managed to say, "for everything."

"Lord, Faye," Palma said. "It's not like we not gone be almost neighbors!"

After Palma had gone, Faye sat for a long time rocking. She didn't turn on her lamp, just sat with Palma's recipes in her lap and read them till she could no longer see that strong, no-nonsense handwriting. On the cover Palma had written, "If you can't fit it in here and dip it out delicious, you don't need to call it food." When Faye went in to put the beans on to soak, she paused, read the label, and then Palma's note: "makes goms of beans," and decided to use them all.

There was enough food on moving day to feed folks all day long and into the evening. It was more like open house than moving day, because there were more people than furniture. Faye never did have an official housewarming, but people came all along, friends and acquaintances both curious and kind, and everyone who came brought something. Yard-sale glasses and a pitcher; a laundry basket and clothespins; a "start" of lemon grass from cuttings of her own (Cliffie); a trowel and ginger root (Father Grattan); a wind-chime mobile made of seashells (Elven). There was a puzzling gift of two fingertip towels from Dawn at work: nice little towels, the matched pair, the velvety kind for show, personalized with embroidery, yet instead of HIS and HERS they announced MINE and MINE in white on navy blue. Dawn gave them to Faye at lunch at work on Tuesday and had her open them so everyone could see. They all laughed. Faye didn't get it.

"Don't worry about it," Dawn told her. "It's better to need something you don't have than have something you don't need."

"Well, I need towels," Faye said. "Thank you."

And they laughed again, so Faye felt she was being hazed, but she couldn't see why.

On the way home that evening she stopped by Palma's. Showed her the towels and watched Palma's face. Palma didn't think it was funny, either. She didn't laugh; she scowled.

"Do you like them?" Faye wondered.

"Who did this?" Palma held one up to her eyes, studying the work. "It's so tight it'll pucker in the wash and dry like a ruffle."

Faye had decided it must be a joke, like "kick me." Maybe if she used the towels it would be like framing a "kick me" sign and hanging it on her wall. "Would you put these in your bathroom?"

"You gotta be kidding!" Palma scratched her head, delicately, speculatively.

"What would you do with them?"

Palma considered. She took the embroidery in both hands and tugged at it, worked at loosening it up, jerking it, finally drawing it on the bias, but it was still tight. "What was that thing thinking of, to do this—herownself, I can tell, look at the back side, tension all a tangle—to a perfectly good piece of terry!" She flung the towel down into the box it came in. "Not even zigzag stitch," she grieved. "It's buttonholed! I'd give anything to have a machine like that, and look how she trifles with her thread."

"Is it about sex?" Faye found the courage to ask. She tried to sound offhand, wise. "Is it cute? Is it an insult?"

Palma looked at her. "Sugar," she said, "Everything in this world is about s-e-x. Whole world! Don't do a bit of good to go around feeling righteous and starchy about it. Don't need to get affronted and confrontated. She sayin' more about herownself than about you. She oughta be more concerned about who been washing up in *her* bathroom than what's hanging up in yours."

"I don't want them," Faye said suddenly. She pushed the box away.

Palma said, "If you mean that—"

Faye nodded.

"—then we can fix 'em. Shootfire can." She got her scissors and cut the monogrammed ends of the towels. "Turn 'em into fingertips or teas," Palma said. She rummaged around in her notions till she found the old card of Wright's eyelet. She crackled the yellowed cellophane off and measured across the towel with the lace. "Plenty to spare," she said. "Enough for both ends. Been saving this I don't know how long. All these menfolk around here . . . when'll I ever need ruffled lace?" She had it pin-basted in no time. "Now, you watch the babies and I'll sew."

She vanished into the other room. Faye could hear the foot-treadle Singer stitching along as Palma sewed. Faye leaned over the playpen to see if she could tell James from John. The first few weeks she had been able to sort out the twins, but now she wasn't sure. James had a freckle on his ear? John had a mole on his fingertip? That wasn't how Palma knew the difference; she had a mother-eye, and insisted they didn't look at all alike.

Elven came in and walked up to the twins; pointed: "James," he said. He reached over and picked him up and handed him to Faye. "And this is Johnny," he said.

From the other room Palma yelled, "Stir my peas! One a'y'all! Stir my peas!" Faye handed the baby to Elven and ran. She was still stirring when Palma came into the kitchen to show her the results. Both towels looked new; no monogram or embroidered remarks on them at all. Palma folded them back into the gift box. She got a plastic bag and put the whole thing in it, saying, "Why don't you just stay on and eat? Plenty-plenty of peas, worlds of 'em, and you know they predictin' it's bound to rain. Zeb'll drive you and your bike home in his truck. He's due. He's long due." She paused. "*Not* overdue," she specified.

Zeb and Palma had been back together since the twins' birth; Zeb was still fishing on the *Palma Forever*. When he was late, she mentioned it; when he was very late, she suffered in silence and kept her shoes on and her handbag handy in case she had to—as she put it—"ride somewhere and identify the body." That was how it was with her, how it would always be. They didn't argue about it anymore, and Zeb did all he could to keep her from grieving.

Faye didn't want to wait for Zeb. "I've got a class tonight." Before Palma could ask, knowing those equivalency sessions were over, Faye said, "I'm going to take watercolor and French next time." Faye tied on her slicker hat. Looked at the sky. "I'll make it," she figured, not that she had a weather eye.

She simply didn't intend to miss another "Life on the Edge" session.

"Supposed to rain all weekend," Palma said, scowling at the sky. She went back inside and turned off the peas. Every step, she grumbled at Zeb. "Of course he don't mind a little rain, man never yet minded a little rain. It can't even blow him off the water, that man."

"Monday too?" Faye said suddenly.

That got Palma's attention. "Thought you was finished paintin'?"

"Shutters and screens to go," Faye said. "But I got plans."

"Plans."

Monday was Faye's day off from the shop. And she was taking a day off from the grocery. Something about the way she announced that, almost a confession, almost guiltily, made Palma suspicious. "You and who else?"

"It's my birthday," Faye said. "I'm going fishing."

"For what?"

"For fish," Faye said. "Fishing."

"On whose boat?"

Faye shrugged. "I don't know. *China Doll* . . . Whose is that?"

Palma gusted her relief. She knew Faye wasn't happy where she worked, was looking; shampooing and sweeping up cut hair and doing towels wasn't a future, but still, she hadn't seemed restless enough to make any sudden changes. Still, she was a person who acted on her feelings. "When the light turns green, that's as green as it gets," was how Faye had explained more than one impulsive moment. "Green ain't no braggin' nothin'," was how Palma countered that. "You eat enough green apples, you'll see what I mean."

But this time she didn't tease Faye or chide her.

"Gals from work?" Palma guessed.

Faye nodded.

"Lord, girl, a smart-painted, brochure-boasted, day-trippin', shallow draft, fringe-awning, bait-and-pole-furnished—"

"Lunch provided," Faye added.

"—party boat! For a minute there I thought you goin' to be doin' it for a livin'!"

A funny look crossed Faye's face.

"Forget I said that!" Palma exclaimed. "I mean that."

Before Dawn could fish, she had to take off her fingernails. Even though she was a nail technician ("Get Nailed by Dawn," her business cards advertised) she didn't use the strong glues and chemicals and techniques on her own hands. "That stuff'll kill you!" she said. "I keep my instruments clean and a fan on, but jeez, did you see that on '60 Minutes'?" She removed her press-on nails one by one and put them in a little compact, snapped it shut, and slid it into her pocket. She and the others had staked out a spot by the stern rail; they had been fishing before, and knew the best spot. Faye didn't join them for long. Even before they reached

the grounds, she felt iffy; by the time the boat paused and the waves began to lift and drop it slightly amid the diesel and bait stinks, Faye
needed to find the bench and sit.

She kept her eyes shut, and from time to time re-dipped her towel in
ice water, and wiped her face.

Sandy broke off a piece of raw ginger root and offered it to Faye, who
didn't open her eyes until Sandy passed the ginger back and forth under
her nose. Then she took only a morsel. The lemony hot flavor was all
right, but the texture—not at all like candied ginger—made her jaw
clench. She did not know whether she was supposed to swallow or spit.
She could not imagine doing either. She was not aware she had groaned.

"There's one on every boat," someone said.

"Usually standing by me," another laughed.

"My first time," Faye managed to say.

A woman rummaged through her mesh tote and found sunglasses.
"Just imagine a horizon inside your head," she told Faye. "Works for me
every time. You just have to fool your ear; that's where you lose it, in
your ear."

"In your ear!" someone echoed, and a few joined in the laugh.

Tracey brought a fish and showed Faye. "Look!"

Faye looked. "It was on your line!" Tracey told her. "We're keeping
the Lone Star cold and the dance floor hot while you're gone."

"You can have it," Faye said.

One of the deckhands came by. "Breathe with the boat," he told her.
He sat beside Faye, and when she opened her eyes, he drew his fingers
apart in front of her face. "Imagine I am stretching a line between your
eyes," he said. "A red string or a blue one, I don't care."

"A green one?" Faye asked. "Like the line at sunset?"

"You like it green? Make it green," he said.

Faye looked. "I can't see a green one."

"Hey," he said. "You're feeling better already."

He started to get up.

"Do it again, please," Faye said. "I really wasn't looking."

He studied her. "All right."

She opened her eyes and watched as he pulled his hands apart, stretching an imaginary line between them. Faye peered. She looked at the air
between them, not at his eyes.

"I see it," she said. "It's blue."

She reached out and, with thumb and index finger of both hands, "picked" the thread from between his hands and held it for herself. "Thank you," she said.

"No big thing," he said.

"Is that all there is to it?" she asked, holding that imaginary thread in front of her face.

"Pull it toward you and take it inside, so it's on the inside, not the outside."

She concentrated. She moved her hands to her temples, as though putting on glasses.

"Still see it?" he asked. "Absolute horizon?"

"Yes."

"From now on, you get to feeling icky, just imagine that line, you'll be fine."

It was nice the way he'd stopped to help her. She shook his hand, just stuck her hand out and shook his. His was rough in the palm, tough like Tom's. Faye glanced at him just an instant, then looked away. "Thank you," she said.

"Let's get fishing," he said, and moved on down the deck, helping others.

Faye sat on the bench a few more minutes. She felt much better. After she was able to think of the horizon line without effort—she just put it in her mind's eye and left it there—she could step to the rail and begin fishing. When she did, Dawn said, "He's cute."

Faye looked around.

"You know who," Dawn said. She glanced down the boat to the area where the hands and mates were helping bait. They were chopping chunks off a block of frozen squid. Faye couldn't look at that. She knew it was silly, but she couldn't look. She had to shut her eyes and think about the horizon again. She didn't like baiting, and she didn't like to see the fish after they were pulled up, caught, but still alive and gaping. She thought she would not bait her lines, just let them be, but in the late afternoon, just before they finished fishing for the day, she caught a good-sized dorado on her bottom line. No bait. She had decided to enjoy the water, just look at the water and the colors in it, and now she had a fish to fight and boat. It was about forty pounds. She didn't have a record, or even the biggest fish of the day, but only one other fisherman had caught a dorado, so that made it special. Everyone gathered around to see.

"Didn't I tell ya?" Sandy crowed.

Faye had been using light spinning tackle, and the deckhand who had given her advice about seasickness helped her boat the dorado. He called it "dolphin."

"That's not a dolphin," Faye said. "Don't say that!"

He looked at her. "But that's what they call it."

"Don't *you* call it," Faye said.

"She's got this thing," Tracey warned him, "about save-the-whales."

"A dolphin's a whale?" Dawn said.

"*That's* not a whale," a child said, pointing.

Faye's fish lay on the deck, its vivid blues and greens fading to gray and yellow. It looked like a light had been turned off inside it. Immediately, Faye's mood crashed from pride to deep contrition. She was glad when they threw it down into the hold on ice.

Faye and Dawn and a man from Pascagoula got their picture in the evening paper, Faye and the man from Mississippi because they had both caught dorado, and Dawn because she jumped into the photo at the last second, for a joke. The man from Mississippi was holding his fish up by a grip on its tail. Faye had her fish across her arms. "It's not a dolphin," she was saying as the shutter clicked.

"Yeah, yeah," the photographer said.

Faye said, "Don't you say it is!"

Dawn said, "Sugar, it's all mahi-mahi by the time it hits the menu." She handed the photographer one of her cards, and said something else to him, another of her jokes about silk, which explains why the photo in the paper didn't have Faye's name at all; he forgot to ask. They just printed the name of the man from Pascagoula and "Dawn of Styles by Raquel" and "a friend," after "a day on the *China Doll*." So Faye's name didn't appear at all. Neither did the word *dolphin*.

Dawn stood on the driver's side of the car, pressing her nails back on. She let Sandy and Tracey haul their cooler of fish to the trunk and lift it in. They waited. Faye's fish was one of the last to be filleted and steaked. She waited too, but didn't watch. The same hand who had told her how to keep from being seasick took care of Faye's fish. She paid a little extra for that.

"But it's worth it," Sandy told her. "Otherwise you won't want to look a fish in the eye, much less eat it!"

Faye planned to take the cooler by Palma's to store in her freezer—but she wondered how she'd manage that, on her bicycle.

At the car, Sandy and Tracey and Dawn were thinking about the problem too. There was not room for Faye's bicycle and the cooler in the trunk, and there was hardly room for four in the car anyway. "Maybe we could drop the fish off somewhere," Sandy suggested. She started back to tell Faye. Faye saw her and ran on across the lot to talk.

"He's going to drop me off, there's room in his truck for my bike," Faye said.

Dawn rolled her eyes.

"I don't know," Sandy said. She tried to mother-hen Faye.

"She's free, white, and twenty-one," Tracey said.

"So am I," Dawn said, "and I wouldn't—"

"Times two," Tracey said. "And you would, too. Only he didn't ask."

Faye said, "He's not my boyfriend, he's just helping."

"Help! Help!" Dawn cried, and got in the driver's side and slammed the door.

"He's actually nice and he knows a lot of history," Faye said.

"Well, what did we learn in school today?" Dawn called.

Tracey got in the backseat. After she had slammed the trunk lid, Sandy got in the front. "Don't mind her," Sandy told Faye.

"Oh, I won't," Faye said.

That made Dawn howl again.

Faye called, "Wait," and Dawn stopped the car and Faye ran to Sandy's window and said, "He was telling me all about the harbor, how it used to be. How the Pass got made."

"Sugar, I saw it!" Dawn said, pulling it into low gear and revving on the floored clutch, and hooting.

"You don't look *that* old," Faye said. Now it was her turn to laugh. But Dawn didn't look so amused.

Sandy said, "Speaking of age, I know somebody's having a birthday," and Faye put her finger to her lips and made the sign for "secret." Sandy smiled. "I do the tax work for your paycheck, you know. Matter of public record."

"Her birthday?" Tracey squealed. "You shoulda told us!"

"How old are you?" Dawn said. She revved it again. And let the clutch up a little, so the car strained to go. Faye made a mental note to jump back, or she'd get covered with grit when they finally roared off.

"I'll be twenty-one tomorrow," Faye said.

Sandy gave her the thumbs-up. "Go for it!" she said, and Dawn took that as a remark meant for her, not Faye. They were off and away in a cloud, kicking up sand. Faye turned her back till the debris settled.

As Faye walked back to the dock to wait for her ride to Palma's, she was thinking, "I'm not going to work tomorrow." She'd never missed;

she'd always been on time. Suddenly she didn't much care if she ever went back. It wasn't the people there, and it wasn't even that bad a job. Faye couldn't figure it. It was sudden. Maybe that's what being twenty-one is, she was thinking.

She felt good. She felt fine. When the man from the boat dropped her off at Palma's, he helped heave the fish into the freezer there. After, he offered to drop Faye's bike off, and Faye too, if she'd care to ride. But she said no. So he unloaded it, set it in the drive on its kickstand. He kept one hand on the seat. She felt strong enough, or bold enough, to look him in the eyes. She thought maybe something would happen, but if it did, it didn't to her. She looked at him again, to make sure. To see if bonding had begun to happen, just from that glance. She couldn't tell. "Well," he said. He didn't hang around. He slid back under the wheel and drove away. She saw his arm pump good-bye in the warm air over his cab roof as he turned the corner onto Delauniere.

Faye stood there. Palma was watching her. When she noticed, Faye relaxed her lips, which she had been pressing together. She couldn't get that puckered look off her forehead, though.

"What?" Palma wanted to know.

Faye smiled. Shrugged. "This is the last day in my whole life I'll ever be twenty." She looked at her watch. "Six hours to go."

Palma shook her head. She knew better than to try teasing Faye. "And then what?"

Faye didn't answer for a moment. She seemed to be thinking it through. She put her hand on the place in the hollow of her throat where fatigue or hunger or bad coffee, the short night and the long day, thinned and sped her pulse. It beat like dread-and-have-to, knocked like opportunity. Dry-mouthed, she said, "I don't know."

PART II

ARIDITY

When Faye got home from fishing on the *China Doll*, there was a notice of attempt to deliver mail. She walked to town the next morning, to collect whatever it was. It had been raining, but was clearing. Still she wore a jacket and took her umbrella. When she presented the notice, the clerk vanished into the back of the office. After a minute he returned with a large cardboard box.

"I didn't order anything," Faye told him. She had not brought her money, to pay a COD.

"It's—no charges," the man told her. He handed it across. The carton was not so heavy, but very large. The return label had Faye's name as addressee. The shipper's name was Replogle. "I don't know them," Faye said.

She didn't want to take it.

"If you didn't order it, and it comes post-paid addressed to you, you can keep it," the clerk told her.

"No," Faye said, as though he were teasing.

"Neckties, thermometers, Christmas seals, you name it," he confirmed.

"I'll bring any neckties back," Faye told him. She lifted the box off the counter and walked with it outside. She could not see over it. She turned her head to the side, rested her cheek along the carton, and navigated by watching where she put her feet. She got safely to the corner. She set it down to wait for the light. As the light went green her way, she looked back at the post office once again, as though someone might be about to call her back. Then she went on. The folded umbrella on her wrist tapped the carton like a drum.

She had gone rather slowly down one block and made the turn into the lane to the beach when she stepped to one side, eased off the roadway entirely to allow someone coming behind her to pass by. The vehicle paused when she did. After a moment she turned to see why. It was Vic Rios. He had parked. He got out and walked up to where she stood.

"Need some help?"

"It's addressed to me," Faye said. "I don't know what it is."

"Maybe you should open it and see. Maybe it would be easier to carry without all the packaging."

If she didn't want it, why carry it all the way home? Faye said, "Well."

Vic already had his little knife out, opened and offered by the handle, the same one she had seen at the Fourth of July picnic. For a moment that made her hesitate.

"Careful," Vic said.

Faye set the box on the sandy shoulder of the lane and knelt to cut the shipping tape. The label was glued across the flap, so she cut a line just through her own name. She didn't like doing that; she drew her breath in.

"Did you cut yourself?"

"No," she said. "Not really."

He backed off a little, looked out through the trees toward the glare over the water. At this time of day there was always that eerie haze off the dry beach, a stormy shimmer that could fool a stranger into raising a convertible top or heading for shelter.

Faye had the box open at last. She had to pull out several pieces of packing, a corrugated brace, and a plastic bag with instructions and a booklet.

"So what do you think?" Vic asked.

"I don't know," Faye said, mystified. "What's a Replogle?"

But then she saw. "Oh!" And reached into the box and pulled out a globe. It was free-standing, with a wooden cradle, not one of the ones with a metal scythe-axis and degrees marked off. This globe was as free as the world itself, within the limits and graces of gravity and taxation, interference and carelessness. She raised it to the sky and laughed. "Oh," she said again.

Then she said, "Who?"

"Maybe there's a note," Vic said.

She couldn't hold the globe and look for the note both. She tried. Vic found the invoice. No price, just "Happy Birthday," typed by someone at the company.

"Is it your birthday?" Vic asked.

The globe's cradle was a warm polished wood, lined with felt so the globe turned silently. "I thought he forgot," she said.

Vic considered that. "Tom," he said. He walked back to his car and got something from his jacket. He leaned into the car and lit his little cigar from the car's lighter. He smoked for a minute, looking out over the marsh, where the inlet kept builders from grading. Faye had helped with that fight; she had carried a save-the-wetlands poster on a stick out in front of the meeting. Now no one could build there. Ever. Faye thought about that. When Vic finally walked back to where Faye was gathering up the packing materials to recycle and re-boxing her present, he offered, "I could run you home."

"Oh, no," Faye said instantly, as though that were out of the question. Which it was.

"You could leave the packing crate with me," he said. "That'd lighten the load."

"I can use the box," Faye said, still not looking at him.

"Well, how about if you carry this," he said, taking the globe out again and handing it to her, "and I'll carry the rest?" He left his car right there to walk beside her.

"It's kind of far," she said.

"My point," he agreed.

When they made the final turn off the pavement—such as it was—onto the sand-and-shell lane, Faye slipped. She didn't fall, but she lost her hold on the globe and it spun out of her arms and down the way ahead of them. She cried out and ran after it, caught it up, and turned back to say, "It's all right," checking the place it had hit, and brushing it gently, blowing sand off so it would not scratch. Feeling with her fingertips for any dent or scar. "Nothing," she said, "not even a scuff. Middle of the ocean. No one was there, it's all right."

"Maybe it's better to have the other kind, with the base attached," he said.

"Nature," Faye said, "doesn't . . . Invisible forces."

"No strings," Vic said.

"That's it," Faye said. "None you can see, anyway!" She forgot and looked at him. He was looking at her. Roasting with speculation, with self-consciousness, she glanced at her shoes. She noticed his. Not deck shoes, town shoes. Half-boots. Dressy. The sand wasn't doing them any good.

"There's a block of sidewalk in a little bit, and then it quits again," she told him. But when they got there, they walked on in the road, side by side. The tracks her bike had made in the sand directed him when she forgot to tell him to turn. Now they were on a road he had never been on in his life, never suspected.

"Who comes out here?" he wondered. There were a few car tracks.

"The mail cart," Faye said. "That's it, some days. Renters, vacationers, in season or on their time-share, but they've all gone for now." She paused, not sure she should tell about the lack of neighbors. They paused, and he lit another cigarillo, from a match he tore from a book. Faye noticed that. That he didn't have a lighter, or didn't use one. They had gone past the shade of the oaks, and the heat, even so early in the day as this, was stinging; his sheer white shirt, fine as the batiste Faye had lost her temper trying to sew for Palma's twins, stuck—transparent with damp—to Vic's skin.

"Who else?" he wondered, exhaling. Looking through a gap in the hedgerow of yaupon and bayonet, past the trilling grasshopper sparrows, toward whatever it was he couldn't see, couldn't fathom.

Faye shrugged. "Palma," she said. "Tom. Friends. Parkers." She offered the last shyly. "A parker or two."

Startled, he swung to face her. "Parkers? They live out here? Ned and the—" he snapped his fingers, trying to call it up. As though he saw the face so clearly. Faye blushed furiously, and started walking on ahead so she didn't have to talk right to him. "You know." Just the way she said it. Over her shoulder. With a wild modesty.

Vic stared. "What?" Looking shrewd.

Then he almost smiled. She walked faster, and decided not to look back again. He said, "Oh. *Those* parkers." He flung his smoked-down cigar away; it landed near some empty bottles.

"It's not a throughfare," she said, quoting the sign posted at the last turning. That's how she pronounced it, "throughfare."

"Thoroughfare," he said.

"Is *that* how? I thought they misspelled it."

This time he did laugh, but not, she decided, unpleasantly. A catbird tick-ticked, flew out in Vic's face, and rustled back into the scrub. From cover it made rattling and crusty and disagreeable noises.

"I know that bird," Faye said, as though that explained everything.

Vic paused at Faye's gatepost and emptied sand from his shoes.

"This is it," Faye said.

"How—" he began.

"How—" she began.

"You."

"No, you," she insisted. But they didn't. Off-time and cranky all of a sudden, they paused at the gate.

"A pink one," Vic said.

"It's not pink," Faye said.

"*This* one?" Vic said. He opened the gate and stood back for her to carry the world through. He followed. At the step, she handed him the globe, which he balanced on one upturned palm, and she bent to pick up the last shell, shake out her door key, and unlock. She put the key back. Completely trusting. It never occurred to her not to.

"Why don't you just leave it in the lock?" he wondered.

She took the globe from him and stepped back.

He waited for her to go in first. She walked to the table she used for studying. The room was moted in shafts of sunlight. She tapped the table. "Here," she said. He got the cradle out of the box and set it there and she put the globe in place. "There," she said. She turned it till the Atlantic and the Gulf rose into view. She put her fingertip on a point just between the two waters. "Here we are," she said.

He looked around.

He seemed interested.

"I'm just starting," she said. She glanced to the door; it was standing open. He took his hat off and set it on the crab-crate table. "How about that," he said, tapping the glass with his knuckle.

"I like it," she said.

He sat on the cedar bench. "So do I," he said.

Pleased, she said, "Everybody does."

He frowned.

Faye sat in the rocker. She did not offer to show him the house; he could see most of it from where he sat, and she felt shy about showing the area where she had made her bedroom. The box Señora Rios had brought, when she and Father Ockham and Mrs. Lockridge drove over, sat in the corner. It had a bedspread, ruffle, shams. The king-size, nine by nine feet, coverlet was larger than the area Faye's cot was set up in. Faye had already decided she would use the fabric to make a bench cushion, and the ruffle for a bit of color at the top of her shower curtain, and maybe some place mats—or maybe she would exchange it all for something she needed, something that fit. The other part of Señora Rios's gift had already gone into service—a coffeemaker and a canister of robust grounds. Faye thought of that now, but didn't offer coffee, because it would take time. She thought Vic would be going soon. She thought he would not waste any more time. The note Señora Rios had enclosed with the coffee said, "Instant, never. Cuban man can wait. Makes it better."

"She shouldn't have," Faye said. "Why does everything—"

"What?" Vic said.

Then Faye knew she had been thinking out loud.

Suddenly it seemed impossible that he was sitting there in her house. She wasn't afraid, not the way she had been, but she didn't have anything to talk about. "Now you're going to have to walk back," she said.

She saw him glance toward the kitchen area, where her secondhand toaster oven, the double hot plate, the camp-size refrigerator, and the slow cooker sat.

"I have two trays of ice cubes," Faye said.

"That sounds fine," he said.

She couldn't decide whether that meant he wanted something to drink or that he thought two trays were enough in general. She decided to fix, not ask. She got up and was busy with that for a minute. Was bringing two glasses of ice water when Tom drove up. He covered the length of the path at a lope and came in the open door.

"I was hoping," Faye said.

"You're famous," he told Faye, and traded the newspaper for one of the glasses of water. Then he saw Vic. They just looked at each other. Vic got up and reached across and took the other glass of water. Faye laid the paper down and went back to her kitchen and cut a lime.

"I guess you've already seen the paper," Tom said, sounding disappointed.

Faye hadn't. Tom had it folded open to that picture of her and the fish. "What?" she said.

Vic waved it off. "I saw it," he said.

Faye took it up and looked. "I'm glad they didn't get the name wrong," she said. She offered lime to Tom first, then to Vic.

Wedges for Tom, and slices in case that was how Vic took it. She didn't know, and wouldn't ask. But Vic didn't take. Faye chose one of the slices and ate the peel. She did not have a glass. She simply ate the fruit. She did not like the taste, but did it to have something to do—she was nervous. She did not know what to do with the pips. She held them in her fist.

"Now Captain Rios won't have to walk back," she said.

"About through?" Tom asked Vic.

Vic leaned back, crossed his legs, rested his arms along the back of the cedar bench. "No hurry," he said.

"At your convenience," Tom assured him.

"I have all day," Vic said. "This is recess."

"You're dressed for court or courting," Tom agreed. "But I saw in the paper which it is."

"Have you got jury duty?" Faye wondered. She had just reregistered to vote. On the form, she had checked the box that she would like to serve, in any capacity, on any panel. "Regular jury or grand jury?" she asked.

Vic gave Tom a look. He set his glass down and stood. "Witness," he said. "Hostile."

Tom seemed to be enjoying all of this. He was still sitting in Faye's rocker. Faye looked from him to Vic and back. She had forgotten all about the globe. She felt the tension between the two men and decided it must be her fault. "Did I say something I shouldn't?"

"This divorce business is killing your mother," Tom said. "Call her. She's lit so many candles it's like Christmas."

Vic tipped his glass and drank the rest of the water.

"More?" Faye said, glad to have something to do. Glad to leave them for a moment. But Vic said, "No more."

And he said it as though he meant it for both of them. Faye glanced around the room. She saw the globe. "Oh!" she said, almost leaping to her feet. "I forgot to say it. Thank you!"

Tom looked. Baffled.

"It's going to sit right here," Faye said. "Don't you think?"

Tom crossed to the table and looked.

"It's perfect," she said. "Tom?"

Vic was almost out the door. "Let's go," he said.

"I didn't even get you a card," Tom said.

"Oh, but they put 'Happy Birthday' in the—on the—" Faye couldn't think of the word. "Papers. Receipts."

"Invoice," Vic said. Tom looked at Vic. "*You*," he said.

"That's it!" Faye said. "They didn't put your name, but that's all right, I knew. I don't need a card."

"I didn't—" Tom said.

"You did plenty," Faye told him. She touched his wrist. He scowled.

Tom and Vic exchanged another look. Faye couldn't read them, couldn't think how to make Tom pleasant again. Finally she said the truest thing. "I knew you didn't forget me."

Faye followed them to the door. They left without much ceremony. The walk was barely wide enough for them to go side by side, but neither one would step ahead, or fall back. Halfway along, Faye heard Tom growl, "Why didn't you tell her—" and Vic put out his hand to Tom's arm, stopping him. They glanced back at her in the doorway. They walked on. "Don't spoil it for her," Vic said. "Let it be. She's happy."

After they had driven away, Faye washed the glasses and put them up. She didn't notice at first, but when she went to get the little plate of limes, she discovered that Vic had left his hat. She ran to the door, but they had gone. She took the lime slices to the refrigerator. Every time she looked across and saw that hat sitting there on her crab-crate table, she felt sad, as though something just right had been spoiled because she hadn't done what she ought. But it was his hat; he should have remembered. Seeing it there gave Faye a little shock. It felt like fear. Palma always said if a person forgets an item, it means they intend to come back; it's like a symbol. They may not even know it. "You might say one thing and do another," Palma would say.

Faye had a policy against fear. And she wasn't going to be like Elven's cat, puffing up and acting like a fool when it caught a glimpse of something it didn't recognize in the twilight. Faye took Vic's hat and carried it over to her front door, hung it on one of the pegs. That was that. Then she thought better. It didn't need to look like it belonged, like it had a place. Even though it was convenient—if he came back for it, she could just hand it out the door to him, he wouldn't even have to come in—she took it down. It didn't need to look so at home.

Not having a thing to prove, she proved it, by trying the hat on, right there in front of her mirror. Lifted the thing off again, it didn't suit her. As she lifted it, a faint aroma—sandalwood? lime? bay?—disturbed her. Something she had not been conscious of, yet that had been, she now realized, an irritant. She looked around; she thought for a moment he was back, had come back and was in the house, so much was that fragrance— she now knew—his signature. She was quite alone. She sniffed around her little cottage as she made sure the doors were locked. The hat itself exhaled that aroma! She stood for the longest time. After a while she raised the hat to her face and looked. It was absolutely clean inside, no oils, no lint or hair; the label had the maker's name, not Vic's. She inhaled. It was odd how that scent—shampoo? cologne?—reminded her. Of something she couldn't remember. Made her sad to the point of tears. She felt her pulse in her teeth, as slow as dread. She felt guilty, as though the mere touching of this hat were trespass. She crossed to the table and set the hat back where she had found it. She wiped the brim, in case her fingerprints had been left on it. She gave it a little poke, and another, till it was as near in its original location as she could manage. Then she ignored it.

She was sorry now she had called Sandy on the way to the post office, and begged off work. She wished she had something to do. She mowed her little lawn, and moved a clump of lilies. Then she walked on the beach. She found three more shells for her border. One was really nice.

She soaked them in the bleach bucket and set them on the back-porch rail to dry. Palma and them had been over on the weekend for cake and coffee, and she had told anyone else who asked that she already had plans. That meant she was free, but she didn't want to be. She walked up to the village, bought a Cuban sandwich and some lemonade, and took it out to the west point to look at the waders in the lagoon. She had her binoculars and field guide, and hopes, but it was the wrong time of day, everything was in silhouette. Faye turned back toward the village. She walked on the beach part of the way, and came up the steps near the municipal pier. She liked the view from the rise by the library, and she took that path through the park. It was going to be a nice sunset.

There was a couple sitting on the bench down on the boardwalk. Children were swinging and sliding in the play area, and a jogger on a taut leash tried to keep up with an eager retriever. They were headed for the water. Faye turned and walked backward, watching to see if the jogger would be able to brake in time. They stopped at the very edge of the rip-rap, as though the dog had finally come to his senses.

When Faye turned back, she noticed the painter. He wasn't working at an easel; he had his things all around on the ground, as he sat working very rapidly at a lapboard. Faye passed, then peeked. She was looking at the painting, not at the one painting it, so she was surprised to hear her name, and see that the man was Father Grattan, in what he called "civvies." No collar, nothing to advertise his vocation.

"I had the day off," Faye said, instantly feeling nervous, though she hadn't told Sandy a lie, about work. She just didn't have a good reason not to go. She had not been to church, either.

"My day off too," Father Grattan said.

She looked at his painting again. He had been working wet on wet, to block in the view and the light, and she knew he needed to hurry on, to catch the sunset. "Please," she said, stepping back, "keep working."

"I'll be done in a minute," he agreed. "Or else I won't. Now or never."

Faye sat on the grass a little way off, and didn't watch. She hoped that was the right thing to do. She looked out to sea through her field glasses and when it got too dark for that, she opened her bird book and pretended to be studying. She wanted to ask him something.

"Look at that! Did you see that?" Father Grattan exclaimed, pointing. Faye looked. "No," she said. "What was it?"

He dumped his rinse water, groomed his brushes, laid things away. "I thought it was that green line."

Faye grieved, "I never have seen it! I look and look! Did you see it to-night? I wasn't looking!"

"Maybe not," he said. "If *you* saw it, I'd say I did too." He shrugged. "Maybe it's like gold; it's the quest."

"Do you always come here?" Faye wondered. "I've never seen you . . . But then I usually work."

"I've painted that stump and those rocks at least forty times," Father Grattan said. He showed her his portfolio.

She had to turn them to the light from the dusk-to-dawn; it gave everything a sort of amber look, but even so, she could tell the colors didn't match reality. The sea looked like glass. Or grass.

"It looks like the prairie at Micanopy," she said.

Flat flat flat.

"The Canadian plains look like that too," he agreed. "Like oceans."

"Oceans of what?" she was going to say, then decided, "Of wheat."

"And corn," he agreed. "And barley and spelt and rye."

Faye looked out to sea. "Oceans of it?" she said.

"And the tide's always in," he added. "Year after year."

"Are you homesick?"

He thought about it. "I—no," he decided. "That's not it."

She looked at the pictures again. Always the sky took most of the page. There were never any people or birds. It was as though he painted at the exact moment when the world at noon is so still, when nothing sings, nothing ventures, and there is no breeze to move you along. She recognized something about his pictures. She put herself in them.

"If you're not homesick," she said.

He recapped the final tube of color. The tubes were tiny, concentrated. He could fit them all in a sandwich bag. He sealed it and put it away in his knapsack. He had a special container for his brushes. They clipped tight, so they wouldn't shift and get bristles bent. "If . . . then . . ." Father Grattan said.

"Sir?"

"If I'm not homesick, then . . ." he prompted.

Faye had a handful of grass she had pulled up. She sorted it, blade by blade. It was light enough; she could see him plainly if she looked.

She wouldn't look. "Maybe you're depressed." She almost whispered it.

"I beg your pardon?"

"In drawing therapy—you know—" she said. Hoping he *would* know.

He waited. He had everything put away now; he sat looking out at the water. He drew his knees up, and wrapped his arms around them.

He didn't talk about drawing at all.

"This," he said, "is when I miss smoking."

"Well, it's not good for you," she said.

He laughed. "I've heard that."

"I took medicine," Faye said.

He looked at her. "To stop smoking?"

Humbly, she admitted, "Because I was depressed."

He glanced at her.

"They said I drew 'desolations,' " she told him. He turned and looked at her. "They said I was depressed because I was angry and wouldn't give in and admit it. I didn't know it. I really didn't know that was how it worked! They told me to get mad and they told me to take medicine for that too."

"Did you?"

"I didn't like the medicine . . . There's other things," she told him. "There's art and walks and swimming lessons and Chinese cooking and driving lessons and French and I'm to keep busy."

"Sounds like it," he said.

"Like Winston Churchill," she said. "Have you heard of him?"

Father Grattan gave her the V-for-victory sign, and she nodded. "Well," she went on, "he laid bricks. Just piles and piles of them, miles and miles, brick after brick. I don't know how long . . . And he painted the same picture over and over, just like you."

Father Grattan laughed.

"Oh," Faye said, for the first time wondering if she'd gone wide of the mark. She gathered her thoughts. "But in between he fought wars."

He laughed again.

"He won them," she said. "He won."

They sat there and watched the jogger and the retriever come back the way they had gone, only this time the jogger was in the lead.

"You knew it already, all that," Faye decided. That was the trouble, Faye was thinking; some of the simplest stuff nobody had heard of, like Becke lines in geology. And then the really hard things, that you'd think might not be common, everybody already knew.

"It's good to be reminded," Father Grattan said.

Faye got to her feet. "I—I just had a question," Faye said. She brushed off her slacks.

"It was a good one," Father Grattan agreed.

"No!" Faye protested. "Not about being homesick. Not personal. Well, that was a—but I meant—"

"You may ask another one," Father Grattan said, smiling.

"I already figured it out," Faye said. "I'm taking watercolor next time, and I wondered if it was better to get the tubes or the—uh—patties."

"Oh," Father Grattan said. "They call them pans . . . I thought you were going to quiz me further on my 'aridity,' like an angel from God."

Faye looked at him. "What's a riddity?"

"My diagnosis," he said. He smiled. " 'Water, water everywhere' and all that." He bent to pick up his equipment. She handed him the portfolio. A whistle screeched. They looked toward the harbor. "I have to go if I'm to make the ferry," he said.

They walked to the slip. It wasn't a busy night; there'd be plenty of room. She was glad he didn't rush on down, to find a seat. "Could I ask one more?" They walked slowly. She hardly limped.

He waited. They had reached the boat. He shifted his pack.

"There's not time," she realized.

"Ride over with me," he said. "They make the return as soon as we get there; don't even have to get off the ferry."

Faye considered. She hadn't ridden alone on the ferry before.

"It's free," he said.

"That," she said. Waved her hands, to show how little that counted. "I brought my money for supper," she said. "But then I just had a sandwich."

She looked at the sign on the chain gate, as the ferryman drew it across. "Children under twelve must be . . ." She made up her mind. "All right," she said. Before he could close her out, she jumped aboard.

"I'm twenty-one," she told him. When he didn't respond to that, she thought his silence was doubt. "Today," she said.

"I believe you," he said. They sat starboard, near the bow, facing the mainland. It was noisy, and there was a tearing wind; no point in chatting.

"It only takes about twelve minutes," Father Grattan told her, when she didn't speak. "Time for one more question."

She nodded. She couldn't think how to ask. She thought over the whole day, and what Tom had said about Vic, about Señora Rios, about divorce.

"Is Captain Rios—"

"Tom?"

"The other one. Is he getting a divorce?"

He made a kind of sighing sound, but more as though it might be exasperating of her to ask than anything else. She moved away a bit on the bench. He laid his hand on hers, to stop her retreating. "Faye," he said, "you're asking to know, aren't you?"

He looked at her.

"I read the papers. I didn't see anything. What are they talking about?"

He thought of many things, from the variety of expressions Faye watched pass across his face, as though he thought of and discarded many answers. Finally he said, "I read about it this morning, that's all. It isn't a big thing. First I've heard."

"*Is he?*" she said.

They were almost to the other side.

"That's not what this is about. It's somebody else's trouble," he said. "Leave it at that, Faye. Or ask him yourself."

He opened his portfolio, tugged at the little cloth strings, and laid it open, sorting through. Then he said, "You pick. Pick one. For your birthday."

She closed her eyes and chose from the pack at random, as though it were a magic trick. "Empty," she said, when she saw it.

He said, "I'll add a bird if you like."

She considered the painting. Again, the flat land and sea, the far horizon, and a sky that took most of the room.

"What kind of bird?" she wondered. "A gull?"

He was busy finding a pen.

"No," she decided, before he could make a mark, or reply. "I'll wait till it returns on its own. It will, you know. They go away before a storm, but that's right."

"You think?"

"I'll call it *Calm Before the Storm*," she said.

"You believe that? How do you know it's 'before'?"

She put out her hand and shook his. "No debris." She pronounced it *deb-riss*. "You haven't been here long enough," she told him. The ferry bumped at the landing, made a slow lurch, then settled. "Pedestrians and bicycles first," the ferryman announced, bored; then, "All ashore that's going . . . Return in five, last run and last call." Last warning. They stepped to the side so the others could go on by. Faye said again, "Thank you," and held up her painting. Father Grattan gave her the V-for-victory, and walked on.

On the way back to the island, she looked at the picture and finally grudged, "You could see it that way." There *were* places where there were no trees visible, there *were* times the sea was flat and like lead, and there might even be times when no birds flew. Or maybe he just needed glasses? Faye decided to mention that, the next time she saw him. She had planned to look up that word—whatever it was he had said his diagnosis was—to see if it had a cure. But she couldn't remember the word.

She got home and put the picture on her wall, above her desk, next to her equivalency diploma. She looked at the globe, turned it to see where Canada was, Father Grattan's home, far away. She took her shower, toweled off, and read the paper while her hair finished drying. She read carefully, every page. She found it on the last page—*Fortner v. Fortner.* Vic Rios wasn't mentioned. Faye recognized the other names—Marnie and Herbert Fortner. It was a brief article. There wasn't much to it; the trial had been postponed owing to the illness of the plaintiff. She wondered which one was plaintiff. Then she remembered how Vic Rios had said, "Witness. Hostile." That didn't tell her much; she didn't know about divorce, but she hoped plaintiff was feeling better, although she didn't see why any of it would make Señora Rios sick enough to die. Tom must have been teasing. Sometimes he did that.

Faye listened to the news at midnight and was asleep very soon. Sound asleep and dreaming when something woke her. Someone knocking at her door, really knocking. She woke so confused she was trying to put her robe on inside out. She couldn't find the sash, kept groping for it as she unlocked the door and flung it open. Anything to stop that racket, that hammering.

It was Vic. She wondered if he had been drinking.

"My hat," he explained. Sober. Coffee-jazzed. Bright. Amused by something. Her hair? She pulled at it, where it always came up cowlicked.

She saw he had left his car backed around, ready to go, motor running, lights on.

"It's all right," she said. Still half asleep. Trying to make sense.

"I saw your light on. I thought you were still—"

She tried to think. "I leave it on," she said. "I—I'm not afraid." She glanced at him to see if he understood that. "I'm *not.* I still forget where I am sometimes; I keep moving the furniture around so I—" Why should she explain anything?

She frowned. Looked at her robe to try to find the sash, and realized it was inside out. She turned her back, took it off, put it on right, and tied it, cinched it tight and made a bow. Vic watched; that made her clumsy. Her fingers untied the bow. Left the sash plain.

"Is Señora Rios—"

"All right, last I heard," he said.

"When was that?" Faye wondered, not thinking how that sounded.

"I talked with her tonight," he said, gentle.

"I'm—" she decided not to apologize, just explain. "I'm still asleep!" She rubbed her face. "What time is it?"

Vic checked his watch. "Late." He shrugged. "Or early."

A terrible thought struck Faye. "She sent you!"

"I came for my hat," he said again. He eased past her, didn't touch her, and retrieved it from the table. She just stood there, blinking.

"Lock up," he said, heading for the door. But he paused, and added, "You're not afraid?" He stood on the little porch and looked everywhere but at her. The stars were faint, misted over. A freighter sounded its horn, calling for a pilot. They could hear the breakers in the roads; that was almost three miles. Moths swirled in the headlight wedges of Vic's car.

"Not ever, usually," she said. And she wasn't. Fear was a goad, not an excuse. She was waking up, in the air.

"You ought not to be opening the door to just anybody. Do you?"

She thought furiously, trying to see where this was coming from, or going. Trying to imagine what right he had to say any such thing. The things she had read about herself, in the old news clippings, came fresh to mind. Was that it? But instead of its shaming her, she got angry. The yard went dark as the moon set behind a cloud.

"You've got your hat," she said crisply. She crossed her arms.

"Now I've made you mad." He seemed to be in a wonderful mood.

She hummed "Row, Row, Row Your Boat." When she tried to shut the door, his foot was in the way.

"I am *not* angry," she said. "I'm getting serene."

"Fooled me," he told her.

"Move your foot," she said. "I'll lock the door now and you won't have to worry."

She shut it firmly, and turned the key. What was he whistling about?

If she had put up curtains the way everyone wanted her to, she would have missed seeing Vic vault her gate. One hand—his right hand—on the post, and over, clean. Didn't lose his hat. He drove off nicely, without raising any sand.

She sat and rocked awhile, and listened to a tape. By the time she went back to bed, she couldn't smell the fragrance from his hat at all. Not by the front door, not by the globe, not on her hands, nowhere.

. . .

On Thursday, in Faye's mailbox, an envelope, addressed by Tom. Inside, just a penciled note on a piece of paper he had recycled from somewhere else, and marked through with a large *X*. Not even hello or good-bye, just one line: "The globe was Vic's idea." Something else had been written there, but Tom had erased it. She took it to the window and held it, trying to see the lasting impression in the strong light.

For several days she tried to imagine what the missing words were. It made her feel differently about the globe, but not about Tom. She didn't know what she thought. She didn't want to believe Vic could have done it. But she didn't want to know, either.

She tried to phone Tom on Saturday afternoon. Señora Rios answered. They talked a few minutes, but Faye did not tell her why she'd called. Faye mostly listened: Tom was never home anymore; he was always away, but he wasn't fishing. That was what Señora Rios had to say.

"What's Tom doing?" Faye wondered.

"Ask God," his mother said. "Ask Him and hope He knows."

On Sunday night Faye had the dream.

She and the Captain were embracing. Not swiftly, or suddenly, but with a darling leisure, comfortable with nearness, powered by and urgent with that very nearness. At first she thought it was Tom . . . And yet something about him—in the dream she leaned against him and drew a deep breath—warned her . . . And yet she didn't mind so much. She didn't—it seemed—mind at all.

It was a nightmare, but she didn't struggle to wake. She slept paralyzed. She listened to what he had to say. It was as though he had been telling her things saved up for a long time, and she had to hear them all. *Yes*, he was saying, *it's all right*, as though he sensed her reluctance, holding her close while he brushed her hair from his mouth. He spoke as though looking down on her, spoke into the top of her hair. The light glinted on the hairs of his hands—she didn't know whose hands they were, but they must be his, it was *his* voice, and yet she leaned against him, pressed her face against his open shirt! The light—which came from everywhere, there was no shadow—glinted off gold—a ring—his hands, decorated in gold, struck her as beautiful; she was ecstatic—yet that ring was cold, bothersome, intrusive in the warmth of the way she felt. Something about the ring . . . If she could step back, to see for sure. If it were Tom! If she were not Faye! Weeping, she turned aside, in the dream.

Her earring caught, scratched his bare skin. He gathered her as she flinched away from hurting him. Assuring her, *No, no.* She placed her hand flat on his chest, in apology, her bare hand with its bitten nails.

All right, he assured her, but she put the other palm flat too, and pushed away. He tried to draw her back, to crush her to him, to make her stay. Struggling free, she sobbed, *You have a wife!*

That voice, amused, almost condescending, talking down, over her head, *It's all right, it's you I want.*

But when she struggled free—and she did—she ran. She got away! But she was caught in great crowds, long lines of people. It seemed to be all of humanity—lined up and leaving—winding toward exits, queued, as though some great drama was over. They were not moving fast; they shuffled off, the sound of their shambling like a great storm. In lock-step forever, all heading toward the same place, up past the rail, past their host, she couldn't see him but she knew he was there, and all the voices mumbling. Faye didn't mumble. At the last moment she cried out, *I won't go that way!* Pushed herself past the others, against the current, and fled. Found a different way out, and the nearer she reached it, the cooler she got, till she could almost breathe again. The enormous mass of people with that furnace of body heat had weakened her, but she had the strength to push open the doors—they were double—and she gave them a mighty push—palms flat in the same gesture she had given to the Captain's chest when she got away. The doors opened easily but heavily. From their first cracking, that cool fresh air came over her. Cold and clean air, once she was outside. Silence.

Faye knew those doors. She knew them in her dream as the doors of the church, not Lady Chapel where she attended now, but Xavier—Ockham's parish. Was one of those people inside, pressing along the other way, her mother? Faye thought she didn't know any of them, all strangers, and they didn't know her. But what if . . . She turned back to see, but the doors were swinging shut, had almost closed, and though she reached to stop them, they sank into place with a final sound. There was no handle. No way to open them now. They were shut against her.

She had no idea what came next. She looked around. There was no way down from the porch she stood on; below her, all around the world—in a dark like the sky itself—stood empty. There was nothing. It was the village, her own place, yet it was empty, in a scintillating blackness like the winter sky. There was not a sound, anywhere. Still, that was not the worst. She could have stood there, she could have stood that, on that blank, black place with everything locked away behind her; that was peaceful, really, but there was worse.

Then she heard it. It wasn't a loud sound at first, just a vigorous rushing. Oncoming. She knew it was going to be terrible, and she braced herself. It came on, louder and stronger, aimed right at her, intended for her, meant to find her and blow her away. A single evil heave of frosty wind, knocking her back toward the building. Again she tried the doors. There was no way. She eased around under the pummeling of that wind, and with her back flat against the building, she faced what tore at her. More terrible than the wind battering her was the knowledge that she was absolutely alone, that she had come out the wrong way, had come out wrong, and there was only this to look forward to—the dark empty sky and world and the pressure of that blow, that could find her in the dark and leave her—as it found her—alone. "Leave me alone!" Faye cried out.

Her own voice woke her. She lay almost panting, trying to reassure herself. Her face was wet with tears. Her hands and feet were cold. She was afraid to move; it seemed impossible for her to move. Slowly the paralysis of terror passed off her, and she sat up, turned her pillow over, and tried the various things she knew to wipe away the effects of nightmare. Nothing helped. She had never known fear that lingered like that. It haunted her. She got up and couldn't even walk. She staggered. She didn't know how to fight the dream, because it seemed to her—on some level she could not reach to change—that it was true.

She went through the cottage and turned on every light. For the first time she felt the negative energy of those dark panes, how they siphoned off privacy and left great chinks in her soul's armor. Faye made up her mind to hang curtains when she could. For the moment, she hung what she had—sheets. She used her paneling tacks and hammer, and simply nailed them over the glass. Along the side windows, where the glazing went from floor to ceiling, Faye rigged up a clothesline with cup hooks, and pinned the massive bedspread Señora Rios had given her. She had to climb up on a chair to reach the top, and she worked very hard to make sure that not a crack of light could escape out, or that a bit of dark—as she now felt it—could get in. She covered her windows with a desperation such as might have motivated a sailor trying to pack oakum and bail at the same time. She worked as though bailing, bailing for dear life. When she finished covering the windows, as she replaced the chair she had been using for a step, she noticed the globe. She started to risk opening the door, to set it outside. She had no pleasure in the globe now. Somehow it irritated, like grit in her eye. But she felt sorry about that, too. Because she had loved it. And sorry for the world. It seemed so mere, after what she had dreamed.

She took the globe out of its cradle and sat with it in her arms, and rocked with it, in her mother's rocker. Didn't think about anything much, or sing, or pray. She wasn't sleepy. She turned on the radio, so there'd be noise outside her head to hear, something to wash out the echo of that gust of wind that still haunted her mind.

When she finally began to relax, it was almost daybreak. She got up and put the world back in its place, and reached over to turn off the desk lamp. She noticed Father Grattan's painting, in which the earth looked no more substantial than water, and the heavens came almost to the bottom of the page, like a shade drawn down, and not a living soul in sight. Faye studied the picture a long time.

PART III

CROSS WORDS

Mrs. Lockridge sat peeling winter squash in the garden of the rectory. It was pleasant in the garden, but that was not why Mrs. Lockridge sat there. Father Ockham had requested that his navy blue suitcase be aired. He had an invitation to the Chancery and would be away overnight. He used to drive up for these dinners and then drive home the same night. He had not needed his suitcase in some years. For two days they had been deciding if this was the suitcase he meant, and each time he said it was, Mrs. Lockridge said she didn't think so. Each of them remembered it as being a different size, so when Mrs. Lockridge came back down from the attic, Father Ockham saw immediately that Mrs. Lockridge was right—it was too large—and therefore he had to say, just as immediately, that it was just right. Mrs. Lockridge remembered why the suitcase had been stored in the attic, but was afraid to say so. It was being aired, on Father Ockham's return from a Council of Churches conference, and because of a domestic or diocesan crisis—Mrs. Lockridge no longer remembered which—the suitcase had been forgotten, had been left out overnight. During that night one of the stray cats had clawed it, which wasn't so bad, really, but he had also marked it with his scent. The scent—powerful, pungent, and, to Father Ockham's tender senses, "worse than skunk"—had resisted every attempt by Mrs. Lockridge to wash it away or neutralize it. After a week of trying, she had scrubbed it all over, inside and out, with white vinegar, and when it had sunned, she had put a paper bag with dry coffee in it—fresh-ground coffee, which she had read somewhere took out the smell of varnish from cupboards—and carted it up to the attic where she hoped it would either "get right" on its own, or be forgotten.

The invitation from the Archbishop had somehow renewed Father Ockham's spirit, and with it his memory. Almost.

"It fits exactly under the seat," Father Ockham had said as Mrs. Lockridge ascended the pull-down steps into the storage area.

"You're not flying," Mrs. Lockridge pointed out.

"Can't hear you," Father Ockham called.

Mrs. Lockridge brought the suitcase down. It was dusty and hazed-over; it looked doubtful. "Won't fit under the seat," she said.

"Not flying," he said.

Father Ockham only needed pajamas and a clean collar, socks, a handkerchief, unders, and his medicine and toothbrush. This case would hold a week's laundry! And towels and shoes. It had wheels and a strap to secure it for a long ride in cargo. It would fit (Mrs. Lockridge was thinking) under a throne, or a house, but not a seat. She had a pride of volumes; she always judged leftovers and their containers at one try. She imagined his little change of clothes slumped down in a corner of this case. She imagined him taking them out—there would be no one to help him, he was traveling on the bus and had been given, as an honor, quarters alone, at the far end of the house, where it would be most quiet—and dressing himself in clothes that reeked of . . . At this point she had come back downstairs and Father Ockham had said, "Perfect!" when he saw it, managing a robust tone of triumph, and then left her with it, saying, "I'll leave you with it," and faded out the side door to go work on his speech in the church office—for he had been asked to introduce the keynoter.

Mrs. Lockridge took the case out in the backyard and gave it a good brushing. She wiped it with a damp cloth and cautiously unzipped it. The coffee had no aroma left. The suitcase had no aroma left either, a pleasant discovery. No vinegar, no cat. Just a staleness that an afternoon laid open in the sun and air would cure. Mrs. Lockridge had propped the case up on the bench and gone back into the house to set some bread to rise.

An hour later she went to get the suitcase. When she looked out in the garden, what she saw made her want to cry, but she laughed instead. Two cats were asleep in the suitcase.

Father Ockham was highly allergic.

Mrs. Lockridge brought out her cleaners and her rag and did her best. She also brought a basket of vegetables and a knife, and her timer. She sat right there and guarded the case while it sunned and dried. Once she had to go back into the house to answer the phone and punch down the bread, and as she came out, she saw that one of the cats had come back, was even then wagging back and forth in a low coil, ready to leap up and resume its sleep.

Mrs. Lockridge did what she usually did. She yelled. And she did what Father Ockham had trained her to do—grabbed a handful of gravel from the nearest source and started firing. Both hands. She settled again and resumed peeling the vegetables for the soup. She didn't notice immediately; it was only later, when she checked to see how much time remained on the second rising, that she realized she had thrown the timer over the wall at the cat, instead of or while throwing gravel. She didn't want to believe that, at first—it sounded crazy—but as she thought it over, she knew that it was so. What clinched it was the timer's chiming when it counted down to zero; she could hear it up in the stonecutter's yard, beyond the fence and hedge. She could hear it above the sound of his chisel. He seemed to be dinking along on something.

Mrs. Lockridge had never minded the work he did; she could only imagine what he was up to, since she had never been over in his yard, but she passed a monument yard on her way to the farmer's market, and she imagined Otto Schimmelpfennig's lot must be something like that—granite in several colors lying around with factory-burnt and painted decorations—crosses, angels, spring flowers, and blank books wide open, waiting for the names and dates of the dead. She thought that was what Otto Schimmelpfennig must be carving in now—someone's dates. She had never liked the sound—or even the thought—of metal on stone. A rake sweeping over concrete could give her shivers. But the noise of his hammer on the chisel—for this was how she imagined it—seemed clean and bright, almost musical, not like the horrible sound his saws made, or that godawful drill.

When he used the heavy equipment—and sometimes she imagined earthmovers and derricks and cranes and sledges and forklifts all beeping and roaring and emitting rotten exhaust—the noise it made enraged her. He had permits; she'd phoned city hall to see. There had even been a few times she was sure there was an illegal jackhammer going. And at night! She had made more phone calls, for Father Ockham's sake. He needed his rest. It did no good to phone the stonecutter, however; he either didn't answer, or didn't hear the phone ringing. She knew the man was deaf, deafer than Father Ockham, and little wonder! So even though he was not using any of those roaring machines, just his musical hand tools, she despaired of his hearing the timer as it signaled. Perhaps it had not even fallen where he would notice it? Perhaps he would mow over it; that was another of the machines he had, and he mowed in such odd patterns (as she imagined, from the sound he made turning and wheeling now away, now toward the rectory) that he couldn't be called systematic, or even a noticing man. She imagined him in a fury, like Thor, thundering and battering the work and world to suit him, great arms like oak, like Longfellow's smith. A mighty man.

She imagined him picking up whole slabs of stone and pitching them around as though sorting out a god's dominoes. She imagined him dark and coarse and, to some extent, simple. She had seen his handwriting; it was earnest, careful, deeply incised. As though each letter he wrote on the page cost as much as if he were cutting it in stone. She imagined above all that he was a bit mad—all those cats, and the hours he worked, the reclusiveness of his habits. Sometimes she heard splashing, an uproarious splashing. She knew he had a pool of some sort—not large, for she could hear it filling; every few weeks he'd let the water run and run. She thought it might even be a tank of some sort, as for hydraulic tools. Did they run on water? She would have believed it except for the stink of diesel when the compressor was going.

In her imagination, the yard was vast, Gothic. He had three lots, no more than the rectory and garden, and the church three more, but somehow it seemed he had more than the lion's share of the block. Even the nuts from their trees fell into his lap; at least half the crop each year landed on the other side of the hedge. She imagined that, too; imagined him out there lining up the nuts and tapping his way along the array, cracking them with his stone hammer. What was the hammer called? She used to know that, she thought, from crosswords. Or was that something else? Some of this, perhaps all of it, ran through her mind that afternoon as she listened to her timer run its batteries down in his weeds.

She made a decision. Took the suitcase into the rectory. Came back and tied a note she had written—not composed, it was far from composed—and a baseball-sized turnip for ballast into a red dishcloth. After gauging elevation and windage with an artilleryman's careful reckonings, she heaved the turnip—it was her finest effort—over the wall toward where his dink-dink-dinking went forth.

A cat screamed. Then silence.

The dink-dink-dink had ceased.

"Please return my dough-timer," she had written. "It was a gift of love. My loaves will over-proof." She waited. And waited.

He had had plenty of time to read that. He could have translated it into thirty languages in the time he had had. She imagined him picking the turnip up, peeling the dishcloth off, and uncrumpling the message, working it out letter by letter, like some beginner trying a tune—right hand only—on a forgotten and atrophied piano.

She listened . . . No semicolons, she said to herself, imagining him reading it; how hard can this be? More leaves twittered down on the breeze. She called that color yellow. She wasn't the sort to sigh, Ah, autumn, old gold. Old lettuce, more like.

She heard him walking back and forth. Pacing rather deliberately. At first she thought he was coming to the fence; then she thought he must be walking out to the front gate—locked to the street side with a BEWARE sign like lightning nailed at eye level. NO USE KNOCKING, it ought to say. But no, not the gate; he turned and walked back along the hedge. His boots—had to be, nothing else so brutish and loud in those unraked and withered leaves—moved and prowled.

He can't hear *that*? she was thinking. The timer went on chiming.

Finally he seemed to arrive—the boots crunched to a stop—very near the timer. She heard him *oof!* as he bent and rustled in the long weeds. She had good hearing. She always had; no pride in it, luck of the draw, but she could hear the seed pods on the weeds as he messed among them, and the change in his pockets, rearranging for gravity. Now the timer stopped chiming. *New batteries,* she was thinking; how long had that been? She was sure they had not run down. But he didn't offer a word as to his intention to give it back. No sign. He walked away. The end?

She thought about the yowl of that cat when she tossed the turnip. Maybe she had killed his cat? She pictured the stonecutter laying the timer on a rough slab and bringing his hammer down. She sighed. "Did I kill your cat?" she called. Loudly enough that Father Ockham could have heard her. No reply. She paced to the other end of the garden and back. She stripped a rosemary sprig into sweet dust.

"I've got all night," she called bitterly. The choir began wrestling with Tavener's "Angels."

She sat and peeled a potato and cut it into fine slices and reached for the next one. She was busy scourging out the potato's eyes when she heard a machine. The bee-hum of the forklift. Ah, well, she thought. Back to work. She gathered up her peelings and took them to the compost pile. When she came back to collect the stockpot and the vegetables, she noticed the glint of the late sun off the forklift tines. The fork was all the way up, aimed her way, as high as it could go, and she could see blue sky between the tines, nothing but blue sky. The machine whirred and eased forward. She stared up at it—as it approached the hedge—and couldn't decide whether she ought to call on God or 911. She decided he *was* mad, and also angry, and she *must* have killed his cat. She had the stockpot and the paring knife and about two quarts of vegetables between her and ruin.

She backed up slowly, because if he drove the forklift over the edge of the wall and tumbled into the garden—she was pretty good at geometry's solids and volumes, but it had been some time since she'd called on her high-school trigonometry—the wreckage would fall almost to the house.

She was all the way back, and easing up onto the bottom step, when the forklift paused; the tines were slowly lowered. A moment later they rose into view again. Mrs. Lockridge was on the third step by then. She noticed it immediately—her red dishcloth. Not flapping, but tied into a bundle. It swung from the near tine, swung on a bit of monofilament like something a spider had dropped. The fork slowly descended; it was obvious she was supposed to go get that parcel. The fork poked through a gap in the cedars.

"Well, of course, you wouldn't throw it back," she said. "Nobody would be *that* stupid." And then, of course, she realized that she had been.

She thought he might try to frighten her, might rev the engine or something. She ran up to the cloth and reached for it. Had to jump a little, but it was easy enough, on that soft ground, to come down safe on her good ankles. She took custody and ran. Didn't even look to see as he cranked it up and backed out of sight. When she got to the steps, she sat by her soup pot and caught her breath. Untied the knot and took out her timer. Put it through its paces to see if it was okay. It was. She almost didn't notice the note. He had put her note back in it. Just her words, the very ones she had pitched over. But he had written in grease pencil, "I keep nice turnip."

Then she was glad she had thrown the largest one. Let him think about that. Vivian Lockridge knew how to toss a turnip. A real hummer.

PART IV

INTENSIVE CARE

When the call came about Señora Rios, Father Ockham was away for the night, and Mrs. Lockridge had already cleared up and gone home, so Father Grattan had his choice: not being a driver himself, he could phone a cab, or go on his bicycle. He did what he usually did when he knew that neither the destination nor the weather was beyond his abilities. For this call, the bicycle. He gathered himself, dressed, and left a note on the kitchen memo to log where he was going.

"Bring your kit," the voice had said.

Tom had ridden behind the ambulance; they were still working over his mother. He could see them. There had not been room for him in there, because they needed to work. His mind had set itself on getting to the hospital, and it seemed to him the ambulance did not go fast enough. At that time of night there was no traffic; they rolled through every light, red or green. But Tom wanted to go faster. In his distraction he forgot himself. His mind drifted off to the conversation he had had with Vic—who was on his way, and it wouldn't be long, he might even get there before the ambulance since he had to come from the island only; he was staying in the house there, the one he had built for Faye, just for the duration of the trial, for those court days, that's what he said, but the case kept being continued because of Mr. Fortner's illness—and Tom, forgetting for the moment everything except that he wanted to be at the hospital at least as soon as Vic, forgot that he was following the ambulance with his mother in it, and swung around to pass. For a moment the ambulance seemed an obstacle. He was alongside the cab, and gave the driver a glance. When she saw him, the driver looked so startled, so full of questions, that it brought Tom back to himself. He gave a little salute, a thumbs-up, and dropped back in line again. He felt ridiculous, but it made him smile. Then he thought of his mother, behind that left-hand cargo door, and he did not forget her again.

They were there before Vic. He found them in emergency, and while Tom was explaining, Father Grattan arrived. They let him through. Vic and Tom had to wait back. "Is she conscious?" Vic kept asking. Every time he did, Tom said, "She wasn't."

They moved Señora Rios immediately to the telemetry unit on ICU. "Massive," they told them. "The first twenty-four hours," they told them. Father Grattan had already attended and had anointed her eyes, ears, nostrils, lips, hands, and feet in Extreme Unction. They all knew that this was not, as it had been in previous attacks, "the beginning of the danger of danger" but was the actual "danger of death," and for an hour after they had settled Señora Rios into her cubicle, they stood outside the glass partition and watched—at first the woman's chest itself, as it barely rose and fell, and then the monitors, whose bright lightnings held their attention to such an extent that their own breathing and pulse began to time itself to those intervals.

"Stable yet?" one or the other would ask.

"Wait," staff told them.

Father Grattan did not go home.

Sometime in the morning, Tom thought to call Faye. She was at Raquel's by then, and she never got calls.

"Some *body*," they teased her, handing her the cordless phone.

When she heard Tom's voice, she ducked out the back door and stood on the stoop to hear what he had to say. She faced Sanavere, and listened. "No, no," she said. And she said, "I'll be there." He didn't think to ask if she wanted him to come get her.

She appeared in the hall of ICU within an hour, and leaned against Tom to remove the bicycle clips from her uniform legs. She hadn't done a thing but get there, throw the bike against the front wall, and run in.

"I could've—" Tom began to apologize. Vic was in with his mother; five minutes per hour, that was it. His turn. So now there was another hour to wait and watch behind the glass.

"I took the ferry," Faye said. She was catching her breath. She looked through the window. "It's bad," she said. More an answer than a question, but hoping it wasn't as bad as it looked.

Tom was as tousled as she was, and he hadn't a ferry ride to blame it on. Vic didn't look much neater. That was when Faye knew it was bad. Señora Rios had been in ICU before. But Vic had never been disheveled. Both brothers needed shaves. Both said they needed coffee, and both wished for something stronger. Father Grattan had gone, but would be back.

Faye bent from the waist, reached for her ankles, shook the kinks out, hung loose. She was straightening up when Vic came out. He turned and looked back as the nurse came to work on Señora Rios. There was not much to be done. She came back out. She told them what they already knew. "Waiting is hard." Told them what they already guessed. "No change."

She directed them down the hall to the private waiting alcove. "There's a coffee machine, newspapers, chairs." But they didn't want to leave; they stood and explained how it had been, in the night, catching Faye up on the whole story.

The charge nurse came and told them about the alcove also. Then they knew that they ought to go there to talk, and not in the hall, but they didn't want to leave Señora Rios unwatched; without discussing it, that was consensus. This made it awkward, for the first time. For Faye wanted to hear how it had been, and what was expected, and if someone stayed, that meant either Tom and Faye had to leave and go to the alcove and sit down and talk, or else Vic and Faye. Even this was not discussed. There was a silent review of options. Faye said, "Why don't you go get some breakfast? I'll stay." Choosing the other option.

By now there were only twenty minutes left till the next visiting moment. And the next report. Not enough time to find the cafeteria and eat. "I had breakfast," Faye said.

"What good would that do?" Vic said. Looking through the window at those monitors.

No one left. They stood there at that window to the point of internal injuries from that hard floor with its hard wax shine, and they didn't talk much, and they didn't take breakfast or lunch, and when the next visit-time came, Tom went in. And the one after that, Vic again, and the one after that, Tom, and then finally Faye would allow them to give up their turn for her, and she went in. She had been wondering if she was allowed to touch; she had watched all day when the nurses came in, had seen how they touched—or didn't—and she decided it was all right, on the right shoulder knob and the right wrist and fingers, and a quick, light pass of her own fingers over the brows, as one might groom one's own, after a walk through mist.

Faye washed her hands first. It seemed like no time at all before her five minutes were up. All the time she was with her, she had talked to Señora Rios; in the hall, Tom and Vic could see her talking. Her back was turned to them, and the way Faye stood by the bed prevented their see-ing their mother's face, but the way Faye was talking—and using her hands—they thought Señora Rios was answering.

"Is she conscious?" they asked, wild with hope.

Faye took her place at the window.

"What were you talking about?"

Faye looked at both brothers. "Stuff," she said. "Anything. Life. Fresh peaches. I don't know, I didn't listen. You know my Spanish isn't that good."

"Did she respond? Why did you talk?"

"She can't read my mind," Faye said.

"How do you know she heard you?"

"She's not dead," Faye said.

The first twenty-four hours passed, and the second.

Another full day, and on the fourth, sometime in the afternoon while the Philippine IV therapist checked the lifelines, Señora Rios stirred. Her hand lifted slightly. Her lips scarcely moved. Her eyelids fluttered and fell shut. The nurse finished her work and came out. "Her daughter?" the nurse said. "She wants her daughter."

Everyone swerved from the nurse to stare in the window, hoping to see those eyes open.

"Daughter-in-law," Vic guessed.

"No, no," the nurse said. "She said *hija*, not *suegra*."

"She meant you," Faye said to the nurse. "She might call a stranger that. She sometimes calls me that." Faye felt embarrassed. She did not want to say one more thing to make an issue of this, for it seemed to her Señora Rios ought to be calling out for her sons. It seemed very clear to Faye that Señora Rios had meant Faye, and that even in her extremity, in her dream, she was not relenting from her matchmaking. Faye was sorry about that. She was sorrier about Tom; she didn't want Tom's feelings to be hurt.

"She probably said *hijos*," Faye said. "These are her sons."

"She said *hija*," the nurse reported flatly, and went on down the hall.

"Medications," Faye said, sorry that Señora Rios had not called out for her sons. They had been right there, ready to hear it, for so long. The schedule of visiting had gradually settled into a routine. It would be Tom's turn next, then Vic's, then Faye's. But when the five-minute portion came around, both men told Faye to go in. Faye didn't want to. She didn't want to take someone's last chance. They were adamant. She didn't know how to argue about it without sounding gloomy. She decided to do what she did about most things she couldn't fix but must endure; she found something to hope for. And did her best. "That wasn't her last word," she said as she went into ICU. "That was her first."

Faye talked and listened and hoped, but Señora Rios didn't say anything.

Faye went home right after that. She had three hours, almost, before her next visiting turn. She told Tom she wanted to run home and get a change of clothes; she had been sleeping at the hospital and washing and wearing, but it was time. She also had some bills to pay, and she wanted to check on her house. Sandy had told her to do what needed to be done, as far as missing work went. They'd manage at Raquel's till she could get back. Faye told her, "Don't manage too well." She picked up her paycheck. Hardly worth cashing with so few hours on it, but she managed to run by the bank. She wouldn't let herself think about why she did it, but she rolled up a dark dress and fitted it into her bookbag, along with a couple of clean T's, a jacket, and her Sunday shoes. She hoped she would not need that dress. She packed as smart as she knew how; she'd run by Tom's from now on, and take a shower there, do her laundry, and get back to the hospital in under an hour. She knew that was all right with Tom. She went there when Vic was "on duty" at St. Joseph's.

Vic had been doing that, going to Tom's to freshen up; not laundry, no, he had bought new clothes, and anything else he needed, he borrowed from Tom. He didn't look so rough ever again, after that first night. Tom, on the other hand, continued rugged.

He wasn't even shaving. It looked as though he had taken a vow. His beard was growing in grizzled. "She won't know you," Faye told him.

"She'll know me," he said.

"She won't admit it," Faye said. And for the first time, in all those days, she saw him smile.

Vic had gone down the hall to the smoking area, a roof terrace at the end of the unit, beyond a mean steel door. This was not a glamour spot—concrete benches, sand in planters for the butts, a general desert for a view—nothing but gravel and tar roofing and, across it, the windsock for the helicopter landing area. There were smokers out there, night and day. Desperately weary nurses and family out for a few minutes in what they settled for as fresh air. It always seemed like midnight, that same alienation, isolation, silence. They smoked like factories, like business was good. Then they took a look around—stubbed out—and went back inside. Vic was glad nobody chatted.

One afternoon Vic saw someone he knew. Not a nurse, though he had begun to know most of them by now. This was a surprise, though as he thought of it, it seemed odd they had not run across each other before.

"Marnie," he said. She had been sitting with her back to the door, looking out at the heliport. There was a chase of sirens, below, as several emergency vehicles rushed toward the back entrance. Marnie didn't even turn. She smoked those long slim ones that looked like drinking straws; she had just lit up.

He crossed to the wall where the planter had been built; no living thing had prospered in it. It had dead stubs, stems of summer weeds, bits of wrappers, half a soda in a can. Vic rested against the wall, his foot up, his heel balancing him away from the wall's weathered paint. That way he had of being hinged. Lean and steely, and absolutely at his ease.

"Captain," she said.

She had on sunglasses, dark gray lenses in tiger frames. She was dressed, as usual, for show. She jiggled one foot on a stiletto heel; beautiful shoes, suede the color of the Stream itself. In the propwash and turbulence of the helicopter, her dress fluttered; it clung to her, then billowed. She caught her skirt with her free hand. She said something he couldn't make out. She raised her hand, signaling him to wait till the helicopter had landed. They watched the blades slow. The grit reached them at last, a flurry of it. She turned her head, shielded her face. Vic looked down, merely, and closed his eyes. In a moment he raised his head. She was studying him.

"Old Madre's ticker?" she guessed.

He didn't need to answer that.

She said, "They should have saved your subpoena. We'll never make it to trial."

"Next time go no-fault," he suggested.

She looked as if she could use a drink, as if she'd had a drink. He checked his watch. "Time to go," he said. He started back.

She let him hold the door for her. They were heading for rooms on opposite sides of the unit; when Vic bore left, toward the east wing, he saw Tom at the end of the hall, watching. Marnie didn't notice him. She started to go west, then turned and called, "Vic!"

"All right," he said, and turned to meet her.

Tom didn't budge. Not good manners, not bad manners, no manners at all.

Vic waited, turned so that Marnie was facing away from Tom, so Tom couldn't see her, as though Tom could read lips, or would. He had been on his way out to the terrace to smoke, and he had his pipe in his hand. He worked on it now, as he waited for Vic and Marnie to finish.

"My apology is about the subpoena," she said. It seemed important to her that he understand that fact. "That's *all* I'm sorry about," she said.

"No regrets," Vic said, in that way he had, that was, in its accent, almost a question, never quite an answer.

"You weren't why it happened," she said. Meaning the affair? Meaning the divorce? Meaning Mr. Fortner's heart failure? She looked around, as though she were standing in the middle of the wreckage of her marriage and life. "You weren't why, I was—" she said. "I—" She noticed Tom. She had to come from so far in her thoughts, she almost waved. Then she put out her hand to Vic's arm. Her fingernails were riveting—tips or extensions, with a band across the natural nail and then black and gold, like jewelry. Her thumbnails actually had little crusts of diamonds.

"Aren't they?" she said, when she saw him notice. She tucked them under, they weren't the point of this. "Listen," she said. He could feel her hand trembling.

"All right," he said.

"*It wasn't you.*" Her voice broke; in a moment she would be weeping, making a real scene. It had only been a few months, and she seemed to have added years.

"It—from the first—it was me."

"All right," he said again.

"He's dying," she said. "This is it."

"I'm sorry," he said. "He could fish."

That helped her somehow. It focused her. "That was it, you see?" She studied him. She didn't seem to think he did see. Both hands on his forearms now, staring up into his face. Tom looked up from his pipe work. "Jealous," she said. "Me," she said. "Jealous of a goddam fish."

"Good luck," he said. She turned to go. His jacket sleeves had marks from her grip. She looked at him, hard. "But it could've been you," she said. As though she feared she had hurt his feelings.

Tom walked that way. She saw him, nodded, but didn't go. Still, she acted a little embarrassed. "We're allowed to talk," she said. "We're on the same side." She forgot for a moment that this was the hospital, not the courthouse. She walked away, down the west hall. At each door she paused, then went on.

"Brother," Tom said, "it's your turn." Shift change for Señora Rios.

Vic glanced at his watch. Glanced toward Marnie Fortner as she went on away. "Maybe Faye—"

"No, she's gone home," Tom said.

Vic had already started after Marnie. Tom caught up, put his hand on Vic's arm. "It's your turn," he said again.

The next day, Tom had come out of the intensive care unit and was standing in the general lobby on that floor, waiting to use the vending machines. He was sorting through change. At first he didn't notice Vic and Marnie, and when he did, he couldn't believe it. They were over in the corner where plastic chairs could be pulled together and a sort of bed made for those who felt they must stay all night, waiting on news. Tom read it wrong; it didn't look as though he got it wrong, though. Vic and Marnie were sitting facing each other, Vic on a chair and Marnie on the table with the magazines, her heels propped on the chair beside Vic's thigh. They had cups of coffee. When Tom saw them, saw Vic stirring sugar into Marnie's coffee with the little wooden stick, he walked over.

He looked at them both. Marnie nodded, put her feet on the floor, put her shoes on. Vic did not stand. "A fine hat and a cigar don't make you a man," Tom said.

Marnie was sober. She reached across and took Vic's hat and also something out of Vic's pocket. She told Tom, "You're right. I have a cigar and a hat and I'm no man."

"Heard it before," Tom said.

"How about this one: We were just talking. Tea and sympathy."

"That's a good one," Tom said.

Vic stood up. Marnie did too.

"You want to make a speech, hire a hall," Vic said.

"This woman," Tom said.

"Nothing about her," Vic warned.

"We're finished," Marnie said, gathering her sweater and handbag. She couldn't get past Tom, though, unless she crawled over the table.

An orderly came. "Mrs. Fortner?"

"Yes!" she cried, then "No!" She pushed past Tom.

"He's asking for you," the orderly said.

They hurried.

PART V

HEROIC MEASURES

Vic said, as though he could change Tom's mind, as though he could read it, "If he dies before they are divorced, she gets nothing."

"*There's* incentive."

"No," Vic said. "She's brought letters and things indicating his wishes about heroic measures. Doesn't want them. The lawyers for the hospital are looking at them now; they have to rule. If they allow it, he can be un-hooked from the life supports. They must have allowed it, if he is able to speak. They must have already taken him off the respirator."

Tom sat.

"It doesn't take long, does it? That's what they said." He forgot and lit a little cigar, exhaled. "They didn't—he didn't want a priest."

Marnie had wound up—in that first heat of moving out, finding her own place, and separating her life from her husband's—with his living will. She didn't know that, at first. She knew where hers was, in the lock-box at the bank, along with both their regular wills. It astonished her to be phoned by Herbert's lawyer and interrogated about the document.

"I don't have it!" she said. "Why would I want it?" She told him to go whistle up a rope, and she wouldn't think about it again.

But she did, of course, because of Herbert's—

"Well, just the whole thing," she explained to Vic, that morning in the waiting room.

"I didn't know it would come to this," she said. "How could I?" She had phoned Vic, left her number on his beeper, and told him she had asked Herbert to settle the divorce suit out of court. It was almost too late for that, but it was never too late. "So I told him," she said, "and he said, 'Toots, you are something else.'" Marnie took that as a good sign, that Herbert still called her "toots." And then he had had the attack. In court! She was weepy when she had phoned Vic; Vic didn't say anything, just, "Yeah," and "So then," and she had talked nonstop, to fight what she knew would be his natural tendency to hang up. She had not been quite sober, but she had her wits about her. All her spunk, all her sparkle, had come to this.

"It's just—" she said. "I don't think I can do this without help," she said.

"What?"

"I found it," she whispered.

He was silent so long she thought the line was dead. She said, "Vic?"

She heard that *bonk-bonk-bonk* of the paging system at the hospital, so she knew he was calling from there.

"Listen," she said. "I'm coming there," she told him. "Just wait. Promise you'll wait."

"I'll wait," Vic said.

She brought it with her, the single piece of paper. "I had it all the time!" She showed it to Vic. "I thought he had it. I forgot how we carried it with us, when we traveled. It was in the map case."

Vic looked at it. *No heroic measures*, he read, *will be taken*.

"Okay," he said, "so give it to his lawyer." He didn't understand.

"Vic," Marnie said. "We made a bet. Last week in court, when I asked Herbert to settle, he said—how did I know he was going to get so sick!—I could either settle—oh, he'd do that!—for nothing, which put me back where I started, or I could bet he'd live to see the jury's decision, let them do it, even if it meant I got everything and he got nothing. 'You're a damn sight cuter than me,' he said." She coughed, cleared her throat, and said, "He's not going to get well enough to go back to court. He's dying."

"Oh," Vic said. "I didn't know."

"But he may not—I mean it could be a long time . . . I mean from his point of view."

Vic thought about it. He handed back the living will.

"This deal you made, gentleman's agreement?"

Marnie laughed. "He changed his will; it was changed the week I moved out."

She could tell she was making Vic nervous.

"Just go with me up there, just go with me to the door," she said. When Vic looked surprised, she said, "No, I haven't been in there. I just get to his door and I can't. I can see him, you know, through the window. But I just . . . You don't have to go in," she said. "Just go that far."

They turned toward the elevator. They went to the administrator's office first. Vic knew where it was. The same olivewood crucifix hung on the wall, the same plants grew in the alcove, as the afternoon he had sat there and signed papers about Faye, after the wreck. There were offices beyond this one; she paced. He took a seat. In a moment, a sister called Marnie's name. Marnie waved Vic off; she went all the way back alone.

Tom said, "So she made monkeys out of both of us." That was his apology. Surprised, Vic said, "Uh . . ." and thought, then said, "I guess you have reason." He got up. Paced. Pinched out the cigar, trashed it, sat again, checking his watch. "What are they doing, you think?"

Tom sat by him, put his hand on Vic's knee. "Tag and release," he said. "Removing the hook and letting him go. Then, maybe in the water for a moment, *momentito*," Tom said, making a trembling motion with his stretched, parallel hands.

They sat and waited. Not waiting for Marnie to come back. Just sitting. They had learned how to judge the passage of time without even looking at a clock, from the disciplines of the nurses and the habituation of their own bodies to the intervals between "no change" and "no change" reports. But this was a different kind of waiting.

Tom drank Marnie's cold coffee. Vic finished his own. Then he bought each of them another cup.

Marnie stood where Mr. Fortner could see her. She couldn't speak, though now he could, but neither of them tried while the nurses fixed things in the bed, raised the head a little, then left the two of them alone. There were no walls, just the glass window and curtains for a sense of privacy. Marnie said, finally, "I'm glad they let you," and touched her own throat. "Is that better?"

"Yeah," he said. The tubes had made his throat raw; his voice was gruff.

"Maybe they're wrong," she lied. She hardly recognized him.

He turned his head back and forth, slowly, for no. "This is it," he said.

Tears were streaming down her face. "Well, I'm sorry," she whispered, when she could. And then, "I'm scared." And she apologized for that, too.

"It's okay if you go," he said. "Mean it."

"No," she said. "No! You're stuck with me."

He reached for her hand, tried to touch her. She moved closer and he held up her hand with the rings still on it—or newly on it. She had put them back on the week they moved him to ICU, so she could visit. Not that she had. Somehow to her they were her proof, "estranged, not divorced."

"Court," he said, remembering.

"Well, it would've been ugly," she said. "Should've gone no-fault," she said. "Fighting over a fish!"

He seemed to sleep. She wondered. She glanced at the monitors; his pulse and other indicators went marching on. A nurse looked in, ducked back out again. Came back with a chair for Marnie and set it up against the back of her knees, pushed hard, and dropped her into it with a tap to her shoulder. "Sometimes it takes a few minutes," she whispered. She ducked out again after adjusting Mr. Fortner's drip.

When she had gone, Mr. Fortner opened his eyes. "Here?" He reached.

"I promised," she said. "Slight detour, but count me in . . . If you get there before I do, just drill a hole and—"

He smiled a little. His lips were very swollen, and a bit of adhesive bothered him; he licked at it. She wet a sponge swab and circled his mouth with it. "Okay?"

He seemed to sleep.

"More candy," he said, not opening his eyes. She touched his lips with the swab again.

"Listen," she said, almost whispering. "Remember that time in San Antonio?"

No response. "I brought that feather," she said. "I've kept it always. I always will." She took it out of her purse and folded his fingers around it.

Nothing.

"I'm sorry," she said. "Herbert, what happened to us?"

He squeezed her hand.

"Are we winning or losing?" he asked. She sniffed back tears, wiped her mouth with the back of her hand. They had given him some sort of painkiller or sedative, because difficulty in breathing makes people anxious.

"Baby," she said, "I think we're gonna win."

"Bet it all," he sighed, and that was it. She didn't have to look at the machines. She felt it, knew it, knew she was alone there.

She was standing in the hall while they did what they had to do. Vic found her there. She had been crying, but she was about done with that. She wasn't sorry to see Vic, but she wasn't glad either. She hardly saw him. The orderly brought her the feather. "Ma'am?"

"Yes," she said, took it, snapped it back into her purse, safe.

They walked to the end of the hall, turned, and started up the other wing, through the double set of doors, and along the hall where Señora Rios lay.

Faye stood at the window, watching. Tom was there too. When they saw Marnie, they knew.

Marnie turned to the window and looked in at Señora Rios. "If she sees me, she'll have another one," Marnie said, turning her back. She reached in her purse for a tissue. When she pulled it out, the feather fell to the floor. Faye picked it up.

"Flicker," Faye said. "Golden-shafted flicker." She handed it back.

Marnie said, "Golden-shafted." She sort of laughed. She wiped it off. "It's never touched down before," she said.

On the flight she took back to Missouri with Mr. Fortner's body—ash by then, safe-sealed in the overhead—Marnie wrote some lists, made some plans. For a few hours she had considered the Neptune Society, but had decided on dry-land burial for Herbert. She thought a stone would be nice; she wanted to write something on that stone, some parting shot. That weakness of hers for the last word . . . His name, of course, but something more than his name. And she wanted, someday, to be buried beside him. But not soon, of course. Not soon.

Marnie couldn't just vanish, like Discord, into the rainbow clouds. She wrote Faye a letter. She sent it to the hospital c/o Señora Rios.

"Don't," Tom said, when he saw who'd sent it.

Vic wouldn't do it either. They told Faye to toss it in the trash. Faye didn't, though; she opened it with a smile. "I'll read it aloud," she offered. She thought it might be fun. She thought it was supposed to be fun. "Do I do 'voices'?" She meant accents. She thought it was a letter of cheer.

"I'm going for a walk," Tom said. But he didn't.

Faye began to read. Unsuspecting. " 'A man and his friend,' " she read, " 'loved the same woman.' " She shrugged. " 'She married the first one who asked her . . . Sometimes she was sad. Sometimes she was happy. When she was sad, the friend cheered her up.' " Faye stopped, and looked at them.

"Mischief," Tom said.

"*Coño*," Vic agreed.

" 'She had a conscience,' " Faye went on. " 'One day her husband came home and found her hanging from the attic stairs . . . The note she wrote said, "I'm sorry." ' " Faye sat down. She didn't look up again. Tom tried to get the papers out of her hands. She jerked them free. Read faster. " 'Her husband took the note and gave it to his friend. "This is for you," ' " Faye finished, in a whisper.

"It's your fault," Tom said to Vic. In Spanish. So it meant *fault* and *lack* and many other things. Vic didn't argue. He just landed a hard left to Tom's jaw, a right to Tom's cheekbone. Tom went down with a certain grace.

Faye ran. Not for help. Away.

That story of Marnie's. Faye had been so proud when she'd said, "I'll read it." She had been showing off. She had been . . . Faye couldn't even think it . . . it took her all the way home to sort it, and on into the night to face it. She had been enjoying their attention, and the way Vic and Tom took care of things and took care of her. She had not thought of it as "using," but the story struck her beyond words. It was an odd thing, to realize that her life was not just about her. It was horrible to her—to the point of actual nausea—to realize that in fact her life had been only about her. That is to say, what she had thought of as life—her active interest, her self. Her precious little skin. Her precious little this, her precious little that . . . She walked and walked, walked on the beach from low tide to high tide and didn't know she was hungry or thirsty or tired.

When she finally walked back into her cottage, she slept around the clock, sometimes waking to drink, to look at the sky—daylight, dusk, and then stars, and dawn, and daylight again. And when she woke for good, she got down on her knees by her cot and prayed. To be nobody's darling. To be nobody's fool. To be Faye, just Faye. And after she'd scrubbed herself clean, dried and dressed, she started on her way.

She wasn't at the hospital for her next visit time with Señora Rios, and she missed the next chances too. Tom had come to almost at once. Vic was gone. So was Faye. Tom would have a black eye and a headache, but he stayed, he was there; it fell to his destiny to be the one, then, when Señora Rios woke from her long sleep. She noticed that eye first thing. She didn't ask. But maybe she knew beforehand, maybe that was why she finally opened her eyes.

Maybe it was as Faye had said, Señora Rios could do everything but read minds, so she had to be awake, finally, to exact tribute, to extract promises, and make things right. It was Vic's turn, or Faye's, for the vigil, but Tom couldn't remember which. Faye had called the nurses and told them she would not be back. Tom did not know what to say about where Vic had gone. Drinking, probably. Señora Rios didn't ask.

There Tom sat when Señora Rios, his weary little mother, opened her eyes and commanded, "Bury me beside my husband."

Tom said, too quickly, "I will." She made him kneel right there by the bed and swear, as she asked him to, and then she let him up. "Go shave," she said.

Marnie's story never got mentioned again. But it, and Tom's answering "Faye went home," when Vic asked about her; "Not my house," Tom added. "The island." Somehow that worked its way under Vic's daily clutter and defenses and landed deep. That night he had the dream.

There was a storm coming. He had changed course, but couldn't outrun it, so he had to make a decision. "Captain," someone said, and he looked and saw the dark cloud. They put the boat about and headed in. It was an unexpected storm, and he wondered about Faye. When he had idled his launch up to the dock on the marsh where she was usually waiting for him with the lantern, she wasn't there. The lights were off everywhere, and he could tell the wind had taken down some lines; he wasn't worried that the house with the blue roof was dark.

He walked through the house, closing windows. Calling her name. She didn't answer. He thought she must have gone out to watch the lightning across the bay. It was a tremendous show, like fireworks. She wasn't afraid of the dark; she wouldn't have taken a flashlight. As he walked back through the house toward the deck doors, he ran into her. Sudden, solid, ran right up against her in the dark. When he exclaimed, said her name, she didn't answer, and he stepped back; she swung. She was cold. She had been dead for hours. Perhaps she had been dead that morning when he left; perhaps he hadn't noticed, had just left, left her hanging. He climbed up, cut her down, and laid her gently on the floor like a fish on deck. He thought, When the next lightning comes, I will see her face. That was when he woke. He was spared that.

He left Tom's almost as soon as he woke. He was still a little drunk and already a little hung over. On the causeway, at the second bridge, the toll collector suggested he turn on his headlights. "You okay?" He studied Vic.

"Okay," Vic told him. He wasn't weaving when he drove on, so the bridge attendant didn't contact the Law.

Ten minutes more and he was there. The house was dark, just as he had dreamed it. The yard lights were on, on a timer. Finally he got out and went in, flicking on lights as he went. He even called Faye's name, but of course she didn't answer. He searched every room. She wasn't there.

He didn't go back to the mainland that night. He didn't show up at the hospital again till almost nine o'clock the next morning. When he walked in, Señora Rios was not there. He couldn't believe it; he counted units, checking on either side of the hall in case he had somehow mixed it up in his aching head. At the nurses' station he didn't even have to ask; they grabbed him, took him by the arm, and led him down the hall, with good news. "In the cardiac step-down unit," they told him. They led him to where Tom sat in a regular chair by Señora Rios's regular bed. "She's awake and asking for you," Tom said. The nurse added, "Already had a bath and breakfast—nothing solid, of course, but we're on our way!"

Faye didn't show up for two more days. She stalled and stalled. Worked at her job at the market, did some laundry, had her bicycle tire fixed, mailed off bills. She was wheeling her bike out to catch the ferry at midmorning when she noticed, across from her gate, the funny tracks. The grass was all crushed down, as though something had been trampling it. Not a parked car; foot tracks in town shoes, or dress boots. Leather soles, smooth, no sneaker treads. And that pile of little stubs. She poked at them with a stick. Black stubs, cigarillos. There must have been a dozen, all smoked down to the nub.

PART VI

STORM WARNINGS

When Mrs. Lockridge stopped by the hardware store to buy a thistle sock for Father Grattan's birthday, she noticed the sign crayoned in neon red on a placard-holder for the next aisle. WE WORK! it announced. MOLE OR MT! HAVAHART! She reached up and spun the sign, to read the other side. WE RENT ♥ HAVAHART ♥ OVERNIGHT OR WEEKLY.

Mrs. Lockridge went around to that aisle and looked. She stood there a long time, thinking. She forgot all about the thistle sock. She walked out of there with a Havahart in either hand, like matched luggage. She opened the trunk and set them in, and covered them with the drop cloth, as though they were contraband. They were hers for a week, and she planned to make the most of them. She pulled up at the Bayshore and bought a pound of haddock and a slab of tuna. "Friday," she said, making plans. She'd use the scraps for bait. Mrs. Lockridge wasn't going fishing.

Mrs. Lockridge had made up her mind. Enough was enough. All fall she had been shooing and defending, but lately she had noticed something else besides the howling of fighting cats. She had heard— definitely—the mewing of kittens. "Well, now," she had said, "we'll see about that." She phoned the Humane Society. They suggested she talk with the county. The county said they'd send someone out. Mrs. Lockridge had a little paper on which she had written it all down: every known feline-transmitted pestilence and plague, every charge of crimes against nature. It took a week for the county's man to arrive, but Mrs. Lockridge used the delay for research. When the officer got there, Mrs. Lockridge had Polaroid snapshots. And of course she had that indictment, like a diary, with dates and damages.

The county's man was a woman. A young woman with a uniform, a badge, and an attitude.

"I am not a dogcatcher," she told Mrs. Lockridge. "I am an Animal Control Officer."

"Even better," Mrs. Lockridge said. "Can you arrest?"

"I follow procedures," the young woman said.

She knew all about the things Mrs. Lockridge had looked up. "We take classes." She hardly glanced at the list. But she studied the sheaf of Polaroids with some interest. "What's this?" She pointed.

"A garden," Mrs. Lockridge said, with a little tone.

The officer said, "Let's go look at the premises."

"They were out there last night," Mrs. Lockridge said. "Digging and scratching things up and growling and clawing and . . . and . . . wallowing!" She led the way.

The officer was looking all around. She wasn't even paying attention to the garden, to the desecrations and wallows.

"Is this a residence?" the officer wondered, her pen poised over a form.

Mrs. Lockridge looked at her. She did not hide her exasperation. "Official residence," she said.

"Official question," the officer said.

Now they were in the back and side yards, right at the ell where the banked wall made the turn. Atop it, the old chain-link—three feet only and looking like hedge with its neatly clipped pelt of hale ivy and grape and creeper vines—and beyond that, on the stonecutter's side, the row of old cedars and junipers and wax myrtles. The officer walked along the bottom of the berm, studying. Passed back and forth, bending, looking to find trails. "You got rats?"

"No *rats*," Mrs. Lockridge said. "Cats."

They paused at a place where the garden soil was upturned, deeply disturbed around a crater.

"Armadillo," the officer said. She looked back across the road, toward that overgrown and scrubby vacant lot. "They commute."

Mrs. Lockridge gave the crater a slight smoothing with the sole of her Ked. "No armadillos," she said. "I just harvested the kohlrabi."

"How do you spell that?" the officer said, putting that in her notes. Mrs. Lockridge told her. The officer wrinkled her nose.

"Heat-resistant," Mrs. Lockridge said. "Father Ockham grew up in the Great Lakes climate."

The officer didn't reply.

"You aren't a gardener," Mrs. Lockridge said.

"I garden," the officer said. She walked along the path between the vegetable and the flower row. Stopped and sniffed. "I smell it," she said. "That's tomcat for sure."

Mrs. Lockridge cried, "There, you see?" and pointed. The herb border lay in shambles. "I can't use those. I can't wash that stuff off. I can't serve that!"

"That's catnip," the control officer said.

"Lemon mint," Mrs. Lockridge said.

"Why would a cat eat lemon mint?" the officer objected. "Look how it's grazed right down to the dirt there."

"And wallowed," Mrs. Lockridge said. She bent and nipped a piece; sniffed it. Offered it to the young woman.

"It's . . . lemony," the officer grudged, "but that's catnip. I guarantee it. You've got enough here to supply the whole city."

Mrs. Lockridge reached over and rummaged under the debris and pulled up the little plastic marker that had come with the plants; it had weathered but could still be read. "Lemon mint," it definitely said. "I have used it for years in the iced tea."

The officer grinned. "Mistakes were made," she agreed. "Be glad it was only catnip!"

Mrs. Lockridge drew a deep breath. Slowly released it. "So you're saying it's my fault?"

Here came a cat! Over the chain-link, balancing a moment on the top, then dropping with a thud. It came right up to the officer. She bent and twiddled her fingers at it; it came up and sniffed, rubbed, and then rolled, as it smelled the herb scent on her hands. She picked the cat up, scratching under its throat. "Definitely catnip," she said. "Pretty boy," she said. "Whose baby are you?" He purred.

"Are you going to take that away?" Mrs. Lockridge pointed at the cat as though she were fingering a criminal from a lineup.

"I can," the officer said. "But why don't I just step over to your neighbor's and—"

"Good luck," Mrs. Lockridge said. She was already on her way to the utility shed for a shovel.

Pansies, she was thinking. I'll put pansies there till next spring, and then I'll transplant thyme and—

The officer said, "Are they home?"

"He doesn't answer the door," Mrs. Lockridge said. "He's—"

"I'll check," the officer said, and, with the cat in her arms, walked around to the front of the rectory and headed briskly for the stonecutter's front door.

Mrs. Lockridge heard her knocking on the side gate, calling "Hello?" and after that, she heard that great brass knocker fall on its striker on the door. It made a sound like the hammer on chisel. It only made it once.

The officer was gone for a long time. Mrs. Lockridge already had the wheelbarrow half-filled with uprooted plants by the time the officer came back. She still had the cat in her arms.

"It's not his cat," she told Mrs. Lockridge.

"You talked with him?"

"Oh, yeah."

"You taking it away, then?"

The officer said, "It's somebody's. You can tell. It's healthy. Cats roam. There's no law against being a cat."

"There's a tag law," Mrs. Lockridge pointed out. "You ought to know that."

The officer said, "I do know it. I also know they lose their collars sometimes. He's got a sort of flat place in his fur, like he's been wearing a collar for a long time."

"Please," Mrs. Lockridge said, disgusted. She resumed work, ripping up herbs.

"I'm going to take him with me, knock on a few doors. He's local," the officer said, running her hand over his coat. "No burrs, no bites. A little bit of fat. He's sleek. Tame. A sweetie . . . You don't know cats," the officer said.

"I know cats," Mrs. Lockridge said.

"Well, it'll go a long way to curing your problem just to get this stuff out." She toed a clump. "Mind if I take a little? My kitty eats it faster than it can grow back." She gathered a bunch, and started for her truck. The cat in her arms leaned over and began grazing and whuffling as she carried him away.

She thought of something. "Your neighbor's cat is up to date," she said. "I saw the papers. He's got it a flea collar and a regular collar with a rabies tag on it, too. Says it's the only cat he's got, the others are just passing though. Probably on their way here to the salad bar."

Mrs. Lockridge tried one last time to make her see. "They pee on the doors! They pee on my car! They peed on the bishop's van."

The officer nodded. "They do."

Mrs. Lockridge did not risk turning the plants into the compost pile. She bagged them for pickup. She double-bagged them, and she washed the shovel and her shoes. She was thinking about buying blood meal when she went to get that thistle-seed feeder for Father Grattan, just scattering the terrible stuff around as a repellent. But she forgot all about that when she saw the Havahart display.

She wanted with all her heart to catch Otto Schimmelpfennig's cat in her garden. She wanted him to have to admit it. She wanted that cat redhanded. If she caught the other cats too, then so be it. She'd carry them in the trap to some safe place where a cat might make a living, and she'd release them. Somewhere they'd have to cross water to get back. She had never seen a cat on a bridge, and she knew they didn't swim.

She thought she had it all figured, and then she wondered if digging up the catnip had been wise; if that was the only reason for the trespassing, maybe she had already cured it. Then she would never be able to catch Otto Schimmelpfennig's cat. She decided to save one clump, or maybe two. Pot them so she could move them around, lure the cat toward the cage, maybe even lay a few sprigs around on the trap itself, like camo.

She didn't even know which cat was his. All kinds had come and gone in that garden, but there had been one she had noticed for several years. Had seen it tidying up after business, raking dirt over its scat, and strolling back to the wall, leaping up, lofting over. It was the largest cat she had ever seen outside of a zoo. Long and rangy, grizzled, with a coat not long yet not short, and a ruff that might be hiding a collar and tag. She had never noticed anything like a tag; she had always been too busy throwing things. When headlights had caught him, he had looked up, not insolently, but without awe; a rather considering glance that always made her want to cry, "How dare you!" And his eyes reflected the light not golden by lamp-glare, but red, as wild as a bobcat's.

She had chosen the Havahart big enough for a bobcat. That was just what she had asked for. The largest one. Friday night she was going to find out if it worked.

Perfect, perfect, perfect, she crooned, when she noticed that it was to be the full moon.

It worked.

She caught a cat, but not that big one. She caught the mother cat, gaunt from feeding kittens, desperate for any kind of food to keep her going, to help her make milk. Mrs. Lockridge thought about it a long time. She already had the cage in the car, ready to drive away. She refused to be sentimental. She refused to consider the kittens lying in a nest of grass. They might mew a few days, but they could survive if they were meant to, or perish. There were enough cats in the world. She was not the sort of woman who'd pay some specialist to come out and rescue five baby possums from the pouch of their road-killed mother. Fifty dollars that had cost her friend Mae. "Possums are not endangered," Mrs. Lockridge had argued. They fitness-walked together, she and Mae. Mae was on a pension, and considered a burger supper at a local drive-in to be a major treat.

Mrs. Lockridge cranked the engine. "No, sir," she vowed. She backed out, drove down the street, turned toward South End and the marsh. "Plenty of mice out there," she said. The mama cat did not cry, purr, or blink. Mrs. Lockridge drove around the block, paused at the driveway to the rectory, and drove past again, around the block. On the third circuit she turned back in. Got out, took the trap back down into the garden, and started to poke it with the stick, the way the instructions showed, to open it "without danger to handler." She laid the stick down. Went into the rectory and got some day-old bread and poured milk over it, warmed it in the microwave, sprinkled it with sugar, and brought it back to the cat. Set it on the ground where the cat could see it, poked the trap open, and stood back. The cat moved out slowly, checking the lay of the land. She didn't do more than sniff at the milk, just went right to the wall, up and over the fence. Mrs. Lockridge felt foolish. She felt compromised. She had already locked up, was going directly home from the garden, and didn't intend to risk disturbing anyone in the rectory by taking the bowl back inside. She left it. Hoped no one would notice. And was grateful, as she backed out and eased her car toward home, that she had not run into anyone in the kitchen when she made that snack. When she came to work the next morning, the bowl was empty and clean-licked. She thought she would scald it—maybe even boil it—and then wash it with the other dishes, but she had read all that about cat saliva. It wasn't fur that folks were allergic to, it was spit . . . . She decided not to keep the bowl. She set it outside, by the recycle bins.

That night, she rebaited the traps as she was clearing up after dinner. She had time, that way, to check and see if she had caught anything before she went home after the eleven o'clock news. She always waited till Father Ockham had retired before she locked up and left. She had some bread left over. She also had some of the tuna scraps left. She used the tuna in the traps, and rubbed the cages all over with bruised leaves of the catnip. The next thing she did, she could not justify or explain to herself. She heated the leftover roll and some broth and scraps, put it in that bowl, and set the bowl where she had left it the night before. She knew that mama cat would eat anything, not like regular cats. She knew, finally, what animal had been eating the birdseed and crumbs she had scattered under the feeder. Vegetable scraps and broth and a little bread might not suit a fighting tom, but that mama cat ought to be pleased to get what she got. Mrs. Lockridge poured it from a height, careful to keep the pan unsplashed. Then bent down and poked her finger in the food, to see if it was too hot.

That was Saturday night.

She was home, she was actually in bed, reading, when a thought struck her. She thought she had heard thunder.

She tried to shake it off, but she woke in an hour and that was the first thing she saw in her mind's eye: the mama cat in the trap again. Trapped all night in the rain. Her kittens cold.

She dressed and went back to the rectory, parked out front along the curb, coasting to a stop and being careful with her door. She tiptoed down into the garden. The mama cat was in one of the traps. And the gray and white grizzled cat, the big one, was sitting by the wall, daintily eating from the vegetables and bread. Mrs. Lockridge knelt down by the other trap and called, "Kitty? Kitty-kitty," in a soft voice. The tom turned and looked at her. Blinked. Resumed eating. The mama cat never moved. Waited. After a few minutes, Mrs. Lockridge used the ferrule of her umbrella to push the release, and the mama cat went free. She did what she had done the night before—leaped to the fence and over, to check on her kittens. The tom came over to the cage where the cat had been, sniffed it, turned, and marked it with his scent.

One good thing from all of that: Mrs. Lockridge could tell that the cage would be large enough, if she could ever get him into it. The other good thing was that as he trotted to the wall and leaped up, balanced, and went over, she could hear his tag tap on the chain-link. She knew then he was the one she wanted. It was just a matter of time.

Now that Señora Rios was feeling better, she was restless. Now that she was awake to enjoy it, she had no company. There was no phone in her room, but as often as she could, she found her way to the phone in the lobby and dialed Tom. The message was always the same. "Come and get me."

Faye was back at work. "I really have to," she explained urgently. "This weekend, I promise."

Vic wasn't hanging around, either, but he didn't answer the phone. From time to time she was able to connect with Tom. "I want to go home," she said.

"It's going to happen," Tom would say. "Tell me what was breakfast." Anything to distract her. He visited her every night, and he was bone-weary, rock-hard, thinner than he had been in his adult life, and he did not smell like a fisherman. If she was sleeping when he got there, he let her. Sooner or later she'd wake, notice his hand holding hers, and she'd grip it. But it would not feel like Tom's hand and she'd raise it to her face, study it, then slowly turn and look at his shoes, his dusty trousers, his sun-faded shirts, so bleached-out they looked frosted across the shoulders.

One day she pointed to his trousers and said, "You building boat?"

If that was a trap, he didn't fall in it. "Did you take your walk?"

"Not boat," she said. "Boat don't need—" She meant to say *argamasa* (mortar) but instead she said "birdlime." Furious with herself, because she had always been very precise with words, she tried again. This time it came out "almonds." Finally she pointed to the white, crusty spatters halfway to his knees and said, "Stewed corn!" Tom took her hand in both his. He told her, "Repairs."

She rested on her pillows, not weeping. Just empty. She would return to herself soon. He had begun to understand. He waited.

"Supper?"

"Not yet," he said.

"Eat mine," she said.

She turned her face away. There was nothing on the wall but scars where tape had been used to put up someone else's get-well wishes. It was a good room, but the window had no view of the south. It felt all wrong to her to be lying there, sleeping against her inner sense of compass; at least Cuba was on her right hand. She could remember that. The side where she wore her wedding band.

She saw Tom.

"I will sleep one more time with my husband."

It was not a question, but it required an answer. She waited. "You have said," she said.

"I have said."

"Then I will not mention it again," she said, as she said every time.

He pushed the wheeled bed table toward her. "This might be something," he said, taking the lid off her supper. "Try."

"I try," she said, poking at it with her spoon.

He sat in the chair to the left of the bed. He leaned his head back. He seemed to be listening to her talk, and then he was asleep. Every evening. Sometimes in the night if she woke and looked, he would still be there like that, in the same position, those cement-dusted shoes and pants stretched out like fence rails, his mouth looking so sad as he slept, one hand dangling over the chair arm, and one fist clenched. But always, when Señora Rios looked in the morning, no matter how early, Tom had gone.

. . .

On Monday morning Mrs. Lockridge was late getting to work. Not late enough to require explanations, but late enough to cause a mystery. She went—as she had begun doing—to the garden first thing and checked the traps. On Monday there was no cat in the trap, but there was no bait either. Mrs. Lockridge mulled that one over all day. It seemed to her nothing could get that bait without touching the plate that sprung the door; anything that had gotten the bait must've stepped on it, that's how it worked. The bait sat on the plate. It was very sensitive. She had tried dropping a pebble on it. But if something from outside had sprung it, the bait would still be there.

A bird couldn't fly in and out without landing somewhere, and it was not the sort of trick she could imagine any snake playing. Or any creeping thing that could climb the mesh sides of the trap—it would take intelligence, it would take a comprehension of what was at stake that gave Mrs. Lockridge chills to imagine—and lean over and lift the bait carefully and ease back out, either with the food in its mouth or after eating it first, and never, in any way, shape, or form, touch that sensitive spring-plate. Mrs. Lockridge thought all day and then, toward evening, imagined a raccoon knowing how. Two or more, actually. They could open hasp locks, turn knobs, fiddle with wires and closures of all sorts. Maybe there were two? One on the outside to receive the food, the other inside. The one on the outside with a stick, ready to poke it down and release his buddy.

She bought some more Polaroid film, just in case.

She wanted to talk about it with someone. Once Father Grattan came into the kitchen and seemed about to tell her something, but didn't, and she thought, I ought to just— But she didn't. The phone rang, and so she didn't. Instead she phoned her friend Mae and asked her to walk; they went to the mall that evening, and it was on the third lap that Mrs. Lockridge told her about the whole thing. "It's crazy, isn't it!"

Mae said, "I'll take them."

Mrs. Lockridge said, "Let me catch them! I haven't caught them yet! Maybe it's not raccoons. Maybe it's—"

And Mae said, "No, I mean the cat and kittens."

That stopped Mrs. Lockridge cold. She found a bench. They sat, and after a moment Mrs. Lockridge said, "If you mean that."

"I do," Mae said. "Somebody ought to."

Mrs. Lockridge considered. "But I don't even know how many. I don't even know where they are! How can I—"

"Follow her," Mae said. "Watch where she goes and go there too."

Mae had ten years on Mrs. Lockridge. Mrs. Lockridge was not a whiner. "You mean climb that wall?"

"Well," Mae said. Which about covered it.

"What if she won't go in the trap again? Maybe she isn't even coming in the garden anymore. I'm not feeding her now. That other one was eating it!"

"She will jump through flaming hoops," Mae told her, "for the right stuff."

That left only one problem: whatever it was that was getting the bait and leaving the traps unsprung. But with the mama and kittens out of the picture, she could go for the tom. "I only have those traps for a week," she said. She and Mae started for the parking lot. They were moving fast.

Father Grattan woke at around two in the morning with a sense that something was wrong. He often did. He habitually did. He would get up, sit in his chair by the window, the streetlight through the lace on the curtain making patterns on his hands. If the window was open, he closed it; if it was closed, he opened it. After some time he would notice that half an hour had passed, or five minutes. It always surprised him how time could do that, could be so vast and so narrow all at the same time. He had had a watch with a glowing dial, but the sea humidity and air conditioning and condensation behind the bezel had finished it off in his first few months here. His bedside clock had red numbers—no face, just digits. Once he woke and looked and it seemed to say 54:17, and he thought, Yes, so, and that was an answer to what time it was; it didn't seem at all impossible, but what it was was that he had set it upside down the last time he looked. What difference did it make, anyway? Just before daybreak he was always awake, and he'd dress and go for his run.

He never remembered the other dreams of the night, only the last one, and he'd take its mood with him out into the street and run it off. Lately he had dreamed the same thing over and over. Maybe it was different in detail, but the impact was always the same. He was somehow in a place he knew, but where he had not entirely intended to be, among people who liked him and whom he liked, crowds of them, masses of them, and they were all dressed for some occasion; he was dressed for running. The place was elegant, spacious, and, to a certain extent, impressive. But he didn't want to be there. He saw where he wanted to be. Yet every set of stairs he took were for show, dead-ended in nowhere, just railed off but nowhere. The elevators weren't really elevators; the doors looked like elevators, but when they opened, there was no way up, just out the other side. The other side was a terrace whose gallery fed back into that same hall. In his dream, he would circle that great glittering place and all the time he was greeting and being greeted, he was eyeing the walls, ceiling, floor for some way to get out. But the only way out was up. And there was no way to get to the next level. The buttons on the elevator said LEVEL.

"You want sainthood," Father Ockham had told him more than once. "Level off."

Father Grattan didn't bother with what the dream meant. He couldn't outrun that, he'd been trying for almost a year. But he could outrun the mood. And he always did. By the time he got back from jogging, he was honed to his usual edge.

So when he ran around the side of the rectory and began his cooldown, he was amused more than surprised to see the ladder against the garden wall, and Mrs. Lockridge's leg vanishing over the top into the hedges. She wasn't gone long. She had a mesh shopping bag in her arms. The mama cat was at her heels. She looked over the wall and fence and saw Father Grattan. Never missed a beat.

"Oh, good," she said. "Take these." She leaned over and lowered the bag of kittens. "There are six!"

Mrs. Lockridge knelt at the top and looked. "Now what?"

"I'll hold it absolutely steady," he told her. "Left leg," he suggested. "Back to the edge, and don't think and don't look down."

Mrs. Lockridge began tucking up her skirts.

"I'm not looking," he told her politely. "Just save yourself. Your modesty is in no danger."

"I can't do it," she said. Now that it was getting light, she felt the height in every atom. "Oh, God," she said.

"You can do it," Father Grattan said. "Or you can wait till Mr. Schimmelpfennig gets up and lets you out the front door."

Worked wonders. Over she came, her left leg groping till it found the step, then her right, and then—the whole ladder trembling with her uncertainty—she eased down foot by foot.

"Two to go," he said cheerfully.

The mama cat jumped down and touched the ground just as Mrs. Lcokridge did. Father Grattan showed the cat the bag. She sniffed and made a little mew.

"Six," he said.

"No wonder she is so hungry," Mrs. Lockridge said.

"Did you catch her again last night?" Father Grattan wondered.

Mrs. Lockridge studied him. "You," she said. "You."

"Yes," he said. "I found her and let her go. "Wasn't I supposed to?"

"I knew it wasn't raccoons!" she said.

"It's not a secret, either," Father Grattan told her. "Father Ockham knows. He sits and watches you out here, dawn and midnight both. He's been quite entertained."

"He hasn't," she said.

"You're solving it," he said. He looked at the mama cat, frantic to get at her kittens. "Peaceably." He looked at her with a growing reproach. "You're not planning any—"

"Adoption," Mrs. Lockridge said. "All of them." She took up the mother cat and stuffed her in the Havahart. "I'll be back in fifteen," she promised.

She settled the kittens in the box she had prepared for them. Father Grattan carried the trap, and Mrs. Lockridge put the box and the mama in her cage on the backseat. "Anything I can do—" Father Grattan began.

Mrs. Lockridge cranked the engine. "Make the coffee," she said. He was already back to the house when she remembered the ladder. It stood against the wall, very shiny. The aluminum took the sunrise like a mirror. She wasn't sure whether Father Grattan was teasing her or not, about Father Ockham's watching. He was a great kidder. She decided to let it go, just leave the ladder. If the old priest said anything, she'd work that out when he did.

She left the Havahart at Mae's for the moment, and let her friend sort it out about how the mama and kittens would be introduced to their new home.

She got back to the rectory in fourteen minutes. As she parked, she was already planning the night's bait. She had two more nights left in the rental, and one trap. The catnip was about gone. The oddest thought crossed her mind; it put her rather out of sorts. It seemed so much simpler than what she had been going through. It seemed ridiculously simple. She felt she must blame the Animal Control Officer for not thinking of it; after all, it was her job. She should've moved all that catnip into Mr. Schimmelpfennig's yard. She had been about to take the ladder back to the utility shed when she thought of that. Looking up, she decided no, she wouldn't make that climb again, and certainly not to put catnip in someone else's yard! But maybe she could tap it out of the pots, and just throw it up and over. But she wasn't that kind of gardener; might as well throw it in the garbage as fling it. Okay, she thought, but she still took the ladder back to storage. She had learned a long time ago that she would do whatever it took. It was a weakness.

When she walked in the kitchen, Father Grattan was pouring the first cups of coffee.

"Not a word," she said.

He raised his cup in tribute.

"Glad we had this little talk," she said.

That was the morning Tom had gone home, showered and shaved, and put on clean clothes. He sat down and, before he had tied his shoes on, fell asleep with one still in his hand, the laces still knotted from the way he had slipped them off, impatient, hurrying. There was always somewhere else he needed to be as soon as possible. He was sitting on the end of the bed, and he didn't fall over for ten minutes or so, then he gradually tipped, slumped, and settled. He dreamed. For the first time in a long time, he stayed deeply asleep so that he dreamed. He found himself in the woods, on a road. He did not know which way to turn. Then he saw Faye. On the same road, but not near. He sensed trouble, and saw the fire sweeping up from the sea.

He called to Faye. *Quick!* but she didn't respond. Again, he called, *There! There!* waving toward the place that was safest. They would meet there. But the danger was between them; it meant risking their lives, but there was no other way.

The flames were too great for him, they came on great and quick and he yelled toward Faye, told her to try to get back to the road, fire on all sides, the road might act as a firebreak. And they made it, made it, huddled there. He covered her with his own strength and the windrush came over, and the heat, and then went on, wide, racing through the woods. Behind the fire there was scorched earth, burnt stumps and char, smoke and smolder.

Spared, there was no obstacle now to their making it to shelter, but Faye called, *Oh, look!* and ran off after something, pursuing it to rescue, some little thing she had her heart set on saving. *I'll meet you there,* she promised. So they made their own way independently, and the way he took was heavy work, slogging through the ruined undergrowth. She seemed to have no trouble; she seemed almost to be airborne, like a butterfly.

When he finally came to the lodge, he heard her before he saw her. Across the lobby. Completely natural, absorbed in her continuing and spared life. She did not seem to feel the weight of their escape, of those moments on the road as the flames overtopped them; those moments seemed to have enabled this separation rather than healed it. She didn't seem to be watching for him at all. He started to call, *Hey!* He wanted to roar it, to see that sweet calm break from her face. He didn't.

She turned and waved, warmly, splendidly, glowingly. Looking all around, not missing a thing. Complete, somehow. A complete picture. Not a thing she had been through—even her smudges and tousles were gone—scarred her or left her in doubt. She was where she was. She had no questions. She was in a little alcove. There was a beautiful soft rug, dark furniture. On a table, a tray with coffee cups and beautiful fruit. The light from the fire—in the hearth, tame, unthreatening—and the light from the windows—beyond which the firestorm rolled on—glinted on silver handles of spoons, shone from gold and brass.

It was like a painting. Like one of those paintings where everyone turns for that moment—dark, dark paintings—and all the faces can be seen as portraits, perfect likenesses, not themselves, but the images of themselves. The others, he knew them also. Their backs had been to him, but they turned, and he saw them. The priests? They were not holding her at bay; she held them.

An attendant, a clerk, left the desk and came to Tom, handed Tom a painting, damaged. The frame had been scorched, a bit of the gold chipped, melted. He took the painting out, laid it to the side, and held the frame up. He moved it back and forth till he had centered them, their backs to him again, and Faye at the center, looking past them all. *This can't be fixed*, Tom said to the clerk, showing him how the gold paint, the gilding, had come off on his hands. *There's nothing I can do about it now*, he told him. He handed it back.

There was something Tom had to do. He did not want to go back out in the night—and darkness had come now—but he knew he must. Nothing so pleasant as here indoors. He was tired, but there were no chairs. All the chairs had been drawn up facing Faye. Every one was taken. He looked at the dark suits, the backs bent forward attentively. And he had that thing to attend to, that obligation, some thing he had begun and had given his word for. He had to cross the lobby. He felt the floor under his feet, the soles of his shoes changed somehow, but not ruined, by the fire. He had to go out the doors facing the sea. There was no light in the sky. A long time before it dawned. He opened the door and instantly an alarm sounded, rebuking him for going the wrong way. But it was the only way he could go. The alarm went on and he stood there, confused.

Tom opened his eyes. He didn't know where he was. He thought it was the hospital, but he couldn't figure it out, why he was in the bed and not his mother. He sat up, stunned, and saw himself in his own dresser mirror. He kept hearing the noise. A real noise, not a dreamed noise. Not the alarm clock, not the telephone. He staggered to the dresser and began searching. Among the things scattered on its dusty surface was Vic's beeper, forgotten for weeks. Tom didn't know how to work it. Pocketed it. Stuffing his feet into his shoes, he ran to the truck. He knew it was the hospital; he didn't even have to wonder. It was either the hospital or Faye; both of them always called Vic first, because it took him longer to come from wherever he was. The beeper sounded again. And a third time, before Tom got there. He would have liked to throw it out the window. He almost did. "Goddammit!" he cried.

Then he realized that if he had not fallen asleep, he would have been long gone for the day; nobody would have been able to find him. No one knew where he'd be except Otto Schimmelpfennig, and who knew to ask him? Maybe it was a mercy, that nap, but an unsparing one.

Tom didn't waste time in parking; he saw the long line at the hourly take-a-ticket, and the congestion at long-term. He braked at the curb on the yellow tow-away and ran up the drive to the front. It was too early for visitors and dismissals. One old guy sat on the bench, smoking, reading the morning news. "Where's the fire?" he called as Tom loped by.

"Hell," Tom said.

"Ain't it, though," the man agreed.

Thursday night, Mrs. Lockridge caught the cat. The gray and white grizzled giant. "You're the man of my dreams," she said. It happened early. It wasn't nine o'clock yet. Even better, the stonecutter was home, was working in his yard. She had been hearing that off and on all evening. Heavy work. Shaping work. Sawing and the—as she imagined it from the odd greenish glow—acetylene. Welding? Some kind of fire-saw? She took the cat in its trap around to the front door and raised that knocker and let it fall. In vain. In vain. She knocked at the gate. Nothing. She walked back to her side of the fence and thought. After a time she decided to give it a try. Got the ladder and set it firm and then changed her mind.

She went back to the kitchen and wrote a note. Father Grattan was away, on calls. Maybe he'd see the ladder, maybe he wouldn't. The note she wrote was for Schimmelpfennig. "Here is your cat. He was absolutely in the garden." She looked at that. It looked—if she did say so herself—a bit meager. A bit thin. What if he said, So what? Oh, if he did! Maybe he was a legalist; he seemed to be. Maybe he would say, You trapped him on the street. Anyone can haul a cat over a wall.

Now, who would? she wondered. But of course she knew the answer to that, too. None of this ever came out in the plus column for her self-esteem. But this might do it, this night might be what it took, and all it took. This might be the end of the problem. She wanted the man to make the fence higher and put that wire on it, angled back toward his own yard. That would do it.

She wrote another note. Explained that in basic English. Found that she was printing it, slowly, as though that would help him read it faster.

"I've turned into one of those women," Mrs. Lockridge said. She blamed it on Father Ockham, as though he were contagious.

"Everybody turns into one of those," Mae said.

Mrs. Lockridge read over the part about making the fence higher. It wasn't clear. A letter would be better. A letter could be mailed anytime.

She wrote the note again, left it like the first try.

Several phone calls—she had to try to track down Father Grattan—kept her in the house for almost another hour. When she finally got out the door, the stonecutter's yard was silent. The greenish light was gone. There was nothing. She had her Polaroid around her neck. She stooped and took a picture of the trap where it sat. Took one from a distance, placing it—so to speak—at the scene of the crime.

Decided to take another, of the ladder against the wall. She walked back to the kitchen and pinned it to the refrigerator with a magnet. Father Grattan always had a glass of milk. He'd see it. He'd get it. Mrs. Lockridge went out. This time for sure.

The cat was lighter than she had thought. Heavy enough, but she was able to lift it in one hand, in the cage, and ease herself up the ladder step by step. Otto's yard was on a natural rise, about five feet higher than the rectory garden, which had been somewhat scooped out, and walled round with cement block and terraced behind with good peat and clay, in an earlier gardener's hope of roses. All that was gone now; the trellises had been overtaken with Algerian ivy and other mistakes. Saplings and cedars grew into a dark wall, solid, dense, with an occasional flutter and unsettling stir that might have been anything, and made Mrs. Lockridge grip like a wren in a gale. Still, she was glad it was dark, for many reasons. It didn't seem as far, in the dark. And it didn't seem as rowdy, swinging her legs over the top. She had slacks, of course, but she didn't wear them to work. That was one of the rules, like line-drying the bed linens.

She had to rest, when she made it over. Just crouched on her hands and knees, gasping. The cat looked around. Reserving judgment.

At first Mrs. Lockridge didn't notice anything. She stood and brushed her skirt off, dusted herself, and stretched the shoulder blade that the cat trap had dragged almost out of its socket. She tried to see the ground. The moon was waning, and she wasn't sure if there was light enough to see pits or boulders. But it was a grassy lawn, mowed occasionally, and the blocks of stone were all very apparent. Mrs. Lockridge took up the trap and walked toward the back of the lot, where the shed seemed to be the focus. She had this all planned, too. She would leave the cat and the trap. In the trap. With the note and the photos in a sandwich bag on top. He couldn't miss it. He couldn't deny it. Of course, he might not find the cat till morning, but she had planned for that too. She had another sandwich bag with crushed ice in it. This had been the hardest part, running that grinder so late, but no one had come to see what or why. She would shake it through the top of the cage into the whipped-topping bowl she had set the bait in tonight. It hadn't been fish bait. The tom liked vegetables? He got vegetables. Every bit of it was gone—squash casserole. She had dashed a bit of extra Romano on it. So she would leave the cat right there, with water, when the ice melted. He'd survive. "Won't you?" she said. The cat wouldn't look her in the eye; sat hunched over, bunched up, miserable, as though the little chip of ice she had accidentally splashed onto his fur had burned like a spark, or bored like a bullet. She had set the trap far enough back that it was entirely under shelter. Not that it was to rain. The moon sailed along through a clear patch, and the clouds were few and far between.

The cat coughed.

She wondered if he needed water right that minute. She looked around for some. A spigot, something. It was an orderly shed, but dry. She saw nothing. She was afraid there might be some sort of alarm she might trip. She didn't prowl. Then she remembered how deaf the man was, and got a bit bolder. She wasn't thinking about the cat by then. She was looking at the stones. There was a scaffolding with some of the work in progress. It wasn't tombstones, she could see that much. Something was cut deep. She felt along it, gathered it into her mind letter by letter—all capitals—and added it up. It didn't make any sense. Then she understood it was Latin. She had turned to go, had bid the cat good night and farewell forever, as she hoped, when the yard lights washed on. Came on with such a sudden flash that she felt them. They buzzed and revved up all around her. It was as bright as a surgery. She couldn't see beyond the first circle of the stones. Most were uncarved, raw. Others had beginnings. A few were done. She couldn't believe her eyes. She didn't even think of making any defense for being there; knew he was there, the stonecutter, was coming toward her. She heard him, beyond the light. Coming down his side steps, one boot at a time. But she hardly dreaded, for looking. Angels, birds, a bear, two dogs, an elephant, a hive and little bee carved around it . . . She sat on a block of stone and looked.

Schimmelpfennig had on welder's garb. A leather apron, gloves, and the helmet and mask. It was tipped up, so he could see to walk. He stood there looking at her. She didn't have a thing to say. Pointed toward the cat in the trap. He walked over and looked in. Put a fingertip to the wire. The cat fell over against his hand, rolled on its back for him. Schimmelpfennig picked up the sandwich bag and opened it. He read the note first. He looked at the Polaroids. Ran through the sheaf of them several times, and read the note again.

He took up his torch, held the lighter; scrubbed it for a spark and lit the gas. Adjusted the flame to a fine point. The flame shot out crisp and material, against the dark. It looked solid. It was beautiful. "Don't look," he said. Thick accent. She was on her feet and running for the ladder when she had that decoded.

She didn't even think to ask for her cage back. She breathed a prayer to the patron of lost causes, and over she went. Her feet hit the rungs in the dark and she didn't waste any emotion hoping for a happy ending. She just went. Had the ladder away and back in the shed and was going up the stairs to the kitchen before she could realize it was over.

But it was. Then she remembered one more loose end. "Ah, the hell with that catnip!" She bagged it for the trash. "Amen," she said. She drove home that night a little early. Listened to the eleven o'clock news on the car radio. She sang along.

Father Grattan had been curious ever since Mrs. Lockridge's report on the things she had seen. "What does that mean?" she said, telling him about the words carved on ribbons. That was what her fingers had felt, that was how it seemed to her. "Maybe it's not in the right order," she said. "Maybe they were just jumbled."

TERRIBILIS EST LOCUS ISTE HIC DOMUS DEI EST CAELI

"No," Father Grattan said. "It's close, but that—" He got the Vulgate. But it wasn't there. Then he asked Father Ockham.

Of course he knew. Looked up over his Lasance's *Prayers* and said, " '*Hic domus Dei est, et porta caeli; et vocabitur aula Dei . . .*' "

"I knew that *caeli* was in it somewhere," she said. She could still feel it in her fingertips.

"Antiphon, consecration of a church," Father Ockham said. "Somebody building a cathedral?"

"Repairs," Mrs. Lockridge suggested.

Father Grattan considered that. "That's what wore out? That's what blew away?" Hard to imagine repairs being needed when stone lasts forever, give or take a few eons. "Vandals," he guessed. "War."

Speaking of war, the Havahart appeared on their front porch on Friday afternoon. No one saw it arrive. Mrs. Lockridge had already taken the other one back. Mae and the cats were getting on fine. Mrs. Lockridge had paid for this trap for another week, but she took it back right away, and didn't wait around for a refund.

When she told Father Grattan about the mysterious return of it from next door he said, "It was empty?"

That was a thought. "Yes, it was empty," she said. Aggravated. There was no note. No word about the incident at all. "Maybe he thought I was going to do it again?"

"Maybe he thought the cat was."

Mrs. Lockridge wondered, but she took it back to the hardware store anyway. On faith.

Father Grattan said, a week later, as that same eerie blue-green light lit up the stoneyard, "What's he up to?"

Mrs. Lockridge had done with the subject.

"Ladder's in the shed," she told him.

But when Father Grattan went, he entered by the front door. Knocked and it was opened. The man invited him through, and they walked out into the work area together. Tom was there. "You know?" he said, gesturing between Tom and the priest, as formal introduction. Off balance, Tom and the priest shook hands. Tom had not expected to see Father Grattan there. He had blueprints with him. He rolled them up and laid them on the workbench.

"No questions," Tom said.

"All right," Father Grattan agreed. They shook again.

Schimmelpfennig looked at them. He could read lips, but there was nothing to read. He had to look deeper. But he already knew Tom's project was a secret.

Father Grattan sat on a stone and looked around.

Schimmelpfennig leaned over and poked at Father Grattan's shoulder. "Okay cat?"

"Okay," Father Grattan said. He could see the gray tom at a screened window on the second floor of the house.

"He hates," Schimmelpfennig said. "Like prison."

"I'm sorry about that," Father Grattan said.

The stonecutter looked around. "No time to make fence."

His accent was so heavy Father Grattan had to work it out. Tom got up and paced. Father Grattan didn't need to see the blueprints to figure out that this was Tom's project. He and Schimmelpfennig walked back toward the house. The carver was doing all the talking. It was apparent that something didn't fit, and that it needed to or nothing else would.

Father Grattan walked along the finished surface, touching the crisp Roman letters Mrs. Lockridge had reported. Tom came back. "Where'd you find this?" the priest asked him, about the quote.

It wasn't a trap; it just assumed that this was Tom's doing.

"Encyclopedia," he said. "It's right."

Father Grattan said, "Yes, it is."

"It's good?"

"Beautiful," Father Grattan said.

Mrs. Lockridge hadn't reported on the color of the stone. It wasn't granite at all, but that was how Father Grattan had imagined it. It was a light stone, sandstone. Tom's truck had a slab of it in back. Father Grattan saw what he had never known—there was a back gate to the lot. All this leaping over walls! The back gate was nothing but a chain between posts. It gave on the other street.

Schimmelpfennig had gone for the key to the forklift. When he brought the machine around, he eased it right up to Tom's truck, and gently, gently he got the slab up on the lift, backed it off. Brought it around to the work area and left it on the lift while he worked.

"Very damn sure?" Schimmelpfennig asked.

Tom said, "I forgot to allow for mortar."

Schimmelpfennig laughed, pulled on his gloves and helmet, and lit the torch. Chipped and burned his way through the stone, just enough, less than a saw kerf would have been, just enough. Wouldn't he know? It was his art. He stepped back. "Trust me," he said.

"Finished?" Tom asked. For answer, Schimmelpfennig cranked the lift and drove it back to Tom's truck and gently loaded the slab on.

Father Grattan wondered how Tom was managing those slabs alone. "You got one of these?" he said, indicating the forklift.

"One of them, two of these," Tom said, holding forth his hands. To Schimmelpfennig he said, "I'll come back."

"Not about this," the stonecutter laughed. No boast, just facts. He'd cut it right.

Father Grattan wondered why they had never heard that laugh before; it was as loud as his machinery. A good laugh, as strong as the man himself. It worked, like his machines, wonders.

Father Grattan wondered if they would find any way to talk. They didn't. So he sat and watched the man work, peeling gracelessness off an angel's wing and throat and tapping in feather vanes with hand tools. It was noisy, but peaceful. Father Grattan forgot all about time and duty, watching. At one point Schimmelpfennig turned to him and pointed to his collar: "Pope?" he asked, pronouncing it *pup*.

"Catholic," Father Grattan nodded.

"Tom?" His *o* had that full *aw* sound. "Very damn good Catholic?"

Father Grattan held out his hand, gave Tom a so-so. "Passing, not head of class," he said.

Schimmelpfennig thought that over. "No dunce," he said. He pulled on his mask, his gloves, picked up his torch.

Father Grattan said, "You?"

Schimmelpfennig lit the torch. "No dunce," he said again. But he knew what Father Grattan was asking. He burned a little off the angel's wing before he answered. "Mama: Martin Luther," he said. "Poppa: Moses." He beat his chest with his free hand. "Me: Tarzan!" And that laugh again, from under the mask, but still large and strong. It rang off the tombstones. He made Father Grattan think of Virgil's ferryman: *Age in a god is tough and green.*

"How'd you and Tom—" Father Grattan said, forgetting that Otto needed to see him speak to understand. "How long have you known Tom?" he asked, when Otto stopped and turned. Otto adjusted the flame. He pushed up the goggles, turned off the torch. It wasn't that he needed to think, to remember. He walked to a particular monument, not large, not small. "Black granite," Otto said. It sounded like he said "Black gray night." It was polished like a mirror with rough edges, like something wet, something just pulled from water. "This," he said to Father Grattan. "For his wife. Chose it just like this." He clicked his fingers, or tried to, but he had on the gauntlets, so it was a symbolic gesture. "*Then,*" Otto said, "the—the—" He couldn't find the right word. "Such a struggle!" he said. Otto clutched his head and shook it, to show Father Grattan how Tom had labored, had stalled, had suffered to find the words for that marker. He made quite a show of it. Then he said, "*Weeks.* Every night he come here, we drank and sat and he stared at that damn rock."

Father Grattan didn't think very much would fit on the rock, a name maybe, dates. "It's beautiful."

"Spanish, English, he puts," Otto said. "I carve like this." He made tiny gestures, thumb to fingertips, nip, nip, nip.

"What did it say?"

"Spanish, I don't know," Otto said, shrugging. "English?" He considered. "It was good! I make a little ribbon for it, only place it fits, right under her name. 'Nola: No longer, no less.'" He studied the effect of that on Father Grattan. "Good?" Gratified, he laughed. "You see? I tell him, 'You come work for me, you're damn good!' He said it was my whiskey . . ." Otto pulled his glove off, keyed open his tool chest, and got out a bottle, gave the label a look, a shrug. Offered it to Father Grattan. "Sometimes we drink his," he said. He rummaged up some plastic cups. "Yes?"

"I must go," Father Grattan said when he finished. As they shook hands, Father Grattan noticed Otto's wrist. The tattoo. He stared. Otto didn't notice.

He had a thought. "Ah," he said, and handed Father Grattan two perfect acorns of that black granite. Finials? Bookends? Paperweights? Something. "Tell nice lady not to throw."

"Lady?" Father Grattan said absently.

Otto pulled his welder's apron up between his legs like Mrs. Lockridge's skirts bunched for fast exit. His parody was wasted. Father Grattan kept staring at the numbers tattooed on Schimmelpfennig's wrist.

"Zip code," the stonecutter said. With that great laugh again. "Dachau."

He let the priest out at the side gate. Father Grattan saw that the mechanism that kept it latched had no actual lock to it. One need only reach over, lift, and shoot the bolt! Schimmelpfennig saw him figure that out. "Nobody thinks," he said. *Tinks.* "So damn smart," he said, hitting himself on the chest, "make it too high to reach, me."

He shut the gate and Father Grattan heard him laughing all the way back.

When Father Grattan told about the cat's being shut in the house, Mrs. Lockridge said, after a quick trip out to the back steps to kick the stockpiled gravel off forever, "I miss him already."

At St. Joseph's, Señora Rios had been prepped for surgery. It had been too risky before, with too great odds against. Now there was no other option. She was weaker, but that very raising of the odds against

her had brought the decision to cut. She understood. Everyone understood. Señora Rios wanted it to be *for* something. Her whole life had
been for something. The things she had been for had set her against others. But she had not been, simply, *against*. It was the things she had been
for that she wanted to carry as her flag into this battle now. She was too
weak to raise her hand. Father Ray and Father Grattan spoke with her.
Father Ockham stepped forward, as they wheeled her down the hall to
the elevator, and walked with her. "May the most just, most high, and
most amiable will of God be done and praised in all things eternally," he
prayed. She couldn't catch it all. At the pause, she said, "Amen." At the
doors, she felt the rolling cot swing around. She was leaving them headfirst. There they all were, her sons, the priests, Faye. Someone else? . . .
She had not seen him in thirty years. She looked for him. "How will he
know me?" she asked, as the doors slid shut.

It would be hours before they would know anything. Tom said, "I
have to work." Everyone else was staying. Faye. Father Ray. Father
Ockham. Vic. Tom said, "You need me, call." He held out Vic's beeper.
Vic looked interested to see it again.

"*That's* where," he said, remembering where he'd left it.

"Okay?"

Vic nodded. "Works for me."

Tom said, "You know the number." He didn't look at Faye.

Vic said, "Maybe someone else will call me."

"They do," Tom said. "How do you ignore them? How do you brush
them off?"

Vic showed him. They walked down the hall. Vic came back. Faye was
gone. Had run down the hall the other way, sprinting through the lobby
to the elevators, to just catch Tom as he was going out the side exit.

"Should I go?" she said. Tom hated this kind of thing. He wouldn't
want to talk it over.

"Look," he said. "Not with me."

"I knew that," she said. She was following him to his truck. He waved
her back. "You weren't like this before," she said.

"Before what?"

"Where are you going? What are you going to do? Why is *there* better
than *here*?"

He laughed, but it wasn't pleasant. "Isn't," he said.

"I don't have to be here," she said.

Tom cranked the truck. "What's stopping you?"

"You're leaving because you don't think it'll work. You think she's going to die," she said. "You're turning into Vic!"

He took her hands off his windowsill by force, peeled them off and gave them back with a little shove. "You don't know," he said. He drove away.

She ran after him. "Neither do you!"

Nothing stopped him.

Tom was sitting with his back to the wall, looking at the dunes. He'd shoved them away, and shoveled them out of the foundations. He had dug deep and he had not built on sand. He was on the lee side of the site, away from the water. He could hear it—louder, if he tipped his head toward the wind. It was rich with low tide. It leaned the sandbur and goldenrod over, combed it out flat on the dune tops, tickled and whorled and tracked the sand with designs that erased and retraced themselves with each gust. Odd weather and an odd sky. Season was almost over. October storms were worst. Something way off, maybe in Africa, was raking and steaming up the sky. A veil over it, not at all cloud, and yet there was some diminishment. The blue was blue, but it could have been bluer. He thought his eyes were tired, burned, like his hands, with lime and mortar dust. But the part of him that had lived all his life on the water knew better. Something. He pushed himself up and walked into the clear and looked. No smoke anywhere. West, things were cleaner, as if the gauze hadn't gotten that far yet. It was noon.

The beeper had not made a noise. He took it out, looked at it. Maybe he was out of range. He thought about that, figured that out. It was on. He wasn't out of range. He went back to work.

The outside was done. Weathered in. The tin roof was a dusty greenish blue. So was the glass in the windows. Tom worked inside. Two steps up on a two-by-six across two ladders, plastering the ceiling, when Father Grattan wheeled his bicycle in and dropped it, and knocked at the open door.

"No news," he said immediately, when Tom whirled to see. But Tom sat down anyway. Indicated for Father Grattan to do the same. The priest didn't, though. He looked around. Found some of the stones he had seen in Otto Schimmelpfennig's yard. Looked till he found the slab that had needed burning down to size. It now fit beautifully, in the floor. A vault cover. There were two.

"You followed me?" Tom guessed.

"Tried," the priest admitted. "Couldn't keep up."

"I saw you."

"I thought you did."

They sat there and talked, then.

"Otto—"

"Did not betray you," Father Grattan said. "I had already figured out what, and why, and Otto showed me, explained about how."

"And where," Tom said, stepping back up with his tools.

"A matter of time," Father Grattan said. Tom worked on, ignoring him.

"This isn't holy ground until this place is consecrated," Father Grattan told him. "Did you know that? You can't just bury her anywhere, like a shrub. There are laws, secular and canon."

"I have a permit," Tom said. "I have a deed."

"Sure," Father Grattan said. He kept looking at those slabs in the floor. The two of them. He had not expected two. He had thought Tom was making the chapel for his mother. Only his mother. "For your mother," Father Grattan said.

"I keep my word," Tom agreed. "I give it, I keep it."

Grattan knelt and cleared off the rubble and dust and bits of construction debris from the stone. Nothing was carved on the slab, on either slab. An enormous blob of plaster splatted to the floor.

"I can help you, I think," Father Grattan said.

"Consecrate?"

"Takes a bishop. Big guns. But I can—"

"Take up bones and keep them under a tent till they oil it up and make it right in here?" Tom looked around. "Unabridged encyclopedia is full of facts. Alpha. Omega. All of it. Just a few questions remain . . ."

"I can plaster," Father Grattan said. He was already taking off his jacket. He laid his collar upon it. Took the board from Tom, loaded up, stepped up to the ladder and began floating, smoothing plaster on, an even skim. A little rough at first, but better than Tom. "I was not always a father," Father Grattan said. "I used to be a son." He was loosening up already, getting the hang of it again.

"He teach you how?"

Father Grattan kept on working. "You judge."

"*Vive?* He still alive?"

"No," Father Grattan said, "he's dead."

"Union?"

Father Grattan laughed. "He paid his dues."

When Tom saw that the priest really could help, and would, he let him.

Didn't try to work alongside. Went on to the next thing. And the next. Trimming out. Then sweeping up, clearing out the extra lumber and mortar sacks. Tom seemed to be trying to finish that day, or would fail trying. Father Grattan shook his head. "No one knows when. She's getting better."

Surprised, Tom explained at the door, "Look," as though Father Grattan had missed something clear as day. Tom said it again, and this time Father Grattan stepped outside and looked, where Tom was pointing. He didn't see anything.

"What?"

"*Tormenta*," Tom said. "Hurricane. Five, six days. Maybe later, maybe not. Good cover, a storm. Any fool can find Cuba in a storm. Some even come home again." He got in his truck, backed it away from the front of the chapel, parked, and came back. Shook the sand out of the doormat.

Father Grattan was astonished. "Cuba?" He looked around at the chapel. He had thought this chapel was *instead of* Cuba. For the first time he could read the cornerstone, now that Tom's truck had left it clear. Father Grattan put out his hand to it and touched.

"I made it," Tom said. "Otto taught me."

In Spanish first, and after that, in English:

> This chappell build by his son
> in memory of Oscar Carrasco Rios, hero,
> in the Year of Our Lord 1991.

Tom touched the stone in two places. First on "son."

"Easy to add *s*," he said. "Maybe Vic will buy a few benches and a . . . what do you call . . ." Tom dipped his fingers in thin air and made the sign of the cross.

"Stoup," Father Grattan said.

Tom looked at him closely. "I know all that," he said. "I was an altar boy." He made a halo with both hands, thumb to thumb, fingertips touching. He lifted his index fingers up, so it looked like a halo with horns. He put it on; it was too small.

"Doesn't fit you," Father Grattan said.

Tom said, "Truth!" He turned back to the cornerstone. "Hero," he said of his father, touching the place it appeared in English and in Spanish. He traced the *h*.

Father Grattan still worked to comprehend. "You are going to Cuba to bring your father's . . . your father . . ."

"Whatever," Tom said. "Whatever I find. She wants to be buried beside him. She'll never quit on it, never will, you know her. No joke. She made me promise, but she didn't make me say where or how!"

"But it's been years. It's been—"

"Long enough," Tom said.

Father Grattan went back into the chapel. He worked a few more minutes. He could not spare another afternoon like this; this was hooky. He worked fast. He was cleaning his tools, putting the lid back on the bucket of mud, when Tom checked to see how far he'd gotten. It was almost done. "Close enough now," Tom said.

"How did you get all this out here?" Father Grattan wondered. "It's a marvel, really. Who else knows?"

"No one," he said. He had bought materials up and down the coast. Had gone out in the *Legal Hours* and docked at strange landings, had things brought to him and loaded on. Had paid cash. "No dots to connect," Tom said.

"It's not a crime to build a church," Father Grattan said. He considered how Tom must have worked, frantically, in the evenings to get the truck back, unloaded into the *Legal Hours*, and everything covered with a tarp before the other fishermen came in. At the hospital parking lot, the truck bed was always empty. Father Grattan had ridden with him.

And that vault cover he had seen Otto Schimmelpfennig loading with a forklift . . . "How did you do it?" the priest wondered.

Tom considered the whole project. "Slow. But soon."

"What if you are found out?" Father Grattan said. He didn't mean by the locals. "What if they—if you—"

"Then put *me*," he said, nodding toward the vault. "Friend," he added, "I need absolute secrecy." He spread his hands to include everything; he didn't make an inventory. "Let me get him here first."

"She has no idea, your mother?"

Tom shook his head. "If she *hates* it, then I'll take him back! and take her later like she thinks I meant when I promised."

"In the *Legal Hours*?"

"It's a good boat."

"But Vic's—"

"His is better, but if they catch me, they'll take the boat. Better for me, not so good for Vic. Mine's okay."

"*Ask him*," Father Grattan said. "*Ask*, at least."

"No!" Tom could roar. "Not till I'm gone! Tell him then." He reached around and locked the door with its button, pulled it shut, then got out his keys and opened the chapel again, pushed the door wide. "Make a prayer," Tom said to Father Grattan. He cut the air with his hands, making a circle, including everything in the chapel's interior, and a larger gesture, that included everything outside the walls, as though Father Grattan would simply walk around the outside and, like an exterminator of termites, proof the foundations against enemies. "Your words are as good as mine," the priest told him. " 'The prayer of an upright man . . .' "

But Tom shook his head as he helped the priest put on his collar and black suitcoat. "I'm not union," he said.

Tom drove on back to town, to the hospital, toward what news there was. It wasn't bad news. She had survived the surgery, and now they must wait and see. "The first twenty-four hours," they told them. Señora Rios was back in ICU. When Tom walked up the hall to the unit, where telemetry tethered his mother and counted everything but the hairs on her head, he had to pass the family room. Tom opened the door and looked in. Faye was there. She looked up when he opened the door, her face bright with the hope of what she had been telling the others. They were facing her, a little group; it was so much like his dream, it stopped him cold. Tom handed Vic the beeper. "I didn't need it," he said.

Vic tossed it up in the air, caught it, tossed it hand to hand, as though it were not fragile or precious. As though Tom's answer did not matter. "No calls?"

"None for *me*," Tom said.

That made Faye laugh.

Except for that, though, she didn't have anything to say to him. Tom went on down the hall to watch his mother through the grid-glass, as she healed.

Father Grattan had refused Tom's offer of a ride. He did what Tom had asked, inside and outside the chapel, and locked the door; it didn't take a key. He didn't leave right away. He walked around the lot, found the survey pins. It was high ground. Tom had chosen well. The scrub and trees began some hundred yards off, and the dunes and ground were well pegged by grasses, vines, and brier. Even as late as this, something sweet bloomed. He broke a sprig, interested. Amazed, really. It looked and smelled like rosemary. He had seen it from a distance many times. It had blended into the general dark weedy cover for which he used gamboge and Hooker's green when painting. He had been very stupid! "You can't just look, you have to see," as Mrs. Lockridge told Father Ockham when he insisted on being given back his car keys. Father

Grattan noticed for the first time the fuselike stems of the vines, the rubbery texture of the purslanes, and the glinting tips of bayonet—all with distinct coloring. Colors he thought it might be worth experimenting to achieve. Perhaps it was the light? Late in the day, a bit golden and thick, but that wasn't it. Things definitely had a surprising distinctness. Not the clarity that comes during solar eclipse, and yet an eerie—

He looked at the sky. Looked around. From where he stood, the chapel seemed to have risen up out of the sea. Not stranded, but grounded. It was good Tom had not made it very tall. It had good proportion and simple dignity. No toy grandeur, either. It was cozy, like a ship, inside. From outside, the impression was of strong lines and angles. And the roof—with its hazy sea-blue-green—seemed to vanish into the sky itself. What was it about the sky? Father Grattan wondered if the leaden overcast was what Tom had seen or felt.

Father Grattan thought of the word *veil*. He felt suddenly that he would like to be back in town, moving down familiar streets toward home. He wondered if this was what Faye had meant about the sense nature gives birds, warning them inland.

He walked around to the sea side of the chapel and stood a few more minutes, looking. There wasn't a bird in sight, but he could hear them, their piercing cries as shrill as children's. The sea was out as far as it could go before the tide turned. It was turning now.

On the way back to town, Father Grattan wasn't really thinking about what Tom had said, and he had business—several calls and a parish meeting, a planning committee and evening service—between him and a moment's quiet time. In fact, he never consciously considered, but as he was leaving the church that night, walking back to the rectory, he saw the lights still on in Otto's stoneyard, and he thought, "I'll take my kit." That was how he knew that he intended to go with Tom to Cuba. That was why he began, from that hour, to carry his prescription medications, his passport, waterproof matches, and a half-pint of brandy in his other pocket, ready as he could be, for he knew not the hour. But he partially cured that, too. He bought a diver's watch. Waterproof. With a compass. Able to withstand pressure. Legible in the dark. "My hurricane watch," he called it. There were instructions in several languages. There was a money-back *garantia*. Father Grattan tossed that in the trash. But when he woke at two, as he usually did, to sit in his chair by the window, he retrieved the *instrucciones* from the wastebasket, uncrumpled them, and, after consideration, placed them in his breviary at the date two weeks away. He was not sure if that was an act of hope or of faith.

He couldn't sleep. He read in bed. Nothing heavy. A little Golden paperback, *Guide to Seashores*. He opened it to the first section. "Advice for Amateurs," it said. There were seven subsections. The fifth one was "Get Help."

Father Grattan turned out the light and went to sleep.

PART VII

SHELTER

By all accounts it wasn't going to be much of a storm, or much of a threat. It seemed for a time that it might simply lose momentum and sling its clouds off with no more than a sigh and not even bother with landfall. Storm warnings went up along the Virgin Islands, but were lifted again as the mass lazed directly north. Faye heard the longitude and latitude on her radio and went and found them on her globe. She touched the islands, spoke their names. They were a thousand miles away, and she had as much chance of making land there as the storm. But she had a savings account, a new one. Just for her plans. When she opened it, the clerk at the bank said, "It's a beginning," and Faye told her, "For a trip."

The teller thought Faye said "Ireland," when she told her where. Faye didn't correct her. She liked to think of it as "Island." But she began to call it "I'll land," and as she studied the storm's path each day, she felt a restlessness and fret like sorrow that she was not on the move too. She always tasted the air, knew from its direction what lands it had crossed to find her, where it was going next.

It was a great disappointment to her when the storm weakened. She was glad for the people in its path, that they were spared. But she answered its downgrade from hurricane status to tropical depression with one of her own.

She still worked two jobs, and since Señora Rios had begun to mend after her surgery, Faye went back to work. She rode over to Sanavere after work and stayed till just time to catch the last ferry home. She liked making her own way. She wouldn't ride with Tom or Vic or any "Tom, Vic, or Harry," as she said, and came and went as she would. Sometimes she stayed at St. Joseph's a long time, sometimes she just looked in. The hospital visits and work had completely knocked her out of her classes. She hadn't been to the library in weeks, and she hadn't been to confession in months, and she hadn't known how tired she was of all of the disruption and stress.

To top it off, the mini-mall where the shop was located had a new manager, and the whole front was being upscaled: canvas awnings, planters with evergreens, and all doors repainted to match each other, with brass hardware and kick plates. There were compressors and hammering, saws screaming through metal, and a dull pounding that was more a feeling than a sound, sauced with the stench of hot tar.

Faye went at lunch and applied at another shop, a nice quiet one, but they didn't need anyone off-season. That was that. But she was so restless. She kept looking.

And then the storm strengthened and the people began to talk about it again. Customers at the market where Faye worked were buying foods in cans, and batteries, candles, and bottles of water. Customers at Raquel's, passengers on the ferry, visitors in the halls at St. Joseph's. There was an excitement, a purpose. Faye wondered if that was all people wanted, if that was enough. She felt the happiness too, the quickening after the dead calm. It was not the weather that had changed, so much as the people. It felt festive.

Another day, and the storm's track across the Atlantic began to straighten. No more wobbles. The newspaper printed a prediction, with the possible path and landfall in little red arrows. They were not in its way, but they were under a watch. A watch, the man on the radio said, means to continue normal activities. Listen for news, but remember, a watch means *possible* danger. Not danger itself.

That was it, Faye was thinking. No one wants danger. Just possible danger. Then normal activities can go on.

Hers did.

At school Elven picked up his pamphlet—everyone got one—on hurricane safety and tracking. Elven had made a tornado in a soda bottle. He made it for his project with two soda bottles and a length of duct tape. Elven had made "an actual tornado." "Waterspout," his teacher had said, trying to keep it local. Everyone saw them now and then. Waterspouts weren't dangerous; tornadoes were. Elven thought danger was just the thing. He called it a tornado. Faye had loaned him a book. Explanations and projects. He made an A-minus on the project. He took it by Faye's and showed it to her. Two taped-together bottles with water inside. He had dyed the water with blue food color. No matter how much he used, he couldn't get it dark enough. "Nossir," Palma had said, when he asked her to buy him "about ten" bottles of black ink at the store. Faye read his report—five pages—and the pamphlet he brought her about hurricanes too.

"Next year," he said, making plans. And there was all this talk of a storm now, making it more exciting. Elven hoped the hurricane was coming. "We'll miss school . . . but not much," he said.

Faye's eye fell on the portion of the pamphlet about what to do if your area gets a warning. Since they were now under a warning, not a watch, Faye thought she should read it. She got about as excited as Elven, but she wasn't sure she wanted to see one, even one homemade for a class project.

Elven could hardly wait. He shook the bottles and turned them over and made the tornado swirl down. It didn't look like one at first; water just rolled and swirled and crashed back and forth in the top bottle and finally began to organize itself and drip into the bottom bottle. All of a sudden, there it was—a strong funnel—sometimes wide and sometimes slender as a needle, and it didn't look like dyed water in a bottle, it looked like the real thing. It looked deadly.

"But a hurricane's not like that," she warned him. "It's—" But she had never seen one either, that she could recall. "It's—"

"What color is the eye?" Elven wondered.

Faye didn't know. She looked through the brochure. Something about the eye . . . AVOID THE EYE OF THE HURRICANE, it said.

"Well, it's not coming this way, anyway," Faye said.

"It does," Elven said, "I'm gonna spit in it. Right in its eye."

Elven gave Faye back her book on tornadoes. "It was good," he said. "But next year I'm making a hurricane. They're bigger. And they're major, major cool."

That night he asked Palma, "What color is the eye?"

Zeb wasn't in yet. Palma had been watching the news all evening. This wasn't anything yet. This was just a little wind and high water. The storm was going to mess up shrimping for a week or so, and he was getting all he could while he still could. He had promised Palma he would run the boat upriver to safe harbor if the storm tracked any closer to them. She wasn't sure how to hope.

Elven asked again, "What color?"

Distracted, Palma said, "Black. Black as a button."

And that was how it turned out—a perfect prediction—for the hurricane made landfall twenty-two hours later, well after dark, and the eye, as expected, passed right over Sanavere. It had been six days since Father Grattan had helped Tom plaster. On the seventh day, as though God was taking a rest, the storm worked to undo creation.

Faye had nailed up her windows. She had taped them inside, great X's she would have to scrape off with a razor blade and scrub and scour to remove, assuming the storm spared her little home. She was not on high ground. No one on the island was. Evacuation had begun that morning, and by the time Faye left, the ferry had already been taken out of service. Water was moving, marching, it seemed to Faye as she stared from the window of Palma's car, and the grass, drowning in the high tide in the surge, lay flat and streaming almost due north as the winds drove it over. Palma had gathered her children first; she had gone back through the house—hastily boarded up by Zeb before he left to take the *Palma Forever* upriver. "Do you have to?" Palma had begged.

"That, or it's sink her, so she won't be washed up or beat to death at the dock." He went alone. Up that same river Ben had drowned in. Palma couldn't think what to take, couldn't choose what to leave behind. Faye helped her pack.

A change of clothes, things for the twins, toiletries. Palma stood in the hall, her hands icy with fear. She covered her eyes, saying, "I can't think!" She had had several days but had believed they would be spared this. In a hundred and thirty years of history there, no storm but one had ever come this close. And in Palma's whole life—growing up at the hammock upcoast on Birdwhistle—she had never seen bad wind or killing high waters. They were working against time. The Law was coming by to be sure folks had gone, but the waters were rising along the causeway, and it would close to traffic as soon as those afternoon tides swept over it.

Faye didn't hassle Palma. She brought another tote bag. "Put your scrapbooks in here," she told her. Palma looked at the bag. "I have a trunk full of pictures!" she said. How could she choose? Faye thought of the story in her tornado book about the woman they found up in the tree, dead, with her marriage license and her Bible still in her arms. She'd run back for them. Died for them.

"Listen," Faye said. "We'll take it all." She helped Palma clear things off the little trunk. Elven carried it to the car. It meant the playpen had to go. The babies were already in the car. One was crying. Faye said, "Palma—" Elven's cat hunkered in its hamper, silent.

Palma stood there at the door. "Lord, what's the use of lockin' it? Come and take it all!" But she let Faye have the key, turn it, hand it back. As she put the car in gear, she said, "We could've got most of it on that boat. Filled it full! Why didn't I think of that?"

"Zeb didn't need to be dragging all that upriver," Faye said.

As they turned and found their place in the line of cars inching along, Palma kept looking back. Faye wouldn't. She rode with her little bundle of things between her feet. She held the globe—in a garbage sack—on her lap. Palma was looking in her rearview when the break came for them to merge into the actual highway. That had taken an hour. "Now!"

But they didn't roll a foot farther. Complete gridlock. "Maybe the bridge's up," Elven said, standing up in the back seat, trying to see around. The gusts tousled the trees and bushes. Wipers couldn't keep up with the rain.

"Maybe it's my daddy! Maybe it's his boat going under."

When he realized what he'd said, he was sorry, but he didn't know how to fix it. "Under the bridge," Faye said, glancing at Palma.

"He'll get there before we do," Elven said.

"This is no laughing matter," Palma said.

The drawbridge was open to let boats through. But not Zeb's. He had passed through hours before. These were the diehards, the holdouts, the doubters, the hopers—a line of them, two and three abreast, a whole fishing fleet and many pleasure craft also, moving toward safe harbor. It looked like the Blessing of the Fleet, except there were no banners and flowers, and no one waved. Most of the yacht yards were empty, and the basin had only a few, bobbing at anchor while their owners made plans. Some chose to sink them. Some chose to anchor far enough from the others that even in a tremendous blow, they'd not knock into anything as they pulled and swung about. The poles wore the full warning: four flags, two red squares with black centers and two red pennants. They stood bold against all that gray sky.

When Zeb jumped onto the deck of the *Palma Forever*, he had noticed Tom struggling to offload something covered in a tarp. He couldn't leave a friend like that. And he knew Tom didn't have a johnboat. He went to help him, and make an offer.

They set whatever it was on the dock. "New engine?" Zeb said. Teasing, not prying. It wasn't big enough for that; it was just something to say. But Tom was touchy. And he was soaked through, under his slicker. It was cheap vinyl, nothing like Tom's usual gear. Lots of things didn't seem like the usual, but then Zeb hadn't seen Tom fishing in a month or more. Occasionally he saw the *Legal Hours* easing out, fueling, but never loading ice. And never selling shrimp or anything when it came back in. If Zeb had been a suspicious man, he might have wondered if Tom had begun to haul contraband. Plenty of cash to fish out of the sea, plenty of grass that wasn't seaweed, plenty of coke that wasn't carbonated. But Zeb knew his man. Or thought he did.

"Whatever it is won't blow away," Zeb said, when Tom did nothing more than grunt. Not even thanks or good day.

"We could travel together," Zeb offered.

"Alone," Tom said.

"All right," Zeb said. "See you there."

"You know where?" Tom gave him a look.

"How are you getting back?" Zeb said. That was what he came over to offer. A ride back. He had driven upriver the night before, and Palma had followed in her station wagon. They had left Zeb's truck and ridden back. Now when Zeb made the *Palma Forever* fast, he could drive himself back to town, meet them at the shelter. Tom hadn't done that. There his truck sat. And he didn't have anyone to help him, the way Zeb had Palma. He didn't even have a striker; he'd fired the last one around Labor Day. People had been talking about Tom, wondering. Zeb always said, "Finest kind." Wouldn't talk about any of them, about Faye or the divorce stuff with the Fortners and Vic's testimony in court that first day, which had ended in Mr. Fortner's being carried out to his doctors.

Zeb asked him again, "How you getting back?"

Tom said, "I don't need." Not hateful, but gentle. With regret. Zeb left him there, on the dock.

Half a league upriver Tom's voice came over Zeb's radio. Zeb picked up his Mickey Mouse and called back.

"Not clear, man. Say again." The signals were blown to pieces by the wind. Too much noise from everywhere, engine, wind, water, and static. Tom tried again.

Something about . . . Zeb couldn't make it out.

At the last moment, Tom's voice, *"Vista."*

"Hasta," Zeb said. He needed both hands on the wheel. The water was surging so strongly it seemed to be pushing him along; he hardly needed fuel.

Tom had his charts out, figuring. It was a matter of timing as much as anything else. Luck was nothing he could help, good or bad. And God would do what He willed. Tom hoped that if he was in the way, it was the right way. He needed to get out soon. The waves and surge were going to be worse later; but he needed to find the eye. To get on the good side of that. He could even ride in it for a way, but crossing it, no, that would be dead stupid. Not worth the risk. He had only run once in weather this bad. They were calling this not the worst storm, but it was bad enough, slow, untidy, and sloppy. A big, wide-open eye, not a little one, focused close. An eye like that could wander. An eye like that could blow you away without blinking. What Tom saw as he calculated was that the whole idea was insane. Below his boots he could feel the bilge pump thrumming. He was a little low in the water, but there was nowhere to leave the other supplies he had. The chapel was not finished; the chapel might never be finished. He took a piece of paper and wrote.

"Otto: Altar base on dock. Cut compartment where I marked it. Zeb Leonard will help you load. Don't discuss it. Obliged. Tom." He put it in a envelope, sealed and stamped it, wrote Otto's address, and walked to the box in front of Lupo's. He stood there a moment and considered. Bayfront had gone under before. They had marked it on the wall of the warehouses, just how high, just how far the sea would go to reclaim its own. The mark was over Tom's belt line. Over the top of the mailbox. But that had been the storm of the century. And this was the same century, he thought. So why not take a chance? He dropped the letter in.

He had cast off; he was revving in reverse, when he heard Vic's boat. Father Grattan was with him.

"*Por Dios!*" He ran out on deck and waved them off. Vic came about, blocking him.

"I'll ram it!" Tom roared.

"Then ram it," Vic said.

Father Grattan said, coming forward to speak without shouting, "Vic's boat."

"*Mi bote es tu bote,*" Vic agreed. "*Mi padre es tuyo.* My father is yours."

"He doesn't mean me," Father Grattan said. "But I'm at your service also."

"Oh, my God," Tom said. "It's a picnic!"

Father Grattan balanced on the rail of the *Blue Lady*, then sprang onto the deck of the *Legal Hours*. "We'll need your charts," he said. Gathering them up. Tom couldn't believe his eyes. But when he saw Father Grattan's watch, that bright yellow, clumsy, beknobbed artifact, he laughed out loud.

He hadn't given a thought to the safety of his boat; now that he was leaving her, he felt troubled. He and Vic talked it over. Finally they decided to moor to the west pier, but anchor in the center of the river. Vic had a thought. They used that anchor too, the one from the *Blue Lady*. Unless the water rose twenty or thirty feet past flood, Tom's boat should stay safe, not float off into the marsh or wind up in the trees or bob like a rubber duck up Main Street and be left in front of Woolworth's like the Ark on Ararat when the tide went out.

"You have another anchor?" Father Grattan asked Vic as they aimed into the storm.

"We won't be stopping that long," he said.

Tom poured each of them some coffee from Vic's thermos. He topped it off with a little cognac. "*Contra mar y viento!*"

"*Jesús y cruz!*"

"God and Harry!"

"Who else did you tell?" Tom wondered. Finishing his drink.

"No one," Father Grattan said. "Nobody on earth," he assured Tom, "knows where the hell we are."

The three of them thought about that as the *Blue Lady* lunged and lurched on. "Well," Vic said finally, "then they don't know we're coming."

Tom brought personal flotation devices for the three of them, but after they thought about it, it seemed rather dainty to imagine themselves bobbing in that sea, worse than useless, and they didn't put them on. "Is there some kind of law?" Father Grattan wondered. For all the crimes they were about to commit, to add that one . . . It was so ridiculous it made all of them laugh.

It was good cognac.

"*Coño!*" Vic suddenly shouted, and beat the wheel with his fist.

"What?"

"I forgot my beeper," Vic said. Tom said, "You'll owe ten thousand virgins a return call!"

Father Grattan didn't get it, but Vic and Tom laughed until they cried.

At the door of the shelter, Agapito's wheelchair hung up. They had to roll him back out and settle him straight on, and then tip the front wheels up a little. He woke, felt the rain on his face where Cassia had not been able to both steer and keep the umbrella completely over him. He looked dapper. He reached for his hat when he saw he was in the building. He looked around at the hall. The trophy cases. The lockers. They were rolling him down the hall toward double doors, open. Carlo walked beside the chair, without a leash. "*¿Votar?*" Agapito asked.

"No, love, we aren't voting," Cassia told him. "There's going to be a storm."

"*Querida,*" he called. He couldn't see her. She was behind the chair, rolling it.

"Here," she said. He called her *querida,* always. It had been a long time since he called her name. She spoke to him every few moments while he was awake, so he would not become frantic. She could not leave him, ever.

"*¡Querida!*" he called again.

"Here," she said.

When they were registered, she moved the chair to the area where they had been assigned. Cassia looked around. She spotted Faye. Faye thought she was waving. Faye waved back.

Cassia beckoned. She stood behind Agapito's chair, her hand on his shoulder. He raised his to touch it.

"*Querida,*" he called. *Beloved.*

"Here," she said.

Faye came over.

"My dear," Cassia said to Faye.

"*Querida,*" Agapito called softly.

Cassia patted his shoulder. "Here," she said.

"May I help?" Faye said, in Spanish.

"Just stand back here," Cassia said, in English. "Right *here.*" She moved so Faye could put her feet right where Cassia's had been. "And when he calls, do what I do."

"*¿Querida?*" he called.

"Here," she said.

Faye put her hand where Cassia's had been, on Agapito's shoulder. Cassia stepped back, directly back, and Agapito could not see her leave. Carlo followed her.

"*¿Querida?*" Agapito called.

"Here," Faye said. She tried to sound like Cassia. She touched his shoulder as Cassia had done. But he grew agitated.

"*¡Querida!*" he called.

"Here," Faye said.

Agapito began to move his hands about in the air, gesturing, touching his face. The rain had dried. He found his hat, held it up to look at it. "*¿Querida?*" he said.

"Here," Faye said, and touched his shoulder.

"*¿Querida?*" Agapito said.

"*Lo siento,*" Faye said. "I'm sorry."

Agapito cocked his head. There was a little tremor in his hands. Faye could feel it in the steel of the chair. "¿*Querida?*" he said.

"Here!" Cassia said, running up, breathless. She had taken Carlo to the kennel area. She had hurried back with her arms laden. So Faye touched his shoulder. But after that, when he called "¿*Querida?*" it was Cassia who answered. She had brought in her "luggage." She set it—a great brimming bowl of flowers—on the floor in front of Agapito. "That's my punchbowl," she said. "Isn't that perfect?" Faye moved away from Agapito's chair. Faye looked at Cassia to see if it was all right for Agapito to see her. Cassia nodded. "He won't know you," she said. "That's all"— she tried to think of the best word—"past." She shrugged.

"They are beautiful flowers," Faye said.

"From our garden," Cassia said. "Did you ever see lilies so late? I couldn't leave them. They have only one day, you know. It was so dark, I thought they might close in the car." She had a thought. "Do you know the science of flowers?" She emphasized *science*.

Faye shook her head.

"I just wondered," Cassia said. "If you—I mean if they never had a speck of darkness fall on them, if twilight never came, would they stay open? Forever? Maybe there is somewhere they could last. One day is not very long."

The evacuation center was filling. Some families had come prepared. They had little televisions that ran on batteries. And another group, several generations, was saying, "How different all this is from what we planned!" They had a birthday cake and candles, lit, and for a moment everyone paused. Listening to them sing. Everybody sang the last line. Then a man's voice called out, "Play ball!" and they cut the cake.

The electricity stayed on another hour. After that, there were lanterns. The managers of the shelter told them they had a generator, but it would be saved to keep the food lockers running. From time to time, new refugees arrived, came down the long hall following the circle of light from a flashlight, and peered around in the gym's twilight, trying to locate family or friends. An occasional gust brought something crashing. Glass crumpled when plywood shutters, nailed for the storm, gave way.

"Will the boats break?" a child of a fisherman asked.

Over in the corner, men played cards. All around the shelter there were little arcs of light, circles of light around which families and friends focused, and nurtured, like ponies at an oasis. Someone had brought a tape player. The music of Abelardo Baloso filled the room.

"Too much!" someone called. A mother, trying to get children to sleep.

Faye wasn't sleepy. After Zeb had gotten back from taking his boat upriver, his family, and Cliffie's, had made a little fort with their bedding, arranged themselves into overlapped strength. Elven and his cousins wound slowly down, but from time to time Elven got up, found Faye where she sat, and said, "When is the eye?"

He actually fell asleep for a time, and Faye thought he might not wake in time to ask it again, but he did. There was a wonderful peace after midnight. The shriek of wind and the constant rush of water on the roof and in the street eased. The trees shook themselves and held still. Elven sneaked away from his parents; they were sitting back to back, each with a twin.

Because of the danger, there could not be lanterns after bedtime. There was just one, hanging near the door, high enough that no one could reach it, and it couldn't fall or be blown down if the storm broke the wall, and make a fire. It lit the hall and the way to the toilets. Elven and Faye made quiet progress toward it. She wanted to see the eye also.

Her head ached. The air in the gym was heavy with candle smoke, lamp fumes, and the exhalation of two hundred people. It was cooler in the hall. The barometer was still low. They moved like sleepwalkers through all those sleepers' dreams. At the front door an official sat in a folding chair. He woke and saw them and said, "No way, José."

"Please," Faye said. "Just a peek."

"What color is the eye?" Elven asked, and his need to know was great. It conveyed itself.

"We're all kids at heart," the guard said, relenting. "Don't go past that line," he said. He stood with the door open. "It could come back at any moment," he called after them, "so you better!"

They couldn't hear a thing. Faye couldn't explain it, but it felt—it had to be because she knew, because they called it "eye"—but she felt it was out there, waiting, moving, watching.

Elven cried, "It's got stars in its eye!" Pointing. She looked up and saw three. She couldn't tell which they were. But they were beautiful.

"Stars in its eye," Elven said as he headed back inside. The man at the door shook his head, amused. "I didn't see 'em," he said. "But what does stars prove?"

"They're still there," Faye said. She and Elven low-fived.

Elven was already light-years ahead. "How'm I gonna do that?" he wondered. "When I make the hurricane next year?"

He ran over to the corner where the pets were cordoned off in their containers and cages. There were dogs, cats, bunnies, birds, fish. He suddenly turned and ran back toward the door. The man was already locking it. The wind had begun again.

"Please," Elven said. "I have to!"

Faye had already gone back to her blanket. She heard the ruckus. She got there in time to see Elven being bodily and forcibly removed from the area, hauled away toward his parents at the other end of the room. As the guards carried him past, not kicking, not screaming, just trying to wriggle free for one last try, he told Faye miserably, "I forgot to spit in its eye!"

Faye had not been worried about Señora Rios, because she was still in the hospital. And when Vic and Tom didn't come to the shelter, she thought they must be there also. It was later in the night that she woke, still sitting up, though she had said she wasn't going to sleep, and she tried lying down, stretching her legs from the sitting cramp. She lay looking up into the dark beams. It came into her mind when she was not thinking at all. *What if they aren't?* Sometimes things happened. Señora Rios could not bear that, Faye thought.

Father Grattan sat braced. It seemed to him he was actually helping to push the sea back as he rode with his shoes flat against the trembling side of the boat. Vic and Tom had never been in anything like this either, but they didn't think there was much they could do to help the boat.

"Truth," Tom said, as he relieved Vic at the wheel. "*Legal Hours* would be on the bottom, dropped like a rock. This is a damn good boat."

"We're on top now," Vic said. But he wasn't boasting.

Father Grattan had noticed the little washers pinned to Tom's sea jacket. He had noticed a similar collection hanging and swinging and tapping against Vic's panel from a safety pin on Vic's key ring. He found another one, a single one, rolling on the deck as tiny as a wedding ring for a sparrow.

"What does AVISE mean?" he asked. "Is it an agency?" The little ring said—he squandered a few seconds of his flashlight's battery life to see—AVISE / WRITE WASHINGTON, D.C., and a number.

"You should ask Faye," Tom said. "Right up her alley. I always let her send mine, that's why I save them. She gets a kick out of it."

Vic turned and considered Tom. Father Grattan said, "Bird bands?"

"Bird bands," Vic said. "Migratory birds across the Gulf, the Atlantic, the Caribbean. They don't all make it."

"Eighty percent," Tom said.

"Make it?"

"Wind up in the belly of a fish, maybe. These did."

"Most of 'em don't," Vic said. "They're down there now."

Mrs. Lockridge had driven Father Ockham to St. Joseph's for the duration. He was not ill; he would be "on call." But he would also be better off there, might even find a bed to sleep in, rather than a blanket on the floor. Mrs. Lockridge didn't think the rectory was in danger. But after the power went off in midafternoon, she decided to pack a few things and be ready to take advice. She made use of the last daylight to roll rugs and set things up on other things, in case water came in. Not many buildings in town had two stories and a basement; the church had built on the highest ground. And built of stone. Still, she pulled the shutters down and secured things. She put the day's mail and the monthly bills in a plastic bag and stored them in the freezer. With the power off, they'd maybe not survive an atomic blast, if the frost had already dripped down into the pan, but maybe, otherwise, they'd make it through. That's where she put her own papers, her photos, and her jewelry, such as it was. In the freezer of her apartment. She always had traveled light. She called her friend Mae.

"Ready as I'll ever be," Mae said.

"Are you staying or going?" Mrs. Lockridge wondered.

"Going," Mae said. "I'm not scared, for myself. But I—"

"The cats," Mrs. Lockridge guessed.

"We're ready, if you're"—She made that little clucking noise, that giddyapp-kick! that indicated she was about to make a joke.

"Goin' my way," Mrs. Lockridge guessed.

"We'll be a-howling and a-scratchin' at the curb," Mae promised.

When the shelter saw the animals Mae brought—wild things, they were called—there was a moment of consultation among the officials, about policy. Besides the cats—for Mae was a habitual rescuer—there was a one-winged mourning dove, a box turtle with a road-cracked and epoxy-mended shell, a grackle with no left foot, and the cat carrier with the mama cat and six kittens. She had also brought her terra-cotta planter with hen-and-chickens. "This was my mother's," she said. She sat on a bench and waited while her case was argued.

That was why Mrs. Lockridge was holding the smaller cage, trying to keep it level so that one-legged grackle wouldn't lose its precarious balance on its perch, when Otto Schimmelpfennig arrived. Mrs. Lockridge wouldn't have known the man, except for his voice. He had been wearing welding garb that night, a monstrous helmet with flaps and goggles, a pair of elbow-length gloves freckled with spark scars from his work, and a leather apron that reached to the ground. She had known even then that he was not the village-smithy specimen she had imagined. He wasn't tall and he wasn't a muscleman. Tonight he looked rather like a diplomat on vacation. His hair was absolutely white, when he took his hat off, and he took his hat off as soon as he saw her. Made a slight bow. She didn't know him at first, but he knew her by sight. He glanced from Mrs. Lockridge to Mae and back. He noticed the kittens. The whole menagerie.

He pointed his whole hand at her, as though reasoning, not accusing. "You got acorn?"

"You got squirrel?" she said, instantly. But she figured him out just as instantly, and stood up so suddenly she tilted the black bird right on its belly. It ruffled and stirred grit on the cage bottom, righting itself. Otto Schimmelpfennig said, "Cat." And held his suitcase forward. Perhaps he had not been sure of its welcome. Perhaps he would simply not have mentioned what it was, if there had been a rule against it? It was an ordinary but not inexpensive Pullman-size piece of Samsonite. He had drilled discreet holes in it, at both ends, and in what appeared to be, to the casual eye, merely ornamental patterns. Mae took all that in at a glance. "You're *him*!" she said. "You're not so bad!"

Schimmelpfennig gave her a little bow.

"There have been worse," he said.

Somehow—and this was the point Mrs. Lockridge was not quite clear on later—she wound up custodian of that cat, the very cat, while Schimmelpfennig beckoned Zeb, and he and Otto found privacy to one side to talk.

"*No*, man," Zeb was saying.

"I zaw it." Otto pointed to his own eyes with his index fingers.

"He was leavin' same as me," Zeb said. He wouldn't believe a word of it till he saw it for himself. "He wouldn't do that!"

He paced away, then back. He was talking, but not facing the stonecutter, so Otto couldn't read his lips.

"Please?" Otto said, and Zeb turned to face him. Still shaking his head, no.

"They're at the hospital," Faye told Zeb when he found her and asked.

She got up and took her shoes off so she wouldn't make any noise as she stepped between sleepers. She bought a little flashlight with her. She didn't know Otto. Zeb said, "This is Faye." As though that were enough. Otto studied her. She studied him. Sidelong. He had high cheekbones, a strong jaw.

"They're not at the hospital," Zeb told Faye. "He went there before he came here. And he says he saw Tom's boat out in the river. At anchor."

"Please don't," Faye said. A general plea, including God.

Mrs. Lockridge came over. It was obvious there was something wrong.

But no matter how they discussed it, no one knew enough of the story to solve the mystery. The last fisherman into the shelter, when he saw the others talking, didn't help things at all. He said, "I saw Vic Rios, but not Tom. He and some other guy. Not Tom," he repeated.

"Where was this?"

"What other guy?"

But there were no answers there. "I was the last one upriver except for them," he said.

He really hated to say it, but it looked as though they had to know. "Headed the other way," he said.

"What other way?" Faye said.

"The wrong way," he said.

In the kitchen, an enterprising refugee had plugged his shortwave into the extra outlet behind the refrigerator on the generator's circuit. He had set up shop. He was speaking some, and listening though headphones. Voices in the wind, bits of this and that. Reports of damage. He could monitor the police band too. Nothing from the coast guard. SOS from a freighter, but nothing from any *Blue Lady* in distress.

The eye passed, and the storm showed its backside. Kicked its way into Alabama and made a run for Tennessee. At least that was the prediction. By four in the morning the fiercest part had gone on; after that it was just a matter of waiting. Daylight came, but no one would be allowed on the streets, owing to flooding, downed wires, and other dangers.

Faye hadn't slept again. She waited her turn and then asked the man with the shortwave to tell her what he knew. He said, "I'll write it all down—or maybe you would? And someone can read it to the people." Faye didn't want to read it out, but she wrote down what he told her. There were reports coming over the radio now too, the regular stations. With the truth came rumor. It became impossible to know what to believe. It was a beautiful morning. Unless you looked down. The ground was a ruin. The streets. The yards. The gardens and stores and neighborhoods. There had been worse winds, worse storms. But how do you judge chaos? Faye watched as several of the men shot rats floating by on debris. Inside the gym, the animals had begun to complain, to cry for attention and exercise. They had made it through, but the ark was not sweet. Faye kept pacing, her overnight in one hand, the globe in its black garbage sack in her other hand.

Word came at about seven-thirty that the causeway and the land roads were out. Faye found Zeb. "I have to," she said. "Isn't there some way?"

"Now, you don't need to be going over there," he said.

"I put everything in my mama's trunk in bags and bags," she said. "I put it up high. I couldn't bring it all."

"Then that's all you could do," he told her. "You couldn't do more than that."

At nine o'clock, Faye got in line for the phone. At ten-fifteen she got her turn. She phoned St. Joseph's. Señora Rios was fine, still recovering. "Do you wish to speak with her?" the voice said. Faye said, "No, no," and hung up. She wasn't allowed another call. But there was no one else to call. Still, she got back in line again, and waited for her next chance. Just before noon she dropped her money in and dialed. Vic's beeper rang. Rang and rang. "It wouldn't have done that if it were wet," she thought. And went to the back of the line again. She didn't want lunch. She had had no breakfast. Several people on line dropped out, to eat. Her next turn came a great deal sooner this time. And this time she dialed Tom's number. "I'm sorry," the recorded message said after a strange noise, "your call cannot be completed at this time. Please try again."

At around one, a television crew was able to fly over the island in a helicopter and send back pictures. Palma jumped and screamed when she saw their roof. "It's still there!" She beat on Elven, she beat on Faye and Zeb and Cliffie. She beat on the man whose little television it was.

Faye was that glad, but when she kept on crying, Palma said, "You can stay with us," and put her arm around her.

Faye never took her eyes off that screen. "It'll be there," she said. But the helicopter had turned and flown the other way, and there was no way to know.

A few minutes later the man with the shortwave called, "Listen to this!" and took off his headset and let the signal run through the speakers. There was a report of a coast guard call, vehicle in tow. Boat people, seeking asylum. Cubans? Haitians? Rescued by a boat that now needed rescue.

"They picked a rough night," someone said. Eleven, including crew, and a report of one dead body. "Haitians," the ham operator said.

"What does that mean," Faye said. " 'Including crew'?"

"That it's not a raft," someone said. Playing for the laugh.

"How many does a boat hold?"

Zeb came up then, and put his hand on Faye's arm. "You don't need to be flustrating yourself like this," he said. "Come eat some lunch with us. You're hollow as a hoop."

"It's them," Faye said. "I know it."

"Eleven Haitian refugees? Asylum?" Zeb reasoned. "That's two days."

"And one dead," Faye said. "Where do they take them?"

"The morgue," he said.

"I mean the others!"

"Depends," Zeb said. Palma was coming to find out why Faye hadn't come to eat with them. She had everything laid out. They were waiting.

"I'll eat," Faye said, "if you'll tell me."

"Municipal docks, if the river's open," he said.

"Not the coast guard—" Faye wondered.

"No," Zeb said. "Road's closed, so it wouldn't do any good."

"Will they be arrested?"

"Detained," Zeb said. "Detained till explained. But it probably isn't them."

Faye sat on the blanket and ate. She took a bite and ate, and took a bite and ate, and took a bite and ate. She smiled when they looked at her, and she answered when they spoke to her. She drank all her tea and said, "No, I'll get it," and walked over to the canteen area, and one moment she was there, and the next she was gone. Out the side door and running. She started a little riot, running like that. Some of the mothers thought it was the milk and ice cream truck, that it had finally come, and they wanted to be in that line at the first, not at the end. Children ran too. But they all dropped out of the chase when Faye turned the corner, crossed Mulgrave, and angled toward the heart of town.

The streets were clearing. The storm drains had done their work on the main streets, but the cross streets were still young lakes. Faye looked back. No one had followed her. She wasn't breaking any law. She wasn't a looter. She caught her breath and went on. It surprised her when she saw the river. Bayfront was under, the low warehouses looking short, a little out of perspective, from being three feet deep. The water had come up the block almost to Lupo's door. She could see on the pavement where it had already subsided. There was no way for her to get to the docks, because the docks weren't there. She would have had to wade, and from what she could see, the water would be almost over her head if she were somehow able to get all the way down to the place where Zeb and Tom usually moored. She turned back, walked the block south, and cut through the alley. Same story with the river, but she could see the *Legal Hours*, standing off where Tom had left her.

The streets were being patrolled. She didn't even turn to look when the bluelight drove by. She was up on Dennison, walking south and east, when the patrol came back. It had turned around. "She's not running, but she's not stopping," she heard one say over the radio.

It was eerie to be out in the empty town, no lights anywhere, and reflections off the lapping water making the buildings look different. Everything looked strange. She couldn't remember how to get back to the school, to the shelter.

The Law stopped her.

Before they could ask her anything, she asked them, "Where do they bring rescuees?"

"They're at the shelters."

"She means refugees."

"Yes," Faye said. "That's it." She gestured south and east, past all the shops and streets, out beyond the docks and channel, toward the open water, a wide gesture that claimed and gathered in.

"Are you a reporter?"

"I'm a shampoo girl," Faye said.

"They'll need it and more," one of the officers said.

"Let's see some identification," the other one said. "What are you doing out here?"

"I don't have any," Faye said. "I'm just walking."

"A tourist," the smart one said.

"Do you know the name of that boat?" Faye said. "The one on the radio?"

"What boat?"

"I heard it at the shelter," Faye said.

"What shelter?"

"Something Street School," Faye said. "I don't remember."

"Get in and we'll drop you off," the driver said.

"No," Faye said.

The other one radioed, asked for information. The answer came back, "*Blue Lady* out of Marathon, in tow. Headed for Key West."

"I'll go there!" Faye cried. "It's family!"

"Get in," the driver said.

A trick, of course, they weren't going to Key West, they were going to the shelter. "Look," they told her as they dropped her off, "nobody's on those roads yet. Just wait by the phone. You'll hear."

They were driving off when Faye thought about the hospital, how she should have asked to be taken there, to wait with Señora Rios. But then she thought that through, too, and realized it was a lot easier to wait with Señora Rios when Señora Rios was in a coma than when she was wide awake and worrying about her sons. The phone lines were as long as before. She found her cot and lay down. She closed her eyes so no one would bother her, but she wasn't asleep. She heard everything going on around her, and when the six-o'clock news came on, she swung her feet to the floor and found her way over to the little group huddled around the black and white TV. Rabbit-eared reception, a bit of a warp to the whole picture. Faye saw the *Blue Lady* being towed in. She could make out Father Grattan, by his clothes. The cameraman had panned across the group of rescued Haitians—"plucked from the sea," the reporter said—and then focused on the pile of ice blankets on the dock, steaming in the warm air. They covered something.

"What?" Faye demanded. "What is that?"

"Jeez Louise," the TV's owner said, when her hand gripped his shoulder so hard. "Your guess is as good as mine. You got a good enough look." He studied her profile, saw it light as she pointed to the screen. "Tom!" she cried, and beat the stranger on his back.

"You know these guys?" But Faye had subsided. The camera quick-panned and the story moved on. More coverage from all up and down the coast; that was all of that particular story.

Palma found her then. Just standing there, arguing with the TV's owner, to change the channel. But that channel was all he could get, rigged like that, and with old batteries too.

"I saw," Palma said, and pulled Faye away. "But I couldn't make out anything. A bad picture."

Faye didn't say anything. She clawed up another quarter for the phone and found a place in line. She shook Palma off, froze her out. What could they talk about? All Faye could think of was that pile of ice blankets, their steam rising like smoke. She knew it was the air temperature that was making them steam, but it was all she could do not to think of it as body heat.

When she got to the phone, of course she dialed the pager beeper. It rang. There was that to consider; that might be good news. But then she imagined no one hearing it, its little beep smothered under the smoking pall, or locked away in a morgue. She didn't torment herself with that thought; it crossed her mind, and then her mind, which had had enough, simply went to black.

Someone else hung up the receiver when Faye fainted. There was a pause. Then they moved her out of the way, and the next customer for the phone stepped up. Faye didn't stir. They carried her to her cot and she slept; she did not come back up into consciousness, she rose from that darkness into sleep, and the sleep was dreamless, seamless. Palma sat and watched her.

"Like sittin' with the dead," she told Zeb. "Look at her!"

"She was wore out like a rag," Zeb agreed.

"If that were close to true," Palma said, "the rest would be easy."

"Looks pretty easy to me," Zeb said.

Palma shook her head. "That's hard rest," she said. "Hard. Only thing harder—we don't hear some good news—be wakin' her to this world."

But she woke easily enough, at first light. She knew immediately where she was, in the shelter. Palma was stirring about, quiet and quick as ever. She had their things packed, hers and Zeb's and Elven's, and Faye's also. Everything was ready. Faye tried to sit up. Zeb and Elven took armloads of things away to Palma's car, to Zeb's truck. People were still sleeping, all around them. She lay back. She whispered, "It's over?"

"We're goin' home," Palma agreed. "You and me both."

"Bob," Faye said.

"That ket was the first thing he packed. We get you on your feet, we're outta here!"

Faye considered. She was still dressed, but they had taken off her shoes. Palma found them and tied them on for her.

Zeb came back for the last load. "You *tell* her?"

"*You* tell her," Palma said.

Faye sat up again. "Tell me," she said.

"Like I said," he said. "Detained till explained."

"Who?"

"Cap'n Rios. All of 'em."

"Detained!" she cried. Palma shushed her.

"Till explained," Zeb agreed, softly. Trying to set an example. It did no good.

"Who?" she demanded. "Who's dead?"

"Not Cap'n Rios," Palma whispered.

Faye whispered too. "Not Captain Rios," she said.

Palma looked at her with a kind of wild and slow-breaking enlightenment. "Not him," she said. "Aw, girl—"

She made Elven and Bob ride with Zeb in the truck. She and Faye talked all the way home.

Faye's cottage had been spared. Some limbs were down, but the surge had not taken the water higher than her step; the roof was still on, the windows in their boards and tape unbroken. Faye unlocked her door and walked right back into her life.

She found that her trunk of things, which she had set on blocks on the highest counter and covered with plastic, and taped and taped, was high and dry. She cut her way into it, and looked inside. The first thing she sought was that envelope from the hospital, the one with her jewelry. Palma had scolded her for leaving that behind—so small, how much space would it take up? But Faye had not been able to decide, among so many things that mattered, which deserved to perish, and which to escape. She had left them all, to be equally at risk.

For the first time in her life she wished that she had a telephone. She set her rooms back in order and raked her yard. She had to start over completely with her little refrigerator; the power had been off, and everything was spoiled. She told herself she was going to the market, but she took the long way, stopped by Palma's with a couple of windfall oranges from her tree. They weren't home. She figured they had gone upriver to get Zeb's boat. She turned her bicycle on the road around the island, not toward the village. She did not tease herself by asking what she was up to; she didn't surprise herself by saying. She just rode, but all the time she

was looking—as she dismounted and made her way past debris—for the blue roof.

"House of Pancakes blue," she thought. Not "madonna blue" and not "morning glory blue." Being critical made her feel more grown up, less at the mercy of her childish curiosity. Of course that was where she was going. Coming back across the causeway with Palma, after the storm, she had noticed it. Tried to blink it from her eye like grit or some other irritant. It was more visible than ever before. Faye didn't mention it, but Palma, who didn't miss much, missed the trees. "Looks like it took a direct hit," she said. "There's quite a gap."

"Where?" Faye said, nearly achieving the tone—innocence—she sought.

Palma had turned and looked at her; almost ran them off the road into the marsh. She didn't say a thing, she just laughed. And shook her head.

That made Faye mad, as though she were being patronized. She got her sunglasses out and put them on, and for the rest of the way kept her head facing straight forward. But under the cover of those lenses, she managed to roam and reckon.

Now she had no one to fool but herself, and she knew better. She was going to that house, and she was going in. She didn't think of it as trespass, either. That's what she said. But she rolled her bike around to the side and laid it over under some bushes, out of view, and when she went in, she didn't linger at the front door—locked—but made her way over limbs and under fallen trunks—everything was piled and balanced and wedged, not just blown over but broken and wrenched, uplifted and slammed. The house had suffered. It hurt Faye to see that it had not been boarded up. It hadn't been tucked in at all. Not one sheet of plywood, not one bit of tape. The windows were gone, blown out. The drapes and blinds swung tattered. The whole back of the house—the decks, the walkway down to the marsh, she could see where it had been, how it had been—gaped and slumped. The edge of the roof had peeled up, and one whole massive oak, which the deck had been built around, had pitched over, limbs punching through the roof.

Faye got down on her hands and knees and eased under the trunk. Stood and dusted off and walked toward the broken doors. She wasn't breaking in; the place was wide open. She stepped across, crunching glass underfoot. She called, but no one answered. She walked in. This had been the living room. This one room was larger than her whole cottage. It made her feel funny, the way she had felt at Seaquarium when she had watched the massive fish drift by, eyeing her; they were as large as boats, and her mere human edible flesh, in this new perspective, felt minnow-frail, vulnerable and inconsequential.

She could not make out how the room had looked in its best days; it was ruined now. The side of the house toward the front door still had window glass, drapes, and dry plaster, but the blowing rains had swept in across the sofas, the tables, and the paintings. She looked at them a little while, each one, as though it could tell her something. They were all paintings of fishing scenes. She straightened them on the walls, gave the sea back a level horizon. Over the mantel was a mounted billfish, its great eye staring, its mouth fierce. It had been mounted so firmly it hadn't moved as the sea came in to reclaim it. It was mounted in mid-leap, and, facing the open door, seemed as though it had kept on fighting. Faye didn't like it.

She found the scent of the house disturbing. At first she thought it was the ruin itself, and then she thought it was the fish, but of course the fish would smell like fish if that were the thing, and this wasn't a bad smell, it was just disturbing. Perhaps that, or because she really was trespassing as she moved deeper into the house, down the hall past the kitchen, toward the bedrooms. The rugs and carpet squelched underfoot. She wiped her feet at the bedroom door. A modern room, impersonal. Perhaps for guests. Another, and a bath, and, at the very end of the house, the master suite.

Damaged on two sides, it seemed impossible, but she stood for a long time, looking. The bed was enormous. And soggy.

She had turned to go when she thought of something. She opened doors. One was to the bath, one was linens. The third door was a closet. It was as big as another room! It had chairs and a dresser. On the lee side of the house, its roof unbroken and dry, the things on the dresser not even moved from a single gust or shudder of the storm. She stepped in. She wished she had brought a flashlight. Her own dim reflection in the wall of mirrors startled her. Faye had been thinking there might be women's things in it, and for a moment . . . She stared at her reflected face, hard-eyed, challenging. Then her chin came up, as though she had given, or taken, a dare. There was another closet, but it was on the ruined side of the house. Over it, the roof had gone, and the door wouldn't open. She had tried. Had got it cracked a bit, and had sniffed the dark air behind it, but she couldn't satisfy herself. Still, that whetted her appetite. She prowled where she could. His closet would do.

Some of the Captain's jackets hung on a pole. She touched a sleeve. It was dry. On the dresser, a brass button, a comb and brush, cologne, a card case, a memo pad and a pen, pocket items. She thought one was a flashlight. She picked it up. It was his pager. She laid it down again, thinking how she had wondered, how she had stood in line, had called that number, had waited and waited for the chance to dial, and it had rung here, in this empty place. It was very sad, very strange to think of that.

In the top drawer of his dresser, not in a box, just bare, as though thrown in, lost under things, shoved to the back, she found his wedding ring. It looked a great deal like hers, only larger in diameter and wider through the band. She looked inside it. There those initials were, his and hers. And something else, engraved.

For a moment she was going to put it back where she'd found it, but then she did a reckless thing. She wrote a note. She tore off a bit of paper from his memo pad and with his own pen wrote, "Have any of your answers changed?" And she rolled the note and slipped the ring around it, and left it on the dresser.

That made her heart tear and race. She slid the door shut and came away from that room. She amazed herself. Wild happiness accompanied her back to the living room. She stood before the fireplace and looked up at the shiny blue marlin. Studied the fanlike spine, the smaller fins. She wondered if it had always been there. She wondered about the words engraved inside the Captain's ring. It did not occur to her they were in Spanish; she read them as English. They were readable, but didn't make sense: *Sin fin*. What's a sin fin, she wondered, looking at the fish, and why would I—would *she*—have had that engraved there? Maybe it was the name of a boat . . . Maybe it was some joke they had shared . . . She wondered if he knew the Twelve Steps to Marital Bonding. We are already past one-two-three, she decided.

She looked around the room. She played a desperate game: she tried to find one thing she had loved before. She tried to find one thing that was "hers." She meant to steal it, steal it from and for herself, steal it back from ruin. The coffee-table books and watercolor pictures and ashtrays—everything large, grand, meant for impressing, no. She dragged the front drapes open to let in more light, but she couldn't feel any attachment, anywhere she looked. Even the drapes were nothing she would ever choose.

She looked at the music cabinet. The power was off, or she would have played a tape, just to listen, to audition and decide. It wasn't fair to judge the music by what she thought the Captain might like, and, when she had ruled those out, settle for the rest as her "own." What was left, anyway?

She left that game off and went into the kitchen and stood for a long time before the cabinets. Their doors had blown open and shut and open and sprung themselves. The glassware and dishes had suffered, here and there. She tugged open a drawer full of linens, another with odds and ends. Her eye fell on an unmatched teaspoon, tarnished, almost black; she picked it out, of all the rest. The bowl of the spoon was like a flower, and the handle had little leaves and flowers engraved. Tarnished or not, she raised it to her lips, touched it to her lips, her tongue. She decided that would be the thing she took. She put it in her pocket.

She shuddered when the wet drapes dragged at her arm as she went out onto the deck again. She noticed the clamp where the telescope had been. She saw the fallen part. She thought it had been a bird feeder, and she walked as far toward it as she could. The downed tree blocked most of the way, but she bent and reached. Almost! She got on her knees and eased down, one leg at a time, into the dark below the deck. The ground was soggy. She had almost room to stand up. Plenty of room to move around, to find the rest of the feeder. She'd take that too. She needed a feeder. Even if it was broken, she would be able to make it work. There!

She had just discovered that the white tube she had been reaching for was not a feeder at all, but a telescope, when she heard the vehicle drive up in front. She wasn't frightened. She wasn't furtive. She set the telescope up on the deck and climbed back up into the light after it, was going to call out, then thought, No, I'll surprise him—for it was the Captain, had to be the Captain. She listened. At the front door, using a key. Of course the Captain.

And then it seemed silly, playing games. She just ducked under the tree to make her way to him, was easing up when she heard the woman's voice.

Faye had been about to speak! What if she had spoken!

The woman's voice said, "Well, it's still a dream house, damaged or not."

"A nightmare house," Vic said.

"But you're insured," the woman said, "you don't have to worry about that." Her voice sounded different, as though she had turned, was walking the other way, now back again. Looking around. Stepping over things. Picking things up, putting them back where they had once belonged. Broken glass crunched underfoot. "I've always liked this place," she said.

"Wait," he said.

Faye listened. She heard his footsteps go down the hall. That's when she remembered the note she had left. She put her hand over her mouth so she wouldn't cry out. Maybe he wouldn't see it. Maybe he wouldn't notice it. Maybe she could get around to the end of the house, through that broken window, and retrieve it! But not yet. The woman was standing in the doorway, looking out on the deck. Faye crushed herself against the trunk of the tree and willed herself invisible.

The Captain came back through the house. She heard him opening and shutting doors. "No one here," he said.

"Of course not," the woman said. "Who'd you expect? Looters maybe." She walked back into the room. "Is your wife—"

"She won't be back," Vic said.

Now Faye could flee. She stood too soon, knocked herself flat under the tree trunk, scrambled up, then crouched again as footsteps crunched over to the door again. Something shifted, fell. Faye imagined it was one of the paintings, the wet plaster finally letting go, hook and all. "Careful," the woman's voice warned.

Faye eased up, turned, and tiptoed away. Jumped to the ground and ran. Full-tilt she crossed the lawn, then remembered she had left her bicycle around the other side. She lurch-loped at sprint-speed, her stiff ankle with its surgical pins hardly a hindrance at that point. She pressed herself against the side of the house. Listening, hearing only her own heavy breathing.

She was below the bedroom window. The intact window. But she wondered, even so, if she might be able to retrieve that note somehow. She was about to try when the front door opened. Vic and the woman both came out.

They walked toward the car. Not Vic's car. A four-wheel-drive car. They went to the back. Groceries, Faye was thinking. Wine, maybe. Luggage.

Faye watched as the Captain and the woman lifted something out of the vehicle. She couldn't make out what it was. It seemed heavy. Whatever it was, it thudded when it hit the ground. Faye couldn't tell if it had fallen or if they had dropped it on purpose. They didn't try to pick it up. The woman laughed and wiped at her skirt, brushed herself off. The Captain reached in the vehicle for a tool; he was working. The vehicle blocked her view. Faye edged out to the corner of the house and squinted. The Captain worked fast. Was it a flat tire? Maybe they had a flat tire. The Captain took off his jacket and the woman held it.

Faye had noticed a faint trail in the scrub beyond the house. Wide enough for a boat trailer. The path went on down to the dock, to the launch ramp. Most of it was underwater, but she figured that it was a real enough road, just a path would do, and this was sand and straw two ruts wide. She wouldn't need that much room. She could bike down that lane and get away; they'd never see her. She had her bicycle up by now. She had one leg across, her foot on the pedal, and was ready to roll, but she took one last look. The Captain had bent to the ground, had picked up whatever it was, and now lifted.

"Make that look easy," Faye heard the woman say. Faye pushed off. Slow going in the sand, but silent. Absolutely silent.

Over her left shoulder, Faye frowned at them. Then blinked. For a moment she didn't take it in, what she was seeing. It wasn't a tire the Captain was lifting. It was a sign. Faye's foot came off the pedal, hit the ground; she paused and stared. The sign was up, a realtor's sign. He was kicking the dirt into the hole he had dug, setting it plumb. Stamped it down with his heel, all around. But when he tested it, it wobbled.

The woman opened her vehicle and got something else—a sledgehammer. "Hit it like you live," she told him. Loud. And laughed again. She couldn't even swing the hammer. She dragged it over to him. Giggling.

Faye could read the sign from where she stood, twisted on her bike, heading in two directions, going nowhere on the sidetrack. FOR SALE. She read it and read it. She thought and thought. Realtor? Realtor! She was so busy thinking, she didn't even notice the Captain raising that hammer and dropping it the first time. The noise was arresting. Faye felt the wallop in her hands where they gripped the handlebars. The blow echoed off the cool side of the ruined house. Faye felt it in her chest. He had raised the hammer again, was about to bear down, when Faye, thinking one more blow that hard would kill her, dropped her bike in the weeds and cried, coming on fast over the littered lawn, "Captain! Victor! Wait!"

BOOK FIVE

THE NATURAL END

notusque medullas / intravit calor
—Virgil

PART I

ALL SOULS

Because the chapel in the dunes was not a church with regular services of public worship, the rituals for consecration could be shortened. Still, it took most of one morning to celebrate the blessing of the cornerstone and the dedication and preparation of the chapel for its first Mass, at noon on the first of November. It was a raw day. The bishop wore his miter secured against squalls. The flames of the twelve candles outside the church and the twelve within danced but did not flicker out.

While the consecration was going on, only the clergy were allowed inside. Non-clergy—family and friends and early arrivals for the Mass—waited under a marquee out front. "If there were holy relics," Faye explained to Elven, who was missing a day of school for this, "they would have spent the night out here in a little tent, and the bishop would have camped with them."

"Relics?" he said. He was going to ask Faye about that when Palma caught him by the arm and pulled him back to his seat. He was thinking about the governor's archaeologists out on the bluff. Elven was glad he had thrown his arrowhead at the sky.

The bishop and Father Ockham marched up to the door of the chapel and the bishop knocked. Once. And again. And the third time. Father Grattan opened the door.

Then the bishop and Father Ockham went inside. They were the only ones. They left the door open.

After the bishop had set the cross in the center of the chapel and had petitioned for consecration, he scattered ashes on the floor, on the cool, mellow stones Otto Schimmelpfennig had cut—and sometimes cut again, for a perfect fit. In the ashes the bishop inscribed the Latin and Greek alphabets in the sign of the cross.

With water, salt, and ashes he again blessed the walls, time on time on time, and came back outdoors and did the same to the weather side, thrice. Then he went back in. Returning to the center of the church, the bishop sprinkled holy water to the four corners of compass and roof.

Then with oil he anointed each of the twelve wall crosses and, going outdoors again, anointed the twelve temporary candles and their holders. Three crosses along each side, east, west, north, and south.

When he came back around the side of the chapel this time, he looked at the little crowd waiting out front and nodded, but he wasn't through yet, that nod was just to let them know he was doing his best. He went inside and began to cense the chapel, its corners, volumes, and intents, three times through its hopes and spaces from one end of time to the next, from eternity to eternity, sweetening and balming, then outside around the whole perimeter, from foundations to rain-shining roof, in a slow, careful perambulation, the smoke hanging heavy as he swung the censer along, Father Ockham proceeding behind him, on his cane, and to the side, Father Grattan holding one umbrella over the bishop, raised high enough to clear his headgear, and another umbrella over Father Ockham as they made their perfect circuits.

That wasn't all, either, but Vic got up and walked. He needed to smoke. He handed Faye his program. Tom and Vic were sitting on either side of their mother. When Vic left, Faye moved over one seat and filled the gap. Señora Rios didn't turn, only reached out a hand and touched Faye's arm, but when she heard the car door, she flinched.

"He's just getting out of the weather," Faye said. "He'll be right back."

Meanwhile the bishop consecrated the altar. Holy water and chrism oil, mixed, applied in seven crosses, then the sprinkling—thrice—of the table with water not mixed with oil. Then the table was wiped and censed.

"Isn't anybody going to sing?" Elven asked his momma. He was beginning to fidget.

"They . . . no," Palma said, checking her program.

"Bet Cap'n Rios be listenin' to the radio," Elven said, looking around.

By then the bishop had made the sign of the cross with oil of catechumens in the exact center of the altar, had blessed the incense and set out five grains—one at each corner and one in the center—and had begun to rub down the whole table with oil and water-and-oil.

At this point, several people waiting under the marquee got up and stretched. But Señora Rios watched as the bishop set the five beeswax candles, one at each corner and one in the center, and lit them. They were slender and burned fast. While the others waiting under the canopy looked around, or read their programs, or watched the sky over the sea, or enjoyed the undertaker's man trying to light his cigarette with one last damp match—which he dropped—Señora Rios sat a little forward in her chair, watching the quick wax melt and run like tears.

After the beeswax had been scraped from the altar and the altar cleaned again, Palma moved in her chair a little, leaned so she could see the altar cloths raised and blessed. Her own hands had hemmed one of these fair linens with an unbroken thread. She had never sewed better. Palma, strict and strictly Baptist, didn't hold with all of this ritual, and yet she leaned. She had learned how to sew with that unbroken thread, had practiced and practiced and estimated and prayed and for several weeks had suffered, wondering if she had measured right, had worked righteously, so it would all come out, in the last stitch, back where she had started, with a little thread to spare. It had. She had Zeb's wrist in her grip when the cloth she had sewn was raised. She knew exactly which cloth was "hers." Zeb could feel the pulse in her thumb, strong against his own pulse.

It had been Faye's portion to sew; she had volunteered and she had been willing, but not able. Her miseries about it had finally—after advice had failed and Faye had failed also—involved Palma, who had done the work without grudging, and with a kind of righteous fire. She would sew, she would bet, as well as any Catholic this side of glory, and if the stitches weren't to show, were to be as fine as the fair linen itself, then so be it, she'd manage that too. And she had. Hallelujah.

Now the ornaments were being blessed. Vic came back, and Faye slid over and he took his seat again. The whole altar, dressed, was balmed with incense. For a moment the cloud hung, then cleared. The bishop and Father Ockham and Father Grattan were coming out. Somehow, though there was no written cue, everyone stood.

The bishop stood, in the door. He spoke to the ones waiting under the marquee, not a prayer, not a homily, but his best caption for the whole day, for any day of awe and gratitude.

"The natural end of sacrifice is to show by the destruction of, or notable change in, the victim"—here Señora Rios took Tom's hand in her left hand and Vic's in her right, and Vic took Faye's—"the sovereign dominion over creation which belongs to God alone."

Father Ockham stepped out and repeated that, in Latin.

Father Grattan, from a card upon which it had been written for him phonetically, read it in Spanish, so that for Señora Rios comprehension came late.

"At last," Señora Rios said, in Spanish, for *Amen*.

· · ·

"Only the beginning," Tom said, standing and stretching.

"Seventh-inning stretch," Faye agreed. She approached Tom carefully on the undertaker's grass carpet; she was not used to wearing shoes with heels. When she got to him, she couldn't think of anything else to say.

"Tom," she said. Vic had gone to the car for another cigar. Señora Rios was surrounded by a group of friends and admirers.

"It's going well," Faye said.

"Great," he said.

She thought he knew he was making her unhappy, thought he probably didn't mind that at all, was even baiting her a little, but she wouldn't quit, she wasn't a quitter, he ought to know that by now. She tried to think of a way through, past, around his defenses. There was a wild moment when she felt angry, felt a sort of flame rush over her and urge her to say or do something mean, anything, just to break through that perfect composure of his. The rains had let up; he walked out from under the tent. Picked the most puddled direction and didn't look back to see if she tottered and splashed after him. Didn't look back when she called his name. Didn't look around, in fact, till her tossed shoe hit him in the middle of his broad back. It left a little sandy mark. He picked up her shoe and, before he handed it to her, gave it a knock on his hand, a little polish on his sleeve.

"Just one question," she said.

She started to brush him off, take that last little mark from his suit. He pulled away, saying, "No." She thought he meant "no question."

She didn't lean on him to put her shoe on; she dropped it on the ground and, tapping her stocking foot clean of sand, managed on her own. It was beyond her at that point to reach out to him for one more thing. She was bruised by the way he had been behaving, but she had felt pain for his pain, and had worked—because of that—on her attitude. She could see it his way; but what could she do about that? She couldn't help the way things had turned out. She turned to go back. She didn't know she had sighed. The undertakers had the catafalque in place; they were opening the hearse, reaching for the small casket.

"What's the question?" Now he was following her.

She started to just keep on walking, but then the perfect thing occurred to her to ask. Before that moment she had wanted to ask something about herself: Did he understand she had not wronged him? Oh, she was so good at that, all that relationship stuff. Hours of that in rehab. She could "relate" like gangbusters. But this question she thought up, this one was inspired. Her anger and hurt perished in the lightning-strike of her inspiration. It came out of nowhere; it never came out of a book. It surprised her. It surprised him. She could tell. She simply said, "If you could say one thing, one word, to your father, what would it be?" They walked all the way back to the marquee before he answered. She wondered if he would answer. Then he said, "*Thanks*. I'd say *thanks*." He put his hand on her arm, guided her around one of the tent stakes and tie-downs. She turned to study him. "To come to that word," he warned her, if she was in the mood to extrapolate, "my whole life."

"I can say it now," she said. "I'll say it to you now." But when she tried, she choked. So they just shook hands, and let go. They were through when Vic came back.

The crowd, which had grown since it was now time for the actual funeral Mass, milled about in the chapel yard itself. It pleased Señora Rios to estimate their numbers; there were going to be too many to fit inside the chapel. This was not going to be a sorry little affair; she had placed an announcement in the paper, in English as well as Spanish, inviting people to remember and honor her husband. She had paid for massive white ribbons and palms to hang on the gates out by the main road, to mark the way down the new tar toward this little refuge in the dunes. Some strangers came, drawn by the decorations, thinking it might be a wedding, curious tourists and sun-seekers put off their golf and beach games by the turn of weather. But then they saw the funeral canopy, the marquee with its little group, and the undertaker's vehicles—Señora Rios's husband's remains lying in state under a simple pall, no flag, no flowers, waiting, not in a casket in the usual sense. What remains, of a hero?

A van drove in, a choir got out. They had come directly from the early service at St. Francis, and were already wearing their robes. They sang their way in. The Mass began.

Late, last of all, a durable old car turned in and mowed into the scrub, parking in what must have been the last available space. Otto. He had been awaited, hoped for, watched for, and despaired of. The seat reserved for him had been—finally, grudgingly—given to another. In fact, he did not even get into the chapel at first. Since his curiosity was more structural than liturgical, he satisfied himself with a vantage in the narthex, but as the congregation settled and sorted, he was able to make his way deeper in, toward the southern windows, and he stood there, one of many standing, throughout. Now he could see, but as it turned out, it was a poor position for quick exit. After the Mass had been celebrated, with full psalms, anthems, collects, and thanksgivings, after the interment, after the stone had been set, it seemed that everyone in the world got out of that chapel before Otto could. He had hoped to speak with Señora Rios; she had written him a personal invitation to the events, and he wished to express his appreciation and official sympathy. But he also hoped to speak with Mrs. Lockridge, and that began to look impossible.

She was tall, but Otto could have found her anyway. He had had time to sort the crowd during the service. Now he caught her eye briefly, candidly, but they both looked away. She was preoccupied with Father Ockham, who was resting, turning his hat in his hands like a steering wheel. He had dropped his cane. Mrs. Lockridge retrieved it, and when she stood, a bit pink from the exertion, she met Otto's gaze again, across the crowd. Father Ockham's cane fell again. Mrs. Lockridge murmured, "Impossible." It did not occur to her that Otto could read lips. He shook his head, but he smiled. She busied herself with her car keys, the cane, and pressed on toward the door, letting the flow bear her on.

When she had almost reached the door, she had time on the threshold to be sure of her footing. She turned then, and found Otto looking at her again. There they stood, on the same stones the cats had caroled on in the moonlight, but this time the subject was not cats or traps or turnips. She and Otto were in their autumn best, crown to heel, dark, respectful, decorous, yet somehow, despite the weather and season, undoused. This time, Mrs. Lockridge did not drop her eyes. Faye could have warned her of the dangers in that, no age limit, but Faye and Vic had gone.

Tom and Señora Rios were the last; she held the umbrella over him as he locked the door. He asked, "Were we proper?" Too late now, if not. Still, he blinked, considering. Honing. "Will it do?"

Señora Rios did not answer. She looked around in the twilight under that great umbrella. Read the cornerstone again. An *s* had been added to *hijo*, to *son*. No one could tell it had been added later. Tom's plan had left room for hope, as well as faith and love. But like most things with Tom, you had to read between the lines.

"It is not Cuba," Señora Rios told him. "But it is close."

"Don't have to do it over?"

"It is enough," she said.

PART II

ADVENT

Señora Rios died thirteen months later, on the day in December that would have been the twenty-third birthday of Cristo Montevidez. Her funeral Mass was said in the church of St. Francis Xavier, and afterward, a smaller procession followed the body to the chapel in the dunes. Without great pomp, but with dignity and honor, Marcela Rios was laid to rest in the vault beside her hero.

Afterward, the *merienda*: a few friends gathered for a light lunch with Vic and Faye. They did not stay long, for Faye needed to rest. Her baby would be born in the new year, around Candlemas. Father Grattan was the final guest to arrive; he had returned to the rectory after the funeral, made a few calls, and at the last minute had canceled the taxi and ridden his bike down to the ferry. When the ferry got to Sanavere Island, he didn't turn toward the village; he rode the other way, the long way, around past the ruins of the old sugar mill, out on the nature preserve, to the graveyard there. Father Ockham had asked him to do something. "A simple matter," he had said. Father Grattan had said, Of course. Of course.

And yes, it was simple, simple enough. He was to lay some flowers on Cristo's grave. Father Ockham had already chosen them. Had kept them in the refrigerator to stay fresh. It only took about a quarter hour more to go the long way around, and afterward, Father Grattan rode on toward Vic's and Faye's. It was a nice house; Father Grattan liked it. Not imposing or showy, as the first one had been, the one with the blue roof.

Faye had wanted to live there, but Vic had not. "Nothing will be the same," she had said. But he hadn't been willing. He wouldn't tell her why, and this stubbornness had precipitated the first quarrels in their new life. Finally, Faye, exasperated by his refusal to discuss reasons, challenged him. "What are you afraid of?"

His efforts to quit smoking had degenerated into efforts not to smoke indoors. Faye followed him outside. They were living temporarily in her little cottage while they argued it out about the blue-roofed house. She picked an orange from her tree and tried to peel it. Vic offered to help, but she raised the fruit to her mouth, bit the skin, and peeled it with her teeth. "If you'd just tell me why," she said.

This most recent quarrel had begun when he noticed that she had been back to the other house again, had brought something else out of it, like Crusoe rescuing one more armload from the wreck. Nothing important. Just something that had been a wedding gift, a set of three crystal whales. When he saw them, he knew she had been back prowling around. And he had asked her not to do that.

The first time she had done it, she'd brought home a double boiler and an egg poacher, though what she needed with either one was beyond him. She also brought a tablecloth and napkins and a basket full of breakfast china. She liked the pattern. If it was fresh and new to her, it wasn't to him, that's how he knew. He recognized it immediately.

"Why do you hate these plates?" she said, when he took exception.

"I don't hate the plates. It isn't safe for you over there, that's all." He wouldn't tell his dream. Not the sort of thing one tells. "If I say so, why isn't that enough?"

But of course she went.

Now it all came to this, this midnight stroll around her yard arguing about three crystal whales, Vic smoking, and Faye viciously peeling that orange.

"I'll burn it to the ground," he said, out of the blue. Not a threat, just a sudden thought—an idea, a solution. He had forgotten for a moment that she was there. Then she put her hand on his arm. He pulled away from her, went to the hedge, tossed the finished cigar over the fence into the road sand.

"You know something I don't!" He didn't respond.

"If you'd just tell me," she said slowly. She made him turn to look at her. She shivered. "Is it something I did?" All her rancor draining away as she considered that it might be her fault. "I mean before?"

She could not stop trembling. He was shirtless but warm; his skin was very warm. She let herself be gathered against him, tucked under his arm against his ribs. Dread kept her shivering. "Was it something awesomely bad?"

"Something terrible might happen there," was all he said.

"It already did," she said simply. The light from their open door was shining softly on her, but he was in silhouette. She didn't know he was crying till she put her hands up to his face.

They didn't say anything. They just held on for dear life. After a time she said, "All right, burn it down, then. But no blue roof the next time."

He thought that over and agreed, saying, "And no pink siding."

"It's not *pink*," she said.

The compromises had been well considered, Father Grattan thought. As he cycled up that day in December, he took time to appreciate the old-fashioned look, the Caribbean style and Key West shutters, the two stories with galleries, the white paint, the silvery tin hipped roof around a central chimney. It wasn't a raw day at all—rather mild, actually—but there was smoke rising. Father Grattan leaned his bike over, pulled off his ankle clips, brushed himself, and started up the walk. Before he could ring the bell, the door opened and Vic hauled him in with a strong handshake. From lifelong habit, Father Grattan gravitated toward the fire.

The mantel was decorated for Christmas, with greens and candles. They had set up a few of their Christmas cards among the greens. When Faye came down to greet him, she had changed from her dressy clothes, had pulled a sweatshirt on over jeans. She had on socks but no shoes. She settled on the couch, drawing an afghan over her swollen ankles. "That one," she said, pointing to a card in the middle as answer to Father Grattan's question about Cassia and Agapito.

Their little sugar cube of a house and its gardens had been lost in the storm, and Agapito and Cassia had moved away. Every day Agapito drifted even farther away; he had almost slipped from Cassia now; his mind could never make up the ground it had lost. He was completely invalid, and lay abed. Cassia had found a good retirement home where she could shelter in the unassisted-living wing, and Agapito could have skilled nursing care around the clock.

Vic brought Faye some cocoa. The others sat in the dining room, drawn up to the table, no more than half a dozen, just the few. Vic and Faye enumerated the choices, including tea, cocoa, coffee, and something stronger. Father Grattan set Cassia's Christmas greeting back in place. "I visit him every day," she had written on the card, slightly uphill. "He still knows me." She had corrected that last part, though, and written instead, "He still loves me."

Father Grattan was slow to turn.

"You need something," Faye invited.

"No," he realized. "I'm fine."

A NOTE ABOUT THE AUTHOR

MARY HOOD is the author of two collections of short stories, *How Far She Went* and *And Venus Is Blue*. She is currently at work on *Survival, Evasion and Escape*, a new collection of stories to be published by Knopf. She lives near Woodstock, Georgia.